LEO, ZACK, AND EMMIE

LEO, ZACK, AND EMMIE

by Amy Ehrlich
pictures by Steven Kellogg

PUFFIN BOOKS

PUFFIN BOOKS
Published by the Penguin Group
Penguin Putnam Inc., 375 Hudson Street, New York, New York 10014, U.S.A.
Penguin Books Ltd, 27 Wrights Lane, London W8 5TZ, England
Penguin Books Australia Ltd, Ringwood, Victoria, Australia
Penguin Books Canada Ltd, 10 Alcorn Avenue, Toronto, Ontario, Canada M4V 3B2
Penguin Books (N.Z.) Ltd, 182-190 Wairau Road, Auckland 10, New Zealand

Penguin Books Ltd, Registered Offices: Harmondsworth, Middlesex, England

First published in the United States of America by Dial Books for Young Readers,1981
Published in a Puffin Easy-to-Read edition, 1997

1 3 5 7 9 10 8 6 4 2

THE LIBRARY OF CONGRESS HAS CATALOGED THE DIAL EDITION AS FOLLOWS:
Ehrlich, Amy. Leo, Zack, and Emmie.
Summary: The new girl in Zack and Leo's class affects the boys' friendship.
[1. Friendship—Fiction.] I. Kellogg, Steven. II. Title.
PZ7.E328Le [E] 81-2604
ISBN 0-8037-4761-6 (lib. bdg.) AACR2
ISBN 0-8037-4760-8 (pbk.)

Puffin Easy-to-Read ISBN 0-14-036199-5
Printed in the United States of America

Reading Level 2.2

CONTENTS

A NEW GIRL

There was a new girl
in Zack and Leo's class.
"Class," said Miss Davis,
"this is Emmie Williams.
Please make her feel welcome
in Room 208."

Miss Davis turned to write
some numbers on the blackboard.
Emmie Williams stuck out her tongue
and wiggled her ears.

No one saw but Zack.

He had tried to wiggle

his ears for years.

"Want to come over to my house?"
Leo said to Zack after school.
"I have a brand-new robot."
But Zack was waiting for Emmie.

"Maybe I'll come later,"
he said.

Emmie came into the schoolyard.

"Hi," said Zack.

"I know how to cross my eyes."

"Big deal," said Emmie.

She crossed her eyes

and looked straight at him.

Then she wiggled her ears.

"See you," she said and

walked away.

Zack went to Leo's house.

He went into the bathroom

and closed the door.

Then he looked in the mirror.

He held his ears with his fingers.

He moved them up and down.

It was no use.

When he took his fingers away,

his ears stayed right where

they were.

"Come on out of the bathroom,"
yelled Leo.

"Don't you want to see my robot?"

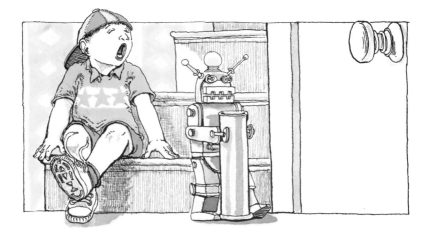

Leo's new robot

could walk and talk.

It could even shoot missiles.

But Zack did not want

to play with it.

"That Emmie Williams thinks
she's so great," he said.
"But I don't like her at all."
Leo shot a missile at the ceiling.
"I think she's nice," he said.
"Did you see how fast she ran
at playtime?
And she knows the names
of all the dinosaurs."

17

Zack did not want to hear about it.

"I'll show her," he said.

"Emmie Williams thinks

wiggling her ears

is the best thing

anyone could ever do."

"Well, that's not so much," said Leo.

He put the robot carefully in its box.

He took off his baseball cap.

Then he wiggled his ears up and down

about twenty times.

"Leo!" Zack yelled.

"You never told me

you could wiggle your ears."

"You never asked me," said Leo.

"It's easy.

I'll show you how."

Zack and Leo practiced

until Zack got it right.

Then they wiggled their ears

at each other

for the rest of the afternoon.

PLAYTIME

It was playtime.

Everyone had a partner

as they walked through the halls

to the schoolyard.

Zack and Leo held hands.

They were always partners

at playtime.

Zack brought out his ball.

It was big and soft,

because it was made out of sponge.

They tried to play catch,

but Leo kept missing the ball.

It sailed past his arms.

It rolled under his legs.

It hit him gently in the nose.

"Leo," said Zack,

"you're a good friend

but as a ballplayer, you stink.

I think I would rather play alone."

He threw the ball at the wall,
and it came back.

Back and forth. Over and over.

He caught it every time.

Suddenly a person
as fast as a streak
grabbed the ball on a bounce.
It was Emmie Williams.
"Who asked you into this game?"
said Zack.
Emmie did not answer.

She took off running
with the ball held close
like a football player.
Zack was getting mad.

"Hey, where are you going
with my ball?" he yelled.

Emmie slid down the slide
before Zack could climb the ladder.

She ran along the seesaw
faster than a tightrope walker.

Then she swung on the swings.

But when she headed for the jungle gym,
Zack was ready for her.
Whap! He grabbed her legs,
and she fell over.
The ball tumbled away in the sand
under the jungle gym.

As they rushed to get it
their heads knocked together hard.
"Ouch!" said Zack.
"That hurt!" said Emmie.

They looked at each other.

They were covered with sand.

They were on their hands and knees.

There was not even room to fight.

Emmie gave Zack his ball,
and they climbed to the top
of the jungle gym.

The schoolyard was empty.
Playtime was over.

"Race you to the school door,"
Emmie said.

They ran as fast as they could,
but it was a tie.

Inside the building

Zack took Emmie's hand.

They were partners

as they walked through the halls

back to Room 208.

HALLOWEEN

It was one week before Halloween.

Zack was going to be Batman.

Emmie was going to be a witch.

But Leo would not say

what his costume was.

"Please tell us," said Zack.

"Is it a superhero?" asked Emmie.

"No," said Leo,

"it's a surprise."

All week long Emmie and Zack

worked on their costumes.

One day they went

to the five-and-ten to buy masks.

Leo was in the checkout line.

He was buying glitter
and silver paper,
but he still wouldn't say
what his costume was.

Finally Zack knew what to do.

He went to Leo's house

and rang the bell.

"Hi, Leo," he said.

"Want to come trick-or-treating

with Emmie and me

on Halloween night?"

"Sure," said Leo.

"There's just one thing," said Zack.

"Only people who tell

what they are wearing can come."

Leo thought it over.

"Okay," he said at last.

"I'm going to be a snowflake."

"A snowflake!" shouted Zack.

"That's really dumb!

That's the dumbest costume

I ever heard of!"

Leo just smiled.

"Oh, well," he said.

"I guess I'll go alone."

On Halloween night
a full moon shone brightly.
Zack and Emmie saw superheroes
walking with pirates,
mummies walking with robots,
and gypsies walking with ghosts.

41

Zack saw three other Batmen.

Emmie counted six other witches.

But they did not say anything

about it to each other.

Suddenly a bright starry shape

came toward them.

As it came closer

Zack and Emmie could see colors

flashing like a million jewels.

"Ooooh, how beautiful!" said Emmie.

Then they both gasped.

It was Leo in his snowflake costume.

They all got to the next house

at the same time.

A lady came to the door.

"What a terrific snowflake!"

she said.

"And what's this?

Another Batman and another witch?"

She gave them all some candy

but she gave Leo more.

45

At every house

the same thing happened.

"Look," Zack whispered to Emmie,

"his trick-or-treat bag

is twice as full as ours."

As they walked along
everyone stopped Leo
to ask about his costume.
People even crossed the street
to look at it.

At last they got to Emmie's house.

As soon as they were inside

Zack took off his Batman cape.

"Hey, Leo, can I try on

your snowflake costume?" he asked.

"You mean this dumb thing?" said Leo.

"NO WAY!"

SHOW AND TELL

Everyone in Room 208

was sitting in a circle.

They were having Show and Tell.

Leo and Emmie had both

brought in plants to show.

Emmie had a potato vine

and Leo had a cactus.

"Class," said Miss Davis,
"these plants look very different,
but many things about them
are the same.

I would like Emmie and Leo
to do a report about plants
for Monday."

"I want to work on the report too,"
Zack said at lunch.

"But, Zack," said Emmie,

"Miss Davis told only

Leo and me to do it."

Zack picked up his lunch box

and moved to another table.

The rest of the week
he would not talk to them.
"He's feeling bad about our report,"
said Leo.

"If you ask me,
he's acting like a dope," said Emmie.

On Monday Leo and Emmie were ready.

At Show and Tell

they showed Room 208

a model of a giant plant.

They told how the roots,

the leaves, and the flowers

helped the plant to grow.

Then they sang a song about plants:

"Oh, the roots are connected

to the stem.

And the stem is connected
to the leaves.

And the leaves are connected
to the flowers.

And the flowers are connected
to the seeds."

Everyone joined the singing.

Everyone but Zack.

He looked like he was going to cry.

After school Emmie and Leo decided
to try to talk to him.
Emmie carried the model of
the giant plant.
Leo took a lunch box in each hand.
When they got to Zack's house,
they could not find him at first.

Then they saw him.

He was sitting in a tree.

He would not come down,

so Leo and Emmie climbed up.

"Don't talk to me," Zack said.

"I don't want you to talk to me."

They sat there quietly

in the tree.

A wind came up and blew the leaves
off the branches.
It began to get dark.

At last Zack started to say
what was wrong.

"Leo was my friend
before he was your friend,"
he told Emmie.

"And he wouldn't even know you
if it wasn't for me.

But ever since you two began
working on your plant report,
you're always together
and you don't like me anymore."
"Why do you think
we're up here then?" asked Emmie.

"Yes, why do you think

we came over?" asked Leo.

"Za—ack, where aaare you?"

It was Zack's mother calling.

"I'm getting cold," said Leo.

"I'm getting tired of this tree,"
said Zack.

"Come on. Let's go."
He climbed down,
and Leo and Emmie followed.
The model of the giant plant
was lying in the grass.
Zack picked it up.

"Hey, this thing's pretty neat.

Was it hard to make?" he asked.

"No," said Emmie, "it was easy.

We'll show you how."

THE ESSAYS OF A.J. MUSTE

Edited by
Nat Hentoff

A CLARION BOOK
PUBLISHED BY SIMON AND SCHUSTER

To the secretaries who through the years
were companions in struggles for freedom, equality, and peace,
and who, incidentally, typed these essays.

A. J. M.

A Clarion Book
Published by Simon and Schuster
Rockefeller Center, 630 Fifth Avenue
New York, New York 10020
All rights reserved
including the right of reproduction
in whole or in part in any form
Copyright © 1967 by Liberation
Reprinted by arrangement with the Bobbs-Merrill Company, Inc.

First paperback printing, 1970

SBN 671-20529-3
Manufactured in the United States of America

Acknowledgments

This book quite literally would not have existed had it not been for Edith Snyder's advice and uncommonly conscientious and diligent work of assembly. Since she is an associate of A. J., her work was one of love—radical love, in the Mustean sense.

Many of these essays were originally published elsewhere, and I would like to thank the following publications for permission to include articles: *Christian Century, Fellowship Publications,* The Hope College *Anchor, New International, Liberation, Pendle Hill Publications, The World Tomorrow.*

Johanna Bosch and James Best of *Fellowship* and Karolyn Kerry of *The Militant* were extraordinarily helpful in gathering some of the writings from which this selection was made.

Robert M. Ockene of Bobbs-Merrill conceived the idea of the book and was of persistent aid to us during its preparation—not only as a thoroughly skillful editor but as a man who fully understands the spirit as well as the letter in the works of A. J. Muste.

N. H.

Contents

Introduction

To anyone who knows A. J. Muste it was no surprise when, at 81, he appeared in Saigon in April, 1966, as the head of a small delegation of pacifists. ("As we have made our voices heard at home, we must also speak to the people of Vietnam. We have sought 'to speak truth to power' at centers where war measures were being planned, where men were being drafted and engines of mass destruction were being made; we now come to the scene where the fighting and slaughter are actually taking place.")

At a Saigon press conference, apparently organized attempts were made—by shouts, by threats, by hurling eggs—to silence the pacifists.

The uproar continued until A. J. rose to state his case. At that point, reported *The New York Times,* "the tumult subsided almost immediately."

Nor would anyone who has heard A. J. talk, privately or at public meetings, have been surprised that he was able, for a time anyway, to create calm. There are some advocates of nonviolence who speak violently, or who stimulate violence in their listeners through self-righteous arrogance. A. J., however, doesn't seek to overwhelm. Constantly, persistently, he tries to communicate. And that means speaking *with,* not only *to.**

---

* Consider this excerpt from a letter written by A. J. Muste and printed in the October 21, 1965, New York *Herald Tribune:*

"The unique thing about A. J.," says Sidney Lens, long active in labor, civil rights and peace movements, "is that you never feel you're retreating when you talk with him. He's about the only radical I know who doesn't threaten other people's egos. In fact, you can talk at him for two hours and he won't interrupt. He'll listen and listen, and, if you don't know him, you'll begin wondering if this old guy has all his marbles. But eventually, he'll make clear what he thinks. Similarly, at a meeting, he can sit as part of the group on the platform without towering over it, and yet he winds up having been the key figure there."

Throughout his long career in the ministry, in labor, in civil rights, in agitating for peace. A. J. has been able to maintain contact with all manner of bristlingly diverse people and groups—sometimes the only person able to do so. As he puts it, "I've always tried to keep communication open between radicals and non-radicals, between pacifists and non-pacifists. It goes back to something very fundamental in the nonviolent approach to life. You always assume there is some element of truth in the position of the other person, and you respect your opponent for hanging on to an idea as long as he believes it to be true. On the other hand, you must try very hard to see what truth actually does exist in his idea, and seize on it to make him realize what you consider to be a larger truth."

"Your editorial . . . 'The Vein of Hate,' points to the frequency in current controversies of resort to blanket condemnations and vicious epithets, suggesting that even militant pacifists 'traffic in their own brand of hate' and inject it into their attacks 'on the individual service men fighting and dying under orders.' I think such attacks are seldom made by those conscientiously opposed to war and regarding nonviolence as a way of life, not merely an expedient tactic. But pacifists are certainly not immune to human weakness.

"My own son enlisted in the Navy during World War II. His mother and I could not be a conscience for him, nor he for us. Each of us had to be true to his own insights and standards. The man who goes into war having seriously thought his way to that decision is on a higher moral level than the smug pacifist who has no notion of the ambiguities and contradictions the decision involves. There is obviously some question as to how many Americans go to war in Viet Nam on this basis.

"However, it remains the fact, as you point out, that the habit of categorizing human beings as 'they' and 'we' is 'central to institutionalized hate.' Never is this habit carried to a more absolute extreme than in war, where it is honorable to slay fellow human beings provided they belong to 'them.'

"The people of Viet Nam have been shot and bombed from various sides for decades. If only *somebody* would stop killing them! No nation or group is more obviously called on both from political and moral grounds to stop shooting and bombing in Viet Nam than the Americans, who instead are daily escalating the war. If we stopped shooting, this might open up the possibility of something like genuine negotiation about other matters."

Because his strength is not the kind that feeds on overwhelming his opponents, A. J. is welcome, and is often a most effective reconciler among peace groups of all persuasions, secular and religious. His name is present on the letterhead of virtually every American peace organization, whether *ad hoc* or long-term, as well as on those of many international pacifist groups.

As one pervasively active pacifist, Bradford Lyttle, explains: "A. J. is the spiritual chairman of every major pacifist demonstration in the country, and often is the actual chairman." Furthermore, in connection with any group, his name is a guarantee of action. "He makes things happen," as a young peace agitator puts it.

"Indignity, human suffering, exploitation," wrote Theodore Roszak in the British weekly, *Peace News*, "call forth no intellectual pyrotechnics from him. Rather, where he perceives injustice, he demands that it stop, for he knows, as all decent men do, that injustice is not necessary for the achievement of anything worthwhile. And if the injustice does not stop, then Muste puts himself in the way of it, directly, immediately, and unflinchingly. 'Very well then, if you say it must be done, do it to me too.' "

A. J., as an act of protest and as an attempt at communication, has climbed over the fence at a missile base in Nebraska. He has been arrested for refusing to take cover during civil defense air-raid drills. He has protested against nuclear testing on the White House lawn and in Moscow's Red Square. He has participated in and helped to plan many other direct action demonstrations aimed at speaking truth to power.

But A. J. is more than a direct actionist and strategist. He is also an analyst—of politics, of nonviolence, of the nature and potential of man and of society. And it is this aspect of A. J., from 1903 to the present, that this book tries to reveal, through sections of autobiography; writings on labor; dissections of the history of radical movements in the United States; explications of international power politics; and probings into the complexities and ambiguities of nonviolence, in theory and in action.

Represented here is the intellectual as well as the emotional evolution of a man who, as was said by Walter G. Muelder, Dean of the Boston University School of Theology, has made the peace movement "an aggressive and dynamic force for social change and has compelled Christian thought to accept full responsibility for the qualitative texture of social life. He did not, like many pacifists, find it possible to stand pat on traditional peace attitudes and static political answers, but has infused the peace movement with a faith that all the institutions of society can be transformed in principle to nonviolent ones. This means that he remains a radical on all social fronts and is not a single-cause pacifist."

And a radical Muste is. "Indeed," states Theodore Roszak, "he is a revolutionary. He has never hesitated to accept that description. As a trade unionist, his designs were radical enough to force his ejection from the American Federation of Labor and to throw him into league with the Trotskyites, though his commitment to open politics and nonviolence was too strong to support that alliance for more than a few years."

And when he returned to Christian pacifism in 1936, Muste's radicalism—his getting at the root of things—persisted. "It was Muste," underlines Professor John Oliver Nelson, of Yale University Divinity School, "who kept the peace movement in this country from becoming a clubwoman's organization. Moreover, he went further than pacifism. He has never believed that if there were no more war man would automatically become good. He feels the heart of man requires radical redemption and his institutions must, as a result, be changed accordingly. A. J. is a devastating reminder to young pacifists of what a real radical is."

And not only to young pacifists. Young radicals of nearly every ideological orientation—and some with, as yet, no real orientation at all—listen to A. J. He is one of those relatively few social activists and theorists over thirty to whom they do listen. "He's much more contemporary in his thinking than nearly all the other elders of the movement," observes David McReynolds of the War Resisters League, whose work keeps him in continual, mobile contact with the young. "You never hear A. J. say, 'When you've been around as long as I have, you'll realize that. . .' He doesn't give you the answers of twenty and thirty years ago."

Moreover, A. J.'s analyses, political and otherwise, are not, as Theodore Roszak emphasizes, those of "a dogmatist or abstruse theoretician. If Americans were but listening to Muste, I doubt they could be bewildered or alienated by him." And, of course, it is the hope of the editor that, through this collection of his writings, many more Americans will begin listening to A. J.

As of now, as Paul Goodman has written in the *New York Review of Books*, "for many thousands of Americans (including myself), and especially for many of the best of the young, A. J. Muste is an authentic Great Man, not a stage hero or an image of public relations. We in America are very much lacking admirable fathers at present—I cannot think of a single person in high public office whom many intelligent persons regard with deep respect—but A. J. is always regarded with respect." People, Goodman continued, "respect and rely on his apparently indefatigable willingness to take his characteristic position in every relevant circumstance; remaining consistent with himself, to be open to improvisations; and especially to *come across*, when the task is his task. He is what he is and people rely on it."

Regarding "the world-wide colonial revolutions of Muste's later concern"—as exemplified here in several contemporary essays—Goodman writes: "Muste's world-traveling knowledge of them has made him, in my opinion, the foremost political analyst in the country." Goodman goes further. A. J., he says, "is a survivor of the days when constitutional and revolutionary politics were real! He flexibly takes part in the para-political improvisations that are now the genuine article, but he can still discuss them in a framework of reasoned theory rather than in sit-in pulpit oratory or go-limp jive."

Theodore Roszak links the thrust of A. J.'s combination of reasoned theory and social action to an American lineage that "runs back through the humanitarian socialism of Eugene Debs to the Populist revolt to the New England Abolitionists (in Muste's case the root-and-branch perfectionism of William Lloyd Garrison but moderated by the human kindness of Whittier). Beyond that, Muste's political ancestry reaches back to the Brook Farmers, to Thoreau, Horace Greeley, Thomas Jefferson and Roger Williams. This is a tradition which might have made America a great and humanly revolutionary force in the affairs of men."

And it is this tradition to which Senator J. W. Fulbright was referring in April, 1966, when in the course of his Christian Herter lectures at the Johns Hopkins University School of Advanced International Studies, Fulbright asked whether America can overcome "the fatal arrogance of power" that has destroyed great nations in the past. "My hope and my belief are that it can," he said, "that it has the human resources to accomplish what few if any great nations have ever accomplished before: to be confident but also tolerant, and rich but also generous, to be willing to teach but also willing to learn, to be powerful but also wise. I believe that America is capable of all of these things, but I also believe it is falling short of them. Gradually but unmistakably we are succumbing to the arrogance of power."

And it is because of his historical knowledge of the effects, within and without, of "the arrogance of power" that A. J.'s wide-ranging analyses through the years remain of acutely contemporary relevance.

It is in his appearance as well as in the radical quality of his reasoned dissent that A. J. is of the American grain. This non-sectarian revolutionary is also, as Theodore Roszak has written, "that same lanky, long-legged, twinkling-eyed old-man-next-door whom John T. McCutcheon always brought into his *Chicago Tribune* cartoons to help the little, typical American boy string up his cracker fish-pole, while telling him about Valley Forge and General Custer and Old Abe Lincoln. One finds Muste's raw-boned, open-faced figure appearing in every advertisement that requires a kindly old grandpa to carve the Thanksgiving turkey. He is all this in appearance, but with an authenticity that redeems the stereotype."

A. J., of course, would tell that boy things about American military history which would stun the *Chicago Tribune*, but what I believe Roszak to mean when he emphasizes the "authenticity" of A. J. in this context is Muste's insistence on being personally responsible for what is done and is not done in his name, as an American, as a human being. And that insistent sense of responsibility used to be much, much more of an operative element in the American ethos than is now the case.

In his acceptance speech of the War Resisters League's 1958 peace award, Muste approvingly quoted the late C. Wright Mills' distillation of that concept of personal responsibility. Mills had urged everyone, especially intellectuals and scientists, to become conscientious objectors to the theory and practie of nuclear deterrence. "If you do not do it," Mills had said, "you at least are not responsible for its being done. If you refuse to do so out loud, others may refrain quietly from doing it, and those who still do it may then do it only with hesitation and guilt. . . . To refuse to do it is an act affirming yourself as a moral center of responsible decisions . . . it is the act of a man who rejects 'fate,' for it reveals the resolution of one human being to take at least his own fate into his own hands."

And that A. J. always has done. After attending the World Pacifist Meeting in India in 1949, A. J. quoted a declaration made by Gandhi nine years before: "No one need wait for anyone else to adopt a right course. Men generally hesitate to make a beginning if they feel that the objective cannot be had in entirety. Such an attitude of mind is in reality a bar to progress. . . . There will never be an army of perfectly nonviolent people. It will be formed of those who will honestly endeavor to observe nonviolence."

A. J.—in his life, his actions, his writings—has made a beginning. To those, and there are many, who have been changed by knowing him, his beginning has helped them, in variously imperfect ways, make beginnings of their own.

"This is an awfully smooth world," says Roy Finch, a professor of philosophy and a former editor of *Liberation*, "and it contains very few men of absolute principle. A. J. has stood so far on that absolute end of the spectrum of principle that he's influenced thousands of people to at least move in his direction, and they have influenced others. Most of us never have to—or don't—take much of a moral stand in the course of our lives. Therefore, we don't build up the collective moral strength of our society. A. J. does. He builds up everybody's backbone."

The value of A. J. Muste—as this selection of his essays reveals —is that he does not simply enunciate principle. He shows us, in each instance, how he came to his principle, how it can be applied, and how it is interconnected with all that we are and do. "We cannot have peace," he has said, "if we are only concerned with peace. War is not an accident. It is the logical outcome of a certain way of life. If we want to attack war, we have to attack that way of life."

So this is not a book solely about peace and war. It is about the way we live now, the way we have been living during the past sixty years and earlier, and the ways in which we must change if—as a country and as part of an international community—we are to go on living at all.

NAT HENTOFF

Sketches for
an Autobiography

Historical Essays, 1891-1960

Part One

1957-1960 On an afternoon in May as a spring rain gently washes the green leaves, in the New York parks, that have come out full in two weeks of continuous sunshine, I sit down with a piece of white paper before me, in a clear space on a slightly cluttered desk. This is the beginning of an effort to write out the story of my life. Since I wanted to check on the time, I turned on the radio to the "Station of *The New York Times*," hoping for some music while waiting for the time signal. Instead I got a woman giving a religious lecture, in a voice that was too sweet at moments when it was not edged with the suggestion of hate which, I fear, too often marks preachers of either sex and all faiths when they sermonize about LOVE.

The voice said: "One may think one needs a better place to dwell in, or more money, or a change of scene. What one needs is a change of view, simply to acknowledge the self-completeness of the Father-Mother God."

Hearing once again—for God knows how many times in seventy-two years—the drivel about not needing a better place to dwell in, but a change of view, and about how simple it all is when you acknowledge self-completeness, or the absolute, or something or other, reminded me of one of the best stories I ever heard in a gathering of theologians—where good stories on both mundane and heavenly themes are not uncommon. This one was told a couple of years ago by an English Quaker—possibly "not without malice,"

1

since most Quakers take a dim view of theology and are reputed not really to know anything about it—and his audience in the little Swiss town of Piridoux consisted mainly of erudite European, Lutheran and Reformed theologians. His story was about a girl of about ten in a devout Church of England family. One evening, as her mother was seeing her to bed, she knelt to say her prayers and suddenly burst into violent weeping. For some time the mother's effort to quiet her was unavailing, but presently the child was able, between sobs, to say: "It's that I just don't understand the Trinity, mother." Mother naturally made several attempts to "make it all clear," but to no avail. The desperate weeping continued. Finally, the mother said: "Darling, I'm going to read you something which you probably won't understand now, but may later, and anyway it may help you. It was written by some very devout and wise men many years ago." Then she read the Athanasian Creed, one of the most abstruse and complicated of all the creeds. And, as she finished, the child looked up, smiled seraphically through her tears, and said: "Oh, mother, *why* didn't you ever read this to me before? It makes it all so plain."

I was also reminded by that Christian Science lecture, about simply needing a change of view, of the bit I clipped out of yesterday's evening paper—and which belongs properly enough in my autobiography, because I can think back to times when my mother, with five children, among whom I was the oldest, must have felt very much like the young California housewife in this story. This housewife set her house afire by placing seven stacks of diapers and dirty clothes in various parts of the house and touching matches to them. (The diapers and dirty clothes with which I have been familiar were not very inflammable but perhaps some of these were the up-to-date, synthetic kind.) Having set the fires, Mrs. Nancy Joyce Stoner hopped into her car with her two daughters and drove off. When a neighbor shouted that the house was afire, Nancy shouted back: "Good. Call the fire department." At this point, she was, of course, behaving ambivalently just like multitudes of supposedly practical and learned people who are setting fires in various places on the planet and who, since they are not completely, or obviously, daft, presumably think there is a fire department that can be called in case of need. But to return to Nancy Joyce Stoner, when the police and Associated Press caught up with her, she gave a most appealing, if not altogether rational, explanation of her act: "I've been doing housework and baby diapers for so long, I just got fed up and blew my stack."

I note with interest and concern that, with all our modern improvements and prosperity, there are still a good many women here in the United States who are situated much as Mrs. Stoner is. Don't tell me they are foreigners. What kind of foreigner would a girl called Nancy Joyce Stoner be? Don't tell me, either, that she probably has a low I.Q. and didn't have much schooling. I can lead you to college graduates with respectable I.Q's who are in the same fix. Nor is there any spiritual or "theological" truth of which life and study have convinced me more utterly than that it is heretical and sinful to say that Nancy Joyce simply needs a change of view and a realization of her self-completeness and *not* "a better place to dwell in."

In a few days Billy Graham is to begin a six weeks' evangelistic Crusade in Madison Square Garden, a mile or so away from where I am sitting. The campaign will cost over a million dollars, more than any such campaign by Billy Graham, or anybody else in history, has cost. We shall see what he has to say about weighty and timely matters.

It is probably somewhat unusual to begin an autobiography with such observations and ruminations about the present, especially when that "present" is as far removed from the beginning as in this case. But it seems to me appropriate. For one thing, we have all heard too many lectures on *The Crisis in the Middle East Today*, which started with the birth of Mohammed perhaps or, in less deplorable instances, with the beginning of the century, and left room at the end for only a few hasty and not too well chosen words about "today." I want to be sure at some point, in a series which obviously cannot go on forever, and which deals with a life which began more than seventy-two years back, to get within hailing distance of where we are and what I am now.

Moreover, though I have not made a study of the matter, I surmise that when a man or woman undertakes to write an autobiography, an important factor is a purpose, which may be more or less clearly defined in the writer's mind, but which in any case relates to the present or immediate past, to the world in which the writer now lives, not the one into which he was born. This is obviously true of any writing like John Henry Newman's *Apologia Pro Vita Sua,* but I think it is also true of others, including those

written by people who have retired pretty completely from other
activities and do not anticipate returning to them. In any event, the
autobiographer is the man at the time of writing, not the child or
youth or even the grown man of earlier periods. The world in which
he writes—and this is much more significant in an era of vast
transitions such as ours than it may have been in the past—is today's
and not yesterday's, and this will enter profoundly into what he
writes, even into what he will observe in his past.

For example, I expect before long to write about "the little
Dutch boy" who, decades ago, walked on the top of a dike one
morning and saw on one side the seemingly boundless sea and, on
the other, the bright green carpet of the meadowland, sunk below
the level of the sea, dotted in the distance with what seemed like
painted toy cattle. The experience was so vivid then, and I was so
shaken anew by the sensations of beauty, of awe, of the horror of
falling off the dike into the sea, of the cattle becoming painted toys
in the lovely shimmering light—that something in me reaches for
my mother's hand, as my hand tightened in hers that morning long
ago. Yet, when I write about it, it will not be "the little Dutch
boy" who writes but—shall we say—a retired agitator who has not
properly retired or—with luck—one who very early in life was taken
on a journey that proved enthralling, and who is still journeying
and, on many days, enthralled.

This is not the first time I have started writing an autobiography,
trying to write about the events and people I have encountered, what
has happened to me inside and outside, and where we are and what
I am now. During the war summer of 1944, I devoted a few weeks
of vacation to the beginning of such an attempt.

Several members of the family were spending that summer in
a western Massachusetts college town near the Berkshires, which we
loved as people who were brought up on the flat and treeless prairie
are, I think, likely to love wooded mountains. We had the free use,
in his absence, of the house of a friend who had for years been
an ardent pacifist, but who concluded that he could not maintain
that position in the face of the Nazi atrocities and the certainty, as he
believed, that this regime would rule the earth for many decades if
it were not smashed, which war alone could accomplish.

I recall that on that occasion also I felt that I had to start by
writing something about the present. Summers are likely to be hot
in the Connecticut River valley towns, and 1944 was no exception.

One waited to go to bed until the earth had cooled and a breeze with the smell of leaves and grass on it began to stir the motionless air. On such a night I lay on a cot letting my mind recall past events. Presently, the clock in the church steeple in the center of town began to strike midnight. One after another, at long intervals it seemed, the twelve notes were struck. It was as if one could see the sound as it started when the clapper struck the bell and watch it float over the trees, enter the open windows, and settle down in the room.

No doubt the effect that church bells, even poor ones, have on me can be traced back to my childhood in Grand Rapids, Michigan, where our family settled after immigrating from the Netherlands. It was a typical small city of the near Middle West in the early Nineties, with only a few traces left of the pioneer and lumber-cutting days; but it was too soon for the changes which come to cities with the accumulation of years, wealth and tradition. In its outward aspects our family life was not uncomfortable, but on the whole drab. Both because there was not much else, and because my parents believed this was just as it should be, the church, especially in the first years when our life was mainly lived within the Dutch community, was the center of social life and culture, as well as of worship and religious training. Sunday certainly was for me, and I think for most other youngsters in that community, *the* high day of the week—a day of "rest and gladness," of "joy and light," as celebrated in one of the Gospel hymns which we learned and sang lustily a few years later, when our jubilation was no longer confined to the medium of the Dutch metrical version of the Psalms. By then, we accepted the fact that God could speak and be spoken to in English as well as in Dutch.

Churches in those days were not open for recreation during the week, partly because most amusements were regarded as sinful, or at any rate as best taken in small doses and in the home. Thus the one day which stood apart, on which you moved into another world, and which somehow made you feel "different" and taller, was Sunday.

Sunday was the day the church bell rang. At least, in our part of the city, the church bell had the hallowed function of calling people to church on the Lord's Day, not the mundane one of telling the time of day during the week. That was done for the important hours by the factory whistles. Thus, Sunday really began for me at 8:30 in the morning, when the church bell sounded the first warning for the recalcitrant and the first jubilant announcement for such as me, that the time for the nine o'clock morning service was approaching.

We lived far enough from the church we attended to have to begin the journey from home soon after "the first bell" sounded. After an interval of about fifteen minutes, when we were about half-way, "the second bell" rang out. The "last bell" would be ringing as we approached or entered the church. Not to be seated by the time the echo from the last stroke of the bell died away was a social and moral error which one simply did not commit. Then there was silence. The preacher, in his Prince Albert, walked to the pulpit; the old organ played as softly as it could. Then the service began. I must have been no older than six or seven when all this gave me a feeling of having entered another world, the "real" world, the feeling, which later I found conveyed in one of the New Testament Epistles, that one had come "to Mount Zion, the city of the living God, the heavenly Jerusalem, to myriads of angels in festal gathering, to the assembly of the first-born enrolled in heaven, to God the judge of all, to the spirits of just men made perfect."

Something of all this the sound of a church bell, any church bell, always brings back to me, and did on that summer night in the Massachusetts town thirteen years ago.

As the spell of the past was broken, I began to muse on what was going on around me. It was the summer of titanic battles in many parts of the world. Nearly all of those whom I had known as young men in the labor and radical movement in the Twenties and Thirties were in the Armed Forces. The United States was allied with Communist Russia, so the adjective was not generally employed in those days. Stalin was often dubbed Uncle Joe. Magazines like *Life* ran articles showing that the Russians were really more like Yankees than any other people in the world. Part of the "treason" of which pacifists were judged guilty was their pointing to the crimes and errors of Stalinism. Indeed the term "Stalinism" itself was virtually forbidden. These things "just sow suspicion about Allies and interfere with the war effort." It is not possible for people to be involved in a great war and to be objective at the same time.

In these circumstances many of the young men to whom I felt most akin were in Federal prisons, or on the way, or recently released, because they had refused to register under the conscription law, or, if they had not drawn the line at that point, refused to do any alternative civilian work under conscription. Some of the older pacifists, when called upon to register a couple of years before, had taken the same position of being unable on grounds of conscience to have anything to do with conscription for war, but we were not prosecuted. I thought of those younger men that night and the next morning wrote about them, in that earlier start on an autobiography. Such men as Caleb Foote, now a Professor of Law at the University of Pennsylvania; Alfred Hassler, for many years editor of the publications of the Fellowship of Reconciliation; James Bristol, then Lutheran minister, recently on the American Friends Service Committee staff; George Houser, one of the eight non-registrants from Union Theological Seminary; Dave Dellinger, another of that company who shocked and did honor to the Seminary; Francis Hall, now with the Bruderhof; Bayard Rustin, one of the editors of *Liberation*, and a key figure in the struggle for racial integration; Ralph DiGia of the War Resisters League; Roy Finch, and others.

A prison is an evil, inhuman place which ravages the spirit of man. Some of the men I knew were then wrestling with agonizing personal problems. Many of them, at one time or another, engaged in hunger strikes against segregation or censorship, and were thrown into solitary. Several of them had wives or sweethearts. They were lonely girls and splendid in their courage and fidelity. They were, the men and the women, like sons and daughters to me, and, as is the case with one's natural children, one longs to help them in specific situations, but most of the time the only thing one can do is believe in them.

One incident which occurred about that time I have often recalled with amusement. I was given permission by the Director of the Federal Bureau of Prisons to visit a number of conscientious objectors then imprisoned in the Federal Institution at Lewisburg, Pennsylvania. The problem of handling people so different from the general run of prisoners, with strong convictions and positive characters, was a difficult one for the authorities. At that time most of the C.O.'s at Lewisburg lived together in a big room where they had a fine opportunity for study, general talk and specific planning about issues which confronted them as individuals or as a group. Instead of being limited to seeing one prisoner at a time with a high desk between us and a guard within hearing distance of anything but a whispered conversation, I was given the unusual opportunity to spend a couple of hours with the men in the big room with no guard nearby, or at least not in sight. We talked, of course, about all sorts of things, but part of the time was spent in discussing the possibility of a fast or a hunger strike, about which a number of them had been thinking for some time. My own contribution to the talk consisted in cautioning that, in the Gandhian philosophy and technique, the hunger strike or fast was a last resort and that motivation and spiritual preparation were of great importance. I left Lewisburg not knowing whether they would go through with the fast and was surprised to read, a day or so later, that it had actually begun. I suppose the Bureau of Prisons officials concluded that I had organized the demonstration; I got no further permits to visit C.O.'s in prison. The circumstantial evidence may well have seemed convincing, but the conclusion was based on a mistake often made in connection with such matters, the mistake of not realizing how impossible it is to "organize" and "lead" a group of conscientious objectors to the well, much less to make them drink. They are not "other-directed" specimens.

That summer I got some distance, perhaps a third of the way, into the reminiscences awakened by the conditions to which I have been alluding. The idea was that in the late summer I should return to New York and take up my work as National Secretary of the Fellowship of Reconciliation—a position which I had assumed in the summer of 1940, after the German blitz attack on Norway, Holland, Belgium, and France, when it became clear that the entry of the Roosevelt administration into open participation in the fighting would be only a matter of time—anticipating that on occasional evenings during the coming months I would work on the manuscript and then go at it again in earnest the following summer.

During the summer of 1945, one of my projects was to take part in a Conference of the Canadian F.O.R. in Toronto and from there, to travel by train to distant Alberta to lecture at what was known as the Alberta School of Religion. The two things I remember about the long trek by train from Toronto around Lake Superior to Calgary were the impressions of overwhelming, inescapable and seemingly boundless space and the casual serving of a big juicy steak at a moderate price in the dining car, at a time when rationing and inflation were putting such things beyond the reach of most people at home.

In the Thirties, peace—even pacifist—sentiment and radical social ideas had been the vogue in Canada, as well as in the United States, and the United Church of Canada actually embraced the pacifist position as the only one compatible with the spirit and teaching of Christ. In that atmosphere the Alberta School of Religion, whose leaders were nearly all convinced and active pacifists, was a respectable and popular institution. Its Summer School, which was its major activity, was housed at the University of Calgary and was attended by a sizeable number of the younger clergy and laity, and able to attract noted lecturers.

When World War II began, public sentiment and official attitudes, both inside and outside the churches, took a sharp turn. With the exception of Richard Roberts, one of the most noted Protestant preachers in the English-speaking world between the Wars, who had been the first Moderator of the United Church of Canada, all or nearly all the well-known pacifist clergy, especially those who had been members of the F.O.R., were driven out of their pulpits, and for some time had serious difficulty in finding any places, however small, where they could practice their ministry.

The Alberta School of Religion nearly foundered in the storm of popular hostility and suspicion toward pacifism. When I went there, in July, 1945, it met in one of the most primitive camps I've ever encountered, twenty miles or so across the prairie from Calgary. The series of lectures I gave was based on the draft of the autobiography which I had composed in the previous summer. I rehearsed my childhood in Holland and youth in Michigan; my conversion to pacifism during World War I; my involvement in the labor movement and some of the historic strikes of the stormy Twenties and Thirties; the brief period of my connection with the Trotskyist movement and my return in 1936 to pacifism.

It happened that the other lecturer at the summer school that year was an Episcopalian clergyman, Joseph Fletcher, who by that time had joined the faculty of the Cambridge (Massachusetts) Episcopal Seminary. In the evening Joe, his wife and I—we had rooms in the shack which presumably was the best on the location— often had hilarious times reminiscing about people and events, or joking about the appointments at the Camp. In the daytime the atmosphere was very different.

Fletcher was a social actionist who made, and is still making, important contributions to the awakening of church people to their social and civic responsibilities. I have not the slightest reason for thinking that he has ever been a Communist or anything but an independent thinker who, whatever the position he might take, stood on his own two feet. Our personal relations have always been friendly. However, his analysis of some developments in the Communist world differed from mine, and he took part at times in peace or other movements which, in my view, were Communist fronts, or at least open to Communist penetration, and in which I felt it was a mistake for pacifists, Christians and democratically minded people generally to participate. As I recounted my own experience with "united fronts" and my analysis of certain aspects of Communism I could sense that Fletcher was inwardly seething.

He made his feelings known to the leaders of the Summer School and it was agreed that we hold an informal session one day after lunch to "have it out." It happened that, not long after we began to talk, the argument focused on Norman Thomas, the well-known Socialist Party leader. Fletcher's animus toward Thomas arose from two sources: Thomas's vigorous and frequent diatribes against Communists and the Soviet Union; and the fact, as Fletcher held, that Thomas was "soft" and uncritical in his attitude toward American capitalism and militarism, and hence prejudiced or blind in his thinking about the Soviet Union and Communism.

I was by no means a thick-and-thin defender of Norman Thomas. I deplored the position of "critical support" of the war which had been taken by him and by the Socialist Party. I still think that one of the tragedies of American politics in our time is that Thomas did not see his way clear to maintaining the pacifist stand, or at least the intransigent anti-war stand, which he took during the first World War. And let me remark here that I am inclined to agree with Thomas that it may well be impossible for him to remain a personal pacifist without the religious faith which he had forty years ago. But it does not seem to me to follow that a clear-cut anti-war stand cannot be taken on political or "socialist" grounds.

While there were also other points at which I could partly go along with Fletcher's strictures, I felt strongly that he—and this was also true of Communists, and practically all Communist sympathizers in those days—had created in his head a caricature of Thomas as a "red-baiter," pro-capitalist, anti-democrat and the rest. I said so at length and with appropriate illustrations. My impression is that most of the Canadian pacifists present wanted to think well of Norman Thomas and were convinced by my eloquence on the subject.

It amuses—though it also outrages—me, that J. Edgar Hoover, the head of the F.B.I., has written of me as one who "has long fronted for Communists." This pronouncement was occasioned by the fact that Thomas and I worked together early in 1957 on a project to have a number of impartial observers present at the Communist Party Convention in February, as we had previously collaborated on a petition to President Eisenhower for amnesty for Communists convicted under the notorious Smith Act. Thomas lost no time in rebuking Hoover for his characterization of me. Communists, and nearly all elements on the "left" in the late Fifties, talked in very different language about Thomas from the way they did in those years.

To get back to Alberta, in July, 1945, a day or two after the episode which I just described, a couple of cars were going to drive from camp to Calgary, returning in time for the evening meeting. I had some thought of going for the ride. After some days of fairly intensive work in an isolated place with a limited group, and without members of the family about, I am likely to feel the urge to walk pavements, see people, buck traffic. But the urge was moderate that day; there was some question as to how much room might be left after those who had to go to town for supplies were seated, and so I was still uncertain. Then a rumor spread—it had been picked up, I think, from a neighbor with a radio, by the camper who got the mail from the box on the main highway—that, a few hours before, an experimental atomic bomb had been exploded somewhere in the United States. So I *had* to go to town to get the news for myself. How could one sit the afternoon out in that lonely spot, perhaps not too unlike the one in which the bomb was tested? How could one rely on the reports of others when they returned hours later?

The long ride into town. The effort to think. The nervous feeling at the pit of the stomach when thinking, or whatever is the proper name for it, becomes visceral. Then the city—the newsstand with *both* papers. Then off into a corner to read and re-read every word. What does it mean? Will there be anything left of Japan, or the world, tomorrow? A year or ten years from now? Shall I rush back to the office in New York? But what to do or say when I get there?

The decision was to remain in camp for the few remaining days of the session and then ride back to the United States, the country which, in a couple of weeks, by the decision of one Harry S Truman, was to catapult the world into the era of atomic war. One of the decisive factors in the world situation today is that it was the United States, "Christian America," which perpetrated the atrocities of Hiroshima and Nagasaki, under circumstances which preclude the plea of "military necessity," for the war had, to all intents and purposes, been won. It was we and not the Nazi swine, as they were called, the Fascist devils, the Japanese militarists or the Russian Communists. No political or moral appraisal of our age is adequate, no attempt to find the answer to its dilemmas and destiny offers hope, which does not take adequate account of that fact.

It provided me with work in the years that followed. So far as writing is concerned, it pushed the autobiography, the attempt to record and evaluate the past, into the background. The book which I was driven to write was one which dealt with Christian pacifism in the atomic age, published by Harper's, in 1947, under the title *Not by Might*.

That I should turn, in a moment of decision, to involvement in action and struggle, from writing an autobiography to writing a "tract for the times," was to follow a pattern which prevailed at all such junctures in my life. It is perhaps high time now to go back to the day early in January, 1885, when that life began and try to trace a part of its course.

As I undertake that effort, I stand aghast at what has happened in my personal life, and in our world, even in that comparatively short span of years since that earlier attempt. It startles me to think that, in that summer of 1945, I was not yet sixty. I did not know in my bones that people reach retirement age and younger men take their place. I did not know either that, when this happens, you just keep on. I did not know in my bones that a being you love and have loved for years on end can die, and that a home can cease to be. I did not then know in my bones that it is possible—just possible—that some day one's own vital powers may fail. Such things are all just talk until they are experienced.

As for the world since 1945, I stand appalled at the list of names that meant either nothing or something innocuous then: Hiroshima; Nagasaki; Bikini; Korea; Dienbienphu; Suez; Hungary; Kenya; Algeria; South Africa; Alger Hiss; McCarthy; Oppenheimer; Japanese fishermen caught in a lethal rain; White Citizens Councils; the H-Bomb; the Intercontinental Ballistics Missile. I, who had so often and so long meditated on war and cried out about its futility, its irrationality, its blasphemy, did not know in my bones even as recently as the spring of 1945 that I should live to see the day when a few professors, none of whom, perhaps, could qualify as a combatant soldier, would sit before intricate machinery in underground laboratories and be able to level the proud cities and the little towns to dust. By the hardly perceptible pressure of their fingers on delicate instruments they can make a shambles of the planet, so that in the minds of those who may survive—assuming they have minds—all those who once claimed the name of warrior—Sumacheril, Attila, Genghis Khan, Napoleon, Hitler, the scourges of mankind, the butchers of history—will seem mere tyros in comparison. How far, far away is all this in years, and in more subtle and profound respects, from a little provincial city in Holland in 1885? How long the journey and to what end?

Part Two

A short time after the advent of the era of nuclear weapons, I wrote, with the eye of imagination fixed upon the physical and psychological evils the scientists, military men and politicians were releasing on mankind: "This is the terror by night, the arrow that flieth by day, the pestilence that stalketh in the darkness, the destruction that wasteth at noonday. This is the abomination of desolation, the great tribulation such as hath not been seen from the beginning of the world until now. This perchance is the Beast of the Apocalypse, who seemed to the ecstatic seer to be leopard, bear, lion and dragon in one, after whom the whole earth wondered and worshipped in terror, crying, 'Who is like unto the Beast? And who is able to war with him?'"

Of the role of the United States in launching this apocalyptic horror upon the world, I wrote at that time: "It has fallen upon this 'Christian' nation, incessantly declaiming against the perpetrators of atrocities, and still doing so, to perpetrate the ultimate atomic atrocity—needlessly*—and so to remove all restraint upon atrocity. This is the logic of the atrocious means. With fatal precision, the means of war become more destructive of physical life as well as of moral standards and spiritual values."

As I write now, in the summer of 1957, I find no reason to change anything in these sentences. The world is all too obviously confronted with the threat of mass annihilation, the poisoning of its air, water, soil and food supplies, perhaps the initiation of mutations which will produce repulsive physical and mental deformities in our children's children, if there be any such. Thus, in this summer of 1957, I am occupied with problems relating to the attitude of

* Needlessly in the sense that the Germans had not come anywhere near producing an atomic weapon, and some of the leading German physicists, including Otto Hahn himself, were deliberately steering research under the Nazis away from that objective. Needlessly also in the sense that the war against Japan had for practical purposes been won before the bombs were dropped on Hiroshima and Nagasaki, so that there was no desperate last ditch situation to render plausible, by ordinary military standards, resort to a desperate measure.

14

the churches toward nuclear war, as that attitude may find expression in meetings of the Central Committee of the World Council of Churches at New Haven; with plans for Gandhian action at the nuclear testing grounds in Nevada when the Hiroshima anniversary rolls around, with hot discussion as to what the ferment in the Communist movement throughout the world may mean for peace and the possibility of a free society on earth, if maintenance of peace makes such a society at least a possibility.

Since I am trying to write an autobiography, the question that intrigues me at the moment is: what is the connection between me today and the baby who was born early in January of 1885 in a small town named Zierikzee, in the province of Zeeland in the Netherlands, to whom his parents, Martin Muste and Adriana Jonker, gave the sonorous name Abraham Johannes?

My mother more than once in later years remarked that during the first year of my existence I cried virtually without interruption all day but slept like a top all night. This was a pattern which I have in some sense followed most of my life, since I am usually sounding off about something a good part of every day and practically never have any trouble about sleeping at night.

As for Zierikzee, when in later years I went back to the Netherlands and told Dutch friends, in answer to their questions, that I was born in Zierikzee, they invariably exclaimed: "Not Zierikzee!" and then let go with a hearty laugh. It seems that Zierikzee is a sort of equivalent of our Podunk. There is in fact a popular song in the Dutch night clubs, the chorus of which starts with "I was born in Zierikzee." It sounds much more tuneful and jocular in Dutch than in English.

My general impression of my early childhood is that it was a happy one—I do not have any conscious memories of extreme terror or desolation such as many children experience. The half dozen incidents during the six years before we emigrated which are vivid in my memory, and which I relive whenever I think of them, are not of that kind, though one of them, as I shall presently relate, was poignant and very painful. If I went to school in those years or was taken to church or taught to say my prayers, I don't remember it.

My father was coachman to a family belonging to the provincial nobility. It was part of his job to bring porridge early in the morning from a communal kitchen, where some food was prepared for well-to-do families, to the home of his employer. When his other duties made this difficult, I was commandeered, at the age of five, or possibly earlier, to fetch the porridge in the morning twilight to the back door of what seemed to me a palace. There was a feeling of considerable but not too intense excitement associated with having to find my way from home to communal kitchen to the palatial residence in the semi-darkness of winter mornings, carrying what was for me a fairly heavy container.

There is a delectable memory of going to some body of water, frozen over in winter, watching the skaters in what seemed to me lovely dances, and drinking a cup of hot chocolate at a stand on the shore.

Altogether unexpectedly, on a morning in early spring, hastening home from some errand, I came upon what seemed to me—and indeed has ever since—more like a painting by a Flemish, Italian or Spanish artist than a real life scene. Seated on a low projection against the wall of a red brick house drenched in sunshine was a black-haired, very dark-skinned mother, probably a Gypsy, nursing a baby at her breast, with a boy of about two, very dark and therefore exotic to me, yet attractive and handsome, standing at her side and leaning against her. The combination of the mother, the children, the soothing warmth, the bright sunlight out of a blue sky, stirred a deep, sensuous delight. I think I can also make out that there was a sort of revelation that people can be strange and in a sense terrifying—where had they come from and what were they up to and where was the man?—yet somehow beautiful and not really terrifying.

It may well have been the same spring, at Easter or Whitsuntide, when my mother sent me out with my sister, a year my junior, dressed in our Sunday best, to promenade around a square in the more fashionable part of the town, through the middle of which, of course, ran a canal. I was carrying a little cane. I have no recollection of getting prepared for the promenade, which must have been quite an operation, or of the walk to that square, or how we got home. But the sensation of being at a certain point in that square, a young gentleman with his sister at his side, properly equipped with a cane, and so "belonging" to "society," was so vivid that thirty years later when I first revisited Holland I was able to go back unerringly to that exact spot.

A St. Nicholas Day eve stands out in my memory. We had really only one room to live in, with alcoves off that room for sleeping purposes. There was a staircase at one side leading to an attic which we never used. Santa Claus was to come down this staircase. Father, my sister and I were in the room, expectantly waiting. Mother was not there, which was, of course, very unusual. As it lies in my memory, there was a kind of understanding that Santa Claus would turn out to be mother and it was this, and not some untoward occasion, which accounted for her absence. Could one be sure, however, that Santa Claus would really come and not skip us and at the same time that mother would turn out to be Santa Claus so that we would not be without her and she could enjoy the feast with us? Presently, there was some commotion on the stair and some baked concoctions, which we called "pepper nuts"—actually they were spiced with cinnamon—began rolling down the stairs and we pounced upon them. Then Santa Claus himself came stomping down the stairs, distributing gifts. He left by the front door and in a moment or two mother came back laughing happily. It was a most stimulating and yet soothing sensation to have a real Santa Claus and a real mother at the same time and in the same person.

The only other incident of this period which I recall vividly, apart from the walk on the dike to which I referred before, is of a very different character. Not long before we emigrated to America, someone gave me a pet bird. We had it only an hour or so when somehow it got out of the cage we had improvised for it. It was in a long, narrow room with a counter running along one side. It had been used as a store before we moved in but was now empty, not being suitable for living purposes. The back door led into our living room, the front door was on the street. There was excitement among the children in the neighborhood when it was known that the bird was flying about in the room. My special playmate from across the street, in his excitement, opened the front door just a crack to have a better view of the bird darting about the room. The bird, of course, flew straight for the crack. The boy instinctively pulled the door shut, but a split second too late. The bird was caught in the door, and when he opened the door again to release the trapped bird, it fell crushed and dead at our feet.

For a moment I was furious and wanted to lash out at my playmate. Then everything else was blotted out by grief over the stricken bird, pity for the creature hurt, the creature that had lived and lived no more.

I do not know what relation, if any, there may be between this incident and the reaction of my whole childish being toward it, and the pacifist convictions of my later years. It is often said that pacifism, or conscientious objection to war, is based upon a literalistic use of the command, "Thou shalt not kill," as if it were an order from outside oneself, an easy rule with which to dispose of a complex problem. There have been pacifists of whom that could be said. But is there not behind the commandment of stone or of paper a command written on the heart and issuing from the heart's own awareness of the preciousness, the wonder of all life and the consequent irrationality and pity of anything that wounds and mutilates a living creature and needlessly snuffs out its life, which issues in that "reverence for life" to which Albert Schweitzer has summoned this generation so horribly addicted to violence?

It was years after the stricken bird lay at my feet that I came to know the lines which A. E. (George Russell), the Irish poet, wrote about one of the goddesses in the old Gaelic pantheon. He has her say about herself:

> *I am the heartbreak over fallen things,*
> *The sudden gentleness that stays the blow,*
> *And I am in the kiss that foemen give*
> *Pausing in battle; and in the tears that fall*
> *Over the vanquished foe; and in the highest*
> *Among the Danaan gods I am the last counsel*
> *Of mercy in their hearts, when they mete judgment*
> *From a thousand starry thrones.*

This is by no means the only place in great literature where we encounter descriptions of the inner commandment of compassion. It is at the heart of the Christian and Buddhist gospels. It is to be found in such unexpected places as Homer's *Iliad,* as Simone Weil* reminds us: "The purest triumph of love, the crowning grace of war, is the friendship that floods the hearts of mortal enemies. Before it the distance between benefactor and suppliant, between victor and vanquished, shrinks to nothing." Whereupon she quotes the passage in which Priam and Achilles talk and gaze upon each other, until "they were satisfied with contemplation of each other."

It was about the time of the death of the pet bird that life in our family entered a period of continuous excitement. Four of my mother's brothers, in the period before or just after my birth, had

---

* *The Iliad, or The Poem of Force,* an article which appeared in the November 1945 issue of Dwight MacDonald's *Politics,* and is now available as a Pendle Hill pamphlet.

moved their families to the United States. They had been poorly paid agricultural laborers in Zeeland. They had not taken up farming in America, but small businesses—groceries, drugs, scrap metal —in Grand Rapids, Michigan, where, in the decades since 1847, thousands of Hollanders had settled. All four of them had done fairly well and were making a much better living than would have been possible in the Netherlands at that time.

Having achieved a measure of security for themselves, they considered the plight of their youngest and favorite sister, my mother, and one of them paid us a visit and proposed that our family emigrate. The brothers were ready to finance the trip. I know from conversations that took place after we had settled in this country that the two arguments against undertaking the venture that weighed most heavily with my parents were leaving the country of their birth and of their fathers, and a doubt as to whether they would ever be able to pay back the (to them) huge loan which my uncles were prepared to make.

All that I remember, however, of the weeks before we embarked on the journey is the atmosphere of excitement that prevailed, in which anxiety, especially on the part of my mother, played a large part, but which was nevertheless somehow welcome. From that time dates my awareness of the fact that I was the oldest child and that an effort was being made to make me understand what my two sisters and my brother were too young to be taken in on, namely that we were entering on a hazardous journey, an awesome undertaking. This was accompanied by a feeling that, although I was a child, I also partly belonged with my parents in carrying responsibility for the younger children.

Suddenly one afternoon in January, 1891, that I remember only as noise, loud talk, seemingly endless running about of neighbors, a journey into darkness took place. We moved out of our house and somehow got to a dock where lay a great steamer which I took for granted was to take us to America. Here I again was engulfed by noise and by people who towered high above me and were perpetually shoving us around—where to I do not recall. I hear whistles, the rattling of chains. I am aware the boat is moving. No doubt I slept.

The boat was actually a small steamer plying the waters which surround the islands which compose the province of Zeeland. It did not take us to America but to Rotterdam. I do not recall the debarking from the small steamer but somehow by that time I had become accustomed in large measure to an environment which was very different from the small town, the quiet streets and the still quieter home in which I had spent my childhood. The sense of a continuous buzzing in my little head, which had dominated the day before, was gone. I could distinguish sounds; there were many more people than I had ever seen before, but they were no longer looming hulks; I could distinguish between them; their hurrying about no longer seemed aimless. I was in a city; I was in the big world; and I was less afraid than excited. I liked to be there.

We embarked on an old Holland-America Line steamer named Obdam which took nearly two weeks in a stormy January to reach Hoboken. We traveled, of course, in the steerage. Families staked out preserves for themselves on the platforms, one above another, which served as beds. Those who were near the wall, as we were, climbed over the families between them and the aisle when the occasion arose. Occasionally soup was passed out, but the migrants had brought their own supplies of bread and cheese with them and, in some instances, cakes, which they occasionally shared with families like ours who had no cakes. Again, it was all new experience; it was adventure and it was to my liking.

There was only one qualification. Mother became ill. Early in the voyage she was removed to the ship's hospital. A vivid memory is of one of the last days of the journey. The storm had abated. My father took me on the deck with him. The ship was still rolling. The sky was not yet clear. The ocean was a blur. We made our way to a window, where my mother's face appeared. We could converse a little. She was not too ill to smile. There was a feeling that everything was going to be all right. It must have dominated the hours that followed very powerfully, because I have not been able to bring to the surface any definite memories of the end of the voyage or the debarkation in Hoboken or the transfer to a hospital on an island in New York harbor, where we were kept for nearly a month because mother was still not well enough to undertake the journey to Grand Rapids.

Here the photograph on the plate of memory becomes clear again. Mother is in one wing of the building. Father and the children are in another, but we know she is near by. The harbor is beautiful. Here I consciously experience for the first time the sensation of the beauty of scenery composed of water, island, and shore. Little tugboats ceaselessly plied the blue waters and left a white wake. We called them "doctors' boats," because it was in a tug that a doctor came each day to see the patients on our island.

Inside the hospital there was delicious food, and more than enough of it. There were corridors in which to play and, as far as my recollection goes, our play was uninhibited. We had, however, been strictly brought up, and I am quite confident we were not noisy.

In our section of the hospital there was an attendant whose name was John. We did not understand his English, nor he our Dutch, but we were friends. John learned that my first name was Abraham. So, when he appeared in the morning, he said, "Hello, Abraham Lincoln," and when he left in the evening it was, "Goodnight, Abraham Lincoln."

We did not know whether Abraham Lincoln was the name of a gadget, a town, or a person dead or alive. It was natural that one of the things we did when we got settled in Michigan was to find out. So it came about that early in life I began to read everything by and about Lincoln that I could lay my hands on. I learned about the boy studying by the light of the hearth in the log cabin. I followed him on the trip down the Mississippi River and I heard him say when he saw a slave sold on the block at New Orleans: "By God, if ever I get a chance to hit that thing, I'll hit it and hit it hard."

Early I learned to chant: "Four score and seven years ago our fathers brought forth upon this continent a new nation, conceived in liberty and dedicated to the proposition that all men are created equal."

In time I learned, of course, about certain distinctions between Lincoln the myth and Lincoln the human being, between the "American Dream" and the reality. Nevertheless, being called "Abraham Lincoln" by John on the island in New York harbor, and passing my youth in Michigan, next door to Illinois, not far from Springfield, in the 1890's when the economy of the Middle West was of course pretty far removed from that of 1865, but when the Middle West, in its own imagination and feeling, still lived in the days of John Brown, the Emancipation Proclamation, the martyred President—all this is part of my inmost being.

There came a morning when mother was well and we all got into a "doctor's boat" and were taken to Castle Garden, which was then the immigrant station, at Battery Park, New York. A later generation knew the building as the Aquarium.

Father left for Hoboken to reclaim the baggage which had been left in storage there. We waited for his return anxiously as the day wore on. What might not have happened to him in this strange land? May it have been a mistake to undertake this journey into the unknown? But no; toward evening father returned, the business taken care of.

Then we were on a train—all night and all the next day and, because of February fog and rain, not much lighter in the day than in the night. I was sick on the train as I had not been on the ocean.

Then, in the late afternoon, we stood on the platform of the Grand Trunk Railway station in the east end of Grand Rapids, where I lived for a dozen years, my parents for over four decades, my sisters to this day. Uncles and cousins are there to greet us. In a pouring rain we drive in a carriage to the home of an uncle. The rain is not so important as the carriage—in America even ordinary people may have their own carriages and are not confined to being someone's coachman if they want to ride and not walk.

Now we are in a warm, brightly lighted room at the home of an uncle. We are eating supper. My mother laughs happily at her brother's jokes. This I recall, but also that there were cousins, girls a few years older than I, who made much of me. By that time the younger children were probably sound asleep. The cousins told me the English words for "table," "chair" and so on, and were delighted when I imitated them precisely. They made me feel that I was the Traveler they had been waiting for.

So the first journey into the unknown had a happy ending. The new country was livable, hospitable, even exciting.

Part Three

You are a boy six years old and you are living on Quimby Street in Grand Rapids, Michigan. The drab frame house is set back in a yard, unlike the houses in Holland, which front directly on the street. In the back there is a considerable garden in which potatoes are planted. There is a street which seems very wide, in contrast to the narrow Dutch streets, and very dusty. There is a wooden sidewalk, but the housewives do not go out to scrub it on their hands and knees. A hundred yards or so to the west the Grand Trunk railroad trains clamor over the crossing, heading for the bridge over the Grand River. Beyond the railroad track is the factory, where your father luckily got a job, a day or two after arriving in the town, at six dollars a week for a sixty-hour week. These are the "hard times" of the early Eighteen Nineties.

We had made the long journey in space from a provincial town in Holland to the Middle West of the United States. I now had to make that other kind of journey—in time—from one language, allegiance, mental environment and culture to another.

Naturally, I did not then reflect upon these matters. The incidents and excitements of the voyage were a pleasing and stimulating memory but not subject matter for philosophizing or planning the course of my future life. Similarly, the events which I am about to recount were at the time experienced but not deliberately or systematically reflected upon. As I look back, however, I am certain that the experience of emigration and immigration, coming so near the beginning of my life, had a good deal to do with shaping its entire pattern and determining my basic attitudes toward the human experience. I think that this is true in spite of the fact that the concept of life which I held in my youth was essentially conservative and static.

The concept of history as movement toward a goal is deeply imbedded in the thinking of Western man. Its source is primarily Hebraic. Abraham is not only the progenitor of Israel but "the father of many peoples." He stands at the beginning of both profane and sacred history because in obedience to divine command he left the city of his ancestors. Unquestionably, this represents a great turning point in man's history. It is in one sense the greatest revolution of all, since it is the father of revolutions and of the revolutionary concept of history as the expression of God at work. History and the daily life of man are, therefore, real and not illusory. If God is to be found at all, He must be found here. Men become co-workers, co-creators, and they are in movement toward a goal.

There had, of course, been nomadic wanderings before Abraham. But they were essentially movements of a geographical character. The tribe moved as a tribe and fought as a tribe, for the immediate purpose of obtaining forage for the flocks. When men settled down, cultivated land, and built cities, they conceived of their society as having been founded by the gods of the place or by divine ancestors. The pattern of life was fixed, as if in the nature of things. The individual could hardly conceive of himself or be conceived of by others as having an existence outside this pattern. His destiny and duty were to remain in the city of his birth so that his sons after him could inherit this same fixed and sacred pattern.

But with Abraham the divine command becomes radically different. What makes a man the true servant of the Most High is that he does not remain in the place of his birth. It has its sacredness and importance but as a point of departure. Through Abraham, man in the Hebraic tradition came to know that his destiny and his God are not ties which bind and confine him. They are ahead of him and are drawing him outward and onward. The crucial thing about men, or societies, is not where they came from but where they are going. The symbol of the Emigrant is born.

What is of even more significance about Abraham than the fact that he emigrated from Ur of the Chaldees is that there was no city, no society or community for him to move into. Had his journey been simply a geographical one to another Ur with another name, it would have constituted no part of the source of dynamic Western civilization.

The fact is that Abraham "went out, not knowing whither he went." He was a fool and a gambler. But he was not a little fool; rather he was a big one, whose foolishness consisted in taking on a Herculean task. He gambled for stakes of such a nature that the gambling itself became the pattern of human history. It created Western society and is still its lifeblood and its reason for existence.

Abraham went out looking for a city which existed—and yet

had to be brought into existence. It was the perfect and holy city—which had to be built and whose "builder and maker is God." Precisely because it was God who built the city, it could be built only by Abraham's faith and labor.

The creative movement in history is not from any city-which-is to another city-which-is. The reality is not what men tend to call the real. Insofar as it is fixed and has a fixating or binding effect on men or societies, it is already becoming unreal and insubstantial. What matters is the movement from the unreal, because unrealized, city-which-is to the city-which-is-to-be, which is more real because the potentiality of realization and completion remains. The city of this world, says Augustine in a memorable passage, "seems to be able to dominate and destroy everything, but it is itself dominated and destroyed by its own lust for power." He might have said, by its own will to exist as it is, to arrogate to itself a substantiality which never belongs to what is but only to what may be. The normative principle, to use a phrase of Martin Buber's, is more real and will prove itself more potent than "the hard soil of political reality" into which it so often seems to attempt to drive its plowshares in vain.

Man the Emigrant is, then, an Immigrant into the city-which-is-to-be. He is "constrained" by that which he has yet to bring into existence. Revolution is permanent, in a much deeper sense than Trotsky realized. Trotsky presumably conceived of *his* "permanent revolution" as the one to end all revolutions.

I shall not dwell on how great a part some such vision as this has played in the development of Western Europe and in the vast movement of the Western European peoples out of the "old world," not only into the Americas but into the rest of the world. There is a passage in the diaries of Christopher Columbus which furnishes a very striking illustration of the point. He says that what impelled him on his voyage over the unexplored deep was not the calculations of the astronomers or the speculations of the philosophers or any other cause, but only "the prophecy of Isaiah that there shall be a new heaven and a new earth in which righteousness dwelleth."

Nor shall I dwell on the extent to which certain aspects of Marxist thought grow out of this concept of history. Up to a point we have a precise and beautiful formulation of the concept in Engels' phrase about the leap from the kingdom of necessity into the realm of freedom, which is the "inevitable" outcome of the historical process—the gates of hell, i.e., of "necessity," shall not prevail against it—but which, paradoxically, must be apprehended by the faith of men and brought to pass by their devotion and suffering.

For the present there is one other aspect of the experience of migration or transition which must be touched upon because of its bearing on my own development. When a man moves from one political, cultural, spiritual environment into another, he does not move out of the old or shed it like a garment. It is forever a part of him. Were he to be completely severed from it he would be a mental cripple, a victim of amnesia. Nor does one put on a new culture in the way one pulls on a new sweater. One grows into it as he builds it. The decisive question is whether there is movement in the direction of the new.

It is a commonplace that in the case of societies considerable alterations may take place in a relatively quiet and undramatic fashion, almost "in a fit of absent-mindedness," as the British Empire is said to have been acquired. In other cases, the transition is profoundly traumatic in character.

The same is true of individuals in their migrations. There are those who are too old when they move or are moved. Their spirits never live where their bodies exist. There are those who are forced out of their original homes by evil eruptions such as have been so common in this century. They, for the most part, never are Emigrants in the true sense since they do not have the complementary experience of Immigration. They are the permanent Exiles. If they are numerous, they remain indigestible elements in the society into which they have been forcibly thrust. If they come to a country like the United States, they are likely, it seems to me, to idealize it. A friend of mine recently characterized a new addition to the Society of Friends as "an over-convinced Quaker." The people I am thinking of are "over-convinced Americans"; and this means that culturally and spiritually they exist in, or rather imagine they are part of, an America which does not exist. They are, therefore, not immigrants as others of the same race who migrated in other days may well have been.

My own experience of absorption into the "new world" was certainly a pleasant and stimulating sensation. As I have looked back upon it and sought to understand its influence on my character and destiny, it has also seemed to me singularly fortunate. It came, of course, at an early age when one is impressionable and to some extent aware of what is taking place—for example, that one speaks a different language, is an object of curiosity, an outsider in some measure—and is also malleable. The ocean voyage had had its enigmas, its apprehensions, its quality of near terror and at times its feeling of bewilderment at being carried along one knew not whither. Yet it had ended well. A place to settle had been found which seemed advantageous compared with the place we had left behind. Might not this experience mark voyagings of another kind than geographical?

The Hollanders who settled in the Middle West in the decades before World War I formed a fairly numerous group in Grand Rapids (without, however, making it a predominantly Dutch center). With the rarest of exceptions, every Dutch family belonged to a church, the Reformed or Christian Reformed, to which it had belonged in the old country. The services and the preaching were all in Dutch.

In the larger population in Grand Rapids the Dutch constituted a lower stratum. The owners of the furniture factories and saw mills were of English stock. Until after the first World War, Hollanders were the cheap labor in the factories, the small shopkeepers in the outlying parts of town, the poor farmers on the land. In my early youth it was still an event when a girl from one of the Dutch families, who well may have been born in the United States, became a clerk in one of the fashionable department stores downtown. The girl's family, for its part, still wondered whether it would not have been better if she had remained in domestic service instead of, for a little more money and a lot more prestige, being exposed to all the lures of life in the English-speaking stratum of the town. Had not their Calvinistic God assigned them their place as hewers of wood, though often highly skilled ones, and would it not be best for the children to remain close to the fold of their humble elect?

There was no semblance of a ghetto, of course. There was no barrier of culture as there was to be later with immigrants from Eastern Europe, and no barrier of color as with Negroes or Asians. The Dutch were considered especially desirable immigrants. Almost without exception they were sober and industrious. Many of them became skillful cabinet makers. They were allergic to unions or "agitators" of any kind.

They were not numerous enough, nor did they have the kind of history or cultural pattern which led them to want to perpetuate a separate Dutch minority over and against the American nation which to them was, in spite of such doubts as I have suggested, a land of opportunity and freedom, the land to which God had led the Pilgrim fathers, a land of peace where youth was not conscripted, and a Christian land, though unfortunately not entirely peopled by orthodox Calvinists.

It was in line with common practice among the Hollanders of Michigan that my father took out his first papers as soon as he was eligible and became a citizen at the earliest opportunity in time to cast his vote for William McKinley in the crucial election of 1896. Voting Republican is a habit which the descendants of that generation who have remained in Michigan still have. In my own youth, one no more thought that a church member could vote the Democratic ticket than that he could beat his wife, or steal, or have extramarital sexual relations.

My brother, sisters and I did not go through the process of naturalization as an act of our own; we were naturalized (in my case at the age of eleven) by my father's act. I remember that it was a step which he did not take lightly. To both him and my mother, who in those days, of course, had no vote, it was a matter for anxious discussion and prayer whether it was the will of God that he forswear allegiance to Queen Wilhelmina and "brave little Holland." But the deed was done, and at the earliest possible moment. Indeed, at that moment, only a little more than five years after landing there, they felt so identified with the new country that I can remember my mother's exclamation of despair when early in the evening of Election Day, before my father got home from work, a newsboy selling an early election extra shouted that Bryan had been elected. Nearly twenty years later, on the afternoon in August, 1914, when the first World War broke out in Europe, one of the old Dutch women sitting on my parents' porch sagely remarked that we could expect such things to happen under a Democratic president.

On this level of transition from one political and cultural home into another, the changes were real and in a sense momentous. There were moments which had a sharp edge to them. I was bruised. But I was spared devastating experiences. What I moved into proved good. The transition spelled growth and self-expression. What lay ahead was not anything one needed to fear in any ultimate sense. What one had to fear was the refusal to move on because of fear or perhaps indifference.

This kind of experience is not so easy or "natural" that one seeks it for itself, and I do not think I welcome change for the sake of being in motion, any more than I have ever cared to travel for the sake of traveling or have ever, for more than very short periods, been a tourist. I may, of course, be mistaken on these points, but the fact is that I have never felt bitter or contemptuous toward that which I have in a sense left behind—certainly not toward people whose views I no longer shared. I suppose I feel that the old was once a part of me; why should I deny or resent it or even be oblivious to it? Where decision is to be made, one's allegiance should be to the city which is to be, the experience ahead. The peril is *not* to move when the new situation develops, the new insight dawns, the new experiment becomes possible. Had my actual experience of transition been either appreciably easier or harder than it was, my basic attitudes might also—so it seems to me—have been different.

My formal schooling began, soon after our arrival in Grand Rapids, in a Reformed Church parochial school run by a somewhat rotund schoolmaster about whom I had the feeling that he was, as I would subsequently have put it, a stuffed shirt. There are two things I remember easily about that school. One is that we were put to memorizing all the verses of the metrical version of Psalm 119, which was chosen because it is the longest of all the Psalms. This suffices to indicate the pedagogical principles which prevailed in this institution of safe and sacred learning. The other memory has to do with one of the older boys in the school, a lad of nine or ten. He was at that tender age distinguished among us because he chewed tobacco. For some reason he had taken a liking to me and I felt that in him I had a sort of protector. One afternoon when we were going out of school he offered me a chew from his plug of tobacco. There may have been an admixture of devilishness with his generosity and a hope that he might witness my discomfiture. If so, he was disappointed. With my urge to be obliging to anyone who is nice to me, I took the chew, but at the same time took off briskly for home. It was not long before I had to seek relief for my stomach behind a lumber pile. When I reached home, Mother remarked on my paleness. I indicated ignorance of any reason for this condition. By supper time I had a near normal appetite, so the incident passed off without further ado.

In a year or two, when my sister was old enough to go to school, we were sent to the nearby public school. The reason was undoubtedly that my parents preferred free public education, despite its non-religious character, to paying the fees at the parochial school for more than one child. Nor did we have to go to a school where Dutch was spoken in order to get along. The fact is that I do not have the slightest recollection of a time after arrival in Grand Rapids when I could not speak English, though there must have been an interval when this was the case. From the time I started in the public school I was the best speller and reader in the class, partly no doubt because in the beginning I had had to concentrate. The teachers made something of this, which served to increase my interest in school.

School was an utter fascination. That apparently there would never be an end of things to learn frequently produced a state of delightful intoxication. I learned with the rapture of the explorer, "silent upon a peak in Darien," that, when I had graduated from the eighth grade, there would be awesome subjects ahead, like algebra, physiology, geology, psychology, not to mention the ultimate wonderlands of theology, predestination, apologetics, eschatology. The words themselves were blessed.

School never started too early in the morning for my taste. The school day always seemed to rush by. The start of vacation was in its way an occasion, but the opening day of school after Labor Day was a much more joyful and momentous one. My impression of my public school teachers is that they knew their business; their classrooms were orderly; they knew how to handle children. They certainly inspired me.

After living for a year or two in the drab frame house we moved across the Grand Trunk railway tracks into a house which belonged to the owners of the furniture factory after whom Quimby Street was named and for whom father drove a team, hauling logs and delivering lumber. Directly across the street was one of the finer mansions in the city, the home of the Quimby family. To the west and on the same side of the street was the sprawling one-story mill from which the music and the lovely smell of lumber being sawed and planed came all day long. Quimby Street came to an end at Canal Street. The considerable strip of land between Canal Street and the Grand River was occupied by the company's lumber-yard, stable and dry kiln.

The Quimby family, in those days, consisted of the elderly and stately widow of the founder of the business; a spinster daughter named Ethel; another daughter, Mrs. Morley, a widow; her son, Lawrence, a handsome youth older than I; and Irving Quimby, an orphan of about my age who was being brought up by his grandmother, the founder's widow. Mrs. Morley was the manager of the factory and, I have no doubt, of the family.

Irving Quimby did not go to public school, at least at that time. He was being tutored by Aunt Ethel. No other family of his social set lived in that part of town. The only available playmates for him were my brother and I. My recollection of the relationship is that Mrs. Morley gave my father to understand that he was under no obligation but that it would be appreciated if Irving were permitted sometimes to come across the street and play in our yard. I always had the feeling that we were doing Irving a favor, and he certainly never gave the impression that he felt that he was condescending in playing with us. He was shy and clumsy at games at which my brother and I were adept.

Irving tended to become tired or bored and took to inviting me over to the mansion in the late afternoon to keep him company. The first time the invitation was extended my mother told me that of course I could not go; the Quimbys would be angry at the intrusion of the teamster's son. I realized afterward that she was afraid that father would be fired for such presumption on our part. But somehow, presumably via Mrs. Morley, word came that if my parents would let me go, it would be not only quite proper but a real kindness.

So, one day I ascended the long flight of steps leading up to the first floor of "the big house." Irving and I turned into a large room at the left, which was the library, and which had shelves upon shelves of books. Irving suggested a book of stories about life at Princeton. This was the first university I knew by name. I have very pleasant, if very vague, memories of the stories, and I still root for Princeton football teams against Yale or Harvard because of those tales.

Soon, however, I found for myself a greater treasure. There were bound volumes of *Harper's* and *Century*, which had been running series of articles on the battles of the Civil War.

For me, as a result of the experience described in the first installment, the Civil War was Lincoln's War. Breathlessly, day after day, I followed the accounts of the battles, marches, sieges. Though the figure of Lincoln and the concept of freeing the slaves dominated the panorama as a whole, I do not remember that I thought of the Northern soldiers as heroes and of the Southern as villains. There were heroes and villains on both sides, but the distinction I made was mainly between the more romantic and the less romantic figures. But this distinction was not really important. The main impression was of a drama of epic proportions being enacted before my eyes.

As I think back, I can still hear the names of battles ringing in my ears: Antietam; the Wilderness; Bull Run; Fredericksburg; Gettysburg; Vicksburg; the battle between the Monitor and the Merrimac; Chickamauga. I can still recall Sheridan riding through the Shenandoah Valley, leaving behind not enough food to keep a crow alive, and Sherman's March to the Sea.

Daily the bugles sounded. Nightly the songs went through my youthful mind, sometimes mingled with the more martial psalms. I marched through Georgia. I witnessed "the trampling out the vintage where the grapes of wrath are stored." I heard the summons: "O be swift my soul to answer Him; be jubilant my feet!" I looked at the men that "are tenting tonight on the old campground" and into their "hearts that are weary tonight wishing for the war to cease."

Such scenes and sounds came back to me in later years when I read Whitman's Civil War poems or Stephen Vincent Benet's magnificent *John Brown's Body*.

In those days I began to take notice of the veterans from the Old Soldiers Home, which was located a mile or so to the north of where we lived. After the noon-day meal, many of them walked the three miles from the Home to what we called downtown. Their route lay partly along the same street that I used going from home to the afternoon session at the North Ionia Street School. I tried each day to summon my courage to speak to one of these awesome figures. When I did, I was usually grumpily rebuffed and this was hard to understand; why should they not be eager to speak of the glorious battles they had fought? Occasionally, one of them talked: "Yes, I lost a leg at Chickamauga," and proceeded to spin a tale. What a day that was!

It was to be quite a few years before I knew that what my heroes went downtown for was booze, and that veterans of wars are not always, not nearly always, heroic noblemen who volunteered to lay down their lives that some great cause might not perish from the earth.

The moral of all this may be that there is no telling what goes into the education of a pacifist.

Part Four

During the past weeks, while I have been looking backward into my experiences as a boy of twelve, explosions have rocked several of the worlds in which I was beginning to develop an interest then, an interest which led to deep involvement in later years.

The Russians, Communists to boot, have beaten the United States in the very realm where Americans were smugly convinced that nobody could teach them anything. They have launched a satellite, their sputnik, into outer space. In so doing they have demonstrated that they are ahead of the United States in at least one crucial aspect of military technology. Furthermore, whatever the relationships of power may be, it is clear that the whole world has been catapulted into the era of "push-button warfare," i.e., of ultimate insecurity.

In another field, what is happening in Little Rock is a startling reminder that the Civil War is not something safely contained in the past. The mask has been torn from the deep-seated racial fears and prejudices which afflict many people in all sections of the country. In the confusion and anguish of the moment, people in Little Rock were called to prayer. There were those who prayed to the God of Law and Order that quiet might prevail and the decrees of the Supreme Court be carried out. There was apparently no clear call to prayer to the God who brought his people out of the land of Egypt, out of the house of bondage and warned: "Thou shalt have no other God before me." No prayer, that is, that the moral sickness and shame of prejudice and segregation might be cut out of our hearts.

In still another field, the press reported on the convention of one of the largest and most powerful unions in the country—the Teamsters. The city authorities of Miami, a Florida resort which has become a favorite location for labor union conventions at which the spokesmen of the proletariat gather, openly suspended their policy of keeping well-known gangsters out of the city for the duration of the convention. When the convention was over, and

their union duties were performed by electing James Hoffa to succeed David Beck as union president, the gangsters were given thirty-
six hours to clear out.

The contrast between the world of six decades ago, which
seemed "to lie before us so various, so beautiful, so new," and
today's world is in many ways so vast that one questions whether
there is any comprehensible relationship between the two and
whether any attempt to articulate a relationship can lead to anything but frustration. Moreover, today's world, not least in America, is sick and in some danger of cracking apart. What does the
life of the individual and the attempt to reflect upon it mean in this
context? A friend passing through an emotional crisis writes: "I
begin this on the day the man-made moon is launched, and I have
just heard its beep on the radio. I am staggered by the gap which
exists between our scientific and our self-knowledge—almost to the
point of thinking we might as well sweep our little problem under
the rug and forget it. What does it matter!"

The qualifying adverb is there, however, "*almost*," but not
quite, at the point of thinking that the attempt at understanding and
communication does not matter. I am indeed persuaded that it would
be enlightening and salutary for Americans today to contemplate
America's image of itself at the turn of the century and immediately
thereafter. I shall attempt to delineate that image, and provide
glimpses of myself, on whose mind that image was imprinted.

I surmise that in the life of every child there are incidents which
reveal a deep-seated behavior pattern; in a crucial and unanticipated
moment the child does what he does without having had time or
often even the inclination to reflect and plan, because this is the
way he is made. With minor alterations, this is the way he will find
he always has to behave.

Such an incident occurred when I was eleven and in the seventh
grade in public school. One afternoon, the big boy in the class, who
was also something of a bully, was called to the front by the teacher
to be reprimanded for some shenanigan. His seat was in the back
row. As he passed my seat, near the front, I surreptitiously stuck out
my foot. He stumbled over it and barely avoided landing in a heap
at the teacher's feet. She had not seen my foot sticking out and
would not easily have suspected me of being a foot-sticker-outer.
She assumed that what had occurred was some more "monkey business" on the part of the other boy—evidence of his lack of respect
for the dignity and authority of teachers—and so he got a double
reprimand.

The other children sensed what had really happened and were consequently aware that there would be excitement when school let out. My recollection is that we did not pay much attention to the arithmetic or whatever it was we were supposed to be doing the rest of the time. When closing time came we marched out, probably with more than the usual angelic innocence written on our faces. One of the teachers stood on the front porch of the frame schoolhouse and watched us go down the sidewalk until we got beyond a high solid fence which hid us from her sight.

I stopped there and so did several other boys. In a moment the big boy arrived and, as he faced me, his pals gathered round. For some unfathomable reason I no longer felt afraid or nervous, as I had up to that moment. He said in a belligerent tone, "You tripped me." I looked him in the eye and quietly said, "Yes, I did." I suppose this development was unexpected to him. He probably had felt I would try to lie out of it, or possibly put up my fists and make the best fight of it that I could. The response I did make took him off his guard. He hesitated, shifted his weight to the other leg, hitched one of his shoulders, then turned and walked away without saying a word. His pals followed him. In a moment the other boys walked off, considerably disappointed.

I have no recollection of what my own thoughts were as I walked home. It was not until twenty years or so later that the incident came back to me for the first time. The fact that thereafter I did at intervals recall it indicates that it had made a considerable impression. It was not, however, until about 1940—that is, about forty years after the occurrence—that it came home to me that it illustrated several aspects of the pacifist philosophy which I had consciously adopted in 1915 but toward which I had, no doubt, an inclination many years earlier.

In amplifying this observation, let me speak in the third person of the little boy in the incident, which has always seemed to me to represent something that happened to me and through me, rather than something which I did deliberately and, as it were, by my own effort. In the first place, the little boy did the unexpected thing. The conventional action in such a situation is that of fight or flight. And the opponent knows by habit or instinct how to respond. When he encounters an unexpected reaction, it is as if an act of what Richard Gregg called "moral jiu-jitsu" has been performed upon him.

In any pacifism which is not cowardice, or at best mere passivity, there must be this factor of spontaneity and imagination. One of the chief marks of our fallen condition is that in a world where no two human beings are exactly alike, we usually behave like figures in a drill. This is true of nations and it is one of the basic causes of war. Nation Number One gets itself a gun or an atomic bomb, not, of course, to do harm to anyone; it is just a matter of security. But the nation at which the gun happens to be pointed feels utterly defenseless again, of course, and must have another gun, and so it goes. It still does when the weapon is I.C.B.M. Well did W. H. Auden pray: "Prohibit sharply the rehearsed response."

Secondly, the Little Boy told the truth. This is also a very revolutionary thing to do. Incidentally, I am not making claims about knowing the truth, or being immune from self-deceit. I am speaking only of a disposition to tell the truth as one sees it in a situation of tension and conflict. It is unusual even in face-to-face relationships. It is not expected at all between nations, in politics or in business. You "give them a sales talk." Yet everyone has experienced what a cleanliness and a healing comes into a situation when nobody is trying to hide anything any more, when the cards are on the table, when what people think privately or will tell to another individual, they also say in the market place or if need be cry from the housetop. I am thinking of what many Southerners will say, for private consumption only, about race; or nuclear scientists about war.

Thirdly, the Little Boy admitted that he was in the wrong. Maybe he should have said it to the teacher in school. However that may be, when the battle was impending, he admitted that he had done the deed. This isn't often done, even in good society. And who ever expects a nation to admit that it is in the wrong? Lord knows what would happen if either Eisenhower or Khrushchev were to have confessed guilt. Yet Jesus held there was no sin like that of thinking one is not a sinner as other men are, no crime like arrogating moral superiority over other men to oneself. And have we not all experienced what a delightful coolness and deep healing comes into a situation when no one is trying to justify himself any more?

Fourthly, the Little Boy in the incident was not afraid. Leave aside the very important question as to how this came about. For the present purpose we deal with the fact. The fact is that he who is afraid, under tension, creates tension in others, makes them afraid. The fact is that men think they must create a world in which they will be what they call secure, i.e., in which there will be nothing to be afraid of. The fact is, also, that there is no such world; the universe is not built like that. Fear never built anything. You have to begin by not being afraid and then you will have the equipment with which to remove the things that are to be feared.

Finally, the Little Boy, having as it were rendered himself defenseless, miraculously found himself safe. Spiritual forces are as real as physical or military. In a way all men know this and at times act upon the knowledge. The trouble is mainly that we want to have both. We want to trust in God and have plenty of H-bombs too, just in case. The fact is, we can't have it both ways. We have to choose on what level, with what weapons, we shall wage the battle, and accept the risks and consequences involved. There are risks either way.

These, then, are some of the things I learned in the course of the years. But they were probably a part of me before my mind apprehended them.

One other incident in my grade school days points to a later interest, that in the labor movement. In the year that I was in the eighth grade, the Trades and Labor Council of Grand Rapids, Michigan, instituted an essay competition for children in the city's grade schools. The subject was Child Labor. The prize was $15 worth of books and publication of the prize essay in the souvenir book issued by the Council, on Labor Day. The principal of the North Ionia Street School, Miss Amanda Stout, whose name went well with her figure and who was a pleasant and noble lady, called me into her office one day, told me I should go into the contest, and expressed the opinion that I'd win if I did. The ideas of writing, of winning, and of books to own, were all delightful. In any case, a boy brought up as I had been had no alternative but to enter the contest, once the principal had proposed it.

I have no idea even now as to what children of twelve or thirteen are supposed to know about child labor—I mean as a subject to write about. Certainly I had practically no idea then. Miss Stout placed in my hands some information about the subject, provided by the Trades and Labor Council. Writing about a subject I could hardly be expected to know much about did not seem too formidable an undertaking to me. After all, by that time, instead of committing somebody's Christmas poem to memory and reciting it at the Sunday School Christmas Festival, I was writing and delivering my own sermonettes on such themes as "Christ as Prophet, Priest and King." So I wrote a moral essay on Child Labor and handed it to Miss Stout. Some weeks later, the matter had gone out of my mind, chiefly because I was full of excitement about going away from home soon, to the Hope College Preparatory School in the town of Holland, twenty-five miles away, to prepare for the ministry, a goal which was eleven years distant—four years of prep school, four of college and three of theological seminary intervening—but which was pre-destined and therefore in a sense already realized. However, one summer day, the announcement came through Mrs. Morley that I had won the prize.

Some days later, she and a representative of the Trades and Labor Council took me to the big bookstore downtown to help me select the books, that is, to pick them out for me. The packages which I carried home included *Self Help* by Samuel Smiles, the standard work of that time for teaching people how to succeed, i.e., make money, by frugality, sobriety and industry. I read it. I have never been drunk. I am, I suppose, industrious—but from preference, not from a sense of duty. My tastes are simple, but I have a considerable aversion to saving, and a strong aversion to money-making.

My prize collection also included Dickens' *Our Mutual Friend*, a novel I was never able to read, and Scott's *Ivanhoe*, which I did read a good many years later and liked. But there were also real prizes. One was an anthology of poems gathered by Agnes Repplier, which helped develop a love for poetry which has been one of life's greatest and most enduring joys. A second was J. B. Green's *Short History of England*, which opened up another field which I have cultivated vigorously through the years and which sometimes tempted me in my youth to desert the ministry and go in for teach-ing history. Finally, there was a volume of Emerson's *Essays*, which was, I am sure, the most seminal influence of all on my thinking. With Lincoln, Emerson was a creator of that "American Dream," which, along with the great passages of the Hebrew-Christian Scrip-tures, molded and nourished my mind and spirit.

Thus I come to another important concern mentioned earlier: the attempt to delineate the image of America; the "myth" which was communicated to Americans in those years before World War I; the attempt, it might be called, to convey what America *felt* like in those days. I have touched upon this earlier in my reference to my introduction to Abraham Lincoln, but now we must be more explicit.

Part Five

If we employed a geographical analogy for America's self-image at the turn of the century, it would go like this:

Here in the center of things is the broad expanse of the United States, varied and beautiful.

> *O, beautiful for spacious skies,*
> *For amber waves of grain,*
> *For purple mountain majesties*
> *Above the fruited plain!*

This was God's country. It was "the new world." It was safe from the rest of the world, behind the great moat of the Atlantic. Because in those days America faced east, we were hardly conscious of the greater moat of the Pacific.

Canada was negligible, a land of prairies, then wilderness, until you came to Hudson Bay and the North Pole, which was a place for American explorers to reach. Of Latin America likewise we were hardly conscious. It was Indian, alien, Roman Catholic. In the dim past there had been Incas and Aztecs to give American historians something to write about. In any case, things were under control down there because of the Monroe Doctrine.

To the east, across the Atlantic, was Western Europe. Toward it our attitude was ambivalent. On the one hand, by ties of blood, language, religion and culture, this was the motherland. We looked up to it, and felt in certain respects inferior. On the other hand, and I think this was the stronger element, Europe was after all the "old world," and as such inferior to the new. We had fought off the Dutch, French, Spanish and English. Now we were engaged in surpassing them. If there were respects in which we were still inferior, this would be remedied when we got around to it. In many ways the old world had made a mess of it, especially in its addiction to monarchy, power politics and war.

Beyond the Europe with which we thought we were familiar was a sort of Slavic no-man's-land out of which strange sounds and cries sometimes issued. You couldn't exactly call Russia, for example, heathen. It was essentially a great question mark.

All the rest, except for fringes colonized by Anglo-Saxons, was the missionary world where "heathen in their blindness bowed down to wood and stone." It was quite generally held that this benighted area would be "evangelized in our generation."

The United States in my youth was, of course, not a static society. We thought of ourselves as moving, progressive, in contrast to the old world. We were in a sense "revolutionaries." But this did not mean that there was a deep feeling of instability or insecurity. Our movement was no longer that of rebels or of the disinherited of Europe, coming over to found a new world and break with the present. We immigrants came into a society where the pattern was supposed to be fixed. The task was to extend it—extend the Union and the industry, faith and culture of New England across the continent. The movement was like that of a great ship toward its destination. I think it is generally true to say that the agrarians and socialists of that era did not think of themselves as aliens seeking to found a new order, but as men who were going to translate the authentic American dream into reality.

It may be noted that, while the country advanced rapidly in technology, the situation was under control. It was the pre-atomic era. We were still applying techniques with confidence and immense energy, not as the subjects or victims of a technological revolution.

The general structure of industrialization and capitalism had been worked out in England. We largely escaped the tension and suffering which marked the Industrial Revolution in Western Europe, a fact which had an immense effect on the character and growth of the American labor movement.

There is one other aspect of America's self-image in that past which we must attempt to portray. The Civil War had, of course, been a traumatic experience. The immediate post-war years were years of strain and scandal. By the eighteen-nineties, however, the image that was communicated to us in the schools, the Fourth of July orations, and in other ways, went like this: we had not fought a war, much less precipitated one, as they were always doing in the bad, old world. God, in his inscrutable Providence, had inflicted upon us the tragedy of the war experience. The nation, North and South, had been crucified on the Cross of War. Did not the Bible teach that "without shedding of blood there is no remission of sin"?

The war had been Christ, "trampling out the vintage where the grapes of wrath are stored." Now all this was over forever. The nation had been saved. The Union was indissoluble. There was no more slavery. Had not the emancipation of the slaves been proclaimed? There was in that period—outside the South—no awareness, I think, of the extent to which the South was isolated, demoralized, bruised and colonialized.

So we were done with war. Lincoln, of course, became the martyr-symbol of the nation, dedicated at Gettysburg to see to it that "government of the people, by the people, for the people, shall not perish from the earth." Movement was evolutionary, but the outlook was utopian. Americans thought of themselves as the chosen people who were to bring the blessings of Christianity, democracy, prosperity and peace to all mankind. Men sang—and believed—

> *Thou, too, sail on, O ship of State.*
> *Sail on, O Union, strong and great!*
> *Humanity with all its fears,*
> *With all its hopes of future years,*
> *Is hanging breathless on thy fate!*

This is the America which, in 1916, followed Woodrow Wilson into the war to end war and secure democracy after, characteristically, having elected him because "he kept us out of war." This is also the America which, four decades later, was still engaged in a tragic conflict over issues which it once thought had been settled forever by the Civil War.

Before I attempt to describe the impact of World War I on this America and on myself, on whom this image of my country was stamped, it is necessary to outline in very summary fashion the events of my life between 1898 and 1914.

In September of 1898 I entered the Preparatory School of Hope College, the institution which the pioneer Dutch Reformed settlers of Western Michigan had founded in 1847. Earlier in 1898, I had been solemnly accepted into membership in the Fourth Reformed Church in Grand Rapids. It was unusual to be received into membership at thirteen, as I was. I was accepted shortly thereafter as a student for the ministry by a higher ecclesiastical body, and granted the small stipend which made enrollment in the denominational prep school possible.

The curriculum, both in the prep school and the college, was heavily loaded on the side of Greek and Latin and Bible study. There-were a couple of competent and inspiring teachers, another couple who were abysmally incompetent and uninspiring, and a larger number who fell between these two extremes. But, on the whole, solid foundations for further study were laid, and I am grateful for what the institution did for me. Moreover, I was not without extra-curricular stimulation. Early in prep school, I was given a job in the college library to eke out my income. This gave me access to books on evolution, for example, which were kept locked away from younger students, and were issued only to college upperclassmen and then only under strict supervision. I remember being scolded by a seminarian from my home church in Grand Rapids for tasting, surreptitiously, of the forbidden fruit. He threatened to tell my parents, which caused me some apprehension, but did not stop me from slipping into the stacks. However, he did not carry out his threat. He also predicted that "all this will come to no good end" and here, of course, he was right.

Graduating from Hope, in 1905, at the age of twenty, I took a year off to teach Greek and English in what was then known as Northwestern Classical Academy, in Orange City, Iowa. There were two cogent reasons for this. One was that at the beginning of my senior year at Hope I had fallen in love, at first sight, with the girl who, later, for over forty-five years, was my wife. Her home was in a town called Rock Valley, in the extreme northwestern corner of Iowa. Though transportation was extremely primitive in that corner of Iowa, I managed to spend longish weekends with her. This involved dashing out of class at noon on Fridays, walking three miles to a railroad station to catch a freight for the heavenly regions, and getting up at four o'clock on Monday mornings to be driven by horse and buggy to a railroad connection for Orange City by one' of Anne's obliging brothers. The other cogent reason for taking off a year to teach Greek and English to the sons and daughters of devout Iowa corn growers was that my closest college friend was to graduate a year after me, and thought it would be nice if I waited a year to enter the theological seminary, so that we could be classmates as well as roommates. Since, also, I loved Greek and English, I think the youngsters did not lose on the deal.

My first trip to the Eastern seaboard was taken in September, 1906, when my friend and I enrolled at the New Brunswick Theological Seminary of the Dutch Reformed Church in New Brunswick, New Jersey. There were two professors and a lecturer on the small faculty who were scholars and good teachers. Otherwise, it was a low period in the school's history. In more recent times the general level of the teaching has been much better. Fortunately, I had time to take graduate courses in philosophy in New York, first at New York University, and later at Columbia, where I first saw John Dewey (who later became a devoted friend), and occasionally heard William James lecture.

On graduation from the seminary in 1909, I was duly licensed and ordained to the ministry of the Reformed Church in America and installed, at the end of June, as the first minister of the Fort Washington Collegiate Church, on Washington Heights, in New York City. The Collegiate Church was the oldest church in the city, going back to the beginning of the Dutch colony of New Amsterdam. There had been, for some years, four congregations in various parts of Manhattan under a common consistory. The chapel at Fort Washington was added in 1909 to take care of the people moving into upper Manhattan.

One advantage of the location was that it was only a few blocks north of where the Yankee ballpark was then located. Another was that Union Theological Seminary was close enough for me to take some courses there. The teachers, like those I had encountered in the philosophy department at Columbia, were in general far superior to those I had met in college and at New Brunswick, and they exercised a profound influence on my intellectual life. This was especially true of Arthur Cushman McGiffert, senior, whose lectures on the history of Christian dogma were far and away the most brilliant I have ever experienced. And "experienced" is the right word, since, for me, McGiffert's courses were an intellectual and spiritual experience. They opened a new approach to the study of religion and new historical vistas, eventually forcing an "agonizing re-appraisal" of the beliefs in which I had been reared. My first encounter with Norman Thomas, then a young Presbyterian minister, took place in a graduate seminar dealing with the authorship of the Johannine writings, conducted by James Everett Frame, professor of New Testament Theology.

The Republicanism in which I had been brought up also received rude shocks from the contacts of that period. These were the years of mushrooming sweatshops, of the terrible Triangle Fire in a garment factory, of the strikes which marked the founding of the garment trades unions, and, in Paterson and more distant places, of the turbulent I. W. W. organizational campaigns and strikes. I had spent the summer of 1908, between my second and final years at New Brunswick, as supply preacher at the Middle Collegiate Church on Second Avenue and Seventh Street, in the very heart of the East Side. For the first time in my life I had really seen, and lived in, slums. I had walked the streets and parks on hot summer days and during the only slightly less oppressive evenings. I had climbed flights of stairs to call on sick and aged parishioners. Sometimes I had been barely able to endure the fetid smells and unceasing raucous noises. This was a very different poverty from that of the furniture-factory workers or even that of the poor farmers of the Middle West during "the hard times," not to mention the poverty that "walks with God and Saint Francis on the Umbrian hills."

The result of this experience was that, although I did not have any direct contact with the strikes and unionizing campaigns of the 1904-14 period and did not attend the I.W.W. or Socialist meetings (both of these groups were regarded by respectable elements in those days much as Bolsheviks were to be later), I read some radical literature and was sympathetically disposed toward the workers in their desperate struggles. I recall an incident in 1912 which illustrates how rapidly my social and political orientation was changing. I had followed with intense interest in the early summer the weeks-long struggle, in the nominating conventions of the Democratic Party in Baltimore, between Champ Clark, then Speaker of the House of Representatives, and Woodrow Wilson, then Governor of New Jersey. When Wilson finally won out, with the support of William Jennings Bryan, who, in those days, was a strong peace advocate, I felt that this was a great victory for progressivism and, of course, looked forward to casting a ballot for Wilson. By the time Election Day came, however, I voted for Eugene V. Debs. I record with satisfaction that I have never subsequently voted for any Democrat or Republican for any major state or national office.

It was not changing social and political views, however, which led to the termination of my ministry at Fort Washington at the end of 1914. By the fall of that year I could no longer acquiesce in giving the impression that I accepted the literal inspiration of Scripture and the whole corpus of Calvinist dogma, at least as then interpreted. There had been a brief period, a year or two before, when it had seemed impossible to hold on to any religious faith at all, but this had passed. I was inwardly more confident than ever that I could, and must, preach the essentials of the Christian faith and strive to bring myself and others to its practice.

The way was opened for me to become the minister of Central Congregational Church at Newtonville, Massachusetts, a suburb of Boston. The first two years in that pastorate were in every way delightful and stimulating. The membership consisted largely of professional people. Preaching to them was a decidedly greater challenge than any I had hitherto met. I was accepted into the circle of some of the leading preachers and theologians of Boston. Spiritually, as well as physically, I felt myself seeing the places that Thoreau and Emerson had looked upon, breathing the air they had breathed. Into this atmosphere, early in January, 1916, our first child was born. She was, naturally, a lovely baby. At heaven's gate the lark sang; the snail was on the thorn, the bird on the wing, God in his heaven, and all was right with the world.

It was into this idyllic situation that the lightning bolt of World War I fell. The war had begun, of course, in Europe in August, 1914, but at first it had seemed remote and American participation unthinkable. As the months passed and the bitter and bloody trench fighting developed, it became clear that the United States would go in, despite protestations that it would not. Thus, along with other Christian preachers, I had to face—not academically but existentially, as it were—the question of whether I could reconcile what I had been preaching out of the Gospels, and passages like I Corinthians:13, from the Epistles, with participation in war.

The observation that in such situations you sometimes "have to think fast" certainly applied in my case. As recently as the late fall of 1914, war had not been a personal problem for me. At that time the Spanish-American War Veterans Post of Washington Heights had held its annual memorial service in the Fort Washington Church and I had been asked to preach the sermon. I had made the expected, conventional observations that war is a terrible and wicked thing and that we Americans are against war, but that when the strong attack the weak, and democracy and religion are in danger, then, of course, as good Christians, we must go bravely, though reluctantly, into battle. I have often reflected since that it would have been difficult to find a more inappropriate event to which to relate such remarks than the Spanish-American war. Certainly, in all the study of the Scriptures through which I had been led in that citadel of orthodoxy, New Brunswick, and in the hotbed of heresy which was Union—in those days—I had never been given an inkling that there might be such a thing as a pacifist interpretation of the Gospel.

How then did it come about that, a year later, I found myself a convinced Christian pacifist? Probably there were tendencies in my basic make-up which helped to produce this result, when the pressure of events necessitated a decision. It is hard to tell whether, or when, the conscious adoption of a pacifist position would have occurred if the situation had not backed me into a corner, where the Yes or No had to be uttered.

I do not think that, during the crucial months of 1915, political or economic considerations relating to war influenced me to any extent, although I did some reading in those fields. The problem, as it presented itself to me, was simply one for the Christian conscience. (I am not attempting here to state the "case" for pacifism. I am simply recalling what happened inside of me as I became aware of where I really stood.) It was a problem which I could not evade because I had been brought up to take religion, specifically the Biblical teaching and Gospel ethic, seriously, and to abhor the sham which enables a person to preach what he does not try desperately to practice. Moreover, my upbringing had given me a definite attitude regarding the struggle which goes on perpetually in the human spirit and in society as to whether the Gospel demand shall be adjusted to the outward circumstances or the recalcitrant reality shall be made to conform to the high ethical demand. I did not believe that there is a pat rule which one can find in a proof text and apply to a complicated situation, thereby achieving perfection. I had received too solid a dose of Calvinism not to have a strong conviction about human frailty and corruption. It was this that had made me aware, long before Freud was more than a name to me, that when a man is sure that he is honest, he deceives himself; when he imagines himself to be pure, he is impure; and when we bask in the glow of the feeling that we love, the fact is that in subtle ways we hate.

But this does not alter the nature of the demand the Gospel places upon us—or, if you prefer, the demand that is placed upon us because we belong to the family of man—that we be honest and pure and that we love all men. The poet who does not agonize to translate the vision he sees truly and exactly into his poem is not a poet. The man who does not passionately strive to be honest, pure and loving is not a man. The temptation to pride and self-righteousness is real and pervasive. The temptation to adapt the Gospel demand to circumstances and to abandon the hard effort to mold one's own life and the world according to that imperious demand is no less subtle and pervasive.

G. K. Chesterton, in a beautiful passage in the volume *Alarms and Discursions,* has stated his version of this law of life:

> Bows are beautiful when they bend only because they try to remain rigid and sword blades can curl like silver only because they are certain to spring straight again. . . . The foil may curve in the lunge, but there is nothing beautiful about beginning the battle with a crooked foil. So the strict aim, the strong doctrine, may give a little in the actual fight with facts; but that is no reason for beginning with a weak doctrine or a twisted aim. . . . Do not try to bend, any more than trees try to bend. Try to grow straight, and life will bend you.

As far as reading is concerned, what undoubtedly influenced me most, during the critical months of inner wrestling, to conclude that I could not "bend" the Sermon on the Mount and the whole concept of the Cross and suffering love to accommodate participation in war, was the serious reading of the Christian mystics. Among the important books on some of these mystics were those by Rufus M. Jones, a leading Quaker. Thus I came to know about Quakers of past and present, Quaker meetings, the Quaker "peace testimony." It was the first time that these things suggested anything to me other than the man on the Quaker Oats box.

My wrestling with these matters resulted in my joining, early in 1916, the Fellowship of Reconciliation, which had been founded at Cambridge University in December, 1914, and established in this country in November of the following year. Thus I became publicly identified as a Christian pacifist.

Part Six

In the United States to which I came as an immigrant boy, and in which I grew to adulthood, the loyalty of the inhabitants to their country was taken for granted. It was not argued—or even discussed. This was true in spite of, and indeed because of, the fact that for great multitudes this was their adopted country.

They had *wanted* to come here and *get away* from other lands. Precious family ties and strong associations of language and culture might bind them to peoples abroad but so far was this from implying loyalty to foreign rulers and the states over which they ruled that the prevailing sentiment was an aversion to these rulers and states, an aversion which did not need to be shouted in meetings or certified by oaths. Anarchists, socialists and other radicals would be the last to bear allegiance to some other nation as against the United States. One's neighbors, or persons who held unorthodox views, were not suspected of being spies. There were no F. B. I.'s or state loyalty boards to assemble dossiers on thousands of citizens.

Many developments, in the months just before and after the United States entered the war in the spring of 1917, were, therefore, as unanticipated and shocking as they were horrible in their nature and in their foreshadowing of trends in American life which have endured and gained in strength to this very moment.

The custom of having people rise to sing *The Star Spangled Banner* at the opening of plays, operas and many public meetings was introduced, and conformity was forced on those who disliked the practice. Military parades occurred frequently, and men were expected to doff their hats whenever a flag was carried by. Many were obviously self-conscious and uncomfortable about it. Salutes and pledges to the flag were introduced in schools. Churches put national flags near altar or pulpit. People appeased the sense of incongruity which this aroused in them by introducing a "church" flag into sanctuaries along with the Stars and Stripes. This has always struck me as rank hypocrisy. The problem is the *presence* of the symbol of nationalism and the state in a church, not the *absence* of a flag with a different color—which, in a Christian sanctuary, cannot possibly add anything to the Cross.

Those who opposed or did not readily accept the United States' entry into the war (especially, of course, if they happened to be of German ancestry) were labeled "pro-Germans." People began to act as amateur spies and loyalty agents, reporting mysterious circles of light in the windows of neighbors living somewhere near the shore, which were assumed to be signals to prowling German submarines. Those who did not buy Liberty (*sic*) bonds to finance the war were suspect, and in not a few Middle Western areas where there were large German settlements, such people were tarred and feathered. As one brought up to think of the Middle West as the liberal, democratic part of the land, in contrast to the aristocratic and effete East, this shocked me. A pacifist and nonconformist felt, and actually was, safer in the East during World War I. Conscription was introduced in the land to which many had fled to escape conscription. At the outset there was no provision whatsoever for conscientious objectors, and many of them, after being forcibly inducted into the Army, were cruelly tortured in barracks and military prisons.

There are a number of reasons why repressive measures were so much more severe and crude during the months of which I am now writing than they were in the corresponding period of World War II. First of all, the war in that earlier period came as a first experience to a people who believed their country had passed beyond war, a people who, for this and other reasons, were imbued with optimism and a rosy view of human nature. When they became convinced that Germans were monsters and that means which they had felt deeply to be stupid and revolting had to be used against such monsters, they experienced a trauma and, in the language now familiar to nearly everybody, had to overcompensate in order to silence their inner resistance and to assuage their hurt.

The war had to be "sold" to such people as a crusade, indeed as the last tragic war to end all war, in a much more naïve and simplistic fashion than was to be the case in the later war. It is now often pointed out that wars conceived as crusades, waged for absolute ends, and thus seeming to require total victory and unconditional surrender, are more bitter and devastating than the wars of an earlier period. The practitioners and expositors of *realpolitik* use this as an argument against what they call "moralism" in politics. And the stand against using morality as a cloak for economic and power factors in conflict and as a means for whipping up savage emotions and an inflexible mental attitude seems valid. But in practice, the argument against "moralism" is used by political theorists and many theologians as an instrument for ruling ethical considerations out of politics and international relations altogether. In much the same way, the doctrine of sin came to be used in the Thirties and Forties (and is still being used to some extent), mainly as special pleading against pacifist rejection of war. This is crass illogicality.

All but the smallest wars today are fought for global objectives and for "causes" or ideologies regarded as absolute—"better no world than a Communist world," etc.—and therefore take on the character of crusades. The instruments with which war is waged have a similar, "ultimate-weapons" character. The preaching of political scientists and theologians against such absolutizing, against self-righteous attitudes, amounts to spitting into a hurricane. None other than the former Secretary of Defense, "General Motors" Charles E. Wilson, said this, in his own pungent fashion, in an interview with Mike Wallace. Having been reminded of the fervent appeals to catch up with the Russians, he said: "I don't enthuse over all-out competition with the Russians. If we mobilized our country into an armed camp, we'd have to preach so much fire and heat to get our people to accept it that we ourselves might be likely to precipitate a war."

The sharpness and crudeness of repression in World War I was also due to the fact that much more resistance had to be overcome than in World War II. For example, the emotional nationalism served to inflame the anti-British nationalism of the Irish-Americans. 1916 was the year of the Easter Rebellion and massacre in Ireland. The Irish were red-hot anti-conscriptionists. The I. W. W. (Industrial Workers of the World) were at the height of their influence and were ardently anti-militarist. The administration arrested all the top leaders and crippled the organization.

There were strong anti-war currents in unions such as the United Mine Workers and the Machinists. The majority of the Socialist Party members maintained an anti-war stand even after United States entry. Eugene V. Debs, who was imprisoned by Woodrow Wilson's regime, is a symbol of the problem of that hour and its harsh resolution by a supposedly liberal government. The intellectuals of the pre-war period were predominantly anti-militarist, as was Wilson himself. Their abandonment of that stand was a painful experience, and not all of them did abandon it. This was true of the

Socialists among them and of such a flaming and eloquent libertarian as Randolph Bourne.

The role of the churches and religious leaders in whipping up enthusiasm for the war was set forth later in a notable book, *Preachers Present Arms*. Leading pulpit orators played much the same role that secular intellectuals, motivated by anti-Nazism, did later in helping the Roosevelt government to bring the country into World War II. By that time the leading clergy were more restrained, and even the neo-orthodox emphasized that a distinction had to be made, even in wartime, between the role of the state and that of the church. By World War II, the larger Protestant denominations had recognized the right of individual conscientious objection to war.

It was, then, in the face of opposition such as I have sketched that an American administration had to tackle the job of securing complete acquiescence and widespread enthusiasm for the war, without benefit of the subtler instruments and the lessons of costly experience which were later to be at the disposal of Franklin D. Roosevelt. The much higher-minded Woodrow Wilson had to deal with more violent tensions and had to use cruder methods.

For the most part the people of Central Church in Newtonville, Massachusetts, welcomed, or at least easily accepted, my espousal of pacifism and my pacifist activities in the first eight months or so of 1916. Toward the end of the summer, as United States entry loomed more distinctly, some warnings came of trouble ahead. The authorities of a fashionable boys' school located near the church thought it advisable not to expose the boys to pacifist corruption and decided to take them to another church on Sunday morning. Pressure from parents was probably the main factor in this decision. About the same time, a small number of the wealthier families in the church ceased attending. As these things became known in the congregation, the tradespeople, and less opulent families generally, began to go out of their way to show their sympathy. It must be said also that the large majority of Central Church families continued to stand by.

But when the United States formally entered the war in April, 1917, the situation changed abruptly. I returned from the great anti-war demonstration in Washington (where I first encountered such pacifist leaders as Judah Magnes, John Haynes Holmes, and the elder J. Howard Melish) to lead a union Lenten service in my own church. The young Swedenborgian minister refused to participate in the union service, even though it was in no sense a political or anti-war service; the fact that I had gone to Washington and had not declared my support of the war on my return made me a traitor in his eyes.

This was not true of the members of Central Church, who still wanted me to remain and to the end defended me against charges of treason and pro-Germanism. Non-pacifist church and pacifist minister somehow managed to make a go of it until the two months' summer vacation intervened to give us a breathing spell.

When I returned after Labor Day, it was clear that the situation was approaching an inevitable break-up. On both sides it was the more painful because there were no personal recriminations.

It was a psychological factor having to do with the pastoral and counseling relationship which was decisive. This did not involve the young men who enlisted or were drafted, with whom I had played baseball as well as discussed Christian ethics. So far as I know, every one of them, as he left, said in effect that he did not know for sure whether I was right or wrong; he himself "had to go," but he hoped I would stick to my "pacifist guns."

It was when some of these boys were wounded and one of them —brilliant, handsome and a noble character—was killed, that the parents and their friends felt that, holding the views I did, I could not adequately comfort them. To tell the truth, I did not feel that I could either. The tension in those days was too great. I resigned. Almost without exception, in World War I, pacifist ministers lost their pulpits or, as in Seattle, in the case of Sidney Strong (father of Anna Louise Strong), the minister "kept his pulpit but lost his congregation," as his son recently put it. (The situation in World War II was very different.)

After my resignation from Central Church, I did considerable volunteer work for a new-born organization (which a little later took the name American Civil Liberties Union) whose director, Roger Baldwin, was a young social worker from St. Louis, himself a Conscientious Objector who served a year's prison term for his stand. After two fruitless visits, marked by the well-known run-around, I located the CO's, imprisoned in their barracks at Camp Devens, near Fitchburg, Massachusetts. Not having been unfrocked, I received some belated recognition from the camp authorities and was able to set in motion activities which eventually resulted in the amelioration of the brutality toward the Camp Devens CO's. We also helped secure some provisions for their better treatment nationally, and even some opportunity, toward the end of the war, for alternative service, which seemed an immense gain then but became a bone of contention among pacifists in World War II.

I helped also in the trials of some of the New England pacifists who fell afoul of the law, and in nearly miraculous fashion escaped being arrested and jailed myself. One thing that helped was that both the Federal Circuit Court Judge in Boston and the Federal District Attorney were true liberals and astute public servants. When they were pressed by patrioteers to get after pacifists and other non-conformists, they answered that it was much better to permit these fellows to let off steam in the open than to drive them underground.

On June 7, 1918, at the annual session of the New England Yearly Meeting of Friends in Vassalboro, Maine, I had a narrow escape. I was speaking to a packed meeting on a Sunday afternoon when I noticed a commotion in the gallery to my right as a man ostentatiously stalked out. I was scheduled to be driven back to Boston by a young Friend immediately after the service. When the closing silence had ended with the ritual handshaking, the young Friend came to the platform and suggested we go out immediately and get into his car, which was parked by the rear door for the trip to Boston. Otherwise, he suggested, "the crank who made a disturbance in the gallery" might delay us. Since I had been delivering a devotional talk, with no special pacifist emphasis, I assumed that if remarks of mine were the occasion of the disturbance, the objection to them would be from a fundamentalist rather than a militarist angle. Regarding argument on the former score as not particularly urgent, I acquiesced readily in a prompt departure.

As we drove out of the meeting ground, I noticed a car approaching from the opposite direction and entering the grounds. Some weeks later, I learned that the other car belonged to the Federal sheriff from a nearby city who had been summoned by the local Baptist minister, self-appointed security agent of the vicinity. He had regarded some of my remarks as treasonous.

The sheriff and his colleagues got out of their car, and leading Friends gathered around. The Baptist minister began a tirade against me, but it had more noise than substance. The sheriff repeatedly asked him to give an exact quotation of something I had said, but he was unable to. Meanwhile, the leading Friends stood by in silence. The affair ended with the sheriff's scolding the Baptist preacher for getting him out on a fool's errand on a pleasant Sunday afternoon. However, if I had been on the grounds, the chances are he would have arrested me, rather than run the risk of being accused of lacking patriotic zeal; and in the atmosphere of the time a conviction on the basis of my writings and general activities would have been almost a foregone conclusion.

The ancient Friends Meeting in Providence, Rhode Island, though not a pastoral meeting in the usual sense, enrolled me as a minister in the Society of Friends and, in return for some pastoral service and speaking, provided us with a home and some expense money. In the basement of that old Meeting House was a large room in which all the progressive and radical magazines and pamphlets of the day were available. On Saturday evenings throughout the war, the various unorthodox, persecuted individuals in the city gathered to talk and, metaphorically, hold hands. To the authorities this was a source of great concern and indeed irritation.

No attempt was ever made, however, to close the library. I am certain that the chief reason for this was that it was sponsored by the leading Friend of Providence Meeting, Charles Sisson. He had been a successful textile manufacturer, and by the time I got to know him he had retired from business and was devoting his time and money, as is frequently the case with Friends, to work for various causes, not least among them peace. He was a quiet man. I cannot believe that he ever in all his adult life raised his voice. But he had clear and strong opinions and, unlike some Quakers, held unequivocally to "the peace testimony," against participation in war. Everybody knew that he could not be swerved by a hair's breadth from his convictions and that his quiet voice could not be silenced. Such was the respect and awe in which he was held in the locality that nothing with which Charles Sisson associated himself could, even in that hysterical time and war-mad city, be molested. This was one of the most beautiful and powerful exhibitions of what Gandhi called soul force that I have ever seen.

Part Seven

It was quite an experience to be, in effect, driven out of a pulpit which for my predecessors had proved a stepping stone to highly distinguished careers in the ministry, and to find myself marked as a pacifist and a possibly dangerous character. It was, however, as nothing compared to the transition from preaching in the somewhat old-fashioned, though sturdy and courageous, Quaker Meeting in Providence to the leadership, early in 1919, of a turbulent strike of 30,000 textile workers in Lawrence, Massachusetts. As one of the good folk in the Newtonville church remarked, "Becoming a pacifist and Quaker in wartime was bad enough, but to go around in a blue shirt and parade on picket lines—this is too much!" What happened in Lawrence was no more of a surprise to anybody else than it was to me.

In the fall of 1918, the Boston group of the Fellowship of Reconciliation rented a house adjacent to Back Bay, but on the wrong side of the New Haven Railroad tracks. The main floor, half a flight up from the street, was made into one large room into which something like a hundred people could be crowded. It was used for pacifist meetings, but also for radical political gatherings which could not find room elsewhere. I remember a warm night when all the windows had to be opened to make it bearable inside and Jim Larkin, the famous Irish labor leader, held forth. He had a voice like thunder. His speech was red hot. All the neighbors in the block, hanging out of their windows, and the cops on the beat must have heard every word as plainly as we who were inside. The cops were probably Irish, and so were quite a few of the neighbors. Nobody interfered. We need not have feared as, frankly, I did, that the next day the police, or men from Army intelligence, would come around to shut the place up.

Harold L. Rotzel, with his wife and their three-year-old daughter, occupied the apartment on the top floor of 99 Appleton Street. The Mustes and our three-year-old daughter lived on the floor below. Harold, a Methodist minister who had been forced to leave his church near Worcester, Massachusetts, and I were members of a loosely organized group of men and women who called themselves "The Comradeship." The emphasis was on the noun, not on the article. Another member was Cedric Long, a young Congregationalist minister who had been unable to get a church on account of his pacifism. Somewhat younger than the three of us was Bill Simpson, who was a striking personality, at the outset more dynamic and dedicated, I felt, than any of the rest of us. After trying, for several years, literally to live without money and without compromising his convictions at any point, during which time he had a powerful effect on all who met him, Bill developed a Nietzschean philosophy and became an enigma to those who had known him.

Two Boston women were prominently identified with The Comradeship. One was a Quaker lady, Ann N. Davis, a member of the wealthy Hollowell family, beautiful in physical appearance and in spirit, unflinching in her pacifism and in support of every struggle for freedom. The other was Miss Ethel Paine, daughter of Robert Treat Paine (who was a descendant of the signer of the Declaration of Independence who bore the same name), and a devout parishioner of the "Phillips Brooks Church," the Trinity Episcopal. Later she became the wife of John F. Moors, Boston broker and Harvard Overseer, and, after Mr. Moors' death, she married the distinguished British theologian and pacifist, postwar vice-chancellor of Cambridge University, Canon Charles E. Raven. Throughout a long life, Ethel Paine poured money, tireless energy, and a capacity for friendliness into the causes of pacifism, racial equality and civil liberties.

Those of us identified with The Comradeship in late 1918 and early 1919 were wrestling with the question of how to organize our lives so that they would truly express the teachings and spirit of Jesus, or, in other terms, faith in the way of truth, nonviolence and love. We were thinking of a place in the country where some members of the community might live and also of places in the city where other members would live, organize cooperatives, and generally enter into the neighborhood life. We talked of a possible economic tie between the community on the land and the community in the city. We were all agreed that we did not want to shut ourselves off from the struggle against war, and for economic justice and racial equality, in the competitive society. I suppose it might be said that this latter was either our undoing or our salvation, depending on how you look at it. This is an important problem and very pertinent to the period in which we are now living. It is, therefore, a subject to which I am likely to return. But for a moment, I shall try to tell "straight" the story of what actually happened.

During that winter, after the November 11 Armistice, Harold Rotzel and I got up about five o'clock every morning for several weeks. When the chill of the apartment made it necessary, we bundled ourselves in our overcoats while we read the New Testament —especially the Sermon on The Mount—together, analyzed the passages, meditated on each phrase, even each word, prayed, and asked ourselves what obedience to those precepts meant for us, then and there. Insofar as we were thinking of an organized future, it was in terms of an "intentional community" along the lines I have mentioned. Indeed, at that time, we, together with members of the F. O. R. and a number of Quakers, *did* constitute a "fellowship of sharing and concern," in a very substantial measure. During most of the period when we were holding the early morning sessions, strikes were not in our thoughts at all; there was certainly no idea that we should become involved. However, in a psychological and spiritual sense, those hours of meditation and self-searching consti-tuted ideal preparation for what we were to face in the nearby city of Lawrence shortly after the start of 1919.

There had been an I. W. W. - led strike in Lawrence in 1912. It had been a general strike of textile workers, textile being virtually the only industry the city had. The names of Elizabeth Gurley Flynn, Carlo Tresca, Joseph Ettar and the Italian poet Arturo Gio-vanitti—and to a lesser extent, Bill Haywood—are associated with that strike. It had been conducted with the flair the I. W. W. had for dramatizing social issues and the human aspects of the labor strug-gle. When the strike had dragged on and starvation had threatened the strikers, scores of Lawrence children had been taken out of Lawrence and into the homes of sympathizers in other cities. The strike had received world-wide publicity.

When rumors began to fly, in January, 1919, that another gen-eral strike was likely to break out, a number of Comradeship people met at "99 Appleton" to talk over the situation. Our discussions about community had sprung out of a feeling that somehow we had to try to translate the ideal of brotherhood into reality. We had also a feeling that nonviolence had to prove itself in actual struggle; otherwise it was a mere abstraction or illusion. I recall that some of us felt the sting of the charge that during the war, while others risked their lives, we had stood on the sidelines and "had it easy." Here a struggle was developing at our own back door. Did our nonviolence have any relevance to the impending conflict? It would probably be risky to get embroiled in this business, and certainly none of us had any experience whatsoever in the field. So, was one to stay on the sidelines once more?

One bleak winter day, three of us, Harold Rotzel (who was then teaching chemistry at Simmons College), Gorham Harris (a member of my old church in Newtonville) and I went from Boston to Lawrence to see for ourselves.

On this visit, and on later visits, we found terrific tension and excitement. This was partly because of the memory of the clashes between strikers and police, the bitterness, of the 1912 strike. There was much more reason for excitement, however, in the immediate situation. A little over a year before, the Bolshevik Revolution had taken place in Russia. Many believed that in the aftermath of the war that revolution would spread, certainly in Europe, perhaps to America. In Winnipeg, Canada, and in Seattle, Washington, there had been general strikes which had received national and international publicity.

We found that among members of the very conservative Quaker Meeting in Lawrence, for example, and indeed in all middle class and native elements of that predominantly proletarian and immigrant section, there was a firm conviction that if a general strike were to break out, it would signal the beginning of the Bolshevik Revolution in America, or at least in Massachusetts—certainly in Lawrence. The workers would seize the city hall, the police station, the mills . . .

We went to see those officials of the great textile companies who would see us. We actually did see William Wood, junior, son of the head of the American Woolen Company, which employed 16,-000 people in its four huge mills. At the outset, the officials had been rather pleased that we were coming to town, because they had assumed that as pacifists we would urge the workers not to strike. When it became clear that we did not condone starvation wages and union smashing, and that, while we opposed violence, we conceived of nonviolence as a form of resistance and not of submission they changed their attitude toward us.

What we found out about the reasons for the impending strike in Lawrence had to do with very specific and painful actualities on the spot and only remotely, if at all, with global revolution. The average wage of textile workers in the city was $11.00 for a 54-hour week. Eleven dollars a week was quite a lot more money then than it would be now. But even then it was miserable pay. With the end of the war, unemployment had set in. The mill owners had proposed to cut hours to 48 per week but not to adjust hour or piece rates; in other words, to institute a more than ten percent reduction in take-home pay. The slogan of the strike had become "54-48," that is, "54 hours' pay for 48 hours' work." Housing conditions were appalling. Moreover, we and our friends dug up facts about unconscionable war profiteering on the part of the industrialists, facts which in later years became common property. We put these facts into a leaflet and passed it out from house to house. This also did not endear us to the mill owners. There was a story, which was true as to substance, that the American Woolen Company had sold raincoats at a good price to the United States Army. The coats had not kept out the rain, so the division to which they had been sold had returned them. American Woolen had promptly sold the lot again out of the front door at a somewhat stiffer price to another division of the Army.

The only union organizations in the mills were a couple of craft locals of skilled loomfixers and spinners, belonging to the United Textile Workers of America, an affiliate of the American Federation of Labor. The men in the craft locals, of English and Scotch and, in a few cases, Irish descent, had no contacts with, or interest in, the great mass of foreign-born workers. The A. F. of L. was opposed to the strike.

The meetings which led to the formation of a provisional strike committee were organized by some middle-aged Belgian, Polish and Italian weavers who had been involved in the 1912 strike, a radical-minded carpenter of English descent named Sam Bramhall, whose command of English made him the chairman, and a number of young men who had been from twelve to sixteen years old at the time of the 1912 strike and were hero-worshippers of the leaders of that strike. One was a Jewish lad named Irve Kaplan, and he served as committee secretary. If he is still alive and happens to read or hear of this account, I hope he will write to me.

Most of these workers were the kind of people who constitute the heart and backbone of every large-scale radical movement: men of devotion, courage, integrity; men of good judgment in matters within the field of their experience, and living close to their fellow workers. Some of them were remarkably well informed, considering the limited character of their education and their lack of leisure for reading. They had the confidence of their fellow workers and, without their mediation, top leadership would have been unable to function.

However, none of these men were able, singly or as part of a group, to provide general leadership for a strike of 30,000 previously unorganized people. Most of them spoke English brokenly or not at all. This in itself was a severe handicap in dealing with liberal groups, whose moral and financial support was needed, or with public officials and mill managements. They had almost no contacts outside the mills and their respective language groups. They had no experience or training in organization techniques or publicity.

No other leadership was in sight. The A. F. L., as I have already mentioned, was opposed to the strike. No socialists from Massachusetts or elsewhere seemed able or willing to undertake the responsibility of leadership in an "outlaw strike," though a leading Boston socialist, George E. Roewer, rendered brilliant and sacrificial service as an attorney, after the strike got underway. The Wilson administration, as we have previously observed, had practically wiped out the I. W. W. leadership.

When Harold Rotzel, Cedric Long and I spoke to meetings in Lawrence in the days before the strike was actually called, it was to tell the workers that we believed in their cause and that we would do all we could to raise relief money in case of a strike. This we did on our own behalf and also in the name of other members of The Comradeship who had "encouraged" us to become active in the situation. The strike was called for the first Monday in February of 1919. We were invited to sit in on strike committee meetings, and we accepted. We were mostly silent observers for a few days, except when manifestos or statements to the press had to be put into English. Each night we went back to Boston to interpret the strike and to raise relief money. When people have been working for an $11.00 weekly wage, some need relief by the end of the first week.

I have said something about the tense atmosphere which prevailed in Lawrence. On the Sunday evening before the strike began, the Commissioner of Public Safety (*sic*) and the Chief of Police briefed the police of Lawrence and squads from the surrounding cities which had been called in to quell the revolution. The Commissioner instructed them to this effect: "If you do not get these people on the picket-line tomorrow morning first, they will get you."

So there was a blood bath on Monday morning. As the vast picket lines formed before the silent mills in the gray dawn, police, on foot and mounted, waded into the lines, clubbing right and left. In at least a couple of cases police broke into homes near the mills, pulled the covers off women in bed and beat them, alleging that the women had been near the line, had thrown stones at the police, and had then fled home. A score or so of those who had got the worst beatings were brought to the little hall belonging to some Polish benefit society which the strike committee had hired as its headquarters. It was after these men and women had been given first aid and reports had been received about other beatings that the strike committee convened to deliberate on the next move.

The reports also showed that the strike was almost 100 percent effective. The decision was to picket the mills again *en masse* that afternoon and the next morning. The next morning and the next, police brutalities were re-enacted.

Before the end of that week, I was asked to become Executive Secretary of the strike committee, which meant taking on the general leadership. Both Rotzel and Long were invited to become voting members of the committee. Some of the reasons for this move on the part of the worker members of the committee I have already suggested. Under pressure of the police brutality and the adverse press in Lawrence and Boston, these local people came to feel a desperate need for a "front," a cover of people who could not so easily be disregarded, discounted and beaten up; of people whose education and contacts might qualify them, in spite of their inexperience, to interpret the struggle to the public and to help in developing basic strategy. Of course, our record of dissent during the war, plus the fact that we had not stopped coming to Lawrence when the police got ugly, had inspired confidence.

The last thing in the world that any of us had expected, when we first went to Lawrence, had been that such a call as this would be made upon us. But when the proposition was made, we clearly had either to undertake the ominous responsibility or else to leave Lawrence altogether. There was no middle course. So we accepted the invitation. It would be more accurate to say that, though we had never learned to swim, we three young preachers and devotees of peace and nonviolence were tossed into a raging ocean—and we swam. I was "leader" of 30,000 strikers of twenty or more nationalities. Harold took over the relief organization. Cedric looked after youth activities, entertainment, and some aspects of public relations.

Cedric was still a youth, considerably younger than Harold

and I, who were thiry-four. He was tall, athletic, handsome, and possessed of a winning smile. He was a pure spirit, a noble being. In later years he was for some time secretary of the Cooperative League of America. One of the best "entertainments" he put on during the strike was a personal one for the benefit of the relief fund. Before he became a pacifist he had been in the state militia. He was a crack shot and had got a heap of medals for his marksmanship. He auctioned off the medals himself one day. Seeing a pacifist sharpshooter auction off his medals made a lot of people feel good, and I guess it taught some of them some kind of lesson about courage and nonviolence.

Union leaders nowadays seldom appear on picket lines—for various reasons. Back in the jungle era in 1919, and for some years thereafter, strike leaders did not ordinarily go out on picket lines, for the same reason that staff generals don't go into the front lines— they would be picked off. However, a few days after we had become full members of the strike committee, the strikers were beginning to wilt under the beatings to which scores of them were being subjected every morning and afternoon. It was decided that something drastic had to be done to boost morale, namely, that a number of local leaders, along with Cedric and myself, should head the picket line on a certain afternoon. It might moderate the police brutality somewhat. If we should be beaten up, the fact that we had gotten it too would nerve others to stay on the line, whatever might come. Utmost precautions were taken to instruct those who were going on the line that day to refuse absolutely to be provoked into counterviolence. This was done publicly so that the labor spies, who infested the strike, and about whom I shall write later on, would carry the word to the police.

Shortly after four o'clock that afternoon, the procession left the hall which served as headquarters, with Cedric and myself at the head. In a few minutes we were on the street opposite the Arlington Mill. As soon as we got there, police on foot, on horseback, and in sidecars swarmed into the neighborhood as if to quell a raging mob that had gotten out of hand. We took one turn back and forth before the Arlington. There were no incidents and there was no shouting. Shortly after we started the second lap, Cedric and I reached a point where a street branched off to the left and then almost immediately took another bend to the left. Thus people on the main street could not witness what happened in the side street.

At that moment, several mounted cops suddenly cut Cedric and me off from the picketers behind us, all of whom were forced by other police to keep walking straight ahead. As soon as we had been shunted into the side street, they began beating us. One of them made the mistake of hitting Cedric at once on the back of the neck and knocking him unconscious, so that he had to be lifted and carried into the patrol wagon, which was conveniently waiting nearby. They beat me around the body and legs with their clubs, taking care not to knock me unconscious, and forced me to keep walking slowly in order to avoid being trampled by the horses.

We were passing a barn that seemed to be shut tight, but suddenly a door opened, an arm shot out, grabbed mine, pulled me into the shed, and slammed the door shut again. In the half light I saw that it was a woman. She could not speak English. She hurried me to a side door of the barn, while the police clamored and cursed outside. She tried to hurry me from the barn into her house, which adjoined it. The police were too quick for her. Some of them had leaped into the yard. They grabbed me, as she tried in vain to hang on. She let go and cursed them in their turn.

The cops got me back on the sidewalk and resumed the systematic beating, with the result that before long I was too exhausted to keep on my feet and was deposited in the wagon by the side of Cedric, who was slowly coming back to consciousness.

In the police headquarters downtown we were placed in separate cells. The one I occupied was at the end of the row. The wall, along which was a wooden bench, the only place to sit or recline, was made of metal. Policemen in relays beat a steady tattoo on that wall. There was a brief interruption when a police captain from Newton, who had been loaned to Lawrence for strike duty and whose son had been a member of my Bible class in Central Church, took his stand before the cell door and looked at me through the bars. He spoke scathingly of the disgrace of a minister of the Gospel behaving in such a way that he "had to be thrown into jail." When he left, hammering on the cell wall was resumed. But shortly before nine o'clock, about three hours after we had landed in jail, we were told that bail had been posted and we could go out. It was an immense relief, for at nine o'clock prisoners were transferred for the night to the prison on the outskirts of the town and it was more or less routine that *en route* prisoners "tried to escape and had to be beaten into submission"—with no witness on hand except the police who did the beating. That is why our fellow committee members had worked so desperately to get the cash before the deadline.

Part Eight

The arrest and beating of Cedric Long and me served to heighten and steady the morale of the strikers. When the case against us for "disturbing the peace" came before the city court about a week later, the judge dismissed it. In spite of the fact that we were acquitted because of testimony which clearly indicated that it was the police who had disturbed the peace, the judge lectured Cedric and me, telling us that Lawrence was no place for young ministers to visit at that time and that we should not be caught again, as we had been the week before, on a picket line.

For several weeks the strike settled down. Management made no special effort to get workers back. In the strike committee, we concentrated on raising funds for relief, bringing influential people from Boston and elsewhere to observe the situation for themselves, and holding daily meetings in several languages. These sessions were study classes in labor problems as well as business meetings.

When, however, the strike had lasted over a month and there were no signs of a break, conditions again became more tense. One night the police mounted machine guns at the head of the principal streets. This was done in spite of the fact that on the workers' side the strike had been remarkably free from violence. Over a hundred strikers were arrested during the sixteen weeks the struggle lasted. Because these cases were heard during, or after the close of, the strike, no one was sentenced to as much as a day in jail or paid even a one-dollar fine. Bringing in the machine guns was clearly an act of provocation. It was hoped that the strikers would resort to violence and that thereupon the strike could be discredited and broken.

This statement is not based on mere speculation. The morning the machine guns appeared, the strike committee met to discuss the strategy for dealing with this development. One of the members got up and made a heated speech, the import of which was: "The police are only a couple of hundred. We are thirty thousand. Let's seize the machine guns this afternoon and turn them on the police."

Very likely, this could have been done. Among the strikers and their families were a good many young men who had been taught guerrilla tactics during the war, and how to operate machine guns. They were bitter enough over the cut in wages with which they had been confronted as soon as the war was over, without the added provocation of having the quarters of the town where they lived besieged with machine guns, as if they were a conquered people.

The three young pacifist ministers who sat there listening to that speech were inwardly shaken and apprehensive as to what might happen. However, one after another, the local members of the committee, ordinary workers in the mills, made remarks to this effect: "The guns were put there to provoke us: why play into the hands of the mill management and the police? It would only discredit the strike. They can't weave wool with machine guns. All we have to do is to continue to stand together." This view prevailed. The man who had made the provocative speech was suspected of being a labor spy. Within two weeks I encountered him in the police headquarters of Lawrence under circumstances which proved that he was either in the employ of the police or in their confidence as an operative of some detective agency. He had made the speech at the instigation of the detective agency, or the police, or both, and the police department had known that he was going to do it.

Strikes in those days, especially those of hitherto unorganized workers, recall jungle warfare. We soon learned that on any strike committee or union executive board there would be one or more labor spies. Let me recount the most startling and illuminating experience we had, in this our first strike, with the phenomenon of labor espionage. After the strike had been going on for ten or more weeks, it had reached a critical stage. Our relief set-up was hardly able to supply even a minimum of milk for children and nursing mothers, and it was a question how long the workers could hold out. At this juncture one John Mach, financial secretary of the strike committee, asked Harold Rotzel, Long and me to meet him for a private conference on the outskirts of town. As financial secretary of the strike committee, John Mach had been in control of every penny that came in for relief and other activities, a total of over $100,000, which was even more money in 1919 than it is now. He had been, and to the end remained, scrupulously accurate and honest in handling these funds. Furthermore, along with two other strike committee members and me, Mach was on a sort of "inside" executive committee which handled confidential matters that could not be taken up in general committee meetings, where we knew spies would be present. Mach, therefore, knew everything there was to be known about strike affairs and plans.

When we met him at the appointed rendezvous he started in by telling us that he was leaving town that afternoon—and for good. Naturally, we threw up our hands and said that this was out of the question. "People will say," I exclaimed, "that you are running away with the money and the word will spread that the strike is lost and that now the rats—the leaders—are deserting the sinking ship." He replied in the most matter-of-fact fashion that this was precisely why he was going, that he was an agent of the Sherman Detective Agency, which had been working for the American Woolen Company in this strike. His employers wanted, at this critical juncture, to create the impression that the relief money was being stolen, and that the strikers would consequently face starvation unless they gave in. They wanted to throw suspicion on us as being about to follow John Mach's example and sell out the strike.

Mach then went on to explain why he was telling us this instead of simply vanishing and leaving us to speculate as to what had become of him. When the three ministers had first arrived in Lawrence, he explained, he had assumed that we also were secret agents, of a detective agency, or of the employers, or perhaps of some government agency. What else could preachers possibly be doing in a strike situation? Incidentally, one of the ways in which John Mach had made himself solid with us all had been by exposing several strike committee members as labor spies. Later we were to discover that it was fairly common for a top labor spy thus to expose lesser agents in order to establish a reputation for devotion, courage and astuteness.

Mach went on to say that he had become convinced some time ago that we were on the level, and that he was impressed. Insofar as it was compatible with his responsibilities as a spy and strike-wrecker, he wished to avoid letting us down. Now a serious situation faced him. A grand jury had been convened to investigate the strike. A plan was on foot to indict me for murder. There had been a fatal shooting in our Italian relief station some days before. It was later conclusively proved in court that the incident had had nothing to do with the strike; it had been the unfortunate culmination of a private feud. But a case was being built up to the effect that the shooting was a result of the strike excitement; the "outside agitator" was, therefore, responsible and should be tried for murder. If this sounds incredible, I must remind the reader that in connection with the 1912 I. W. W. strike in Lawrence a similar case had been framed against two leaders, Joseph Ettor and Arturo Giovannitti, and that they had been kept in jail for over a year before the prosecution dropped the case.

Why was Mach warning us about the plan at the very moment when he was about to deliver a mortal blow against the strike? He explained that if an indictment was returned against me and he was called on to testify at the trial, he would have to say some things which would tend to incriminate me. He had, after all, been practically living with me for over two months and if in all that time he hadn't got some kind of "goods" on me, this would be bad for his reputation as a spy and reflect adversely on the usefulness of the spy agency to the Lawrence employers, who were paying a lot of money for "service."

Mach next proceeded to give us certain information—such as his "real" or other name, and places where he filed reports—which would enable us, if he testified, to prove that he was a spy and thus discredit his testimony. This would not be a reflection on him, but would only show how clever we had been to catch him.

In order that readers may grasp the full significance and the complexity of this spy's behavior, I have to add that a week or so before this episode which I have been describing, John Mach and I had spent almost an entire night together discussing strike strategy. He had tried persistently to convince me that, in order to get national publicity, get relief money flowing in again, and so on, something dramatic had to be done. His proposal had been that we stage a parade not confined to the mill section of Lawrence but moving into the principal street, which we had been forbidden to do. It was a virtual certainty that a clash would occur in which somebody would be killed—the police would see to that. Then they would have an extremely plausible case for murder against me. In other words, in his professional capacity, John Mach had been trying that night to build a case against me, although later as an individual who was convinced that we were on the level, he was willing to put information into our hands to save me. Whether he would have given us this information if I had assented to his proposal and had been indicted as a result of bloodshed incident to the forbidden demonstration, I am not certain. I think it is quite possible that he might have. The ability of human beings to perform in one capacity acts that they would abhor in another, to show understanding and mercy in one situation, while in another performing horrible atrocities, is frequently seen. The behavior of sensible people, including Christians and devotees of other faiths, in war is, of course, a case in point.

The nature of the labor struggle of the past can be understood only if we grasp the role the labor spy played because of the very nature of his job. Ordinarily, a professional spy did not confine his reports to straight statements about what strikers or unionists among whom he was placed were saying or doing. Most of the time, this would have been humdrum stuff, and employers would have soon stopped paying for information which they could pick up in other ways. Consequently, the labor spy's reports were nearly always highly colored, full of hints that workers were planning to blow up a plant or injure or kill somebody. Management would then decide to hire some more "operatives." But the process did not stop there. If spies were to constantly report that something violent and exciting was going to take place, and it never did, this would be bad for the spy business. So they went on, as John Mach did, to try to provoke the violence which would seem to bear out the accuracy of their dire warnings.

How had Mach gotten into this business and, specifically, why had he been regarded by the Lawrence workers as so eminently trustworthy that he had been given a key position in the strike? His background was Polish. It appears that he had picked up some training in intelligence service in the Kaiser's army before World War I. Some time before 1912, he had migrated to the United States and turned to employment with private detective agencies. At the close of the 1912 I. W. W. strike in Lawrence, which had been successful in its immediate objective, the employers had taken on several hundred labor spies and given them jobs in the plants as a means of breaking up the I. W. W. organization. John Mach was one of these spies. He operated, presumably under direction, in such a way as to help effectively in undermining the union and at the same time establish for himself the reputation of being a staunch unionist, a hater of capitalism and the bosses. His technique was to pose as an ardent syndicalist and perfectionist who could not tolerate any deviation from the highest standards. If some treasurer or collector of shop dues was ten cents off in his account, Mach would pounce on it in the membership meeting and make a big thing of it. He would do the same if some worker or union organizer said something which deviated, or seemed to, from orthodox class-struggle ideology. The effect of these tactics was to sow suspicion and thus undermine morale. Time would be consumed, with the result that most of the rank and file who had to go to work in the morning would leave the union meeting before the important business had been reached. This would be transacted by John Mach and a handful of others whose business it was to sit it out. Mach was never blamed for the disorganization, boredom and disillusionment. He was the shining example of the man who held up the noblest standards, who would not let anyone get away with carelessness or other sins, and who was always the last man still on the job at membership and committee meetings.

During World War I, John Mach had had a job somewhere in the intelligence department of the U. S. Armed Forces. But when the 1919 strike broke out in Lawrence he had promptly been hired and sent back to continue his union-wrecking activities. When the workers, especially the Polish ones, who had known Mach in 1912-13 saw him again, they hailed him as a comrade and hero.

The postscript: A couple of years after the close of the 1919 strike, when I was general secretary of the Amalgamated Textile Workers of America, John Mach came to see me. He offered his services to the union as a spy against employers. Whether he had experienced a conversion and now wished to place his talents and training at the disposal of the righteous cause; or whether he planned to play both ends against the middle and make money from management and unions both (which has sometimes been done); or whether he had been instructed to set a trap for me, perhaps similar to the one he had attempted in 1919, I do not know. I told him that his proposal was not one I cared to discuss. He did not press the matter and walked away. I have never seen him since.

Part Nine

Let me go back for a moment to the day the machine guns were mounted on the streets of Lawrence. In the afternoon, at about two o'clock, those of the strikers who could crowd into the one hall which would hold fifteen or sixteen hundred people, all standing and packed as closely as possible, met there, as they did every afternoon when the weather did not permit an outdoor meeting. The air was electric, as it is whenever large numbers of men meet in a crisis in the midst of a struggle. Speakers addressed them in several languages. Then it was my turn to try to explain the policy of refraining from violence, refusing to be provoked, which had been decided upon by the strike committee in the morning. The strikers had, of course, to be persuaded that it was a sound policy and to follow it enthusiastically; otherwise their morale would be hopelessly undermined. Men and women who, many of them, had already been clubbed on the picket line, whose savings had long since been used up, whose children no longer had shoes to wear to go to school, had to accept bitter defeat or a split in their ranks which could lead only to early defeat—or else they had to embrace non-violent resistance.

When I began my talk by saying that the machine guns were an insult and a provocation and that we could not take this attack lying down, the cheers shook the frame building. Then I told them, in line with the strike committee's decision, that to permit ourselves to be provoked into violence would mean defeating ourselves; that our real power was in our solidarity and in our capacity to endure suffering rather than give up the fight for the right to organize; that no one could "weave wool with machine guns"; that cheerfulness was better for morale than bitterness and that therefore we would smile as we passed the machine guns and the police on the way from the hall to the picket lines around the mills. I told the spies, who were sure to be in the audience, to go and tell the police and the mill managements that this was our policy. At this point the cheers broke out again, louder and longer, and the crowds left, laughing and singing:

> *Though cowards flinch and traitors sneer,*
> *We'll keep the Red Flag flying here.*

I have had other such experiences which have convinced me that the often expressed idea that Americans cannot understand nonviolence, as Indians (for example) do, is erroneous. Under certain circumstances, American workers will practice nonviolent resistance, as the Negroes of Montgomery, Alabama, did in their bus protest.

As the John Mach incident illustrates, desperate efforts to break the strike did not cease merely because it was conducted peacefully. The attempt to provoke mass violence having failed, terrorization of the leaders was again resorted to. More or less friendly newspaper reporters from out of town hinted that my life was in danger and that, since the strike had dragged out so long that it could not end victoriously, no harm would be done if I left town. Not long after these warnings, a group of men, some of whom were reliably identified as members of the Lawrence police force, in the middle of the night entered the hotel where I occasionally stayed and broke the door of the room which I had rented for the week. It happened that I had left town that afternoon unexpectedly to go to New York for a conference with officers of the Amalgamated Clothing Workers Union. Surprisingly, no spies or plainclothesmen had seen me leave town, or if any did, they had decided to keep it quiet. So the thugs missed their prey.

That night they did succeed in routing out a young Italian organizer, Anthony Capraro, who had been loaned to us by Sidney Hillman, the A. C. W. A. president, along with Harry J. Rubenstein, a Paterson silk worker who had been greatly influenced in his thinking by Daniel De Leon, founder of the Socialist Labor Party. Capraro was an engaging, if somewhat erratic, youth who was a fabulously eloquent talker in Italian. I remember vividly, in those days of failing relief funds, a meeting of angry Italian grocery and meat-market owners who had advanced more goods to the strike committee and individual families than they could afford and who were demanding cash to wipe out these debts. Capraro was sent to their meeting to talk the situation over. I had no idea what he or the storekeepers had been saying to one another during the early stages of the meeting, except that the latter were in a rage. Presently, Capraro broke into a speech. In a few minutes the audience became quiet; a little later tears began to roll down the cheeks of some of them. Pretty soon they were taking out their pocketbooks and putting bills into a hat as a contribution to the relief fund. Their action, which we publicized, served temporarily to stimulate others to contribute and enabled us to hang on a couple of weeks longer.

Capraro had been involved in another incident which had a direct bearing on his terrible experience the night the thugs broke into our hotel rooms. Carlo Tresca, a lovable fighter for freedom for several decades, had been one of the leaders of the 1912 I. W. W. strike in Lawrence, and probably its most dramatic figure. In addition to the general animosity of Lawrence authorities to the leading figures of that strike, Tresca was the object of special resentment on the part of the officer who in 1919 was chief of police. In the earlier strike, Tresca on one occasion had marched at the head of a procession of strikers who were approaching a point beyond which the police had warned them not to go. On the line marking the forbidden area had stood the future chief of police, with several officers behind him. Tresca, according to reliable accounts, had simply kept marching straight ahead, and, when he came up to the officer, had given him a resounding slap on the cheek with his bare hand. The officer had been so nonplused, as had been his aides, that they stood aside and let Tresca and his cohorts pass through.

This was an insult which some time had to be avenged. Tresca had been told to keep away from Lawrence if he was concerned about his health. The ban still held in 1919, and we were repeatedly warned not to bring him to Lawrence to address the strikers, or there would be "trouble" for him and the rest of us. Tresca was, however, a hero, especially to the Italian strikers. As the bitter days wore on, the effort to keep up their morale became more and more difficult. There were rumors that Tresca did not support the strike, or he would have come to Lawrence to help. We decided that he should come to address a mass meeting but that it would have to be arranged secretly so that he would not be injured. Capraro was in charge of the ticklish job of getting him safely into Lawrence and out again, without any of the numerous remaining spies getting wind of it.

Tresca was spirited into town. He saw a number of key people and urged them to keep up the struggle. In the evening he was brought by a back door into the hall where we had our mass meetings. As soon as the hall was filled, the doors were locked, lest any spy, having got wind of what was happening, should summon the police. The ovation when he climbed on the platform was tremendous. He spoke, received another ovation, embraced us and left again by the back stairs. Only after we knew he was safely out of town were the doors unlocked so that the happy strikers could go home and the less happy spies report to headquarters.

We had thought that there was going to be trouble, and there was. It was only a few days later that the strong-arm squad broke into my room—to find it empty. Then they routed out Capraro and took him in a car into the country. They gave him a frightful beating and left him senseless in a ditch near Andover, a town adjoining Lawrence. Fortunately, it was a comparatively mild spring night. Tony recovered consciousness as day began to dawn, and crawled out of the ditch and onto the road. As he was crawling along the road, a milk-wagon driver noticed him in time to avoid side-swiping him. The driver carried him to a nearby house, where the people took him in and called a doctor.

A short time before this, there had occurred an incident which I relate here, since it had a bearing on the eventual settlement of the strike. The strike had been in progress a good while when Henry Endicott, founder of the famous Endicott-Johnson Shoe Company, first interested himself in it. He had been the wartime labor commissioner of Massachusetts (I am not sure this was his exact title) and trouble-shooter for the Federal government in strike situations. He still occupied these posts in 1919. He had the reputation of being a progressive capitalist, and regarded the labor relations policy of the New England textile corporations as a relic of the Dark Ages. Through our attorney, George Roemer, a couple of us were in contact with Endicott, who, in turn, was in touch with Calvin Coolidge, then Governor of Massachusetts. The problem was that the strikers could not advance a proposal to arbitrate without this being interpreted as a sign of weakness. The employers did not want to consider arbitration at all. Endicott assured us—and I have no reason to think he was not honest with us—that Coolidge would issue a statement calling on both sides, as "good Americans," etc., to agree to arbitration, so that peace might be restored to the Commonwealth. If the strikers responded by indicating their willingness to arbitrate, Coolidge would bring pressure to bear on the manufacturers.

Coolidge *did* issue what seemed to be a strong, clear appeal for arbitration. Not without some difficulty, we persuaded the strike committee to issue a statement accepting arbitration. But Coolidge never issued another statement, although the manufacturers ignored us and him. Nor did we receive any indication that he had brought any pressure whatsoever to bear on them.

We had been tricked by Calvin Coolidge. Some time after the strike was over, John A. Fitch, for many years an honored member of the faculty of the New York School of Social Work, told me that when Governor Coolidge had issued his noble-sounding appeal for industrial peace and arbitration, Fitch had written the Governor expressing his approbation and urging that, since the strike committee had accepted the proposal, Coolidge now do his utmost to bring the manufacturers into line. Coolidge had replied that Fitch was badly mistaken, that the strike was a Bolshevik revolt and not a bona fide strike at all, and that you could not deal with such people. Coolidge's arbitration appeal was a piece of duplicity. It is natural to assume that the employers knew this all the time, either because he had confided in them or because they knew their man without having to be told in so many words what he was up to.

A few months later, Coolidge became a national figure, destined for the Presidency, as a result of his breaking of the Boston police strike. A little episode in connection with the near-strike of the police at Lawrence, which took place that same summer, deserves mention here. After the close of the Lawrence textile strike in the middle of May, Cedric Long took to writing anonymous memos to the Lawrence policemen, dealing with their wages, hours and working conditions. He showed that these were not much better than those of the textile workers whom they had so frequently clubbed in preceding weeks. Cedric himself had "received some education," as we used to say, at the end of a policeman's club, and I suppose that these educational letters of his constituted a case of heaping coals of fire on the policemen's heads. Anyway, the policemen got a considerable improvement in their pay and working conditions.

As the days passed, and the question of arbitration was left hanging, it became increasingly difficult to keep the strike going. The American Woolen Company opened a couple of its mills in other cities. In Lawrence, it offered any workers who would come back an increase in piece or hourly rates to compensate for the cut in hours from fifty-four to forty-eight per week. The temptation to return as individuals, without gaining recognition of the right to appoint shop grievance committees, became very strong. On the week end, at the close of the fifteenth week of the struggle, we held a series of conferences and mass meetings in a final effort to keep the workers out on Monday. It was well known that the first day of the new working week was crucial; if they did not stampede back into the mills Monday, they would remain out the rest of the week. We succeeded. The workers, with only a handful of exceptions, had the magnificent courage to remain on strike.

However, on Monday afternoon, the completely trustworthy members of the strike committee held a long conference and decided that we had no right to call on the workers for further sacrifices. The following week end, therefore, we would make no special effort to bring pressure on them. There being no settlement in sight, we anticipated that on the following Monday the workers—those who were not on the company blacklists—would go to work; all would be over, and the strike lost.

Some weeks earlier, a convention of textile workers from Lawrence, New York, Paterson, Passaic and a couple of other centers had set up an independent union, the Amalgamated Textile Workers of America. I had been elected national secretary. The Lawrence committee decided that it was my job to go to the other locals and prepare them for the shock which the collapse of the Lawrence strike was sure to cause them. On a lovely Tuesday afternoon in the middle of May, therefore, I was disconsolately making my way to the railroad station to take the train to Boston, and thence to New York. I was walking down the street on which was located the little hall where for four months we had held our daily strike committee meetings. As I approached the hall, I noticed a large automobile standing in front of the building. It was unoccupied. I slackened my step, wondering what that car, standing on the otherwise deserted street, might mean. I had just come abreast of the car when the door of our hall opened and a man whom I recognized as a friendly milk dealer, who had probably saved many babies' lives because he had sold quantities of milk on credit to the strikers, stepped onto the sidewalk. He recognized me at the same instant and motioned to me to come over.

"Lamont wants to see you," he said. Lamont, who was not related to the J. Pierpont Morgan partner, was the head of the American Woolen Company Mills in Lawrence. "What does he want to see me for?" I asked. The milk dealer answered that the only possible reason could be to talk about settling the strike.

He had arranged with Lamont to bring me to the latter's home in Andover shortly after five o'clock. It was then about two. We agreed that I should keep out of circulation during the interval, since it would be catastrophic to have it leak out that there might be a settlement and then have the hope dashed.

We met again at five, and he drove me into the spacious yard of Lamont's home. All about were trees in blossom. Lamont drove into the yard directly behind us, having approached from another direction. There, on the lawn beside the cars, the three of us met. The moment he laid eyes on me, Lamont began to excoriate me as "the outside agitator who has brought all this needless trouble and suffering to Lawrence." When he paused for a moment, I said, "Is this what you brought me here for?" He said, "No. How can we settle this damned strike?" It appeared that, at the very moment when we felt we had to give up, the mill management had decided that, with orders coming in again, they could not hold out, either.

I replied that, of course, we two couldn't "settle" it. The conditions were well known: a twelve percent increase in hour and piece rates, and recognition in all departments to shop committees, through which the union would have a voice in settling grievances. Lamont said that the American Woolen Company agreed. I asked him if he could speak for the other mill corporations also. He answered that he did. Then I told him that it would be necessary for the management of each mill to meet a committee of strikers from its mill on Wednesday morning and formally assure the committee that our terms were accepted. He agreed. We parted without shaking hands on it.

When I showed up later that evening in the relief station, where the strike committeemen usually got together informally, they thought they were seeing a ghost. By that time, I was supposed to be well on the way to New York. When I told them of the encounter with the milk dealer and Lamont, they were sure, at first, that the strain of the long weeks of strike and the anticipation of failure had been too much for me and that I was out of my head. I stuck to my story and seemed on the whole sober and in my right mind. When someone who had slipped out to telephone the milk dealer came back and confirmed my story, it was finally accepted.

Even so, the joy was restrained. These workers, who had gone through so much this year, and in 1912 and earlier, were not sure that the managements were not up to some trick. They were not going to let their joy really break out until the committees had met the managements and confirmed the settlement. Early Wednesday morning, word was passed around that workers were to meet by mills. The report of the meeting with Lamont was given. Committees were selected and went off to their respective mills. They returned promptly and reported that in each case agreement had been quickly reached.

That evening there was a great outdoor mass meeting, where the strikers as a body formally ratified the settlement and authorized those who were needed to put the machinery back in operation after a sixteen-week lay-off to return to work the next morning. They sang:

> *Arise, ye prisoners of starvation. . . .*
> *We have been nought; we shall be all.*

And that was that.

Part Ten

The two years or so that followed the termination of the Lawrence
textile strike in May, 1919, actually marked a continuation of that
struggle and further wrestling with the problems which it raised.
I have mentioned that while the strike was still on textile workers
from Lawrence, Paterson, Passaic, New York (silk weavers), Brook-
lyn (knit-goods workers) and a couple of lesser centers met in
convention and organized the Amalgamated Textile Workers of
America. It was not affiliated with other unions, or with the American Federation of Labor, which recognized only one union in any
trade or industry. In this field, the A. F. L. union was the United
Textile Workers of America, which in practice limited itself to
skilled workers, and which had given no help to the Lawrence
workers in their desperate struggle. However, the Amalgamated
Clothing Workers of America, under the presidency of Sidney Hillman, gave considerable assistance.

Hillman was then a very young man. Helped in part by the
stimulus to the manufacture of clothing supplied by the war, the
A. C. W. had gained some notable victories and achieved a solid
organization which was never afterwards to be seriously shaken,
and which has long been what might be called one of the showpieces
of the American labor movement. The A. C. W. stood for a militant
industrial unionism, and had a socialist or revolutionary vision and
ultimate objective. Its Italian and Jewish leaders had behind them
youthful experiences in the socialist and labor movements of Poland,
Russia, Italy, and other countries, and were convinced that capitalism
could not really solve the problems of the working people. At the
same time, believing in the need for political action, they rejected
the out-and-out syndicalism for which the Industrial Workers of the
World (I. W. W.) had stood. The A. C. W. leaders, while believing
that political and economic (or labor union) action both were indispensable parts of an effective working class movement, nevertheless held that each arm of the movement had its own function
and should develop according to its own genius or character. Ac-

cordingly, from the very beginning, the A. C. W. sought to give order and stability to the relationship between union and management, and introduced innovations such as providing full-time "impartial chairmen" for the clothing trade.

The Amalgamated Textile Workers of America had, almost completely, the outlook, approach and methodology of the A. C. W. Hillman cherished the idea that some day there might be a union which would embrace all workers who made clothing, starting back in the textile plants, and encouraged our infant organization partly because it might fit some day into that pattern. He was, however, shrewd and far-sighted and did not want to jeopardize the union of clothing workers by being tied in with textile workers until it had been demonstrated that a viable and stable union of the latter was a possibility.

The two and a quarter years that I served as general secretary of the A. T. W. were made up of week after week of unremitting, desperate effort to establish a beachhead (as we would now phrase it) of unionism in a chaotic industry, during a period of social ferment, postwar economic crisis and anti-labor hysteria.

I do not recall a week when there was not a strike on somewhere in our union, which before long embraced locals as far west as Chicago and neighboring towns in Southern Wisconsin. There was no strike without labor spies; no strike in which we did not encounter arbitrary, and usually violent, conduct on the part of the police; no strike, hardly even a union meeting in those days, where raids by Attorney General Palmer's men were not carried out or at least threatened. One of the results was that idealistic and courageous young men were attracted to the A. T. W., and served as organizers and strike leaders for a bare subsistence. A good many of them, I recall, as I check over the list, certainly had that "lean and hungry look."

One of them was Evan W. Thomas, brother of Norman, who headed activity in Paterson, then the country's leading silk center, for about a year. Evan had been imprisoned and tortured as a conscientious objector during the war. The Paterson city jail was a pleasant place compared to Leavenworth, and naturally held no terrors for him. After Evan left the union post, he worked his way across the whole of the United States for a year or more, gaining firsthand experience of conditions in many industries, and among hoboes. It was not until later that he received his degree in medicine. Along about 1937, we were again in close contact with each other,

in the Fellowship of Reconciliation, and to a greater extent in the
War Resisters League. During a considerable part of the time from
1937 to 1952, Evan was also our family physician. The fact that
he did much to make life comfortable and happy during those years
for my wife Anne, and that she had as deep an affection for him as
I have, is not least among the reasons which endear him to me.

No intellectual or pacifist seeking an outlet for idealism, but
a worker in the mills at Rockville, Connecticut, was James Dick,
the mainstay of the A. T. W. local there, as long as there was one,
and, after an interval during which no union could be maintained,
a mainstay of the United Textile Workers organization. Jimmy
Dick and his family subsequently lived at Brookwood Labor College
for a number of years, where Jimmy was superintendent of grounds
and buildings. In my life I have encountered many men and women
like him, who have spent most of their lives as wage earners, have
comparatively little formal education, but who had clear heads and
intellectual interests, who constantly risked their jobs for the sake
of the union, gave endless hours of voluntary labor to the cause,
displayed good judgment and common sense, were utterly dependable in difficult times, and did not consider themselves "any great
shakes."

One afternoon in the summer of 1920, one of our organizers
in Passaic telephoned the national office in New York to say that a
strike was brewing in the big Forstmann Woolen Mills, that there
would be a meeting of union members after work at five-thirty, and
that I should be there. What followed was typical of most of our
union meetings in those days.

A good-sized hall was filled with workers when I arrived, and
I started to speak about what to do in case a strike seemed necessary.
Two burly policemen stood at the end of the middle aisle in the
back. How many detectives and labor spies there may have been,
no one knows. I had been speaking for only three or four minutes
when the two policemen plodded down the aisle and planted themselves in front of me. One of them said: "Orders is you can't speak
here"—meaning in Passaic. I asked whether this meant that if I
went on talking they would arrest me. They indicated, a bit hesi-
tantly, that it did. I asked if they would permit me to explain this
to the audience. They were nonplused at this, said, "O.K.," and
took their stand some distance away.

I launched into a discourse on civil liberties, on how wrong it
was to interfere with meetings such as this, and then eased into

further talk about the conduct of a possible strike. After some moments, the police advanced again and repeated: "Orders is you can't speak." I asked a little more specifically if this meant that, unless I stopped talking, they would physically force me to stop if I did not submit to arrest. This proved to be a problem about which they had no "orders is." So, after a moment's hesitation, they said they'd have to phone the chief.

I was very certain that under the conditions which then prevailed, they would come back with definite orders to arrest me at once. I talked fast in order to get in all the necessary instructions and answer questions raised by the workers, who were thoroughly enjoying the situation. The policemen did return with a clear answer to the question I had raised, and escorted me into the patrol wagon, which had been waiting outside all the time.

The final evidence of the arbitrariness and illegality of the whole business came when I was ushered into the office of Captain Turner, chief of police, at city hall. He politely bade me sit down. Then he looked at me for a moment and said: "Now that I've got you here, I don't know what to do with you." It seemed that the commissioner was out for the evening and the captain did not want to get involved in any unforeseeable difficulties.

It happened that I had planned to go on to Paterson for a union meeting after the meeting in Passaic. I suggested to Captain Turner that he just let me go to Paterson—on the same kind of mission for which I had come to Passaic. He at once agreed, and proposed that I stop in Passaic on the way back! But I explained that I had a wife and a couple of children in New York who lived a rather hectic life and would be nervous if I didn't get home until the middle of the night, or not at all. With that, Captain Turner yielded still further and agreed that I should go home after the Paterson meeting and that he would let me know whether or not I was wanted back at all. To this I demurred, stating that it was necessary that I have a clear understanding as to whether union meetings and organizers could be arbitrarily interfered with at the whim of the police and the employers. When I went back to the Passaic city hall, two days later, I was informed that there was no charge against me, but neither was there any assurance that I would not be interfered with the next time I came to town.

Not long afterward, in Paterson, there was a silk workers' strike. Norman Thomas came out to join the picket line when the police tried to make picketing impossible. Before long, Norman, Evan,

I and most of the local leaders were in jail. We spent a number of hours in stimulating, and sometimes hilarious, discussion before being bailed out. When we appeared in court a few days later, the charge against us was again dismissed after the damage of interference with the strike and intimidation of the workers had been done.

During the same period, in an effort to arouse public opinion against this treatment, a civil liberties meeting was held in Passaic, with Norman Thomas as the featured speaker, as, to his undying credit, he has been so many times on similar occasions. A few minutes after the meeting got under way, as Norman was reading the Declaration of Independence, the lights went out. The police were responsible. Somebody—Norman himself like as not—remarked that consigning the Declaration of Independence to darkness was just what was happening in Passaic. In the midst of such conditions, accompanied by a serious depression, the effort to establish that beachhead of unionism in the textile industry had only the most meagre and precarious success. So far as Lawrence itself is concerned, nine months or so after the termination of the historic strike, the mills closed down completely for lack of orders. It was months—I have not checked how many—before they opened up again at all. It was still longer before they were operating at anything like full capacity. When small numbers of people were taken back, as work was painfully resumed, the mill managers took care that there would not be among them a single person who had been active in the strike and in the union afterward. Some years later, the attempt to build a union had to begin again from scratch— except for the memory of a heroic struggle which inspired young workers to try, in 1924 and later, what their older brothers or parents had done in 1919.

One other episode of the A. T. W. history during my time as general secretary deserves mention. We were one of the American unions invited to send delegates or official observers to Moscow to constitute what later was to be known as the Red International of Labor Unions. This was during the chaotic formative period of the Communist movement in this country, when various groups were involved. It was, and is, my impression that probably two of the seven members of our national executive committee were members of one or another of these groups. They did not press for favorable action on the invitation. I am sure that if I had recommended such action it would have been adopted and, as the general secretary, I would have been the delegate. Though it was then not altogether clear what the proposed meeting was to do, I was opposed to our participation. When a couple of years later the R. I. L. U. was under way and William Z. Foster was urging American unionists to affiliate or cooperate with it, I was opposed. This may be the first instance of my "long collaboration" with Communists, and Communist fronts, which J. Edgar Hoover has in his records.

One of the reasons why I felt it inadvisable to send a delegate to Moscow was simply that since we had not been able to build a viable organization at home, why pretend we had any title to a role in building any kind of world organization? Maneuvering with what amounted to paper organizations (a practice to which Communists have regrettably been addicted) always reminds me of the fact that one of the very first unions in British labor history, which had only a handful of members even there, was known as the Grand National Consolidated Union of Great Britain, Ireland and the World.

Part Eleven

When I resigned as general secretary of the Amalgamated Textile Workers of America, in the summer of 1921, and moved to the newly established Brookwood Labor College, forty miles north of New York, to become its educational director, I was thirty-six years old. Ahead lay another twelve years of continuously exciting pioneering in labor education, with Brookwood as its center; efforts at stimulating and cleaning up the pre-C. I. O. labor movement; the break from Brookwood in the midst of the Great Depression, followed by involvement through the Unemployed Leagues in the desperate struggles of the depression victims; the attempt to provide non-Communist radical leadership in economic and political spheres; ventures in united fronting with Communists, followed by a drastic break; eventual conversion to Marxism-Leninism and collaboration in the leadership of the Workers Party of the U. S. A., a section of the Trotskyist Fourth International; participation in violent struggles in the West Virginia and Illinois coal fields and in the sit-down strikes in automobiles, glass and rubber, which revolutionized the American labor scene and established the C. I. O.— which has by now, alas, become institutionalized and perhaps incapable of radical action—the break with Trotsky, and the return to religious faith and to pacifism in 1936.

Other years, toils, experiments and risk-takings have followed. It is hard to realize these latter years already number twenty-two. But now, before starting on the Brookwood story, I want to say something about what goes on inside of me, or what goes on in that part of me which I am able to project onto a mental screen and contemplate. I want to comment on some of the drives or convictions which are behind the decisions I make and which determine the road I take.

Earlier, I wrote about a group of radical Christian pacifists who were loosely associated in what we called The Comradeship. We were in one sense a left wing of the Fellowship of Reconciliation, but not in any degree a faction which caused tension and organizational conflict. We felt the need of spiritual discipline, both individual and corporate, and were engaged in frequent intensive discussions as to the forms of common discipline. All of us as individuals set aside times for Bible study, devotional reading and prayer, and attended church services. We observed certain standards about the kind of work we would accept and the use we made of whatever income we had. Wherever a number of comrades lived near enough to one another, they practiced many things in common and engaged in some form of check on one another.

We were, of course, affected by the revolutionary ferment of the times, as well as by the visions of the prophets of a new heaven and a new earth, where righteousness would prevail and every man would sit under his own vine and fig tree, and none should make them afraid. We were also imbued with the idea (to use a formula common in those days) that we should order our lives today as if the Kingdom were already here. I can recall being appalled by socialists who proclaimed the advent of the classless and warless world and, in the meantime, lived as capitalists. We were accordingly concerned to establish what is now called an "intentional community," but which, in those days, we spoke of simply as a community. We were looking around for suitable rural sites and also had the idea that, alongside settlements on the land, there should be cooperative houses in cities where some members would live and seek to affect the day-to-day life of the neighborhood. We thought of an exchange of products between rural and urban sectors of the community as a sound economic measure. I suppose that among intentional communities in existence today the Bruderhof (Society of Brothers) comes closest to what we were groping after, though not exactly a parallel.

No community came out of those discussions and tentative explorations. The main reason was that at the critical juncture early in 1919 when the war was over and steps to realize the community idea might have been taken, a large percentage of those of us who were then footloose and eager and vigorous were drawn into the Lawrence strike. It is important to note that those who were most involved in that absorbing struggle did not break away from the rest of the group and were not cut off by it. On the contrary, it was in a very real measure this group of radical Christian pacifists that provided backing, leadership and a certain spirit to the Lawrence struggle. We continued to regard ourselves as a spiritual community, whether we lived in Lawrence or Boston or farther away. The fellowship among us was constant. There was never the slightest doubt that our families would be taken care of if any of us were injured or jailed. In the feverish atmosphere of a mass strike, amidst the practical decisions that had to be made daily about matters in which we had had no previous experience and which involved "compromises" of a kind which would never arise in an intentional community, we were, on the one hand, under a real, though not externally imposed, discipline of the group and on the other hand, materially and spiritually sustained by that fellowship.

I can see in retrospect that in some of its aspects the labor education experiment at Brookwood was a spiritual child of The Comradeship. Neither Harold Rotzel nor Cedric Long participated directly in that project, but it had substantial financial support from individuals in the radical pacifist group. Most of the comrades felt, I think, that Brookwood was an outgrowth and expression of their ideals. William and Helen Fincke, members of the Fellowship of Reconciliation, the former a Presbyterian minister who had been forced to give up his pulpit during the War on account of his pacifism, owned the estate which housed the School. Had they lived in or around Boston instead of New York, they too would have been part of The Comradeship. Certainly my own spiritual roots in the early days of Brookwood were in this group rather than in the labor movement into which I had recently come.

We did not make our living at Brookwood by farming or industrial work on the place. But faculty and students alike carried out a manual-work schedule. In the earliest years, virtually all meals were eaten in the common dining room. We devised our recreational and cultural activities without benefit of movies and such, and the results were invariably exhilarating and often creative. The life was simple, even rugged, especially in the beginning. Standards were not at all conventional or "bourgeois," and on the whole an effective group discipline prevailed. There were no conventional religious observances, but the group was unquestionably a dedicated one and a sense of spiritual comradeship existed which is felt to this day by dozens of the old graduates.

However, it must quickly be added that Brookwood was essentially a labor school and that its standing ground was that of radical "laborism" and not religious pacifism. In my own case it served in this respect as a transition. For, though I returned to religious faith and pacifism after abandoning them for a time in the Thirties, after 1919, when The Comradeship was interrupted in trying to form a community, I never again came close to helping to found, or to joining, an intentional community. My activity has been in the labor movement and in other organizations and movements seeking to effect changes in society, or a part of it, rather than to build an image or nucleus of a more ideal community within the larger society.

For me, I believe this has been right. I have no regrets or misgivings on this score.

In the first place, it seems to me that if we start with the concept that human beings are of infinite worth—because they are all children of God or on some other ground—and profess to conceive of mankind as a family which should live as a family, then our only valid objective is the transformation of society, not the building of a shelter for the saints or a secular élite within a corrupt social order, which in effect is assumed to be beyond redemption. There have been periods and regions where a civilization was indeed in process of disintegration and where it therefore would have been unrealistic to try to patch it up or even to think that an acceptable social order could be possible before the existing structure had been eliminated. It may be that the attempt to build communities which serve partly as refuges, and partly as nuclei of a new way of life, is useful in such circumstances. But even then it is not likely to be the only possible recourse.

Religious people in such a time see apocalyptic visions and embrace an apocalyptic view of history. I surmise that some form of apocalypticism is a conscious or unconscious part of the mentality of those who are drawn into intentional communities, whether they are religious or not. In our own day, many people are attracted to the Jehovah's Witnesses and the Seventh Day Adventists. These movements are growing. I think it must be granted that as dissenters from the prevailing culture they are pretty effective. There is no question that their members find an intense and deeply satisfying fellowship in their movements. It is also true that in these denominations there are standards regarding the use of income and a degree of economic sharing which one does not find in the more respectable churches. But these people do not live in communities of the kind we usually associate with that term. They live much more in the mainstream of urban or rural life, and mingle more constantly with other people than communitarians generally do.

The same may be said of the early Christians, and it will certainly not be contended that they were not effective or that they did not achieve *koinonia* of a remarkable kind, even though they did not live in some Middle Eastern or Italian Rifton or Primavera settlement, but rather in a second- or third-century equivalent of London, Paris or New York. "See how these Christians love one another," their neighbors used to remark.

Is there not something "precious" and "fragile" about many "community" experiments, in comparison with these past and contemporary movements? I have puzzled over the question of whether many community experiments are not outlets for certain types of intellectuals and disoriented middle-class people which are therefore inherently incapable of expansion beyond very narrow limits.

In the second place, the justification of an intentional community as a factor in the transformation of society, rather than as a shelter from society, would be that the community was a model of how society should, and eventually might, be organized; in place of a competitive economy here we have a model of cooperative economy. The great problem that confronts us in this realm stems from the development of technology; how, in a super-technological civilization, keep the human spirit from extinction, and generate brotherhood? It is possible that some of the European "communities of work" are making some contribution to the solution of this problem. It does not seem to me that any of our recent American experiments have solved it. On the other hand, the consumers' cooperative movement and some producers' cooperatives have, in my opinion, made a contribution at this point. If I understand the situation, it would also be correct to say that the more viable "communities of work" in Europe owe their existence largely to the fact that people simply needed to make a living. Another question that puzzles me, therefore, is whether an economic problem may be solved more effectively if it is tackled from an economic base or urge rather than by a group which feels (or thinks it feels) a sense of community and brotherhood, and then turns to the problem of making a living which will be consonant with that motivation.

If intentional communities seem not to give a convincing clue as to how to adjust positively to modern technology, how to make it serve true human needs, and not just foster immature or perverse desires, another weakness seems to me to be that they do not make nearly so decisive a break with the prevailing economic system as their members want to make, and apparently think in many cases that they have been able to make. In one way or another, most communities depend on subsidies or contributions from those who make, or who have made, money in the prevailing economy. Fairly often, some of their members take jobs outside the community. The communities have to buy and sell within the price system; they have to own property, and so on. I do not intend by these observations to express moral condemnation—except where living in a community makes people feel more morally superior to those outside than is warranted by the facts. But it seems to me doubtful whether the communities give us a model of how society generally should, and can be, organized.

Thirty years ago, there were enthusiastic consumers' cooperators who rejected labor organization and political activity as unnecessary or immoral because they involved social struggle. All that was necessary, according to these enthusiasts, was steadily to bring the economic order within the cooperative orbit, to buy up one sector of enterprise after another: the retail cooperative stores would combine to set up a wholesale co-op; the wholesale co-ops would start producing their own food, manufacturing their own furniture, and so on. One day capitalism would vanish, and the surviving capitalists would be transmuted into cooperators. It seemed to me that this theory ignored a good many aspects of reality and in particular the social power-structure.

In somewhat the same way, certain communitarians seem to think that the one effective as well as "pure" way to build a new society, and put an end to the social ills which afflict us, is for more and more communities to be built; after a while (probably a long while), everyone will be living in communities. This also seems to me an oversimplified view. There is the dominant fact of our time that the nuclear arms race and the power-struggle between super-states may simply wipe out whole nations, or even mankind, including the most ideal communities. I believe that economic, political and cultural struggles against war and its causes are necessary struggles in which we try to involve masses, and which may affect the decisions of government and the structure of society as a whole. There have to be similar struggles to end economic exploitation or, for example, the racial pattern in the South. The persistence of that evil pattern can work havoc on a community such as the one called Koinonia. The community can help to battle the pattern, as Koinonia did, but formation of communities is not the only means that has to be employed.

To cite another instance, Vinoba Bhave, in India, has carried out a notable activity by diminishing the exploitation of landless peasants and eventually altering the pattern of land ownership and thereby the whole social and political structure. He has employed the method of *Bhoodan,* getting landowners to give a portion of surplus land to those who have none or little. He has not used the ordinary political methods of getting laws passed, and so on. I believe that this experiment is highly significant and that it should be approached with a fresh mind and a desire to penetrate into its full potentialities. In the meantime, however, India lies under the threat of war. The conduct of its government in foreign affairs is an important factor in determining whether the *Bhoodan* movement survives. Moreover, forces are at work within India which may lead, for example, to its going Communist. Fumbling and often corrupt as are the economic and political measures which are used in trying to deal with these problems, I do not see how one can simply turn one's back on these measures. The problems entail too much suffering for people today and perhaps for the generations to come. I am sure that many are called to involvement in these struggles—the effort, as Buber phrases it, to "drive the plowshare of the normative principle into the hard soil of political reality."

One other consideration which has kept me from being drawn again toward community life is that the impulse which draws a good many in that direction is an ascetic one which I do not share. I do not contend that asceticism has no place in human life. I believe that it is a vocation to which some are called. I believe that in some it has borne rich spiritual and social fruit, despite the fact that it is usually based on what I believe to be a profoundly wrong separation between body and soul, flesh and spirit, and a classifying of the "flesh" as evil. But as our own contemporary American life so revoltingly illustrates, the temptation merely to amass things and to live for "kicks" derived from "conspicuous consumption," while half of mankind lives on the edge of starvation and "Christian" nations practice the atrocities of brutal racial discrimination and preparation for nuclear war, is so strong and prevalent that any critique of asceticism must be made with reservation. I read not long ago that a surprising number of American troops in World War II carried copies of Thoreau's *Walden* in the hip pockets of their fatigues. There they would read such counsels as these: "A man is rich in proportion to the number of things which he can afford to let alone. . . . Beware of all enterprises that require new clothes."

My own vocation, however, has certainly not been to asceticism as it is usually understood. This is because I have a deep-seated conviction that the aim and the essence of life is love. And love is in its inmost nature an affirmation, not a negation; an embracing and being embraced, not rejection and withdrawal. In the degree that it is there, joy blossoms forth. Love in its very nature also implies discipline. Indulgence is the opposite of love. Moreover, love in its very nature implies the capacity for sacrifice, in other words, non-attachment as far as material goods, or popularity, or simple bodily pleasure in eating or making love, or the enjoyment of beauty in art and nature are concerned. But this is not the same as loathing these things or feeling guilty about enjoying them when they are bestowed upon us.

But I must not pursue these matters further now. The main point is that my work for four decades has been mainly in social movements, in economic and political struggles. I am aware of the limitations of such activity. It has, furthermore, its own peculiar temptations, to some of which I have fallen prey. But I believe that these struggles are important and that my place is in them. What I have come to believe increasingly is that they must be carried on by nonviolent methods, and in love; and I trust that the reader will keep this in mind as I write about the years, at Brookwood and later, when I wavered in this conviction.

Part Twelve

In the spring of 1921, a conference took place at an estate near Katonah, New York, in northern Westchester County, 42 miles from Grand Central Station, as the legend on the New York Central station in the village pointed out. I attended as semi-official delegate of the Amalgamated Textile Workers of America of which I was still general secretary.

There were other trade unionists present or in close touch with the conference group. Of these James H. Maurer, then, and for a number of years following, the President of the Pennsylvania Federation of Labor, was both the most outstanding and the most typical of the group. Miss Franca Cohn, for many years Educational Director of the International Ladies Garment Workers Union, and Abraham Lefkowitz, a leader of the American Federation of Teachers which was then in its hectic infancy, were other prominent figures among the trade union officials who took an active part in the support and direction of Brookwood Labor College. Lefkowitz managed to be a pretty militant unionist and a vigorous and persistent critic of the New York City Public School system, while at the same time, through outstanding qualities as a teacher and administrator, rising to become the principal of one of the city's finest high schools.

Some of Brookwood's labor union supporters were, like Maurer himself, active in the Socialist Party. All had something of a socialist background and would be classified as socialists with a small "s." They were first of all, however, labor union people who had come out of the ranks of workers and were concerned to press union organization and to carry on the day-to-day struggle for improved working conditions, shorter hours, better wages, and status in the mill, mine or school-room. From this standpoint, they were "practical," "down to earth." Most of them, as I recall, indulged in the habit of broadcasting this fact to all and sundry.

At the same time, they were militants, severe critics of the narrow craft unionism of the American Federation of Labor, and visionaries who believed we needed a new social order. They contended that the workers would never solve their basic problems unless they strove for a radical reorganization of society, and that such a reorganization was possible. Though they held offices in unions, they were not at all typical bureaucrats. Except for some of the A. F. L. craft unions, such as those in the building trades, their unions were not institutionalized and did not have substantial treasuries. The unions were in process of ferment and growth. There was no big gap between the officials and the rank and file membership.

Above all, the men and women I am talking about and with whom I worked closely for a decade or more at Brookwood, in the general field of workers' education, and in various phases of labor organization and strike activity, were people of integrity. They had their shortcomings, in a few cases distressing or irritating ones, but they were solid and clean, incapable of playing cheap politics, though by no means political babes or bunglers. In the circumstances of that time, when organizing workers in unions was regarded as extreme radicalism and was fought bitterly by employers, police and other agencies, these people were engaged in continuous conflict and frequently encountered defeat and frustration; nevertheless they remained personally unembittered and wholesome. Partly because of the kind of people they were, and largely because the Communist Party—which was struggling to be born in those days—pursued for the most part an erratic and divisive policy in the unions, none of the trade unionists I am writing about, though temperamentally militant and radical, were drawn into the Communist movement in the turbulent Twenties and Thirties.

They came to the conference at Brookwood in the spring of 1921, or became involved in the project shortly afterwards, because they had a passionate interest in workers' education. In some, this grew out of their own consciousness of having had inadequate schooling and of being handicapped by that, both in their union activity and in their personal intellectual lives. The younger strike leaders and trade unionists to whom older leaders looked to back them up in local unions and on shop or pit committees—children of working-class families—had for the most part been compelled to go to work on graduation from the eighth grade, if not before. Quite a few of the latter were recent immigrants, or the children of recent immigrants, and accordingly had language difficulties. There were practically no facilities in those days, even in the big cities, not to mention the steel or coal towns, where young adults could supplement their curtailed school training.

But it was not only, or even chiefly, this situation which led progressive unionists to explore the possibilities of workers' education. They wanted the more capable younger unionists to learn about many things in an atmosphere which was friendly and not hostile to unionism. They wanted them to have a picture of the human struggle through the ages, some concept of the working of the economic system, a life-philosophy which integrated satisfaction of basic psychological needs with devotion to the cause of a new social order, with practical and, if need be, sacrificial and risky daily work for such a new order in working-class districts throughout the country. Thirdly, the pioneers in workers' education wanted young workers to acquire what we now call "know-how" in certain fields: how to keep minutes and write resolutions; how to conduct a meeting; how to organize a strike, provide relief, secure fair publicity for the cause, and so on.

These pioneers were well aware that if you educated people, taught them to think critically, they would presently be criticizing unions and union officials too. But the progressive unionists of that period were themselves virulent critics of many A. F. L. policies, and were glad to get recruits for the critical ranks. Moreover, as I have mentioned, they were not "bureaucrats," with settled jobs in well-to-do and institutionalized unions and consequently not inordinately afraid of criticism directed against themselves. It may be added that they were not anti-eggheads. On the other hand, they did not want the students who attended local classes or came to Brookwood for resident study to become professionals or intellectuals. They wanted them to go back to the shop or mine, to be active in local unions, perhaps, in time, to be elected to higher union offices but to "remain in the struggle"—not to acquire an itch to get on the pay roll—to retain a fighting edge and a dynamic idealism.

Of another type involved in the founding and development of Brookwood were professional people or intellectuals who were also pioneers in their way. They were path breakers, for one thing, of the adult education movement which, in a relatively short time, burgeoned in connection with public school systems, the universities and colleges, in the form of extension systems, schools of "general studies," etc., and in all kinds of voluntary private associations, as well as in some of the more forward-looking unions. The Socialist Party, which had been a vigorous and growing force in the decade and a half before the outbreak of World War I, did carry on adult or workers' education on a considerable scale, and the Rand School of Social Sciences was a flourishing enterprise in that period. There was, however, no such elaborate development of Marxist and other "social science" classes and varied cultural activities in connection with the young Socialist movement here, as was the case on the continent of Europe and to a considerable extent in Great Britain. In the United States, in general the traditional concept of education prevailed: namely, that one went to school for a longer or shorter period in order to "prepare for life," which meant for the job associated with one's "station in life." Then one proceeded to live and, by definition, "schooling" was behind one. This tended to be true even in the case of professional people and teachers, but especially of people in other categories. This attitude toward "schooling," which was taken over from the medieval and European tradition, was confirmed in this country until the period of World War I by the exigencies of frontier life. Frontier living was democratic and there was accordingly a strong determination that *everybody* should have some schooling; but equally the time for that was short and after that everybody had to get to work. In the new period, adult education became part of the American scene.

The social scientists who shared in building Brookwood were also distinguished by the fact that they recognized the role of labor organization in American life, believed that this role was fraught with potentiality for good in the adjustment of democratic ideas to a society moving from the pioneer into the industrial era, and wanted to contribute to the growth of unionism and the interpretation of its role to the general public, the intellectual community and the press. The most important beginning of this relation between social scientists and labor unions had been made by John R. Commons in the Economics Department of the University of Wisconsin. Either as students under Commons, as research assistants or fellow-teachers, or in more indirect ways, most of the professional people actively interested in Brookwood and in other workers' education developments had been substantially influenced by Commons.

World War I marked, of course, the first break of this nation out of its isolationism and initiated a kind of "return" to Europe. It served in turn to develop new contacts with Europe on the part of American unionists and intellectuals. These contacts for obvious reasons were more numerous and close with Great Britain than with continental European peoples. Such early supporters of Brookwood as Arthur Gleason, a researcher and exceptionally able writer, and Walton H. Hamilton, then at Amherst in what soon came to be

known as the Meiklejohn era and who went on to a very distinguished career as an economist at Brookings Institute and Yale, had
come to know and to be greatly influenced by such pro-labor British
intellectuals as R. H. Tawney. They had also seen Ruskin College,
a resident labor school situated at Oxford, and the more radical
London Labor College, as well as some of the local labor education
enterprises sponsored and nurtured by the Workers' Education Association with which the scholarly and greatly beloved Bishop
Charles Gore had cooperated and which, in the Twenties, had the
famous Archbishop William Temple as its chairman.

Men like Gleason and Hamilton were ready to give counsel and
enthusiastic backing to any similar ventures in the United States. It
may be mentioned at this point that such men were not dogmatic
Marxists but neither were they dogmatic anti-Marxists. They did not
have a concept of "objectivity" or "neutrality" in education, which
would have made them shy away from an educational venture which
was oriented toward the labor movement, which indeed felt itself
a part of it, and which was dedicated to changing the status quo
rather than conforming to it. At the same time they wanted the work
in such an institution to maintain high educational standards and to
proceed in the spirit of intellectual integrity and inquiry, not of
dogmatism. This was an approach with which the trade unionists of
whom I wrote earlier were in hearty agreement. It was the approach
which we sought to maintain at Brookwood and I think we succeeded rather remarkably in doing so.

Obviously neither the American Federation of Labor nor most
of the other unions of 1921 had more than a superficial, if any,
interest in such experiments. When they got under way the A. F. L.
officials were profoundly suspicious. The few unions which had
some interest, in a few cases a very real one, were in industries such
as textiles, clothing, mining or steel, where unions had tough going,
or had been unable to establish a foothold at all.

There had to be some people to bring the unionists and the pro-
labor social scientists together and to provide working capital, if a
resident labor college was to get going in the United States. Four
persons—two couples—then lived on the estate known as Brookwood and were hosts to the conference I referred to in the opening
sentence of this essay. One couple, as I have previously mentioned,
were William and Helen Fincke, pacifists and members of the
Fellowship of Reconciliation, which was then a little over five years
old. Bill or "Dad" Fincke, as he was known to the students at the

progressive school they had launched at Brookwood a couple years previously, was a Presbyterian minister who had been briefly the Director of the Presbyterian Labor Temple in New York.

The Finckes had been joined during the 1920-21 school year by another couple, M. Toscan Bennett and his wife, Josephine. Toscan Bennett had been a successful corporation lawyer in Hartford, Connecticut, and a founder of a Labor Party in that state. Josephine had been one of the militants in the women's suffrage movement along with her neighbor in Hartford, a Mrs. Hepburn, mother of Katherine, who a few years later became a famous actress. Common interest in education, as well as other causes, brought the Finckes and Bennetts together. The conference which led to the founding of Brookwood Labor College was called after the two couples had concluded, largely, I surmise, at the instigation of the Bennetts, that a school which would serve the labor movement more directly than the progressive prep school which the Finckes had headed was desirable and might be feasible.

The 1921 conference of trade unionists and educators decided to found a resident labor college and authorized the Finckes and Bennetts to serve as an organizing committee assured of full moral support. Among other things, they were instructed to secure an educational director.

A week or so later the Finckes came to see me and implored me to take the post. It did not take me long to make up my mind. The situation in the textile industry, and in the American Textile Workers itself, was not one which promised growth. I had never intended to become a labor official. I believed that my background, training, and so-called talents were such as to enable me to be much more useful in a workers' education venture than in the textile union post.

Early in the summer our family moved out of a New York apartment to a cottage on a low hill on the 42-acre estate at Brookwood, an idyllic place to bring up children. The family included two girls, one about five years old, the other three years younger.

The Finckes, Bennetts and Mustes set about producing promotional literature, devising a curriculum, looking for teachers. Before school opened, late in September, the Finckes had moved to a house a few miles away as a result of personality conflicts with the Bennetts, though they continued their support of the school and their most devoted support of the Mustes. A few weeks after school opened in September, Josephine Bennett left Toscan and went abroad. Toscan was in no position to contribute much to the func-

tioning of the school. At the time these were heavy blows. In retrospect, one may venture the opinion that it was an advantage to
have the situation clarified early rather than late and for one to be
given the opportunity to shape, in so far as any one individual ever
can shape, an enterprise to which I was deeply committed. In any
event, there was steady support from the educators and unionists
who had helped to launch the school and from the unforgettable
first class that registered in September, 1921.

Part Thirteen

Late in September, 1921, Brookwood Labor College opened its doors to its first class. We started virtually from scratch. There were a few traditions and a couple of the older students from the Brookwood School for progressive secondary education, which had operated on the estates during two or three preceding years. But that was all.

We contemplated at the outset a two-year course. The first year would be devoted largely to enabling the students to make up for what they had missed in academic schooling; the second would be devoted to more specific training for activity in the labor struggle. There were some twenty students in that first class. We hoped by the following autumn to be able to house about twice that number. Some forty-odd students, with about ten teaching and secretarial personnel, some of them with children, made up the community after the first year and throughout the rest of the twelve-year period when I was connected with the institution.

At the beginning, the equipment consisted of the Main House, situated on a lovely hilltop, which inevitably reminded visitors of the Washington home at Mount Vernon and which somehow conferred a kind of respectable status and dignity on the school; a two-story farm house and a barn at the foot of the hill that was crowned by the Main House; a small rambling cottage on your right as you drove up the hill; and another on your left, across a little brook, on a knoll where it was surrounded by trees which hid it most of the year. During the first year, the faculty consisted almost entirely of single people. In fairly rapid succession, we added a two-story brick women's dormitory (architecturally not exactly in keeping with the older buildings) and three faculty-houses (after an interval a fourth) along a ridge on the far side of the brook, which fitted beautifully into the landscape, and were fine residences by the standards of those days, though not in a class with the many palatial country homes in the vicinity.

The students in that first class were to a remarkable degree typi-

cal of the classes that followed, and the fact that the school established itself both as an institution in the eyes of the labor movement
(or rather the progressive section of it) and of academic circles,
and as a viable community in its internal life, must be credited
largely to them. They came to an institution which had no precedent
in American life, which might or might not outlast the year, and
where living conditions were fairly rugged. Except for the fact that
a few of them knew something about me because of my involvement
in the 1919 Lawrence strike, they had no idea who their teachers
would be. They made the venture of chucking their jobs and journeying to get a "labor education" mainly, of course, at the instigation and recommendation of the progressive labor leaders to whom
I referred earlier, who in turn were taking a chance that the experiment would work out.

If the members of that first class had been questioned as to what
"made" the school and the year for them, I surmise they might have
emphasized certain extra-curricular features, namely, Anne Muste
and our daughters, Nancy and Connie, who were, let the reader take
my word for it, angelic beings. Nancy did, in fact, play an important part in our public relations with the people of Katonah. We
sent her to the public school in the village. Most mornings, she rode
down there in the sidecar of the motorcycle of Stacy May, one of our
instructors, a protégé of Walton Hamilton at Amherst. Since we had
the reputation, as did the school which had preceded the labor college, of being "red," there were suspicions that we must be a "free-
love colony." One look at Nancy was enough to dispel any such
notions, and to convince all who were not dead set against being
convinced, that "they must be nice people up there on the hill."

"In the interests of truth," as the old Quaker said, perhaps I
ought to add that the trade of thirty-five people was quite an item
for the tradespeople, and that we paid our bills, a fact that also
helped to establish our good reputation.

I might also mention a quirk in the politics of Westchester
County at that time which came to the aid of one of the students of
that first class, a miner whom I shall call Tony. He was an immigrant from a part of what is now Yugoslavia and thus, by accident,
was an "enemy alien" during World War I. He had registered as
such and worked throughout the war in the Ohio bituminous coal
fields, thus technically serving in an essential war industry. Whether
by design or accident, however, he had had no subsequent contact
with the draft authorities during the war. To the bureaucrats there

was, therefore, a gap in his papers, though he had been doing exactly what he probably would have been required to do if his behavior had been "regular." Each time Tony appeared in the court to apply for naturalization, the United States commissioner suggested that they had better wait until the discrepancy in this foreigner's record was cleared up, and the judge agreed.

This was expensive business for a coal miner. Tony came to me with his problem, wondering whether he might not get his citizenship in Westchester County. The County in those days was solidly Republican, and Northern Westchester was solidly solid Republican. The only things the politicians were concerned about was Democrats. It is true we were all regarded as "socialists" of one kind or other, but a few socialist votes wouldn't have hurt, even if they had been counted.

Accordingly, when I went to the Republican boss of Northern Westchester with Tony's story, he readily assured me that he agreed that this fine young man should be admitted to citizenship, and said that "we" would "fix it up." The next time naturalization hearings were held in White Plains, Tony and I went down. The United States commissioner once more suggested postponement of Tony's case "until this suspicious gap in the man's record is cleared up." At this point Mr. Boss arose and said, as an immediate hush fell on the room, "Your honor, we have with us this morning a distinguished citizen of our county, an educator who is director of a very interesting school in our part of the county, and I think he is in a position to shed light upon this case." Whereupon I shed my light, after which the judge asked the commissioner whether in the light of the information provided by these two distinguished citizens of our county (the boss and me) it did not seem clear that Tony should be granted citizenship. The commissioner agreed. It did not cost Tony a penny.

The class was typical in that a considerable range of occupations was represented. There were naturally textile and garment workers, but there were also machinists, a member of a craft union of coopers, and even a couple of bituminous coal miners from Ohio. Miners from that state and from Illinois, Pennsylvania and West Virginia constituted a considerable percentage of the student body as time went on. They were a sort of balance to the garment workers, who came out of very different geographical, national and ideological backgrounds. To these garment workers and others, the miners were, I suppose, a kind of aristocracy of labor. They were "real workers," evoked images of the French miners in Zola's novels, and were types of native American radicals. After the first year or two, the building trades and railroad workers also were represented in the student body. It was, I think, in its second year that our first class was joined by a young Englishman who had spent several years at Oxford, then gone to France because he had been attracted to the syndicalist movement there, come to the United States and worked for a year or more as a migrant laborer, and then to Brookwood for "graduate" study. Subsequently, he worked here for many years as a labor journalist.

Except for an occasional youngster, the average age range was twenty-one to thirty, with several, usually, who were older. They were, in other words, mature men and women who already had several years of work experience behind them. They ranged culturally from people who were orthodox and devout church members from isolated and backward villages to extremely sophisticated people who read Marx and the great Russian novelists; who attended Provincetown Playhouse in New York and saw the O'Neill plays before they came to Broadway; saved pennies to get standing-room admission to the Metropolitan Opera House; and went to *avant garde* dances in Greenwich Village on week ends.

Having such people live together in a smallish community where they went to classes, worked, ate, had most of their recreation, and roomed together presented its problems, and was for some a harrowing experience. I shall never forget a young Pennsylvania miner, one of the noblest and most sensitive human beings I have ever met, who had made a living as a coal miner for years while giving leadership to his local union; and who, when he came to Brookwood, had no view of life, or information on which to build one, except what he had received from the priest of one of the Slavic Orthodox churches in a backward mining town. What he heard in my own class in History of Civilization, which started with pre-history, and from other students in bull sessions, shocked him terribly. After a couple of weeks, he came to me and almost wept as he exploded: "Everything I have believed is a lie, if what I am being told here is the truth." A young man with less integrity and guts would either have gone back home or taken it all complacently, waiting until he thought he had got his bearings. But he could neither run away nor take ideas lightly, as if they did not have what we would now call "existential" meaning.

Some years before this, I had learned one of the great lessons of my life, namely, that it is important really to listen to people. Most of us, most of the time that we are conversing with people, do not listen to what they are saying but are thinking of what we are going to say next. I am sure that the main service I have rendered many people, in the most varied situations, has been simply to listen. I told the young miner on that autumn afternoon, as we watched the setting sun set the leaves on the maples and oaks outside the window in flame, two things. One was not to take anything on anybody's mere say-so, to keep on thinking for himself. We, on our part, did not want to tell him, or anybody else, what to think. The other suggestion was that he write his priest, if he wanted to, or talk with him when he went home for the holidays. Later, he did talk with his priest, and what the priest told him must have reassured him, for he developed into a self-assured, highly intelligent student and, to use a trite phrase, a well-adjusted individual.

The educational process at Brookwood was deadly serious, continuously stimulating to teachers as well as students, and therefore a lot of fun most of the time. For the most part, the faculty members were academically well-trained people, had had some university teaching experience, or could easily have had college teaching posts. I do not think that any of those who held regular positions at Brookwood ever felt any urge to take conventional teaching jobs.

I used to say in lectures on workers' education, in those days, that the difference between the educational problem in high school or college and at such a place as Brookwood was that in the former you had students who did not know anything but knew how to say it, whereas at Brookwood you had students who knew a great deal but did not know how to say it. To put it in more accurate and restrained terms, a very large percentage of college students in those days had had little experience of life, education in their case having run ahead of experience, and consequently ahead of thirst for education. Most of our Brookwood students had already acquired a good deal of experience: they knew a lot about industry, politics, labor relations, and what the economic system meant in its impact on human beings. They knew, therefore, that they were ignorant of much that they needed to know. Their thirst for knowledge was what can only be described as "terrific."

When it came to the so-called tools of learning—composition and the rest—instruction often had to be pretty elementary. When it came to content, classes were often a medium of mutual education for instructors who had theory and students who could bring the test of experience to bear on theory. I think that those who were well-acquainted with the work of Brookwood would agree that, except perhaps for the least competent quarter of each class, the work was on a par with upperclass work in a good college or university.

Before turning away from the class of that pioneering 1921-22 year, I must again place on record my gratitude to them. They were a very large factor in "making" the school, both in the literal sense of building roads, making houses livable, and serving food, and in the sense of demonstrating its ability to educate workers and to develop a community with a high morale, in which people experienced deep satisfaction and grew in intellectual and moral stature. They established Brookwood's reputation. They impressed potential and actual contributors. The labor movement and the workers' education movement owe them a substantial debt. I owe them a lot myself.

There were also teachers at Brookwood, as has been hinted from time to time. During the first year, there were two young instructors, Stacy May and Eli Oliver. Remaining as English teacher from the former Brookwood School was the distinguished and beloved Sarah N. Cleghorn, "Aunt Sally," who wrote a number of the finest labor poems in English literature. It is appropriate to note now that she was a relative and intimate friend of the recently deceased Dorothy Canfield Fisher, who was an early friend of Brookwood and who, in the period following World War II, served as national chairman of the Committee for Amnesty for Conscientious Objectors. Aunt Sally's health was somewhat precarious at that time (despite which she survived for nearly four decades) and she left before the first year was over to join the Finckes in laying the foundations of Manumit School.

Her place was taken by Josephine Colly, a leader in the then infant movement to organize a teachers' union and a brilliant teacher, who remained one of the key staff members for nearly a dozen years. There were two other full-time staff members during the Twenties who remained for long periods. One was David J. Saposs, who had studied under John K. Commons at Wisconsin and had contributed to Commons' monumental labor history. His reputation as one of the nation's most eminent historians and analysts of the labor movement, here and abroad, grew during his years at Brookwood. The other was Arthur W. Calhoun, who taught sociology and economics. Calhoun had been at Clark University during the golden era of G. Stanley Hall's presidency, a colleague there of the young Harry Elmer Barnes. Both of them remained productive and unrepentant "rebels" and provocative and stimulating teachers. The continuity in service of these three people and myself, and our ability, despite considerable differences of temperament and opinion, to work with each other and with younger staff colleagues as a team had much to do with the effectiveness of Brookwood.

The educational process was also helped greatly by a steady stream of visitors, most of whom gave one or more formal addresses and engaged in protracted talks with faculty members and students. Hardly anyone was ever paid for these lectures. Those who came did so primarily because they were interested in the "experiment," and they often made us feel that they owed us something for the privilege of intruding upon our time. A list would include such diverse people as Paxton Hibben, Harry F. Ward, Powers Hapgood, William Z. Foster, Henry R. Linville, for many years head of the Teachers Union (now Guild) in New York, and Joseph Schlossberg, of the Amalgamated Clothing Workers. Visitors from abroad included John Strachey, at that time a Communist, later a Labor member of the British Parliament, and later still a member of the "shadow cabinet"; André Philip, French economist and Socialist leader, who was, for a short time after World War II, a member of De Gaulle's cabinet; J. Olson, the Norwegian Labor Party editor at whose home Leon Trotsky lived during the years of his exile in Norway (though Olson was not a Trotskyist); and that delightful English labor author and cartoonist, J. F. Horrabin.

From the academic world came such people as Harry A. Overstreet, then a philosophy professor at the College of the City of New York; Everett Dean Martin, the social psychologist who taught at Cooper Union; Harry Elmer Barnes, then at Smith; Horace Kallen; Reinhold Niebuhr, who was beginning to make a reputation as a theologian; Sumner Slichter, then at Cornell, I think, later for many years at Harvard, and whom some people considered the nation's foremost economist.

Still others on the list would be Abraham Epstein, responsible probably more than any other individual for the social security laws now on our statute books; Father John A. Ryan, of the Catholic Social Welfare Council; Norman Thomas; Roger N. Baldwin; Bertram Wolfe, later a noted anti-Communist lecturer, but at that time a Communist Party educational director; J. B. S. Hardman, who for years headed the Amalgamated Clothing Workers' educational department; Oscar Ameringer, labor journalist of the Progressive Miners of Illinois and incomparable *raconteur;* and such labor stalwarts as James H. Maurer; Phil Ziegler, of the Railway Clerks; Fannia Cohn, of the International Ladies Garment Workers Union; John Brophy, then head of District No. 2, United Mine Workers; Abraham Lefkowitz; Robert Fechner, of the International Association of Machinists; and John Fitzpatrick, joint leader of the great 1919 steel strike, and for many years the militant head of the Chicago Federation of Labor.

There may have been dull moments at Brookwood. If there were, I have not been able to recall them as the figures of its first class and of the visitors through the years have paraded before my eyes.

Part Fourteen

Although we sought to achieve high educational standards at Brookwood, the school did not have a body of economic and political doctrine to inculcate. We deliberately sought to stimulate intellectual controversy. On the other hand, we were not academic, in the usual sense of that term, in our approach. We did not conceive of objectivity in the realm of social studies and the humanities as a stance apart, from which one observed social processes as one observes an amoeba under a microscope. We held, as I still do, that any educational institution is placed in a specific social context. There is a constituency which uses its products and whose needs it must in some fundamental sense serve. Such objectivity as is possible to achieve, for those who work in an educational institution, is reached by recognizing this fact and by trying to make allowance for biases rather than ignoring their existence.

Another result of our basic approach was that, as students and teachers, we did not think of ourselves as temporarily withdrawn from the labor struggle while preparing for future activity. Geographically, we were off in a somewhat idyllic country setting, and the students were away from their jobs and day-to-day union activities. But psychologically, we were participants in the economic and political movements of that time. Students continued to attend local union meetings if their homes were near enough to permit it. Others might travel farther if there was a crucial policy decision to be made in their unions, or a strike in progress.

The school did not, of course, as an organization have representation at labor meetings or seek to influence policy. However, not long after the school was launched, the teachers and other staff members were organized as Local 189 of the American Federation of Teachers, which was an affiliate of the American Federation of Labor, though certainly not a favorite child of its officials. Among the more or less conflicting, but invariably somewhat uncomplimentary, ideas about teacher unionism which typical "labor skates" had in those days were these: that teachers were too dumb to know how to conduct a labor union properly; that it was not altogether respectable for teachers to be organized like plumbers and plasterers; that these smart teachers would introduce strange and probably subversive ideas into the unions. As union members, nonetheless, Brookwood teachers gained experience and exerted influence as delegates to city central trade unions and state federation of labor conventions, as well as to national gatherings of the A. F. T.

One of the younger members of the staff wrote of some of her experiences:

When appeals for miners' relief went out in the bitter winter of '28, we canvassed Katonah village for clothing and spoke at nearby union meetings for contributions. With another member of the staff, I even tackled the notoriously tough Westchester County Building Trades Council and collected a heaping truck-load of clothing, and their promise to send money. Further acquaintance with labor officialdom was afforded when I became a delegate to the New York Central Trades and Labor Council. I stood up before those hard-boiled bureaucrats and proudly took my little oath of membership, only to be promptly disillusioned by the interminable, futile, smoke-spittoon sessions of that august body.

To some extent, all the Brookwood faculty members functioned as participants in the labor movement; some were involved in many ways. A time was to come when the extent and nature of such involvement would be a subject of intense controversy among us, but this was not the case in the early period. This is, therefore, an appropriate moment to deal with labor and political developments in the early Twenties, culminating in the LaFollette-Wheeler Presidential campaign of 1924, the only campaign of any kind, so far as I can recall, in which I actually took the stump on behalf of a candidate for public office. I have never been a candidate for public office myself, though periodically the idea that I should run for Congress, or even for the Presidency, as a pacifist or peace candidate has been advanced. Occasionally, I have played briefly with the idea. At some point in these reminiscences I should perhaps try to state my attitude toward the electoral system in a democracy. Suffice it for now to record the rebuke that was administered to me in the course of the 1948 Presidential campaign by an elderly lady of distinguished lineage in one of the Southern states who was an ardent pacifist. I had written her that, apart from other considerations, I had not been born in this country and therefore could not be a Presidential candidate, or at any rate could not serve if elected. She shot back a note saying that was "a very picayune and nationalistic excuse."

To return to the Twenties: World War I was followed by a depression and by vicious attacks on organized labor. I have already touched on some aspects of this situation in my accounts of the 1919 Lawrence strike and the vicissitudes of the Amalgamated Textile Workers. The combination of post-war depression and of extreme reaction, marked especially by a determination to wipe out the start made in union organization in mass production industries during the war, led to a number of gigantic struggles. They were generally pictured in the press as efforts of the forces of law and order and of the American (and Christian) system of free enterprise to beat back the onrushing wave of revolution. This picture was supposed to justify the anti-Red crusade launched by the Department of Justice in March, 1919, when one A. Mitchell Palmer (a graduate of Swarthmore College, alas, and a life-long Quaker) became Woodrow Wilson's Attorney-General, and laid the foundation for certain basic attitudes on the question of dealing with political dissent. These attitudes have since been more subtly and thoroughly applied by the F. B. I. under J. Edgar Hoover. (To offset the reference to Palmer's Quakerism, I should no doubt mention that Hoover was under the ministerial and pastoral care of the same Presbyterian minister in the national capital as was President Eisenhower. Each of the two religious bodies to which I belong ought to shed a tear for the other.)

The assiduously cultivated notion that the social upheavals of the time were caused by the onrushing wave of revolution was also held by many to justify the terroristic activities of an organization which appeared on the American scene about this time—the American Legion. Actually, the struggles of the period were defensive actions on the part of workers against efforts to beat down wages and, above all, to smash unionism (except in a few skilled trades), so that the power of finance and management should remain uncurbed in industries which had expanded and profiteered during the war.

One of the titanic conflicts was the steel strike of 1919. It was this strike which made a national figure—and for many years a widely respected and admired one—of William Z. Foster. With strong support from such incorruptible and militant unionists as John Fitzpatrick, then and for many years afterwards president of the Chicago Federation of Labor, Foster proved to be a magnificent organizer and agitator. He came out of a syndicalist, I. W. W. background. I think that those of us who knew him in those days felt that he had the ruggedness, straightforwardness, humanitarianism and essential foundation of personal independence (anti-tyranny, anti-state and so on) which we associated with the best of the Wobblies.

Not long after the end of the steel strike, Bill made his first trip to Moscow. Shortly after his return, he came to Brookwood and talked to the students and teachers. He made a favorable impression on quite a few. He was, after all, a "hero of labor" in the American sense, and he had been to the land of the revolution and had talked with the mysterious and fabulous persons who had "made the revolution." One of the questions in the minds of all labor activists at that time was whether Bill had joined the Communist Party. He sought to create the impression that he had not. I have carried with me all through the years a vivid recollection of my feeling on that day nearly forty years ago. I have lived it over again at fairly frequent intervals since. It was a feeling of uneasiness, certainly not of hostility in any personal sense. I felt that there was a human being inside him, but that it was under restraint, hidden somewhere. The element of straightforwardness was now lacking. There he was, over there, and here was I. It would remain so. Politically, we were not on the same road.

This impression, that Foster had put on blinders, had, so to speak, been shut in upon himself, was to be fully confirmed by later developments. John Gates, who left the Communist Party early in 1958, and who, like many others, had been an ardent admirer of Foster, the labor organizer (Samuel Gompers, John L. Lewis, Philip Murray were also in that category), points out in his important book, *The Story of an American Communist*, that in Foster's later years he paid practically no attention to the social and political struggles going on in the United States or elsewhere, but always seemed to have plenty of reserve energy left for internal party controversy and power struggles even after he had been stricken with a bad heart. He was uninterested in America, and pointed to the fact that his books had been translated for Communists into Russian, Chinese and many other languages. "He lived in a make-believe world of his own and, though more typically American than most party leaders, he was also strangely remote from his own land and people." I am reminded of a line, having to do with another matter, by a poetess who was a Communist in her youth: "Never lie blind within a dream."

The period after World War I was marked also by a bitter

strike of miners whose lot had been temporarily eased during the war but who, at least in the case of the soft coal workers, were cast back into the misery of low wages, episodic employment, perpetually hazardous work and company village life which was to remain their lot until New Deal days. Also involved in desperate defensive battles were sections of the railroad workers. The four operating Brotherhoods—engineers, firemen, conductors and trainmen—constituted a special case, but the railway shop workers and maintenance-of-way men were in much the same position as the workers in big industry. They still had to battle for bare recognition and some security in labor-management relations. As for the operative workers, when in those days anti-unionists disparaged workers, suggesting that if they had bathtubs they'd only use them to hold coal, we proudly pointed to the fact that tables of the parentage of enrolled college students showed a larger percentage of locomotive engineers than of any other vocation.

The consequence of the inability of workers to make progress by economic action was, as usual, a turning to political action. Leadership in this turn came primarily from the Railroad Brotherhoods, who were not affiliated with the A. F. L., but A. F. L. railroad workers in such unions as the Machinists also played an active part. At a meeting held in February, 1922, in Chicago, at the invitation of the Brotherhoods, there were present also representatives of the Farmer-Labor Party; the Non-Partisan League; the Committee of 48 (originally Teddy Roosevelt Republicans); church groups, such as the Methodist Federation for Social Service, the Church League for Democracy and the National Catholic Welfare Council; and the Socialist Party, which was led by the New York attorney, Morris Hillquit, and supported by such Social-Democratic figures as Victor Berger, who had been a congressman from Wisconsin, Daniel Hoan, Milwaukee Socialist leader and many times mayor, and James Oneal, journalist and leading anti-C. P. pamphleteer.

The Chicago meeting formed an organization called the Conference for Progressive Political Action (C. P. P. A.), which should not be confused with the Conference for Progressive Labor Action (C. P. L. A.), which came into being several years later and in which I was to play a much more active part.

The C. P. P. A. had in it a good many people, including the Socialists, who believed that an independent political party should be established on the lines of the British Labor Party. It was faced with the ever-present problem of the anti-independent-political-action stance of the A. F. L. The outcome of prolonged discussion and manifold maneuvering during the years 1922-24 was postponement of the issue of a new party, but agreement at the C. P. P.-A. conference in St. Louis, February, 1924, that in the 1924 elections C. P. P. A. should set up candidates for President and Vice President, Congress, state legislatures and other offices, candidates "who are pledged to the interests of the producing classes and to the principles of genuine democracy in agriculture, industry and government." The specific proposals of the platform that was eventually adopted were not Socialist, or very radical, but the Socialist Party was accepted as part of C. P. P. A., and the platform contained little or nothing with which Socialists could disagree.

Here a brief additional comment on Socialist Party participation in this movement needs to be made. We have pointed out that the C. P. P. A. was the result of a movement to the left among labor people under the pressure of unemployment, wage cuts and vicious attacks on unionism. S. P. participation in what was not a specifically Socialist political program marked a move to the right so far as the Party was concerned.

The Party had been growing and seemingly headed for an important role in American life in the decade before World War I. When the war came, and especially as the United States itself was drawn in, the Party had had to face the war issue. It is an issue which has been present ever since and which, in my opinion, neither the S. P. in this country nor its counterpart anywhere else has ever satisfactorily resolved. The European Socialist movement had been vocally internationalist and anti-war before 1914. Internationalism and anti-militarism had been deeply ingrained in Socialist life, and accounted in considerable measure for the hold Socialism had on the European masses. This fact was amply demonstrated by the traumatic effect of the collapse of the anti-war stand in the great parties of Germany, France and Great Britain in 1914, and the ascendancy of national loyalties over international working-class solidarity in these movements.

The S. P. in this country officially maintained an anti-war stand, and its leader, Eugene V. Debs, became an immortal hero of the anti-war movement. To a considerable extent, also, the Party continued to have popular confidence and support—whether because of or in spite of its anti-war stand—as the vote of nearly one million, cast for Debs while he was still in prison in 1920, demonstrated.

However, this vote was less than four percent of the popular vote, as against the six percent Debs had received in 1912.* Moreover, the anti-war stand of the Party had caused bitter and exhausting internal controversy and led to the defection of a large percentage of its leading intellectuals.

The war was hardly over before the controversies centering around the Russian Revolution and the S. P.'s relation to the world Bolshevik movement split so-called right-wing and left-wing Socialists wide apart. The Communist Party eventually emerged out of this turmoil, and from then until now, the two have expended considerable energy in fighting each other. Thus we come in this period upon another characteristic of radical political life in the United States. Occasionally, there has seemed to be an approach to something like a mass socialist or labor party. But most of the time, the radical movement has been sectarian. It may perhaps be argued that objective conditions in this country make the development of a revolutionary, socialist, labor party—perhaps any kind of "third" party—impossible, and that the sectarianism which has marked the political left is essentially an effect, rather than a cause. At any rate, it was under these conditions of weakness that the S. P. turned toward the C. P. P. A., for the time being resolving the perpetual problem of whether to plug away at building the S. P. itself, or to regard it as a ginger group in a broader and less radical political party, in favor of the latter.

The C. P. P. A. nominating convention met in Cleveland on July 4, 1924. The candidate nominated for the Presidency was Robert M. LaFollette, Sr., Senator from Wisconsin; for Vice-President, Burton K. Wheeler, Jr., Senator from Montana. There was immense enthusiasm and hope, as I recall. I was there as a delegate, probably from Local 189, American Federation of Teachers. LaFollette was an "ideal" candidate for the occasion. His labor record was excellent. He had long been a spokesman for the dirt farmer. He had made Wisconsin a pioneer in political measures seeking to preserve democratic processes in an increasingly centralized society. His record of voting against United States entry into the war had endeared him to idealists, including pacifists, and it was not a serious handicap in gaining popular support at that juncture, when the

* I am indebted for such figures (and for refreshing my memory on other points) to David A. Shannon: *The Socialist Party of America;* Macmillan, 1957.

revulsion against "the war to end war and save democracy," which was to become nearly universal in the decade following 1924, was already under way.

I rode back in the sleeper to New York from Cleveland with three or four other delegates. One of them was Fiorello H. La-Guardia, then a Republican congressman from Manhattan, who had been one of the big figures in the convention. No one ever met the Little Flower without being impressed by his gusto, his wit, his essential honesty and dedication. If there have to be politicians, let them be LaGuardias!

A further big boost was given to the campaign when in August, the A. F. L. abandoned its traditional non-partisan policy and endorsed LaFollette and Wheeler. As always in such situations, however, the A. F. L. did not go all out, and some prominent international union presidents supported the Democratic candidate, John W. Davis; others, like John L. Lewis, backed that great Republican leader, Calvin Coolidge.

As I intimated a while back, I stumped for LaFollette. David K. Niles, who was then associated with the Ford Hall Forum in Boston, and later a member of the Roosevelt entourage, was head of the speakers' bureau, and recruited me to make a number of speeches in Middle Western states, and especially among the Dutch communities in Western Michigan where I had grown up. They were as solidly Republican as Southern whites have been solidly Democratic, and I don't think I made much of an impact, though the count was eventually to show that LaFollette had not done too badly. One of the meetings was in Holland, Michigan, site of Hope College, my *alma mater*, which had graduated me in 1905. It was the first time I had been back in the town since I had committed a whole series of crimes, such as getting fired from a church for my pacifism, getting arrested on the picket line in a strike, and haranguing strike meetings in a plain shirt and without a tie. There was a good turnout at the meeting and a friendly reception. The head of the English department, who had once regarded me as his star protégé, refused to attend. The next day, he did make a concession, as I was later informed, saying that he was pleased to learn that I had not "ranted, but talked common sense—more or less."

One other aspect of the 1924 campaign should be mentioned, which also helped to establish its appeal for labor and other voters. Such organs as the *Saturday Evening Post* tried to pin the Communist label on the LaFollette campaign. There was no basis whatever for such an accusation. As early as December, 1922, Communists had been excluded from the C. P. P. A. The next year, they had turned their attention to the Farmer-Labor Party, captured and wrecked it. The C. P. P. A., in its platform, opposed "equally the dictatorship of the plutocracy and the dictatorship of the proletariat." The campaign textbook quoted LaFollette as characterizing the Communists as "mortal enemies of the Progressive Movement and democratic ideals."

No doubt the most convincing evidence that the Communists were excluded is in an exchange which took place between Foster and the ailing S. P. leader, Debs. Foster wrote to Debs, rebuking him for "complete capitulation to this petty-bourgeois reformer," LaFollette. "The petty-bourgeois united front is now complete from Hearst to Debs." Debs answered: "You may be right in your criticism of my position, and I may be wrong, as I have often been before. Having no Vatican in Moscow to guide me, I must follow the light that I have, and this I have done in the present instance."

LaFollette polled 4,861,471 popular votes, or seventeen percent of the total, and got the vote of Wisconsin in the electoral college. He ran a strong third generally and was second in eleven states in the Middle and Far West, including California.

In many respects, it was a terrific showing. But the A. F. L. announced that the election results showed that "the launching of a third party had been wasted effort." In Chicago, in February, 1925, the C. P. P. A. met and decided that without labor support it was neither possible nor sensible to try to form a labor party. It would take a long time to analyze what this teaches about politics in the U. S. A. As was remarked in another context: "Maybe it ain't logical, but it's so."

Part Fifteen

Another phase in the life of the post-World War I labor and radical movement deserves attention. The social shake-up which accompanied and followed the war, the contacts with the European labor movement, the hope that after the war there would be a new world "fit for heroes to live in," and consequently a new kind of labor movement—these and other factors which produced the upsurge in labor education, and other developments with which we have dealt, were reflected in the field of labor and radical journalism. In many ways, the most typical event in this field was the founding in 1921 of the monthly magazine *Labor Age*.

From the beginning, its editor—described in the early issues as "executive secretary and manager"—was Louis F. Budenz. As most of our readers will be aware, Budenz in later years became one of the most noted strike leaders and mass organizers of the depression period, an important factor in trying to found an American Workers Party with a revolutionary goal. He was briefly—and uneasily—a Trotskyist; thereafter a sensationally publicized recruit to the Communist Party, U. S. A., and editor of the *Daily Worker*; and after that an equally sensationally publicized convert back to the Roman Catholic Church in which he had been brought up; and an "expert" in exposing Communism and Communists for the benefit of the Un-American Activities Committee and the Department of Justice (I do not mean to suggest that the juxtaposition of conversion to Roman Catholicism and becoming an informer for the agencies mentioned is anything more than a statement of a fact which happens to be true in this particular case).

My first contact with young Louie Budenz, who, along with Roger N. Baldwin, had fairly recently moved from St. Louis to New York, was related to his editorship of *Labor Age*. The contact was occasional and of a minor character for a year or two. Gradually it became much closer, and in time we became pretty intimately associated in writing on radical problems and in a number of desperate and dramatic strikes, until our paths diverged again very sharply, when he joined the C. P. I think my memory is accurate in recalling that after he joined the C. P. I saw him only once, in a casual encounter in a train going to Chicago when we passed the time of day standing briefly in the aisle of a car. When he left the C. P., I sent several messages to him indicating that I should like to have a talk with him. I feared that he would be tempted to go into the informer business, and I felt that I might be able to dissuade him. In any case, I wished to make the effort. I have every reason to think that my messages were delivered, but I never received a reply. Whether the decision not to reply was his own or that of his religious or secular counselors, I do not know. However, this is running ahead of our story.

When I went recently to the New York Public Library to have a look at early issues of *Labor Age*, I could not find an entry under that name in its voluminous card catalogue of periodical literature. I had been told many times during the years that there was a file at that library, so I called one of the attendants to my aid. She glanced at cards in a couple of cases and said: "You have to look for that under Intercollegiate Socialist Society." I told her that if it was so listed it was by mistake; that *Labor Age* had not been a publication of the I. S. S.—that very flourishing society (in the 1910-20 period) of students, faculty members and other intellectuals who held socialist views (though they were not necessarily Socialist Party members), and of which Harry W. Laidler early became the executive director. In its golden days, the I. S. S. had had associated with it, in one capacity or another, such a galaxy as Randolph Bourne; Bruce Bliven (later editor of the *New Republic*); John Dewey; Paul H. Douglas (now Senator from Illinois); Zona Gale; William Ellery Leonard; Robert Morss Lovett; Alexander Meiklejohn; Vida Scudder—that gallant soul who apparently fitted equally well for decades in left-wing circles, in the Episcopal Church as a devout worshipper and a near-saint, and on the faculty of Wellesley College as an extraordinarily able teacher of English Literature; Ordway Tead, later chairman of the Board of Higher Education in New York City and department head in the respectable publishing firm of Harper and Brothers; Charles P. Steinmetz, the electrical wizard to whom General Electric hung on, though many of its directors must have been irked by his outspoken Socialism; and Alexander Trachtenberg, who later made a career of publishing Communist literature.

When I told the attendant that *Labor Age* did not belong under

I. S. S., she replied positively, but without emotion, as if simply stating a fact of life: "If we have it there, that is where it belongs." It turned out that she had a case, though I think there should have been a separate listing for *Labor Age* also.

I had completely forgotten, though I must have known about it in a general way, since I was on the board of directors which launched *Labor Age*, that it had grown out of *The Socialist Review*, an organ of the old I. S. S., and thereby hangs a little tale of the vicissitudes of labor and radical journalism which is worth recounting.

The January, 1921, issue of *The Socialist Review* announced that in the next issue there would be an important announcement about the future of the magazine. The next issue—and it proved to be the last—was dated April-May, 1921. It reported that as long ago as the summer of 1920, i. e., when the post-war period had set in, it had become clear that the magazine could not be published efficiently as part of the work of the Intercollegiate Socialist Society. It was impossible for I. S. S. to do justice to its other activities—issuing pamphlets, building chapters in the colleges—if it also tried to do the arduous job of getting out a magazine. A magazine should be published by a board whose main business was just that. These people should be "representatives—official and unofficial—of advanced labor, socialist and other groups." As to content, "while more narrowly socialist problems should not be ignored, far more attention should be given to the problems of labor unionism, problems of increasing importance with every passing day."

The setup of the new magazine, which was to have been called *Age of Labor* but carried the title *Labor Age* when its first issue finally appeared in November, 1921, was clearly such as to give promise of fulfilling its purpose. The chairman of the board was James H. Maurer, president of the Pennsylvania Federation of Labor, who served also as chairman of the Workers' Education Bureau and before long was to serve also as chairman of the board of Brookwood Labor College. Jim, who had to have a spittoon handy at any board meeting he attended and was an expert marksman, had an impregnable place in the second echelon of the labor hierarchy, though he was feared and suspected by the A. F. L. brass. At the same time, he could be counted on not to try to put brakes on the adventurism and radicalism of any enterprise to which he gave his name and, invariably, serious attention.

The treasurer of The Labor Publication Society, which put out

Labor Age, was Abraham Baroff, also treasurer of the International Ladies' Garment Workers Union, one of a company, numerous in those days, who had emigrated from European ghettos, worked in the garment-district sweatshops, educated themselves, organized unions out of nothing, and proved capable administrators, and who never got far or long enough away from the shops and from the East Side or Brownsville slums to acquire the psychology of bureaucrats.

The secretary was Harry W. Laidler, who contributed a summary of labor news of the month to early issues and was the link with the I. S. S., which at about that time changed its name to the League for Industrial Democracy. The board of editors included Roger N. Baldwin; Stuart Chase, who was one of the members of the brilliant team that had formed the Labor Research Bureau; Evans Clark, and David J. Saposs, all of whom contributed articles to *Labor Age* in its early years; Max Danish, then an administrator and later for many years editor of the I. L. G. W. U.'s official organ; Harry W. Laidler; Prince Hopkins, scion of a wealthy California family, a psychologist and friend of Budenz, who contributed a long series of articles which sought to popularize psychology for worker readers, and who was also for some years the magazine's financial angel; Joseph Schlossberg, general secretary-treasurer of the Amalgamated Clothing Workers of America, a type similar to Baroff, a charming and lovable person who could make an eloquent and impressive speech on any occasion for thirty minutes, but who almost invariably kept on going for another hour or so; and finally Norman Thomas, who was then still a pacifist and the editor of the Fellowship of Reconciliation's magazine *The World Tomorrow*, but who before long was to move rapidly into the role of leader of the Socialist Party which he held for so many years.

It may be worthwhile to name some additional people who served on the reorganization committee, which made the bridge between the old publication and the new, or served on the board of directors of the new, to illustrate the wide spread of people who in those days, in contrast to later years, could still collaborate on an enterprise which had ideological and political implications. There was, for example, Morris Hillquit, the very capable lawyer, who in this period, when Debs was largely incapacitated by illness and before Norman Thomas came to be recognized as such, was the leader of the Socialist Party. There were such people as Florence Kelley and Harriet Stanton Blatch. There was Leonard Boudin, who came later to be known as an attorney for Communist cases, and James Oneal, who was the S. P.'s most pungent and persistent anti-Communist polemicist. Others included Charles Ervin, a breezy character who had edited the *Socialist Call* (daily) in the days of its prime and was entering on a career as public-relations man for Sidney Hillman and the Amalgamated Clothing Workers of America; J. B. Salutzky, then in one of the left-wing groups that preceded the crystallization of the C. P. U. S. A., who, as J. B. S. Hardiman, soon was to become editor of *Advance* (the A. C. W.'s official organ) and one of the keenest and most controversial analysts of American labor and radical movements; and Fannia Cohn, an indefatigable crusader for workers' education, who headed the flourishing educational department of the I. L. G. W. U. and, like Jim Maurer, managed to play a leading part on the boards both of Brookwood and the Workers Education Bureau, which was closely tied to the A. F. L. and much more cautious and conservative than Brookwood.

The coming together at an opportune moment of such a group of sponsors, of an editor, Budenz, who passionately wanted to edit such a paper and was prepared to do it for a bare living wage, and an "angel," Prince Hopkins, produced *Labor Age*.

A perusal of the issues of the magazine from 1921 through 1924 amply demonstrates that it was capably edited, that it covered remarkably well the activities and the problems of the progressive labor movement in those years of ferment, experimentation and unceasing struggle against reaction, and that it had more than nominal support from the people who counted in the movement, consistently enlisting them as writers.

A bare enumeration of some of the articles will have to suffice. William Z. Foster, in one of the earlier issues, contributed an article replying to "An I. W. W.," in which he denounced dual unionism, an interesting point in view of the part he was to play later—when the Moscow line required it—in organizing the C. P.-dominated "industrial unions." Said Foster· "American workers are tired of chasing Daniel De Leon's rainbow of a blue-printed dual union movement. . . . Dual unionism as a settled program will soon be a thing of the past in the U. S."

Warren Stone himself, president of the Locomotive Engineers, wrote the article on the Plumb Plan—public ownership and democratic management—of the railroads. John Brophy, president of District 2 of the United Mine Workers of America and symbol of the anti-Lewis forces in that union, did the article on the "Miners' American Plan"—again public ownership.

Evans Clark, who later became one of the country's foremost economics researchers and, in his old age, an editorial writer on *The New York Times*, wrote an article on labor banking in February, 1923, when the Locomotive Engineers, who had their own bank in Cleveland, bought into one of New York's fair-sized banks, the Empire Trust. Said Clark, uncharacteristically going out on a limb: "Labor is now definitely ready for financial power through the control of credit." Ten labor banks, he ventured, was not much, but it was a beginning!

In November, 1922, Frank H. Gilmore, executive secretary of the newly formed Actors Equity Association, wrote an article entitled "A Volcano On Manhattan Isle." It described the exciting strike which had just been waged for the actors' right to organize. *Labor Age* celebrated by having on its cover that month a picture of a lady in flowing pink garments, no doubt meant to represent a beautiful actress. Inside were poor prints of two star actresses, Ethel Barrymore, who was a vice-president of Actors Equity, and Elsie Ferguson, a board member; apart from their supreme artistic merits, both deserve to be enrolled as heroines of American labor for having defied convention and placed their immense prestige behind this crucial battle for the right of professionals to organize, and the responsibility of recognizing that they too were laborers, and not some sort of superior beings living in an artist's utopia.

My own connection with *Labor Age*, which later came to be regarded by Communists, and others as well, as a Musteite organ, was not a close one in the early days. The same was true of my relation with Budenz (the files through 1924 give evidence that the connection with the magazine and its editor became closer and closer). It was not until May, 1923, that I contributed an article. It was entitled "Enter the Labor Spy," and it recounted some of my experiences with the species in textile strikes. My next article appeared in November of the same year and was more significant. It was entitled "A Bird's Eye View of European Workers' Education." It was based on my attendance at a workers' education conference in Belgium during the summer of 1922, and it outlined the extent of workers' education, and the various ideological trends in a dozen countries.

In February, 1924, an editorial dealt approvingly with the more radical concept of workers' education exemplified at Brookwood, and hailed the establishment at Brookwood of the Washington's Birthday Conference on Workers' Education, an institution which, under different auspices, exists to this day.

Shortly afterward, in April, 1924, the lead article was by me: "Workers Education: What's It All About?" It was a programmatic statement of a philosophy of workers' education, and was accompanied by a display of pictures of Brookwood. Thus were signalized the facts that *Labor Age* and Brookwood were actively supporting each other and that, in certain important fields, Budenz and Muste were becoming a team.

Mention should be made of the fact that in the same period (from 1923 through 1924) anti-war material became more prominent in the magazine. This was, of course, the period in which peace sentiment and "pacifism" began to sweep the United States. The fact that *Labor Age* took up the cause was, however, another sign that at that time, when unionism in the A. F. L. was tending to settle down to narrow economic interests and the progressive forces were encountering hard sledding, *Labor Age* devoted itself increasingly to broad social issues, though eschewing the path of "dual unionism," and thereby went into "the opposition."

One of Budenz's own articles of about this period must be cited here, since it is a clue to much in his thinking at the time and in his later development. On the basis of a trip to the Middle West, he did a piece on "What Main Street Labor Thinks." Throughout, he paraphrases what workers had said to him. Referring to such "socialist" ideas as public ownership, he remarks that "in the past such ideas have come to us loaded down with Europeanisms." He goes on: "It was American liberty and American institutions that I was interested in. The Socialists have been talking about these things of late—perhaps too late. From out of their ranks have come the Communists who can think only of Russia. Every time they want to tell us how to carry on our fight, they must first find out how Lenin did it. . . . I have nothing against Mr. Lenin. But I am a free American citizen and I have been taught for several generations to keep away from foreign entanglements and ideas."

It would not be possible to find a more exact and complete statement of what I think was the core of Louis Budenz as a political being, of what he felt in his bones and wanted to live and die for, than this paraphrase of what he said American workers had said to him. He was emotionally a radical. He was enthralled by the American Revolution. He thought of himself, I surmise, as a combination of Patrick Henry and a Minute Man, carrying forward the American Revolution in the twentieth century. He had only the slightest interest in theory, and was inclined to regard theories as "Europeanisms." He was impatient of any jargon which tried to talk to the American worker in any language but his own.

I think that this is the thread of consistency in Budenz's political career. There are reasons to think that this thread was eventually broken when he left the C. P., but it was not, in my opinion, before that. An American revolutionary movement was certainly what we strove for in the Conference for Progressive Labor Action, and in the American Workers Party, which grew out of it. Budenz left the Workers Party U. S. A. (Trotskyists) and joined the Communist Party at the time when that party was talking about carrying forward the "American" revolution, and I do not doubt that he believed he could strengthen that tendency. He remained in the C. P. during the war, when it certainly backed national policy and could be thought of as getting ready to carry the New Deal to its goal after the war. He left during the period when Earl Browder was being ousted and the C. P. renounced "American exceptionalism." It was no longer talking the American language but falling into "Europeanisms."

As to what has come after, speculation and judgment must wait.

Part Sixteen

Earlier, I observed that although LaFollette polled around five million votes in the 1924 Presidential election, nothing in the way of more effective political organization came of it. The American Federation of Labor had broken precedent by endorsing LaFollette and Wheeler; many of its members and even some of its leaders had shown a strong interest in independent political action, perhaps on the model of the British Labor Party. But it turned firmly back to Samuel Gompers' essentially apolitical syndicalist philosophy, which in politics confined itself to a policy of "rewarding your friends and punishing your enemies," who were running for office on the tickets of one of the major parties.

This was only one of many indications that 1924 was a turning point marking the end of the post-World War I period of social upheaval and experimentation. In Europe the key factor was Germany, as is again the case today. With the Dawes and Owen Young plans, American capitalist interests and the Republican Party began the process of rehabilitating the German economy and preparing the German state for the role of providing a military balance against France to the west and Russia to the east. This was the year when it finally became clear that no Socialist or Communist revolution was impending in Germany.

In the United States, Calvin Coolidge was eletced to the Presidency and what was *then* called the New Capitalism developed. This was a capitalism which had overcome the boom-and-bust cycle. It had also eliminated any need for class struggle, since under it employers and labor had a common interest in ever-expanding production. In the 1928 election its propagandists promised "a chicken in every pot and an automobile in every garage."

Business propagandists went to Europe to induct the tired and old-fashioned industrialists of that continent into the mysteries of their craft, and European trade unionists were brought over here to be instructed by A. F. L. leaders in the techniques of labor-management cooperation. Some of us have lived through that period and the ensuing inexplicable (?) depression of 1929 and after, as well as that second World War which had supposedly been rendered impossible by the victorious war to end war which preceded it. The victory over war itself was indeed supposed to have been sealed by the Kellogg-Briand pact of that same year, 1928, which outlawed war among civilized states forever. In our minds, there remains a hard residue of skepticism about the built-in guarantees against depression of the People's Capitalism of today, and the cultural significance of its bigger cars in bigger garages and TV sets in the bedroom as well as the parlor. There remains in our hearts skepticism and foreboding about the balance of nuclear terror, with its built-in guarantees against another world war.

To return to 1924, this was the year that William Green was elected, at the Atlantic City convention of the A. F. L., to succeed the deceased Samuel Gompers. Green was a miner from Ohio who had once been something of a militant and idealist, as anyone who tried to organize miners in the first quarter of this century had to be. He had become secretary-treasurer of the United Mine Workers, as John L. Lewis' stooge. By 1924, Green was to the labor movement what Calvin Coolidge was to the American political scene—an incarnation of perfect mediocrity, who was therefore an ideal instrument for stronger men who knew what they wanted and dared to go after it. There was, of course, one glaring contrast between the two: Green was as voluble as Coolidge was taciturn. Coolidge's one very precious contribution to the American language was his reply to Mrs. Coolidge, who asked him, one morning when he came home from church, what the minister had preached about. Coolidge answered: "About sin." Hoping to get a little more information, Mrs. Coolidge asked, "What did he say about it?" Calvin answered: "He was against it." Now Green, if asked a similar question in public, would have talked about it in rolling periods, packing in the maximum number of clichés, for forty minutes. In that time he would have conveyed exactly the same amount of information that Coolidge conveyed in five words.

The A. F. L., as "prosperity" returned, entered upon a period of stodgy class-collaboration. Union membership paradoxically declined in spite of "good times." What militancy there had been disappeared, except in the garment trades, textiles and soft coal, which did not benefit from the miracle of the New Capitalism. But these were sick industries. Efforts at organization, unsupported by the more stable unions, almost invariably failed. There were bitter internal battles between Communists and other elements. The non-Communist progressives had a tough time of it. The prevailing trend in the A. F. L. hierarchy was marked by complacency, stolid conservatism and obscurantism.

One of the most flagrant instances of the attitude of the executive committee of the A. F. L. was its condemnation of Brookwood Labor College in 1928. Brookwood had weathered its first two or three experimental years and by 1924 was firmly established and was recognized as the leading workers' educational project in the country. Students in the regular courses represented an increasing number of unions and more of them came on scholarships from their local or national unions. During the summer we put on one- and two-week institutes which were entirely financed by union bodies and, in a number of cases, attended by top officials. These were in no sense radical unions. Included among them were the United Textile Workers of America, the Women's Auxiliary of the International Association of Machinists, the Women's Trade Union League, and some of the unions in the Railroad Department of the A. F. L. Our connection with the trade unions was real and increasingly close.

Encouraged by this support, as well as by our reputation in progressive academic circles, in 1927-28 we actually announced a campaign for a two-million-dollar building and endowment fund. As I look back now and reflect on what two million dollars meant in those years, the idea strikes me as having been on the fantastic side. Had we raised anything like such an amount, the enlarged resident school and the greatly enlarged extension work which would have been made possible would have made Brookwood the dominant factor in the workers' education movement, where it was already a substantial force. In view of prevailing conditions, the program might have proved unrealistic even if the country had not, in a year or two, gone into the tailspin of the depression. As it was, the campaign did not get off the ground at all, in considerable part because the executive council of the A. F. L. (or some key figures in it) decided that Brookwood was dangerous and ought to be cut down to size.

The announcement of the condemnation voted by the executive council came without any warning, like a thunderclap out of a cloudless sky. On August 18, 1928, *The New York Times* and other papers stated that, on the basis of a partial report by Vice President Matthew Woll, the council had urged all affiliated unions to withdraw support from Brookwood, keep students away from it, etc.

Woll's report was not published and has not been made public to this day. Only recently have I been informed that even now, after thirty years have elapsed, academic researchers who want to write on the period are not permitted to see the document. From statements made by Woll and others it appeared that the charges were that "doctrines antagonistic to A. F. L. policy were taught at Brookwood"; also that "anti-religious doctrines" were being promulgated, and that "pro-Soviet demonstrations" had occurred there. One specific allegation was that at a May Day observance at the school the picture of Samuel Gompers had been displayed along with those of Eugene V. Debs, Marx and Lenin. This was true. The composition of the student body being what it was, some of them were as irked by having Gompers' picture on the wall as others were by Lenin's, but it was in accord with the catholicity we observed in these matters that both were there and that the whole student body took part in the meeting. We were given to understand that, in the eyes of the A. F. L. magnates, the fact that Gompers' picture, like the others', had a border of red ribbon around it constituted an additional affront.

It happened that on the summer night when the news about the A. F. L.'s attack on Brookwood broke, I was in Paterson, New Jersey, along with the officers—Roman Catholics, conservatives in their social philosophy, and completely loyal to the A. F. L.—of the United Textile Workers of America. Paterson was then still a silk-weaving center of some importance. It had a history of bitter and continuous labor-management conflict. Union organization had been bedeviled for years by a conflict between locals of the U. T. W. and an independent union of silk workers known as the Associated Silk Workers. The U. T. W. was eager to bring the Associated into its fold and had called me into the situation as a moderator of meetings between the two unions to lay the basis for merger. At the time, the leaders of the Associated were mainly young militants with whom Evan W. Thomas and I had worked closely in 1920-21. They had, by 1928, joined the Communist Party, but at that moment the C. P. favored unity of workers in the established—mostly A. F. L.—unions, so I had the confidence of the Associated leadership also. What these youths did at a later point in the negotiations, when the C. P. line abruptly changed, I may recount later. At the moment it was the A. F. L. officialdom which launched the bomb—to the vast surprise of the leaders of their own union in the textile industry.

The attack on Brookwood was, as a matter of fact, essentially an attack on the progressive trade-union leaders of the time, whose role I have described already. The college had at that time ten labor directors. These ten had ultimate control of its policies, because they had a clear majority of the votes on a board on which faculty, alumni and students were also represented. The chairman was Jim Maurer, whose abilities were so great and whose loyalty to the trade union movement so indubitable that despite efforts of reactionaries to oppose him, he was repeatedly re-elected by overwhelming majorities. Other board members included Fannia M. Cohn; Rose Schneiderman, president of the Women's Trade Union League; John Fitzpatrick, head of the Chicago Federation of Labor; John Brophy of the United Mine Workers; the editor of the official journal of the Brotherhood of Railway Clerks; the editor and vice-president of the International Association of Machinists; an official of the American Federation of Teachers, and one from the United Textile Workers.

The Brookwood board naturally protested against being publicly attacked without a word of warning (a gross violation of trade-union ethics), and asked for a copy of the Woll report and a hearing before the executive council. President Green's response to this request, and to a flood of protests which poured into the A. F. L. office from all quarters, was: "I will refrain from taking any decisive action in this case until after the members of the executive council have had ample opportunity to acquaint themselves with the protests filed and the requests made for a hearing by the board of directors of Brookwood College." It was a typically weasel-worded statement, which sounded moderate and democratic, but did not commit Green to anything except acquainting the members of the executive council with the simple request from a group of important unionists to see the evidence against them and to be given a hearing before being further pilloried as traitors or irresponsible dupes.

The Brookwood board was never given a look at the Woll report. It was never given a hearing. Instead Green wrote to a couple of them that he would be willing to talk privately with one member at a time, a suggestion which was indignantly repudiated. In the fall, Green sent out a communication to all affiliated unions, making the warning to withdraw support from Brookwood final.

It should be mentioned that the action against Brookwood directly affected the American Federation of Teachers, a supposedly autonomous international union, which, according to firmly established procedure, the executive council should have consulted before taking even preliminary action. This was essential both because the charges had to do with educational theory and practice and because the educational status and livelihood of the members of Brookwood Local 189 A. F. T. were threatened. The A. F. T. protested vehemently and persistently, only to be completely ignored.

Since this was a Presidential election year, the 48th annual convention of the A. F. L. was held late in November at New Orleans. By all usual standards, the American Federation of Teachers and the Brookwood Board of Directors should have been granted an appeal to the convention. But this would have required revealing the evidence on which the attack against us was based and hearing the dozens of labor unionists who had been students at Brookwood and who would have refuted charges of "Communism," "disloyalty to the labor movement," and teaching of "anti-religious doctrines." So, rather than arrange for an appeal, the higher-ups sent word during the early days of the New Orleans convention that the Brookwood case was settled. Brookwood was no longer a trade-union concern and it would not come up at the convention at all! However, there was an immense amount of interest in the case, and if it had not come up, many would have gone away with the impression that the executive council had no real evidence, that it was trying to weasel out, and that the unions could safely disregard its action and continue to patronize Brookwood. The situation required the kind of witch-hunt that had marked A. F. L. conventions for several years.

The witch-hunt was precipitated by P. J. Shea, a vice-president of the Street Car Men's Union. An agreement made by that union with the Mitten interests in Philadelphia was widely regarded as having played outrageously into the hands of the street car company. It had been severely and effectively criticized by Brookwood graduates at a Pennsylvania Federation of Labor convention. When the education committee's report came before the convention, Shea indignantly asked why Brookwood had not been mentioned either in this or in the executive council's report. This gave Matthew Woll an opening for an extended speech. His "investigation" had demonstrated that Brookwood was "a breeding ground for Communism." He devoted ample space to branding John Dewey, who led the ranks of educators who were outraged by the content and manner of the attack on Brookwood, as himself a "Communist propagandist." He quoted me as having said that "capitalism is not a just social system," and calling for "control of the world by producers." Not a single hint was given of the hundreds of communications which questioned or condemned the Woll report, or the fact that none of the accused had been permitted to see it.

Even in this lynch atmosphere it was impossible to shut off debate entirely. President Thomas F. McMahon of the United Textile Workers, which had expelled Communists from its ranks only a couple of months earlier, said that his union had implicit confidence in Brookwood. Toby Hall, a veteran of labor struggles in Pennsylvania; Charles L. Reed, a Brookwood graduate and delegate of the Salem, Massachusetts, Central Labor Union, who charged the executive council with cowardice for not giving Brookwood a hearing, and several others got the floor. This was becoming a serious debate, and the steam roller swung into action. President Green made a speech in which he complained that some union men always seemed to think that the executive council consisted of a "bunch of fossils who are always wrong and the enemy always right," which in those days came very near being the case.

When the secretary-treasurer of the American Federation of Teachers, Florence Hanson, moved that I, one of the A. F. T.'s vice-presidents, be given the floor, she was told that she was out of order at the moment but that she could make the motion later. Later, when she stood up repeatedly directly in front of President Green she simply was not recognized, and there the matter ended, as far as the New Orleans convention was concerned.

Enough leaked out for it to become known that the allegedly damaging material in Woll's report came from one (possibly two) students at Brookwood, during 1927-28, on scholarship from the Railway Carmen's Union. There is considerable reason to think that at least one man was sent for the express purpose of gathering material that would furnish a basis for an attack to curb Brookwood's growing influence, and with it that of other progressive elements in the labor movement. However, it is conceivable that a man coming out of a very conservative and fundamentalist environment would be genuinely shocked by an institution where labor practices, political and economic theories, practices and philosophies were all possible subjects for study and criticism; where the frankest discussion of all kinds of questions went on all the time; where there were Communists and Socialists, as well as "pure and simple trade unionists," in the student body; where we did sing the *Internationale* and the *Red Flag* from time to time; and where the general atmosphere was certainly critical of the kind of methods and theories of a large section of the A. F. L. officialdom that led to the attack on Brookwood and the infamous way in which it was carried out. In the case of other students who experienced this shock—much as innumerable students have experienced similar shocks in academic institutions—they came to us and we fought out the intellectual battle while assuaging the emotional stress. In this case the man said nothing to his fellow students or to his teachers, but sent "inside" reports to Matthew Woll.

The progressive elements in the unions, and educators generally, continued to support Brookwood. We had two or three excellent years following the A. F. L. blast.

As for the Communists, the *Daily Worker* stated on August 8, 1928, when the news broke, that "there are no Communists on the staff of the school. Its teachings are known primarily as class-collaborationist." The *Daily Worker* also opined, correctly, that the A. F. L. officialdom (called "misleaders" of course) preferred to control workers' education through the Workers' Education Bureau which, in the face of opposition from progressive quarters, had adopted the policy of permitting the executive council of the A. F. L. to control its policies.

On the next day, the Young Workers (Communist) League joined the A. F. L. in warning worker students away from Brookwood, stating: "Brookwood is no more Communist in spirit than the Executive Board of the A. F. L. itself. We have always found that this institution has consistently functioned as a cloak for . . . the reactionary labor fakirs. . . . The Y. W. L. will continue its struggle against Brookwood and its ideology and will make every effort to destroy whatever influence it may have among the working youth."

Part Seventeen

The A. F. L. attack on Brookwood was a symptom and symbol of important developments which heralded big changes in many fields. The mere fact that the event occurred in 1928 in the thick of the Hoover boom, and only a year before the Big Bust of October, 1929, suffices to illustrate the point.

In my own work, it resulted not only in my remaining at Brookwood for several years, but also in the founding of the Conference for Progressive Labor Action and the renewal of my direct involvement in labor struggles and labor politics of a sort. At the outset, the C. P. L. A. was chiefly concerned with combating corruption and racketeering in unions and with stimulating organization in the mass production industries, which had been totally neglected by the A. F. L. After a few years, the C. P. L. A. moved from advocacy of an American labor party somewhat along the lines of the British to the effort to establish an American "revolutionary" party, transforming itself into the American Workers Party. In 1935, the A. W. P. merged with the Communist League of America (led by James P. Cannon and Max Shachtman), which was composed of the followers of Trotsky who had been expelled from the C. P. some years earlier. The name of the new organization was Workers Party U. S. A., a section of the Trotskyist Fourth International. I was its general secretary. Concurrently, there was exciting activity, from 1932 on, in the Unemployed Leagues and in great strikes such as the one at Toledo Auto-Lite and the early sit-down strikes in automobiles and rubber, which led to the birth of the C. I. O. and its fantastic growth under the New Deal.

In 1928, I still thought of myself as a Christian, though I was not particularly active in any church or even in the Quaker meeting to which I belonged, and as a pacifist. In politics, I voted for the Socialist Party candidates at election time, without being a Party member, largely because I could never get up much enthusiasm for electoral activity as against education on the one hand and direct labor struggle on the economic field on the other. I had begun a running battle with the Communist Party, which was to last for years, chiefly because I felt that the Party's policies in the trade-union field were usually inept, contrived and disruptive.

A few years later, I had become a Trotskyist Marxist-Leninist and had accordingly ceased to think of myself as a Christian and a pacifist.

If I try to recall and to communicate to others how the change came about, I think first of what was certainly not the most important factor, namely the reading matter to which I turned increasingly in the late Twenties. I have recounted my excited introduction in 1915 to the writings of the mystics, mainly Christian, and of the Quakers and Anabaptists, and the effect they had on leading me to become a pacifist and conscientious objector in World War I. In the late Twenties, for the first time I began to read fairly extensively in the literature of Marxism, including Marx himself, Trotsky and Lenin. In the early and middle Twenties, my reading had been mainly of historians such as Beard, Spengler, and the post-World War I "Revisionists"; Guild socialists such as G. D. H. Cole; and the pioneer sociologists and social psychologists of that time.

I never became in any sense a scholar in Marxist and Leninist literature. To a large extent this is, frankly, due to a lack of zest and capacity for that sort of thing. I do not regret this as much as perhaps I should, because those who are Marxist-Leninist scholars differ about as widely as do the less learned as to what the masters taught, and because Communist politicians have been able to use Marxism-Leninism for very diverse purposes, including some shameful and brutal ones. In saying this I am aware, of course, that power groups and individuals in power have also used other systems for varying and questionable purposes. In any event, I turned to these books and periodicals in the late Twenties as I had turned to the mystics and early Quakers a dozen years earlier, not out of academic interest but because I faced conditions and problems about which I felt I had to make decisions. The result of the reading was in each case *acted out* rather than written about.

In the earlier crisis, the problem had been what attitude I could take toward war which would be consistent with what I had been preaching and what I believed to be the meaning of the Gospel. In the late Twenties and early Thirties, I was part of the labor movement as an educator and in other roles, part of the movement for political and social change, in the midst of the Great Depression. How was one to analyze what had happened? What could replace the existing regime which would hold out greater promise for men? By what instrumentalities was the old to be removed and the new world brought into being? What could one say to the unemployed and the unorganized who were betrayed and shot down when they protested? What could one say in answer to their question—what to do? What did one point out to them?

Well, not the Church. That seemed to me more and more obvious, in that crisis of three decades ago. I was, of course, one of those to whom the support the churches had—well-nigh unanimously—given to World War I, and their persecution of the few pacifists, had been mournful and searing experiences. While I did not feel personally bitter about that experience, I suppose the fact that I did not avail myself of the opportunities to go back into preaching which opened up fairly soon after the war was over and the tide of revulsion against it began to rise, itself indicates how greatly I had lost faith in the Church's relevance. By 1928, when war was not the issue, the prevailing sentiment in most of the leading American Protestant denominations was pacifistic and a large percentage of the leading preachers were pacifists.

But when the issue was that of the economic system, the class structure of American society and related matters, once again the churches were identified with the *status quo*, middle-class in composition and coloration; and with rare exceptions they seemed to me irrelevant. I recall that, in answer to the question often asked as to the attitude of workers and the labor movement toward the churches, I used to say in those days that on the continent of Europe the labor movement was largely hostile to the churches and Christianity; in Great Britain in the main quite friendly; whereas in this country workers were simply indifferent: they did not have the European Marxist animosity toward religion, they just felt it was irrelevant.

Nor could one point out to the unemployed and unorganized, the starving and persecuted, the stodgy, unimaginative, and passive labor movement of that era. A new labor movement with a different philosophy clearly seemed indicated. Under the circumstances, a philosophy emphasizing economic determinism, the decisive role of class struggles in human history, the enervating and corrupting influence of religion, the need of revolutionary action toward a revolutionary goal, the role of a vanguard party of dedicated revolutionaries, had an immense attraction for many of us.

There are two or three specific factors which greatly influenced my thinking and my emotional reactions which should be mentioned. In the first place, when you looked out on the scene of misery and desperation during the depression, you saw that it was the radicals, the Left-wingers, the people who had adopted some form of Marxian philosophy, who were *doing something* about the situation, who were banding people together for action, who were putting up a fight. Unless you were indifferent or despairing, you lined up with them. In the interests of an objective review of the situation, it must be said that in many cases these doers and fighters were Communists, or those set in motion by them. So far as my experience goes, in any specific situation where there was a militant non-Communist Left, it could stand up to them, in spite of the often vicious tactics used by the C. P. But if there was a vacuum, the Communists filled it. Without them the unions in the mass production industries would not have been built. On a larger scale, the Communists are filling a similar vacuum in many parts of the world today. They cannot be replaced by wailing about it, or by another vacuum.

Secondly, it was on the Left—and here again the Communists cannot be excluded—that one found people who were truly "religious" in the sense that they were virtually completely committed, they were betting their lives on the cause they embraced. Often they gave up ordinary comforts, security, life itself, with a burning devotion which few Christians display toward the Christ whom they profess as Lord and incarnation of God. Later I was to mourn the wastage of so much youthful devotion and its corruption, among Communists and others, which I had witnessed, as it were, from the inside. Yet the beauty and attractive power of commitment to that which we profess to believe remains—and it plays a considerable part in the contemporary world struggle.

Besides, the Left had the vision, the dream, of a classless and warless world, as the hackneyed phrase goes. This was a strong factor in making me feel that here, in a sense, was the true church. Here was the fellowship drawn together and drawn forward by the Judeo-Christian prophetic vision of "a new earth in which righteousness dwelleth." The now generally despised Christian liberals had had this vision. As neo-orthodoxy took over, that vision was scorned as naïve and utopian. The "Kingdom" was something to be realized "beyond history." And again, the Communists are those who today are able to convince vast multitudes that they do cherish the ancient dream of brotherhood realized on earth and have the determination to make it come true. This is a measure of the fall of what is called the Free World. The liberal Christians were never, in my opinion, wrong in cherishing the vision. Their mistake and, in a sense, their crime, was not to see that it was revolutionary in character and demanded revolutionary living and action of those who claimed to be its votaries.

What had become of my pacifism when I became a Trotskyist? I surmise that not a few of my associates of that period would say that I never ceased being a pacifist at heart and therefore never was a true-blue Marxist-Leninist—and there is something to that. At any rate, I never abandoned certain ethical attitudes which had been and are now a part of my "pacifism," and which soon led to altercations with The Comrades. Indeed, one of the things that drew me into the Trotskyist movement was the fact that Trotsky was not implicated in the crimes which Stalin perpetrated as he concentrated power in his own hands. Trotsky, moreover, in those days made trenchant criticisms of the violations of socialist or revolutionary ethics of which Stalin and Stalinists were guilty. I discounted, for the time being, Trotsky's views on "terrorism" and his complicity in the shooting of the Kronstadt sailors when, at a critical point in the early days of the Revolution, they had revolted against bureaucratic tendencies in the Soviet government. At a later point, I shall return to these questions of ethics which led to altercations with The Comrades. At the time, however, as will also be documented later, I did fully embrace the view that only revolutionary action by the working class and other elements, under the leadership of a vanguard party, could bring in a new social order; and that revolutionary action did not in principle exclude violence; that violence in taking over power would almost certainly be necessary and hence justified.

In a certain sense, there is no "explanation" for the fact that one who had been so deeply convinced a pacifist as I was and who, furthermore, had seen some remarkable instances of nonviolence in American labor struggles like the Lawrence strike, ceased to hold that position. You simply have to take it as one of "the facts of life." (No doubt analysts could come up with interesting and perhaps startling deductions.) Insofar as I can make this episode intelligible to myself and others, the "explanation" goes like this: I have to *experience* ideas, rather than *think* them. I have to learn what they mean in practice, have to act them out. Also, as I have indicated before, life, or at least responsible living, means to me being involved in the struggle against injustice and tyranny. It means acting "politically," trying to help build a new world, or new social forms.

A reviewer of a book about Albert Camus says of him that "he has not swerved from his determination to reintroduce the language of ethics into the language of politics," and this expresses a compulsion I have felt ever since 1915.

In the Thirties we faced a terrible situation. The ultimate betrayal, the sacrifice of my inner integrity, would have been to stay out of it, not to resist, not to be on the side of the oppressed. I did not know how to apply nonviolence effectively to the situation. The effort to apply Gandhian methods to American conditions had scarcely begun. Pacifism was mostly a middle-class and an individualistic phenomenon. The churches certainly were not giving illustrations of spiritual force, of true community, which might have had a nonviolent but transforming influence. For a time, I tried to reconcile my Christian pacifism with involvement in the struggle as it was then taking shape. Gradually, as I said to someone in that period, I came to feel that I was more and more a caricature of a Christian pacifist, and only a half-baked revolutionary, and that I had to choose. I chose revolution, recognizing that it might involve violence. (I did not, having given up my pacifism, think that I could remain a Christian.)

It is perhaps of some historic value to note that one of the people with whom I discussed my break with pacifism in those days was Reinhold Niebuhr, who did not make the same break until a couple of years later. Afterwards he recalled our conversation in a public discussion he and I held before the students of Union Theological Seminary early in World War II. I invited him to follow my example in coming back to faith in nonviolence.

As this suggests, I do not essentially regret that course I took (not that regret would do any good). But I put the theories of "lesser evil," of "realism," of the inescapability or necessity of violence, of revolutionary dictatorship, and so on, to the test of experience. I am not beguiled by contemporary expressions of them. I know in a far deeper sense than I did thirty years ago that you cannot overcome violence by violence or establish democracy by dictatorship. I am sure my earlier experience has been helpful to me in my attempts to help develop nonviolent methods and a more revolutionary pacifist movement in later years. If people tell me that there is no clearly defined nonviolent way to deal with a situation, then I answer that we have got to experiment and find one. God knows we have experimented long enough with other methods.

The recent review of a book about Albert Camus, to which I

have referred, also says this of him: "He has remained a man of
the Left . . . But he is aghast at the decadence of the Left in France
and elsewhere at a time when perhaps only a strong and moral non-
Communist Left could save Europe and offer an alternative to
sovietization of Asia." I too continue to consider myself a man of
the Left, and I agree completely with the attitude attributed to Camus in the other sentence in that quotation. I would add two points.
One, without a strong and moral non-Communist Left we shall
not escape nuclear war. Two, a moral Left has to be an essentially
nonviolent one. This will enable us, in a phrase of Camus', to be
"neither victims nor executioners."

Part Eighteen

Brookwood Labor College had been founded by progressive trade unionists, and by educators and liberals sympathetic with the labor movement who worked on the assumption that the movement was capable of a certain amount of self-criticism. It might not welcome criticism enthusiastically; some of its more conservative and powerful leaders certainly would not. But it was hoped that they would tolerate it.

We have seen that as the country entered the Coolidge-Hoover era, the official labor movement, the American Federation of Labor, was placed on the defensive and its leaders took a more and more conservative stance. They reacted with increasing bitterness and even viciousness against those who were vocal in opposition to this trend, criticism in itself being regarded as evidence of disloyalty. One result of this trend was the A. F. L. attack on Brookwood. We may note in passing that the A. F. L. was not content to warn its members not to have any commerce with heretics but increasingly insisted on telling them what they should think. This it accomplished by placing control of the Workers Education Bureau of America in the hands of top A. F. L. officials, and by threatening the Bureau with ostracism if its officers resisted the move. Regular conventions of the W. E. B. were then eliminated. None was held for four years. Textbooks on the Workers Bookshelf were subjected to A. F. L. censorship. The idea that labor might need a "culture" of its own and could not depend on the cultural material provided in the universities was condemned.

Spencer Miller, Jr., was the executive secretary of the W. E. B. throughout this period. During his student days at Columbia he had been a protégé of the well-known historian Charles A. Beard. In the beginning he had been suspect among labor bureaucrats as an intellectual, but he collaborated faithfully with them in all the moves we have outlined. It is just possible that he did this without feeling that he was seriously betraying his early training and some of his educational principles. But these should have led him

to attempt a mediating role. Actually, it is on the record that he contributed to the attack on Brookwood and other progressive labor-
education projects, reporting to A. F. L. President William Green
that "Mr. Muste" was controlling the flourishing labor-institute program in many places, "without seeking W. E. B. co-operation." An
objective assessment of the situation might well result in the conclusion that an attempt by Miller to play a mediating role would have
proved futile. But I felt very strongly in those days (as did many
others) that Miller paid too high a price for the survival of the
W. E. B. and the retention of his role in it. Nor have I changed my
conviction on this matter.*

I was, in 1928-29, in the position of "having no choice" as to
the next move. Brookwood could no longer serve as an educational
and inspirational center for progressive unionists operating within
the A. F. L. structure and accepted, however reluctantly, within it.
If Brookwood and the various local educational institutes staffed
largely by its graduates were to continue to have a base, we had to
help the progressive laborites, who did not choose to acquiesce in
the trend but would not follow Communist leadership, to develop
some sort of coherence and structure. The progressive laborites
needed Brookwood's help in dealing with the same problem. This
was the background for the founding of the Conference for Progressive Labor Action at a convention held in the Presbyterian Labor
Temple in New York on May 25-26, 1929. I suppose at the time I
would have regarded as laughable a prediction of the circuitous
route I was to follow in the intervening years toward becoming, in
1937, the director of that same Labor Temple.

The May C. P. L. A. founding convention was preceded by the
publication in the February issue of *Labor Age,* then still under the
editorship of Louis Budenz, of a "Challenge to Progressives," written by myself. It had sixteen points and it is worth mentioning the
principal ones, both because many of them forecast what the C. I. O.
would strive for and achieve in the boisterous organizing cam-

---

* A useful and well-documented study of these developments has been published
by the New York School of Industrial and Labor Relations at Cornell University.
It is written by James L. Morris, an Assistant Professor of the School, and is
entitled *Conflict Within the American Federation of Labor.* It is of current as
well as historical value at this time, when the A. F. L.-C. I. O. is in a period of
defensiveness and of pretty thorough identification with prevailing political policies. Whether, in face of the threat of nuclear war and developments such as
automation, it will again adopt an attitude of "opposition" and creativeness, is
one of the most important questions before the country today.

paigns of the Thirties, and because others foreshadow issues which the A. F. L.-C. I. O. failed to resolve and faces, in an acute form, today.

The first and major plank was the organization of the unorganized in the basic industries into industrial unions, a job the bureaucrats had neglected both because it was difficult in that reactionary period and because, in their hearts, they feared what unionization of millions of industrial workers would do to their own jobs and to the structure and philosophy of the labor movement.

Another plank called for an end to the denial of union membership to workers for racial, political, economic, social or religious reasons. Racial discrimination in the unions was a colossal scandal in those days. We opposed expelling Communists merely for being Communists, and denying them the right to run for office. I would not, for a moment, underestimate the problem which the C. P. created in the unions; nor was the C. P. under any illusion that we supported its trade union policies. As a matter of fact, the C. P. L. A. (the "Musteites") in those years was constantly stigmatized in the C. P. press as the worst traitors to the working class, the most dangerous allies of the bourgeoisie and what-have-you. But I am convinced that the C. P. would not have got far in this country if it had not been for the general lack of social vision in the labor movement and the practice within the movement of racial and political discrimination.

Another major C. P. L. A. emphasis in those days was on unemployment benefits and other forms of social insurance. One of our most ardent supporters was Abraham Epstein, heroic and tireless pioneer of the movement for social insurance in the United States, who, on this account, was regarded as a dangerous radical by the official labor leadership, though he was essentially very moderate in his political orientation.

Along with such proposals, which now seem eminently sensible (even "old hat"), were others which are still controversial in the labor movement. C. P. L. A. advocated formation of a Labor Party on essentially British Labor Party lines. We urged recognition of the Soviet Union by the United States government. This is now, of course, a long accepted fact, and the labor movement, which had formerly denounced the proposal as proof of Communist sympathies and "playing into the hands of the Russians," heartily supported the World War II alliance with Joseph Stalin. But this support has not prevented today's labor leaders from adopting a nationalistic, rigid, emotionally charged attitude toward problems of Communism and Soviet policy which causes them to line up in support of a mad nuclear arms race and the "cold war," and in opposition to cultural exchange with Soviet countries.

One other plank in the "Challenge" to progressives needs to be mentioned. It advocated a "definitely anti-imperialist" and "anti-militarist" labor movement, one which would become internationalist in spirit and action by encouraging "a closer union of all the workers of the world."

Some trade union progressives who had supported Brookwood and *Labor Age* did not come along into the C. P. L. A. They had questions about the wisdom of trying to organize what amounted to an opposition within the A. F. L. They were also confronted with the fact that their own trade union posts would be placed in jeopardy if they defied the top leadership. Nevertheless, the C. P. L. A.'s labor base was far from negligible. James Maurer served as vice-chairman, as did Carl Holderman, an official of the Hosiery Workers Union and later, for many years, head of the C.I.O. in New Jersey. A. J. Kennedy, one of the heads of the Lithographers Union, was treasurer. Members or business agents of the Machinists, Jewelry Workers, Railway Clerks, Hat and Cap Makers, Amalgamated Clothing Workers, Teachers, Sleeping Car Porters, and other unions served on the executive board. Moreover, C. P. L. A. had strong, though unofficial, Socialist Party support, as is evident from the presence of Norman Thomas on the executive board, and even more from that of James Oneal, editor of the *New Leader* and the leading anti-Communist theoretician in the S. P. at that time.

With sharp struggles going on in a number of unions, including one against the autocratic leadership of John L. Lewis in the United Mine Workers, and with sorely exploited workers in textile, steel, mining and other fields spontaneously revolting and crying desperately for sympathy and leadership, it was inevitable that C. P. L. A. activists, including myself, other Brookwood faculty members, and our graduates, should be drawn more directly into organizing and strike activity than had been the case earlier. This involved taking responsibility for raising relief funds and, more importantly, for strike and union strategy, which would not normally be regarded as functions of a "college," even a labor college. It was perhaps also inevitable that in time this would lead to controversy and conflict in the school. However, at this point I wish to recall an event which took place in the summer immediately following the founding of the C. P. L. A.

Not only were a number of its own officers, including myself, involved, but also all the Brookwood faculty members, in one way or another. It was an event which, in spite of the tragedy which was part of it, was an immensely exhilarating instance of collective action, and of people from many different backgrounds being fused into a joyous fellowship, as well as of individual heroism and self-sacrifice that lent it a noble and even idyllic aspect. I am referring to the Marion, North Carolina, textile strike of 1929.

Nineteen twenty-nine was a year when Southern textile workers could no longer endure silently their poverty, undernourishment, chronic strikes and humiliation.* One of the resulting strikes was that at Gastonia, North Carolina. The Communist-infiltrated National Textile Workers Union was involved in that strike, and the local police chief, Aderholt, was shot—by whom was never definitely established—in a mélée which occurred when he and some of his men were challenged while trying to enter the union grounds at night and without a warrant. Many strikers were living on the grounds, partly in order to be safe from violence at the hands of police and goons. Further notoriety accrued to the Gastonia strike when seven convicted men jumped bail and sought asylum in Russia. One of them, Fred Beal, returned later to serve his time.

Marion, at least the part which tourists saw, was a lovely, slumbering town in the Blue Ridge Mountains. In the other part were a couple of mills and the shacks of the workers who toiled in them—white workers, but certainly regarded by the "better" people as an inferior breed, if not sub-human. Communists had nothing to do with the strike which broke out in the Marion mills that summer. Officially, the A. F. L. affiliate, the United Textile Workers, was in charge. Extremely cautious, it sought to discourage any strike, not knowing how it could provide relief. A Hosiery Workers organizer who was a Brookwood graduate gave what help he could. The C. P. L. A. kept another Brookwood graduate on the job. When the strike came, an emergency relief committee was set up, to which many organizations, such as the Y. W. C. A. in Southern towns, and renowned individuals such as Sinclair Lewis contributed.

The strikers were church folk. If you had been near the grove

---

* An account of the condition and activities of Southern labor in this period, including the story of the Gastonia and Marion strikes, was set down in *When Southern Labor Stirs,* by Tom Tippett, at that time director of Brookwood's extension work, who played a key role in the Marion strike. Later, Tippett was for many years associated with the extensive research and educational program of the International Association of Machinists.

in which their mass meetings took place, you would have thought that a camp-meeting revival was going on. The union songs were sung to the tunes of spirituals and evangelistic Gospel hymns. I think it was in Marion that summer that the old spiritual *Jacob's Ladder* was first adapted to include these lines:

> *We are building a strong union,*
> *Workers in the mill.*

In these meetings there was a fusion of personal and social religion, the old and the new, which to people like myself was inexpressibly poignant.

Some weeks later, in a private session, not attended by any strikers, a vague agreement was reached with the management of the Baldwin mill which seemed to give some guarantee that there would be no discrimination against most of the returning workers. It was accepted by the strikers as a pretext for calling off the strike, since they and their friends had come to the end of their resources.

When the workers did go back, most of them were not rehired at all. The ones who were rehired were mercilessly speeded up, amid constant taunts. The result was unrest, and one night the people on the night shift walked out spontaneously. They waited near the mill for the day shift to arrive. In the meantime, the local sheriff and his deputies were in the mill, which suggests that there was a deliberate plan to provoke trouble. They came into the road in the early morning. The mill superintendent came out and called to "loyal workers" to come into the mill. No one would. The superintendent spoke to the sheriff, who told his men to fire tear gas at the crowd a few feet away. A crippled sixty-five-year-old worker, blinded by gas, grappled with the sheriff, either in anger or in fear. The deputies fired at the crowd which was running away from the tear gas. Thirty-six strikers were wounded in the back, twenty-five of them seriously. Two died at once, four later—all shot in the back. Not a single deputy or mill official was scratched.

To multitudes the Gastonia strike had the connotation of "violence." A police officer was killed, *perhaps* by a striker. In Marion, six workers were shot in the back, running away from tear gas. To multitudes at the time this did not spell "violence," and probably would not even now, in the same way that the killing—perhaps accidental—of one police chief in Gastonia did.

Besides, Communists were in Gastonia, and Communists spell "big trouble" wherever they go, don't they? I do not need to be

reminded at this late hour that Communists are not Christian pacifists or Gandhians. But, may the Marion story remind us that the
jungle violence which has often marked American labor history was
there independently of the C.P. and that it remained, during the
Thirties, a prevailing accompaniment to labor's efforts to establish
the elementary right to organize, including episodes in which Communists did not figure at all. Those of us who have learned not
to trust or condone violence as a means of resisting oppression and
achieving social change must not fall into the trap of having our
attention diverted from the violence, and the provocations to violence, which are perpetrated by those who oppress and seek to
prevent change which endangers vested interests.

On October 4, a beautiful autumn morning, a funeral service
was held for the murdered strikers. The Reverend James Myers,
then secretary of the industrial department of the Federal Council
of Churches, had tried to find some parish minister in the Carolina
hills or Piedmont cities who would officiate at the funeral. None
had been willing. The ministers of the dead in the mill village
churches, whose living depended on the mill owners, did not even
dare to attend. So Jim Myers and I conducted the service. Some
local strike leaders and an official of the United Textile Workers
spoke.

Suddenly, in the midst of the services, a venerable bearded
figure stepped out of the crowd onto the platform before which
lay the bodies of the dead. He was a mountain preacher who had
come down out of the hills, like some Amos, who retained the
prophet's suspicion and scorn of "advancing" civilization and who
had refused to accept the "easier" lot of preachers subsidized by
mill owners. Without any preliminary talk, he fell on his knees,
raised his long arms to heaven, and prayed:

> O Lord Jesus Christ, here are men in their coffins, blood of
> my blood, bone of my bone. I trust, O God, that these friends
> will go to a place better than this mill village or any other place
> in Carolina.
>
> O God, we know we are not in high society, but we know
> Jesus Christ loves us. The poor people have their rights too.
> For the work we do in this world, is this what we get if we
> demand our rights? Jesus Christ, Your son, O God, was a work-
> ing man. If He were to pass under these trees today, He would
> see these cold bodies lying here before us.

O God, mend the broken hearts of these loved ones left behind. Dear God, do feed their children. Drive selfishness and cruelty out of Your world. May these weeping wives and little children have a strong arm to lean on. Dear God—what would Jesus do if He were to come to Carolina?

Then the man from the hills walked away, as if in a trance. Some of the bodies were taken elsewhere for burial, but one was buried in the shabby cemetery adjoining the Baldwin mill. Many of us followed this body as it was carried to its grave. As it was lowered into the grave, the undertaker asked if there was a minister present. No minister of the kind he had in mind was there. After a tense silence, I stepped forward. Somebody took down what I said, and some years later showed it to me: "We consecrate this worker's body and give it back to the earth from which it came. He has fought a good fight in a noble cause. He will rest in peace."

What Mr. Baldwin, the owner of the mill in which these men had been sweated and crippled, said, when reporters told him about the casualties and fatalities at his sheriff's hands, was this: "I think the officers are damn good marksmen. If I ever organize an army, they can have jobs with me. I read that the death of each soldier in the World War consumed five tons of lead. Here we have less than five pounds and these casualties. A good average I call it."

Part Nineteen

In 1933 there occurred a rift that led to my departure from Brookwood Labor College, after twelve years as teacher and educational director. In the main, I will present only certain aspects of this episode, largely personal. I do not have available, at the moment, material for the thorough description and analysis which, in view of Brookwood's place in the history of workers' education in this country, it perhaps deserves. However, some of the political angles are dealt with elsewhere in this book.

As the reader knows by now, I have more than once found myself engaged in controversies over policies which seemed to me to involve issues of conscience, and which led to the severing of certain political, religious or personal ties and the making of other connections. In every such instance, except the Brookwood controversy, I had the feeling that I was moving ahead on a straight course, as it were, and in the direction in which I should be moving. There was also the feeling that inwardly I was having an experience of growth, of a maturing. This was so in spite of the fact that there were grave risks for myself and my family and considerable emotional stress. Moreover, I came out of all these other experiences of conflict with the feeling that I had behaved as well as I was capable of doing, and had no reason to reproach myself for having slipped into bitterness or unfairness.

The Brookwood struggle of 1932-33 was, in a number of ways, exceptional. The issues were more complicated than they had been when, for example, I espoused pacifism before World War I, or became involved in the labor movement after that war. The personal emotions and strains at the time of the Brookwood break were more intense. This was, no doubt, largely because Brookwood was a pretty closely knit community, where the lives of faculty members and their families and of the students had been intimately bound together. It was not as if a church or school or union were being torn while the individuals involved lived in different communities and had family refuges. This time the community itself was disintegrating.

It should certainly be borne in mind, also, that the Brookwood controversy culminated at a time when the whole American community was going through one of the most traumatic experiences in all United States history. The A. F. L. attack on Brookwood came just one year before the crash of 1929. During that school year, and for a couple of succeeding ones, Brookwood had the most vitality, I surmise, in its history. But the depression deepened. Brookwood, like other institutions, experienced a severe drop in income. Issues of policy were exasperated because problems of who should be dropped, and so on, arose. The whole political atmosphere was highly charged. Truly symbolic of many factors in the situation was the fact that the break became final and a considerable percentage of the staff, the Mustes, and the majority of the students left Brookwood on almost the same day in March, 1933, that the newly elected President Franklin D. Roosevelt closed the banks of the nation. Quite a few things were falling apart!

I have speculated occasionally as to whether my age at the time of the Brookwood breakup, namely 48, had something to do with the severity of the experience and with the fact that I was inwardly somewhat less assured than in earlier and later crises. When younger, one probably has more resilience and more zest for adventure. When a man passes the middle period, if he has experienced no personal breakdown, he probably knows that life holds no ultimate terror. He is sure to have acquired a certain toughness and immunity to shock. Moreover, when a man passes his fifties, he no longer has "dependents," in the same sense that wife and children are dependents before the children have grown up and started to establish families of their own.

This much reference to family matters makes it appropriate to mention another item. I was 48 when we left Brookwood and it was only a little over three years later—which is almost unbelievable to me as I write it down now—that I had completed the "detour" which saw the Conference for Progressive Labor Action organize the Unemployed Leagues (the unemployed organizations inspired by the C. P. were called Councils), transform itself into the American Workers Party, and merge with the Trotskyist Communist League, taking the name Workers Party of the U. S. A.; and then saw the Workers Party, at the instigation of the Trotskyist elements in the merger and against my firm opposition, make what I regarded as a fake union with the Socialist Party—a major element in my breaking with the Trotskyists in the late summer of 1936.

The age at which I left Brookwood is said for a good many to be a "dangerous" one, bringing with it strains, and perhaps catastrophes, in marital and family relationships. I think it is accurate to say that there was none of this in our case. The family at that time included Anne Muste and the two daughters who have been previously mentioned, and my son John, who was just past six when we moved away. For each of us it was a painful experience, but we bore it together. Within the family circle there was no storm, only mutual support against the storm we had run into.

As is suggested by the above summary of the rapid changes in the 1933-36 period—at the end of which I found myself back in the Christian church and the pacifist movement—my hunch at the time of the Brookwood break that I was not moving ahead on a straight road was correct. It was natural, under the circumstances, that I should feel somewhat uncertain as to whether I was inwardly maturing. I hit accidentally on the term "detour" in writing of the period between my leaving Brookwood in 1933 and breaking with the Trotskyist movement in 1936. The more I reflect upon it, however, the more accurate and descriptive the term seems. You come to a "detour" after you have been rolling along pretty smoothly and steadily for a good while, though there may have been some warnings of delay ahead. Then the block in the road looms, and you simply go ahead. You have to take the detour, frustrated as it may make you feel. There is likely to be a certain excitement about the detour, but the going is rougher than on the highway. There are likely to be moments when you wonder whether the road leads anywhere or will ever hit a highway again. But if it is a proper detour, it does.

Let me turn now to a very summary statement of the issues which, as I view it, brought about the split in Brookwood. When the reactionary trend in the A. F. L. made it virtually impossible for the progressives, in workers' education or other fields, to maintain a base within the A. F. L., they had to try to develop a base which would be prepared to incur the hostility of the A. F. L. leadership but, at the same time, be independent of the Communist Party. Brookwood, on its part, had to help build such a base or die for lack of a constituency from which students could come and into which they could return to carry on the labor struggle. I have mentioned the historic and tragic Marion strike as an illustration of how Brookwood faculty members and students combined schooling and direct organizing and strike activity. I have also indicated how, in the beginning, Brookwood and the Conference for Progressive Labor Action worked together—Brookwood, of course, emphasizing the educational job and the C. P. L. A. that of organizing and of strike activity.

As always happens when a split takes place in an organization, people divided in various ways; but the objective facts seem to me to show that the decisive dividing line in the faculty and staff was between those whose primary interest was in an institution devoted to education in some sort of relationship to the labor movement, and those whose primary interest was in labor action during those strenuous years before the C. I. O. got under way and who wanted to relate Brookwood and the educational process going on there *directly* to the day-to-day battles in mining, textiles and steel, and automobiles—the great unorganized industries of that era.

One of the ways in which the division expressed itself was in the tendency of the latter group, to which I belonged, to emphasize extension courses and to suggest that it might be advisable, if trying to maintain a resident institution in Westchester County under depression conditions absorbed all the energies we had and all the money we could raise, to sell the Brookwood property and to move the school to less expensive quarters in an industrial center. The former group characterized any proposal to dispose of the Brookwood property and drastically reduce the resident academic work as an abandonment of the purpose for which Brookwood had been founded.

The latter group included David J. Saposs, who taught labor history and problems for many years; Josephine Colby, who had been on the faculty even longer, and was an unusual English instructor; Helen Norton, teacher of labor journalism, who had become the wife of Mark Starr, who had first come to Brookwood from the Labor College movement in England and had started on his long association with the educational work of the International Ladies' Garment Workers Union; and Katherine Pollack, who later was for many years on the research staff of the C. I. O.

The former group included Tom Tippett, director of extension work; Lucille Kohn, an instructor, though not in residence, who had been one of Brookwood's most consistent supporters during the years, and continued as a major figure in the workers' education movement in connection with Labor Summer Schools and the Amer-

ican Labor Education Service; Cara Cook, librarian and tutor, later
in executive positions with the Womens Trade Union League and
the New York Teachers Guild, affiliate of the American Federation
of Teachers; and Cal Bellaver, Illinois miner, who, after graduation,
had become superintendent of grounds and buildings, and subsequently had a career as a labor organizer.

The one thing the members of the latter group were clearly
and firmly united on was the emphasis on action and *direct* involvement in the labor struggle. (On other matters, as became clear in
later years, they held varying views.) It had been at a meeting of
the Brookwood faculty and student body in connection with an
exposition of the "action" issue that I used Bernard Shaw's familiar
sentence: "Those who can, do; those who can't, teach." It was not
a pointless or purely gratuitous remark. I think the record shows
that the members of our group had inclinations and aptitudes which
made it easy for us to mingle with workers and to function in labor
battles and controversies—perhaps in certain forms of "labor politics"—which members of the other group did not have to the same
extent. But in the circumstances it was an expression of arrogance
and malice on my part, the only time I can recall having been consciously malicious in such a situation. I regretted it then and I do
now. It was one of those moments in a controversy when you sense
that it cannot be "patched up" any more. Josephine Colby, I know,
was deeply wounded by my remark. After the break came, she went
to the Soviet Union to teach English and died there some years
later, after experiencing the hardships of life in that country in
the Thirties—experiencing them, I am sure, with great fortitude.

The relation between Brookwood and the C. P. L. A. and my
own relation to the two, including major responsibility for money
raising, also figured. Louis Budenz, who was executive secretary of
the C. P. L. A., held that it was wrong of me to limit my involvement in organizing campaigns and strikes by putting in time on
Brookwood. My critics at Brookwood were equally convinced that
the time I spent in C. P. L. A. work was highly injurious, if not fatal,
to Brookwood. I believed that the two should function together.
In the showdown, it was my critics at Brookwood who forced the
issue.

There were underlying ideological issues which were not by
any means fully discussed or perhaps even realized at the time. The
best way to indicate them, in a very cursory way, is to point out
that, with two exceptions, all the leading faculty figures on both

sides in the 1933 break before very long found positions in the Federal government or in unions which idolized Roosevelt and, after Roosevelt's "quarantine the aggressors" speech in 1936, supported his foreign policy and, eventually, United States entry into World War II. It is contemplation of that fact that convinces me, after all these years, that a split would have taken place at Brookwood later even if it had somehow been avoided in 1933, and that my own course at the time was the right one for me and the one consistent with my basic impulses and convictions—even though that was not altogether obvious at the time and involved taking the "detour."

It may be argued that if the Brookwood faculty had arrived at a compromise in 1933 and I had concentrated on the school rather than on the C. P. L. A. and its successors, Brookwood might have survived, might have been supported by the unions born under the New Deal and become a flourishing C. I. O. training school. It could be said that this would have been the realization of the aims and dreams of the progressives who had founded Brookwood: a militant labor movement based on industrial unionism, and so on. This evaluation would have a measure of validity. Certainly this is what many people felt in the early days of the great C. I. O. unions, including the trade union directors of Brookwood who reluctantly cast the deciding votes against me in the situation where the faculty was split in two and the great majority of students and alumni were with me.

It is, however, doubtful whether, on the basis of an adjustment in 1933, these rosy anticipations would actually have been realized. The years from 1933 to 1939 (when the war broke out in Europe) would have been, financially and otherwise, rough ones for Brookwood or any resident labor college. Any progressive or militant worker worth his salt was needed on the job in those hectic years. The minds of leaders were preoccupied with the daily struggle. There were also constant internal battles over leadership and policies in the nascent unions into which Brookwood, insofar as it might have retained influence, would inevitably have been dragged.

All such considerations are, however, of minor significance. If, in this sense, Brookwood were to have "flourished," I would still have been out of it. To have become identified with the New Deal, with the C. I. O. top leadership and, presently, with support of the war—this would have been for me the abandonment of my deepest convictions and the collapse of inner integrity. In this context, my instinct that those who disagreed with me wished to carry Brookwood in a conservative direction seems to me to have been validated. This remains true, though, as I have mentioned, some of my own supporters at the time were also drawn into the New Deal orbit, and into acceptance or support of the war. Of necessity, my "detour" had to be to the Left.

This is the moment to return to an earlier observation about *two* exceptions among those who for a considerable period played a major role in Brookwood's history. I have in mind, along with myself, Arthur W. Calhoun. He was no longer at Brookwood when the crisis came, having been dropped a couple of years before in another crisis. I suppose that the main causes of that earlier disagreement had been my apprehension that, after the A. F. L. attack, some of Calhoun's policies could result in Brookwood's becoming a "captive" of the C. P., and Calhoun's apprehension that steps I wanted to take in order to prevent that would carry the school in a conservative direction—if not make it a "captive" of the A. F. L.

However that may be, Calhoun subsequently made it clear that his fears had, in the main, been mistaken and that in the 1933 battle he would have been on "my side." Alone among major Brookwood staff people, he and I remain rebels, unequivocal opponents of war, and fundamentally dissatisfied with the course the world is taking.

Due to the break itself and to the circumstances of the time on which we have touched, those who attempted to carry on at Brookwood after the break were frustrated and, after three years, had to give up the effort.

Thus we come to the end of the story of Brookwood. It is a satisfaction to recall that although the controversy was truly a fierce one and feelings were deeply stirred, it was carried on in an essentially decent way, without the chicanery which often characterizes such events. I think it was not long before whatever personal bitter feelings there had been were washed out. It is one of the minor ironies of labor and political history that in the years from 1937 to 1942, when I was back in the pacifist movement and a vocal opponent of the war, I was the one who was quite often visited by agents of the F. B. I. and the Federal Civil Service Commission inquiring about my former associates. Though, for the most part, I feel that I have to refuse to have any official dealing with such political inquisitors, in these instances I spent quite a few hours explaining to agents—not so well informed as most of them are now —the differences between Communists, socialists, syndicalists, and what-have-you, and assuring them that my former associates in a fairly radical labor educational enterprise were people of good character and could be trusted not to try, or even want to try, to overthrow the government by force and violence.

Part Twenty

The year and three quarters (March, 1933-December, 1934) which began with my departure from Brookwood was marked by intense and almost uninterrupted participation in the mass struggles of that period—it was also the first year and three quarters of F. D. Roosevelt's first term—and equally intense and seemingly continuous involvement in political discussion and maneuvering. The political activity I shall describe later. Here I want to describe a few incidents in the mass struggles which may serve to communicate something of the atmosphere of those days and to identify the role played in them by a number of figures with whom readers may be familiar.

I happen to be writing this on the thirtieth anniversary of the great crash of October, 1929. This may serve to remind us of the great contrast between our time and the 1933-34 period. The actual conditions were still much the same as in the panic years. Only the atmosphere was different, because there was an impression that the situation was now mobile. But where things were going was still wholly unclear. It was not, it should be noted, until 1936-37 that deep inroads were made into the hosts of unemployed, that the unions in the mass industries succeeded in establishing themselves, and that the sustained climb to high levels of production got under way. It is well to recall that this was also the time when the Roosevelt administration began to push the defense budget up and worked out the foreign policy which was bound to bring the United States in due time into World War II.

It requires a considerable effort of imagination even for those who lived through the depression to make that experience vivid again. Perhaps younger readers can get some idea of what it was like if they will imagine that the nation was in a state of civil war—civil war which was not sectional as in 1861-65 and therefore did not present the picture of two organized armies in formal battle, but which was a war nevertheless, a war in which every city and section of the country was rent with deep cleavages and in which there was a good deal of fighting, though the guns were almost entirely in the hands of the police and the National Guard. Another useful comparison is with Southern cities today, where racial division puts up barriers through which there is hardly any real communication; paralyzes the respectable and moderate sections of the community and makes them feel and act like helpless onlookers at a mad battle; makes the supposed guardians of law and order the armed foes of the oppressed; and creates continuous and almost unbearable tension which, now here, now there, erupts into open violence.

One of the ways in which men and women sought in this period to defend themselves was by means of various kinds of organizations of the unemployed. Those which were directly organized by the Conference for Progressive Labor Actions and its successor, the American Workers Party, or in which these organizations exercised substantial influence, as I have mentioned, were called Unemployed Leagues. They were to be found in such widely scattered parts of the country as Seattle; Los Angeles; St. Louis; Southern Illinois; West Virginia; Pittsburgh; Allentown, Pennsylvania, and in North Carolina. The Leagues, for the most part, had to act directly in local situations, in preventing evictions (for example, moving furniture back into homes as fast as sheriffs moved it out), compelling authorities to raise the amount of relief a little bit, preventing discrimination against active members of the Leagues, and so on. The Leagues therefore had to have strong local backing and leadership, though outside organizers could be helpful. Since appropriations had to come out of state funds, the next step was to organize State Unemployed Leagues, which sponsored marches on state capitals. Efforts to set up national bodies also had to be made, but it is obvious that in a situation where League members often literally could not pay five cents a week dues, no formidable state or national structures could be built. The genius of all the unemployed organizations was in organizing direct action on the local level.

On July 4, 1933, in the State Fair Grounds at Columbus, Ohio, the National Unemployed League was organized. Hundreds attended the convention and there were moments when it seemed touch and go whether it would break up or not. There were representatives present of the Unemployed Councils, which often were under Communist influence and direction. They proposed the usual merger, or at least "united front," and that was a ticklish matter to handle in a gathering largely made up of politically untrained people. One of the C. P. youths present was John W. Gates, as he has mentioned in his autobiography. Later he became a C. P. leader and editor of the *Daily Worker* and is now one of the many who have left the C. P., and one of the considerable number who have seriously criticized it and have renounced some of their former views.

The main threat to the Columbus convention came from another source, not clearly identified, but almost certainly a few operatives of some detective agency hired either by political figures or by business interests to provoke a riot and thus break up the convention. The effort failed, basically I think because of the hold certain leaders had over the rank and file of the unemployed on account of the sacrificial and vigorous way in which they had backed local struggles. One of them was William Truax, a former sub-district mine-union official who knew the Ohio scene thoroughly. Another was Arnold Johnson, a recent Union Theological Seminary graduate, who had begun work in a Columbus church but soon found his energies entirely absorbed in Unemployed League work. Johnson was one of the Workers Party leaders who later joined the C. P. and who, unlike Gates, for example, is still in it. Much as I have differed with him through these years on his views and activities, I do not doubt that throughout, as in 1933, he has acted on the basis of deep inner convictions and with no qualms about paying a steep price for being true to them.

I think it was almost immediately after I left Columbus that I was driven by one of the Unemployed League local leaders to Toledo, where one of the early struggles that led to the founding of the United Automobile Workers Union took place. It was a strike against the Auto-Lite Company, a big producer of certain automotive parts and accessories. The head of the company was also the dominant figure in one of Toledo's big banks, which had gone bankrupt, as a result of which hundreds of families were in the direst circumstances.

Some days earlier, Louis Budenz, who had gained new fame as an organizer and leader of mass demonstrations of hosiery workers in Kenosha, Wisconsin, had come to Toledo as representative of the C. P. L. A. I think none of those who had a chance to observe Budenz' work in those days would question the verdict that he was a genius at organizing mass activities. Though in many respects a weak person, and certainly not physically impressive, he was transformed the moment he got up before a crowd, and was able to fire it with enthusiasm and determination. In a mass situation he was also personally courageous.

Not as a result of deliberate planning on anyone's part, but as an expression of the pent-up suffering of many years and the resentment of large sections of the Toledo population, including Auto-Lite employees, the latter with numerous allies had attacked the Auto-Lite plant in the late afternoon, a few hours before I approached Toledo in a car that seemed ready to fall apart at any minute. Practically every window in the front of the big plant had been smashed. The militia had been rushed in when the police were unable to cope with the situation. They stood the crowd off and eventually drove them back some distance with tear gas. As we neared the city, the sky was occasionally lighted up with flares sent up by the soldiers to enable them to see whether fresh attackers might be gathering behind the trees or in nearby streets. After I got into town and contacted some of our C. P. L. A. people, we went to the scene of battle. For some time I stood behind a tree within sight of the militia, contemplating that eerie spectacle and wondering whether the soldiers might try to encircle the neighborhood and round us all up. They did not. By the middle of the night everyone was pretty much exhausted and moved away, leaving the soldiers "in peace."

I am not sure at the moment whether it was in connection with the Auto-Lite strike or another strike in Toledo during the same period that there occurred an incident involving Charles P. Taft which merits recording. Taft is the well-known civic reformer and churchman, brother of the late Senator Robert Taft. At the time of this incident he was one of the Federal mediators sent to Toledo to seek the termination of one of those bitter struggles which preceded the organization of the U. A. W. In Toledo we had a local group of remarkable young radicals, a number of whom continued through the years to be active in the labor movement. One of them, Ted Selander, was particularly active on the picket line and as a general organizer. One afternoon he was arrested and taken to the city jail. It was pretty general practice in those days (not only in Toledo) for the police to rough up strikers who had been arrested. Because of Ted's prominence, we feared he would be badly beaten if he was not released on bail before nightfall. Finding that we did not seem to be making progress with police officials, I decided to telephone Charles Taft, who knew me personally.

At first, when I asked him to call the chief of police and show an interest in Selander's prompt release, he said that this was not the sort of thing a Federal mediator could properly take up. I told him that there might be bitterness and a serious flare-up of violence if Selander were badly hurt, and that this might well have a bearing on the prospect of an early settlement. He granted that this was so, and said that he would see what he could do. Selander was released shortly thereafter.

However, in the course of our telephone conservation, Taft had remarked that there was no justification for the strike anyway, the context making it clear that he thought little or nothing of the workers' side of the case. I began to reflect on this and concluded that this was a queer attitude for a supposedly impartial mediator to take, and that under the circumstances he could not be expected to deal fairly with the case for the workers. On further reflection, I decided I could not let this pass. At the very least, I should be in a precarious position if it became known that I had been aware of the mediator's attitude in advance and had kept it to myself. A couple of the strike leaders with whom I conferred agreed that something had to be done.

I called Taft again and reported this to him. He conferred for a moment with colleagues in his hotel suite and then asked if I was willing to come up in a couple of hours for a conference. He also asked me not to do anything further until then. I agreed.

When I stepped into the mediator's suite at nine o'clock I found already there not only Charles Taft but another Federal mediator, the editors of the local papers, the representatives of the national press services, and a couple of special writers who were in town. One of them was the famous columnist Heywood Broun, who was a good friend of mine.

Taft reported, with complete accuracy, what he had first said to me over the telephone and our subsequent conversation. I have always respected him for this. He could simply have denied that he had said anything of the sort, claiming that I had "misunderstood" him; most politicians probably would have done just that. He had made a bad slip, and he risked his prestige in that gathering by frankly admitting that he had. Then he went on to say that he really did not consider himself disqualified as a mediator and that it obviously would be bad public relations and might have an adverse effect on the strike negotiations if the situation were made public. He therefore suggested that I say nothing in public, though without seeking to bring special pressure or pleading to bear on me, and asked the newspaper editors and reporters present not to publish anything about the matter, even if I did make a statement. All of them indicated that they would keep still, except for Heywood Broun, who said it seemed obvious to him that if I made a statement it would be significant news, and he would have no choice but to report it. I said that I would have a statement within an hour.

In the statement I reported what Charles Taft had said in the original telephone talk (omitting any reference at that time to the later conference) and expressed the opinion that this might well disqualify him for serving on this particular case, pointing out that in any event the workers and the general public should know the facts in order to be able to judge for themselves. Neither of the Toledo dailies published a thing, nor did the press services carry a word. Consequently, no paper carried a news story. Heywood Broun duly reported the matter in his next column, which did not, however, appear in print until four days later, a week end having intervened.

After the close of the Auto-Lite strike, which had naturally received a great deal of publicity and had intensified the jitters from which Middle Western employers suffered in those days, I went to central and southern Illinois to report on the strike, especially to our groups in the mining towns. It was soon apparent that I was being followed. Much of the trip was made in the company of two young miners, one of whom, by some stroke of luck, had a new car. One lovely summer morning we arrived soon after dawn at Belleville, Illinois, not far from St. Louis. We drove to the outskirts of the town, where there was a struck metal plant. Everything was quiet there. The plant was closed down tight. A couple of strikers were stationed nearby as observers. We talked to them briefly and then my companions and I sat down on a soft grassy spot, quietly conversing. Incidentally, one of my companions that morning was a handsome young miner, Jimmy Cross. He is the James Cross who later became president of the Bakery Workers Union, which was expelled from the A. F. L.-C. I. O. because he and the union failed to "clean house" in accord with the ethical-practices requirements of the federation. I think that Cross is the only Brookwood graduate who achieved personal wealth and adopted the style of living which we had associated with the most deplorable type of labor leadership.

All the time—an hour or so—during which we had been in that pleasant spot, a police squad car had been parked near by, and three policemen had stood or sat around in leisurely fashion, just like ourselves. We might have been two groups taking it easy in a public park. Then the three policemen came over to us, asked who we were, looked at our C. P. L. A. membership cards, which were red, in the fashion of those days, and announced that we were under arrest.

After some hours in the cells at police headquarters, we learned that there were two charges against us. The first was vagrancy: being "without visible means of support." This was absurd, since I had money enough in my pocket for train fare back to New York and one of us had proof that he was the owner of a new car—and not the cheapest on the market at that! The other charge was violation of the "Treason Statute" of Illinois, i. e., conspiracy "to overthrow the state of Illinois by force and violence." The statute was a left-over from the anti-labor hysteria following World War I. This was, of course, a very serious charge, and so bail was set at twenty thousand dollars in my case, and at ten thousand dollars each for the two young miners.

We spent three or four days in the county jail—not knowing for some time whether any of our friends were aware of our plight. However, they did know and under the leadership of Agnes Burns Wieck got this fantastic sum of forty thousand dollars, most of it from an elderly German-American with a radical background in Germany, who had prospered even in those hard times as a junk and scrap dealer. Agnes Wieck, mother of the writer David Wieck, was a fiery and highly effective leader in education and organizational work among the Illinois miners.

American Civil Liberties Union lawyers from St. Louis stepped into our case, which also had the backing of the influential St. Louis *Post-Dispatch*. The vagrancy charge was quietly dropped at the preliminary hearing, but I was held on the "treason" charge, in spite of the fact that the hearing had been comical.

The arresting officer, having testified that we had been doing nothing illegal or in any sense disturbing at the struck plant, was asked why he had arrested me. He answered: "I thought that any preacher who was traveling around like that so far from his home must be up to some mischief." He may have had something there.

The treason charge hung over me for nearly a year. Then the A. C. L. U. was informed that it had been dropped. Our friend the junk dealer, who had fled from Germany to escape persecution, had not forgotten his youthful experience in his prosperous old age. Up to the time he came forward and offered the bail, he seems to have had no contact with radical activity over here. He risked more than money in suddenly appearing out of nowhere with nearly forty thousand dollars. He got his money back, and then returned to the obscurity of an aged junk dealer's life.

Part Twenty-One

As has been pointed out previously, under the pressure of the economic collapse and other national and international developments in the early Thirties, the elements which had composed the Conference for Progressive Labor Action and which had concentrated on combating corruption in the unions, on organizing the unorganized workers in the mass industries, and on organizing the unemployed, were driven to a more radical theoretical position. They felt that structurally their movement should seek to transform itself into a revolutionary political party.

In the latter part of 1933, a well-attended conference decided to set up a provisional committee to establish the American Workers Party. Our program was based on the Marxist philosophy of class struggle, though not on Marxism-Leninism as a metaphysical doctrine. It asserted that the United States was in a revolutionary period, and that only when the workers and other progressive and exploited elements took power under leadership of a democratically organized revolutionary party would their problems be resolved. It also declared that, for different reasons, neither the Communist Party nor the Socialist Party could fill the need of the time or showed any likelihood of becoming fitted to do so. There was no alternative, therefore, but to try to launch a new party. Finally, we stated that the struggle for liberation from exploitation and war is basically an international one and that consequently we were concerned about the formation of a new International, finding both the Third International (Communist) and the Second (Socialist or Social-Democratic) hindrances rather than aids in the task of building a new order.

Here, then, we had a movement of activists who had acquired considerable prestige in the carrying out of mass activities and were widely trusted among the workers, moving toward theoretical definition and political organization. In this same period, the American followers of Leon Trotsky had been undergoing changes. They had started, of course, as Marxist-Leninists, deeply concerned about purity of doctrine, and involved in persistent controversy with the C. P. over points of philosophy and program. As members of the C. P., they had belonged to a political and highly disciplined group. Some years earlier, they had been expelled from the C. P. For a time they fought to get back, but in 1933 they had given up and announced that a new revolutionary party had to be formed in the United States and, following Trotsky's lead, that a new International had to be constituted. At the same time, they felt that they should cease to live the life of a sect. "The time had come," according to one of their two top leaders, James P. Cannon, in his *History of American Trotskyism*, "to transform our whole activity, to make the turn to mass work." It was in a sense inevitable that these two streams—the A. W. P. and the Communist League of America, as the Trotskyists called themselves, should come together.

It was the C. L. A. which, in 1934, approached the A. W. P. and suggested merger. I have mentioned some of the mass struggles in which the A. W. P. was involved. The C. L. A. had played a crucial part in the brilliant strikes of the Minneapolis teamsters in May, and again in July-August of that year. We in the A. W. P. spent a lot of time that year in discussions as to whether, and on what terms, we should join the C. L. A. Anyone who reads Jim Cannon's book (Max Shachtman, by the way, was the other top C. L. A. leader) will learn that the C. L. A. spent a lot more time on internal wrangles with those whom Cannon and Shachtman regarded as sectarians, on merger with the A. W. P. and other issues. On looking back, one wonders how so much strenuous and often dangerous mass work got accomplished along with so much talk and seemingly interminable program drafting. Somehow it did. The upshot was that at a joint convention on December 1-2, 1934, a merger was consummated, and the Workers Party of the United States was formed with a Declaration of Principles which, according to Jim Cannon, "was characterized by Comrade Trotsky as a rigidly principled program," i.e., as fulfilling the requirements of Marxism-Leninism as interpreted by Trotsky. Cannon had been sent to France a couple of months before by the C. L. A. to get the Old Man's approval and his directives for the future.

We who came into the merger from the A. W. P. knew something, but as the event proved, not nearly enough, about a new development in the Trotskyist movement called the French Turn. It was so called because, quoting Cannon again, it was "the turn taken by our French organization to join the Socialist Party of France as a body in order to work within this reformist party as a faction."

Enough was known by us to cause us, in the months before the merger, to ask the C. L. A. negotiators whether their plan was, as soon as they had merged with us to form the Workers Party of the United States, to come forward with the proposal that we execute a "French Turn" here, dissolve the W. P. and enter the Socialist Party. We were assured that the French Turn was for France, where there was a very big S. P., an advanced revolutionary crisis, etc., and not for general application—certainly not for the U. S., where the merger would be a section of "a new International with a clean banner" which we would not want to lower again or have confused with another. We accepted these assurances.

But this did not prevent Cannon, Shachtman, and most of the other former C. L. A. leaders from raising, early in 1935, the question of entry into the Socialist Party here. Cannon's own account, in the book already referred to, makes it abundantly clear how much time and effort was then consumed for an entire year in internal discussion over this issue and how the mass work to which we had supposedly dedicated ourselves suffered. Trotskyists never slackened their efforts to "educate" the dissidents (such as the Oehlerites) in their own ranks and the politically backward Musteites, in the Bolshevik soundness of entry into the S. P. In the spring of 1936, they achieved their objective, at least to the extent of getting a substantial majority of the membership to vote to join the S. P. So the Workers Party of the United States ceased to be, and the banner of the Fourth International went underground.

I opposed the move to the bitter end. Cannon's explanation of my failure to become a true Bolshevik is largely a personal one. He reveals that he always had a certain liking for me, which, to tell the truth, I reciprocated. But, "Muste had started out life as a preacher. That put two strikes on him to start with." He says this more in sorrow than in anger: "Muste was, you may say, the last chance and the best chance, and even he, the best prospect of all, couldn't come through in the end because of that terrible background of the church. . . . To peddle the opium of religion . . . is an occupation that deforms the mind."

The rationale for going into the S. P. was that just as a radical development had taken place among the Musteites, so important changes were also taking place in the Socialist Party. Left-wingers were developing there. They were not at the moment attracted to our new party. It would not be sound Bolshevism to ignore them. The way to get them was to go into the Socialist Party, educate them in true Bolshevism, and presently, with their help, take over the Socialist Party or take them out of it into a new revolutionary party with another set of initials.

Let us give an illustration of what we thought, according to Jim Cannon, of those we were joining and preparing to educate. The leaders of this important Left Wing of the Socialist Party were "philistines to the marrow of their bones, without tradition, without serious knowledge, without anything at all." How they could call themselves "Militants" was to Jim an unfathomable mystery.

Nevertheless, these nobodies were drawing prospective recruits into the Socialist Party and away from us. "The Socialist Party was in our way. We had to remove that obstacle from our path." Since these things have to be done gradually, and neither internal conditions in the Workers Party nor the attitude of the S. P. permitted the true Bolsheviks to join the latter outright, in a transition period the Cannon-Shachtman program included forming "Trotskyist fractions in the S. P." and sending thirty or forty of our members to "join the S. P., and work inside it in the interests of the Bolshevik education of the Left Wing."

Toward the end there were "two small hurdles" to jump over before our French Turn maneuver could be completed. There had to be a Workers Party convention and "we had to get permission from the heads of the S. P. before we could join it." At this stage Cannon-Shachtman began negotiations with the leaders of the Militants briefly characterized above. From these negotiations, Muste, who was making a "fetish" of organizational integrity, was excluded. So we must perforce depend on Cannon's vivid description.

The negotiations with the Militant leaders, "these papier-mâché heroes, were a spectacle for gods and men. . . . In all my long and somewhat checkered experience . . . I never encountered anything so fabulous and fantastic. . . . They were all transient figures, important for a day. . . . They were ignorant, untalented, petty-minded, weak, cowardly, treacherous and vain. And they had other faults too. They were in a quandary over our application for admission to their party. . . . Yet they were the leaders of the Left Wing of the S. P. and we had to negotiate with them all, including Norman Thomas who was the head of the party nominally, and who, as Trotsky very well explained, called himself a Socialist as a result of a misunderstanding."

But, Cannon continues, a Trotskyist "will do anything for the party, even if he has to crawl on his belly in the mud." So, though "they wouldn't allow us the honor and dignity of joining as a body," we eventually "gained admission by all sorts of devices and at a heavy cost. . . . We received no welcome, no friendly salute. . . . Not one of the leaders of our party was offered so much as a post as branch organizer by these cheapskates . . . not one. . . . It was a shabby business . . . the way they received us." It does not seem to enter Cannon's mind that even if the whole idea of entry into the Socialist Party was not a "shabby business," the way in which he and his colleagues carried it out was. I thought it a "shabby business" then and I still do.

As for the balance sheet on the results of the maneuver, the Socialist Party was, of course, torn with dissension and weakened, but then it "was destined in any case to be torn apart," according to Cannon. Even if this is true, it did not help radicalism in the United States to have it done in this way. Within the Socialist Party, Trotskyist leaders "adapted themselves a little too much to the centrist officialdom." Too much time was spent in "palaver and negotiations with the leaders of the New York Militants group . . . who had absolutely no real power in the party and whose strategic position was a transitory one rather than that of real influence over the ranks of the party." Mass work was largely neglected. In about a year, the Trotskyists were out again.

However, according to Cannon, they had twice as many members as before entry. I cannot vouch for the accuracy of that figure, as by that time I had long severed my connections. But, even if taken at face value, this reminds one of the minister, in the old story, who moves to a new parish with ten children of his own and is able to report that the Sunday school enrollment has doubled. How soon were many of the new recruits demoralized in new factional struggles, while mass work remained neglected? And if, in the Workers Party, we had stuck to mass work and wooed the younger elements in the Socialist Party by different means from the devious ones we used, would we not have won them away from the Militant leaders, who, according to Cannon himself, had no real influence over the ranks of the party?

Cannon also claims that it is because they had closer access to liberals as members of the Socialist Party that they were able in 1936-37 to involve John Dewey and others in setting up the Trotsky Defense Committee, arranging the famous inquiry about Stalinist persecution of Trotsky in Mexico. Personally, I feel that this is preposterous; and it is certainly arguable that Trotsky was so great a figure, John Dewey and the others on the committee were such courageous liberals, and the Workers Party in those days had enough contacts among intellectuals, to have made these things possible if we had attended to our own knitting instead of going through the complicated and boring adventure of getting the Socialist Party out of our way.

The other claim Cannon makes is that in California, where he went to live for reasons of health, Trotskyists did good mass work in the 1936-37 maritime strike. I cannot vouch for this, but it may well be. Both groups that formed the Workers Party had done notable mass work before merger. After the merger, as Cannon states, "We should have had a year or two of constructive work, uninterrupted by differences, conflicts and internal fights. But history didn't work that way." History got a big assist from Cannon and Company. What might have happened if the pre-merger understanding that we were not proposing a French Turn here had been kept is obviously a matter for speculation. The deterioration of the American Left in the years since could hardly have been worse than it has proved to be, and I am convinced that the kind of in-fighting and maneuvering which went on in the Workers Party, and which was by no means confined to it, had a good deal to do with that deterioration.

Other significant developments in the period under discussion included the defection of Louis Budenz and Arnold Johnson to the C. P., under highly dramatic circumstances. Here let me add, in order to avoid misunderstanding, that my observations about the entry of Workers Party members into the Socialist Party in 1936 and the conduct of certain Trotskyist leaders then should not be taken as a criticism of the recent entry of Independent Socialist League members, most of whom were at one time Trotskyists, into the Socialist Party. It is no secret that I harbor some doubts about whether and how the recent merger contributes to the reconstitution of an American Left. But the two "entries" are far apart chronologically and even farther apart in political terms. It is naturally not entirely excluded that the present can draw certain "lessons" from the past in such matters; but they do not lie on the surface, and nobody should try to draw neat inferences about my views on the current scene.

Part Twenty-Two

On October 2, 1935, the day the New York section of the Workers Party, much the largest section in the country, had its crucial discussion on the "entry into the Socialist Party," two events suddenly erupted. The first centered around Leon Trotsky, the second around Louis Francis Budenz.

The Musteites, it will be recalled, had merged with the Trotskyist organization on the understanding that there was no plan to execute another maneuver shortly and go into the S. P. Accordingly, most of the opposition to the move, when it was proposed, came from those of us who had come from the American Workers Party, though some of the latter favored the application of the so-called French Turn to the United States. (Later I came to suspect that some of these may have been "plants" sent into the A. W. P. by the Trotskyists or converted and told to stay in the W. P.) However, there was also a considerable number who had belonged to the Communist League of America (Trotskyist) who opposed entry into the S. P. With these we were naturally in close contact as the hour of decision approached.

Important meetings of this kind always convened from one to three hours late. Partly this was from ingrained habit, partly because there was always furious caucusing to be done at the last minute, and sometimes it took time to line up the comrades. I arrived at the meeting place, on a Saturday morning, ahead of most of the leading people. One of the Trotskyists of long standing showed me a cable which had arrived that morning from Trotsky, who by then was living as an exile in Norway, in a small town called Hoenefoss, near Oslo. He and his devoted wife lived there in the home of a delightful couple named Knudsen who were leading members of the Norwegian Labor Party, which had a consistent record of militancy, of regard for internationalism and support for Socialists who had been persecuted in other countries and forced to seek asylum.

The telegram from the Old Man, as Trotsky was usually called, simply stated that in his opinion the Workers Party should now make the entry into the Socialist Party and that he hoped all comrades would see it that way. But to true-blue Trotskyists this meant that the W. P. was ordered to enter the S. P. and the comrades were expected to see it that way, or at the very least to accept it and shut their mouths.

So my friends were placed in a sore dilemma. Having staked their revolutionary insight and virtue on the proposition that the S. P. entry would be a betrayal of the revolution and of the Fourth International, and having relied on us to help them save the cause, they could not quite reverse their position in the discussion that was about to open and say, in effect, that in obedience to Trotsky's order they now recognized that white was black and vice versa. On the other hand, they had to carry on their opposition in such a way as not to lay themselves open to the charge of insubordination and to leave the way open for acceptance, in the case of most of them, of the S. P. entry. Meanwhile, they were, of course, well aware that Cannon and Shachtman knew about the "orders" they had received and would plant barbs of sarcasm in their hides—privately, if not publicly; later, if not then.

I felt sorry for my allies. I was considerably amused by the development. And I did some perspiring inwardly as I absorbed a hard lesson. I do not recall the details of how my friends walked on eggs in the ensuing debate.

It was not long before I became convinced that Trotsky controlled his followers about as autocratically as Stalin controlled his, though of course Trotsky did not have at his command the crude disciplinary instruments which Stalin had in such abundance. Moreover, much as I admired, and still admire, Trotsky in many ways, and agree with him at a number of points in his controversy with Stalin, I suspect that if he had come to power in the Soviet state, his reign, too, would have been a bloody one. This is partly because, as I see it, he would have been dealing with forces which would have pushed him into actions he might have preferred not to commit, as is the case to some extent with any head of state. But it is also clear from Trotsky's own writing that he was not, even in a remote sense, a pacifist, and that he had no scruples about violence and even terrorism when his objectives demanded them. He was a much more complicated character than Stalin, and there was an element of charm, gentleness, and softness (in the better sense of that term) in him that was apparently totally lacking in his great antagonist; but, as is often the case, this did not exclude a capacity for ruthlessness and for glorying in that capacity. His destiny (and in considerable measure his virtue) lay in that he did not achieve power.

The other thunderbolt that hit on that October morning in 1935 was the announcement in the *Daily Worker* that Louis Budenz, Arnold Johnson, and a couple of lesser lights of the Workers Party had joined the Communist Party. According to Budenz' own statement, in his autobiographical *This Is My Story,* he had actually joined three months earlier (and he may possibly have done so even before that). In any case, the announcement was obviously timed to cause consternation in Trotskyist ranks and to show the Trotskyists that their merger with the Musteites was not going to pay off so handsomely as they might have hoped. No doubt it was thought in C. P. circles that fear would develop that more former A. W. P. people might go over to the C. P.; perhaps even Muste himself was secretly negotiating with them to follow his old fellow-agitator, Budenz.

If there were such expectations, they were not fulfilled. I have no reason to think that any W. P. people suspected, even momentarily, that I would defect. But obviously, in view of the telegram from Oslo and the announcement in the *Daily Worker,* my position in that day's debate was, organizationally speaking, a shaky one. We were, naturally, defeated, though not by too big a vote. I have made it clear that I thought, and still think, that the S. P. entry was a mistake and a grave violation of working-class ethics.

This is the place for me to expand a little on my relations with Budenz and to set down some evaluation of his character and role. One enters upon such an undertaking with some hesitation, knowing how subjective one's judgments inevitably are and how little one may understand the inner workings of a person with whom one has worked fairly closely over a considerable period. We all have to make such evaluations, however, in order to determine our own political course and our association with others.

For younger readers, let me recall once more that Louis Budenz is the man who gained considerable notoriety by joining the C. P. and working in it for ten years, 1935-45, as editorial writer on the *Daily Worker*, editor of a Chicago C. P. organ, and in other fairly important posts; even more by a dramatic return to the Roman Catholic Church into which he had been born, under the tutelage of Monsignor, now Bishop, Fulton J. Sheen; and still more by becoming an ardent anti-Communist campaigner and a source of more or less select information for the House Un-American Activities Committee and other such agencies.

In some moods, one would say that Louis was fundamentally a "good guy" and a pleasant person. He certainly was not, in my experience, a vicious person. I do not think he has the temperament of an inquisitor or persecutor, or that it was natural for him to make up stories out of whole cloth. If, as has been alleged, he departed from the truth, my guess is that he did so from weakness, because his imagination ran away with him, or from a desire to please whomever he was with, rather than from a vicious impulse to get people in trouble. He was at no time in his life under the influence of an ultra-rigorous ethic, one that did not allow some latitude in a "good cause." He was not a scholar or profound thinker and made no claim to being one. Nor was he a political analyst. For the most part, he operated on the basis of intuition and impulse. His genius was as a tactician in labor struggles and propaganda campaigns.

It seems to me that he suffered from considerable insecurity, which kept him from meeting issues straight on. He needed people about him to lean on, both emotionally and in work relationships. On the other hand, he overcame his insecurity when he mounted a platform to make a speech, or led a strike, or marched at the head of a picket line. Since he was short, the phrase "little Napoleon" came readily to the lips of people who saw him in such settings, where few could match him. His insecurity seems to me also to explain in large measure the fact that he has spent much of his life either in the Roman Catholic Church or in the Communist Party, has seemed somehow to be at home in both groups and palpably restless and bereft of moorings during the quarter-century from 1920 to 1945, during which I worked with him fairly continuously.

That Louis landed in the C. P. at all was somewhat surprising. He had long regarded it as a foreign importation. He had been a severe critic, as were others of us, of its erratic and opportunistic trade union policies. He cannot have been comfortable with the dialectical materialistic philosophy. Restraint irked him. I was not surprised to read in his autobiography a statement telling about his reaction to sessions of the national committee of the C. P. shortly after he joined: "I was immediately conscious of the suffocating air of conspiracy which surrounded these sessions."

That he joined the C. P. when he did, is, however, perfectly understandable. The Party in 1935 was moving into the Popular Front period. It was seeking to adapt itself to American conditions and using American revolutionary traditions and slogans in its speeches and literature, something which Louis consistently advocated all his life. Moreover, this was the heyday of C. P. growth in all directions and especially in the unions, where Louis was eager to work. It was a big operation. Obviously, Louis was flattered. He was pushed to the front and used as a "front," as he later pointed out. It was again in keeping that he should leave the C. P. when the "American line" was being abandoned and preparations being made to dismiss Earl Browder, who had been chief.

In the meantime there had been the Soviet attack on Finland and the Hitler-Stalin pact. That, outwardly at least, he should have remained true to the C. P. in spite of such events can perhaps be explained only by the fact that he had, in his own words, an "intense desire to close my eyes to things I did not want to see."

In this context one puzzles over a phase of his contact with the Roman Catholic Church, which I did not fully realize until, recently, I re-read some portions of *This Is My Story*. His first contact with Fulton Sheen, according to this book, was in 1937, less than two years after Louis had joined the C. P.! Louis had written some pieces suggesting that the C. P. would gladly work with Catholics, and that Catholics might well collaborate with the C. P. In those days he hoped—or so he alleges—that the time might come when membership in the Roman Church would not be a barrier to admission into the C. P. Sheen promptly wrote him a long letter, citing chapter and verse from C. P. literature as to why there had to be eternal enmity between Communism and the Church.

Louis indicated that he would like to talk to the Monsignor, and shortly thereafter they met for luncheon in the Commodore Hotel in New York. For a while they talked politics and sparred. The Monsignor suggested that the *Daily Worker* publish his critique of Communism! Then, according to Louis' account, after a pause, the Monsignor said: "Let us talk about the Blessed Virgin." He proceeded to do so. Louis says, a little before this, that this period represented "the lowest ebb in my religious life." Now, as Sheen spoke of Immaculate Mary, "immediately I was conscious of the senselessness and sinfulness of my life as I then lived it. The peace that flows from Mary . . . flashed back to me with an overwhelming vividness."

Yet he remained in the C. P. for eight more years. One may

guess that when he wrote his autobiography, after having again become a practicing Catholic, he read back into the meeting in the Commodore some of the emotion which he felt while under the spell of his return to his spiritual home. Even so, since I feel certain, in the light of all I know, that Louis had a deep emotional experience back in 1937, it remains an enigma how he could have remained active and a recognized, apparently completely convinced spokesman of the C. P. for so long. His frequently expressed contention—that he continued during those years to believe that cooperation between Catholics and Communists could be achieved—strikes me as either a rationalization after the event or an instance of the kind of superficial, purely tactical and non-philosophical thinking of which he was capable at times.

His final return to the Roman Catholic Church came in 1945, after the change in the C. P. line already referred to. In tender passages which, I feel sure, reflect his true feelings, Louis ascribes the return largely to the prayers of his parents. Speaking of those prayers, he writes that "Mary Immaculate was brought to the aid of this man who had succumbed to the vanity of this world. Great is the faith that can put such trust in the Mother of God."

Just as he had remained in the Workers Party, in 1935, for some time after he had secretly joined the C. P., so he remained in the C. P. for at least four weeks, according to his own account, after all the arrangements for his return to the Catholic fold had been made. These no doubt included some understanding relating to his forthcoming "exposure" of the C. P. and his associates of the past decade. He did his work and attended meetings at the *Daily Worker* during those weeks and "fingered the rosary in my pocket as I did so."

I have not intended at any point in this account to ridicule religious mystical experience, either in general or as mediated through the Roman Catholic Church. The individual's political behavior is another matter, and is subject to ethical judgment. After it became known that Budenz was leaving the C. P. and joining the Catholic Church, as I said earlier, I made several attempts to see him. I wanted to talk with him, partly from the vantage point of one who had returned to religious life nearly a decade before, because I feared that he would become what is popularly known as a "red-baiter." He did not make any response to my messages.

In *This Is My Story*, Louis writes about an incident that occurred, before he became well known in the labor movement, in

Rahway, New Jersey, where he lived for many years. A mayor who had been a Socialist and who was a friend of Louis' had been carrying out some reforms which angered some elements in the city. A mob formed one night and threatened Louis. They beat on his front door and vowed to throw him in the river. He writes that under this threat he was "cold-sweatedly disturbed" and then adds: "I resolved that thereafter in any crisis I would be at the head of the crowd rather than ahead of it." Certainly he was at the head of a crowd a number of times in later years. I have pondered over this sentence many times. I leave the reader to do likewise.

The Problem
of Discontent

1905 * The inevitable fruit of all life and progress is dissatisfaction and unrest. Over the dull clod broods absolute contentment. Infuse life into it, let it progress but a little, and in silent, mighty restlessness it struggles up from the dark earth, and grows into leaves and branches, flowers and fruit. Even the death sleep of the winter cannot calm its unrest, but ever, after the resurrection of the spring time, it struggles outward and upward again into the pure, mysterious ideal of its Maker. The dumb multitudes whose only prayer is for the daily bread, whose only suffering is the meek and voiceless anguish of the brute, these feel no mental unrest. But for the men and nations who have been swept into the current of an advancing civilization, there is no peace forever. Progress perpetuates itself by the hardy seeds of unrest which it sows. Witness the seething ferment of the present industrial world—the bold aggression of the higher classes, the fearless resistance of the enlightened lower classes. Or again that gigantic discontent of unfolding national life which has brought about the Russo-Japanese war, the latest conflict of the Titans and the gods. History, with its mighty empires and colossal ruins, its victory and defeat, its progress and retrogression, is but the tragic story of human unrest.

The same principle of discontent manifests itself in the life of

* His first published work, this essay was delivered by A. J. Muste as the Commencement Day address at Hope College, Holland, Michigan, and later appeared in the Hope College magazine, *The Anchor*.

the individual who has begun to live and develop, and as its field of action is here narrower, so its intensity is greater. For the man who thinks, there can be no honorable peace. Before him lies the vast domain of knowledge—one glimpse of that mighty dreamland, and the restless, adventurous spirit of the pioneer is upon him. Or again, who dares sit idle in the midst of this great humanity with its sadness and imperfection, its unallayed thirst for freedom and its hope deferred? Greatest of all, the soul of man demands an explanation of itself, the crushing problem of the universe is upon him, and the heart's insistent clamor for a knowledge of the things it sees in the night time beyond the thousand orbs of light. For nowhere does this dissatisfaction become so intense as in matters of religion. By some relentless law thought begets doubt. And oh, the utter anguish of that hour when in its troubled restlessness the soul loses its grasp also on those eternal verities by which alone we dare to live. Not that one ceases to love his early faith; it is inseparably linked with childhood memories of mother and of home. Nor does one cease to respect it: the forefathers lived by it, and were they not earth's noblemen? But the soul is powerless against its own discontent.

What is the solution of this problem of unrest? Why this eternal restlessness? Where is surcease from sorrow?

Wearied with struggle, men have sometimes gone forth into the desert to do penance for their insufficiency and to find in the stillness and the loneliness, if it might be, some answer to their questioning. They abandoned living in order to solve the problem of life; and the same temptation to exchange a life of action for one of thought comes today to the men who, in the depth of their philosophic doubt and unrest, have lost the courage to live. Cowards are they all! And the solution of the problem of human restlessness lies not in thought but in action, not in rest but in struggle.

In the physical world the law is clearly illustrated. The plant works out the life-principle of unrest that abides in it, through its constant struggle with the earth that would hold it forever in bands of darkness, and with the powers of air and sky that wrestle with it in the night and in the storm, and by that very struggle it grows at last into the princely sentinel of the forest stream, the spirit within it being satisfied anew each summer by the growth and loveliness that it has taken unto itself from the conflicts of the winter and the spring. Thus, too, mankind has learned to satisfy its discontent by battling with it. Awakened from its enchanted sleep of ignorance and dissatisfied in the relentless grasp of a dead church, sixteenth-century Europe was forced to struggle for release, and in that struggle achieved its liberty. For human unrest is not some unrequited pain whose stifled cry goes up into the void and is unheard forever. Rather is it the vital principle of progress planted deep in the soil of our common humanity. In a world of sin it could not be otherwise; there must be unrest before there can be progress. And thus in labor and in sorrow mankind works out the long problem of its redemption.

How clearly this shows the duty of the educated man of today. Not in a life of retirement and contemplation will he find peace or a solution of the vexing problems of life. The deep unrest of his soul is a divine call to battle. Let him plunge boldly into the conflict then. Let him be "with the van and the freemen" in humanity's varied struggle. Thus will he most truly advance mankind's development, for the world's silent appeal is for an act, not a philosophy. Men who can slay the demon of corruption that stands guard over the halls of our legislature, men who can lead nations in the gigantic battles of modern statecraft, men who by the silent compulsion of action and of life can teach the efficacy of true religion—these humanity summons to the conflict. Let them gladly answer, for in the stress of the world's battle discontent shall pass away into action and be no more.

But not only will the life of action and of usefulness furnish a natural outlet for man's restlessness; it will furnish also the surest means to solve those vexing problems of morality and religion which most deeply stir the faith and calm of the educated mind. Character is built by action rather than by thought. Contemplation does not beget virtues. But out of the elements of the daily struggle we mold at last conceptions of justice, parity and truth and build that temple of morality which is the chosen seat of true religion. Finally, it is only through the conflict into which his unrest urges him that man at last finds God. Revelation is powerless if it enlightens only the reason. Nature shows only some inscrutable force which forever baffles the mind and overawes the spirit with its mystery and power. All the labor of philosophic thought and contemplation has availed only to reason away the elemental instincts of our being or to create some lifeless, loveless God from whom the soul revolts. And even faith, without works, is dead. Only when it can enable us to enter fearlessly upon our God-given portion of labor, trusting somehow that good shall come of it, can it demonstrate its power to lay hold on God. And as faith is valid only when it leads to action, so its ultimate satisfaction is found only in the active life. In the monotony of each day's burden-bearing we learn to know a Power that answers unvoiced prayer. When we fall back, weary of the bitter strife with sin, we hear the whisperings of a sustaining Love. In the hour of pained affliction we meet the Man of Sorrows. And upon the child that stumbles bravely at its task falls the benignant radiance of a Father's smile. The god of philosophy is an abstraction. The God of experience is Personality, Power and Love. In the stress and agony of conflict we feel his living presence. At our side in the battle rides a sustaining Power.

How strangely wise and simple, after all, is Heaven's decree. The eternal unrest of humanity and the discontent of the soul urge men to action, and in action is the principle of all progress on the part of the race and the ultimate warrant of peace to the individual. Thus does life's simplest law summon us to the conflict. Therefore —the battle! until each weary soldier file away to where:

"Beyond these voices there is peace."

Pacifism
and Class War

1928 It is expected perhaps that an article dealing with pacifism in relation to class war should consist of an exhortation to labor organizations and radicals to eschew violent methods in the pursuit of their ends, together with an exposition of the use of pacifist methods in labor disputes and social revolutions. If there is such an expectation, this article will be in large measure disappointing. Chiefly, because in my opinion much more time must be spent than has yet been given to clearing away some exceedingly mischievous misconceptions before we can think fruitfully about concrete non-violent methods of social change; and because there are very, very few individuals in the world, including the pacifist groups and churches, who are in a moral position to preach non-resistance to the labor or radical movement.

Practically all our thinking about pacifism in connection with class war starts out at the wrong point. The question raised is how the oppressed, in struggling for freedom and the good life, may be dissuaded from employing "the revolutionary method of violence" and won over to "the peaceful process of evolution." Two erroneous assumptions are concealed in the question put that way. The first is that the oppressed, the radicals, are the ones who are creating the disturbance. To the leaders of Jesus' day, Pharisees, Sadducees, Roman governor, it was Jesus who was upsetting the people, turning the world upside down. In the same way, we speak of the Kuomintang "making a revolution" in China today, seldom by any chance of the Most Christian Powers having made the revolution by almost a hundred years of trickery, oppression, and inhumanity. Similarly, society may permit an utterly impossible situation to develop in an industry like coal, but the workers who finally in desperation put down tools and fold their arms, they are "the strikers," the cause of the breach of the peace. We need to get our thinking focused, and to see the rulers of Jewry and Rome, not Jesus; the Powers, not the Chinese Nationalists; selfish employers or a negligent society—not striking workers—as the cause of disturbance in the social order.

A second assumption underlying much of our thinking is that the violence is solely or chiefly committed by the rebels against oppression, and that this violence constitutes the heart of our problem. However, the basic fact is that the economic, social, political order in which we live was built up largely by violence, is now being extended by violence, and is maintained only by violence. A slight knowledge of history, a glimpse at the armies and navies of the Most Christian Powers, at our police and constabulary, at the militaristic fashion in which practically every attempt of workers to organize is greeted, in Nicaragua or China, will suffice to make the point clear to an unbiased mind.

The foremost task, therefore, of the pacifist in connection with class war is to denounce the violence on which the present system is based, and all the evil—material and spiritual—this entails for the masses of men throughout the world; and to exhort all rulers in social, political, industrial life, all who occupy places of privilege, all who are the beneficiaries of the present state of things, to relinquish every attempt to hold on to wealth, position and power by force, to give up the instruments of violence on which they annually spend billions of wealth produced by the sweat and anguish of the toilers. So long as we are not dealing honestly and adequately with this ninety percent of our problem, there is something ludicrous, and perhaps hypocritical, about our concern over the ten percent of violence employed by the rebels against oppression. Can we win the rulers of earth to peaceful methods?

The psychological basis for the use of nonviolent methods is the simple rule that like produces like, kindness provokes kindness, as surely as injustice produces resentment and evil. It is sometimes forgotten by those whose pacifism is a spurious, namby-pamby thing that if one Biblical statement of this rule is "Do good to them that hate you" (an exhortation presumably intended for the capitalist as well as for the laborer), another statement of the same rule is, "They that sow the wind shall reap the whirlwind." You get from the universe what you give, with interest! What if men build a system on violence and injustice, on not doing good to those who hate them nor even to those who meekly obey and toil for them? And persist in this course through centuries of Christian history? And if, then, the oppressed raise the chant:

> *Ye who sowed the wind of sorrow,*
> *Now the whirlwind you must dare,*
> *As ye face upon the morrow,*
> *The advancing Proletaire!*

In such a day, the pacifist is presumably not absolved from preaching to the rebels that they also shall reap what they sow; but assuredly not in such wise as to leave the oppressors safely entrenched in their position, not at the cost of preaching to them in all sternness that "the judgments of the Lord are true and righteous altogether."

As we are stayed from preaching nonviolence to the underdog, unless and until we have dealt adequately with the dog who is chewing him up, so also are all those who would support a country in war against another country stayed from preaching nonviolence in principle to labor or to radical movements. Much could be said on this point, but it is perhaps unnecessary to dwell on it here. Suffice it to observe in passing that, to one who has had any intimate connection with labor, the flutter occasioned in certain breasts by the occasional violence in connection with strikes seems utterly ridiculous, and will continue to seem so until the possessors of these fluttering breasts have sacrificed a great deal more than they already have in order to banish from the earth the horrible monster of international war.

We are not, to pursue the matter a little further, in a moral position to advocate nonviolent methods to labor while we continue to be beneficiaries of the existing order. They who profit by violence, though it be indirectly, unwillingly and only in a small measure, will always be under suspicion, and rightly so, of seeking to protect their profits, of being selfishly motivated, if they address pious exhortations to those who suffer by that violence.

Nor can anyone really with good conscience advocate abstention from violence to the masses of labor in revolt, unless he is himself identified in spirit with labor and helping it with all his might to achieve its rights and to realize its ideals. In a world built on violence, one must be a revolutionary before one can be a pacifist; in such a world a non-revolutionary pacifist is a contradiction in terms, a monstrosity. During the war, no absolute pacifist in America would have felt justified in exhorting Germany to lay down its arms while saying and doing nothing about America's belligerent activities. We should have recognized instantly the moral absurdity, the implied hypocrisy of such a position. Our duty was to win our own "side" to a "more excellent way." It is a sign of ignorance and lack of realism in our pacifist groups and churches that so many fail to recognize clearly and instantly the same point with regard to the practice of pacifism in social and labor struggles.

Things being as they are, it is fairly certain that if a group of workers goes on strike for better conditions, other methods having failed, they will commit some acts of violence and coercion; some evil passions will be aroused in their breasts. Shall the pacifist who has identified himself with labor's cause therefore seek to dissuade the workers from going on strike? (I am of course confining myself here to a question of principle, leaving out of account questions of the expediency of a strike in given conditions.) My own answer is an emphatic negative, because I am convinced that in these cases the alternative of submission is by far the greater evil. Appearances are deceiving here, and the human heart is deceitful. There is a certain indolence in us, a wish not to be disturbed, which tempts us to think that when things are quiet all is well. Subconsciously, we tend to give the preference to "social peace," though it be only apparent, because our lives and possessions seem then secure. Actually, human beings acquiesce too easily in evil conditions; they rebel far too little and too seldom. There is nothing noble about acquiescence in a cramped life or mere submission to superior force. There is as vast a spiritual difference between such submission of the masses and the glad acceptance of pain by the saint, as there is between the sodden poverty of the urban or rural slum and the voluntary poverty of St. Francis "that walks with God upon the Umbrian hills." No one who has ever inwardly experienced the spiritual exaltation and the intense brotherhood created by a strike, on the one hand, and the sullen submission of hopeless poverty or the dull contentment or "respectability" of those who are too fat and lazy to struggle for freedom, on the other hand, will hesitate for a moment to choose the former, though it involves a measure of violence.

Here it may be well to point out that, as a matter of fact, the amount of violence on the part of workers on strike is usually grossly exaggerated; and that, on the other hand, practically every great strike furnishes inspiring examples of non-resistance under cruel provocation and victory by "soul force" alone—victory through patient endurance of evil and sacrifice, even unto death, for spiritual ends. I have witnessed these things repeatedly. More than once, I have exhorted masses of strikers to fold their arms, not to strike back, to smile at those who beat them and trample them under their horses' feet, and the strikers' response has been instantaneous, unreserved, exalted. I have also appealed to police heads to call off violence-provoking extra forces and to employees to discharge labor spies, and have been laughed at for my pains.

Much of what has already been said bears upon the special problem of the Communist, with his frank espousal of terrorism, his conviction that no great and salutary social change can be accomplished without violence and that the workers must therefore be prepared for armed revolt. Our whole focus on this problem also is wrong unless we get it clear that violence inheres first in the system against which the Communist revolts; that they who suffer from social revolt in the main reap what, by positive evil-doing or indifference, they have sown; that practically every great revolution begins peacefully and might proceed so, to all appearances, but for the development of violent counter-revolution; that the degree of terrorism employed in such an upheaval as the French or Russian revolution is always directly proportionate to the pressure of foreign attack; that in general the amount of "red" terrorism in human history is a bagatelle compared to the "white" terrorism of reactionaries. The question is pertinent as to whether the "Lord's will" is done by the servant who talks about terrorism and practices very little, or by the servant who talks about law and order and practices a vast deal of terrorism.

Most discussions assume that on this point of the use of violence there is a fundamental difference between the conservative and radical wings of the labor movement, and between Socialism and Communism. There are important differences between these elements, but the contention that they differ *in principle* on the use of violence, in the sense that the absolute pacifist attaches to these terms, cannot be sustained. Among the unions in the United States, many of the more conservative ones practice violence in industrial disputes more extensively than do radical unions. Gangsterism in the American labor world is not an invention of the Communist unions, though the latter have not refrained from employing it.

The Socialist parties do not commit themselves in advance to the inevitability of violent revolution, but neither do they promise to refrain from the use of force to defend a Socialist order if they deem that necessary. If Ramsay MacDonald, for example, is to be called a pacifist because he favors the League of Nations and disarmament—though he helps to keep the British navy in trim when he is in power, and tells Indian revolutionists he will have the British army shoot them down if they go too far—then it will be difficult to prove that Stalin and Litvinov are not entitled to the same designation.

All this does not mean that the labor movement is not confronted with a serious problem as to the means to which it will resort to advance its aims. Many times employers, on the one hand, and workers, on the other hand, are approached by the most crude and self-defeating psychological methods. Money is spent on gangsters, for example, that might well net a thousand fold better return if devoted to the education of workers and of the public. Violence begets violence by whomever it is used. War is a dirty business and entails the use of degrading means, whoever wages it.

The labor movement in New York City has recently given a striking illustration of the law, upon which the pacifist so often insists, that the means one uses inevitably incorporate themselves into his ends and, if evil, will defeat him. Some years ago, employers in the garment trades resorted to the practice of employing armed gangsters to attack peaceful picketers. It became impossible to send men and women on the picket line to meet such brutal attacks, so the union also resorted to hiring gangsters. Once you started the practice, you had to hire gangsters in every strike, of course. Thus a group of gangsters came to be a permanent part of the union machinery. Next, it was easy for officers who had employed the gangsters in strikes to use these same gangsters, who were on the pay roll anyway, in union elections to insure continued tenure to the "machine." The next step in the "descent to Avernus" was for the gangsters on whom the administration depended for its tenure of office to make themselves the administration—the union "machine." In the meantime, the union gangsters naturally came to a gentleman's agreement with those hired by the employer, so that both sides were paying out large sums of money to gangsters no longer doing any decisive work in strikes or lockouts; both sides had likewise to pay graft to the police so that they would not interfere with their private armies; and the rank and file of union members, having come to look to gangsters to do the real picketing, no longer had the desire, courage or morale to picket peacefully, appeal to strike-breakers to join them, and so on. The whole process, working itself out so fatally, and from the aesthetic viewpoint so beautifully, had not a little to do with the deterioration undergone by these unions in which the bitter left-right factional strife was rather a symptom than a cause.

Those who can bring themselves to renounce wealth, position and power accruing from a social system based on violence and putting a premium on acquisitiveness, and to identify themselves in some real fashion with the struggle of the masses toward the light, may help in a measure—more, doubtless, by life than by words—to devise a more excellent way, a technique of social progress less crude, brutal, costly and slow than mankind has yet evolved.

Trade Unions
and the Revolution

1935 This essay makes no claim to finality. It is an attempt to raise questions and provoke discussion rather than to provide definitive answers to the question of the role which unions and other mass economic organizations may play in the working class revolution in such a country as the United States.

Two other preliminary observations are required. In the first place, though confining ourselves here in the main to discussion of mass organizations, we are not implying some theory of "spontaneity" of the masses. It is our position that the leadership of the revolutionary Marxian party is indispensable for the success of the proletarian revolution.

In the second place, important as it is in certain respects, we are not dealing here with the question of the A. F. L. vs "independent unionism." The question we are posing is: regardless of how this issue may be resolved, what role will unions and other mass organizations play in the revolutionary crisis?

One of the more able of the younger American historians of the labor movement has frequently made the assertion, in private conversation, that there would never be a proletarian revolution in a country where a strong trade union movement had been built up. He based his contention on the fact that these unions themselves become great vested interests clearly tied up with the capitalist operation of industry; that the officialdom constitutes a privileged group which develops close relations with the employing class and a psychology similar to that of the latter; that the tactic of compromise, "give and take," progress by slow degrees, becomes ingrained and sets up a resistance against risking all on a throw of the revolutionary dice, and so on; and that these unions gain such a hold upon the workers, come to seem so indispensable, that the workers will not act independently of them even in a major crisis.

The evidence in support of a part of this contention is very strong. The way in which the unions in western Europe and the United States survived the war and post-war crisis—in fact, came out of it with enhanced numbers and prestige—as well as the doggedness with which the German workers clung to the unions when these were forced to retreat and quite obviously were no longer able to offer any substantial measure of protection—much less to solve the crisis—sufficiently illustrate the hold of the unions upon the workers. Some form of inclusive organization through which to carry on the immediate struggle, offensive or defensive, on the job, the workers are bound to seek or cling to, so long as they have any opportunity to struggle at all.

It is not necessary, either, to dwell upon the conservatism which has characterized trade unionism in Germany, England and the United States—for example, the enormous difficulty experienced in shaking, even a little, the entrenched trade union bureaucracies, etc.

Are we then forced to accept the conclusion that, on the one hand, the unions cannot be uprooted and, on the other hand, cannot be expected to play a progressive role as the crisis deepens for the working class—that in order to protect themselves against the assaults of the employers, the workers have as it were encased themselves in a suit of armor which, in the last analysis, weighs down the workers themselves, prevents them from breaking their way to liberty, keeps them rooted to the ground while the reaction showers its blows upon them?

There is indeed no escape from this conclusion—unless it is conceivable that revolutionary Marxists can take the leadership of the unions away from the trade union bureaucrats with their limited vision (even where other vices do not exist), and from the social democrats with their reformist, parliamentarian, pacifist, social-patriotic outlook. But, if this possibility has come to seem remote, just barely conceivable, almost in the realm of miracle, this gives us a measure of the extent to which the Communist International (i. e., the Third) and its sections have failed to function as revolutionary Marxian organizations, and of the consequent calamity they have brought upon the proletarian movement.

The "normal," the to-be-expected course is precisely that the influence of the revolutionists over the mass organizations should grow and presently become preponderant. As the crisis of the capitalist economy becomes deeper and more intense, the masses are set in motion. Instinctively, we might say, they fight back against the attempts to lower their standards. The struggles become more bitter. The illusion that employers and workers have mutual interests tends to break down. The state comes out more and more openly against the workers, no matter how elementary their demands. The struggle is waged on a constantly broader front. More and more workers are drawn into strike actions. "General" strikes break out in localities or industries and the strike organizations have to intervene in governmental functions, such as maintenance of supply services, of order in the strike area, etc. All this is elementary and has been observed often enough.

Such situations open the door wide for the politically developed workers and for the revolutionary party, provided that the latter has not pursued a course in the unions which has discredited it and left it isolated. The developing actions which we have referred to require energy, initiative, the will to struggle, courage, capacity to organize large-scale actions, ability to sway masses in motion, to arouse mass enthusiasm, interpret the subtle changes in mass psychology, and a political outlook on the part of the leadership. But the conventional trade union leadership is, to put it mildly, not distinguished for these qualities. They will try, but they cannot hold back the masses from struggle. As the struggle extends and sharpens, they must call for or, with as much grace as they can muster, accept aid from the radical elements, or be pushed out of the picture entirely.

At this point it should prove both interesting and useful to introduce a somewhat detailed description of how this process worked out in certain dramatic episodes during the Auto-Lite strike in Toledo in 1934. It is common knowledge that this strike was on its last legs owing to the indifference of the A. F. L. leadership in automobiles, the inexperience and passivity of the local union leadership, etc., and that it was brought back to life by militants in the union and in the Lucas County Unemployed League under the leadership of Workers Party elements. Mass picketing and demonstrations, in defiance of injunctions, culminated in "the battle of Toledo," during which ten thousand Toledo workers, enraged at the brutality of special deputies, stormed the Auto-Lite plant, etc.

The revolutionists had begun to talk up the idea of a general strike of all Toledo workers to compel the Auto-Lite management to settle with the union. The idea got an instant response among the workers. The Central Labor Union, an A. F. L. body less reactionary and bureaucratized than similar bodies in some of the larger cities, but not in the remotest sense "Red," was compelled to take cognizance of the agitation. It appointed a Committee of Twenty-three to take a strike vote of the locals affiliated with the C. L. U., with the understanding that the organization of a general strike, if the vote were favorable, rested in the hands of the Committee. As a matter of fact, out of the one hundred or so local unions, over ninety-five voted in favor of such a strike in support of the Auto-Lite workers, and only one against.

The vote having been taken, the disposition among the C. L. U. officials was to do nothing definite about it. As the Auto-Lite Company dragged out the negotiations, however, the workers began to press for action. The officials then resorted to a characteristic device. They called for a big parade and mass meeting to be held on a Friday night. This would serve to let off steam. They did not dare, however, to offer the demonstration openly as a substitute for general strike action. They had to give out the impression that it was in preparation for the strike, that at the mass meeting probably a final call to strike on Monday would be announced.

The spirit of enthusiasm and militancy was running high among the workers. The local union leaders had to bend to it. A few days before the mass meeting, for example, they asked the present writer, known to be a Workers Party member, to be one of the speakers. As the demonstration day came nearer, however, the employers and the higher-ups in the A. F. L. put on the screws. Things must not "get out of hand" at the meeting, since there must not be a general strike. There must be simply a parade, with a very brief meeting at the conclusion at which three or four safe C. L. U. officials would speak briefly and prosaically. Then the crowd would be sent home—without any mention of general strike. A few hours before the parade started, the writer was accordingly informed that he would not be called upon to speak; after the parade the crowd would be "too tired to stand and listen to speeches."

The parade exceeded all expectations in numbers and enthusiasm. The mass meeting opened peacefully with a few remarks by the chairman of the Committee of Twenty-three. The next speaker talked in an uninspired manner. To test out the sentiment of the crowd, someone called out to the speaker, who was carefully staying a thousand miles away from that subject, "What about the general strike Monday?" The speaker played dumb. But the crowd quickly demonstrated that the general strike was the one thing in which it was interested. The question was shouted from all directions at the speaker. In a few minutes he gave up the attempt to speak. The same question greeted the chairman of the meeting as he tried to introduce the next safe and sane functionary. The crowd insisted on an answer to its question. The bureaucrats had none to give. The uproar increased. The meeting was thrown into turmoil. The bureaucrats threw up their hands in despair and walked out on their own meeting. The more astute ones perhaps conjectured that the crowd would leave too, and thus the strike issue would be downed.

That is, of course, what would have happened if there had been no experienced revolutionary mass leaders present who had the confidence of the workers, or could at least get their attention, and who knew what to do in such a situation. They were present and acted promptly. Sam Pollock, picket leader, Unemployed League official and party member, took the chair and quickly got the attention of the workers. One speaker after another got up, as per agreement, and hammered home the messages the workers needed and wanted to hear: "General Strike on Monday unless the Auto-Lite Strike is settled by then. Spread this word around over the week-end. Do not go to work on Monday, but wait for orders from the Strike Committee. Disperse quietly when this meeting is over; let no one provoke you." While this was going on, someone came to the platform and said to me: "You fellows have all had your say. Why can't a man who has been in the trade union movement here for twenty-five years have a chance?" It developed that he was the editor of the official organ of the Toledo C. L. U. He was given his chance to speak, as I would not have been if his fellow-officials had remained in charge of the meeting!

The general strike did not take place, because on Saturday the final negotiations were started which, on Monday, ended in a settlement between the union and the Auto-Lite firm. Had the strike occurred, representatives of the Unemployed Leagues who would have been party members would undoubtedly have been added to the Committee of Twenty-three. Militants would have been put in charge of picketing. Known party leaders would have been drawn in for consultation and would have wielded increasing influence. An enlarged strike committee on which militant rank and filers would have predominated would have been elected in the shop meetings. As the struggle became more intense, the same thing would have happened with the strike that happened in the mass meeting—leadership would have slipped out of the hands of the bureaucrats, utterly incompetent and unwilling to handle such a situation, and the militants and revolutionists would have taken it up.

Furthermore, if the strike had occurred, including the transportation system, the light and power plants, etc., the strike organization would have had to give orders to, interfere with, in greater or less degree replace, the mayor, the police, the health authorities, the public utilities commission, etc. To the extent that it did so, it would have foreshadowed and approximated a Soviet, a workers' council—an organ of workers' government as against the organs of capitalist government. And we can think, of course, of developments such as these we have sketched occurring not in a single locality, but in an entire basic industry and over a wide territory, eventually on a national scale.

It is suggested, then, not only that the unions, Unemployed Leagues, farmers' organizations, may under the leadership of revolutionary Marxists be prevented from becoming bulwarks of reaction, but may, as the struggle for power sharpens, be transformed into or be directly instrumental in helping to form the organs of workers' power.

It must be understood, of course, that this will involve the bitterest struggles for control over the mass organizations, for leadership within them. The fact that we have presented our illustration from Toledo in a simplified and abbreviated manner does not imply an underestimate of the violence of this internal struggle.

It is likely that there will be many variations in the process. In a mining region, for example, the union membership and the working population will be nearly identical. The union is the agency through which the miners habitually handle their economic, political, cultural problems. The election for the Council of Action (Soviet) in that region may very likely take place in the miners' union meeting. The same sort of thing may take place in a farming community which has a militant farmers' union.

In cases where the union organization is not fully responsive to the developing situation and the moods of the workers, the shop organizations may take the initiative with the mild approval or toleration of or even in opposition to the union bureaucracy. In general, as the struggle develops and nears a climax, the masses will get into motion, take things into their own hands in the establishments. It is to be expected, however, that this rank and file participation will in general reflect itself in the union organization. The reflection is likely to be uneven. The union machinery may in many instances prove too cumbersome, the control of the officialdom too rigid, so that the workers will have to proceed independently of them, as the pace of events quickens. This would be especially likely to happen in the case of long-established organizations of the highly skilled workers. Generally speaking, however, we cannot conceive of an advance of the working class to a point where it can enter upon a struggle for power, without an advance in the economic organizations in the direction of industrial unionism, a class struggle philosophy, rank and file control, close contact with the shop and the happenings there, etc.

In connection with all this, it is important to remember that the unions became repositories of an immense amount of information about the operations of industry—technical, engineering, administrative, etc. This also makes them exceedingly important agencies in the process by which the control of the workers over industrial operations is made actual and productive of efficient operation amid the difficulties of the period when workers' power is being consolidated.

The alternative to the general conception we have sketched is to suppose that the unions are peculiar to an earlier period in capitalist development; that they are no longer able to function in the interest of the workers in the period of capitalist decline and collapse; that, therefore, the workers must abandon them or that they will in fact be wrecked by the capitalist reaction.

We cannot accept this perspective. In the first place, as we have already suggested, the workers have demonstrated a remarkable tenacity in clinging to their unions. Whatever may happen to this or that union, or any number of unions, the workers do not wish to abandon the union movement but to broaden it, increase its militancy, etc. So long as capitalism endures, organization of some kind on the job to deal with the boss is indispensable. Instinctively the masses fight to defend the unions, the right to strike, etc. If the mass economic organizations are smashed, what in practice can that mean except the establishment of Fascism?

From the other direction, the question arises: if the general trend is, as we have indicated, toward the broadening of the mass organizations, increase in their militancy, acceptance of Marxian leadership, struggle on a broader scale and a higher and higher political plane, etc., then is it not likely that the unions as a whole will, so far as the industrial sections of the country are concerned, become the workers' councils, the instruments of workers' power? Thus the Central Labor Union—now, of course, with workers of all categories in its affiliated unions—becomes the Soviet of a given city; and the national, union-federation convention, with its delegates from all industries and sections of the country, becomes the industrial part of the national congress of Soviets.

Theoretically, it seems to me, this possibility cannot be excluded. The "seizure of the factories" by the Italian workers, under the direction of the General Confederation of Labor, comes to mind in this connection. When a body such as the British Trade Union Congress calls or sponsors a general strike in support, for example, of the miners, the conflict almost from the first moment takes on the character of a direct clash with the state, which either places the leading union body in a hopeless dilemma, or leads to revolutionary steps, depending on the character and the aims of this same leading body. Other things being equal, a movement of the workers, with the full sanction and under the leadership of the organization through which they have become accustomed to carry on their struggles, would seem to have more promise of success—starting out with a ready-made machinery for communication, action, etc.— than a movement where this condition does not exist.

Much more attention must be given, both to the analysis of this possibility and to the details of seizure of power where this condition prevails, than has yet been given to the subject, to this author's knowledge.

It would be far from safe, however, to assume confidently that such a condition will exist. The trade union organization as such, while being drawn into the current of revolutionary action and in the main supporting, may not be ready or entirely fitted to conduct the movement, even assuming that the revolutionary party has the dominant influence in it. The union organization is, after all, primarily economic rather than political, and not in the first instance equipped to deal with the larger national and international political issues. Furthermore, it is entirely possible that the pace of development in various unions may vary, as I have suggested at an earlier point in this article. The revolutionary party must give a great deal of study to these questions and be prepared, as the actual crisis develops, to deal in accordance with the facts of the situation and the actual forces at its disposal.

For the present, we conclude with brief practical suggestions. First, the slogan "Deeper into the unions" (whether they happen to be A. F. L. or independent) must be applied by the party and all its committees and members much more thoroughly and enthusiastically even than heretofore. Second, in every strike situation the policy of drawing in the broadest forces—all the unions, unemployed organizations, political parties and groups—must be carried out, in order to break down trade union provincialism; to politicalize the struggle; develop class consciousness; face the workers with the problems of conflict with capitalist governmental agencies, etc. Third, the greatest emphasis must be placed on drawing the employed and unemployed organizations together, forming Councils of Action on which these and also the more militant farmers' organizations are represented, to prevent the division of the working class into employed and unemployed; to insure the broadening of all struggles; and, again, in order to accustom the working masses as workers, and not as craftsmen, skilled or unskilled, etc., to confront the employers and the state.

Return to Pacifism

1936 In recent years, I have been a part of the labor movement and of its left wing. I have accepted fully the Marxist-Leninist position and metaphysics. I have regarded the working class movement as the one effective agency to bring in a finer social order. I have believed that it was the most dependable, indeed the one really dependable, force to maintain world peace, or at least to abolish war—since it would abolish capitalism which begets war. It has seemed to me the expression of practical idealism, the "religion" which was able to call forth in its members the devotion and self-sacrifice which characterized the early Christians, for example. I have said to those who claimed that they desired to obey the teachings of Jesus in our time that they *must,* in spite of all its shortcomings, identify themselves with this movement or at least wholeheartedly support it. I do not now repudiate all this. But, in addition to rejecting some of it, there are a number of things that I would put in a different way and some things that I would add.

Take first the issue of war and peace. No one can spend a few weeks in Europe, as I did this summer, without feeling the overpowering urgency of this issue, and being appalled by the nightmare of whole populations living day after day under the threat of the outbreak of a general war, a threat which hangs over them like a sword suspended on a single gossamer thread. If we are to be realistic, we must say, as so many who are not ordinarily alarmists have said, that unless dynamics and methods hitherto not widely employed be found, war will come, possibly before many months, certainly before many years, and that when it comes it will be of an unimaginable horror and will wreak incalculable destruction. It seems to me now that one must be a romanticist capable of flying in the face of all the evidence to believe that such a war, under modern conditions, will be the portal to socialism or higher civilization or whatever one may prefer to call it. Rather must it set back the clock for generations, if, indeed, it does not involve the total eclipse of Western civilization.

If we are to continue being realistic, then we must state next that the labor movement by itself, using the approach and the methods which it has hitherto used, is not a dependable agency to prevent or abolish wars. That applies to all wings and tendencies of the movement.

So far as the reformist wing, trade union and socialist, is concerned, in 1914 it became an instrument of the respective warring imperialist powers, recruiting the workers for slaughter on the plea that a distinction had to be made between (relatively) "good" and (relatively) "bad" imperialist nations, and by other such specious arguments. In the post-war period, and particularly in recent years, it has failed to put up an effective resistance against the armament programs of the capitalist governments, and where it has been in office, as today in France, it continues or even exceeds the military preparations of its predecessors in office. Trade unions everywhere are still entangled in the contradiction of being "against war" but not scorning, often welcoming and avidly seeking, jobs for their members in war industries.

Nor is there any ground for looking to the Soviet Union and the Communist International under existing policies and leadership. These vociferously propagate the conception that there are two kinds of capitalist powers and that it may be quite all right for revolutionists and peace lovers and Christians to fight in the army of the better kind—fight just one more war to end war, one more war for "democracy," one more war against Fascism. They have openly endorsed and supported, moreover, the war preparations of certain powers, such as France, and this not only now when there is an administration which has some title to be called democratic in its sympathies, but also under a Laval. They hold that if a war should break out in which the government of the United States happens to be on the same side as the government of the Soviet Union, it will be your duty and mine loyally to support "our" government in that war.

Nor can I see that those who adhere to a thorough-going Marxist-Leninist position on war—that, as the lesser evil, the workers in each country must strive for the defeat of their own government in a war—give us any more dependable agency for preventing war. The Marxist-Leninists, of whom the Trotskyists, with whom I was until recently connected, constitute the main force, have in the first place what amounts to a fatalistic position—another war will certainly come, as capitalist collapse proceeds. They support rather than combat the psychological attitude which leads to war by espousing and acting on the view that violence is the only way to achieve fundamental social changes.

Such radicals are involved in the contradiction of abhorring war as the ugliest fruit of an outworn economic order and yet "welcoming" that war as giving them the opportunity to hasten the collapse of capitalism. Their formula for putting an end to war is to "transform the imperialist war into civil war"—which seems pretty much like saying that by this road, as by the one the governments of the great powers are traveling, we come to that war which will indeed be both international and civil, fought not merely along certain clearly defined national boundary lines, but inside every nation—in every city, every hamlet, every street—that war which can hardly mean anything except collective suicide.

If we turn away for a moment from the question of war and peace, in its restricted sense, we are confronted by the fact that the movement has, since about 1924, suffered an uninterrupted series of defeats. The defeats of the Chinese revolution, the smashing of the Chinese Communist party by its one-time ally, Chiang Kai-shek, and the triumph of Hitler in Germany, followed by the total annihilation of the labor movement in the classic land of Marxism, constitute the great landmarks, in the East and West respectively, in this history of retreat and disillusionment. Nor can the reformist wing of the movement, when you take a broad, world view and mark the trend of the period as a whole, point to decisive progress and triumphs. Daily also it becomes more obvious that the Soviet Union itself, "the homeland of the working class," is in a serious plight. The Russian state has in recent years come to depend for the safety of its frontiers upon these very weapons—military forces and military alliances—which have so often proved to be nothing but preludes to war and agencies of insecurity.

The devoted members of any movement, among other reasons because they have experience of what is fine and true in the movement, are apt to rationalize away its defeats as merely superficial and temporary. Personally, I have had to conclude that it is inexcusable, after all that has taken place in the labor movement since 1914, not to be willing to study the whole situation afresh, and as deeply and thoroughly as possible. There is reason to believe that this attitude is becoming more common.

One who has lived within the labor movement is compelled, it seems to me, to admit that it has not only suffered external delays or setbacks, something which might be of little or no significance for a great movement, but that there has also been a declension from basic principles and an internal deterioration. Consider, for example, the evidence of internal collapse presented by the external collapse, without one gesture of resistance, of the mighty German labor movement, in all its branches, at the advent of Hitler. No sane mind can believe that if that movement had meant one-tenth of what it once meant and was still thought to mean to its millions of members, this could possibly have happened. Consider the divisions which mark and so often gravely weaken the movement; the bitterness and virulence with which internal controversy is carried on; the methods used in dealing with opponents within the movement which are often devoid of any shred of honor, decency or fair play, which do not differ in any essential respect—be it said with shame—from the methods employed by militarists and Fascists. Or look again for a moment at the supposedly revolutionary wing of the movement, those who sit in the seat of Lenin.

The basic Leninist concept of world revolution they have abandoned, "for the time being," it is sometimes said. But it does not take a very profound mind or an extensive knowledge of history and Marxism to realize that such an idea cannot be put away in a drawer for a few months or years and then be taken out, dusted and put to work where it left off. The Leninist concept of fighting against war has been abandoned. Obviously the Leninist concept of party democracy can by no stretching of words be said to obtain in a party which, wielding the machinery of a totalitarian state, and in a situation where expulsion from party membership means subjection to grave economic penalties, expels not less than 300,000 members in one operation; puts tens of thousands of political opponents into jail or concentration camps; and executes the remaining outstanding leaders of the October Revolution after a "trial" to which representatives of the socialist and trade union movement are refused admission.

If one looks squarely at these and many other such facts touching all organizations in the labor movement, then I think one is driven to the conclusion that the root of the difficulty is moral and spiritual, not primarily political or economic or organizational. Inextricably mingled with and in the end corrupting, thwarting, largely defeating all that is fine, idealistic, courageous, self-sacrificing in the proletarian movement is the philosophy of power, the will to power, the desire to humiliate and dominate over or destroy the opponent, the acceptance of the methods of violence and deceit, the theory that "the end justifies the means." There is a succumbing to the spirit which so largely dominates the existing social and political order and an acceptance of the methods of capitalism at its worst.

And wherever one turns, on a large scale or small, in greater or less (usually greater) degree, one sees the working out of the judgment which the Christian conscience would pronounce upon such motives and methods.

Take the development in the Soviet Union during and after the great October Revolution—not in order to single it out for criticism or condemnation, but precisely because it is the most significant event in our own epoch and must be understood in more than a superficial manner both by the Church and by the working class movement. You achieve a revolution by violence, though admittedly by a relatively small amount of it. You proceed to build the defenses of violence around your revolution. You create a great machine for war, repression and terrorism. You develop a Cheka, a system of espionage, numerous revolutionary tribunals. You exalt ruthlessness into a major virtue. You deliberately become—temporarily, you tell yourself, of course—callous about the individual human life. What do you get? Certainly, something which is, as yet, far removed from socialism. And no one can deny that the machinery for repression which has persisted now gives evidence of becoming, like every machine, a vested interest.

Take another illustration from a common experience in trade unions. The employer uses violence against peaceful pickets in a strike. They fear to go on the picket line and so the union engages strong-arm men in its turn. Having done so in one strike, it feels compelled to do so in the next, and the next. The appropriation for gangsters becomes a regular and a big item in the union's budget— a steadily mounting one because, among other things, the employers' gangsters and the unions' strong-arm men are very apt to come to an understanding, in businesslike fashion, to do as little work for as much pay as possible, thus necessitating higher and higher pay in order to get them to do anything. Presently, the union's gangsters, sensing another avenue for gain, assert themselves in the union's internal affairs, in elections of officers, for example—unless, indeed, some group in the union, possibly the "machine" in office, has already bought their services for internal purposes. The next step is that the gangsters may dispense with intermediaries and simply make themselves the officers of the union. In any case, the union has become corrupted, its members demoralized, its effectiveness for advancing the cause of the workers destroyed.

To cite one more illustration: under the "end justifies the means" theory, "anything goes" in dealing with the "class enemy"; but those whom you regard as reactionaries in the labor movement you deem to be, in effect, "agents of the bourgeoisie" and "tools of the class enemy." Therefore they also must be ruthlessly crushed, and by any means. Thus the methods, standards and motivations of war are introduced inside the labor movement, with consequent divisions and weakening. Presently, within your own party, within your own faction of the party, and so on, almost *ad infinitum,* the view arises that other parties and other factions are "objectively considered" simply agents of the enemy. The necessary saving conclusion that a moral and religious spirit must be infused into this, as into every relation of life, is not drawn. Until it is, I believe that the movement will be cheated of its goal.

Let no one think that I am standing outside of all this, observing and passing judgment. I was judged. Begin by assuming that, in some degree, in some situations, you must forswear the way of love, of truth, must accept the method of domination, deceit, violence—and on that road there is no stopping place. Take the way of war and there is war—not only between nations, classes, individuals—but war, division and consequent frustration within your own soul. Thus, it seems to me that we have to say and practice, much more devotedly and consistently than we have yet begun to do, that peace is indivisible and that pacifism must be, is, religious— is religion!—or it will prove to be but a broken reed when the moment of crisis arrives when we have to lean upon it.

"Peace is indivisible," not only in the geographical and diplomatic sense in which Litvinov has so often and justly used the expression, but in the sense that the way of peace is really a seamless garment that must cover the whole of life and must be applied in all its relationships.

Every pseudo and partial pacifism breaks down. Is it the pacifism of those who are against international war but who would, and do, use every form of coercion and violence in order to hang on to their own property and prestige and the system which gives them comfort? Lenin was absolutely right when he said that this pacifism simply served as a cover for war preparations. The pacifism of those who are against all wars except just one more war for what they regard as an absolute end? The pacifism of the unions which are against wars but build battleships and guns in the unexpressed hope that they will somehow be smashed, or rust away, before they are used? The pacifism of those who are against international war but idealize and glorify class war? The pacifism of those who are against war but who are motivated by prejudice, fear, contempt in their relations with people of other races? All of these, I can see as plainly as my own hand under my eyes as I write, are either utterly invalid or have the most temporary and limited validity and in any case survive no real crisis.

Pacifism—life—is built upon a central truth and the experience of that truth, its apprehension not by the mind alone but by the entire being in an act of faith and surrender. That truth is: God is love, love is of God. Love is the central thing in the universe. Mankind is one in an ultimate spiritual reality. Now, either such an affirmation is a mere form of words or it represents an essentially religious insight and experience—though its validity is verified in every form of human association, even that of thieves, where there must be "honor," some shred of trust, of each taking the other as an end and not a means, if the group is to "function" for a brief moment.

Such an affirmation one must accept, and make, first in one's own soul. If it is not there, it exists only in formulas and abstractions. The individual must therefore be won and saved. But since it is precisely to love, to the apprehension of our unity with mankind, to the kingdom of God, that we are won, we must carry this dynamic and method into every relationship—into family life, into race relations, into work in the labor movement, political activity, international relations.

Surely no one can have visualized, in even one brief instant of insight, the abyss to which we are being carried by the dynamics and methods we have been employing, without agreeing that at least nothing could be lost by trying Christ's way of love.

I believe that one who holds such views as I have described

must live and work in fellowship with those who hold like views in such an organization as the Fellowship of Reconciliation. He must also, I am convinced, work in and with the Church. For the religious man can, less than anyone, live as an isolated atom. Nor can each of us go about organizing little private churches. That, too, expresses division and not unity. It may be indeed that the Church everywhere will finally identify itself with the status quo, but that day is not yet. Even if it is to come, we must, after the example of Jesus, work from within and not without, though it lead to crucifixion. We must fulfill rather than destroy.

But let there be no mistake. Since the issue is finally and fundamentally religious, the church failing to meet it will receive the most terrible judgment of all. Of how many church buildings and organizations, in our day, has not the prophecy uttered by Jesus about the institutions of another day already been fulfilled?—"There shall not be left here one stone upon another that shall not be torn down." When we contemplate what has happened, must we not bow our heads and acknowledge once again that "the judgments of the Lord are true and righteous altogether"?

On the other hand, if the Church, or any substantial minority in it, will take seriously the gospel of the Lord whom it professes to serve and apply it persistently and in love, we can, in all soberness and calm, assert that never since the early Christian centuries has such a door been opened as now when, for the first time since that epoch, mankind is struggling to achieve a world civilization and waits, as never before in its history, for leadership possessed of dynamics and power adequate to such a task.

Sit-Downs
and Lie-Downs

"The American Federation of Hosiery Workers did not plan or instigate the nonviolent or 'lie-down' picket demonstrations but the union will support to the limit all those young men and women who are so deeply convinced of the justice of their cause as to undertake this courageous form of peaceful protest.

"As a rule men and women hesitate to adopt the tactics of a Gandhi in an industrial or civil dispute for fear of seeming to make fools of themselves. The fact of the matter is that nonviolence is a tactic that requires perhaps a higher type of courage and devotion than is called for in ordinary physical combat.

"The trade union movement is hopeful that the possibilities of employing nonviolent tactics will be fully explored in connection with labor disputes. Labor almost always gets the worst of things when rough stuff is used in strike situations."

—Statement by Alexander McKeown, National Vice-President, American Federation of Full-Fashioned Hosiery Workers.

1937 An event of the greatest significance for those who believe in the way of nonviolence occurred recently. A great national labor union, the American Federation of Full-Fashioned Hosiery Workers, which is itself a department of the United Textile Workers of America, and affiliated with the Committee for Industrial Organization (C. I. O.), adopted at its annual convention a resolution providing for the appointment of "a standing commission to study the merits and possibilities of using nonviolent resistance in labor disputes and that the commission be instructed to propagate its findings among the membership, and be requested to continue its study of this philosophy."

This action was an outgrowth of the actual experiment in nonviolent resistance ("lie-down picketing") carried on in December, 1936, under the leadership of a Fellowship of Reconciliation member and another student of Richard Gregg's writings. Both are members of the Hosiery Workers Union and active participants in the strike which has been in progress since October at the Berkshire Mills of Reading, Pennsylvania. The most encouraging feature of this entire development is that the initiative has at each stage come from the ranks of the workers themselves and not as the result of more or less artificial stimulation from without.

The reference to "lie-down picketing" naturally brings to mind the matter of the "sit-down," which has figured so largely in the news during recent weeks. Many who are ordinarily sympathetic with organized labor are inclined to condemn this method as flagrantly illegal and as a peculiarly unfair device which enables a very small minority to hold up not only the employer but their fellow-workers against their will. I am convinced that this view leaves many important factors out of consideration. Space permits us to mention only a few of them.

As was demonstrated in one instance, in Flint, when the workers in the department in which the sit-down occurs are not pretty unanimously for it, it is impossible to put it into effect. Also, the sit-down technique lends itself in a special sense to furnishing an alibi to workers who are themselves afraid of discharge if they join a union, and who do not know how the strike is going to come out. They often sign petitions indicating that they are anxious to go back to work at the same time when they secretly hope the sit-down may succeed and lead to better conditions! In such a situation, who is subject to judgment and who is doing the coercing—the sit-downers, or their less courageous fellow-workers; or is it the corporation which controls a man's job and his family's livelihood and has him so intimidated that he may sign up with a company union at the very time he has joined a bona-fide union? And this of course suggests that in all such situations it is exceedingly difficult to tell how many men are really for or against the union. Or rather I think we can safely say on the basis of experiences in the railroads, the garment trades and many others, that an overwhelming majority of the workers in any industry will almost certainly flock into the union the moment they feel sure that this will not subject them to the displeasure of the employer.

Consider another phase of the problem. The General Motors Corporation for years refused collective bargaining, now the law of the land. It stocked at least some of its plants with gas and guns and spent nearly a million dollars in a couple of years for labor spy service. Do the laws governing private property cover a plant made into a private arsenal? When men sit down inside such a plant, so that these weapons cannot be turned against them, while a dispute over union recognition goes on, are they so obviously violating property rights and breaking the peace? Or are they safeguarding property and preserving peace?

To whom do the G. M. C. factories "belong"? To a few officials who perhaps own very little stock? To the 300,000 stockholders who have practically nothing to say about the labor policy which leads to the sit-down? To the DuPonts who probably do exercise predominant influence over this policy and who raked in $250,000,000 in a few years, on an investment of about one-third that amount? To the municipal, state and national government which help the corporation to function? To the purchasers of General Motors cars, who may not like to have their money spent for labor espionage and resistance to collective bargaining? Or does the worker himself also have some "property right" in his job?

We must surely face the fact that the concept of property rights is in flux. There was a time when any strike, any form of picketing, was regarded as an infraction of property rights, because it interfered with production, with a supposed right of an owner to use his property in disregard of any social restrictions. It is not inconceivable that the sit-down may come to be regarded as no more an invasion of property rights than ordinary forms of strike and picketing.

It must be noted also that the sit-downers observed very strict discipline and that practically no actual damage was done to property, and that on the whole the evidence tends to show that the sit-down method lends itself more readily than other types of picketing to nonviolent techniques.

That so little actual violence and no loss of life occurred, in a situation so "loaded with dynamite" (both literally and figuratively) as that in Detroit, Flint and their vicinity, is to be credited in part to the rigorous discipline which the strikers imposed upon themselves. The restraint which General Motors appears to have exercised in not insisting upon having the men driven out of the plants at the point of a bayonet was another factor. Chiefly, however, thanks seem to be due to Governor Frank Murphy. His position—that if the forces of the state are to be used, they shall be used simply to maintain order and to see that private individuals or groups do not use violence against each other, not to weight the scales against the workers—is eminently sound. Above all we can subscribe to his view that violence itself is an evil, a poison which corrupts whatever it touches. Bring it into a situation and all other issues become more complicated and are made harder of solution. Keep it out and all other issues are simplified. Even property will in the long run be safer!

We do not wish to leave the impression, however, that the sit-down is, from the point of view of our Fellowship philosophy, on the same level as the "lie-down picketing" or that it fully exemplifies the spirit of nonviolence. There was, alas, altogether too much readiness to resort to violence on the part of strikers, as well as others, in the G. M. C. situation, even if violence seemed "necessary" and likely to produce "results." It is, in large degree, on physical possession of property and physical coercion of the non-striker that sit-downers depend, though the spiritual qualities of men who will subject themselves for over forty days to the stern rigors of a sit-down must by no means be minimized.

The leaders of the Reading lie-down experiment, on the other hand, were definitely moved by the spirit of love, even toward their enemies. They openly depended upon the appeal to the higher sentiments and feelings of others rather than upon physical means for success. The action of the Hosiery Workers convention therefore opens up a glorious opportunity for all who believe in the way of love and nonviolence to propagate our message in the ranks of the workers. Let us pray that we may make full use of that opportunity. It will require very clear and responsible thinking on our part to devise techniques of nonviolence. It will also involve identification in knowledge, in spirit and in action with the underprivileged and oppressed so that we may, without hypocrisy, speak to them of "the better way" and may win a hearing when we plead that evil means can never lead to good ends.

The True
International

1939 At the beginning of 1919 I was a devout Christian pacifist. I had been compelled to resign from my pulpit, a year or so before, because I could not give up or agree to keep silent about my convictions for the duration of the war. I considered myself, however, a faithful member of the Christian church and fervently hoped that its eyes might be opened to the sin which it had, in my opinion, committed in blessing war. It will be remembered that, as one of a group of Christian pacifists, I was involved in the Lawrence textile strike of that year. Our leadership at critical moments in that sixteen-weeks' strike involving thirty thousand people, in the tense and turbulent months immediately following upon the armistice, was uncompromisingly pacifist. The power which carried me, with no previous experience whatever in labor or strike activity, through the severe labors and the nerve-wracking crises of that strike had been accumulated during the preceding weeks when Harold Rotzel and I got up on cold mornings in Boston to pray and study the Sermon on the Mount together, verse by verse.

Ten years later, at the beginning of 1929, I was in my eighth year as director of Brookwood Labor College, then probably at the height of its prestige and usefulness—although (or perhaps because) the American Federation of Labor had, the previous fall, warned its unions against giving any support to this "Communist institution" and also against the wiles of one John Dewey of Columbia University, whom the A. F. L. designated as the principal

agent of the Bolshevik International in this country! Brookwood
was not in any sense a Communist institution, but personally I was
moving rapidly along the road which made me become an inwardly
convinced Marxist-Leninist—though critical of the official Communist party's course—and eventually a leader of the Trotskyist movement. I no longer considered myself in any sense a member of the
Church. It was to me nothing but a peculiarly pernicious bulwark of
a reactionary status quo. I rejected the Christian world view utterly.

Today, at the beginning of 1939, I am again a Christian pacifist.
Though in my own thinking and feeling there is no separating these
two terms as I define them, nevertheless I am first and foremost and
altogether not a member of a secular anti-war movement, but a member of the Church of those who trust for redemption in the love of
God and in Christ.

When, in obedience to the counsel of the editor of *The Christian
Century,* I searched my "intellectual experience to discover, if possible, a single fundamental insight which comprehends and explains" my changed outlook, I thought of a number of answers to
that question which one might to good purpose state and explain.
For example, I was self-sufficient in 1929. Now I know that I was
not and am not; that I live by the grace of God and stand straightest
when I am on my knees.

In 1929, I believed that the way to bring in a new world was
basically—virtually exclusively—a matter of "social engineering,"
changing "the system," economic, political, social. Today I recognize that we neglected too much the problem of what happens inside
the human being. Whether there can be a democratic society, for
example, depends in the final analysis upon what human beings are,
whether they are capable of making moral decisions and therefore
of building and maintaining a free society.

Still another clue to my changed outlook occurred to me. It has
to do with the question of ends and means, whether or not evil can
overcome evil. In those days our group of Christian pacifists was
in all matters of economics, politics, international affairs unsophisticated and poorly informed. But, on all important issues—the real
causes of the war, what led the United States into the war, the unreliability of propaganda, the kind of peace which would follow
the war—we sensed the correct positions! Nearly all informed people now accept as a matter of course the positions which, twenty
years ago, informed people ridiculed our pathetically uninformed
group for holding. In 1929, I was much better informed than ten

years earlier. But I was coming to believe that the way to true democracy and brotherhood and peace was that of dictatorship and hate and repression and violence. Presently I was brought up hard against the realization that by that very pragmatic test which I had chosen, the method did not produce the desired results and that, furthermore, I was undergoing an inner deterioration and was reduced to judging events and making decisions by purely *ad hoc*, opportunistic standards.

I am, however, setting aside all these valid and, I think, important answers to the question directed at us, because while I was meditating upon them, there flashed into my mind the recollection of three events and the fact that they were significantly related. First, I remembered those mornings with Harold Rotzel in the house on Appleton Street in Boston and the little Christian pacifist comradeship to which I belonged just at the close of the war, and the Society of Friends which had welcomed me into its membership and ministry in those days; and how one had the sense of having found the true church, felt with mingled awe and gladness that he had "come unto Mount Zion, and unto the city of the living God, ... to the general assembly and church of the first-born who are enrolled in heaven"; and how, in that fellowship, fear melted away and strength and endurance were supplied according to need, though the need was sometimes immeasurable.

Next, I remembered that during my years of absorption in the secular revolutionary movement it had been the doctrine of "The Party"—the nature, structure, functions of the revolutionary party—which had enlisted my deepest study and concern. I recalled those moments when the sense of "belonging" to a comradeship that had burned away self-centeredness in devotion to the task of making heaven real on earth by building "the workers' world" brought again joy and strength. I recalled also that what came to hurt the most, and really forced me to try to think things through again from the beginning, was to find pettiness and duplicity and self-indulgence and ruthlessness and a lack of human sensitiveness and of moral standards in "The Party" itself.

Last, I recalled the circumstances and the form of my "re-conversion." It was in Paris in the beginning of August, 1936. I had begun in very tentative fashion to re-examine my beliefs and to consider what I should do on my return to the United States some weeks later. However, at the time I was sightseeing, with no conscious purpose except to see sights. One who is seeing the sights of

Paris for the first time must see some of the churches. Casually, one afternoon, I walked into one of them. It was being repaired. There was a certain impression of solidity about it, but it had too many statues of saints for my taste. I sat down on a bench near the front and looked at the cross. Without the slightest premonition of what was going to happen, I was saying to myself: "This is where you belong"; and "belong" again, in spirit, to the Church of Christ I did from that moment on. I felt as if the hand of God had drawn me up out of those "titanic glooms of chasmed fears" of which Francis Thompson sings and had catapulted me back into the Church.

Even as these events were passing before me, I was saying to myself: "You see how it is. What you have all along been seeking is what the Marxist calls 'The Party' and what the religious man calls the 'True Church' and that is indeed the crucial question of our day: what is the instrument by which the revolution is to be achieved, the Kingdom of God established? We cannot go on as we are. The great deliverance must come. But how? Where is The Party? Where is the True Church?" I could not rest without an answer.

Lenin, it is interesting to note, was really concerned about two things: the nature and structure of a revolutionary party and how the party might acquire state power. The great split of the Russian social democratic movement into Bolshevik and Menshevik wings was not over a great philosophical or economic issue but over the question of a highly centralized party, such as Lenin was determined to have, versus a decentralized, "democratic" party such as the Mensheviks wanted. It is a patent fact that in the Fascist or Nazi, as in the Bolshevik, scheme, the idea and the fact of The Party are all-important. Are we not all in Christian circles rediscovering the "Church"?

Let us return for a moment to Lenin. It is astonishing how many of the remarks of the True Church are included in his doctrine of The Party. The Party must be revolutionary. The existing order is corrupt; it is also unable any longer to function; it is doomed. The Party must therefore aim to overthrow it, not to come to an understanding with it. The Party stands over against "the world" therefore. It is despised, it is weak, it is in a hopeless minority, it is outrageously persecuted—until the day of revolution dawns. Then when the more imposing and less intransigent parties stand paralyzed before a world falling to pieces, The Party will fill the breach.

The Party is the instrument of God—of destiny at any rate, of those "historical forces which make the triumph of socialism inevitable." A force which makes for the reign of righteousness and brotherhood, to which the individual must surrender himself utterly, and which cannot fail—that comes close to being a definition of, let us say, a Calvinist God. The Party accordingly cannot really fail. "Fear not, little flock." It has the deposit of the truth. It cannot do wrong, since at a given moment nothing can be nearer right than the instrument of historic destiny.

There can on these terms be only one true party. The individual member, if he be a true member who has no will but The Party's will, will find ineffable joy in its service. Without The Party, the proletariat is lost. Of itself, through its own experience, without being led and for its good manipulated by The Party, it will not rise to revolutionary heights and be able to save itself. "The basic error," Lenin wrote, "is the idea that political consciousness can be developed in the workers from within. . . . Political consciousness can only be impressed on the workers from outside," and through The Party, of the elite, the elect, through the "ecclesia."

The Party, Lenin contended, must be international, universal, in scope and in essence. Violently he contended against the leaders of the Second International who thought in terms of a British, Dutch, German, Russian party affiliated to the International. There could be only one International party, with British, Dutch, and so forth sections, but sections without autonomy. "One, holy catholic Church." When finally The Party triumphs, history as we know it comes to an end, or rather history begins for the first time. Man will pass, in Engels' great phrase, "from kingdom of necessity into the kingdom of freedom."

It was, my masters, a magnificent attempt to sketch and create the True Church for which men long and, because of its daring and its partial truth, and because of the apostasy of Christ's church—not least in Russia itself—it was given to Lenin's church to have power for a season, and to win many devout adherents, and to be the midwife for the "historical forces" in one of the great hours in human history—and Lenin has become an ikon.

Why is Lenin's party failing, its members in the United States today, for example, being engaged in recruiting for the United States army, and why can we not accept it as the true church? Of the many things that need to be said in answer to that question, I must confine myself to mentioning two. For one thing, Lenin rightly discerned that if you are to exercise control over the flux of the historical present, you must believe that you have a position out-side and above it; and that if you are to have the strength and the courage to break down the pillars of this temple and in three days to build another in which the goal of all history will be achieved, then you must be in league with destiny itself. But this, as I have already suggested, is to speak of God, the true God, the Almighty. Then, as Lenin did, you have to wage relentless war against all those you regard as false gods, which for Lenin meant above all against Christ. But then, also, the question is obviously raised: is your God verily God? And, just as in the case of the human being the question as to whether he is "really" human has to do with his character, so the ultimate question about your God has to do with his character.

This leads to a second and closely related question. If you have The Party which is international, universal, the depository of the truth, the sole instrument for the redemption of mankind, without which there is no salvation, which can brook no rivals since to do so would be to deny its divine commission and to turn mankind over to destruction—and this party is composed of human beings albeit "the elect"—how can you prevent such a party from becom-ing the instrument of unspeakable pride and tyranny and hence tearing itself to pieces? Obviously you cannot, and your advice to the inner circle of your party, "Don't make the mistake the leaders of the French Revolution made and get to killing each other off," will go unheeded if you begin as Lenin did by assuming that the character of its members, save in the one respect of self-effacement for The Party, is not of first-rate importance and that the party may employ any means in order to achieve its end.

The positive phase of the answer to this most crucial question about the International Party or the Universal Church is stated in the classic chapter on Karl Marx in J. Middleton Murry's recent *Heroes of Thought:*

"To keep alive within any human society the sense of the reality of Good and Evil as absolutes, independent of the convention of the society, or the ordinance of the secular state, is the function of a church. . . . Therefore the institution of the church is precious, but precious only in so far as it asserts and justifies in act the claim to possess an authority superior to that of the secular state, because derived from its knowledge of the absolute Good, which is God. . . . Further, it is self-evident that there is but one safeguard against the abuse of this authority of the church, namely, that the absolute

Good in obedience to which its authority consists should forbid persecution, and command non-resistance to evil. This the God of the invisible Christian church does command."

The only true God is not the God of impersonal historical or economic forces which "automatically," apart from the human agents, and regardless of the quality of the human agents, redeem society. To think this is to try "to abolish the problem of human society, which is the problem of human nature." The true God is the God of love who can and does redeem men. This God is revealed in Jesus Christ. The true church is the "ecclesia" of those redeemed by infinite love. It must seek to redeem the world and must assert that it is the channel of the grace of God without which there is no salvation, and that to it are entrusted "the keys of the Kingdom of Heaven." But it can rightfully do this only in the degree that it exercises no violence except that of a love which will not be gainsaid and which is ever ready to die for sinners, and if it is in itself a true community of love.

What has been said reminds us, of course, why it is that the Church has so largely failed and why multitudes have turned in their passionate hunger for a truly redeeming church to "The Party" of Lenin, or Stalin, or Hitler or Mussolini. Too often when it has dared to claim divine authority the Church has sought to exercise power by worldly means. Often it has not dared claim to be an instrument of historical forces, much less of the Everlasting God, the Creator of the ends of the earth. Instead of challenging its members and subjecting them to a mighty and joyous discipline, it has tried to be a sanctified Rotary Club or League of Women Voters for them. It has not laid claim, as its Lord authorized it, to being the True Scarlet International of those who "have washed their robes and made them white in the blood of the Lamb" and among whom is neither Aryan, Negro, Slav, Japanese, or Malay, since all are one man in Christ. Instead, all of its branches including those called "catholic" have been in effect mainly national, state-worshipping or picayune provincial sects.

How explain the return to such a church and a sense of coming back to one's eternal home in thus returning? Let two remarks suffice. In the first place, at the moment the visible church is by way of becoming a more faithful replica of the invisible. It is a magnificent portent that the figures in our world today which symbolize challenge to the state, the final refusal to make a bargain with totalitarianism, are not, as would probably have been the case a few years ago, secular radicals, but religious, Christian, church figures such as Martin Niemoller and some of the Roman Catholic bishops of Germany. And it is many centuries since the sense that the Church is in essence universal, ecumenical, and must in fact become so, the conviction that the Church must redeem and rule the world in Christ's name, has been so strong as it is today.

But more important than this, there is no greater presumption than that a man should undertake to build his own church, and since community, communion, is of the essence of life, no more heinous sin than that of schism. There is One God and One Lord Jesus Christ. There is despite all its divisions and disfigurements and sins but one Church, one Christian movement. In it one must, one does, humbly and joyfully take his place. What branches may yet be lopped off from the Church, what changes in outward form may come, what stern prophetic denunciations the Lord of the Church may call upon us to utter, God shall reveal. It is palpable error to think that getting out of the Church of Christ, and joining one of the internationals which aims to replace it, will bring salvation to us or to the world.

The World Task
of Pacifism

1941* It is a common thing to hear people of practically all schools of thought say that what is going on today is not a war in the ordinary sense of the term but a revolution. One of the leaders of the younger generation of pacifists said to me recently that for the most part our pacifist movement is not aware of how profound and sweeping are the changes that are coming and that, as a consequence, we pacifists are still approaching our tasks with a narrow and provincial vision and on a petty scale.

On the other hand, Gerald Heard has said that the pacifist movement alone can qualify as the "receiver" for the bankrupt Western world, which faces extinction unless pacifists are prepared to "take over" presently. I believe this to be a sober statement of fact. I shall try to explain why and how it is so.

The order of life to which we have been accustomed in the Western world is very evidently breaking up. This is true of its spiritual and cultural and also of its economic and political aspects. In life these are never really separated, but for convenience we may deal with each for a moment.

Out of Renaissance and Reformation grew a great impulse for

* This essay was published some time before the United States' entry into World War II, a development A. J. Muste was prophetically certain would take place. For the duration of the war, A. J. Muste served as National Secretary of the Fellowship of Reconciliation and when the call came for men above forty-five to register for the draft, he was one of sixteen leading pacifists who refused to do so.

the liberation of the human spirit and its various cultural expressions, a movement largely justified in its efforts, one example of which was the freeing of economic, political and intellectual life from ecclesiastical fetters. From this point, however, there was a tendency to set man at the corner of the universe—despite fervent protestations that the anthropomorphic must be given up in favor of the scientific or of some other outlook—a tendency to conceive of man as really the highest form of moral being and to put any thought of God, of moral Being beyond man, out of the picture. Whenever man is thus cut off from the living source and end of his being, which is deep within and yet infinitely beyond himself, disaster overtakes him and his societies, as is now again the case. Man, whose spirit was to have been freed at last from ancient restraint and superstition, has not for centuries found himself less free than he is today: a cog in a machine in our own industrialism; a pawn in the hands of a totalitarian state under Fascism; or the tool of a totalitarian party under Communism. Men who think it childish to bow the knee before God and to be humble followers of the gentle Jesus do bow the knee by millions before Hitler, Mussolini, Stalin, a favorite movie idol, an impersonal trade union, a political or a business boss. Many of the most sophisticated and sensitive spirits in our day who cannot degrade themselves to that level fall into disillusionment or cynicism, the mood of being able to "see through" everything and everybody but no longer able to "see anything in" anything or anybody.

This is the result of inexorable spiritual law. "If there is no God," exclaims one of Dostoievsky's characters, "then I am God." And when men come to believe that, when they really believe there is no objective Good for which they can live; no law of reality to which high and low are truly subject; no One in all the universe more honest, more dependable, more capable of living in and building up a free society than they are themselves, then they cannot respect and trust themselves or one another. The bond of community is broken and life flies apart.

Equally, in a political and economic sense, our world is falling in pieces. We have productive machines to furnish the material means for the good life in abundance; but we fail or refuse to devise ways for distributing these goods in equitable or brotherly fashion, and so the machine is periodically clogged by its own output. There are just two ways to meet such a situation. One is to take the brakes off the machine and distribute the goods. We have everywhere rejected that course; therefore we have to put brakes on so that the machine will not be completely buried under its own products. That means an end to any form of "free enterprise," individual or cooperative. The State is the only agency available to put on the brakes, so everywhere we get rapidly increasing state intervention in the economic process, in order to limit production by crude methods such as plowing under cotton, burning coffee and leaving fruit to rot beneath trees; or by more subtle methods such as tariffs and production quotas.

But the supposed remedy aggravates the disease and causes a further contraction of the economy. For nations to try to be self-sufficient, grow all their raw materials and manufacture all their goods is as uneconomic as it would be for Texas to try to have its own steel industry and for Pittsburgh to insist on raising its own wheat. Rivalries between sorely pressed nations become intense and all devote increasing capital and energy to unproductive war expenditures. This "puts the unemployed to work" on producing war implements which no one can eat, wear, or live in, resulting eventually in still further contraction of production and more complete collapse.

Not a single country in the Western world has broken away from this circle. In one nation after another, therefore, the point has been reached at which the pressure on the masses is so severe that no organ of criticism or opposition can be permitted to exist. A war-time "communism" must be instituted to ration out the few goods that remain and to prepare for a death-struggle with some other national unit. That means dictatorship, totalitarianism—deadly uniform throughout, except for the color of shirt it wears! If the unemployed, whom we in the United States now are "putting to work" in arms plants and military camps, presently walk the streets again without jobs, it seems certain that nothing on earth will prevent the emergence of an American dictatorship.

War will not stop this process of disintegration; it is fatuous to hope that it can, even momentarily, given a victory by the "right side," halt the process so that a new beginning may be made. This is true whether we look at the matter from the ethical and spiritual or from the politico-economic viewpoint. In the former case, war is itself an extreme expression of our disintegration, our inability to meet difficulties except by increasingly brutal strife; and, as experience has demonstrated, neither the poverty, exhaustion, disillusionment and humiliation of defeat, nor the nationalistic exultation and the moral let-down of victory contribute to the healing of the nations. Similarly, in the economic and political realm, war is the inevitable expression of our failure and refusal to face our real problems and to institute sane solutions. War can only serve, as World War I and its aftermath have made clear for all who do not close their eyes, to accelerate fearfully the process of impoverishment and breaking up.

The best chance—in fact, the only chance we have left—to stop the movement of disintegration and to begin building on sounder foundations without first passing through a period marked by chaos and incalculable woe, is an early peace. Such a peace is, however, conceivable only if nations were to recognize that war offered no way out of any real problem and if they were to turn their attention seriously to dealing with those economic and cultural conditions which we have described and which constitute the roots of war. Obviously, that would mean that the present rulers would be converted to what might be called a realistic pacifism or that other leaders who did take that position would come to the front. And this in turn clearly implies that a great responsibility such as we alluded to in the beginning would be placed on the pacifist forces.

Unfortunately, the chances that events will take this turn are not bright. If the war continues, an appalling situation will obtain at its close. This will be true, as I have elsewhere tried to set forth at some length, whether it ends in a nominal British victory or a nominal German victory or in a stalemate of complete exhaustion in which neither side pretends to have won a victory. An increasing number of non-pacifist observers accept in private conversation if not in public utterances this analysis of the future.

Assuming that Europe is not reduced to utter anarchy, we are likely to be confronted with a revolutionary situation. We recall that this was the case at the close of the last war. At that time there was, in the defeated countries, a revolt against those who had been in command during the war. They were held responsible for the distress that had overtaken the masses and were considered unworthy of the trust of leadership. To whom then did men turn? They turned to the Communists and Social Democrats who had in one degree or other been opposed to the war, who had pointed out its danger and futility even while war was going on and who had been the first to agitate for peace. Nor was this phenomenon confined to the defeated countries. In France and Great Britain, also, the Socialists, Communists and Labor Party people, including such pacifists or near-pacifists as Ramsay MacDonald and Philip Snowden, were given the trust of the people and rose to positions of responsibility. A moment's reflection will indicate that it was bound to be. People experiencing disillusionment with war, finding that its fruits turn to ashes in their mouths, inevitably reject the leaders who were instrumental in leading them into war and whose prophecies of its blessed results have been disproved; and by the same token they must turn to those who were on the other side and who were clear-sighted enough to see the outcome, and brave and honest enough to tell what they foresaw.

In its essentials, the situation after the present war will present the same characteristics. There will, however, be two important differences. In Europe, the revulsion against war and against those who are thought of as war-makers will be practically as great in countries that are nominally victorious as in the others. It seems inconceivable that anywhere the regimes that were in control at the opening of the war should survive its end. Even apart from the factor of distrust and resentment felt against the leaders who took them into the war, the conditions will differ so vastly from those to which people have been accustomed that they will only fumble in their efforts to deal with them. Witness how these same regimes, even in the democratic countries, fumbled the ball after the last war!

But there will be an even more important difference. The Communists and Socialists of various hues, to whom the masses turned at the close of World War I, rejected imperialist wars, but in varying degrees they accepted violence and war, offensive or defensive, if waged on behalf of the proletariat. War between nations could achieve no good; but war between classes and the setting up of a temporary proletarian dictatorship based on force were seen as instruments of liberation. But the events of the post-war period in Russia and elsewhere have, to put it mildly, thrown grave doubts on this thesis. I doubt whether anyone who comes to the masses—fed up with the horrors of war—with the gospel that they can now turn to civil war in order to set up an iron dictatorship which will give them a utopia on the Russian model will actually be regarded as a savior and liberator. It is indeed not impossible that Stalin might become the "receiver" of a bankrupt Europe—much more likely, perhaps, than that it should be Churchill or Roosevelt or even Hitler—but that would be an indication, not that new hope had inspired the masses of Europe, but that they despairingly had accepted a debased Bolshevism as preferable to utter chaos.

The movement to which alone men might turn with hope, in

the conviction that the journey into a new day had indeed begun, would need to have certain characteristics. It must be a movement which renounces war and organized violence of all kinds and which had made it clear beforehand that this was its stand. It must be a movement which renounced dictatorship, which summoned men to a life organized around the principle of cooperation and not of coercion or individualism. It must be a profoundly religious movement. For men will no longer be able to believe in the too simple and mechanical notion that if you will only set up a new system, all our problems will be solved. They will not really be able to believe that a new world is possible unless they can believe that new men can be created, that they themseves can be delivered from imprisonment in the self and become conscious of unity with the whole, united with God, with moral reality beyond themselves. They will need a faith that transforms and saves them, gives them eternal resources to live by and values to live for.

But this simply means what Gerald Heard has said in effect, namely: only the Christianity of Jesus—only religious pacifism—can build a movement which goes to the root of evil in man and in society, a movement which men will trust and which can take over when the war is ended or has run its course.

A searching question immediately arises. Should the religious pacifist movement think of itself in these large terms as a mass movement for achieving social change by nonviolence? It seems to me increasingly clear that we can no longer evade the responsibility and the challenge. If we do seek to evade it, we shall no longer be able to believe in or respect ourselves. Either we believe our own words when we say that love, nonviolence, community form the basis on which all human association must be founded—and in that case we must do our utmost to achieve such an order, especially when the multitudes will be asking, "To whom else shall we go?"—or we do not really believe what we say. In that case we ought, of course, to stop saying it. Furthermore, we would be forced to admit that our pacifism is indeed the escape from social and political realities which our critics charge. Those of us whose roots go down into the Jewish-Christian prophetic tradition cannot evade the call to pray and work for the realization of the Kingdom of God on earth.

To put it in another way, either we ought to resign from the world and abandon political activity altogether—quit voting, quit working against conscription laws or for provisions for conscientious objectors in draft laws, and the like—or else we must resolutely carry out the political task to its end, the organization of all life on true foundations and for worthy ends. We cannot keep on saying, in effect, to the disinherited and oppressed: "We suffer with you; we hope that your wrongs may be redressed; we share your dream of a world in which men shall live together as brothers. But we are opposed to violence. If, therefore, you resort to violence, we shall have to stand aside."

We must indeed resolutely refuse to be tempted to violence: that is the short cut which invariably turns out to be the blind alley. But if we leave it at that, then, in effect, as our critics have pointed out, the disinherited are condemned to the choice between acquiescence in tyranny or resorting to violence. We pacifists must go on to show that evil can be overcome and a new order built in the spirit by the method of nonviolence.

Or we may look at our dilemma from still another angle. Obviously there will be, during the war perhaps, and at its close certainly, a vastly increased need and demand for the pacifist work of relief and reconstruction in which the Society of Friends has pioneered and which has so profoundly won the confidence of all peoples. It is unthinkable that this work should be abandoned, and failure to extend it enormously, whether through existing or new agencies, would be pretty nearly equivalent to abandonment. But how maintain separate relief and reconstruction under the conditions which will prevail then in Europe and elsewhere? Will relief which is not reconstruction be anything but a mockery, a business of trying to stop the tide with a board fence? Will not the reconstruction require to be general in scope, including housing, transportation, and all the rest? And how will it be possible for American Friends Service Committee workers to draw a line between rebuilding houses and helping to build an order of life which will make houses something more than shelters for driven cattle or ravening wolves? Have we not always said that it was not material goods we were bringing to men, except in a secondary sense, but a demonstration or at least a symbol of a new way of life? What are we to give men when they have despaired of other ways of life and hold out their hands in hope? I see only two choices: to retire from the field and shamefacedly to admit that we have been only playing at building life on truth and love; or humbly to undertake leadership of the new world, and seek to build our vision into economic and political reality, as, for example, did William Penn.

But is not all this a fantastic kind of day dreaming? Is it even remotely possible that the religious pacifist forces, the Christian forces, should measure up to such a challenge? It is of course possible that we may fail through our own fault; that for lack of faith and discipline the salt will lose its savor, the light be hidden under a bushel or extinguished. To that problem we must return in a moment. But before the Western world can or does begin to rebuild, it may break up as utterly as did the western Roman Empire; in this event small groups of pacifists might serve as little islands of safety and sanity and faith in a black sea of barbarism, as did the monasteries in the beginning of the Dark Ages. For this also we must be prepared, if it should come; but we have not yet arrived at that point. Assuming then that, in the post-war period, we might be given the chance to provide leadership in building a new order and that we ourselves are prepared to undergo the severe disciplines, physical, intellectual, and spiritual, which that would entail, is there any possibility that the forces of nonviolence may in some degree meet the situation?

Several observations may be made in answer to that question. In the first place, the fact that we are now few and that the self-styled realists do not think that they need to take us into political consideration is not at all decisive. In the nature of the case, the revolutionary element remains small, little noticed unless it be to visit persecution upon it, so long as men still hope that the world can go on much as it has done or that they can wake up presently as from a nightmare and find themselves safe in the old bed. For the majority of people, to turn to those who say boldly that the old order must go on and that men must build on new and divine foundations would mean to admit utter inadequacy and to accept blame for apostasy and insensitiveness. They may not come to that until the bankruptcy of the forces of the old order can no longer be hidden.

Secondly, we are appreciably stronger than we were a score of years ago, not only in numbers, but in intellectual comprehension and spiritual development. When we consider that in theological writing and discussion it is the non-pacifists rather than the pacifists who are on the defensive, when we note the advance in dealing with the problem of the conscientious objector both in the church and in the nation, and observe the widespread interest in activities of the American Friends Service Committee, we need not despair.

In the third place, every period of upheaval in history has revealed that there are men and women of great technical, organizing, administrative ability who cannot adjust themselves to a new order and who in one way or another sabotage it. There are, however, not a few such experts and technicians who have long known that the old order was thwarting them and stultifying them in the exercise of their abilities, and many who have no objection to placing their technical and other talents at the disposal of the forces of the new day. There have always been military leaders who have readily transferred their services to the regime which has overthrown that for which they had fought for a lifetime. Our own best scientific, engineering and organizing minds often devote themselves now to forging diabolically effective instruments of slaughter and destruction. Many such brains will continue to do so as long as men believe that war is a possible solution for social problems. Let men once come out from under the spell of that delusion, and we shall be surprised at the resources both in ordinary human beings and in the intellectual leaders which will be released for the work of building a new world, resources which men will joyously put at the service of those who have been the prophets and pioneers of the new order. Indeed not a few people who themselves are not pacifists already ask for the opportunity of putting their talents at the disposal of the work of Friends.

Fourthly, the Gandhi movement in India is giving the world an example of the use of nonviolence on a mass scale. Not only may we pacifists learn much from Gandhi and his followers in building a mass nonviolence movement in this and other Western countries, but we may hope that people generally in the Western world will be impressed by this oriental example, as the futility and waste of violence becomes more obvious. Furthermore, cooperation between Eastern and Western nonviolence movements may well come to have a decisive influence on world events.

It may be fruitful to observe in passing those fundamental characteristics of the Gandhi movement which must also, I believe, mark the growing pacifist movement in the United States. First of all, it is a religious movement. It is based upon convictions about the very nature of life and the universe, convictions held not merely by the mind but by a moral commitment of the whole being to the practice of them. Pacifism, with Gandhi and, if not with all his followers, certainly with those who constitute the inner core of his movement, was not a tool that you pick up or lay down, use today but not tomorrow, use in this relationship and not in some other. It was a way of life. You cannot really practice pacifism unless you are a pacifist, and likewise, in the measure that you are a pacifist, it becomes unthinkable ever to practice violence whether physical or spiritual. Hence also the program of personal training and discipline is an indispensable part of the movement.

It is an economic and social movement. These elements are symbolized in Gandhi's program by spinning. About some aspects of Gandhi's economic program I am dubious—for instance I am not convinced that it is necessary or desirable to go back to a pre-machine economy—but such questions may, for our present purpose, be put to one side. Three elements implied or suggested by Gandhi's emphasis on spinning are, as I see it, essential to an adequate non-violence movement.

First, any movement which undertakes to give leadership or help in building a better world must give much attention to the ordering of the economic life. It must clarify its thinking as to the kind of economic order to strive for. It must decide how much socialization is possible without the creation either of a totalitarian state or of a political machine which, besides crushing the liberty of the individual, could fail in the narrow economic sense because of bureaucratic administration and attendant red tape, the deadening of initiative and the accompanying temptation to evade responsibility. It must not only invent, it must experiment with schemes for a more decentralized, human and cooperative way of living.

The second essential symbolized by Gandhi's spinning plan is the expression of our basic philosophy of life in the economic sphere now rather than some day in the future when a new system is established. To postpone action has been the prevailing tendency among Socialists and Communists: "The day will come when socialism will be established and then we'll be socialists. Meanwhile there is not much that can be done to alleviate the evils of the present order and you personally go on living and doing business much as any capitalist might." One difficulty with this approach is that workers are hungry and cold now and they cannot wait until the revolution to do something about it. But there is a deeper and more subtle difficulty, which may be put this way: If you say that men cannot live as socialists until socialism has been established—or as Christians until a Christian world has been achieved—then you are saying in effect that non-socialists can build socialism and that people who are not Christians except in a theoretical sense can build a Christian order of life. That has an implication which the social democrats never faced squarely, but which the Communists saw clearly and accepted: namely, that if the new system does not represent the general convincement of the people, it has to be set up in the first instance by violence and that human beings must be regimented in the new environment until they are psychologically reconditioned and adapted to the new system. But the Russian experience has reminded us that, in this realm also, violence and coercion are self-defeating and that the product of regimentation is not a finer man, but a degraded human being. We are driven to the conviction that men who are autocrats and lovers of power in their own souls will not build a democratic world; men who are essentially self-seekers will not build a cooperative commonwealth. It equally follows that men who have entered into the spirit of community will inevitably be driven to seek to give expression at once to their inner spirit in economic relationships. As the early Christians, the Franciscans, the early Friends illustrate, there is always creative experimentation in the economic life where there is genuine and fresh religious experience.

Gandhi's spinning program has a third important element for those who seriously desire to build a nonviolence movement. It shows that manual work has important effects on the individual spirit and that corporate manual activity is a powerful agent for unifying pacifist groups within and also for unifying them with their non-pacifist neighbors, especially workers and farmers.

Gandhi's movement, finally, is a political movement. It expresses the determination of the masses of India to free themselves from the yoke of British imperialism without violence and without hatred for the oppressor. For our present purpose it is not necessary to elaborate this point except to observe that, in addition to developing mass resistance to war, a Western nonviolence movement must make effective contacts with oppressed and minority groups such as Negroes, share-croppers, industrial workers, and help them to develop a nonviolent technique, as Gandhi did in the India National Congress.

Our conception of the ultimate, major task of the religious pacifist movement will necessarily have an important influence on our ideas about the strategy of the movement in the immediate war crisis. Discussion of the attitudes and activities of pacifists in time of conscription and war indicates that there are some who incline toward an activist and militant and others to a more quietist pacifism. The latter would discourage direct opposition to the war activities of the nation, urging concentration on works of mercy and reconstruction. This reconstruction must be such that it will not antagonize people, but that it will illustrate the underlying spirit of love which animates us, and enable us to survive without being subjected to fruitless suffering until such time as the masses recover from their war-mania and are able to weigh calmly our counsels about national and international policy.

It seems clear to me that we must indeed do our utmost to remain in fellowship with our own countrymen and fellow-churchmen. We must seek to identify ourselves with their need and suffering. If community is to be temporarily broken, it must be they and not we who do the cutting off, and even then we must harbor no ill will and be on the look-out for opportunities to be helpful to them in simple human ways. It is also clear that we cannot engage in sabotaging the activities of our fellow-citizens who feel called to fight. We seek to wean our fellows from the desire to make war, not to interfere from without with their war-efforts or to destroy their property. Our non-cooperation with the war-effort of the nation, if enough were moved to participate in it, might of course at some stage have a decisive effect upon that war-effort; but this would not be the result of a positive and deliberate destructive act on our part but simply the result of our inability to cooperate with what seems to us an evil and ruinous course. Besides, it would not be an act of disloyalty to our own country but of obedience to a higher law and to a sovereign "not of this world."

Furthermore, the negative act of refusal to support war is only one part of pacifism, of the way of love and nonviolence. Never can we abate our efforts to give positive expression to pacifism in cooperative living and brotherly service.

I am, however, equally clear in feeling that in time of conscription and war, we cannot retire for practical purposes from political activity, from attempting to influence the nation's course, especially when there are still certain democratic channels available for doing so. The movement as a whole should not, it seems to me, become quietist and non-political. That might be merely an expression of an isolationist or escapist attitude, neither of which expresses the true spirit of community with our fellows.

For one thing, there will always be concrete issues on which we must speak or run the risk of being traitors to the truth. Civil liberties will be abridged; minorities may be persecuted; labor may be denied its rights and the masses may be made to bear an inordinate share of the costs of war. Certainly the fact that one may not be able to speak out on such matters without having to suffer for it, or without offending many, would hardly be sufficient cause to excuse silence. Periodically, in a war situation, the question comes up as to whether an effort should be made to negotiate a peace or whether the war shall go on until our own nation is in a position to dictate a peace. Periodically, the question of war aims or peace terms will or should be raised.

We have already pointed out a more fundamental reason why the pacifist movement cannot, save at peril to itself and mankind, retire from the arena of political discussion. In that arena the process of education and miseducation is going on all the time. Silence may contribute to it as well as speech. The extent to which the masses will have confidence in us and turn to our leadership after the war will depend upon whether we have given practical demonstrations of love and of our ability to build and organize. But it will also depend on whether by our analysis and interpretation of events we have demonstrated our intellectual capacity for leadership, our ability to see that war was futile before that became common knowledge, and our courage to speak the truth when it is unpleasant and dangerous to do so. It is impossible to read, for example, the early history of the Quakers without realizing that it was precisely because they could not be silenced, because they continued to bear witness to their faith and to oppose personal and social sin even when multitudes were offended, that those multitudes at last said in effect: "Obviously these Quakers are serious. We have come upon a strange species of human being who refuses to compromise the truth or to be clubbed into silence. Consequently, we shall have to adapt ourselves to this strange phenomenon. With this man who refused to try to buy immunity, we shall have to compromise, give him special exemptions and a peculiar confidence!" This may indeed be a good time to recall George Fox's words, written in 1667: "The cry is now amongst them that are without, 'where is there a Quaker for such and such a trade?'—Oh! therefore, Friends who have purchased this through great sufferings, lose not this great favor which God hath given unto you, but that ye may answer the witness of God in every man which witnesseth to your faithfulness, that they may glorify your Father on your behalf."

Here I think we have put our fingers on what must be foremost and basic in our shaping of pacifist policy in time of crisis. Probably we are not all called upon to bear our witness in the same way. Some will be led to a more militant course, others to a quieter form of witness. The former must take especial pains to make sure their only motive is love; the latter that they are not unwittingly influenced by fear or a tendency to avoid difficult and complicated issues. All who have committed themselves to the way of love and nonviolence must remain in fellowship and unity with each other, not thinking of themselves as more orthodox or honest or useful pacifists than those who put the emphasis in a different place. The fact that this spirit of unity and mutual confidence has obtained between non-registrants and registrants has been very heartening. But most important is it that all of us should be deeply and unreservedly committed to that life "which taketh away the occasion of all war." We should realize that that life is the hope of the world, the one means of salvation. Our task is always the positive one of witnessing to that life and of practicing it.

The problem which confronts us at any moment is never: to what extent can we compromise with existing economic and political institutions, adapt ourselves to the demands of the world? Our problem always is to bring the state and other institutions of the world to adjust themselves to the demands of the Christ spirit, to the way of life which His truest followers incarnate, though in order to accomplish this we have no weapons but those of reason, love, humility, prayer, and willingness to die for our faith. In outward appearance, the point at which we arrive by these contrasting processes of the world adapting itself to us, or of adapting ourselves to the world, may at a given moment be much the same; but the direction in which we are going as we pass through that point will be the decisive matter. If we are doing the compromising, there will be no end until our power is gone. If the state is being made to adapt itself to the demands of the spirit, then, to mix the metaphor, it is clear that the yeast has not lost its fermenting power and the lump will yet be transformed into wholesome bread.

All this has, finally, an important bearing upon the question of alternative service under the conscription act. One of our best loved leaders who earned his right to speak and be listened to by his sufferings as a conscientious objector in the last war, has said: "There is of course no absolutely consistent and final position in this complicated world; but there are only two approximately consistent positions under conscription: either you accept conscription—and then you may as well do what the government forces you to do—or else you refuse to be ordered and put it up to the government to leave you alone or put you in jail."

With what is aimed at in this drastic saying, I am in thorough accord. If our readiness to render what is called alternative service arises out of an intellectual blurring of the issue between totalitarianism and democracy, between conscription by the state and voluntary service to society; if it arises from a desire to make it easy for the government to carry forward war which we profess to regard as evil and suicidal; or if it arises from an unconfessed and unfaced impulse to avoid unpleasantness and persecution for ourselves, a desire to have our fellow-citizens say with a sigh of relief, "These pacifists are harmless and jolly good fellows after all"; or if from a desire to hold our young people organizationally in the membership of some denomination or sect—then there would, in my opinion, be no important difference of principle between such alternative service on the one hand and non-combatant or even combatant service on the other hand. In that case a handful of absolutists going to jail or to their death as did the uncompromising pioneers of Quakerism would do more for religious pacifism and for the salvation of mankind from the curse of war than thousands of so-called pacifists in alternative service camps.

But I do not believe we are confined to the choice among submitting to conscription; a form of alternative service which amounts to submitting to conscription because in effect it is a device to smooth the way for the war-machine and its Fascist trends; or going to jail. There are those who will not be true to the Inner Light unless they follow a course such as that of the non-registrants, which leaves the government no alternative except at once radically to alter its own course or send these men to jail. From the beginning it has been my conviction that these men rendered a great service to the cause of pacifism and democracy and prophetic religion. Our movement would have been poorer and would, I think, have won less regard even from those who oppose us if we had not produced such "absolutists." Fidelity to conscience at cost to the individual in the face of general opposition and disapproval still has power to win the respect of men who also have "that of God" in them. Every man has in his own conduct a line beyond which he will not go, no matter how absurd it may seem to others to draw the line at just that point, the point at which he must stand with Athanasius or Luther against the world, and say, "So help me God, I can do no other." There are known to be COs who registered but also consider themselves "absolutists" and who will refuse to accept anything but that complete exemption from compulsory or assigned service which is available to British "absolutists" under the law in that country. If such men take this course as a result of mature reflection and an unreserved commitment to the leading of the Spirit, I believe they will do a great service. Personally, I should wish to be morally identified with them.

This does not mean, however, that acceptance of alternative service necessarily and under all conditions represents a compromise with evil, "making the best of a bad business," taking shelter and keeping still until the storm blows over. The issue is sufficiently fundamental to warrant consideration. From one standpoint, it is impossible to exaggerate the importance of war-resistance, of total refusal to have any part in war. Some of our critics, referring to this phase of pacifism, speak of it disparagingly or with violent condemnation as "merely negative," and sometimes we are a bit intimidated by them. These critics, in most instances, do not mean that they want us to abstain from war and in addition do something else. They themselves are not ready to do this "merely negative" thing and sometimes just because this "merely negative" thing is so hard and would have such decisive and positive repercussions! In a sense, the nations cannot solve, they will not even face, their real problems so long as they think resort to an armament boom and presently to war constitutes a "way out." To say that refusal to participate in war and so to help remove this tumor from the body politic is "merely negative" is the same as applying that description to removal of a tumor from the body physical. Of course it is negative and in itself not sufficient, but in the first place, unless this is done the patient will die and in the second place, if it is done the life forces in the organism can flow unimpeded and can do the positive job of making that organism vital and effective again.

Nevertheless there is a sense in which war resistance is only incidental in the pacifist way of life, in the life of love and non-violence. To break out of the hard shell of the Self, which is all the time seeking to defend itself against its brothers and therefore commits aggression against them; to know in one's inmost being the unity of all men in God; to express love at every moment and in every relationship, to be channels of this quiet, unobtrusive, persistent force which is always there, which ever goes on, after "the tumult and the shouting dies, the captains and the kings depart"— this is the meaning of pacifism. This is the love which binds man and maid together; which all through the ages has held the primary social unit, the family, together; which underlies the patient and beautiful labor of the multitudes who year after year plow the ground, sow the seed, reap the harvest, bake the bread, make the clothing, construct the buildings; which leads the dying soldier to give his last cup of water to his dying comrade, even to his dying foe. This it is that must always find expression even where on certain issues we must stand against our brothers and accept the bitter fact that Christ came to bring "not peace but division," even sometimes between mother and child, lover and beloved. On this account, in a world which in a sense is always committed to misunderstanding and division, under the dominion of an evil spirit, we have all the time got to be insisting on our right to "alternative service." Even if we were all thrown into jail or concentration camp, we should have to devise ways of rendering "alternative service" there and proclaim our right to give food and drink to our "enemies." And even when we accept complete separation from our fellows, pursue the "negative" way of refusal to participate in evil to the point where men slay us, from our point of view it means nothing unless that also is an expression of love for and unity with "that of God" in them. "If I give my body to be burned and have not love, it is worthless."

Thus the individual pacifist, at every moment, and especially in every crisis, is confronted with the twofold need of resisting human customs and institutions—coming "out from among them" and being "separate"—because he must "obey God rather than men," and at the same time creatively and at whatever cost serve his fellows. The pacifist movement must of necessity, I think, help the individual at both points. If it fails to provide channels for the positive and sacrificial service of human need, it will fail its youth as truly as if it became slack in its resistance to war. Looking at the matter from the standpoint of the movement itself, it must deal vigorously and imaginatively with the problem of "alternative service" since its responsibility is to say to the world in Christ's name not only "War is not the way, " but "This is the way; walk ye in it."

From such an analysis of the problem, certain conclusions as to the character of constructive pacifist service inevitably flow. In the first place, it must be civilian service, for we have to exemplify a way of life which excludes war, "takes away the occasion of all wars." In the second place, it is important—personally I am prepared to say essential—that the service be under private auspices and control and not under a civilian department of the government. The basic reason for this is that the service projects must grow out of and must express the spirit of religious pacifism; otherwise we are making no distinctive contribution. If this requirement is to be met, the religious pacifist bodies will have to be in charge of the life of the camps. This will apply to the organization of the actual work program of the camps which can express or deny the basic pacifist attitudes, make or break the pacifist purpose of the enterprise. It will apply also to the educational program of the camps, which also will inevitably tend to produce either more convinced and disciplined pacifists or less convinced and disciplined pacifists. Another reason why it is important that camps be under private auspices rather than civilian departments of the government is that, in an age when the tendency toward totalitarian state control is so powerful and prevalent, and when conscript service is inevitably tied up to regimentation for war purposes, no greater service can be rendered to society than keeping alive the spirit of voluntarism, the principle of free association, thus providing a demonstration of how morale can be developed and society served by non-state or non-governmental bodies and without resorting to conscription.

The third characteristic of the work-projects must inevitably— so it seems to me—be that they cost the individual CO and the pacifist movement something substantial; they must represent a sacrifice rendered to our fellows, an identification with them in self-denial and suffering, a sacrifice on behalf of our principles and faith. The longer I reflect upon it the more convinced I become that unless the Public Service Camps do quite clearly represent a sacrificial contribution on our part, they will not only bring no positive results, but will throw discredit upon the whole religious pacifist movement in the eyes of the masses. Not only must we not ask for government funds for maintenance of CO's, administration, and education in the camps; we must, it seems to me, refuse them. "Alternative service," government financed and controlled, would not be a genuine pacifist alternative at all. It would represent an almost complete absorption into the program and machinery of a government engaged in war preparation, and probably war, and tending increasingly toward dictatorship. We are well aware that large numbers of our CO's would be unable to accept such service, and would go to jail instead. So far as the religious pacifist movement is concerned, we could not cooperate with such a program without greatly weakening and obscuring our witness. It would mean that in effect the National Service Board for Religious Objectors, for example, and the various Service Committees, would become government agencies instead of agencies of the pacifist movement. Grave issues in the realm of church-state relationships, in addition to all the other considerations we have named, would obviously be raised. Certainly the religious pacifist forces should not themselves initiate a movement in this direction.

On the other hand, work-camps in which, because we are willing to pay for the opportunity, we can hold before men the vision of the world-task of pacifism, challenge them to voluntary discipline and weld them into a joyous fellowship, may make a great contribution to the achievement of that world-task which it has been the aim of this paper to suggest.

Where Are We Going?

1941 The President of the United States began the year 1941 as he ended the year 1940—with a plea against a peace based on appeasement of the dictators; and in this we agree with him. His alternative was to give the green light to the Churchill cabinet for an all-out war against Germany, in which the United States would take a great and decisive part and which would not end until, as was the case in 1918, the United States and Great Britain were in a position to dictate the terms of peace. The only alternatives he sees are a military victory for the Berlin-Rome-Tokyo axis or a military victory for the Washington-London (and many fondly hope Moscow) axis. There are certain considerations which move the President toward the course he has mapped out and which move multitudes of Americans to follow him, even though it becomes daily clearer that this will mean the complete involvement in war which they profoundly dread. One set of considerations expresses itself in such phrases as these: "British imperialism may be bad, but Hitler's aggression is much worse and we live in a world where we have to choose between evils"; or, "a Hitler victory would be such an unmitigated evil that anything is worthwhile which gives the most promise of preventing that." The other considerations anticipate that a victory for the "democracies" will furnish, not "in a distant millennium," but, as the President boldly proclaimed (address at the opening of the Seventy-seventh Congress), "in our time and generation," the basis for a world of free expression, free worship, freedom from want, and freedom from fear!

Let us analyze these trends of thought briefly. Upon a clear understanding of them hangs the ever-lessening chance we have of remaining out of the conflict in order that this nation may do a work of reconciliation and healing and rebuilding in a mad world.

If people who contrast the British and German roles in the war mean that certain values suggested by the term democracy are preferable to certain values represented by the terms Fascism, Nazism, or some other form of totalitarianism, we readily agree with them. We too want to preserve democracy and above all make it more real. We want to see Nazism wiped out; we do not speak of wiping out Nazis because we see no evidence that killing off people who hold certain ideas, or are temporarily spell-bound by them, is an effective way to get rid of those ideas.

Before we go on, therefore, from a concern to save and extend democracy to the conclusion that we should, in one or another form and degree of intensity, enter the war on the side of Britain against Germany, certain questions need to be faced: Is the regime in Britain (meaning the Churchill cabinet and the forces and interests it represents) in a decisive sense fighting the battle of democracy, civilization, and Christian faith, or is it fighting the battle of empire? Just what will be the difference between a peace written by Churchill-Roosevelt (plus Stalin?) and a peace written by Hitler and associates? Or, assuming for the sake of argument that Britain is fighting the last ditch battle for democracy and civilization, will war accomplish the desired result?

Americans were drawn into the last war because they became persuaded that it was essentially a war for democracy against autocracy. During the later 1920s and the early 1930s, when we had an opportunity to appraise the matter in the sober light of "the morning after," most recognized historical scholars and a considerable majority of our people became convinced that we had been mistaken and that the war had been about imperialist interests and some curious provisions of secret treaties that we did not learn about until after the horrible orgy of war was over. We were convinced that the vindictive and impossible peace of Versailles showed pretty clearly what the war had been about. Educators who taught these things in the post-war years now tend to denounce as irresponsible and indifferent to democracy students who still believe

what they were taught then and who consequently find it difficult
to become enthusiastic over another war!

What of the present war? How square with the idea of democracy the persistent refusal of the Churchill cabinet to state its war
aims, even in face of the demand from millions of its own people?
What did Britain promise Mussolini in the months when he was on
the fence and such earnest efforts were being made to persuade
him to become one of the leaders in the war for liberty? What is
the British Government now offering to Franco, whom in effect it
supported, in his war against democracy in Spain? It has been
reported in highly reputable journals, and never denied, that Sir
Stafford Cripps, on behalf of the Churchill cabinet, offered Stalin
de facto recognition of his occupation of the small Baltic countries
and an equal seat with Britain at the peace table. If true that Britain
has offered him this recognition of his occupation of three little
defenseless countries, how much stands in the way of recognition of
his conquests in Poland and Finland? Is it credible that a peace
primarily concerned with the preservation of democracy, the values
of Western civilization, and Christian faith, will be written at a
council table at which Stalin has an equal voice with one or two
other men? Or, to put it another way, people who hold that a
realistic attitude requires Stalin's presence at the peace table cannot
consistently take the position, at least not on ethical grounds, that
they could under no conceivable circumstances sit down with Hitler.
And how explain in terms of democratic war-aims the refusal of
the present British regime to grant freedom to India or the jailing
of nonviolent followers of Mahatma Gandhi? Or the effort to keep
some seventy million people in the East Indies and Malaysia under
French, Dutch, and British rule?

The evidence seems to point as clearly as in the last war to a
conflict between two groups of powers for survival and domination.
One set of powers which includes Britain and the United States,
and perhaps "free" France, controls some seventy percent of the
earth's resources and thirty million square miles of territory. The
imperialistic *status quo* thus to their advantage was achieved by a
series of wars including the last one. All they ask now is to be left
at peace, and if so they are disposed to make their rule mild though
firm. In the *Statement on the American Churches and the International Situation* adopted at the *Biennial Meeting of the Federal
Council of Churches* occurs an incisive comment on this point: "To
profess a love for peace is no great virtue in those who control so

disproportionate a share of the world's wealth that to retain it is their principal concern. Peace which means merely an undisturbed exploitation of power and privilege is not true peace, but only an interlude which inevitably provokes revolt. To seek, through power, to maintain a status quo of inequality and injustice may be no less evil than to invoke force to change it." The "satisfied" powers have, however, refused to make any basic change in the distribution of power and privilege. (Giving away, as at Munich, something that does not belong to you and then hurrying home to speed up your armament program, so that you can take it back in six months, or so that you will, at any rate, not have to give up anything you consider a vital interest of your own, is not a fundamental departure from the old game of power politics.) These powers have always sought to maintain a preponderance of armed strength, and they broke their thrice-recorded promise to disarm after the last war and the disarmament of Germany. They are now armed and arming to the teeth in order to retain their control, even if that means a world war. On the other hand stands a group of powers, such as Germany, Italy, Hungary, Japan, controlling about fifteen percent of the earth's resources and one million square miles of territory, equally determined to alter the situation in their own favor, to impose their ideas of "order," and armed to the teeth to do that, even if it means plunging the whole world into war.

Yet, even if all this is true, many persons believe that there will still be a significant difference between a British and a German victory which makes it worth our while to risk war for the sake of the former. Let us glance for a moment, then, at the three possible outcomes of a war fought to a finish. That finish may be a German victory, or a British-American victory, or a stalemate of utter exhaustion.

There may be what the history books will call a German victory: a coalition of dictators combines finally to put an end to the dominance of French and British imperialism. There is always much that is sad and horrifying about such a collapse of empires and, in part, of the cultures associated with them. That was true of the collapse of Babylonia, Persia, Greece, Rome. It is not true—all history is there to support this assertion—it is not true that the collapse of these empires meant the end of civilization and religion. It would be more nearly accurate to say that these empires had to give way in their turn in order that civilization and religion might survive and break through to higher developments. And what reason is there to suppose that the French and British, and for that matter we in the United States, have developed an imperialism that has the attribute of immortality?—of which it never will be said:

> *Far-called our navies melt away;*
> *On dune and headland sinks the fire.*
> *Lo, all our pomp of yesterday*
> *Is one with Nineveh and Tyre.*

Though this should happen, it would not mean the end of civilization and religion. Those who say that the end of the "plutocratic democracies" has to come are probably nearer right than those who think that for practical purposes the fate of the Kingdom of God on earth is identified with the fate of the British Empire. Nothing will be changed by calling the former "appeasers" or saying that "they talk just like Hitler." "The judgments of the Lord" are still "true and righteous altogether," even though they are terrible and their human instruments appalling. And the judgments fall unfailingly upon men and nations who will not repent.

I do not mean for an instant to minimize the evils of a totalitarian victory; nor do I think that Nazism embodies progressive tendencies. The point is that Western imperialism as a whole, whether in its totalitarian or its "democratic" manifestations, is no longer able to serve the cause of human progress. Its moral prestige has vanished. Its economy no longer functions; nowhere, for example, is it able to put its unemployed to work save by the artificial and suicidal device of an armament boom. The war, so far from holding out any promise of halting this disintegration, is itself a result of it and in turn can bring about nothing but an acceleration of the break-up—unless now at the eleventh hour nations will stop fighting and completely reverse their course. In the context of an exhausted Europe, a Nazi victory will mean utter chaos on the continent or the setting up of some monstrosity that might be called Commu-nazism and which will have none of the early idealism of the Communist movement about it. Furthermore the disillusionment would spread to defeated Britons, as it has so largely infected the French, and English civilization as we have known it would go under. From such a prospect we shrink, and rightly so.

Let us suppose, then, that we get the alternative the President offers. We pursue, as in the last war, a course of interventionism and once again the outcome is a British-American victory. There will then be another Woodrow Wilson to propose an idealistic Fourteen Points as the basis of an armistice. Clearly, President Roosevelt has already cast himself in that role. There will also be another Lloyd George and perhaps a Clemenceau to accept our President's proposals and promise to write a peace based thereon. But no matter what the personal motivation of these men may be, they will not be able to write such a peace. No British statesman involved in this war will be able to stand against the demand which will arise that, this time, the job must be finished and it must be made forever impossible for "the Huns" again to bring woe to mankind. If, in the post-war let-down, it should seem to be necessary, the man who will then be the war-dictator of England will not hesitate to order a "Khaki election" any more than Lloyd George did in 1918, in a period when there was much more democracy left in the world and much more of a basis for democracy than now. But suppose, for the sake of argument, that some measure of restraint is exercised in the peace. Will exhausted Great Britain be able to maintain or enforce that peace? Britain and France together could not do it the last time. Will the United States keep a huge army of occupation in Europe to feed starving millions until some semblance of order is restored and the ghosts of a debased Bolshevism or utter anarchy are laid?

Look at the picture from another angle. Defeated Germany, after such a war as is now being waged, will be relatively in the same position as Russia at the close of the last war. Actually the position will be much worse, partly because the economic disintegration of our Western world has gone much further than it had in 1918, partly because even the horrors that marked the debacle of agricultural Russia will seem mild compared to what will happen in a complex, close-packed, urbanized German population facing disillusionment and humiliation for a second time in a generation.

And what of "victorious" Britain itself, which will, relatively, be in much the same economic position as was Germany at the close of the last war, when the soldiers return to a devastated land, to a Britain with not a customer left in Europe? For there will be no one on the continent who will be able to buy anything for a long time. As J. Middleton Murry points out in a recent issue of the British *Peace News:* "The idea that you can change over simply from war-production to peace-production in a great exporting country like this is an illusion. The vast destruction of shipping, the swift formation of economic blocs from which our trade will be virtually excluded, the collapse of the financial machinery of international trade, will make the absorption of our vast conscript army into peaceful production impossible." So the "victory" will turn to ashes in the mouths of the British masses, who will swiftly realize that the only real "victors" in the sense of world-trade and power politics will be Uncle Shylock, from across the seas, who will be wanting his "garden-hose" and ships and guns back—or, in lieu of them, rubber and tin which Britain will need so much more desperately—and/or, possibly, Comrade Stalin, if he succeeds for long enough in keeping everybody else fighting, with Russia on the sidelines. Unless there is a reversion to utter anarchy for a period, then obviously this situation will require in Britain also an iron dictatorship, possibly of a predominantly Bolshevik, possibly Fascist, hue, if there is any appreciable difference left between those two. Any moderate Laborite seeking to handle that situation will play as pathetic and futile a role against this Commissar for Britain as Kerensky played in Russia in 1917.

It is needless to dwell on the point that if the war ends in a stalemate of complete exhaustion, the situation will still be essentially the same.

The nations at war are like men fighting each other desperately on a slippery, inclined plane. Their only salvation is to quit fighting and singly or together get off that plane. If they do not, they will land presently at the bottom of a precipice, and the question as to which is on top or which was a shade more virtuous will be pretty nearly an academic question, because they will all be dead.

Recently we have been assured in many quarters that this is too pessimistic a picture, based on too literal a following of what happened in the last war. This time, "things are going to be different." The chief reason given for this hope by progressives in the United States is that this time the British Larbor Party and trade union forces will play an important part. They will raise a real, perhaps decisive, voice at the peace table. They will not permit the old order to return, but will insist on the end of privilege and the building of a socialist order.

Some of us remember that much the same thing was said by British laborites and their friends at home and abroad during the last war. Lloyd George promised "a land fit for heroes to live in." Mr. Churchill, so far as we recall, has not yet spoken in such glowing terms; but Mr. Roosevelt has outdone Lloyd George, for the land he pictured, in his January 6 address to Congress, would be fit for saints as well as heroes to live in. What reason is there for the British laborites to think that they will get, out of their collaboration with the Churchill cabinet, what they so patently and tragically failed to get out of collaboration with Lloyd George, that Bevin, if he outlives the war, will not die of a broken heart as Arthur Henderson is said to have done when the Disarmament Conference over which he presided collapsed?—"not only or even chiefly," as H. N. Brailsford pointed out, because of Germany.

Since the answer to this question is so crucial, great importance attaches to Harold Laski's recent book, *Where Do We Go From Here?* Laski has dealt very honestly with the problem. He asserts that as yet there has been no significant shift in the balance of economic power in England, no breaking down of "privilege." If the war were to end now, British labor would have experienced a setback, or a virulent civil war would break out to prevent that. Only if some significant social changes are begun during the war is there any real assurance, says Laski, that there will not be chaos or reaction after the war. He names some of these changes: the Trades Unions Disputes Act passed after the 1926 General Strike, which seriously curtailed union activities, must be repealed; steps toward equalizing educational opportunity must be taken; there must be beginnings of socialization in finance and some basic industries; and India must be freed, for you cannot effectively claim to be fighting for democracy when forty million Britons hold three hundred and fifty million Indians against their will.

What reason is there to think that these steps will be taken? Laski replies, in effect, that the British workers and unions will not keep on fighting much longer unless this is done, so that they may feel confident that it will be economic democracy and not pseudo-democratic plutocracy which "wins the war and the peace." Surely this is the slenderest and most pathetic of threads on which to hang so great a weight of hope. For, under the terrific pounding which Britain is now undergoing, there is no more chance—short of spiritual rebirth—that fundamental progressive social changes will occur than there was in Germany under the terrific economic and psychological pounding which the German people underwent from 1929 through 1933. If the British workers are to keep on producing at top speed and fighting off the invader, as they are exhorted to do, they will be unable to give a moment's thought to basic changes of a progressive character in the social structure. The moment production slackens a little and they stop to insist that something "revolutionary" must be done, a mighty cry will go up: "Surely you do not want to slacken the pace now and let Hitler win. Anyone who rocks the boat now is a slacker, a Fifth Columnist, an emissary, conscious or unconscious, of Hitler—Stalin. We must devote all our energies now to winning the war or there won't be an England any more—Tory, Labor, democratic, socialist, or what have you." At the very moment, as I write, the newspapers are reporting that more drastic conscription of labor is contemplated in Britain and Bevin is being called upon to see to it that his working class mates "play the game," i.e., submit. Incidentally, those who look to Bevin as the instrumentality for achieving a peaceful socialist "revolution" in Britain will do well to remember that he was the most powerful person in the British Trade Union movement in 1926, when that movement abandoned the general strike on which it had entered in support of the sorely distressed miners, and left the latter to carry on alone until exhaustion forced them also to abandon the struggle. It was this backing down of the British Trade Union Congress which gave the Tory government, under Stanley Baldwin, the opportunity to put over that very Trade Union Act which Harold Laski, echoing the view of millions of British workers, says must be repealed before the latter can have any confidence that Toryism is really threatened.

"But surely great changes are going on, in spite of what any one may say or wish—a levelling process, the boss and his workers sleeping together most democratically in the underground shelter." That is true. Furthermore, there will be a lot more of this, as there has been in Germany, where the business of "everybody sacrificing for the national effort" has gone much further, and women and girls, as well as men, are conscripted. There is always "communism" in a besieged fortress—the more desperate the siege the more complete the "communism" among the survivors. There was "communism," levelling down, in Russia during the terrible years after the war, blockade and revolution. Many, in Russia and outside, believed that it was the beginning of the golden age of the communism of social justice, equality and brotherhood for which men have longed through the ages. But it was not. It was the communism of a beleaguered nation, "military communism" as the historians later called it, which is not the road to a truly socialized order, but a road which leads away from it to the pit. As J. Middleton Murry says in the recent article already quoted: "War-socialization is the diabolical antithesis of peace-socialization; and it cannot be changed to peace-socialization except by an effort of social imagination on the grand scale, to which the war-mentality itself is the chief obstacle."

Murry goes on to say: "We will ask our generous progressive friends to come out of their dream world. There is no social justice to be found by marching through the shambles of modern war. Justice may be lovely; but the vision of justice that appears at the end of the vista of war is a phantom, and worse—an angel from hell. The true goddess of Justice is the goddess also of Peace. By that sign you may know her." It seems to me there is no gainsaying that. The moment the British workers, for example, begin to think seriously of a just social order, for England and for other lands, they will begin also to think of putting an immediate end to the war. One quite simple and elementary reason why that is so, we have already indicated. In war you postpone consideration of progressive social changes; all energies must be concentrated on maintaining national unity and winning the war, and that means maintaining the status quo, except insofar as all elements, and especially the masses, are subjected to regimentation for war purposes. The moment you begin to think seriously about eliminating inequality and exploitation at home and contemplate putting some real effort into that, you take some attention and energy away from the war effort. Then you are accused of being consciously or unconsciously an agent of the enemy, a defeatist, and so on. Inevitably at that point you take one of two courses: you yield to the clamor, throw all your energy blindly into the war effort, and consequently postpone again the struggle for social justice; or you decide that the struggle for social justice must not be postponed, even at the risk of weakening the national war effort. If you choose the latter course, you are inevitably driven to seek an end to the fighting in order that you may be free to give yourself to the really important job. You see clearly then that the longer the waste of resources and the disorganization of economic life—your own and the enemy's—goes on, the more completely you are sawing off the limb on which you are sitting; i.e., undermining the material foundations, not only for a new social order, but even for as decent a one as you had when the war began.

You then see the truth which both the Christian prophets and the most penetrating revolutionists have always pointed out: that your real "enemy" is not the other human beings across the border or the persons of another race against whom you have been inflamed. In the deepest sense, the "enemy" is not a person, someone whom you can shoot and thus "solve" your problem. You realize that you are living in a civilization under a political-economic system of which your nation and the enemy nation are alike a part, and which is going to pieces. It may once have served progressive human ends, but its foundations were largely laid in greed and injustice and violence; and, at any rate, it is now everywhere unable to function unless basic economic changes are made. You recognize then that in those countries where the economic deterioration has gone furthest, the most horrible manifestations of cruelty and tyranny are certain to break out, just as a cancer may disfigure one part of the body though it is essentially a disease of the organism and not of one isolated part of it. You will realize, however, that you and your fellow-countrymen are not an essentially different breed of humans from the enemy and that, unless you repent and gain an entirely new view on the whole matter, you will behave just as he does when hunger, chaos, and humiliation overtake you. You will see clearly also that war—so far from being even a temporary and partial solution of the problem of capitalist-imperialist decay—is both an outgrowth and an expression of that decay and an agent for terribly accelerating it. You will see, finally, that insofar as the evil which is overcoming the masses is incarnated in individuals, it is incarnated just as much in the rules and privileged interests of your own country as of other nations; that rather than face the real economic issues at home—putting the unemployed to work, for example—they involve you in war with an enemy "out there" who must always be disposed of first before honest and basic reforms are instituted at home. You will then deal with these "enemies" at home, not indeed by turning the guns on them and "transforming the imperialist war into civil war," but simply by laying down your weapons, ceasing the manufacture of bombers, refusing to cooperate with those who think war is the solution of the nation's ills. But, if you threaten to do that, a mighty cry will ascend to heaven that the enemy people will not hear about it or, if they do, will simply seize the opportunity to sweep on to the conquest of the world. It will be the age-old human cry of those who are deprived of ease, prestige, privilege, power which they have cherished—such as those who sought very hard to come to an understanding with Hitler himself, in order that they might hold on to these things without having to fight.

It is not claimed that a refusal to continue fighting, such as we have sketched, will provide a cheap and easy way to Utopia or even to a fairly tolerable life in the near future. There is no cheap and easy way out. But the assumption that the German people are a special breed of semi-humans who do not react to love and hate, good and evil, as do other men is patently without foundation. The trouble with the world today is that they have reacted just as men usually do in similar circumstances. In the end radically different treatment will produce different results. We have only to remember how the Russian Revolution put the fear of God into rulers and privileged groups for years to get an idea of what might happen—and at not too distant a date—if some people dared to risk a revolution of good will and nonviolence. In any case the only alternative left is suicide.

All this has an important bearing on the role of those progressive but non-pacifist British churchmen whose chief spokesman is the Archbishop of York. These men are to a considerable extent responsible for the exceedingly enlightened provisions for conscientious objectors in the British conscription act and for the fact that, in face of increasing popular pressure, the government appears in the main to be adhering to these provisions. They are greatly concerned about the ecumenical movement in the churches, insisting that the Christian Church is supra-national, that Christians cannot pray for a victory of their own nation in war since they cannot ask for themselves what they are not equally ready to ask for others, and that the church as such cannot bless war. They point out, furthermore, that an economic order based on private ownership and exploitation of basic resources is largely responsible for war and for the other woes of our age, and that, after and even during the war, genuine efforts to abolish privilege and develop a brotherly economic order must be made. This is a great advance over the position taken by any equally representative group of churchmen anywhere in the world during the last war. We may truly be grateful for it and recognize this as a good omen of the part the Church of Christ may eventually play in building a true world community.

But while these men hold that the Church as such must not bless war and that Britain is largely responsible for the emergence of Hitlerism and the outbreak of another war, they accept the common assumption that for the moment the British nation has no alternative except to fight; and that a British victory is, in the political realm, that "lesser evil" which will provide the foundation for

a better world, the achievement of which would be ruled out by a
Hitler victory. When all is said and done, therefore, they are involved in participation in war with all the ethical problems which
that raises for Christians. There is also the fearful risk that, although
they recognize much more clearly and concretely than in the past
that we must work for a world community, the war which they
reluctantly condone will, by its process, shatter the possibility of
achieving world community in our day and, quite possibly, for
decades to come. They recognize that England must repent of her
share in bringing about the war; but is not all continuance of war
itself a terrible evil of which the nation should repent? And how
can men be said to repent unless they cease doing the evil thing?
To say in effect that a nation must repent of a course which has led
to war, but that for the time being it must leave off speculation
about past sins and mistakes and bend all energy to winning another war, seems to be assuming that, in God's economy, "*tomorrow* is the accepted time, the day of salvation." Such a fallacy is
disproved by experience which teaches that the period following
a war is one of moral relapse, not of repentance and new birth.

To return to our political argument, President Roosevelt, as we
have pointed out, sees but two courses open: that which leads to a
military victory of the Rome-Berlin-Tokyo axis or that which leads
to a military victory of the London-Washington (and Moscow?)
axis. He brands as appeaser those who call instead for an effort to
start peace negotiations. It is assumed—and I do not question the
sincerity of the President and many others in these matters—that
if the United States goes all-out for support of Britain, we shall be
playing the role of liberators of oppressed peoples and saviors of
democracy. There are aspects of the situation, however, which throw
serious doubt on that assumption.

Many competent students of history and international affairs
are convinced that, in the early months of 1917, the first World
War had reached a stalemate and that if the European powers had
been left to themselves they would have had no alternative but to
seek a negotiated peace. Such a peace, based on a recognition by
all the powers involved that war offered no solution to their problems and that neither side was in a position to impose cash or other
indemnities on the other, might have led to a relatively sound economic settlement and to serious moves toward disarmament. But
British propaganda and American interpretation of our own "interests" as a sea-power persuaded us that such a negotiated peace

would really be a German-dictated peace. Therefore, we intervened
on the side of France and Britain and made it possible for them
to dictate a peace in 1918, a "solution" which by general admission
was about as bad as it could be.

There are not wanting signs that World War II may have resolved itself into a stalemate. Major General John F. O'Ryan, testi-
fying before the House Foreign Affairs Committee, recently said:
"It is conceivable that in our own interest we should enter the war
and prevent a stalemate." Recent weeks certainly cast doubt on the
possibility of a decisive German victory; but a decisive British victory involving an invasion of the continent, a defeat of the German
land forces, the taking of Berlin, may also be beyond reach and certainly will require a terrific effort. Practically all experts doubt that
it can be done without actual air and naval aid and an expeditionary
force from the United States.

Admittedly it would not be possible today or in the immediate
future to get the American people to consent to another expeditionary force. President Roosevelt feels compelled to give solemn
and explicit assurances on that point. It is quite possible that, in
view of the actual or alleged threat in the Pacific and of other
circumstances, it will not be possible to win popular consent in this
country to the policy of an expeditionary force at any time. That
would mean in effect, whatever the conscious intention may be, that
we would not give Britain the ultimate help needed for a decisive
and final victory over Germany—which, incidentally, might leave
Britain in virtual control of Europe and Africa and a dangerous
naval and commercial rival to this nation. But, unless Britain wins a
decisive victory soon, the "arsenal of democracy" might furnish
arms to Britain until both Germany and Britain were exhausted,
and a British "victory" would be purely nominal. Britain as a world
power would have passed from the scene. The United States as a
world power would have gotten rid of both its European rivals,
Britain and Germany; it would have piled up huge armaments of
its own while supplying Britain; and relatively its position as a
world power might be vastly strengthened.

The least that can be said for this analysis of the actual role the
United States is playing in the game of power politics is that it
cannot be dismissed with a mere shrug of the shoulder—if only
because it follows closely at some points the pattern of our role
in the last war when, in spite of our expeditionary force effort, we
suffered much less than the European nations and were able, for

example, to impose moral equality on Britain. There is good reason to think that there are hard-headed realists in Washington who read the picture in the same terms as those we have set forth and who therefore hold that, in any case, the English-speaking nations and their dependencies will be run from Washington and not from London, after the war is over. According to these analysts, the real point of the Lend-Lease Bill is not so much aid to the British Isles in warding off the specific threat of German invasion as it is giving the President a free hand to intervene by means of various forms of "aid"—"short of nothing"—in Canada, Africa, Australia, the East Indies. Negatively, the purpose would be to keep these areas out of German hands; positively, the effect, if not the conscious aim, would be to make the United States "the arsenal" and the dictator, not only over North and South America, but over English-speaking nations and their dependencies or subjects anywhere, and especially in the lands bordering on the Pacific. The attempt would be made within this empire to maintain a modified capitalism which would engage in economic combat on a huge scale with countries under a totalitarian economy. It would, of course, engage also in feverishly building up armaments in preparation for World War III.

It may be noted, as our analysis in an earlier section of this essay suggests, that even if Britain wins an apparent victory in the present phase of the World War, she may nonetheless have to accept subordination to the United States in the post-war period. The United States, for example, will unquestionably be able to impose naval inferiority on Britain just as, after the last war, we were able to demand equality and thus put an end to more than two centuries of British naval superiority. The economy of the British Isles will be at the mercy of the United States by the same token that her war effort can continue only if this country becomes its arsenal. It would be interesting to know whether British statesman do not see this prospect and believe that the post-war world will be much the same as that of 1939, except that Hitler will have joined the Kaiser in Doorn or will have committed suicide. Or whether some of them see it and are making plans to repudiate any obligations to the United States after the war, on the ground that Britain fought our war for us and any price we may have paid was cheap, and to gird for an intensified economic war against us as well as other survivors, as happened after the last war. Or whether, finally, some of them—those for example who have supported Clarence Streit's

Union Now proposals—see the situation, welcome it, and are consciously working to hasten the process. The circumstances surrounding the coming of Lord Halifax as British Ambassador to the United States while retaining a seat in the British Cabinet would fit in with this interpretation. He was escorted to a British warship by Winston Churchill, in person, transported across the Atlantic in that warship and then met at the United States Naval Academy by the President of the United States, in person, and driven in the President's car to Washington—as the President might have met his own Secretary of State, or the Chief of Staff of his own Army, in an exceptional crisis. Was not this intended to give notice to Hitler and the American people of a virtual merger of British and American forces for the duration of the war? It may well have been also, for those who have eyes to see, a forecast and symbol of the post-war line-up.

On this interpretation, the people of the British Isles are indeed "fighting our war," not as well as, but instead of, their own! We are playing the same role, that of keeping our rivals fighting until they exhaust themselves, which Stalin is playing in Europe and also in Asia, where the Chinese Nationalists receive enough help to keep fighting Japan but never enough to win a decisive victory. Can any Christian who retains a measure of objectivity contemplate with anything but horror and shame the moral state of a post-war United States when, after such an adventure, we return to "normalcy?"—when the new American empire takes shape, when the masses realize what the second crusade for democracy and English-speaking culture was really about, and another "Ohio gang" is in the saddle?

If there is any validity to this analysis, an astounding reversal of supposed roles is involved. Then the honest democratic elements (I am not speaking of agents of foreign powers or isolationists) who urge that the United States keep out of war, and that the possibility of an early negotiated peace be explored, are the realists, the friends of Britain, the defenders of democracy and of the values of Western civilization. On the other hand, those who advocate military aid to Britain, short of war—or short of nothing—are dupes, not indeed of a foreign power, but of American capitalist and imperialist interests. They are, furthermore, the enemies of the British people and are unwittingly helping to dig the grave of democracy. "The shoe is on the other foot" in very truth! Our theological friends who never tire of telling us that nations always act on the basis of self-interest are certainly obligated to consider very carefully whether the United States may not be acting in its interests as a world power, and whether that may not mean acting in the interests of its privileged classes.

If we admit that there is some likelihood that the above analysis is correct, then the least to follow is that the possibility of a negotiated peace should be once more diligently and honestly explored before the United States is committed to complete involvement in the war. Granted that such an exploration involves risks, surely no one thinks that the Roosevelt administration's present course involves no ambiguities, imponderables, or risks!

Actually we should go beyond exposing the unhappy and sordid "realism" that may be masquerading behind the interventionist idealism for which the Administration stands. God calls nations as well as individuals to serve him. He summons this nation today to a course of Christian realism. The political expression of this course would begin with an admission that we carry a full share of responsibility for the tragic state of the world. Surely the absence of any faintest note of humility and penitence in the President's recent addresses is ominous. Christian realism would lead us to renounce war preparation and war as obviously suicidal; to offer to surrender our own special privileges; to participate in lowering tariff walls, in providing access to basic resources on equitable terms to all peoples; to spend the billions we shall otherwise squander on war preparations, and war, for the economic rehabilitation of Europe and Asia, for carrying a great "offensive" of food, medicine, and clothing to the stricken peoples of the world; and to take our full share of responsibility for building an effective federal world government.

People sometimes tell us that "you can't get the United States to make such a proposal." If not, what does that reveal about our own moral position? What, besides our own "interests," are we fighting for in that case? People exclaim that "Hitler would not accept." If we are so certain that he would not, why has someone not made the offer during the eight fateful years since 1933? It would have been so perfect a way to put Hitler finally "on the spot," not with other nations (which does not accomplish much) but with his own people. Or, men exclaim that Hitler would interpret such a proposal as a sign of weakness and would march blithely on to world conquest. Let us assume for the sake of argument that nothing can be done with Hitler. Then it follows inexorably that the problem of statesmanship today is that of driving a wedge between him, or his system, and the German people. There are two ways in which that may be attempted. The first is by military might. So long as we use that way, the German people will be solidified behind Hitler, since they believe—and who shall say without good cause?—that on this basis the only alternative to a victory with Hitler is "a fate worse than Versailles." Furthermore, we separated the German people from the Kaiser by such means and we got Hitler in the Kaiser's place. What monstrosity shall we get in Hitler's place?

Some nation must come forward to reject the idea of a Berlin-Rome-Tokyo military triumph and equally to reject the idea of a London-Washington (Moscow?) military triumph. Inevitably, either spells a dictated peace again, for where there is a victor and a vanquished, there is someone who can write terms and someone who must accept them. Nor have we any moral or historic right to lull ourselves with the promise that if we can only win, we shall establish a righteous peace. As someone has recently put it, if any-one "thinks that conscience, which is not strong enough to prevent a war, will be forceful enough to condition the peace treaty, then he has lost all right to speak to the illusions of even the most naïve form of pacifism." There must be no "appeasement" of the pesent "democratic" regimes and the interests which they represent. These regimes did rule the world before 1914. They were the victors in 1918 and ruled the world again after that. They, above all, are responsible for the catastrophe which has overtaken mankind. They have demonstrated their incapacity, and we reject a peace dictated by them as boding no good for mankind. They are the "Christian" nations who cried, "Lord, Lord," who had "Moses and the proph-ets," and professed to be their followers. Not one whit less than "the publicans and harlots" of international life do they need repentance.

We must have done, then, altogether with the old game of power politics and must begin to play an entirely different game. A great nation such as ours must propose a peace negotiated by peoples on such a basis as we sketched a moment ago.

As Harold Laski correctly pointed out, in the book on which we have already commented, if a people is to have any ground for hoping that a new world may be achieved after war, it must begin shaping such a world at once. Specifically, that would mean recog-nizing that we here in the United States are hypocrites or else utterly incapable of rational thought if we make ourselves believe that we really are interested in stamping out the Hitlerian doctrine and practice of racism while we retain our "Oriental Exclusion" laws and continue to subject millions of Negroes to Jim Crow laws; confinement in ghettoes; exclusion from universities, clubs, and churches; discrimination of the rankest kind in jobs and even in the military forces that are to stamp out the evil of racism. So long as this situation obtains, we make it clear that we are interested not in stamping out racial discrimination and injustice but in maintaining our own brand in comfort and security. Likewise we show ourselves to be hypocrites, or incapable of rational thought, if we tell ourselves that we shall create a new and decent economic order after the war; when we have been proved no more able than any other nation to put our unemployed to work, except by the device of an armament boom, and when we conscript life at the same time that we ease up limitations on profits on war orders. Thus we make it clear that we are not interested in ending exploitation and insanity in economic life but in having our own brand of exploitation and insanity dominant.

Does anyone honestly believe that if, by a great national effort, we had put an end to racial prejudice and discrimination; had put our unemployed to work; had been ready to participate honestly in providing equitable access to the earth's resources, for all peoples, instead of vainly seeking to protect ourselves behind tariff and immigration walls—that it would have been possible for Hitlerism to emerge? Does our hesitation to embark now on such a pioneering venture spring from a genuine fear that the German and Japanese people will prefer what they now endure to such a prospect of deliverance? Do we believe that God will not answer our prayers for peace? Or, do we suffer from "the panic caused by the prospect of answered prayer"? For, "the answer to the prayer for universal peace involves disarmament, the surrender of all foreign possessions, and the displacement of competition by the fullest cooperation—exactions to which Christian faith is at present apparently unequal."

Are there risks involved in the course which we propose? Undoubtedly. But our choice is between certain mass suicide if we cling to the method of war or being willing to risk something for an alternative that holds at least some promise. And there is Christ's promise that those who have even "a little faith" shall by the grace of God's Spirit remove mountains.

Postscript June 25, 1941

While American citizens were reflecting upon the events which followed President Roosevelt's May 27 speech—including the sinking of the *Robin Moor,* the President's blistering denunciation of the German government for this act, and the outbreak of fighting between the British and the collaborationist French forces in the French mandate of Syria—news of the German invasion of Soviet Russia in the dawn of Sunday, June 22, broke on the astonished world. Those who exclaimed, when the Nazi-Soviet pact was signed in August, 1939, that "anything can happen" in the world we now inhabit, have been proven good prophets. It would be foolhardy for anyone, including the ruling inner cliques in the world's capitals, to claim that he could give an adequate and rational analysis of the present situation and forecast the course of the fighting. But in the midst of the bewildering confusion there are three observations which can be confidently made.

First, nowhere in the world do the common people know what is going on behind the scenes and nowhere do they exercise any real influence on the decisions being made. This holds good also for the United States, where the President states publicly, and without apology or even explanation, that he and "our military and naval technicians"—not Congress—are making plans to use our armed forces to see that aid gets to Britain "and all who, with Britain, are resisting Hitlerism or its equivalent with force of arms." Since China was prominently mentioned in the May 27 address, as among the nations resisting aggressors, it would appear that the President is prepared to use American armed forces in the Pacific as well as the Atlantic, if in his judgment the need arises.

Second, the war is spreading relentlessly and ever more rapidly. More and more millions of human beings are drawn into the vortex. The United States is the one great power not involved in open "shooting war," and we are obviously drawing nearer the brink. On June 23, a columnist in the New York *World-Telegram & Sun* wrote: "To an experienced eye there can be no doubt, after reading innocent but censored letters from young naval officers, that we have already sunk Nazi submarines." Is there anyone who would be greatly surprised if, in a month or a week or in twenty-four hours, that statement were verified?

Third, as the war spreads it makes less and less sense, partly because wholesale destruction of life, property, and values is insane, but also because it is increasingly obvious that what nations fight for is survival and domination by whatever means. Thus, Winston Churchill—the moment Stalin and Hitler have fallen out—can point to his record of more than twenty-five years of denunciation of Bolshevism and efforts to break Russia, declare that he "will unsay no words" that he has spoken about Communism, and then declaim: "All this fades away before the spectacle which is now unfolding. The past with its crimes, its follies, and its tragedies flashes away." He sees the soldiers of the Red army "guarding their fields which their fathers have tilled from time immemorial . . . guarding their homes, where mothers and wives pray." Then, suddenly remembering, I suppose, that yesterday Bolshevik Russia was "Godless," he says, "Ah, yes, for there are times when all pray"— except, it appears, Germans and their allies.

He promises, "Any man or state who fights against Nazidom will have our aid. Any man or state who marches with Hitler is our foe." Thus as in the last war did the Russia of Nicholas, so in this one the Russia of Stalin takes her place among the saviors of civilization, the defenders of democracy and of the Christian faith! Unabashed, Mr. Churchill speaks of the "valor and constancy" with which the Czarist armies fought to "gain a victory from all share in which they were, through no fault of ours, utterly cut out." Is there any doubt that if Japan should "see the light" and desert the Axis, British and American official opinion about "the Japanese devils" would also change overnight?

The longer the war goes on the more senseless it becomes, because the chances fade away for anything but an abysmally disastrous outcome. In the past it has been suggested that if Stalin succeeded in staying out of the war, he rather than Churchill or Roosevelt or Hitler might be the receiver of a bankrupt Europe. What are the alternatives now? There is the remote possibility of a Russian victory or at least a failure of Germany to win against Stalin. In that case Communism will sweep Germany—and, in a sense, with British and American aid. Or Germany may win and, in that case, Nazism will dominate Russia at least for a time. Or this may be the beginning of mutual slaughter of Germans and Russians on a titanic scale, ending in a stalemate of complete exhaustion. What can that mean but the descent of another Dark Age on Europe?

The war becomes increasingly senseless, because even if the

London-Washington axis "wins" the war, the possibility becomes ever more remote that it will establish a tolerable peace. No responsible British or American statesmen give any indication that, in winning the war, they will resist the demand: "This time we must not make the mistake we made the last time and be too easy on the Huns. We must smash them, so they can never raise their heads again." As a matter of fact, British and American leaders make it clear—in the language of diplomacy of course—that they fully share this purpose. Thus, Anthony Eden in an address on May 29, obviously calculated to form part of the same pattern with the Roosevelt pronouncement of May 27, pays lip service to the idea that in a "system of free economic cooperation" which the Washington-London axis will institute, after having firmly established control of sea and air (and perhaps most of the land surface of the earth), "Germany must play a part." Then Eden proceeds, much more firmly and precisely: "But here I draw a firm distinction. We must never forget that Germany is the worst master Europe has yet known. Five times in the last century she has violated the peace. She must never be in a position to play that role again. Our political and military terms of peace will be designed to prevent repetition of Germany's misdeeds." In that same address, Mr. Eden dismisses, with a smugness and self-righteousness that seem utterly tragic, any notion that "the democracies" might have selfish and questionable aims of their own: "It is obvious that we have no motive of self-interest prompting us to economic exploitation of Germany or the rest of Europe. This is not what we want nor what we could perform!"

Mr. Churchill certainly does all in his power to arouse and encourage the spirit of vengeance and witch-hunting which was manifested in the hundreds of letters which, according to *The New York Times* of June 17, were received by the London *Daily Mail* in answer to a query raised in connection with the Kaiser's death as to what should be done with Hitler, "when the Nazis have finally been defeated." The largest section—twenty-five percent—of the correspondents want to see Hitler "exhibited in a cage—proceeds to be given to bombed victims." The death penalty, "to be treated as a lunatic," or "to be handed over to the Poles or Jews" *(sic)* were other suggestions. Churchill approaches ever nearer Hitler's justly detested vituperative vulgarity in painting Hitler as a "monster of wickedness," and the German armies as composed of "the dull, drilled, docile, brutish masses of the Hun soldiery, plodding on like a swarm of crawling locusts," and in promising to make "the German people"—note that phrase—"taste and gulp each month a sharper does of the miseries they have showered upon mankind."

Noteworthy, too, is the fact that there is no serious talk among responsible statesmen today about disarmament or drastic reduction of armaments after the war, but instead frequent declarations that we must look forward to maintaining vast armed forces for an indefinite period.

Faced with such developments, there are apparently multitudes who confidently expect that all will be well because not Mr. Churchill but progressive British laborites and churchmen will write the peace if Britain wins. I cannot imagine a more extreme and tragic example of wishful thinking than thus to assume that when Churchill has become the greatest national hero in all British history by winning the war, it will be possible to say to him: "We could not win the war without you; but we have known all along that you were a Tory old fogy, a tough imperialist, and a vengeful militarist, not fit to give the British and the world a good peace. We do not need you for that and we shall now take command!"

Indeed the Archbishop of York himself, leader among the non-pacifist churchmen of Great Britain, has already in effect admitted that there is no substance to this dream and, in a recent article in *The Churchman* (summarized in *The Christian Century* for June 25), has outlined peace terms which outdo Versailles. Though visualizing an eventual permanent settlement in which all nations, including Germany, take part on equal terms, he says Germany must first be punished as the guilty nation. It would have been better if, after the armistice in 1918, there had followed "a march across Germany and a temporary occupation of Berlin." The interim settlement this time "should be in part penal." One suggestion which deserves careful consideration is that during this interim period, "the ancient German nations should be reconstituted as they were before the rise of Bismarck"—!

And what is ahead for the United States? It seems clearer each day that we shall be the next nation to seek world domination—in other words, to do what we condemn Hitler for trying to do. The avowed position of the Roosevelt administration, and of all "interventionists," is that if Hitler wins this will make complete militarization and dictatorship necessary here in order that we may successfully engage in a life-and-death struggle for survival with Hitler and his allies or henchmen.

And our course will not be fundamentally different if we win the war, and we and our allies (or more accurately dependents, since we shall have in our "arsenal of the democracies" the guns without which even Britain admittedly cannot survive) dictate the peace. Both internal and external conditions will indeed make this inevitable unless we are prepared to reverse our present course. As for the latter, the world after the war will obviously be a sadly disordered one. It is hardly to be expected that no "threat" to American supremacy or American interests will exist anywhere in such a world. We shall be told by all who believe that security lies, in the last resort, in armed might that, in such a world, our only safety lies in making or keeping ourselves "impregnable." But that means being in a position to meet any potential combination of enemies, and that, in turn, means being able to decide by preponderance of military might any international issue that may arise—which would put us in the position in which Hitler is trying to put Germany.

The internal situation, after a devastating war which leaves us with a huge national debt and in a world where the struggle of nations for existence, trade, etc., has been intensified, will be dominated by this consideration: if, in peacetime, in the richest and most favorably situated nation on earth, we could not find work for our unemployed save by resort to an armament boom, peacetime conscription and war, the forces and leadership which led us into war will not, on the morrow of victory, by some magic know how to solve this problem under seriously aggravated circumstances. They will fear revolt of the masses if the armies are demobilized and the armaments industries dismantled. Accordingly we shall be told that the "unlimited emergency" continues and that the wartime dictatorship must continue. Surely it is only mental blindness or self-righteousness that can enable anyone to contemplate with anything but horror what such dictatorship, armed to dominate all the seas, will mean for the United States or for the world.

Under these circumstances, we of the Fellowship of Reconciliation are as firmly opposed as ever to American entry into the war. So long as America is not in all the way, a remote hope remains that we may yet choose a course of dynamic peace action. This does not mean that we have any sympathy for the position of those who believe in war and violence for their own purposes, but whose concern about the interests of Germany, Japan, Russia, or some other nation leads them to oppose American entry and perhaps even to sabotage American war efforts.

We see no hope for the world in a Hitler victory and a so-called "peace" based upon it, nor in an "armistice," which would be simply a state of suppressed warfare during which new and vaster power combinations would aim feverishly for a greater and more brutal conflict. Neither do we share the views of those who, equally with the Roosevelt administration, believe in colossal armaments and are concerned to build up an "impregnable defense" for American soil and national interests, but who hold that our "national interest" is best served by a foreign policy inclined toward "isolationism," and by keeping out of the war *now* so as to be better able to fight Hitler later, if we deem it necessary. We do not impugn the motives of these citizens any more than we do those of the Administration and its supporters. But, insofar as the debate between these two camps is one of military strategy, it is not a concern of religious pacifists. For the rest, we do not believe that vast armaments in the hands of such opponents of the Administration will, in the long run, go unused or are any more likely to be used for human welfare than the present Administration is able so to use them. Furthermore, these opponents have given no indication that they have a satisfactory economic program and that, therefore, they too may not eventually prove instruments for the establishment of an American form of Fascism.

In a world in which "isolationism" is no longer possible, which is inexorably driven to seek some sort of political, economic and spiritual unity, the only genuinely hopeful alternative to an attempt at world domination by one nation is a dynamic pacifism inspired by and moving toward a Christian universalism. We must do our thinking as members of the one human family in God, not as those who are first of all servants of any national state. Our own nation must confess its share of responsibility for the present hurt of the world. It must be prepared to sacrifice a substantial measure of its own irresponsible right "to determine whether and when and where our interests are attacked and our security threatened." It must publicly announce, as deep down in their hearts the masses everywhere sense, that war is suicide and that it must be renounced now while there is yet time.

The Council of the Fellowship of Reconciliation, at its June meeting, sent a letter to the President, outlining some of the main points of such a dynamic peace as we envisage:

"The basic principles of a peace which would command our 100 percent support would include:

1. That no attempt be made to fasten sole war-guilt on any nation or group of nations. Instead, all people should take up the works of repentance in a common effort to halt the break-up of civilization and to build a good life which the earth's resources and modern technology make possible for all.

2. That all peoples be assured of equitable access to markets and to essential raw materials; and also that immigration and emigration be internationally controlled with a view to the welfare of every nation. If, for example, this should require the progressive lowering of tariff barriers, the United States would do its share in achieving this end.

3. That there will be immediate and drastic reduction of armament all round and that steps to move from an armament-and-war economy to an economy of peace be taken as rapidly as possible.

4. That the United States offer to invest the billions that it would otherwise devote to war preparations and war, in a sound international plan for the economic rehabilitation of Europe and Asia, and in order to stay the inroads of famine and pestilence which otherwise threaten to engulf mankind.

5. That the United States take its full share of responsibility, with other nations, for the building of federal world government along some such lines as those of our American union.

"A peace proposal like the above would differ radically from a peace dictated by the totalitarian powers, and equally from a peace dictated by victorious democratic powers as in the last war. It would differ also from an armistice entered into only because of war weariness or fear of war's consequences. It would bring a new and creative element into the picture. When we remember with what joy the masses hailed the bright promise which seemed to be held out by President Wilson's Fourteen Points, and that the masses now are far less enthusiastic about what war can bring them than they were two decades ago, there is surely a possibility that to such dynamic peace action there would be a tremendous, spontaneous response which dictators, militarists, and exploiters everywhere could not ignore."

Since the crisis is so desperate, we may not cease to speak, work, and pray for this peace so long as one ray of hope remains. If the one way of true peace is rejected, an "unlimited emergency" in very truth confronts the Fellowship of Reconciliation and all who reject the way of violence and war. We must discipline ourselves to endure privation and persecution if they come. Daily, in humility and love, we must show forth toward all men and in all relationships the power of that life which "taketh away the occasion of all war." We must, throughout the land, and all the lands, be welded together in faith in the Eternal, and in those "little fellowships of the holy imagination, that keep alive in men sensitivity to moral issues," and which have repeatedly demonstrated that no tyranny or terror can destroy them, and out of whose fidelity and travail a new world presently comes forth.

War Is the Enemy

1942 It would be pertinent at this time to explain the underlying philosophy of those who, in the face of the present world situation, hold to the way of nonviolence, with a view toward clarification rather than argument. It is a prerequisite of fruitful thought and discussion in such a crisis that we should think of each other, pacifists and non-pacifists, as fellow-searchers for truth, not as intellectual adversaries. In each of the diverse positions which men hold there will be something that is valid, that represents an effort to respond to the situation, a fidelity to the truth as they see it. Recognizing this is a way of achieving at-oneness with our fellows.

At-oneness, however, must not be confused with appeasement. The truth is often hard and harsh. There is sometimes a tendency, therefore, to refrain from stating issues sharply and clearly, to gloss over differences, perhaps on the pretext that "our agreements are so much greater than our differences after all," and that bringing out the issues and facing them "does not make for reconciliation." Similarly we often hear it said that in the church or religious meeting, or elsewhere, "controversial issues" ought not to be discussed.

Grave dangers may lurk behind these plausible suggestions. No reconciliation—within a single human soul, between man and wife, in a family, an industry, a nation, or between nations—was ever built on a lie or a half-truth. "Ye shall know the truth, and the truth shall make you free"; conversely, aught but the truth leads to slavery and strife. Have we not all experienced this many times? What a

healing coolness and balm come into any situation the moment nobody is pretending any more, nobody is holding anything back. Even
though it be a very difficult situation, the poison has been sucked out
of it when those involved speak their minds freely.

For the individual, salvation, reconciliation with God, begins
with the bitter experience of facing the truth about himself, shedding all pretense and evasion, and crying out, "God, be merciful to
me, a sinner." In our relations with one another, although it ill
becomes us to try to beat our version of the truth into our neighbor's
brain with arguments, we owe it to him to bear faithful witness to
the truth as we see it, holding nothing back and in nought equivo-
cating. And any parent knows that making oneself agreeable to a
child is not the same as loving him.

Sometimes, behind our reticences, there is a subtle snobbish-
ness, a feeling of "why bother to discuss with him or tell him what
I think: he wouldn't understand anyway." There is no greater
honor a man can pay his fellows, no greater service he can render
them, than to share with them such truth as has been vouchsafed to
him. And, as for the proposal to avoid "controversial issues," usually
it amounts to a counsel of despair, for if an issue is a real one there
are bound to be differences of opinion; it is bound to be "controversial."

Much the same observations apply to proposals that a mora-
torium be declared on the discussion of certain matters for a certain
time—for example for the duration of the war—and that during this
period pacifists should devote themselves exclusively to "works of
mercy and healing." That pacifists should be not mere talkers, but
practical friends and helpers, and especially in wartime, can hardly
be too often or too emphatically stated. We have no desire to obstruct
our fellow citizens in the performance of what they regard as their
patriotic duty. "There is a time for silence," and probably many of
us talk too much. We are not all called to perform the same tasks
in the same way. Nor must we press impatiently for immediate results, like the child who sows his seeds one day and digs them up the
next to see if they are sprouting. Having given witness to the truth
as best we can, we must be content to let it make its own way in the
minds and hearts of men.

But the idea that in wartime there might be a general mora-
torium on the preaching of our philosophy and gospel, including their
application to the immediate concrete situation, and that this somehow would make for reconciliation, seems to me unsound. Let us

suppose that the religious-pacifist analysis of war, of its effects, of
its evils, is suspended. Obviously that does not mean that people will
have no other ideas presented to them, that no analysis of current developments is attempted. It does mean that what the religious pacifist
regards as false and dangerous ideas are presented, but no criticism
and no alternatives. Why should we regard such conduct as democratic, or as loyal on our part to our fellows? We hope that some
day men will experience a great revulsion against war, will lay down
their arms, and cease to trust those who advocate or acquiesce in the
method of war. If in that hour we try to tell them of a better way
will they not ask, "Why did you keep still while we were engaged
in senseless slaughter? And why should we have any special confidence in you who took pains to keep your counsel until everybody
agreed with you?"

Surely the time to witness against tragic, self-righteous distortion of the truth is at the moment when it is widely proclaimed and
believed. Moreover, silence and passivity in the presence of false-
hood, injustice and oppression, and the waging of war, is likely to
mean that for a momentary and delusive sense of unity with our
"own folk" we pay in the coin of alienation from the victims
of injustice and from God's children on the other side of the border.
And the reconciliation with our own people is certain to be temporary and unreal; we have not really done them a service when, by
our silence, we permit the impression to stand, for example, that we
acquiesce in the version of the Japanese mentality and character
which prevails in so many American circles today. For what men
need is not that other men should agree with their ideas or be indulgent toward them. What they need to save them from "the hell of
fire" is to be able to believe in themselves, in truth, in an inexorable
moral order, in the God of Love. Men always have been helped so to
believe by the sight of men who were true to themselves, who refused to blunt "the Word of God which is a two-edged sword," who
could "hate" father, mother, wife, child, their own life, for God's
sake. These men, though in their life they may have been rejected
and crucified, have always been the great reconcilers, the centers
around which human societies were built.

Often it is true we cannot speak or act where conflict rages and
evil is being done, because we do not love enough. We know that our
eye is not single, that we are not disinterested, that we desire the
satisfaction of setting somebody right rather than the right itself.
It is true that while we are in this condition we cannot speak, or

that if we do, we merely bungle or destroy; our only course, then, is to change our condition.

The reconciliation which must take place in our own minds and spirits, whether we be pacifists or non-pacifists, is promoted when we try to think through each problem with our fellows with something of that innocence and freshness and childlikeness and humility which, Jesus taught, is the gateway to truth and felicity. In other words, in each moment we seek to divest ourselves of any notion that our knowledge is sufficient and final; of prejudices; of inappropriate emotions. The moment we find resistance and resentment against an idea stiffening our mental attitude, stridency creeping into our voices, we should examine ourselves. It will be the signal that there is something in that idea which we have not yet been willing to take fully into account. Our highly emotional "certainty" that it is absurd will really mean that deep down we are not sure of our own position.

Our unwillingness to be reconciled to truth, which is a manifestation of God, to accept it in its fullness and with our whole mind ("Thou shalt love the Lord thy God with all thy mind") is one of the fundamental causes of division in life, of the divided self, the divided human family. On the other hand, almost nothing can do so much to increase our spiritual health and power, our effectiveness in the work of reconciliation, as to discipline ourselves to discern and renounce our prejudices. When we think of our insights as having finality, as something to be possessed and defended, we set up a wall against God who is the Source of Light and whom we can receive only if we become infinitely receptive like little children.[1]

[1] So important is this matter that I want to call attention to a psychologist's presentation of it. Dr. Trigant Burrow, Scientific Director of the Lifwyn Foundation, in an article entitled "The Human Equation" in *Mental Hygiene* for April, 1941, speaks of a "subtle attitude of secret self-propitiation . . . a delusive sense of personal approbation" in people and in social groups as a most pernicious danger to society. "There is no question but that" such a "one-sided ideology leads to a two-sided wrangle . . . There would be no question of a two-sided wrangle, individual or social, if man's *total powers of observation* were brought to bear" upon the situation. The self which thus tries to justify itself and which sees itself standing over against others, rather than indissolubly bound to others, both limited and sustained by them in the attempt to apprehend truth, necessarily sees the world, any problem, in a partial, distorted way, not as a whole and objectively. Furthermore, it is a divided self, it cannot function with its whole, undivided attention, cannot *give* freely, unreservedly, *to* the situation. It has been, says Dr. Burrow, "the outstanding finding" of his "laboratory of human biology that *the brain of man*, unlike other organs in the body, *does not now operate as a function-*

Now in the degree that we have divested ourselves of inner resistance to the truth and have developed a readiness to receive it from whatever source, we are also enabled to "speak the truth—in love." We can hope that our fellows may see and come to welcome the light that we have. And we can let our testimony go forth, let our light shine, and not, out of a secret cowardice or false modesty, which is also "self-propitiation" and self-indulgence, put our light "under a bushel, but on a stand so that it may shine to all that are in the house."

It does not, however, follow that disinterested love invariably wins an immediate and predictable victory. That has not, alas, been the Eternal Father's experience with us; and in this as in other respects, "the servant is not above his Master." There is no reconciliation through the medium of any partial love, but only through a love that is prepared to pay the final price, which lasts unto and through death. The final price is not always required; often it is, and always the readiness to pay must be clearly demonstrated. Certainly, until individuals and nations are prepared to sacrifice as much in practicing reconciliation and nonviolence as they sacrifice in the pursuit of war, we cannot reasonably expect an end of wars. It is a fact, as well established as any in history, that human enmities are healed and human communities are built through the process of costing, sacrificial love. The apostle Paul spoke, not of a remote theological dogma but of this demonstrable truth when he wrote to the Ephesians: "Ye that once were far off are made nigh *in the blood of Christ.*" He who would save men and heal strife first must unite in himself both reconciliation and a new order. He must "create in himself, of the two, one new man, so making peace and reconciling both in one body unto God through the cross, *having slain the enmity thereby.*" To what as yet uncalculated sacrifice, in prayer, in giving, in witnessing, in renunciation of war, in service to human need, are we called in order that in us the world's enmity may be slain!

From this vantage point, then, let us consider for a moment the problems confronting our own nation and all the world's peoples in this grim hour. Many sincere persons are saying: "We are faced

---

ing whole." He has only a "specialized, restrictive use of his part-brain." He must supplant this with "the total function of man's brain." How? "Applying universal principles to a universal situation, man needs to adjure his habitual partitive approach to the problem of his behavior, and to *encompass this problem of his own making with the whole of himself.*" (Italics by A. J. Muste.)

with a terrible dilemma, a choice of diabolical evils. We know what it means to resort to war, war under modern conditions and with modern weapons, war on the planetary scale which is required to stop Hitler and the other aggressors. We recognize that we share to a large extent in responsibility for things having come to their present pass. But, as things stand now, we cannot believe that anything except decisive defeat in war can stop the sweep of the utterly inhuman, brutal dictatorships. The possibility of a hegemony of Nazi might and the Nazi philosophy of life over the world, over our own children, for a generation, many generations, possibly centuries, seems to us an evil so monstrous that it is better to resort to war on the chance that we may prevent it than to stand aside from the conflict. We have no illusions about war or about our own superior virtues; therefore we believe that we can fight without bitterness and hate. If, by the grace of God, we win, we shall make a wiser, more Christian use of our victory than we made the last time. We believe the English-speaking world has learned a bitter lesson as a result of the last war and of the peace which we lost following that war. We shall not make those mistakes again."

It would require a whole book even to begin to deal with all the problems presented here. We must therefore confine ourselves to a brief statement of what seem the basic elements in religious-pacifist criticism of this position. We take the points in the preceding paragraph in reverse order so as to come last to the most fundamental issue.

In the first place, we believe that it is a dangerous delusion to think that if the United States and its allies were to win, we should make a much better use of our opportunity than we did the last time. This argument assumes that the course followed ever since the last war was a major factor in bringing on the outbreak of the present war. Yet, since the outbreak of war in 1939, the United States has followed step for step a course similar to that followed in 1914-1917. The result is that we are again completely involved in total, world-wide war. Every indication seems to point to our following the same familiar pattern from this point on, i.e., to aim at a decisive military victory, one which indeed will cripple our national enemies much more completely and give us a much greater relative superiority than before. But we tell ourselves that, having arrived with fatal precision at that point, a miracle will happen. The momentum acquired in the terrific plunge downhill into which the nations are pouring all their energies will disappear as if by magic.

We shall suddenly get off this road and strike out boldly in another direction. What reason have we to believe this? Surely we have a right to ask for concrete evidence.

When we examine that concrete evidence, I think we find either that it is very shaky or that it points in quite the opposite direction. For example, men cite the better treatment of conscientious objectors and the extent to which civil liberties are being preserved in Britain and the United States. But it cannot be denied that these things occur within a general context of increasing concentration of power in the executive, regimentation of the entire population, and the gearing of all energies to war purposes, and that it is these developments that are decisive. Furthermore, the period after a great war is always one of catastrophic spiritual let-down; and we see no good reason for supposing that it can be otherwise this time.

Will those who write the peace this time, whoever they are, have more favorable conditions with which to work than did Wilson and Lloyd George? To ask the question is to answer it in the negative, though it is safe to say that few have even tried to imagine and none can really visualize what conditions will be after many more months, or years, of war and blood-letting; after the subjugated peoples of Europe turn upon the Germans and wreak vengeance upon them (avowedly a part of Allied strategy); after pestilence, famine, social chaos have done their work. If the job of policing the situation proved too much after the last war and ended in the debacles of 1929 and 1939, what reason to expect a different result now?

Furthermore, responsible leaders quite frankly pitch their objectives much lower than did the statesmen of the last war and of the "peace." Their frankness may be to their credit, but we cannot safely discount the significance of their announced aims. So able and temperate an expert in international affairs as John Foster Dulles has said of the Atlantic Charter: "In its present form, it falls far short of the conceptions of President Wilson, and *short even of their expression in the Treaty of Versailles.*" During the last war, we said that we must disarm Germany and that we too must promptly disarm, since not to do so could only mean further war. This time, our statesmen frankly say that we do not think in terms of no more war following the present one; that we must disarm "the aggressors" even more completely than before; "make it impossible for them to raise their heads ever again," while we remain "suitably protected." This can only mean American-British military domination of the earth. It seems to us to require a grave arrogance, or a great simplicity, to suppose that in the context of the post-war situation this can spell aught but disaster for us and for mankind. Altogether the prospect for a "better peace" is scarcely so promising as to constitute a convincing reason for participation in war.

In the second place, a word about the contention that war can be waged without hate and bitterness. People come back from England and report that they have not encountered a single trace of these emotions. It may be that our penchant for seeing and hearing what we want to see and hear plays a part here. Certainly expressions calculated to stir up hate and contempt for a people are not absent from Mr. Churchill's references to Germans. Dr. Arthur Salter, M. P., stated in the House of Commons recently: "Open retaliation and revenge are now being advocated in the highest quarters. No apologies are being offered for the indiscriminate bombing of women and children. Now we have photographs showing whole streets of working-class houses being blown sky-high by our bombs." It is evident that hatred for the Japanese has been fairly general in the United States in recent weeks. The training in our military forces is not based on the theory that teaching our young men to love their enemies is the best way to make good soldiers of them.

If it is true that people do all that modern warfare requires without being aware of any emotions of hate and anger, feeling quite composed and virtuous and "sweet," it is evident that we are faced with a grave psychological and moral problem. This would not be the first time that such a phenomenon has been witnessed. The men who tortured and killed the victims of the Inquisition did so "for the greater glory of God," and out of compassion, in order to save the souls of those victims! The amazing and dangerous situation into which we may now be moving was suggested by the columnist who recently urged that we need not grow hysterical with hate as we did in the last war, and went on to say that, while it might become a military necessity to blot out whole Japanese cities by bombing from the air, we should do so calmly and objectively, with no poison of hate in our hearts. But what has happened here? As Professor Harper Brown, of Wellesley, pointed out in a recent discussion, a complete splitting of personality has taken place. There is no relationship between what men feel and what they do. If this process continues there will be no limit to the deeds we may perform, the havoc that may be wrought, while all the time we experience no inner turmoil, feel quite composed, even congratulate ourselves on the fact that we do not experience the emotions which in ordinary mortals accompany the performance of acts of destruction, deceit and killing. Under other circumstances that would be regarded as an advanced form of insanity. Perhaps the ordinary mortal who is not free from rages and hate when performing the acts of a soldier is, after all, a better integrated personality and nearer to a state of grace, whether from the standpoint of the psychologist or of the gospel. And what will be the personal and the social reactions as the divorce between inner state and outward act becomes more complete—and in that hour of awakening and return to reality when men contemplate with unveiled eyes what they have done "for the greater glory of God" and in "love" for their enemies?

We come thus to the most crucial question. Men of goodwill recognize how terrible is the dilemma, but choose war because, in spite of everything, it seems the only way to prevent the establishment of a diabolical, demoniacal tyranny over all men, the only chance to build a decent world again. Here, we are face to face with the problem of calculating the consequences of our decisions and actions in complex social situations; and at this point all of us, pacifists and non-pacifists alike, suffer from the limitation that we are human and fallible and can see only a short distance ahead and calculate only a few of the consequences of our decisions, and these only imperfectly. Political campaigns and wars and treaty-making seldom are what they appear to be or accomplish what the actors in them professedly or actually seek to accomplish. If, therefore, non-pacifist friends assert that I may not be fully aware of the consequences of my refusal to support the United States government in war, I readily agree that this is so. But neither can they calculate the consequences of their actions; certain it is that in helping to release the terrible forces of modern warfare, they release forces over which they have no control, and to judge by the experience of the last war, they may live to regret the consequences bitterly.

Are we then utterly without guide and compass in this wilderness? Are we condemned to mere guess-work? Aldous Huxley has given an answer to that question in his remarkable recent book, *Grey Eminence:* "It is by no means impossible to foresee, in the light of past historical experience, the *sort* of consequences that are likely, in a general way, to follow certain *sorts* of acts. Thus, from the records of past experience, it seems sufficiently clear that the consequences attendant on a course of action involving large-scale war, violent revolution, unrestrained tyranny and persecution are likely to be bad."

Another way to put the answer would be to point out that, in the more restricted realm of personal relationships, we are guided by our moral codes and moral impulses. We do not deceive, steal, assault, blackmail, even though it looks as if the immediate consequences in a specific situation might be favorable. Whether we think of moral codes and impulses as expressions of an objective moral order or simply as representing what the race has found by experience to be good in the long run, does not in this connection make any important difference. The point is that, in a real sense, conscience, the Inner Light, is the only guide among the complexities of life. What we know surely, and the only thing we can know, is that evil cannot produce good, violence can produce only violence, love is forever the only power that can conquer evil and establish good on earth.

Here I bear witness for a moment out of personal experience. Like most of the others in the small Christian pacifist group during the last war, I was ill-informed about economics and politics, utterly unsophisticated. Now, when I hear my non-pacifist friends, including many who consider themselves conservative and substantial citizens, talking about "choice between evils," and the need of being "realistic," when I hear them say that we must first get the situation in hand by violence and only then can we set about building a brave new world, I can close my eyes and feel that I am hearing the communists who, for a time, converted me to Marxism-Leninism!

Two things emerged out of my experiences, as pacifist and later as Marxist-Leninist, which greatly influence my outlook today. The pacifists of the last war, ill-informed and unsophisticated though we were, somehow sensed what the war was really about, sensed the unreliability of the war propaganda, sensed what would come after the war. Later, when I had ceased to be a pacifist, I became much better informed. But presently I found that, although I was much more experienced in analyzing what lay just ahead and taking the next step, my grasp of the total development in my own life and in the world became more and more fumbling; I drifted into a complete opportunism which brought outward confusion and inner disintegration. The only explanation I have for this experience is this: the law that evil can be overcome only by its opposite, i. e., by a dynamic, sacrificial goodness, is so basic in the structure of the universe, so central for an understanding of life and history, that if one stands at that center he sees things in clear focus. He may not know much, but that much he will see clearly. Contrarily, if one moves away from that center, he may know and see vastly more, but it will be out of focus, blurred.

Secondly, Lenin taught me that if you are going to be "realistic," you must be thoroughly realistic. If the success of your movement may depend on violence applied effectively at the right moment, then it is criminal to prepare "too little and too late." You must accustom your people to the idea of violence, you must acquire weapons. Since in war the offensive may be the best defense, you must be ready for that too. From this experience I became convinced that, in spite of all the brains, the vast energies, the titanic sacrifices that went into the revolutionary movement, the effort to establish democracy by dictatorship, brotherhood by terrorism and espionage, fullness of life by war and violence, would leave you with dictatorship, terrorism and strife, not with the fair goals of which men had dreamed. The end could not be divorced from the means; the means thwarted and corrupted the idealistic end. All the leading early revolutionists in Russia, except Lenin and Stalin, were liquidated by assassination or exile; no fewer than three million peasants were destroyed in the forcible collectivization of agriculture, and the Russians are so far from having achieved the classless society of which ancient seers and modern revolutionists and proletarians dreamed that an analysis of statistics published in the Soviet press reveals that the upper eleven or twelve percent of the population receives approximately half of the national income. (This differentiation is even sharper than in the United States, where the upper ten percent receives approximately 35 percent of the national income.) Demoralization and defeat overtook the modern revolutionary movements in all other important centers also, as for example in Germany, often spoken of as "the classic land of Marxism," where the degeneration of the whole movement of social protest and revolt had gone so far that when Hitler came to power it did not offer even a gesture of resistance, violent or nonviolent.

Few would question the analysis of the relationship between means and ends in this case. In the 1920s and 1930s, people were practically unanimous in pointing out that World War I had failed miserably to accomplish what good people had believed it would; and college faculties still contain many members who are troubled about the "souls" of their students, because the students still believe what the professors told them about war a few years ago. Again we ask: what reason have men to believe that, "this time," it all will be different?

So much for the negative side of our position. Now for the positive proposals.

It is significant that friends who have often said to us, "Almost thou persuadest me to be a pacifist," now are saying that a great deal of thought must be given at once, even though the war so far as the United States is concerned has only begun, to the problem of "a just and durable peace." It is inevitable that reasonable and conscientious men should feel this concern, for obviously the only justifiable end of war is a "good peace," a peace that does not sow the seed of future war. Unless men can believe in such a goal, war, wholesale slaughter, becomes utterly irrational and completely immoral. It would then, beyond a shadow of doubt, be "the sum of all evils."

We have already stated our disbelief in the likelihood that we can follow the same fatal path as in the last war and then, suddenly, at the moment of victory for "our side," strike out in an entirely new direction to a durable and tolerable, not to mention a noble, peace. Before the United States entered into war, the religious pacifist could only say: "Go not to war, keep the sword in its scabbard; instead of drifting into war, take the initiative in offering to the world a creative, dynamic peace, a way out of this fearful impasse of a military victory for this Axis or that." It seems to me the only thing we can say to our nation now is: "Stop the war, put up your sword before it is too late altogether. Instead of automatically going through the old motions, be imaginative, be creative. There is no hope in a peace dictated by 'totalitarian' powers; nor in a peace dictated by 'democratic' powers. That has already been tried and proved disastrous. We are incurring stupendous risks in trying that course once more; let us rather take some risks for a new course. O, our country, pioneer again—this time on a world scale; for mankind's sake, try the way of reconciliation."

In political terms, such a policy would express itself in an offer by the United States to enter into negotiations immediately with all nations, Axis and Allies, based on such terms as the following:

1. The United States will take its full share of responsibility, with other nations, for the building of federal world government along such lines as those of our American union.
2. Instead of seeking to hold on to what we have, which is so much more than any other people have, the United States

will offer to invest the billions which otherwise it would devote to war preparation and war, in a sound international plan for the economic rehabilitation of Europe and Asia, and in order to stay the inroads of famine and pestilence which otherwise threaten to engulf mankind.

3. In the coming peace no attempt shall be made to fasten *sole* war-guilt on any nation or group of nations. Instead, all people should take up the works of repentance in a common effort to halt the break-up of civilization and to build the good life which the earth's resources and modern technology make possible for all.

4. All subject nations, including India, the Philippines, Puerto Rico, Denmark, Norway, France, Belgium, Holland, and subject peoples on every continent, must be given a genuine opportunity to determine their own destinies. In those few cases where a people are clearly not yet ready for self-government, their affairs should be administered by the federal world government with a primary view to the welfare of such people and to the granting of full self-determination at the earliest possible time.

5. All peoples should be assured of equitable access to markets and to essential raw materials. To this end, concerted action to adjust and ultimately to remove tariff barriers should be undertaken. Immigration and emigration should be internationally controlled with a view to the welfare of every nation. There is a direct and infinitely tragic connection between (a.) the fact that since 1914 there has been no *free* movement of population and labor from one country to another and (b.) the *forcible* uprooting of millions by brutal discriminatory legislation and by war. Stifle immigration and you get refugees.

6. To give a lead in furthering democracy, the United States will undertake to establish equality of opportunity for all within its own borders: to begin with, a national program should be established to provide decent housing for all who now lack it; to make unused land accessible to those who will till it; to encourage cooperatives for the maintenance and revival of the initiative of our people; to provide adequate medical and hospital service and equal educational facilities for all, including Negroes and Orientals.

7. The United States will repudiate every form of racism in

dealing with all minority groups and, as an initial move toward reconciliation in the Far East, repeal the Oriental Exclusion Act. It will call on Germany and other countries similarly to renounce racist doctrines and practices.

8. There should be immediate and drastic reduction of armaments by all nations, and steps to move from an armaments-and-war economy to an economy of peace should be taken as rapidly as possible.

We readily admit that, from the standpoint of "power politics," national aggrandizement—any materialistic interpretation of history—this seems a fantastic proposal. But any proposal made by idealistic non-pacifists seems to us quite as untenable. They believe, for example, that a wedge ultimately must be driven and can be driven between the German people and Hitler and Hitlerism. There can be no good peace, they say, until the demons have been driven out of the souls of the German people. For the present, however, they believe that military means must be used to that end. But to say to the German people: "The world has no realistic choice except a military victory, decisive, crushing, of your side or our side" is to tell them the same thing that Hitler tells them. This is what keeps them fighting behind Hitler, as practically all observers admit; for, on that basis, they believe that the only alternative to a victory behind Hitler is "something worse than Versailles." They might as well keep on fighting, since they face hell in any case and there remains the outside chance that they might win and then let the rest of the world find out what it means to be the underdog. There is, furthermore, the ghastly record of what our "success" in separating the German people from the Kaiser by military means amounted to: it gave us Hitler in place of the Kaiser.

This brings us to another dilemma. Our proposal for a dynamic peace at this time is dismissed by non-pacifists as "unrealistic." It would require an impossibly great change of heart in the German people and others. The American people, too, would have to rise to heights of repentance, faith in spiritual forces and moral courage, which it is felt unreasonable to expect. But isn't that what people generally have assumed would take place after the war and a "democratic" victory? For obviously, unless a spirit of humility and repentance, a high spiritual imaginativeness and courage animate the victorious peoples; and unless the German and Japanese people feel that they can trust us and are freed from fear and resentment and the inverted egoism of an inferiority complex—unless the world experiences a spiritual re-birth—there can be no good peace after this greatest and most destructive of all wars. We cannot believe there will be. But what shred of evidence is there that conditions at the end of a long war to the finish will be favorable for such a re-birth, more than conditions today? Is it not rather that, every day the war drags on, fresh evidence appears that we have not the will nor the strength to "turn again and be saved"? And, when was the law repealed which warns men, even as it woos their spirits—"Now is the accepted time; now is the day of salvation"?

If we do not wait until the spiritual energies of this generation are utterly exhausted to offer proposals for a creative peace we may yet find salvation. It may not seem likely, but when we think of the deep-seated reluctance in the hearts of all peoples to go to war, the inability of all the modern machinery of propaganda to arouse any enthusiasm for war in their breasts, it is not impossible that one of these days the utter futility and irrationality of it might seize upon millions, that they would lay down their arms, and walk home. When we remember with what joy the masses, in 1917-18, hailed the bright promise which was held out by President Wilson's Fourteen Points, and by the Russian Revolution in its early idealistic days, there is a possibility that there would be a tremendous, spontaneous response to such dynamic peace action by the United States which could not be ignored. Why, in any event, should so many Christians be so sure that the way of reconciliation would not work?

Even as these words were being written, the fall of Manila, Singapore, Rangoon, Sumatra, Java stunned the Western world. With fearful dispatch an end has been made to white supremacy in the Orient. Whatever the future course of the war, that has been settled. These developments cause many people to feel that, for the time being, there is no basis left for any imaginative peace proposal by the United States. The Axis Powers, Japan in particular, would inevitably regard such a move as a sign of weakness or even cowardice on our part. They feel that world domination is in their grasp, after decades of defeat and frustration, and nothing except crushing military defeat can keep them now from driving on to the attainment of that prize.

If we are prepared to make proposals looking toward a genuine peace only when we clearly have the upper hand, we cannot expect our national enemies to do otherwise. In that case there is nothing to do but fight to the bitter end. It is now plain just how bitter that end will be. If the full strength of the people of the United States, of the millions and hundreds of millions of Russia, China, India, the Near East, South America, as well as the desperate ultimate efforts of Great Britain, Germany, Italy and Japan are to be thrown into this war before an end is made of it, the war must eventuate either in a stalemate of complete exhaustion or in the "victory" of one group of embittered peoples over another group of despairing peoples. Both will have been brutalized by the most hideous warfare in all the tortured course of human history, and both must dwell on a devastated planet of which it will indeed be said that "the whole creation groaneth and travaileth in pain together." This is not a goal for which human beings can fight rationally. Verily, if there was ever an occasion when it seemed wise for adversaries to agree quickly, this is it.

Nor is it utterly fantastic to suppose that, precisely now, when they feel that the stigma of inferiority has to some extent been removed from them and that they could negotiate as equals with equals, the Japanese and the German people may be more willing and better able to discuss a just peace than before. There is no evidence that they are intoxicated with victory as nations sometimes have been. It is reasonable to suppose that, whatever may be true of certain of their leaders, multitudes in these as in other lands are well aware that the costs of prolonged conflict will be incalculable. A chance to sit down together with other peoples of the earth in friendship, and to work together at utilizing the earth's resources and modern technology in order to build the good life for all, offers them more than Hitler and the Japanese militarists—even if victorious—can bring to them. By offering them that chance we on our part will gain more than a victory of the United States, Britain and their allies can bring to us.

And if, finally, the nation and the world are not ready to try this way and we pacifists find ourselves a minority which seems to have no immediate political influence, seems indeed to be quite irrelevant, to belong as it were to another world, what then? That will not alter our course. As Howard H. Brinton has reminded us so effectively in his recent contribution to the Pendle Hill Historical Studies, "Sources of the Quaker Peace Testimony," our pacifism is not primarily that of objectors to war or of peace propagandists. We believe that there are rational and pragmatic arguments to support our pacifism; but it rests finally upon "arguments based on the direct insight of the soul into the nature of Truth and Goodness, an insight interpreted as a revelation through Divine Light and Life. According to this view, a certain way of life is intuitively recognized as good and war is seen to be incongruous. This argument is primary, because the Divine Light is not only the source of knowledge but the source of power. The Light shines deep within at the springs of the will." Wherefore, God helping us, we can do no other.

We are sustained indeed by the evidence which history affords that "the little fellowships of the holy imagination which keep alive in men sensitivity to moral issues" and faith in the Eternal Love may indeed be more effective than surface appearances indicate. Sometimes they may have been the carriers of the seed out of which sprang the harvests that have nourished nations and civilizations. If God's peaceable Kingdom is ever to come on earth, it must, as Isaac Penington wrote in 1661, "have a beginning before it can grow and be perfected. And where should it begin but in some particulars [individuals] in a nation and so spread by degrees? Therefore, whoever desires to see this lovely state brought forth in the general must cherish it in the particular."

Or, as one said many centuries earlier: "Ye are the salt of the earth; but if the salt have lost its savor, it is thenceforth good for nothing."

Yes, though we be driven still further "out of this world," into seeming futility, confined to very simple living in small cooperative groups and, for the rest, giving ourselves to silence, meditation, prayer, discipline of the mind and spirit, we shall hold to the way. The trouble with the world today is precisely that men have come to believe that "the only means which work are material ones, and the only goal attainable is material. The world as perceived by the untrained physical senses is reality and the way to master that reality is through physical force."

The result is that tremendous material energies are at our disposal, but our souls are empty and exhausted. Developing a consciousness of the reality of spiritual things and generating moral power are the supreme need of such a world. It may well be that now, as in other such crises, this cannot be done save through small groups of men and women who austerely renounce outward things, strip down to the bare essentials, and give themselves to the task of "purifying the springs of history which are within ourselves," and to "that secret labor by which those of a little faith raise, first of all in themselves, the level of mankind's spiritual energy."

There have been other minorities: for example, there was that party in Germany which had seven members when Hitler joined it a score of years ago, but which dared to aim at becoming the majority, and at wiping out all opposition so that there would never be a minority again; and there is that minority, of which we seek to be a part, to which the Word was and is spoken: "The Kingdom of God is at hand; repent and believe the good news. Go into all the world and preach the good news and make disciples of all the nations. Fear not, little flock. It is your Father's good pleasure to give unto you the kingdom. And lo, I am with you alway, even unto the end of the age. For God hath not given us a spirit of fearfulness, but of power and love and discipline."

What the Bible
Teaches About Freedom

1943 More than three thousand years ago there was a group of people who were being persecuted as a minority.

Through most of their history, before and since, they have been a persecuted minority. They still are. They are the Jews.

Long ago these people made a tremendous discovery about what true religion and true religious leadership are. You can find the story in your Bible.

They made this discovery during a time of great trouble, while they were exiled from their own land. But there were persons and events in their past that helped them in thinking the thing through, and in telling about what religion is they tied the story up with this past.

They tied it up with Moses and an earlier experience of exile and deliverance in which he played a big part.

Moses lived in a period of dictatorship. His people were slaves. The bosses made them work under a speed-up system, and committed horrible atrocities, such as trying to kill all the boy-babies born to the Jews.

Moses himself was saved from such a death only because his mother hid him in a reed basket in the Nile River. There he was found by the daughter of the Pharaoh, which is what they called their dictator in Egypt. (Notice how much *Pharaoh* sounds like *Fuebrer!*) The princess took Moses to the royal palace and had him brought up as her own son.

When Moses was a young man he became curious about the Hebrew slaves, and one day went to the brickyards where some of them were working. The first thing he saw was an Egyptian boss hitting a Hebrew laborer. Moses was a powerful young man. He lost his temper. He hit the boss—and killed him! He buried the body hastily in the sand, and went back to the palace.

But a fire had been kindled in Moses' heart, a fire of concern about his people and their suffering. The next day he went back to the hot brickyards. Then he learned two things that those who try to help their fellow men often discover.

He found, first, that slaves often spend as much time and energy fighting each other as they do fighting their common oppressors, and second, that slaves do not always welcome their deliverers. They get accustomed to being slaves. They cling to the ills they have, as Shakespeare pointed out, rather than fly to others that they know not of! Even after they have been freed, if freedom brings hardship, they may want to go back "to the fleshpots of Egypt."

This time Moses found two Hebrews fighting each other. When he rebuked them, they turned on him and said, "Who made you our boss? Do you mean to kill us as you did that Egyptian yesterday?"

Moses feared that in order to turn suspicion away from themselves they would tell the Egyptians that he killed the boss. He concluded that it might not be healthy to stay around those parts, so he ran away.

On his flight he met a young woman and her sisters who were having a hard time getting water for their flocks. Moses still felt in a fighting mood. He drove away some shepherds who were bothering the women. Later he fell in love with one of the women, and presently they were married. Then—so the Bible goes on to tell—his father-in-law gave him a job and he settled down to a nice comfortable life, raising a family and feeding the flocks of his father-in-law Jethro.

Only, after a while, God came into the picture. What was the sign that God had come? It was a bush that burned and burned and did not stop burning. Moses had had a fire kindled in his heart once, but it went out, or at least died down. God is the Being whose heart does not stop burning, in whom the flame does not die down.

What was God all burned up about? The voice that came out of the bush said, "I have seen the affliction of my people that are in Egypt and have heard their cry by reason of their oppressors." It was the physical, economic, and spiritual suffering, the injustice, the degradation to which actual people were subjected here on earth, that caused God concern.

And the proof that God had entered into Moses, and that Moses had really been "converted," was that he had to go back and identify himself with his enslaved people—"organize them into Brickmakers' Union Number One"—and lead them out of hunger and slavery into freedom and into "a good land, and a large, a land flowing with milk and honey."

At the head of the Ten Commandments stand these great words: "I am the Lord thy God which have brought thee out of the land of Egypt, *out of the slave-house.* Thou shalt have no other God before me"—before this God who is in the hearts of his prophets as the Eternal Flame that will not let them rest where there is injustice and inequality until these have been done away with and men set about building God's House instead of the slave-house.

To be religious, the Hebrews discovered, is to get out of Egypt into Canaan; to refuse to be slaves or contented draft-horses; to build brotherhood in freedom—because that is what men, the children of God, were created to do!

And religious leaders are those who identify themselves with the oppressed, so that men may carry out this, their true mission in the world.

The world and human beings are so made that you can't organize life securely on injustice and oppression. All kinds of things happen to "ball things up." The top dogs always get to fighting each other about the spoils. Besides, men really can work efficiently only in freedom, and if oppression is pushed beyond a certain point, men either stop producing anything to speak of, or, because they don't find living and having children worth while, they may even just die off (as happened to the slave population in the Roman Empire)— or else they revolt.

So, in a way, the oppressed always go free. And, very often, the minority gets its chance to become a majority.

What happens then, when the tables are turned? What usually happened was simply that the tables *were* turned. The "minority," the oppressed, promptly proved that they were humans, too, made in the same mould as the oppressors, and started to behave very much as their former exploiters had done.

That happened in the history of Israel, too. There came a time in Canaan, the Land of Promise, when the Hebrews decided to be like other peoples, who had kingdoms and empires. They began to organize armies to fight, plunder, and rape. At first, of course, this was just in "self-defense," to make themselves "secure." But it wasn't very long before they became frankly imperialistic. *The kingdom was not completely established until the time of David. His son, Solomon, was already an arch-imperialist.* Nothing could satisfy his appetite, as illustrated by his thousand wives and concubines, symbols chiefly of his *political* alliances and ambitions.

But exploitation and imperialism do not work for the former underdogs, either. Under Solomon's son—it worked that fast—the Hebrew kingdom already was split in two! Before a great while one of the parts was destroyed. The other led the existence of an ancient Belgium or Czechoslovakia—one of the little countries on whose soil big countries like to do their fighting. Presently this Hebrew kingdom also was shattered and the people driven into exile.

Still later the wheel turned again, and under the patronage of a benevolent monarch named Cyrus a little band of Hebrew exiles went back to the dear homeland. One of those who went back was a priest named Ezra.

When Ezra first thought of making the long journey through territory infested by robbers and hostile armies he decided to ask the king for an armed escort. But then—much like Gandhi—"he proclaimed a fast!" For he said, "I was ashamed to ask of the king a band of soldiers and horsemen to help us against the enemy in the way because we had often told the king, 'the hand of our God is upon all that seek him for good.'" Ezra was not like the clergyman who, after Britain passed through a crisis, wrote, "We must give fervent thanks to Almighty God for delivering us and now we must be careful not to be caught in such a defenseless position again."

These events in the life of the Hebrew people were taking place at a time of turmoil in the history of the ancient world. Presently Alexander the Great appeared and conquered Palestine. Under some of his successors the Hebrews had to endure horrible persecution again. Of course, there were Fifth Columnists among the Jews, and these helped the infamous Antiochus Epiphanes get control over their people. There were others who refused to toady to the conqueror, and met his attacks with non-resistance and non-cooperation, and died as martyrs. But there were still others who said this was not enough. You must fight fire with fire, give the conquerors some of their own medicine. So there was a heroic revolt led by the Maccabees, and the Hebrews were an independent nation again.

This time they said that although they must have a king, the people would elect him. They would be democratic about it. But alas, the old business of the oppressed behaving like oppressors as soon as they got into power occurred again. The first king in the new line, Simon, was murdered by his son-in-law, who nevertheless did not succeed in becoming king. So Simon's son, John Hyrcanus, succeeded him and promptly set out on a career of conquest which included forcing the Jewish religion on conquered peoples!

Members of the Jewish ruling class quarreled among themselves, and presently made the mistake of inviting Pompey, a Roman general waging war in those parts, to arbitrate their dispute. Pompey brought their land under the control of the Romans.

By the time Jesus was born, Judea was ruled by Herod, a puppet of the Roman Caesar. As his first act of kingly power, Herod put to death all the old aristocracy. He introduced a spy system like Hitler's Gestapo or Stalin's Ogpu. Herod assassinated Mariamne, his own wife, her mother, and three sons.

Not many decades after Jesus died, Jerusalem was razed to the ground, Palestine devastated, and the Jews scattered in an exile from their country which was to last for eighteen centuries. This was after a war against the Romans in which Jews fought each other about as bitterly as they fought the foreign dictator. As one Jewish scholar has recently put it: "Amidst a terrorism comparable only to that which took place later in the French and Russian revolutions, the Jewish state, like a building burning from within and without, collapsed in the flames of war."

It was in such times that Jesus lived. He knew the history of his people which we have sketched; it was a part of him. You cannot understand him unless you see him in the midst of all this.

One thing that was not true of him is that he told his people simply to submit to dictatorship and oppression. No one could have been more un-submissive to human laws, institutions, and dignitaries than he. No one ever learned subservience or false humility from him.

He began his public career with the proclamation: "the Kingdom of God is at hand." It was like someone saying today, "the revolution is here; the end of the reign of oppressors, native and foreign; the beginning of the rule of justice and brotherhood."

If Jesus had been safe and respectable, the powers of his time would not have put him away as they did. Rulers are almost always somewhat dumb and often very dumb, but not that dumb.

What Jesus objected to was not the great religious act of human beings moving out of Egypt into Canaan, out of bondage and insecurity into freedom, security and peace. What grieved him was that men were forever moving out of bondage—*into bondage!* They escaped from the violence of another to fasten the chains of violence on themselves. This terrible evil circle must be broken.

Jesus said: "It is really very simple. You cannot expect Satan to cast out Satan. You cannot overcome evil with evil. Evil can be overcome only by its opposite, good."

Now let us see if we can describe in our own language, in terms of our own problems, how Jesus believed men could overcome evil and injustice in such a way as not to fasten new chains of tyranny and injustice on themselves.

This may sound sentimental or positively crazy to you. You may think that if large numbers of ordinary Negroes have to begin by loving the white enemies who oppress them and Jim Crow them, we may as well stop talking about nonviolence as a method for liberating the Negro people. But Jesus is still a mighty force after nineteen centuries. It may not be wise to dismiss him as a fool. Besides, the leaders of most of the great religions have said much the same things about the power of love over brute force that Jesus did. Let us see how much common sense there may be in these teachings.

When we cry out for justice and equality, on what do we base our demand? We say that racial discrimination is contrary to the findings of science and the principles of reason and religion. Men— all men—are human beings, members of one family, children of one God. Discrimination denies men their standing as human beings, shuts them out of the family, deprives them of the moral dignity with which God clothed them. So runs the argument for democracy and equality.

For Jesus, who saw all men thus as brothers, the worst sin is the denial of brotherhood by drawing lines that shut some in and others out. When people think of Jesus' symbol of wickedness, they do not think of robbers, or prostitutes, or bloody tyrants, or Quislings like the publicans of his time who became tax-gatherers for the foreign dictator. Jesus' symbol of sinfulness was the Pharisee. The Pharisee was a good and respectable man; a devoted churchman and an ardent patriot. But the Pharisee set himself apart from other men; he prided himself on his separateness from them. He prayed: "God, I thank thee that I am not as other men are . . . or even as this publican." But suppose that the publican in his turn had turned around and prayed: "God, I thank thee that I am not as other men are—or even as this Pharisee"? Then he would have been a Pharisee too, shutting people out, putting them in a lower rank.

We cannot have it both ways. Either there is a fundamental kinship among all men—in the old Quaker phrase, there is "that of God" in every man—or else there is not. If there is not, and we are not all fundamentally the same breed, then there never can be any real understanding among men. They simply think and feel differently. In that case, whenever any real difference develops among them, men can only fight it out and those who prove the strongest, most clever, and most ruthless will always be on top. There will be no point in crying over it or getting up a lot of moral indignation about it. There is no question of morals between a tiger and a cobra, or between two-legged animals that belong to essentially different breeds that have no kinship with each other.

Another thing, if men are not members of one family in God, then the pattern of human society will always be that of domination—subordination. There will always be some top dogs and many underdogs. And then Hitler and all the imperialists and exploiters and exponents of racism are right and the idea of a democratic society is bunk, as they say it is.

But if the oppressed Negroes and their white friends today accept the biblical, democratic concept of the kinship of all men and reject racism, then we have to be governed in our own actions by this fact of human kinship or we shall only be plotting our own defeat.

That means that we must always remember that our enemy, the exploiter, is not an abstract word—not a nation or race or class, for example. A nation, race or class cannot have pneumonia or chickenpox, cannot be warm or cold, cannot cry or laugh. Only human beings can. And these who injure and degrade us are human beings, very much like ourselves. Our strategy must always be based on that fact. The human in us must try to reach and touch the human in them.

Our object always will be to build up a family relationship, a brotherhood and a democratic society with them; to put an end to separateness and to the top-dog-underdog business. When the Japanese took Hong Kong from the British, they put white men in front of the Chinese rickshas, and then made a point of putting colored folk—Chinese, Hindus, Filipinos—in the seat, telling the white men to "hurry up." People in this country who had never been much shocked when Chinese coolies were used like animals were shocked very much. The Japanese broadcast the news throughout Asia and many colored people chuckled and thought that it served the dirty white men right.

They were both wrong. Nothing really had changed. It is no better and no worse for white men or colored men to be humiliated and exploited. The only worth-while objective is to have them walk together as brothers; to destroy the pattern of domination and slavery altogether.

One of the brilliant young Negro writers recently said it—"The fallacy is that the Negro is a problem both *in vacuo* and *in toto,* where in reality the Negro is only an equation in a problem of many equations, an equally important one of which is the white man. To know and understand and love the Negro is not enough. One must know and understand and love the white man as well. . . . It was in this direction, in the direction of knowledge and understanding and love that I had come a little way." That is J. Saunders Redding in the closing pages of *No Day of Triumph,* which is a terribly realistic and not at all a sentimental book.

The emphasis on problem rather than conflict, on understanding rather than victory, is another technique that flows from Jesus' teaching that we must love the enemy because he is our brother. Ordinarily when differences occur, we get all emotional and hysterical about it. We think in terms of God's hosts versus the Devil's, the good versus the evil, the people who are "perfectly willing to listen to reason" versus those who "don't understand anything except force"—we and our side being, of course, God's host and the good and the rational! The Hebrews of old were always doing that. They blamed the devilish Egyptians and Babylonians. If only they would behave better, or were not on top! The prophets always came back at them and said: You should repent first; that is, change your focus on this thing. You and the Babylonians and Egyptians are all in the same boat, all faced with a problem. Devote your energy to solving it.

The oppressor is always involved in the same perplexing and calamitous situation with the oppressed. How obvious that is in the situation in India today. The whole future of the British in the war and afterward is tied up with what they do in India. How true it is also of whites and Negroes in this country today. The Negro problem is the white problem. The white problem is the Negro problem. So we can always include the "enemy" in our strategy—the enemy as a human being—and the Negro can say to white folks today: "Here we are in this mess. Obviously, it cannot go on this way. We cannot continue to accept this discrimination and degradation, even though submission to it seems to have certain initial advantages, and resistance may bring suffering upon us. But neither can you continue to practice this discrimination that has brought us all to this sorry pass, and the continuance of which can lead only to more woe. Let us then face our common problem together."

Thus to recognize the essential humanity of the enemy and to see, as Gandhi has emphasized, that the changing of his will and his spirit is involved in all real overcoming of evil, is also to recognize that the enemy in the situation is one's "other self." It is, in the practical, social sense, to obey the great command: "Thou shalt love thy neighbor—including the Samaritan, the publican, the enemy—as thyself."

From this flow two other basic approaches in overcoming evil which Jesus taught and practiced.

Man must be true to himself, to his moral dignity, to the spirit of God in whose image he is made. When a man has lost all respect for himself, he is no longer human. That is why men strive so desperately to keep a little self-respect. But a man who grovels before another, or before laws and customs that degrade him—as Hitler's laws degrade the Jews and Jim Crow degrades the Negro—is wounded in his self-respect. If he continues to grovel, his self-respect, his essential self, will die.

What do men do under these circumstances? Too often, unless they can sneak out of doing so, they do obey the evil laws and submit to the degrading customs. But sneaking does not make for self-respect either. So very often, when they think they can succeed in a revolt, and perhaps even put themselves on top and bind oppressive laws on others, they strike back. They demand justice from an evil government or institution and, as Gandhi puts it, they say: "We will hurt you, if you do not give this." When they do not like certain laws, they "break the heads of the lawgivers."

Where he or his own nation or group is the victim, nearly everybody believes that it is a noble thing thus to strike back. Every nation and race reveres as liberators and heroes those who were successful in thus striking back. Of course, those who struck back and lost are not remembered or, if remembered, are probably regarded as rash fools. Of course, too, the liberator of one people or group is likely to be regarded as a scoundrel by another. However, probably everybody would agree that those who consider themselves grievously wronged and enslaved and who strike back are morally on a higher plane than those who submit to evil in a cowardly or passive fashion.

Nevertheless, fighting back against laws and customs that degrade men is not a solution. Suppose, as often happens, you are not strong enough to organize and fight back? Must the crucifying of the human spirit go on? Does wrong become right if the wronged are weak?

If Negroes in this country today were to resort to violence in order to achieve liberation, it would serve chiefly to give Fascist forces the excuse to take power openly. Does that mean that Negroes must continue to submit to being Jim-Crowed? Do the preachers, Negro or white, believe that the God of Moses and Jesus desires this?

Furthermore, as we have already shown, fighting back does not change things essentially. At most it may reverse the role of the top dogs and the underdogs. J. Saunders Redding, whom I quoted a moment ago, wrote in the same book about the Communist movement: "What I had seen of it did not convince me that it was interested in broadening the basis of human relationships but rather that it aimed only at transposing them, so that those at the top—the rich and the mighty—would come to the mud at the bottom. It seemed not to be interested in leveling barriers of caste and class and race but only in scaling them. Surely this imbruting struggle is not all."

Faced with the wastefulness and futility of violence as a means of righting things in a fundamental way, many say that the oppressed—as for example the Negroes today—should stick to gradual, democratic ways of amending laws and customs. Unquestionably this procedure has its place, and an important one. Efforts of Negro organizations and their friends along these lines must continue and be strengthened. In dealing with certain conditions ordinary educational, legislative and judicial processes are all that need to be used.

There are, however, other spiritual and social issues that cannot be met satisfactorily, or at all, in this way. Henry David Thoreau, the great American exponent of nonviolence and civil disobedience, pointed out one of the difficulties in the days of the Fugitive Slave Law. Such a law, he said, "requires you to be the agent of injustice to another." By obeying it while you work to amend it, you become an evildoer and a supporter of evil. The very fact that you are ordinarily a law-abiding and conscientious person actually may make your influence for perpetuating this evil greater. "Those who, while they disapprove of the character and measures of a government, yield to it their allegiance and support are undoubtedly its most conscientious supporters, and so frequently the most serious obstacles to reform."

As there are laws and customs that require one to be "the agent of injustice to another," so there are laws and practices that directly and deeply bind and degrade one's own spirit—the laws, for example, that at various times have forbidden Christians to practice their religion or teach it to their children. Also, the law that makes one man an agent of injustice to another may serve to destroy the self-respect and the soul of this other if he yields to it.

The laws against the Jews in Germany, for example, if enforced or accepted degrade both Germans and Jews. The same is true of those who practice and those who submit to Jim Crow in the United States. Every time such laws are obeyed the deepest sin is committed, the Spirit of God is denied and trodden under foot. It will not do to say: "I will obey, submit, but hope and work for change."

What is one to do then? Those spiritual leaders whom we most revere have given one answer: Refuse to obey or conform to such laws as deny love and brotherhood. The most sacred law and custom of Jesus' own group was that relating to the Sabbath. Jesus broke it openly, unmistakably, completely. When the three young men in the Book of Daniel were told they must worship an idol, they said: "Be it known unto thee, O King, that we will not." When Daniel was forbidden to worship his God as he had been accustomed to, "he went into his house and he kneeled upon his knees three times a day and prayed, as he did aforetime." If the law is of such a nature that it requires you to be the agent of injustice to another, declared Thoreau: "then I say, break the law."

Often men are afraid to break such taboos and laws as Jim Crow today. They tell themselves and others that it is dangerous, that it will make trouble and breed anarchy if the law and practice are violated. Gandhi calls the idea that such a law must be kept a "superstition." He is exactly right, for superstition means making something real and sacred out of something that is unreal and unholy.

He adds: "So long as the superstition that men should obey unjust laws exists, so long will their slavery exist. And a passive resister alone"—that is, one who will not cooperate with, who breaks the law nonviolently—"can remove such a superstition." Jesus said essentially the same thing about his people's Sabbath observance: "The Sabbath was made for man, not man for the Sabbath."

It is our timidity and blindness that makes us observe man-made law while we break God's law. We keep up Jim Crow practices, for example, because, whites and Negroes alike, we think only of the unpleasant and dangerous results that might follow if we do anything else. We simply do not see the frightful sin we constantly commit by acting upon the Pharisee's principle of excluding and degrading others: "God, I thank thee that I am not as other men are."

If we really did see the truth, in the light of God's law, it would become impossible for us, from that moment on, to observe a single Jim Crow law or practice. We would be impelled to act on Thoreau's challenge: "Let your life be a counter-friction to the machine. . . . Cast your whole vote, not a strip of paper merely, but your whole influence." A minority is powerless when it conforms to the majority; but it is irresistible when it clogs with its whole weight. As with the early Christians, ". . . They only can force me who obey a higher law than I. They force me to become like themselves."

Before such faithfulness to God we might find unbrotherly institutions crumbling much more easily and quickly than we had supposed. For it is not God, not anything in the true nature of life or the universe, that sustains them, but only the fact that we uphold them by our support, active or passive.

If for the oppressed and their friends the conclusion to be drawn from the moral dignity and kinship of all men is the duty of non-conformity with evil laws and practices, the conclusion for those who have privilege and power is that they must not eat the fruits of their position in smugness and peace. It is when we realize that they do have consciences and refuse to permit them to slumber that we deal with the privileged in the one way that recognizes their moral worth and our kinship with them.

Here again we confront a basic problem in social action. Generally, the oppressed take one of two attitudes toward the privileged. Some obsequiously accept injustice and even regard the oppressor as a benefactor. He is "such a nice boss." So the master is morally justified; he tells himself that he is waxing great and rich, not at the expense of his victims but "for their own good." Or else the oppressed pour out their scorn, hate, and thirst for revenge upon the master group. Again the latter continue to feel morally vindicated and secure: "The underdogs are no better than we are; they simply want to put themselves in our place."

Often both of these attitudes are found side by side in the same person. Many a Jew in Jesus' day would bow obsequiously to a Roman dignitary and then spit out of the corner of his mouth at him when he was past. Jesus did not spit out of the corner of his mouth at the conquerors of his people; neither did he do grovelling obeisance to them.

Space does not permit consideration of the many instances in the Gospels when Jesus confronted people, especially the privileged and mighty, with the moral realities of their position and the hypocrisy that underlay it. For example, to his home town people who expected a flattering speech from the home town boy who had made good, he administered a rebuke to their nationalism and to all group pride: "There were many lepers in Israel in the days of Naaman the Syrian; to none of them was the prophet sent, but to this foreigner." To the virtuous, he said, "This publican is justified before God rather than you"; to the philanthropists: "This poor widow who has contributed a penny has given incalculably more than you all." So must we find ways to keep conscience, in those who impose discrimination on Negroes, awake and hurt, with the hurt that heals in the end because it makes the oppressor whole and unites him with those he has injured.

We have to understand that when we speak to the conscience of our fellow men, we have to come with truth and with principles, not with half-truths and expediency. There is often timidity and evasion in the way Negroes and their friends present their case. They want such and such improvements in the condition of the Negroes, but they suggest or permit it to be understood that this does not mean equality in *all* respects. We are going to "do justice" to the Negro, but things will remain very much as they have been. And we give various reasons why it would be prudent or clever to introduce these reforms. And truly there is a good deal of ground for such arguments. Herbert Agar, editor of the Louisville *Courier-Journal*, writes in *A Time For Greatness:* "We can no longer think in terms of what we are willing to 'do' for the colored peoples of the world. That is not the question. We must force ourselves to understand that the question is whether *we* can join the human race in time, while the white man has still the chance to be treated as an equal in a world where the people of his color are a small minority."

But all this misses the main point. The real question, the only question, is whether or not we believe the great truth that God taught Peter in the vision on the housetop and that caused Peter later to say: "I am a man"—not a Jew or Roman or Greek—"and God hath taught me not to call any man common or unclean." Whether we shall so act that we can say honestly as did the Early Church: "In Christ Jesus there is neither Jew nor Greek"—white, black, yellow, brown. In Christian teaching and in democratic concepts there is *no moral basis for Jim Crow,* for segregation of any kind, no basis for anything but complete brotherhood. In the face of that all questions of expediency pale into insignificance and all half-measures are mockeries. In face of that, the attitude of the churches and of Christian people, North and South, smells of the same hypocrisy that Jesus was constantly exposing in his contemporaries.

We have to confront these Christians with the stark question—whether, in this matter of Jim Crow, theirs is the program of the man who says, "I am a Christian, therefore," or the program of the man who says, "I am a Christian, but." So long as men can believe that there is some moral justification for Jim Crow it can endure. As soon as the churches quit pussy-footing on the issue and men know that Jim Crow has no ethical and Christian justification, its end will be in sight.

Especially oppose evil in yourself. Much of the time men generate no real power in combating an evil because they are not really against the evil at all. In the United States today, for example, we are against racism when practiced by Hitler and the Japanese militarists, but we practice it ourselves against Negroes. We are against occupation and rule by a foreign power in Belgium, Norway, and so on; but we want it to continue in India. We are against concentration camps, but we put our own citizens of Japanese descent into them. Such things show that we are not really against these evils at all; we are simply against those results that happen to inconvenience ourselves. No wonder this device of casting out Satan by the power of Satan gets us nowhere.

This is why the great teachers of nonviolence always have taught their followers that before they can really fight to overcome evil, they must purify themselves. It is common knowledge that the United Nations have suffered tremendously in this war because in their treatment of the Negro and in other respects they have not practiced the democracy they preach. They have enabled the Japanese to pose before millions of Asiatics as "liberators" from white domination. No one can estimate how many American and British lads have had to die and will die from our failure to destroy what Gandhi calls "the canker of white supremacy."

The Negro people also will be strong exactly in the proportion to which they put their own house in order and remove from their own midst the evils they condemn when practiced by white men. Among Negroes, as among other exploited groups, there are those who will exploit their own people as ruthlessly as any outsider does. Negro leadership is often guilty of selfishness, smugness and pettiness. Many Negroes are as self-seeking and cynical as those who oppress them. Unless they develop a tremendous moral and spiritual dynamic themselves, Negroes will not be delivered from Jim Crow. Will the Negro churches meet this challenge?

Care enough to be willing to die in order that the evil may be overcome. This is the law of the seed, Jesus pointed out, which bears no fruit except it fall into the ground and die. This is the Way of the Cross.

Few expressions are used more often than the saying: "If a man would save his life, he shall lose it; he who loses his life, shall find it." Yet people will not face up to the truth and the inexorability of that law they talk about so often. They want an easy, cheap, painless way out. Let any Negro reader of these lines, or white friend of the Negro people, sit down some time for five minutes and ask himself how often he has been willing to die that Jim Crow might be abolished—yes, how often he has been willing to risk a little unpopularity, a day in jail, the loss of a job. White people generally have bad consciences about Jim Crow and want to "do something about it"; but as soon as it appears that this may result in some disturbance, they draw back. They think God will be indulgent; that in this case there will be remission of sins without shedding of blood. But if there is any sense in the Christian symbol of the Cross at all, this cannot be.

There will be suffering, there will be a fearful price to be paid for removing Jim Crow. There is always the choice of inflicting suffering upon others or taking it upon ourselves. The Christian way is to refuse to cooperate with evil and to accept the consequence. The consequence is the Cross. Only as Negroes and whites who are concerned with abolishing the denial of brotherhood as represented by Jim Crow take up the Cross of suffering can Jim Crow be done away with. When we are ready for that, God himself will give us victory.

This idea that evil cannot be overcome by inflicting suffering in the effort to stop it, but by accepting suffering unto death rather than acquiescing in the evil, profiting by it, or obeying its command, seems to many sheer "moonshine." If we reflect for a moment, however, we shall see that it is sober realism.

For one thing, as Gandhi has pointed out, unjust laws and practices survive because men obey them and conform to them. This they do out of fear. There are things they dread more than the continuance of the evil. So long as there is still something the oppressor can take away that we fear to lose, or selfishly cling to, his power over us continues. So long as we are still afraid of death we can be bought off. We are not yet hard enough to overcome evil. That is why so much thought and effort are expended in trying to drug or paralyze the fear of death in the soldier. So also when we become true, i.e., fearless, nonviolent resisters, we have the courage against which evil cannot stand. The degree of suffering we, Negroes and whites, can endure for our cause of establishing brotherhood without qualification in race relationships will determine the measure of our success. Gandhi said, "Who is the true warrior—he who keeps death always as a bosom friend, or he who controls the death of others? . . . That nation is great which rests its head upon death as a pillow. Those who defy death are free from all fear."

Back in 1933 when Hitler already had come to power a great statesman whom most people would consider more "practical" than Gandhi stated the same truth. Thomas G. Masaryk, the first president of the Czech Republic, expressed confidence that democracy would prevail. "How can it most speedily be brought about?" he was asked, and answered, "Follow your convictions. Do not merely talk your politics. Live them. Tell the truth and do not steal. Above all, do not be afraid to die."

To put it another way, the capacity to suffer unto death on behalf of our fellows is the real power that makes human life possible, and creates and maintains human society. If it were the regular thing that in a pinch the mother sacrificed her babe in order to save herself, the human family long since would have ceased to exist. Not even animal life, for that matter, can be sustained on that basis of each for himself and the devil take the hindmost. Thus it is that whenever love that will suffer unto death is manifested, whenever a true Crucifixion takes place, unconquerable power is released into the stream of history. The intuition that says that God has been let loose on the earth when such devotion is manifested is absolutely sound.

This is the true road to liberation. Chiefly, mankind must always depend on its minorities, on the downtrodden, to show the way, since the privileged are too much bound by their vested interests. Gandhi, in India, practiced nonviolence on a great scale. If the Negro churches of this country were to give the lead to their own people and their friends in the use of this basically Christian way of redemption, it would constitute another great step toward the achievement of a revolution greater and more beneficent than all the revolutions of the past.

Germany—Summer 1947

1947   The real author of this article is André Trocmé, travelling secretary of the Fellowship of Reconciliation in Europe and pastor of the French Reformed Church of Le Chambon-sur-Lignon, who sheltered refugee Jewish children in his school in the Occupied Zone; helped Jews to escape from France into Switzerland; and was himself imprisoned by the Pétain regime. Last July, during the two weeks I spent in Le Chambon, André lectured one evening about his trip to Germany from which he had but recently returned. Sitting on a hard, backless bench in what used to be the shed of a farmhouse recently acquired by Collège Cévenol, I took the notes which provide the framework and much of the material of this article. At the time I did not know whether I should get a permit to visit Germany. Eventually I did and spent a week there in August. But André had spent four weeks and, of course, started out with a much more intimate knowledge of Germany's history and people than I have.

André began by drawing on the blackboard a circle with a bull's-eye in the middle. He said one cannot be objective about Germany or Russia without great pains. You shoot too low or too high, too far to left or right before locating the bull's-eye.

First, it is almost impossible for a Frenchman not to have a feeling of pride, as a victor, on entering Germany. "They got what was coming to them."

Then you go about and see that practically every large city in Germany is flat. Germany is now dusty, unclean, unkempt. Contrary to the old days, it is when you get back into France that you feel you are crossing into an orderly land. Among the occupation forces there are few who do not come to feel some pity for the Germans. You watch a Corpus Christi procession in the Ruhr. If the men and children look fairly healthy, the women, who deny themselves food to make this possible, are like phantoms. Kassel, a city of a couple of hundred thousand, has one hospital, in an underground shelter. There are so many mutilated veterans that every train carries a car reserved for them. The roads are full of people wandering about trying to find some food or fuel in the country. A good many live off the black market. An American Pall Mall cigarette is worth forty to fifty cents on that market. But peasant surpluses may be exhausted before long and then the basis for the black market will be gone. In North Germany in particular, into which eleven million Germans have been driven from the Sudetenland and the Russian zone, conditions are desperate. Five or six families live in a single house.

You reflect on such things and there is danger that your pity may become too unrestrained. Germans are given to self-pity. There are unrepentant Nazis. Many Germans are still unconscious of the suffering they inflicted on the rest of the world. Not a few are convinced that the victors are deliberately and slowly killing off several million Germans: "The whole of Germany is now a concentration camp worse than Buchenwald" is a typical statement. "There people were at least killed swiftly. Here we are starved to death slowly."

There is, then, a German "problem." And so we must "re-educate" them. The Americans, said André, carry on this work of re-education with "the greatest conviction, naïveté and incompetence." The whole thing is built on the racist assumption that the Germans are inferior.

In the U. S. zone de-Nazification is pursued most seriously. Recently there were still forty-five thousand suspected Nazis in concentration camps. They are not well-treated. Tribunals work so slowly that many have no hope of ever getting out. These camps are breeding grounds for future Nazis.

"Democracy" is largely a sham. Thoughtful and well-informed people told me that it would have been better if no pretense of instituting democracy had been made. At least democracy would not have gotten the bad name it now has. André told of an incident in the French zone. Huge posters announced that free elections were to be held and democracy established. Everybody ought to vote. The first act of the newly elected Landtag was to ask the occupation authority, in the politest terms, to do something about the bad food conditions. Of ten newspapers in Baden, nine did not dare to print the news for fear of offending the authorities. The Socialist Party paper did print the story; the next day it was suppressed for good!

Under such conditions the German people are nearly impotent. Young people, for the greater part, see no future for themselves or their country. Siegmund-Schultze told me that of a hundred or more young people he had interviewed recently, not one had voted in the elections. Some simply saw no use in it. Others said, "How do we know conditions won't change in a couple of years and then, if we voted wrong, we'll be out of luck?"

One result of all this is that great numbers of Germans, especially youth, hope that the United States will fight Russia soon and are eager to help. There is no question that the Russians are bitterly hated. There are the eleven million evacuees. Prisoners of war, I was told on the most reliable authority, are not sent home from Russian labor camps until there is practically no muscle left on their bones. Multitudes do not return at all. Furthermore, war between Russia and America seems inevitable, so why delay it until Russia has the atomic bomb? And the Americans would of course feed German soldiers who fought for them well.

Of course, many Germans know how Germany would be crushed between the two great powers and converted into an utter shambles in such a war. But desperate German youth often reply, "Well, what is *your* alternative?"

Siegmund-Schultze believes that the German states should proclaim their complete neutrality in any future war and stick to it whether or not the powers recognize this status, and he has found some response to that suggestion in German official circles. It is, I believe, a sound idea if only because such neighbors of Germany as the Czechs and French would have a very different outlook if they were once convinced that they need not fear another German attack. It is that fear which has so much to do with their pro-Russian orientation now. Unquestionably the voluntary adoption of a war-renouncing course by Germany would have a good effect also on public opinion in the United States and might encourage a good many to advocate following this example. Having said that, we must, however, also recognize that for the Germans the step, as far as immediate political results are concerned, might be a mere gesture. The decision as to whether there would be an atomic war in which, in spite of her neutrality, Germany would be crushed between Russia and the United States, would still rest with these two powers.

Let me refer in closing to the bright side. Finally, said André Trocmé in his lecture to us at Le Chambon in France, you hit the bull's-eye about Germany and the Germans. And then this Frenchman, who suffered in his own flesh and in that of his loved ones at the hands of the Nazis, began to recite a sort of modern version of Hebrews XI. He spoke of Wilhelm Mensching, our Fellowship of Reconciliation chairman in Germany, who never once said, "Heil Hitler." I met Wilhelm Mensching, too, a few weeks ago in his home at Petzen. A German Lutheran pastor, he is also in the noblest sense of the term a revolutionist. You look into his eyes and you know at once that he simply could not say Heil Hitler—or Heil Stalin—or Heil any earthly lord. You know that you are in the presence of one of the "truly great" who, wherever they go, "leave the vivid air signed with their honor." I had the same feeling when, a couple of days later, I met Pastor Herman Maas, another of our FOR leaders, in Heidelberg. He, who had known long years of suspicion and persecution, had just passed his seventieth birthday but he has the vitality of a man of fifty. Now the tide has turned for him. Every decent element in Heidelberg had turned out to celebrate his birthday and the ancient university had given him an honorary doctorate of theology.

But let André resume his roll-call: Karl and Eva Herrman; Karl, professor of crystallography at the University of Marburg, two years in concentration camp for helping Jewish families; Herman Stoer, teacher at Stettin, refused military service, condemned to death. The court was so moved by Stoer's story and his attitude that it appealed to Hitler personally to save him. Hitler refused and Stoer was beheaded. Taber, one of the very inner circle of the Nazis, still remorseful, said that if only the matter had not gone to the Fuehrer himself, they would have saved Stoer somehow.

General von Thaden, German governor in Liége, courageously defended the Belgian population from Nazi cruelties. After the war he was invited back to Liége and fêted by the population. General von Scholtitz, governor of Paris at the time of the liberation, who was ordered by Hitler to destroy Paris and refused. He barely escaped execution and lives in honor now in Baden-Baden. A former S. S. man in one of André's audiences said to his former comrades publicly: "What makes me sad is all this talk about collective guilt. I don't know such a thing. I know only personal guilt. I was a Brown Shirt. It was a mistake and a sin. Before you, I confess my guilt. What we suffer is the boomerang we threw at Europe and which has come back to us."

"The youth of Germany," said André, "who recently were still children, are not guilty; and I found them marvelous. In no country have I met youth so sympathetic and so ready to understand our message. And at this moment when they are ready we send them corporals. Can we bring them something besides kicks in the face? German youth are not yet pacifists, not because they are unable to become pacifists but because pacifism has not yet been brought to them. Such Germans were expecting the revelation of the sons of God and they are deeply disappointed that from nations they supposed more Christian than themselves there comes much the same thing as they have had in Germany.

"The present opportunity is unique. For one or two years German youth are ready to become radical religious pacifists. We must hasten to bring them a 'constructive Christian extremism.'"

My own last moments in Germany were unforgettable. The German customs official who examined my baggage was a powerfully built man with a face that was both handsome and full of integrity and gentle strength. When he saw the word "clergyman" on my passport after "occupation," he pointed to it questioningly. I happened to know the German word for pastor. His face lighted up. He looked casually at the bag I had opened for inspection and then closed the lid, saying in German which I fortunately understood: "I think you have no secrets in there"—then a pause—"not even an atom bomb." When I made clear to him as best I could the regret and shame many of us felt about the atomic bomb, he indicated that he understood. Then we looked quietly into each other's eyes and there was *"Auf wiedersehen—goodbye,"* spoken as if we had been lifelong friends. The conversation must have been overheard, or word was passed along, for when I returned to the coach in which I was riding and stood leaning out of the window, waiting on that beautiful Sabbath evening for the train to move across the border into Holland, I noticed that porters and trainmen, one at a time, sauntered down the platform, and each one, as he came to my window, glanced up for a moment and said, "It's a nice day." And so it was—a nice day.

I know that I owe it to that customs official and his children and to the German men and women on André Trocmé's roll-call to do all in my power to persuade our Fellowship and all its friends to see to it that we do send the message of pacifism and reconciliation, and not atom bombs, to the new generation of German youth.

Theology of Despair

An Open Letter to Reinhold Niebuhr

1948 Dear Dr. Niebuhr:

I have just finished reading your editorial, "Amid Encircling Gloom," in *Christianity and Crisis** and the "Editorial Notes" immediately following. The experience has saddened and dismayed me, not alone because of the defeatism and despair that pervade both, but because of the *justification* for despair and even suicide I found there.

In the editorial you point out that "our possession of a monopoly in atomic weapons and our fear that the monopoly will run out" in a few years make it possible that Americans may plunge into a "preventative" war against Russia, and certainly make it likely that they will not exercise "the forbearance without which it will be impossible to prevent present tensions from breaking out into overt conflict."

You warn that we shall have to walk the tight rope of avoidance of such a course even while we "defend" ourselves by both military and political weapons—atomic not excluded—against communism, a counsel which is no whit different from that which we may hear from enlightened secular sources! Aside from this, what do you, widely regarded as America's foremost theologian, have to say that might avert the tragedy and lead men out of the "encircling gloom"?

What you offer is a variation on the only text about which you

---

* April 21, 1948.

ever preach or write any more, though there are so many other texts and—I venture to say—more Christian ones, in the Scriptures. If the world is plunged into war, you say, "it would be indeed the final ironic and tragic culmination of the pretensions of modern man." Men drawn into war, though not wishing to be, "would merely"—what does that assumption-laden, emotion-ridden word "merely" signify in this context?—"illustrate the human predicament confessed by St. Paul in the words: 'For the good that I would I do not. . . .' "

As befits a Christian prophet, you warn that in these circumstances "we face not merely a Russian or communist peril but the threat of a divine judgment." But you do not conclude, as did the prophets that were before you, by calling upon your hearers to repent, act and so flee from that judgment. Instead, you finish with a solemn statement which, I am bound to say, makes little sense if taken at face value: "We are drifting toward a possible calamity in which even the most self-righteous assurance of the justice of our cause will give us no easy conscience."

Here is an illustration, it seems to me, of your tendency to blur all distinctions, in disregard of your own insistently proclaimed doctrine that there are relative differences that matter. What the sentence just quoted does in the political realm—on the *existential* level, shall we say?—is to convey to people the subtle suggestion that they are paralyzed, under a judgment which they cannot escape, that in the now-so-familiar phrase, "there isn't anything they can do about it." They will feel when they go to war that it is right, necessary, or even holy—and yet they will not have easy consciences! They will not have easy consciences, and yet they will feel self-righteous! That is the human condition.

So there is no true tension, but only *anxiety,* or a pervading sense of futility, for tension in the biblical sense is surely characteristic of a situation where man stands before his God and makes a *decision.* Here, no decision is possible any more. The important decisions have all been made, or are being made, but always by something or somebody else. (I do not mean to say that you deliberately try to convey this subtle suggestion of paralysis and helplessness, but I believe it is the effect of your writing. And a confession on your part that this might be another illustration of how men do the evil which they would not—a confession I well know you are humble enough to make—would not do a thing to mend matters.)

The habit of utterance which seems to me to have grown upon

you, and which dismays and disturbs me so, is illustrated again in the editorial note about the Palestine partition question in the same issue. After pointing out that in spite of what the Jews endured at Hitler's hands, they have been grievously wounded again "and not even the Stratton bill has been passed as a balm for those wounds," you conclude: "The whole situation is almost too tragic to contemplate. But the whole world situation has become so tragic that the perplexities of this particular problem only engage a fraction of our conscience." There it is again. The tragic plight of the Jews. What to do? It can "only engage a fraction of our conscience."

Sandwiched between these two items is your comment on Jan Masaryk's suicide. It seems to me very revealing. You recall that many people felt that Masaryk's willingness to become foreign secretary of a communist government, in spite of his well-known aversion to communism, demonstrated a lack of inner integrity. But, you assert, "he proved himself in possession of a final resource of such integrity by taking his life." You recognize, of course, that "suicide is not an ideal way of coming to terms with the issues of life," but, not being a "perfectionist," you are certain that men cannot attain the ideal anyway. And, having reached the point where the battle against "perfectionists" has become practically your sole occupation, now for the third time with rather obvious avidity you seize the opportunity to emphasize the complete hopelessness of man's estate and to pour sarcasm upon "the pretensions of modern man." Young Masaryk "proved his loyalty to his father's political ideas by violating his father's scruples against suicide," and from this you conclude, "that men may be forced into a position in which they can maintain the integrity of their soul *only* (italics mine) by taking their life, points to a dimension of human selfhood which makes nonsense of most modern theories of 'self-realization'!"

I am not suggesting that Jan Masaryk may not indeed have been truer to his father's ideals and to his own attachment to democratic principles by committing suicide—if that is what occurred—than he would have been by continuing to serve in the communist government of Czechoslovakia after the coup. But the assertion that suicide was the "only" way of proving the integrity of his soul is, I think, a very revealing one. So is the fact that every tragedy as it passes in review before you is the occasion for just one comment: that it proves the validity of a theory of human depravity or, more accurately, futility.

The upshot of the business is that Jan Masaryk commits suicide—and it is really the only thing he can do. On the larger scale of world politics the conclusion likewise is that mankind—or at least western civilization—commits suicide in atomic war. When it comes to a show-down that is the only thing it can do! Surely it is not altogether inappropriate to raise the question whether something like a "death-wish" is not operating here. The one positive element in the situation is that the thesis of man's utter futility has been vindicated!

This philosophy of fatalism and "inevitability" has its parallel in the Marxist-Leninist-Stalinist dogma of the "inevitability" of war between "the workers' fatherland" and the capitalist-imperialist world. That dogma also is linked to a low view of human nature and an essentially fatalistic one. It declares that man and his history are chiefly, if not entirely, the product of economic forces. According to this view of things, also, the living human beings in Russia, the United States, and elsewhere are essentially spectators at a tragedy of which they are also, alas, the victims, but which, nevertheless, they have no alternative but to play through to the bloody end.

The parallel does not end there. All is happily resolved—in theory—after the "inevitable" catastrophe has taken place. In the Marxist case, the solution is "within history," in the free society which grows out of "the dictatorship of the proletariat." In the other case, the resolution is "beyond history." Actual human beings, living and suffering, killing and being killed, today are offered "pie in the sky" under both systems!

One other observation remains to be made about how your thesis works out in contemporary affairs. In essential matters—support of the Marshall Plan, the need of fighting communism and Russia by both military and "peaceful" means, and so on—your political position today cannot be distinguished from that of John Foster Dulles, who is Thomas E. Dewey's choice for Secretary of State. For you, a Socialist who knows how to make use of certain parts of the Marxian analysis, who has been the nemesis not only of conservatives but of liberals for these many years, this conjunction certainly should give pause.*

Considered as a political phenomenon it is not an accident that Reinhold Niebuhr, the radical, and John Foster Dulles, the Wall

---

* I do not, of course, reflect on Mr. Dulles as a person, in which capacity I consider him both admirable and attractive.

Street attorney and one of the chief architects of the bipartisan foreign policy of the United States, should now be virtually a team. For, if war is "inevitable," whether on the basis of the Marxist class war and materialistic interpretation of history, or on the basis of the theory of human depravity and the necessity of exposing "the pretensions of modern man," in actuality the war will be between Stalinist Russia and imperialist United States, for "communism" on the one hand and "free enterprise" on the other. Let me emphasize that I am not saying that war is "inevitable," only that *if* there is war, it will be this kind and no other. These are the elements that have an "interest" in making war and that possess the resources with which to make war.

However, in lining up the masses of people for war, these elements must have at least the acquiescence of the Church and of Christian leaders, if not their unequalled blessing. They must have, in both the conservative and the progressive camps, men who are regarded as idealists but who, being practical, know that you have to meet Soviet military might with American military might, including atomic bombs, even while they also use other means; "practical" idealists who will not seriously interfere with war preparations; who are, whether conscious of it or not, and despite disclaimers, pretty well convinced in their hearts that war *is* inevitable. —Hence the constellation of Niebuhr and Dulles.

To Jan Masaryk, there was open another way than suicide to prove his integrity: open refusal to serve in the post-coup cabinet, and a public statement, either in Czechoslovakia or in exile, of the reasons therefor. This probably would have had little immediate or obvious political effect. Many would have regarded it as a foolish gesture, or even as an exhibition of addiction to "perfectionism." He might have lost his life in that case, too. But, as it is, his suicide served only to dramatize what the discerning already knew and the American government had already accepted as the basis of its policy, namely, that in the final analysis Soviet totalitarianism will not compromise on essentials. Had he been killed for public repudiation of the Stalinist course, democracy and truth would have had a martyr, Bohemia perhaps another Jan Hus.

The world does not have to go to war and commit suicide, either. But it can escape that calamity only if there are those who do not believe that catastrophe is inevitable; who do not believe that you have to line up with one side or the other in the "cold" war; who are willing to pursue a course that will seem politically ineffective and foolish in the estimation of "the wise of this world"; who will not, indeed, ask for victims or executioners, in the name of any cause or theory, but who will be prepared to lay down their own lives if the call comes, since they have learned, from the most authoritative of all teachers, that most infallible and inexorable of all laws: unless the seed falls into the ground and dies, it bears no fruit; but if it die, it brings forth much fruit.

The Scriptures are not simply an extended commentary on the single text, "Vanity of vanities, all is vanity." We read in them the commandment, "Be ye perfect as your heavenly Father is perfect," and the promise, "Behold, I make all things new." Even Paul declared, "I can do all things in him that strengtheneth me." Pacifists verily need to be on guard both against the error of over-simplification and the sin of self-righteousness, but it does not follow that nonviolence as political strategy and pacifism as a way of life are invalidated. For Christian leaders to reject them may be in truth to condemn the Church and our age to futility and doom.

Pacifism
and Perfectionism

1948 Why has the Christian Church not renounced war?
Atomic and germ warfare have appalled the Church's leaders. No
authoritative statement by any major church body attempts any
longer to prove that war itself is compatible with the will of God
or the teaching and spirit of Christ. The First Assembly of the
World Council of Churches at Amsterdam in 1948 expressed deep
concern over the inability of the Church of Christ to take a unified
stand against war, challenged the concept of a just war, and called
war a "consequence of the disregard of God." Now the discussion
of the hydrogen bomb, with its destructive potentialities a thousand
or a million times that of the Hiroshima bomb, has posed the problem still more sharply. Yet still the overwhelming majority of the
churches do not declare their irrevocable refusal any longer to
sanction or support war, and the numbers of the Christian pacifists
increase only microscopically if at all. Any exploration of the
reasons for this must undoubtedly take into account the entangle-
ment of the churches in the existing social and economic order, as
well as the fact that vast numbers of church members are Christian
only in a superficial sense.

But overshadowing even these is the influence of such men as
Karl Barth, Emil Brunner, Reinhold Niebuhr and the large number
of unquestionably sincere, learned and devout Christian thinkers
and leaders who follow them in an interpretation of the Christian

Gospel that rules out pacifism, either as a general philosophy of life, or as a practical absolute in the present situation. Though there are considerable divergences of view among them, the basic tendencies they have in common may for purposes of brevity and convenience be grouped under the term neo-orthodoxy. Without attempting to recite neo-orthodoxy's full indictment of liberal and other theologies, its attitude toward Christian pacifism may be summarized briefly as holding that the latter falls into the error of Perfectionism in its concept of personal religious experience and the moral life; into the error of Utopianism in its concept of human society and the goal of history; and into the errors of Sentimentalism and Oversimplification in its political strategy.

The impact of the neo-orthodox orientation and mood in Christian thinking and policy today is enormous, especially in the student bodies of theological schools and among the younger ministers. Moreover, quite irrespective of the numbers of adherents it may attract, its criticism merits serious consideration.

Pacifists in particular do well to heed it. It is perfectly true that a good many of us have had a soft, sentimental, naïve view of things. Our political analysis often has been superficial. Tending to minimize the power of tyranny and to underestimate the depth and extent of depravity in certain persons and systems, we have tended also to assume that there were comparatively cheap and easy solutions for international problems.

Moreover, we pacifists need to take the neo-orthodox criticism to heart in judging ourselves as moral beings and professing Christians, that we may be kept from self-deceit, from pampering ourselves, and from arrogating virtue or moral superiority to ourselves.

I am, however, convinced that in essential respects the neo-orthodox teaching and mood are un-Scriptural, not fully Christian, and a source of the gravest danger to the Church and to mankind today; and in this and succeeding articles I wish to deal with these shortcomings, considering in order the doctrine of Perfectionism as it relates to man's personal religious experience, moral life, and ethical standards; then the nature of society and the goal of history; and finally problems connected with the use of love and nonviolence as social and political strategy.

Basic to neo-orthodoxy is a well-known Christian doctrine that has come down through Paul, Augustine, Luther, and Calvin: the doctrine that we are saved by grace through faith and not by our

own efforts. Both from a theological and a psychological standpoint
this is a sound and extremely useful doctrine, and one that should
play a very important part in Christian pacifist thinking.

The person who undertakes to attain perfection in terms of
some individual standard invariably finds that the standard is never
deep enough. Only a love that does not think primarily of itself,
that has the sensitivity to feel the need of others in concrete situations which cannot be blue-printed beforehand, is adequate to human need. To be "perfect" or "whole" is precisely to be unself-
conscious, that is, perfectly spontaneous.

Furthermore, there is always an element of competition in this
business of keeping the law and striving for individual perfection—
"I thank thee that I am not as other men are"—which itself is the
deepest kind of violation of the law of life or community.

To make it the aim of life to strive for one's own perfection by
one's own power and wisdom involves an assumption of self-
sufficiency. But man is a creature, a dependent being, not self-
created. He cuts himself off, therefore, from the source of his being
when he considers himself self-sufficient. That applies both to his
relation to his fellow men, and his relation to his universe or God.
The idea that the individual, somehow isolated from his fellows and
God, can have true merit or even reality, is adjudged completely
unsound equally by Christian theology and modern psychology.
Modern psychologists and the great Christian mystics agree that the
source of evil is the "I," "mine," "me," and that "nothing burns
in hell but self-will."

For those who are not accustomed to biblical terms, this doctrine
may be expressed as saying that the assumption that we are "saved"
—which is to become integrated, or achieve serenity—because we
live a good life is true only in a secondary sense. Taken as a primary
factor, it is contrary to all human experience. The baby born into a
home does not first have to do something to make himself acceptable. For him the great basic fact is that he is accepted. For multitudes of humans born into tolerably normal homes this remains the
case right on into their adult lives. Home, as someone said, "is the
place where, when you have to go there, they have to take you in,"
and do.

It is the fact that the child is thus accepted, loved, cared for, and
trained before he has acquired any merit that makes it possible for
him to grow up into an acceptable human being. He is saved by
"grace." There is conclusive evidence that the people who grow up

to be notably unacceptable and anti-social are those who, in infancy and childhood, suffered deprivation of love. There was no "grace" to accept them for what they were.

Now the core of Christian evangelical teaching and preaching is just this: "You—any man—are accepted of God before you make yourself acceptable, and even though you are not acceptable. You always have been; you always will be. 'Like as a father pitieth his children, so the Lord. . . .' Cease, then, from running away from your true home. Stop this agonized striving to be something in yourself. Accept yourself, as you have been accepted. Pause to realize the grace available to you, the love that begat you, the energizing spirit that seeks to invade and flow through you; accept it, take it, yield yourself to it. Only believe. God is he who, when you have to go there, has to take you in, and has all the time been waiting to take you in, as the parable of the Prodigal Son portrays."

Certainly the New Testament offers no way of salvation save this of simple trust in the everlasting mercy and unmerited grace of God.

But it is equally certain that the New Testament never so much as hints that this implies any lowering or compromising of the standard to which men are called to conform or that God's grace is not equal to enabling man to live according to the will of God!

The true evangelical position is surely that stated so admirably by Karl Holl:[1]

"It is all the more astonishing that on the basis of such a conception of God, which seemed to dissolve all morality, Jesus nevertheless built up an ethic, and the most exacting ethic conceivable at that. . . . The meaning is clear: pardoning grace overcomes, because at the same time it encourages and humbles. It creates an inner affection, a feeling of gratitude which must find expression, and for which the highest is not too much to do. . . . From this follows the most splendid feature of the ethic of Jesus, namely, the naturalness, the spontaneous character of the action, which he supposes even in things most difficult and self-denying. . . . God takes the initiative: with his forgiveness he creates something quite new, out of which arises at once a real, close, and warm relationship to God, and with it at the same time a morality which ventures to take even God himself as its model."

Let us dwell for a moment on these crucial items in Christian

[1] *Distinctive Elements in Christianity*, by Karl Holl. Charles Scribner's Sons.

experience. First of all, the demand made upon man is the utmost, as Holl remarks, namely that the man saved by grace shall take even God himself as his model. "Be ye perfect, as your Heavenly Father is perfect." "If any man would be my disciple, let him take up his own cross and come after me."

And how steadfastly there runs throughout the New Testament the note of joy, elation, confidence, achievement, victory. It is a triumph song of the accepted sinner who becomes acceptable. "Beloved, now are we the children of God and it is not yet made manifest what we shall be. . . . Everyone that hath this hope set on him purifieth himself even as he is pure. . . . Whosoever is begotten of God doeth no sin, because his seed abideth in him: and he cannot sin because he is begotten of God." (I John: 3)

True, we love only because he first loved us; but we do love, and thus we have passed out of death into life. What a difference between the feeling we get from these and other typical New Testament passages and that derived from so much in the neo-orthodox writings, which sometimes impress one as all based on a single text: "The good that I would I do not; the evil that I would not, that I practice. . . . Wretched man that I am, who shall deliver me?"

For in this very passage the apostle does not end with the cry of despair, "Who shall deliver me?" but with the cry of gratitude and victory, "I thank God through Jesus Christ our Lord." And he makes it plain that the victory has, among other things, its revolutionary and transforming moral results and would have to be dismissed as spurious and not fully Christian if it failed to bear such fruit. "The ordinance of the law" is to be "fulfilled *in* us." If we still "mind the things of the flesh" then we are not Christ's. "We are debtors, not to the flesh, to live after the flesh; for if ye live after the flesh, ye must die." Only "if by the Spirit ye put to death the deeds of the body, shall ye live."

The moral life is a paradox truly enough and we are greatly in the debt of neo-orthodox theologians for having brought the paradox back into the focus of our thinking and preaching. But they get their paradoxes twisted around, I think. It is true, as they insist, that even where grace abounds, sin still also persists. (They seem to me sometimes to come very close to saying that where grace abounds, sin abounds much more!) But this is not the Christian last word; it is the statement of the paradox in its negative, noncreative form. The Christian, scriptural, creative statement of the paradox is ever: *"Where sin abounds, grace much more abounds."*

The negative and essentially non-Christian version of the paradox runs: "When I am strong, or think I am, I am weak and do not realize how weak I am. Truly, 'even the youths shall faint and be weary and the young men shall utterly fall.' When I am pure, then I am impure. When I am wise, or think I am, then my mind is closed to knowledge and wisdom. When I love, I hate in subtle ways. When I seek life, or think I have it, I lose it."

Most of us fail to dwell sufficiently on this truth, but we fail equally to dwell on the positive and creative statement of life's experience. "When at last I know I am weak, I am strong. Then I find myself the channel of the spirit of him who 'giveth power to the faint and increaseth strength to him that hath no might.' When at last I know how impure I am and no longer seek to evade or escape the humiliating and bitter realization of that, then I am purified 'even as he is pure.' When I no longer regard truth as an achievement or possession of mine and am no longer defensive about my opinions and ideas, then my mind is liberated and truth can enter its open door. When I recognize in what subtle ways I am tempted to seek my own and to hate others, then I cease to hate and do accept and love my fellows. When I lose my life, I find it."

All of this is so clearly the Christian message of redemption that for all his pessimism Niebuhr cannot avoid pointing to it. Thus in his latest book he says that the New Testament "promises a new beginning in the life of any man, nation or culture which recognizes the persistence and depth of man's defiance."

Daniel Day Williams, in his book *God's Grace and Man's Hope*,[2] in similar vein declares: "God does transform rebellious and self-sufficient men into persons who can begin to love their fellows"; and he adds the very important observation: "The power which works this transformation is *released in the depths of the personal life just at the point where man finds his own self-righteousness shattered.*" (Italics mine.)

Thus Christian humility, the abandonment of human "pretension" to which Niebuhr summons us, is the "moment" in which we experience the transforming power of God and are born anew of his spirit. It is not the moment in which we experience as final or decisive our own helplessness and corruption. When we become obsessed with human helplessness and corruption instead of being caught up in transcending them by the grace of God, we are

2 Published by Harper and Brothers, and quoted by permission.

still preoccupied with self, still self-centered and, therefore, still self-righteous. That heart that is "deceitful above all things" arrogates virtue to itself because it "knows," as "other men" do not, how self-righteous we are. If we do not end with the experience of the grace and power of God as that which overcomes and blots out our preoccupation with our sinful selves, we are but giving another demonstration of the pretension and corruption of man.

Not only in its presentation of the nature of the Christian experience of salvation is the neo-orthodox position open to important criticisms, but also in its teaching with respect to the moral life and experience: what men ought to do and can do.[3]

The opening sentences of Dr. Williams' *God's Grace and Man's Hope* read: "The Christian religion has always created hope in the human spirit. It has produced men who lived in the world of affairs with a unique expectancy." He proceeds then to criticize Reinhold Niebuhr and certain other theologians for cutting this "nerve of hope." Similarly, the neo-orthodox orientation and mood tend to cut the nerve of moral action in the individual, largely as a result of what it has to say about sin.

As they use it, "sin" appears to refer to two different things: the ordinary, garden variety of sin, which is the failure of human beings to do what they ought to do; and a sort of primal curse that rests upon man and history and binds them with a chain of evil, quite apart from any choices of good and evil on the part of individual human beings or groups.

Dr. H. D. Lewis of the University of Wales has stated one type of criticism of the neo-orthodox presentation of sin as a "mysterious cosmic disaster" so effectively that it would be foolish to attempt to improve upon it and unfortunate to paraphrase rather than quote him:[4]

"A sinfulness which is as much that of the race as of the individual, which depends on a freedom quite different from the power to choose between good and ill, which is 'introduced into the human situation,' and made inevitable by a 'force of evil prior to any human action,' is devoid of relevance to the conduct of indi-

[3] I ask the reader to keep in mind, however, what has already been said about the religious experience: what God does for man, and the source of the dynamic for moral action.

[4] *Morals and the New Theology,* H. D. Lewis, Harper and Brothers, New York, 1949, p. 68.

vidual lives; and for that reason alone it must stand discredited at the bar of ethics."

To this Dr. Lewis adds:

"The upshot of Niebuhr's doctrine is the presentation of sin, as many are only too prone to regard it today, as some mysterious cosmic disaster, some vague blot upon the universe which we just cannot conjure away, something also on account of which we must all bow our heads in shame, and, in particular, something towards which we should adopt certain religious attitudes and about which theological doctrines have to be formed. The preacher must stand in his pulpit at appointed times to pronounce himself 'agin it,' and to announce the way of salvation. But none of this appears to touch the individual in the conduct of his life, and however much he may be induced to give formal assent to his own involvement in the sins of the world, he remains fundamentally serene in the assurance that it does not really concern him for the simple reason that there was nothing he could have done about it."

To agree with this criticism is not to say that man's lot is not in certain aspects a tragic one. He is a finite creature whose days are as grass. He cannot transcend his finiteness. The circumstances of his life are often desperate, his social environment depressing and corrupting. Suffering of many kinds is likely to fall to his lot. But the issue of the moral life is not whether man can overcome his limitations and escape suffering: it is how he meets suffering (and pleasure as well), and whether he can and does fulfill the will of God for man, equipped and situated as he is.

In dealing on the plane of moral conduct with the very real problem of human sin in its proper sense, the extreme neo-orthodox emphasis on human impotence and corruption is a dangerous distortion.

Thus, if man is to acknowledge the existence of such a thing as moral life and moral responsibilities, then he must have some genuine freedom of choice. If in fact he cannot choose to do the right thing, then he is not free, any more than he would be if he had no power to choose the wrong. Either man cannot be so impotent as many neo-orthodox utterances make him out to be, or he is not a morally responsible being.

Similarly, this overemphasis on human impotence and corruption is irreconcilable with the basic character of the moral consciousness itself: what happens in the "moment" when we experience the "sense of ought," the feeling that one "must" do this or that. To quote Mr. Lewis again: "As deep rooted an assurance of the moral consciousness as any" is that "the 'sense of ought' carries with it the assumption that I can, not that I cannot." Moral responsibility becomes a fantasy if we say in effect that the moral consciousness means: "You ought to do this, because—or although—you cannot." If I cannot, that is the end of it.

Men may and do have questions about what is right. They may choose wrongly in some instances, by mistake.[5] But moments come that require a moral decision, and man finds himself confronted with an inexorable "ought," the will of God made known to him. In such a moment he knows perfectly well the difference between telling the truth or a lie, accepting a responsibility or dodging it, dwelling upon an impure thought or facing it for what it is and rejecting it. No amount of sophistry enables him, if he chooses the evil, to say later, "I could not help it." The categorical imperative is precisely: "You could help it."

This is so indubitably the case that Niebuhr, for example, on occasion clearly supports this position. "The chain of evil," he declares, "is not an absolute historical fate." And he asserts that the "self is always sufficiently emancipated of natural necessity not to be compelled to follow the course dictated by self-interest. If it does so nevertheless, it is held culpable both in the court of public opinion and in the secret of its own heart."

But this is not the prevailing impression left by the Niebuhrian pronouncements. Instead, there is here another striking instance of Niebuhr putting his finger on a very sore spot, an important psychological and spiritual fact, but using it on the whole in a negative and defeatist rather than a positive and creative way.

Thus he points out correctly how in simple subtle ways we delude ourselves as a result of social and class bias and the like, and his castigation of liberals and pacifists is largely merited. But, clearly, if self-deceit is an incurable defect of the human mind and spirit, then the neo-orthodox theologians themselves are also subject to it. Consequently, their criticism of others can be dismissed on the grounds either that it is an expression of self-deceit or that there is nothing anybody can do about it in any case. If, on the other hand, the criticism has validity and point, it is precisely because the possibility

[5] There are serious difficulties at this point, and with some of the problems of "compromise" and the like that will be dealt with in a later section.

of rising above it exists and men ought, therefore, to accept and utilize the criticism. But it is the self-deceit the neo-orthodox theoreticians tend to emphasize rather than the fact that in some sense the human spirit sees through its own devious ways; the self-deceit rather than the "grace" that prevents us from resting comfortably in it.

We live in a time when the individual is in danger of becoming a cipher. He is overwhelmed by the vast and intricate technological machinery around which his working life is organized, by the high-powered propaganda to which he is incessantly subjected, and by the state-machine on which he is increasingly dependent and by which he is increasingly regimented in peace and war.

In the face of such circumstances the individual *must* be able to believe in his own essential dignity and in his ability somehow to assert it. Instead, the neo-orthodox position has the effect, to use Dr. Lewis' vivid formulation once again, of drying up "the very springs of individual responsibility . . . in an apathetic surrender to oppressive doctrinal fictions." The neo-orthodox version of the religious experience of grace and justification, the extreme alienation of man from God so as to "veil the nature of God altogether from the eyes of man" and to make the Christian revelation wholly mysterious, "an insoluble enigma expressible only in paradox and antimony," also supports this contemptuous view of man and human powers that gives support to the most dangerous trend of our times.

Moreover, by making the process of salvation a wholly irrational one, it gives support to the idea that man must find salvation in the irrational. This is the notion that was used so effectively by the Nazis and is embraced by all reactionary movements, and that appears in a somewhat different form in the worship of the monolithic party, and the immolation to it of the individual's reason and conscience, which we encounter in communism.[6]

[6] We cannot restore the Russians to sanity except by recovering our own; we can overcome materialism only by renouncing it, and practicing brotherhood. Only the nonviolent can apply therapy to the violent.

But to ask a nation like the United States at the peak of its wealth to be willing to become poor, or at least poorer, so that others may cease to be poor, or at the peak of its power to renounce its power, is to ask a miracle comparable to that of atomic fission. Human experience suggests that such a new order can come only if there comes into being first a fellowship of persons who in themselves and through their fellowship embody the new order and who become its completely committed witnesses to all the world.

The Communists have in their International such an instrument, and every

Having said all this, however, it is important also to take some of the central admonitions of neo-orthodoxy humbly and seriously to heart. A discussion of the experience of grace and the demands of the moral law necessarily must issue in personal application. Intellectual speculation upon these matters may help, but it cannot take the place of decisions taken in "real life," on the "existential" level. The great sin is not in the intellectual distortions that may characterize speculations about these matters, but in the practical distortions of life as God meant it to be—the failure even to will the good, much less to do it—of which we are guilty. Here each of us must be his own critic and no one's else. The only real "answer" to what neo-orthodox theology has to say about human corruption and moral impotence has to be given by our lives, individual and corporate, by the Church of Christ and by the members of that Church. And who is equal to that challenge? As someone remarked recently, at the close of a long discussion when a feeling of deep humility had settled on the group, "That's where Niebuhr has us!"

What do we who contend that Christian theology cannot dispense with a doctrine of perfection have to say at this point?

In the nature of the case perfection can never be a claim. To claim perfection for oneself except in a society of the perfected would be to set up an ego that arrogates virtue to itself, the very root of imperfection. Moreover, the possibility of perfection arises precisely in the moment of true humility, when one has yielded oneself to God, and has ceased to make any claim for oneself.

The question as to whether in fact perfection can be achieved is one of those questions that should not be asked because it cannot be answered. The question cannot be answered in the negative because perfection is what God asks of us and we cannot place limits upon what "his grace made perfect in weakness" can accomplish. On the other hand, as soon as we begin to talk about perfection as an achievement of actuality, all the difficulties already stated emerge.

Nevertheless, perfection as the demand God makes upon us cannot be ruled out. "If ye keep my commandments," said Jesus, in the solemn closing hours of his life, "ye shall abide in my love, even as I have kept my Father's commandments and abide in his love. . . . I am the vine, ye are the branches; he that abideth in me

---

day bears fresh and startling witness to its effectiveness on a world scale. Obviously an International of Love and Nonviolence is needed, and this is what the Christian Church in principle is and in practice ought to be.

and I in him, the same beareth much fruit. . . . Verily, verily, I say unto you, he that believeth on me, the works that I do shall he do also; and greater works than these shall he do."

As the neo-orthodox theologians point out, the revelation in Christ stands in judgment over our achievements as well as our failures, and even in our righteousnesses, which are "as filthy rags," we stand in need of forgiveness. But we stand under judgment precisely because we should and could have done what we failed to do. And the word of forgiveness is necessarily accompanied by the charge, "Go and sin no more." Forgiveness in its most basic aspect means this: that God will not let us drop out of the moral universe; he will not free us from the requirement that we be his children reborn in Christ.

In every important sphere of life the passion for perfection is the indispensable binding and transfiguring element. What would man's intellectual life and science be like but for the insatiable effort to wrest from the universe its innermost secrets? Suppose the scientist, instead of sitting down austerely before some phenomenon, trying a hundred "solutions" if necessary and discarding in the process some of his oldest and most cherished ideas, were to tell himself, "Well, man is but a poor, fallible creature. I am bound to deceive myself anyway. . . ." Clearly it is the passion for perfection, expressed in the iron determination not to be deceived, which alone makes man's science possible.

The same is true of the artist's desperate, agonizing effort really to "see" a landscape or a human face and transfer it to canvas; of the composer's straining to hear the exact harmonies of his symphony; and of the poet's longing for the word, the phrase, the sonnet that expresses his soul. And as with the artist, so with the artisan. Many have commented upon the frustration suffered by multitudes of human beings because the world seems no longer to need their craftsmanship.

So it is with human relations. How accurately the child senses whether there is genuine integrity in the relations of grown-ups to him and to each other! How desperately we need truth in all group relationships and how swiftly and surely the lack of it produces tension and frustration! How deeply each of us feels the need of giving and receiving love from parent, child, wife, husband, friend! And when all has been said that can be said by modern theologians or psychologists about our ambivalent and self-deceiving egos, we still long to give and to receive love, and not any substitute. And we actually have experienced enough love to know that it has to be genuine and whole; that, as in Tennyson's homely yet perceptive lines, "In love, if love be love, if love be ours, faith and unfaith can ne'er be equal powers"; and that we cannot tolerate even "the little rift within the lute that by-and-bye will make the music mute."

A civilization that has blurred the ideas of obligation to the highest moral standards and accountability to God has no bond to hold it together. A generation that believes itself condemned to moral impotence is doomed to moral impotence and to disintegration.

So it is, finally, in the deepest and innermost realm of all, that of religious experience, that the soul of man thirsts for God, not for a lesser being, and will not rest until it finds its rest in him. "My soul thirsteth for God; yea, e'en for the living God." Even *my* soul . . . for the *living God*.

There it is, as it was yesterday and will be forever. That "thirst" and its quenching in the water of life that proceeds from God and becomes in us as a well of water springing up into eternal life is what religion and all our theologies are about. Nothing else finally is worth writing about. There would be no human life if this binding element of the thirst for perfection and its satisfaction were not in it.

There is, of course, a better keyword to use here than the term "perfection." The keyword is "commitment" or "surrender." It is the purity of heart, the integrity, of which Jesus spoke. It is Kierkegaard's concept, "Purity of heart is to will one thing."

When our theological discussions are ended as when they began, the one overarching question remains: Are we willing to make this unconditional surrender to the will of God as it is revealed? Are we willing to make the unequivocal and complete commitment of all we have and are to his service? Christ stands before each of us and says: "Will you take up your cross and follow me?"

And the first and gravest difficulty is simply that we will not say yes to that question, as Tertullian suggests in a notable passage:[7] "The state of faith does not admit of necessities. No necessity of sinning have they, whose one necessity is that of not sinning. . . . For [otherwise] *even inclination can be pleaded [as a] necessity having of course an element of compulsion in it.*" (Italics mine.)

We are warranted, therefore, in humbly asking those of our

---

[7] *De Corona Militia* II, pp. 91-93. Cited by C. J. Cadoux.

fellow-Christians who frame, or accept, elaborate and distorted doctrines about man's general inability to do the will of God and adhere to the ethic of the gospel, whether they are in this way rationalizing their own disinclination to obey the gospel at some very specific point—in not renouncing war, for example, when deep in their hearts they know there is no longer any way in which it can be reconciled with the gospel. Yet who among us is not stricken with shame by the knowledge that he, too, is holding back part of the price of complete commitment that God asks? What is there for us to do in face of the ghastly need of our age and the disaster that threatens it but pray unitedly for the spirit of repentance and faith, knowing that all things are possible to those who believe and are willing to submit to the baptism of the Holy Spirit?

Communism
and Civil Liberties

1949 In beautiful, wealthy and almost solidly Republican Westchester County, just north of New York City, not in the wicked cities, the "wild west," or the "backward south," but in the land of respectability, on two successive Sundays late this summer angry mobs stoned and overturned automobiles, injuring 150 people who had committed the "crime" of attending a concert given by Paul Robeson, a great singer and an avowed Communist. At least some of the 800 police who were present to keep order joined the mob in shouting imprecations at the "Communists."

Two months earlier, in July, several thousand teachers and other school officials, gathered in Boston for the annual convention of the National Education Association, passed a resolution urging that Communist Party members be barred from employment in the public schools. The resolution was carried in an atmosphere of intense excitement, impatience with any expression of negative opinion, and insistence on putting the thing through before the regular order for this action had arrived.

The action of the NEA is typical of action being taken currently by many governmental and private bodies, and the Westchester riots were an ominous symptom of the now widespread anti-Communist hysteria. Increasing numbers of teachers and other public employees must sign "loyalty oaths." Communists are barred from teaching in public and private educational institutions, and in many instances a "Communist" may be merely a Wallace voter or anyone else with an unorthodox idea. The United States Senate unanimously agreed this summer to bar any Communist youth from holding a fellowship under the Atomic Energy Commission, even for research that has no connection whatever with military security, while the Department of Justice is seeking to convict the top officials of the Communist Party in a trial under the Smith (Gag) Act in New York City. State legislatures throughout the country are considering proposals to outlaw the Communist Party, and immigration authorities are deporting Communists who have lived in this country for many years.

My deep concern for these things does not grow out of any sympathy for the Communist point of view. I believe that the world Communist movement and the Communist-dominated regimes in Russia and other lands present problems of the utmost seriousness for all who value the democratic way of life and want to see it maintained, improved, and extended.

Regardless of what may be true of some forms of communism in theory, communism as a cultural and political manifestation in our day is a form of totalitarianism. To stop its spread and to abolish it as a way of life and as a political dictatorship is therefore the necessary and urgent purpose of believers in democracy.

Added to this is the fact that Communists constantly resort to deceit and violence, and that they believe this to be the only realistic way to work for "the revolution"—a new social order—in the kind of world in which we live. The seriousness of this is not altered by the fact that multitudes of Communists are utterly and magnificently sincere in giving unquestioning obedience to the monolithic Party through which alone, they are persuaded, a new world can be born. They do use deceit and violence at the behest of the Party; they do conceal and lie about membership in the Party; they do penetrate organizations of all kinds for ulterior purposes and without hesitating to resort to the most egregious chicanery.

Finally, and most exasperatingly, while Communists vehemently insist on their "democratic freedom" to speak, write, and organize, they do not maintain these civil liberties in Russia or other Communist-dominated lands, and are frankly bent upon replacing "bourgeois democratic forms" with the "dictatorship of the proletariat," in the United States and other democracies. In the United States the C.P. actually supported the prosecution of Trotskyists in Minneapolis under the Smith Act in 1941 and, at recent "Civil Rights Congresses" (*sic*), refused to join in urging pardon for these Trotskyists, while demanding that all "progressive" elements join them in the bitterest protests against the current prosecution of Communist Party officials under this same Act. It is completely understandable that non-Communist Americans should exclaim: "Why should a democratic country commit suicide by practicing tolerance toward the intolerant?"

Why then do pacifists, who in their rejection of all violence are in a sense further removed from Communists than any other elements in our country, contend against the current anti-Communist measures and plead for full liberties of speech, press and association for Communists and fellow-travelers?[1]

The first reason, I suppose, is the obvious futility of the typically sweeping repressive measures now being resorted to, their failure to do what they are supposed to do. For example, let us concede that Communists are disloyal and anti-democratic, and an insidious danger by reason of their concealment of their adherence to the Party and its ideas. The argument then is that, by requiring loyalty oaths of government employees and teachers, by barring Communists ("advocates of the overthrow of the government by force and violence") from government posts and teaching positions, we can "smoke out" the Communists and thus deprive them of the opportunity to spread their doctrines and influence surreptitiously.

Plainly such reasoning is faulty. The Communists will not hesitate to take the loyalty oaths, and simultaneously they will take stronger measures than ever to conceal their identity whenever that may serve their purposes. Morally they will feel that they are more than ever justified in doing so, for these very repressive measures will seem to confirm what they have all along contended: that the exponents of civil liberties—and more particularly the governing elements in the so-called democratic countries—do not believe in civil liberty in principle any more than they, the Communists, do! In other words, in order to smoke out the Communists, we institute

---

[1] In this article I am not dealing with the measures taken against illegal or violent *actions* of Communists or other subversive groups. Pacifists do not necessarily accept uncritically all that the duly constituted authorities may do in this field, but this is not the urgent issue before the American people today. For the sake of the present argument it will be assumed that counter-intelligence operates against Russian spies in this country, that laws against violence in labor disputes or public demonstrations in which Communists may be involved are enforced, and that *actions* involving the betrayal of military secrets, treason, or threatening the forcible overthrow of national or state governments will be dealt with under the laws existing for the purpose.

measures that convince them they were right all the time in believing that democracy is an illusion and a farce, and make them take greater precautions against being smoked out. This hardly seems the way either to win Communists to faith in democracy or to protect society against their deceitfulness.

Consider the proposal to bar Communists from teaching positions. The democratic or libertarian standard for engaging or retaining teachers is simply that they should be professionally competent, without regard to their religious or political beliefs or lack of them. Professional competence, putting the matter in very summary fashion, means a knowledge of subject matter, skill in communicating it to others, and an attitude of wanting to help pupils learn to think for themselves.

Now it is argued by a good many usually sober and balanced people that the fact that a person becomes a member of the Communist Party in itself constitutes conclusive evidence that he or she cannot have the balanced, objective, unemotional attitude essential in a good teacher. The political views of Communist Party members, say these critics, are bound to affect their teaching improperly. Thus two members of a University of Washington faculty committee that considered charges against fellow professors, two of whom eventually were discharged from their posts, said in a minority report that "active membership in the Communist Party is an overt act of such reckless, uncritical and intemperate partisanship as to be inimical to and incompatible with the highest traditions of academic freedom and responsible scholarship." The obvious—and at the same time profound—comment on this statement is the one made by Henry Steele Commager, the distinguished Columbia University historian: "If membership in the Communist Party—or in any other organization—does paralyze the critical sense or produce bad teaching or worthless scholarship, it should not be difficult to prove this."[2]

By adhering to a pragmatic approach, judging each case on the merit of the evidence produced about the individual's record, we would avoid adopting the policy of guilt by association and intention which is contrary to the American tradition and characteristic of procedure under dictatorships. Abandonment of an important element in democratic process might be too high a price to pay, even if it were the only way to accomplish the objective of eliminating

[2] *The New Republic*, July 25, 1949.

some undesirable teachers, but to make this sacrifice when there is another simple way to gain the desired result surely suggests that hysterical emotions rather than reason are the source of our current reactions.

In the second place, as has been suggested, the cost of the prevalent repressive measures is too high. The mere cost in dollars and cents is a far from negligible item. Since the Communists are not going to expose themselves voluntarily, it becomes necessary to set up bulky and expensive investigating machinery. Under the Feinberg Law in New York State, every school board in the state has to examine the loyalty of all the teachers in its jurisdiction. Of course, it will be deemed hardly sufficient to do this once in each case, certifying a teacher as loyal for the rest of his professional life. And presently, as experience has shown, it becomes necessary to have investigators to check on the investigators. Politicians, moreover, who serve on federal and state committees on so-called un-American activities have patronage, publicity, and other reasons for wanting their work extended and their staffs enlarged. Seldom if ever does such an agency consent to go out of existence, or even to have its appropriations cut.

The point becomes sharper when we consider this item of cost from other angles. How many Communists have been discovered and removed from government jobs or university teaching positions? Professor Thomas I. Emerson of the Yale Law School pointed out at a conference of the American Civil Liberties Union this spring that fifty persons in federal posts—none of them top-echelon positions in any sense—out of a total of 2,300,000 have been discharged as a result of the loyalty tests! At the University of Washington a very long and searching study found three Communist Party members on a faculty of over seven hundred.

Looking at the problem from another angle, Professor Commager, in his *New Republic* article, makes the flat assertion: "No instance has yet been produced where a Communist on a university faculty actually did harm to students or to scientific truth." He goes on to point out that we have, as yet, no reliable evidence as to the advantage which follows from such an investigation. Professor Commager then makes the interesting suggestion that the University of Washington should, in a year or two, set up a careful study to determine the answer to that question. "Will it then appear that competent scholars are more eager to join its faculty . . . ? Will parents breathe more easily . . . ? Will students come to the campus more gladly, and will their learning and morals show an improvement?"

The current procedures are costly and dangerous also because they tend to divert attention from the really important reasons for the existence of incompetent teachers, and are actually likely to help perpetuate and nourish the sources of the evil. Any informed American must realize that the number of Communists, competent or incompetent, who may have positions in the educational institutions of the country, especially the public schools, is infinitesimal compared to the incompetents who owe their jobs to the influence of groups like the American Legion, Chambers of Commerce, churches (Catholic in some communities and Protestant in others), political machines, or just plain dumb school board members—all regarded as one hundred percent American and unquestionably anti-Communist.

And in the final analysis, surely the inadequacy of teachers is due to inadequate pay and the low esteem in which the job of teaching is held by large sections of the American populace! Certainly there is no reason to think that the present anti-Communist hysteria and the measures that flow from it will do anything to remedy these tremendous evils. On the contrary, the result easily may be aggravation of them.

If once we abandon the clear and simple test of professional competence and decree that some racial, religious, or political test is to be applied to teachers, then in various parts of the land it soon will be difficult for Negroes or Jews or Roman Catholics or agnostics or trade unionists, as the case may be, to obtain or hold positions in the schools or other public institutions. If people who regard Russia and communism as a supreme menace are justified in applying *a priori* political tests and the doctrine of guilt by association and intention against Communists, then why should not equally sincere and equally disturbed people who think Roman Catholicism is the supreme menace apply such tests and doctrines against all Roman Catholics?—Provided, that is, that they have the power to do what they want. In the defense of civil liberties there can be no exceptions, or there will soon be many.

We have it on the authority of the ardent anti-Communists themselves that Stalin and the Communists are trying to produce social strife in America, while the Communists claim that they need only give a little assistance to tendencies that are inherent in our "fake capitalistic democracy." Are we not doing a good deal to prove them right, and thereby playing directly into Stalin's hands? Certainly the growing tendency to "purge" all nonconformist thinking represents a rending of the very fabric of American life.

Even so, a good many people who share misgivings about these repressive measures are not inclined to oppose them wholeheartedly unless they see an effective alternative method of "stopping communism." It is important to discuss whether such an alternative exists.

Communism, which involves the abrogation of the civil liberties that are so important a part of the "American way of life," can come to prevail in this or any other country under two conditions.

The first of these is the continuance of economic injustice and insecurity and racial inequality. This is the soil in which communism and other forms of totalitarianism flourish. To combat communism effectively, then, we must remove these evils. Otherwise, we shall prevent communism only at the cost of civil war and setting up the kind of Fascist totalitarianism that existed in Germany, Japan and Italy.

Contrariwise, the provision of such reforms as genuine equality for Negroes and other minority groups would create in this country a sense of such moral and social well-being as would cause members of minority groups, and millions of others, to laugh Communist propaganda off the stage. The churches, I suggest, ought to ponder the possibilities of an immediate large-scale campaign against all segregation and discrimination as perhaps the most effective single contribution they can make to the campaign against communism both in this country and abroad.

The second pre-condition for an anti-democratic regime is a situation in which people become afraid of change and of the democratic process that makes peaceful change possible. Unhappily, this already has happened to large sections of the American public. There are a good many groups—employer, veteran, church, political—that all along have had more real faith in conformity, and in some form of authoritarianism, than in nonconformity and democracy; and, as always happens in time of crisis, such underlying beliefs are coming to the surface. In this age of persecution, terror, and atomic war, millions of people who thought they believed unconditionally in humaneness, liberty, and peace have gone through an experience of shattering disillusionment. Though many shrink from admitting it, even to themselves, they have concluded that ours is not an age in which these things can be; that survival demands readiness to resort to the most "realistic"—i.e., ruthless—means.

Ultimately I think this poses for American libertarians of all kinds the hard choice of renouncing war or giving up the democratic way of life. I do not want to press that issue now. Suffice it to remind our fellow libertarians who are not yet convinced that this drastic choice must be made; that it will be very difficult to develop a morale for the defense of democracy when democracy is a vanishing quantity. In such circumstances the advantage is bound to be with the totalitarians who have no scruples or inhibitions and have all along contended that democracy is on the way out. Democracy cannot be saved by "rear-guard action." It has to be positive. Democratic nations can be saved only by living their creeds radiantly and imaginatively.

For pacifists, at any rate, the way seems clear. We shall oppose all the current repressive measures. We shall seek to allay hysteria. We shall defend Communists against repression and violence by every nonviolent means open to us, even if that means that portions of the public lump us with the Communists. Many of us, if placed in similar situations, surely will want to follow the example of Dr. Miriam Brailey and two other Baltimore pacifists who, at the risk of their jobs, refused on August 1 to take the "loyalty oath" under the notorious Ober Act, which a Maryland judge pronounced unconstitutional some days later. And we shall continue resolutely to oppose war with Russia and appeal for a nonviolent solution of the controversy between Russia and the United States.

To avoid misunderstanding, let me observe in conclusion that this is not an argument in favor of refraining from criticism of communism and of Russia. Freedom of expression for "the thought we hate" implies equal freedom *and responsibility* to say that we do reject the thought and why. There is no inconsistency in opposing the State's attempts to "control thought" and in criticizing regimes that do the same thing.

Nor do we advocate "united fronts" or organizational collaboration with Communists. Communists have made it abundantly clear that they do not believe in civil liberties in principle and for those with whom they differ essentially. The problem is whether those who *do* believe in freedom of utterance will grant that freedom to those who frankly would destroy it if they had the power.

Toward solving that crucial problem, Communists obviously cannot contribute. And I think many well-meaning Americans would feel more secure now, and would be more willing to risk the great adventure of contesting communism on democracy's own ground, and by strictly democratic means, if the line I have indicated had been drawn more clearly and consistently in the past. These people now feel that they have been duped. Communist propaganda for civil liberties has turned out to be propaganda for communism and Soviet policy. These people now conclude—mistakenly of course—that all propaganda for civil liberties is therefore suspect; and some of the "intellectuals"—fellow-travellers, innocents and collaborators—are partly responsible for that conclusion. As a result, we lack support we desperately need in the supreme crisis for democracy in our own country and elsewhere.

The corollary of this observation is that it is essential in the struggle against totalitarianism that all the elements in educational circles, farmers' organizations, unions, churches, women's organizations, and so on who are unequivocally committed to the principles of free expression and association should find a way immediately to put themselves on record against the current repressive activities, and for a positive and imaginative practice of democracy, and then should devise effective ways of working for these ends. Communists and fellow-travellers and other kinds of authoritarians cannot do this. Unless the democratic elements get to work at once, the cause of freedom is doomed—in other words, the authoritarians will have won.

Korea:
Spark to Set
a World Afire?

1950 Two short paragraphs in the opening pages of *Newsweek* for July 10, 1950, when placed side by side, vividly suggest the mixed feelings that the American people have about the war in Korea; at the same time they outline the complicated character of the situation and the problems it presents. The first of these paragraphs appeared originally in *Newsweek* of April 24, 1950, and was reprinted in the later issue as proof of the prophetic powers of the editors.

It can't be officially admitted but the U. S. is trapped in South Korea. Its efforts to reform Syngman Rhee's government and build a satisfactory anti-Communist bulwark have been a dismal flop. Yet the U. S. can't get out without handing the country to the Soviets. Any such retreat would have a disastrous, perhaps fatal, effect on anti-Red morale throughout Asia. So, unpleasant as the outlook is, the U. S. will have to hang on.

The second paragraph opens the magazine's special section on the Korean War. It is headed: "Uncle Sam Takes Role as World Cop," and says:

Never before had the United States risked so much in defense of freedom. Never had the American people seemed so firmly united in their approval of an audacious national policy. Never had the nation's prestige risen so high in the part of the world still free to admire courageous knight errantry.

331

On the one hand, we are "trapped in South Korea." On the other hand, Uncle Sam has become the brave and glamorous cop on the global beat. We are knights errant in a crusade for freedom. Our prestige among free peoples has never been so high. Never have the American people been "so firmly united in their approval of an audacious national policy."

When North Korean troops crossed the Thirty-eighth Parallel into South Korea and a couple of days later, on June 30, President Truman ordered American ground troops into that country, the "cold war" ended. Admittedly Russia and the United States now are engaged in a power struggle, matching military might with military might, all around the world. Politically, the Truman administration has committed the United States to World War III, which is to say, to all-out war with the strongest weapons that may be available, whenever in the opinion of the White House and the Pentagon the developing world situation, the "security" and the "interests" of the United States, require it. If the actions recently taken in Korea, Formosa, the Philippines and Indo-China, in accord with the President's policy statement of June 27, 1950, were "inevitable" and required by the "national honor" of the United States, at another moment all-out war will similarly be "inevitable" and required by the "national honor."

Psychologically and spiritually, the American people, if they accept this explicit extension to the entire planet of the "Truman doctrine" of "containment of Russia and communism by force," have also committed themselves to World War III.

To say this is not to say that all-out war will break out next week, next month, or even next year. Chronologically, full-scale war may still be some distance away, though even in this sense the situation is ominous. Commentators have suggested that the "real" beginning of World War II was the Japanese invasion of Manchuria in 1931, with the failure of the democratic nations to take collective action against it, or Mussolini's attack on Ethiopia in 1935, or the Spanish Civil War in 1936. These events took place thirteen, seventeen and eighteen years respectively after the Armistice of 1918. Korea of 1950 is less than five years after V-J Day! Thus has the pace of world events in the Atomic Age been accelerated.

Clearly we need to get the best possible understanding of the present world situation, of what underlies it, of how we should react to it, of what may yet be done to avert catastrophe or to salvage what is worthy of preservation from the whirlwind being produced by the wind men have sown.

Korea was "liberated" from the Japanese at the end of World War II. Under a wartime agreement between the United States and the Soviet Union, the former occupied the southern end of the peninsula and accepted the surrender of the Japanese forces there. Russia functioned similarly north of the Thirty-eighth Parallel. This arrangement was to remain in force only until a unified and independent government could be established for the whole country.

Each occupying nation functioned according to its own pattern during the transition period. The Soviet Union ruthlessly eliminated the Japanese business men and landlords. They promoted the organization of unions of peasants and industrial workers and, so far as North Koreans were permitted to exercise economic and political power, such power was in the hands of these unions. Industries were transferred from private to public ownership. Land was widely distributed to the peasants. All this was done under the guidance of the Communist Party, which was built up rapidly under Moscow leadership and which, in its disciplined fashion, exercised final power in the unions, the government, among the police, and later the army, and so on. Dissenting elements were purged.

In South Korea, the American forces from the outset worked largely through Syngman Rhee, elder statesman and symbol of the Korean independence movement, especially to the outside world. He had lived in exile for many years. His thinking was in terms of nineteenth-century Western democracy and a free enterprise economy and he was out of touch with the masses who had lived in Korea during the harsh Japanese occupation and with the ideas, including Communistic ones, which had spread among them. On Rhee's advice the distribution of land to the peasants was for the most part postponed until a Korean government should be established. Any peasant could see the difference between the land policy in South Korea and that in the north. The American Occupation had directives to encourage organization of workers and peasants but Rhee did not want strong bona fide unions, and the Occupation authorities (military) were primarily concerned with maintaining order. The presence and intense activity of Communists in the unions seemed to them to offer sufficient warrant for following Rhee's line of suppressing independent unions and encouraging company unions.

All Koreans, in the meantime, were agreed upon one thing, namely, that they wanted a united country with its own independent government. This was ostensibly also the objective of the two occupying powers. The continued division between the industrial north, with a population of about nine million, and the food-producing south with a population of twenty million, was and is economic and political nonsense.

Russia and the Communists advocated, in both North and South Korea, the setting up of a coalition government in which virtually all parties would be represented. They were intent, however, on keeping out of the coalition, if possible, groups such as Syngman Rhee's which were intransigently anti-Russian and anti-Communist. Experience in European satellite countries has demonstrated that the strictly disciplined Communist Party always dominates such coalitions and, before very long, openly takes over.

For a time, American policy in South Korea also favored the coalition idea, though the Occupation authorities wanted the Communists kept down and wanted a government in Korea which would not be "unfriendly" to the United States.

The two men on whom the United States depended to carry through the coalition policy in South Korea were a popular non-Communist leftist, Lyuh Woon Hyung, and Kim Kiu Sic, an American-educated, highly respected Presbyterian elder who had been vice-premier in Syngman Rhee's government-in-exile. The two met for the first time on June 14, 1946, at the home of a political adviser to U. S. Commander Lieutenant General John R. Hodge. For a time discussions proceeded hopefully. Then worker and peasant discontent with the policy previously described expressed itself in strikes. Syngman Rhee's tough youth corps and Korean police, largely retained from the brutal Japanese regime, joined with American troops in violent suppression which led to riots and more suppression. Mass arrests and police raids shattered the unions and all leftist parties. Lyuh remained independent but the remnants of his party felt they had no alternative but to go underground and join the Communists. Both Kim and Lyuh denounced as a farce the election of a provisional South Korean legislature that was held under these conditions. In response to Kim's demand that the elections be annulled General Hodge appointed some centrists to seats in the legislature and hope for a moderate government was kept flickering. In the spring of 1947, when the U.S.-U.S.S.R. Joint Commission reconvened in an attempt to establish an all-Korean government, Kim and Lyuh tried once more. But on July 19 a rightist assassin shot down Lyuh on the street in Seoul. Hopes for a moderate course came to an end. The United States was committed to the support of Rhee's regime.[1]

It was in the context of such developments that the Russian sponsored government was set up in North Korea and the United States-United Nations sponsored government in the South. Russia withdrew her troops in December, 1948, except for a military mission numbering about 3,500. The United States withdrew her troops in June, 1949, except for a military mission of about 500. Both have supplied military aid to their respective "puppets."

It is only when this background is kept in mind that anything like a balanced view of the developments which occurred toward the end of June is possible. So far as the immediate situation in Korea is concerned, the weight of the available evidence seems to be with those who charge the North Korean republic with being the "aggressor." However, it is notoriously difficult in such situations to determine which "incidents" among many precipitated the conflict and who is "responsible" for such incidents. Each side engages in what the other side regards as "provocations," and the "incidents" well may be just that. The North Korean government has made no secret of its conviction that Korea should be united and could be united only under a coalition regime that would be called that but actually would be Communist-controlled. It has proclaimed its duty to "liberate" the oppressed South Koreans, by force if necessary. Communists have engaged in intensive and often violent activity against the Syngman Rhee regime in South Korea.

That regime on its part has continued to pile up a sorry record. William Costello, director of news broadcasting for the Far Eastern Division, Columbia Broadcasting System, who recently returned from a four-year tour of duty in Asia, writes of "a motley assort-

---

[1] A detailed running account of these developments may be found in files of *The Compass*, July 13, 1950, and in preceding and following issues. The series was written by Hugh Deane, who served in U. S. Navy for four years as a Japanese language officer, wrote broadcasts to the Orient for the Office of War Information, and visited South Korea in 1947-48. Other newspapers and periodicals have furnished abundant corroborating documentation.

ment of expatriates, collaborators (with the former Japanese occupation), Fascist reactionaries, professional assassins and confused intellectuals,"[2] in speaking of the Rhee regime. The regime's purging of Communists was carried out in such a way that the public hates "Syngman Rhee's police; thousands of Korean peasants who have suffered from the brutality and rapacity of the police would welcome an opportunity to turn on them." Syngman Rhee, whose party was decisively defeated in an election some weeks ago but who still wields power, has proclaimed his intention to "liberate" the poor North Koreans. On July 14, Brigadier General William L. Roberts, head of the U. S. Military Mission in Korea for twenty-six months, stated, according to an Associate Press dispatch to *The New York Times,* July 16, 1950, that the South Korean government did not get heavy military equipment before the recent large-scale fighting broke out chiefly because it had a strong desire to attack North Korea. "This placed us in a skittish position," General Roberts explained. "To prevent the South Koreans from attacking, we gave them no combat air force, no tanks, and no heavy artillery."

Clearly, North Korea is, in the immediate sense, the "aggressor." Its troops are on South Korean soil and engaged in obviously well planned military operations. Pacifists, of all people, will not regard this lightly. Neither is there evidence that in the immediate situation on the Thirty-eighth Parallel the United States engaged in any provocation. But one can hardly be certain that the Rhee regime engaged in none. One suspects that he may have wanted intervention to save his regime and may not have made much effort to prevent a situation that would lead to intervention.

The union which the North Koreans, on their part, offered is unquestionably one that would have involved Communist control; but maybe the ordinary Korean would prefer that to long-drawn-out war or another occupation.

Whatever further analysis may show, what we have already recorded makes it clear that American troops in Korea are hardly engaged in a perfectly simple police action to save an innocent pedestrian, on a lawful and beneficent errand, from a bandit. There is surely reason for questioning whether the calculated risk of global war is rational or right under the circumstances.

The steps taken by the United States in the Korean crisis are justified primarily, however, as "police" or "collective security" ac-

2 *The New Republic*, July 10, 1950.

tion against an "aggressor." It is declared that Russia, through its puppet North Korea, is engaged in "aggression" against South Korea and the democratic or "peace-loving" nations. North Korean troops are on South Korean soil.

It is conceivable, the argument continues, that Russia or North Korea, or both, have genuine grievances, but that these should not be adjusted by unilateral military measures. Differences among nations should be settled by diplomacy and negotiation, preferably through the United Nations. "Peace-loving" nations must demonstrate unmistakably that no nation can get away with an attempt to settle some crucial issue by force.

Many hold that this case for "police" action is practically unassailable, because of the stand taken by the United Nations Security Council. The United Nations, they contend, as the organization set up to maintain peace had a clear duty to order North Korean troops to cease fire and retire behind Parallel Thirty-eight. When this order was disregarded, the Security Council called on the United States and other nations to furnish military aid to stop the "aggression." It is under United Nations auspices, therefore, that the United States is proceeding to take the necessary "police" action. General MacArthur, pursuant to a United Nations request that the United States designate a commander in Korea, has been so designated. The United Nations flag flies beside the American flag over Korean battlefields. "The case," people say, "is as simple as that."

At the outset it is worth noting that, even if the case were essentially as described by the exponents of American policy, the action being taken is military and not "police" action in the usual sense of the term. Soldiers and bombing planes are fighting against other soldiers and against civilians. The "police" do not look and act like London bobbies, or New York's "finest." It is war and it may be the spark that sets off World War III, as indeed is generally admitted. Whatever the merits of any argument that the war is a righteous one, we deceive ourselves by describing the fighting in Korea as being analogous to police action.

Another important aspect of the Korean situation is that in a very real sense this is a civil war, attempting to achieve national unity under one or another of two competing regimes. That comparatively little attention has been paid to this fact is unfortunate and probably symptomatic, since it is another instance of a pattern that shows up in nearly every recurring crisis, especially in the Orient. Such a war raged in China for many years. One is going on openly in Indo-China and another just below the surface in Iran.

Less than a century ago, the United States was embroiled in civil war in which national unity and competing economic systems were basic factors. The issue of foreign meddling in that civil conflict was a very sore one. Most Americans would agree that it would have been most unfortunate if Great Britain had intervened, as influential elements in that country wanted. The North would certainly have regarded intervention as an act of war. Perhaps Americans ought to ponder this analogy between an episode in their own history and what is taking place in Korea rather than concentrating exclusively on the "police" action analogy.

The fact is that neither the United States nor the United Nations would have intervened in the Korean civil war today if they did not regard it as an episode in the power struggle between Russia and the United States. The "national interests" and the "security" of the United States are involved and it is assumed that these are paramount considerations for any nation.

It has long been recognized that domination of Europe by one power would harm the "interests" and imperil the "security" of the United States. Germany under the Kaiser and again under Hitler sought to establish itself as such a power on the European continent. The United States "had to" fight two world wars to prevent that. If it had not done that, it would have become an "inferior" power.

The "interests" and "security" of this country are involved, it is argued, in Europe, in the Pacific and in fact all over the world. The place of Germany in American propaganda as the threat to world peace has been taken by Russia. President Truman, in the policy statement of June 27, 1950, makes this perfectly explicit, and he groups with the United Nations "police action" in Korea other moves that are frankly American moves in the global conflict with Russia. Thus he announces that an American fleet is being sent to Formosa, and that the deposed Nationalist Government of China now located on that island—whose representation in the United Nations the United States still recognizes and defends—has been ordered not to carry on military operations against the Chinese mainland held by the Communists. "The determination of the future status of Formosa"—which for the present is made a *de facto* military base and ward, or puppet, of the United States— "must await the restoration of security in the Pacific."

This is frankly on the ground that "the occupation of Formosa by Communist forces would be a direct threat to the security of the Pacific and *to United States forces performing their lawful and necessary functions in that area."* (Use of the term "Communist" here, of course, serves as a warning both to Russia and to the Chinese Communist government which admittedly is the functioning government on the entire Chinese mainland and has plenty of grounds for contending that Formosa belongs to China.) The functions of American troops so far away from home are "lawful," presumably on account of the American victory over Japan in World War II, and "necessary" for American "interests" and "security."

John Foster Dulles pointed to the same kind of consideration in a radio address on his recent return from Korea and Japan.[1] He had gone to Japan to discuss a projected treaty between that country and the United States. Spokesmen for the Administration had made it clear that in connection with such a treaty a prime consideration must be the "security" of Japan against Russian attack. Since, with the consent if not on the initiative of the United States Occupation authorities, Japan had written a clause into its constitution eliminating any military establishment whatever, it also had been made clear that the United States would "have to" provide Japan with the "security" which an unarmed nation would "of course" lack. This in turn meant bases for the United States in Japan.

Against this background, Mr. Dulles pointed out that Russia already held the island of Sakhalin to the north of Japan and that Korea is very close to the southern part of Japan. "Thus, if the Communists have . . . Sakhalin . . . also Korea . . . Japan would be between the upper and lower jaws of the Russian bear. That obviously would make it more difficult to provide the Japanese people with security." And according to current American foreign policy the United States must furnish the Japanese with this "security," since the "security" of the United States takes in the whole Pacific area, and Japan, as everyone knows, is in that area. There is good reason to suppose that the Kremlin's move to consolidate the Russian position in Korea, i.e., on the Asiatic mainland, may have been made to counter the American move to consolidate its power position in Japan.

Thus it is that realistic consideration of the Korean crisis and

[1] *The New York Times,* July 2, 1950.

how to deal with it must give adequate weight to the basic fact that two vast, dynamic powerful nations—the Soviet Union and the United States—armed with more destructive and diabolical weapons than nations have ever possessed in the past, are locked in a struggle of power all around the world. The governments and the peoples of these countries are admittedly seeking to defend and promote the "interests" and "security" of their respective national states. Each group contends that in so doing it is acting in the best interest of other peoples and on behalf of a way of life which alone is truly good, whereas the other nation is acting against the interests of mankind and toward an evil and enslaving way of life. Unbiased observers question and discount the claims of each in this regard.

In fact, on occasion each nation disregards the sacredness of its own "faith," the need of defending it against those who will not embrace it, and keeping itself separate from such people. Thus Russia and the United States were themselves allies in war not long ago. The United States during the war sent more than eleven billion dollars' worth of lend-lease material to Stalin's Communist dictatorship and thus helped to save the Communist dictatorship from destruction.

Moreover, whatever these "interests" and this "security" may be, the conflict undertaken in their behalf periodically leads the United States to help build up yet another nation whose people Americans later must war against because this nation has become a threat to American "interests" and "security." Thus we helped to build up Japan in the Thirties and sent munitions to its warlords; and then we sent American boys to fight the Japanese and to be killed, in some cases with American shells. In much the same way the United States fought Germany in World War I, helped rebuild German military power even under the Nazis, then fought Germany again, and now once more is engaged in rebuilding it.

In the course of World War II we helped make Stalin co-victor in the greatest war in history and thus saved the Russian dictatorship. Now, on behalf of these same American "interests" and "security," American boys must war against Koreans and tomorrow perhaps against Russians. Indeed we admittedly are killing North Koreans in order to limit or weaken the power position of Stalin and the Russians. It is hard to avoid asking whether this power struggle between rival nation-states is not totally irrational.

Moreover, when we are dealing with this power rivalry, the

case for each nation appears equally good or bad, as one chooses to put it. If the United States "must" expand across an entire continent and in political or power terms "must" make the Atlantic and the Pacific and assorted seas including those around Japan, Formosa and China into American lakes, why "must" not Russia expand across an entire continent and build up "security" zones in eastern and central Europe, in China, Korea, perhaps in Iran and a few other spots? If the United States has any business in South Korea, why not Russia in North Korea? Or, one might even say, if the United States has interests in Japan and its security requires American troops there, why has not Russia interests in Mexico and Canada and why might not her security require the presence of some dependable Russian or at least Mexican and Canadian Communist troops there? Or if Russia ought to keep out of Mexico and Canada, why should not the United States keep on its side of the Pacific? If another gun or A-bomb in the Russian arsenal is a threat to this country, why is not another gun or A-bomb in the American arsenal an equal threat against Russia?

Moreover, in this context the question of who is the "aggressor" in any specific action is always, from one standpoint, a very minor one, though each nation tries very hard to fasten that label on its adversary. The question is minor because in the nature of this power rivalry each nation is an "aggressor" against the other and invariably is so regarded by the other. If one makes a move that alters the power situation, the other "must" make a countermove. If it is to the "advantage" of one to hold a certain territory, or to have a certain government in office in another nation, it automatically becomes the "advantage" of the other to change the set-up. On this level, the debate between two nations or groups of nations is a debate about power. It will be settled as such "debates" always are, in terms of power, which is to say on the battlefield.

There is considerable opinion in American political and military circles to the effect that this is the situation, but it is coupled with the conviction that in such a situation the only thing a nation can do is to fight. The exponents of this view, if reminded that nations may lose as well as win and in the end that each does lose, probably would contend that this is still the proper way for a nation to behave or that in any case it is the only way a nation can behave. They go on to argue that this time the United States will win precisely because it and the nations allied with it have taken decisive "collective action" in time. This the "democratic" nations, it is said, failed to do against the Japanese warlords in 1931, and against Mussolini, Hitler and Franco a little later.

In the first place, the United States starts off at a considerable disadvantage. What people mean when they say the United States was "trapped in Korea" is partly that the military preferred not to try to hold Korea against Russia and very likely do not believe that it can be held if Russia is determined. It is easily available to Russia and Communist China by land. It is very far away from America and approachable from American bases only by tying up sea and air transport that might at any moment be desperately needed elsewhere. It is good terrain for the kind of guerrilla war at which Communist-trained North Koreans are adept.

Secondly, in Korea, China and Indo-China, the United States is intervening in civil wars a very long way from home. The nation that does this is virtually always highly unpopular, to some extent on both sides.

Third, this is intervention by a "white" nation, identified with Western conquest of Asia in the past, and if there is one thing certain about the Asiatics it is that they want Westerners out of there. Fourth, American "intervention" is on the side of unpopular regimes such as that of Bao Dai, Chiang Kai-shek and Syngman Rhee. Tied up with such regimes the United States is at a disadvantage compared with Russia, which is for immediate abolition of them. The experience with the support America gave to the Nationalist regime in China seems to prove pretty conclusively that the Asiatic masses cannot be kept from going Communist by military measures.

One or two additional comments may be made at this time on the idea that America and its allies will stave off a war or win it because they are applying force in time. The first is that it is a speculation to argue that Mussolini, Hitler, and the Japanese militarists would have been "stopped," if only "collective" measures had been applied at the start. It is quite possible that a show of force would have halted these "aggressors" temporarily, at this point or that. But if fundamental political and economic difficulties had not been remedied, the conditions that produced Nazism in Germany, for example, would have broken out in another place and in another form as surely as an overcharge of steam will blow out a boiler at one spot if not at another. The assumption that the Western nations, if they had stopped Hitler in the Saar, would have proceeded to remedy the evils that begot and nurtured Nazism is not supported by history, or by the recent behavior of these nations after they gained a complete victory over the Nazi regime.

The argument stands on shaky legs in another respect. Russia today is hardly a totalitarianism "on the make," in the early, comparatively feeble stage of expansionism, like the Japanese in 1931, Italy in 1935, or even Hitler in the middle Thirties. The effort to contain Russia and Communism by force has been, with only a brief interval, the policy of Western nations since the Revolution of 1917. There seems little reason to believe that the policy on which—or in spite of which—the Stalinist regime evidently thrived, from 1917 to 1939, under the power relationships of that period, will prove magically successful in 1950 when the Russian power position is, relatively and absolutely, vastly more favorable.

It is entirely possible, of course, that a sufficient show of force might result in a temporary stabilization of the relationship between the United States and the Union of Soviet Socialist Republics, and the possibility that open warfare may be confined to Korea cannot be finally ruled out yet. However, the history of the last five years of Russian expansionism and persistent prosecution of the "war of nerves" does not give grounds for optimism. It seems at the moment more likely that as in Korea, so at other points, the pace of the conflict will be stepped up.

Even if a temporary stabilization should take place, however, this will not prove that Russia can be intimidated into backing down and making real peace, any more than Russia is going to be able to intimidate the United States, if for example it should experience a decisive defeat in Korea, into giving up rather than redoubling its preparations for the ultimate showdown.

Such a showdown would be with atomic and possibly biological weapons. Presumably the United States still has the advantage over Russia in atomic stockpiling. Winston Churchill and others see this advantage as offsetting the disadvantages of the long lines of communication to which we have referred, and voices are raised in Parliament and Congress suggesting that it might be best for the United States to drop a few atomic bombs on North Korea if that country and Russia do not shortly—and after solemn warning—abandon their "aggressive" conduct. If, it is argued, this is the only way to prove that "aggression" must stop, it would be better than to undergo virtually unendurable tension throughout another period, only to have an all-out war when Russia is no longer at a disadvantage in atomic armament.

It is to be feared that this line of reasoning will have an increasing appeal as time goes on for many people, including some in authority. Nevertheless, to resort to atomic bombing or the serious threat of it in Asia would be playing straight into Stalin's hands. It even may be that the Kremlin deliberately might be baiting President Truman to add the atomic bombing of Korea to that of Hiroshima and Nagasaki. For the Asiatic and African masses such an act would forever "prove" the Stalinist contention that it is the Americans who are the ruthless warmongers who will stop at nothing. It might hasten rather than postpone general war. It would not eliminate the ultimate showdown, even if it did postpone it, and it would insure that that showdown would be even more savage than otherwise.

We conclude, then, that in the context of the power conflict, global war is the outcome and that there is no assurance that in this war the victor—if there should be a victor, and whatever "victory" might mean—will be the United States.

As indicated earlier, Americans are concerned also about political and moral issues in connection with the present crisis, and it is necessary to say something more about two of them. One is the element of "aggression" and the question of whether men and nations are not bound, at almost any cost, to end it; the other has to do with the menace of Communist totalitarianism.

We have said all that needs to be said in this connection for present purposes about North and South Korea. Here we have to consider briefly the charge that in the world generally and in Korea in particular Russia is the "aggressor." The writer certainly has no doubt that Russia is an aggressor. But the reader will recall what was said earlier about the power rivalry between the United States and Russia. "For isolationists," as someone once said, "these Americans certainly do get around."

Consider also that the United States is a nation that has, or thinks it has, preponderant power. It is extremely wealthy. Its citizens have large amounts of capital they want to invest. Consequently, it does not want to be disturbed; the *status quo* suits us Americans and we just want everything to be quiet and peaceful. We are convinced that our super-armaments exist only to maintain the peace, and not to enable us to hang on—even at the risk of a world war—to what we have. It seems obvious to us that anyone who wants to upset this ideal situation is an "aggressor," a bandit and a Bolshevik.

But there are impoverished masses who are determined to up-set this situation and we have given no indication that we might be willing to lower our standard of living even temporarily in or-der to help raise theirs. Russia, on its part, does not see itself as we do. It sees itself as "the liberator of colonial peoples"—who often agree with that estimate rather than with ours—and as a rising, healthy nation destined to take the place of an older nation that refuses to adapt itself to the new age and is destined to follow Babylon, Rome and Britain into oblivion or insignificance.

Nor can the situation be altered by citing the Russian refusal to accept the Baruch plan, its walking out of the United Nations be-cause other nations refuse to recognize the *de facto* Communist government of China, and so on. Let it suffice to put it that Russia refuses to accept majority decisions in a United Nations dominated by non-Communist nations. Then let us ask whether the United States would become a "law-abiding" member of a United Na-tions dominated by Communist nations. If so, why do we still back Nationalist China's representative in the United Nations and let him vote sanctions against Communist North Korea, while refusing to recognize the *de facto* government of the most populous nation on earth?

We seem to be "trapped," to use *Newsweek's* expressive phrase. To let Russia go on is to invite war, but to stop her by force also is to invite war. Either course would be an episode on the way to World War III.

All this has a vital bearing on what is happening in and to the United Nations. The course it has taken cannot be characterized in the political and moral sense as simple, clean police action, though many individuals intended it to be and many more wished it to be. But even if it were, Russia does not accept it as such. In fact, therefore, we have civil war, not police action. Moreover, it is global war, and even if it is in some degree a righteous or even holy war on "our" side, if it runs its course the human race may be doomed and democratic and Christian values destroyed.

The United Nations also, then, is "trapped." It might well have been regarded as a laughing-stock by much of the world if it had not called for military action in Korea. But by calling for such action, it transformed itself into a war agency. It has in fact decreed that World War III shall be known as the United Nations' War Against Communism. On that basis the masses in this country are to be led to accept, and already have largely accepted, the atomic war they have dreaded and against which they have felt a deep moral revulsion ever since Hiroshima Day in 1945.

In the absence of resistance, or the readiness to resist to the limit, an attempt might be made to impose Communism on the American people and, in the ordinary sense of the term, it might succeed. "Appeasement" is no more likely to work in dealing with the Kremlin than it did with Hitler Germany.

To all who believe in Christian and democratic values, as we do, the struggle against totalitarianism of all kinds is a very important one. Nevertheless, two world wars have proved that war does not stop Communism. On the contrary, war gives Communism its chance. The psychological tension, the social upheaval and the material destruction of war prepare the soil in which Communism flourishes.

Moreover, to multitudes in industrially backward countries, Communism represents their means of liberation from feudalism, landlordism and colonialism. The United States unfortunately has often lined up with regimes which maintain or at best are very slow to remedy the very evils that the masses are determined to end. The surest way to turn Asia over to Stalin is to make the struggle against the Communist way of life synonymous with war waged by American troops on the soil of Asiatic countries.

More fundamental still is a consideration that arises from the very nature of democracy and the Christian way of life. War, even atomic and biological war, conceivably may be an instrument to serve the purposes of a totalitarian regime, though it is more likely to destroy every nation that uses it. But war, certainly in its modern form, can only poison and destroy democracy. Christians or humanitarians who take up atom bombs belie their own professions, cause a rent in their own souls, and inflict an abysmal spiritual defeat upon themselves.

To sum up the situation with which the American people are now confronted:

1. The United States is engaged in a shooting war in Korea.
2. Back of the war in Korea is a titanic, global struggle of power between Russia and the United States. *Politically* World War III has started, although some time may intervene yet before it becomes all-out war. For the American people the question is whether to get out of this war or to stay in it. Each individual American must answer now the

question of whether he will or will not take part in atomic and biological war.

3. In this war the United States suffers under a number of handicaps and can by no means be sure of victory—whatever such "victory" could bring.

4. The moral position of the United States in this conflict has serious weaknesses. It was the United States which in 1945 made the unilateral decision to launch atomic war on the earth. That, having done so, we recoiled and, at least while we thought we had the monopoly of the bomb and the know-how of its construction, we wanted to bring about international control, does not erase what we did at Hiroshima and Nagasaki and all it means in political and moral terms. When Russia decided unilaterally to build its own stockpile, to accept control on its own terms and at a time convenient to itself, and in the meantime to take the "calculated risk" of "having" to use the atomic bomb when its "interests" or the cause of "world liberation" require it, the moral position of the Russian regime became bad, shockingly bad. This does not wipe out the fact that the American moral position remains bad, shockingly bad; it underscores it. And there are other weaknesses in our moral position, too, such as our failure to use our resources and technology to raise the world standard of living, and our hoarding food or letting it rot while others starve.

5. There is no longer a quick, easy, fairly cheap solution. We are now so far down the road to war that going on and turning back are both fearful operations. The enemy, Russia, is powerful and determined, as is the United States. The power struggle having reached the stage it has, the Russians will take advantage of every "weakness" on the part of their enemies. Furthermore, Communist totalitarianism is itself a monstrous evil which humanity should resist.

The broad, strategic problem, then, is this: If the West fails to resist, Communist totalitarianism may overrun the earth. If the West continues to resist by the means of modern warfare, this will lead to global war and chaos or to the general triumph of totalitarianism. Whatever the physical outcome, spiritually the totalitarians would win.

The make-the-best-of-both-worlds "solution" is that the United States should keep up its military "security" and not let Russia or its satellites get away with aggression. At the same time, we should improve our political program: stop supporting undemocratic regimes in Asia, have racial equality at home, and so on.

This is the proposal of all the many varieties of liberals. It is not new. It is what liberals have been advocating for four decades. Riding these two horses going in opposite directions does not work. When they try or pretend to do both, nations always put their money and moral steam first into H-bombs and other armaments, and never have enough left to do anything adequate about economic rehabilitation and social change. Moreover, military "necessity" leads to alliances with the very elements that oppose all idealistic or progressive measures. With each succeeding war a larger percentage of liberals line up for war in the final showdown. This is what both the Communists and the political and military leaders in the liberals' respective countries calculated the liberals would do.

The painful and frightening tactical problem that emerges is this: suppose a people like the American people were to decide to draw back from being implicated in the atrocity of atomic war, adopt a policy of creative use of their resources and skills for truly liberating mankind, and rely on Gandhian nonviolent resistance. Would not the Russian Communist leaders, at least at first, distrust their sincerity? If during the period when we were not yet organized and trained for nonviolent resistance, we did not "keep up our military defenses" and refuse to "let Russia get away with aggression," would we not be running a fearful risk?

The honest answer to that question is an unqualified yes. This is the ultimate sense in which we and mankind are "trapped." We are sunk if we do not change our course radically and promptly. But we have to try to change under the most difficult circumstances, when it actually may be "too late" to change.

What does the pacifist say to this? In the first place, this argument that to attempt a radical change of course now is fearfully risky is the ultimate, most subtle and most debilitating temptation. For Americans today it represents the snake that hypnotizes the bird into impotent rigidity. To change the metaphor, it means seeing a man who is about to step over the edge into a chasm and not telling him to stop and turn around before taking that next step, because, even if he tried to save himself, there would be no certainty that someone might not push him over. The truth is that the lateness of the hour, and the consequent viciousness of the trap in which we are caught, should lead us to summon all our energies now, without another moment's delay.

But metaphors are of only limited value and always partially misleading. Basically the pacifist answer—the Christian answer, the answer of all great religions—is this: the problem is ultimately a spiritual one. Shall human beings survive as human beings, shall a truly human existence continue on this planet, or shall man descend below the level of the brute? Shall *men* destroy *man* or shall men continue the work of creation—creation of a true civilization? If it helps to envision the problem, let us say that the question is whether Communist totalitarianism shall drag the democratic and Christian peoples down to its own level or whether, spiritually, they will refuse to bow the knee to it, to call on Satan to cast out Satan.

If the American people today had the imagination, courage and faith to launch the true human revolution, placing itself at the service of mankind and practicing nonviolent resistance to aggression and dictatorship, the price would be high, and it might be too late to avert vast catastrophes anyway. But for a nation to lay down its life for mankind and truth, in an attempt to lead the world to a creative solution of the appeasement versus "war-to-end-war" impasse, would be an utterly different historical deed from that of a nation which joined other nations in atomic suicide and to greater or less degree goaded them into it. If a nation were willing to risk destruction for peace and truth, man as a human being rather than a brute would have reasserted himself. Humanity as a spiritual reality would live. Truth, decency, honor, courage would still live on earth in the midst of madness. In time, civilization could be rebuilt on firmer and more beautiful lines than ever. In a profound sense all the suffering and the travail of men might be redeemed.

And there is a possibility that if the Russians and Communists faced a more profound revolution than their own, espoused by men as ready as they to die for their faith—but refusing to kill or to hate—the catastrophe of world war might be averted and the menace of totalitarianism soon dispelled. We have contended for years against political naïveté in dealing with the Russian leaders and the Communists. But they are human beings, and sometimes we forget that, as perhaps they often forget that we are human too. It is tremendously important that Americans realize the extent to which they give occasion for such doubts. Perhaps someone has to be very deeply and courageously human in order to enable others also to be true to themselves. And, on a quite simple and elementary level, the ordinary Russian does not want atomic war any more than the ordinary American.

If there is no nation to follow the course we have suggested, then the pacifist would say that it is all the more important that smaller groups of people—Christians, pacifists, whoever they may be, all over the world—should follow that course, and keep mankind as a spiritual entity alive in the midst of the catastrophes and the moral disintegration that will sweep over men and nations. Finally it is all the more important that *one man,* even if he stood alone, should stand apart, refuse to join the compulsive march of the armies, and continue to be a man rather than a dictator, or a conscript in atomic war, or a passive automaton.

A program of action on this basis would include the following:

1. Support of efforts to bring about a cessation of hostilities in Korea and mediation of the issues in that situation and all the issues that underlie the East-West conflict. Pacifists should, however, feel under a deep sense of responsibility in dealing with specific mediation proposals. They have a moral right to refuse any support to American military measures and to insist that the United States should cease waging or preparing for war, withdraw from the power struggle and adopt a policy of creative service to mankind. The moral right of pacifists to set forth this radical gospel is conditional on their making it clear that they issue the same call to Russia and other nations, and on their being frank with their American fellow citizens as to what it may cost to pursue this course.

    But pacifists are on dangerous ground when they back up political maneuvers, well-meaning and attractive as they may be, which proceed from an entirely different philosophy. They should scrupulously avoid putting the United States "on the spot" vis-à-vis Russia in connection with proposals which essentially aim to achieve a bargain between governments which still are pursuing their respective interests and security, and continue to rely on military force. Jesus said, to the covetous man who wanted Jesus to compel his brother to divide an inheritance, "Who hath set me to be a judge and divider over you?" The rule should guide pacifists in their attitude toward the claims of conflicting nation-states. Mediation and reconciliation may not be the same thing, and it is reconciliation that is needed. Appeasement and renunciation are not the same thing at all. It is renunciation that we call for because there is no hope either in appeasement or in counter-violence.

In the absence of a basic resolution of the power struggle mediation moves always will be tinged with consideration growing out of that struggle; a nation will welcome or reject mediation according as it interprets its own "interests" at the moment. This will apply also to governments which proffer mediation. The danger of another Munich must be remembered. If hostilities should be suspended and some kind of mediation begun, we should continue to watch critically to see whether the basic power struggle is being eliminated. Otherwise, the "breathing spell" will be used only to prepare more adequately for war.

2. Urging that the United Nations promptly cease to serve as a war agency. Participation on one side in the war between great powers can only destroy the United Nations. The United Nations should exercise the only power it is capable of exercising, the moral power it has as the voice of the longing of men for peace. It must keep calling for an end to hostilities and for exploration of peaceful means of resolving conflicts. At this stage in the global conflict, this may offer slim hope; that is all the more reason why that slim hope should be kept alive and that the one political world body that might be an agency of peace not be transformed into an agency of war.

3. Advocacy of abandonment by the United States of the war method, and adoption of a nonviolent program, including racial equality at home and abroad, and a concentrated effort at raising the standard of living of the masses, especially in the so-called backward countries and in the lands of our "enemies." Uncle Sam, the soldier, should get out of Korea, Japan and the rest in order that Uncle Sam, the friend and enormously skilled fellow worker, may get in.

4. Strenuous efforts to bring the challenge of pacifism to as many individuals as possible and to get them to declare clearly and publicly—in their families, neighborhoods, churches, unions, before draft boards, etc.—their refusal to serve in armies, to be conscripted, to make or transport

munitions. They should make it clear that they are as ready to defend human life and democratic values and to oppose aggression by nonviolent means as they are determined not to take part in war. Such open and public adoption of the "conscientious objector" position is essential because so long as the White House and the Pentagon believe that in a showdown the people will "go along" with military measures, these agencies will continue to prepare for war and to wage it. The only basis on which Truman could do otherwise would be if he took a CO stand. We believe he should—that it is the wisest, most patriotic and human thing to do. But Truman is under no greater moral obligation to do that than is any one of his fellow citizens.

5. Individuals and groups who reject the way of war should go patiently about weaving strands of human fellowship wherever they may be; easing suffering; seeking to remove injustice and inequality; building the community of man in accordance with the purpose of God. They should train themselves as "soldiers of nonviolence" striving to deal with conflict situations. They should become missionaries, preachers of the gospel of nonviolence and truth, all over the land and the world—not least to Communists and peoples behind the Iron Curtain. Thus, by the word and by the deed, they would build the International of man, the World Community, which alone can stand in an Atomic Age that can dissolve national powers and all institutions that limit and exclude, and that set man against man anywhere on the earth.

On the eve of the meeting of the United Nations General Assembly on September 19, 1950, a leading liberal columnist, alluding to the situation in Korea, wrote: "For the first time . . . the international organization has taken direct action to enforce its decrees. It is now a body with power. It can immeasurably increase its prestige and influence as it resolutely supports the forces acting in its name."

The major criticism that has been made of this pamphlet is that we have failed to take account of the epoch-making significance of this collective action in Korea to maintain world law and enforce peace against an aggressor. Alfred Hassler in an article entitled "Cops in Korea" in the magazine *Fellowship* has set forth important material answering this question. Since human beings sometimes do develop blind spots in their thinking, however, I have to take a new look at the Korean situation and at its "police" and collective-action-to-enforce-peace aspect.

It is interesting to note that the soldiers and the so-called "man in the street" for the most part refer to what is happening in Korea as war. The Russians and the Communists, they say, showed their hand in Korea by resorting to open fighting. They have to be taught a lesson by the United States. If they should resort to similar sniping at other points, as in Iran, then rather than permit American strength to be gradually sapped by military engagements in various quarters of the globe, the United States should once and for all put an end to the Russo-Communist threat by attacking Russia itself. This is the prevailing view of ordinary people in this country today.

It is the liberals and socially minded people, including some pacifists or near-pacifists, who emphasize the UN involvement and contend that this gives an entirely new character to the situation or at least means that in a clumsy way the world is moving toward a reign of law and an orderly administration of it.

It is essential in such situations to keep our eyes fixed upon what is actually happening rather than on what people say about it. For example, the United States is increasing its military budget by billions of dollars. There is no pretense that these vast new forces are even nominally UN contingents or are being brought into being as a result of UN deliberation and decision. Nor will anyone contend on reflection that the existence of this tremendous military establishment will not exercise a great influence on future UN deliberations. Russia, of course, has not in any degree relaxed its rearmament efforts under the impact of the "police" action taken against her satellite, North Korea.

Preceding and during the UN sessions the foreign ministers are meeting frequently to bring about a big increase in the military establishments of the western European countries. This includes the rearmament of Western Germany, a segment of that nation whose military power and militarism we have "had" to destroy at vast cost in blood and which now for a second time we are rebuilding.

A few miles from Korea itself lies Japan. That country's militarism we likewise "had" to destroy recently. With the enthusiastic and eloquent approval of the American Occupation, including General MacArthur, a clause was written into the Japanese Constitution in which war and war preparation are renounced forever. Now it is proposed to make a peace treaty with Japan which will place "no restrictions on rearmament." It is expected that the Japanese government will then "invite" the United States to use Japan freely

as a military base. If the Japanese government should not be ame-
nable, "economic aid, such as that provided by the Economic Cooperation Administration, could be withdrawn."[1] That the war-
renouncing clause in the Japanese Constitution will be scrapped
is taken for granted.

Two observations may be made in conclusion of this survey of
international developments. In the first place, power and authority
have not really passed from the hands of Molotov, Acheson, Bevin,
Schumann, into the hands of Trygve Lie. No real step in that
direction has been taken. The struggle between two vast coalitions
of states, each arming as rapidly and extensively as it can, dominates
the international scene. Russia may suffer a set-back in that struggle
in Korea, as it did a year or two ago in Berlin. That will be an
incident in the war and no more a termination of it than the Berlin
air-lift proved to be. We have dealt with the arguments that, on
one side, the war is a righteous one and that, from the standpoint
of the anti-totalitarian powers, the situation has improved because
they have taken joint military action "in time," as was not done
against Mussolini, Hitler and the Japanese militarists.

The second observation is that, even if it is thought necessary
to regard the situation from the UN angle, we then have a UN
split down the middle in a civil war. If it has taken all that has
been required to "restore order" where only half of a very small and
backward country—with some backing but not overt military supporting action from a great power—is involved, what will be the
nature of the "police" action when either Russia or the United
States, or both, should believe that their "interests" are decisively
involved? The idea that there is such a thing as a "world" force or
an "impartial" force which can compel either of these powers to
"obey the law" is an illusion.

We are left with the basic problem of war as a means of dealing with conflict and of the underlying spiritual and economic
causes of war in the modern world, and we shall do well to keep
our eye on that ball. The basic forces are at work at "the rice-roots"
in Asia, the basic decisions are made there and in Moscow, Washington and a few other capitals, not at Lake Success. And to say
this is not to disparage the United Nations or to be indifferent to
it. It is, on the contrary, to express very deep concern for it and for
ordinary human beings all over the planet and to offer the prayer
that they and the UN may live and truly flourish.

[1] *The New York Times,* September 16, 1950.

Of Holy Disobedience

1952 A book has just been published in this country which the French writer Georges Bernanos wrote in Brazil, where he had exiled himself because he would not remain in France under Nazi occupation. It is entitled *Tradition of Freedom* and it is a hymn to freedom, an impassioned warning against obedience and conformity, especially obedience to the modern State engaged in mechanized, total war.

In the closing pages of this work, Bernanos writes:

> I have thought for a long time now that if, some day, the increasing efficiency of the technique of destruction finally causes our species to disappear from the earth, it will not be cruelty that will be responsible for our extinction and still less, of course, the indignation that cruelty awakens and the reprisals and vengeance that it brings upon itself . . . but the docility, the lack of responsibility of the modern man, his base, subservient acceptance of every common decree. The horrors which we have seen, the still greater horrors we shall presently see, are not signs that rebels, insubordinate, untameable men, are increasing in number throughout the world, but rather that there is a constant increase, a stupendously rapid increase, in the number of obedient, docile men.

It seems to me that this is a true and timely warning. It might serve as a text for a general appeal to American youth to adopt and practice the great and urgent virtues of Holy Disobedience, nonconformity, resistance toward conscription, regimentation, and war. For the present I want to use Bernanos' words as an introduction to some observations on the discussion regarding the absolute and relative role of these "virtues" which goes on chiefly among pacifists, members of the Historic Peace Churches and similar groups. I think it will be readily apparent, however, that the principles set forth have a wider bearing and merit consideration by all who are concerned about the maintenance of freedom in our time and the abolition of war.

Most believers in democracy, and all pacifists, begin, of course, with an area of agreement as to the moral necessity, the validity and the possible social value of No-saying, or Holy Disobedience. Both pacifists and conscientious objectors draw the line at engaging in military combat, and most of us indeed at any kind of service in the armed forces. But immediately thereupon questions arise as to whether we should not emphasize "positive and constructive service" rather than the "negative" of refusal to fight or to register; or questions about the relative importance of "resistance" and "reconciliation" and so on. It is to this discussion that I wish to attempt a contribution. It may be that it will be most useful both to young men of draft age and to other readers if we concentrate largely on the quite concrete problem of whether the former should register, conform to other requirements of the Selective Service Act which apply to conscientious objectors and accept or submit to the alternative service required of them under the law as amended in June, 1951; or whether they shall refuse to register, or if they do register or are "automatically" registered by the authorities, shall refuse to conform at the next stage; and in any event refuse to render any alternative service under conscription. We deal, in other words, with the question of whether young men who are eligible for it shall accept the IV-E classification or take the more "absolutist," non-registrant position. (For present purposes, consideration of the I-A-O position, the designation used for draftees who are willing to accept service in the armed forces provided this is non-combatant in character, may be omitted. The IV-E classification is the designation used for persons who, on grounds of religious training and belief, are opposed to participation in any war. Those who are given this classification are required to render alternative service, outside the armed forces and under civilian auspices, and designed to serve "the health, safety and interest of the United States.")

Two preliminary observations are probably necessary in order to avoid misunderstanding. In the first place, in every social movement there are varied trends, or emphases, and methods of working. Those who hold to one approach are likely to be very critical of those who take another. Disagreements among those within the same movement may be more intense, or even bitter, than with those on the outside. I suppose it can hardly be denied that every movement has in it individuals whose contribution is negative, and that such individuals do not all come from within one wing of the movement. Objective evaluation also leads to the view that the cause is forwarded by various methods and through the agency of diverse individuals and groups. But this does not mean that discussion within the movement of trends and methods of work is not useful and important. Even if it were true that each of several strategies was *equally* valid and useful, it still would be necessary for each to be presented and implemented clearly and vigorously in order for the movement to develop maximum impact.

Secondly, in what I shall have to say, I am not passing moral judgment on individual draftees. But, although a pacifist minister should not pass moral condemnation on the young man in his congregation who in obedience to his conscience enlists or submits to conscription, we do not deduce from this that the minister should abandon his pacifism or cease to witness to it. Similarly, that in the pacifist movement we support various types of COs in following the lead of conscience does not rule out discussion as to the validity and usefulness of various strategies. It is one thing for a young and immature draftee to follow a course which amounts to "making the best of a bad business," and for others to give him sympathetic understanding and help; it is very different for pacifist organizations or churches to advocate such a course, or to rationalize it into something other than it really is.

As some readers may be aware, the writer has advocated the non-registrant position. The majority in the pacifist movement probably believe that it is preferable for COs to accept or submit to the alternative civilian service which was required under the World War II Selective Service Act and is again required now under "peacetime conscription."

The varied considerations and arguments which currently enter into the discussion of this choice confronting the youth of draft age tend, as I see it, to fall into three categories, though there is a good deal of overlapping. One set of considerations may be said to center largely around the idea of Christian or human "vocation";

a second set has to do with the problem of "the immature 18-year-old"; the third with the relation of the pacifist and citizens generally to military conscription and the modern power-state.

The argument for accepting alternative service, under the first category, has been stated somewhat as follows:

God calls us to love and serve our fellowmen. This is, for Christians and other pacifists, a matter of vocation. If, then, the government in wartime, or under peacetime conscription, requires some service of mercy or construction from us which is not obviously and directly a part of war-making, we will raise no objection to undertaking such work. We may even seek, and shall certainly be grateful for the opportunity to demonstrate our desire to be good citizens and helpful members of society, and to show a reconciling spirit.

This question of the meaning and implications of Christian or human vocation in the context of military conscription clearly needs careful analysis.

The question of his vocation does not or should not arise suddenly for the Christian, or for any morally sensitive and responsible individual, when Congress enacts a conscription law. The committed Christian presumably has been engaged in an occupation and a way of living which he believes to be in accord with the will of God. This need not be some unusual or spectacular occupation. A Christian farmer, factory worker, miner, teacher, raising a family and giving an example of unselfishness to his neighbors; his wife maintaining an unobtrusively wholesome Christian home; the children walking in the footsteps of such parents—all these may be following a true Christian vocation.

Then war, or peacetime conscription, comes along. If these people are pacifists, they hold that direct participation in war or in combat training is inconsistent with a Christian profession and calling. They must, therefore, refuse such participation. At this point, the government tells those of them who come under the draft that they must nevertheless render some civilian service within or under the conscription system. In most cases this will be something different from what they have been doing and will involve temporary removal from the home community.

It has for some time troubled me that a good many pacifists of draft age seem ready to acquiesce in this situation and that, furthermore, many who are not directly affected by the draft seem to feel at such a time they must immediately find something else to do than that which they have been doing—something that is often referred to as "meaningful" or "sacrificial." Was what they were doing so definitely not meaningful or sacrificial? Unfortunately, this is very likely the case in many instances. But it does not follow, as is seemingly often assumed, that this justifies going into some entirely new work, a "project," as we say, perhaps preferably relief work which has some connection with the war effort, something which society will regard as the "equivalent" of support of the war effort. Certainly the fact that a young man of draft age has not been following a meaningful or Christian vocation does not automatically or by itself constitute a warrant for submitting to conscription for so-called civilian service. It may well be that God calls him at this juncture to put meaning into the life he has been living and into the work he was supposed to be doing.

It is certainly incumbent on us to search our hearts as to whether this rush to get into other jobs and to go to distant places may be motivated by fear of men and of the authorities, by a desire to be thought well of, by a dread of the social displeasure or actual legal punishment which might fall upon us if we were to continue quietly in the home town at the work which we had been doing when war fever, if not outright hysteria, seizes the people. "If I were still pleasing men," said St. Paul, "I should not be the slave of Christ."

I am convinced that our thinking in these matters is often distorted. Fundamentally, God calls men and women to "be fruitful and multiply and replenish the earth and subdue it and have dominion" over the animal creation—to sow the grain, weave the cloth, build the homes and the temples to the Eternal. That is what most people should be doing most of the time. In fact, unless they did, even the armies would soon have to stop in their tracks! War comes along and breaks into this normal life of human beings. That it does this is one of the gravest indictments of war. To resist this breaking up of orderly family and community life—not to yield to the subtle and insistent pressure to do something "different" under the tacit assumption that the normal cannot be meaningful—is one of the great services that may be rendered by the people who believe in nonviolence and reconciliation. "In returning and rest shall ye be saved, in quietness and in confidence shall be your strength."

It is sometimes said that it is important for pacifists to make it clear that they can face hardship and danger and are ready to suffer, if need be, on behalf of their convictions. Granted that this is true, it by no means automatically follows that draft-age youths should submit to conscription or that other pacifists, on the advent of war or conscription, should leave what they are doing for other work. It well may be that the most challenging opportunity to display courage, hardihood and readiness to suffer will be found precisely in the community in which one has been living, and in trying to do the ordinary things about which we have been speaking. There is reason to think that some Congressmen may have been influenced in supporting the "deferment," or virtual exemption, for COs under the original 1948 United States Selective Service Act because they were convinced that few who claim to be COs would have the nerve to stand up against the pressure if they tried to go their normal way in their town or college, while others were being drafted and forced to leave home or school. Obviously, only a pacifist who was leading not a self-indulgent but a disciplined life, who was ready to face danger and suffering and who deeply loved his fellows, could follow such a course. It is possible that some leave the home or college environment not because they wish to face hardship but because they yield to the temptation to try to avoid it.

Let us, after these preliminary observations, try to determine how—from the standpoint of the concept of Christian vocation— the pacifist may judge the action of a government which requires so-called alternative conscript service of him or of his children or fellow-pacifists. There are, so far as I can see, only three possible verdicts. One is to say that the government is demanding that these conscripts shall at least temporarily *abandon* their Christian, or true, vocation for work to which they clearly are *not* "called." A second is to say that the government is competent in these special circumstances to determine, and has correctly determined, that the alternative service to which it assigns COs constitutes their Christian vocation for the time being. The third possibility is to reason that when the government thus forces a Christian into another occupation, it is performing an unwarranted and sinful act, but that the Christian's duty in such a situation is to practice non-resistance. It, therefore, becomes his vocation to undertake the work which is imposed upon him, not because it is somehow good in itself but because non-resistance to evil constitutes Christian behavior.

The first case is easily disposed of. If the individual is convinced that he is being forced out of his Christian or human vocation into something which requires him to disobey God or conscience, he has no alternative but to refuse to comply with the State's demand, perhaps to resist it nonviolently, and take the consequences. He probably will be forced out of his accustomed place and work anyway, but his non-conformity, or non-cooperation with the State's demand, at this point becomes his true vocation.

The second possible decision is to hold that, in the context of conscription and provided it does not require service in the armed forces, the State may determine what one's Christian vocation is. Some of the Mennonites' statements and those of some other pacifists seem to me to fall under this head. The position seems to me a very precarious one and I question whether Mennonites, for example, can maintain it as consistent with their own theology and Christian ethics.

It is essential in the Christian concept of vocation that the "call" is from the Spirit speaking in the heart of the believer. And the believer must always remain in a position where he can be free to respond to the prompting of the Spirit. But, under a conscription regime, how can this be? The position taken by Jehovah's Witnesses that they cannot submit to conscription because they must always be free to "witness" to the faith is, in this respect, surely a strong and impressive one. It has a bearing, incidentally, on our earlier general observations about Christian vocation. It seems to me that Christian pacifists need to give much more thought than they have to whether in, this particular respect, the Witnesses, so far from being eccentric, are not taking the clear and consistent, centrally Christian stand. The fact that the Witnesses hardly can be classified as pacifists in the usual sense of the term does not affect the relevance of this question for pacifists and for Christians generally.

In Mennonite thought, government, the State, though it is "an ordinance of God" to curb sin, is itself by definition sinful, not Christian, not a part of "the order of redemption." Where, then, does the State get the competence, or the mandate to determine, of all things, the *Christian* vocation of a *believer?*—And particularly the war-making arm or department of the State? If the war department or its adjunct, Selective Service, is qualified to determine Christian vocation as part of its conduct of, or preparation for, a war, why, then should not the labor department tell Christians where to work in peacetime?

There remains a third possible position, namely, that the State is undoubtedly doing an evil thing in taking the individual out of the work to which he feels God has called him, but that the principle of non-resistance to evil then comes into operation and submission to this evil becomes the vocation of the persecuted Christian. Given certain premises, there is logic in this position, but it is nevertheless open to serious question. In the first place, non-resistance to an evil should not mean cooperation with it. "Depart from evil and do good" is the law. Pacifists in general, and Christian pacifists in particular, have to ask whether, in conforming with any of the provisions of a draft law and especially in rendering conscript service regarded as of "national importance" by a war-making state, they are not helping conscription to run smoothly; helping thus to force conscription on millions of youth and thus in turn promoting war, since conscription is an integral part of an armaments race. The phenomenon of increased tension between nations when they lengthen the compulsory service period for youth is a familiar one. This, of course, raises the whole question of our evaluation of the meaning and role of military conscription, to which we shall return later.

In the meantime, one or two comments need to be made on the phase of our problem under discussion. If what is really happening is that the war-making state is inflicting an evil on people, forcing them away from their vocation, subjecting them to a measure of persecution, then it seems we ought to keep this clearly in our own minds and ought not to let the government or the public assume that we think otherwise. The expressions of "gratitude" which we have sometimes heard addressed to government for "permitting" pacifists to render alternative service seem inappropriate. We cannot have it both ways: accuse the State of the grave sin of invading the realm of Christian vocation and at the same time thank it for doing us a "favor" by making the invasion less than total. The State is not doing God or Christian people a favor in recognizing conscience, though that is what most United States Congressmen think they are doing in making some provision for COs. The pacifist who in any way encourages this notion is in danger of helping to give currency to the idea that conscience is a private whim which legislators may see fit to indulge for prudential reasons, as long as those who are afflicted with this peculiarity are very few in number. If non-resistant pacifists get off the high ground of patiently bowing the neck to Caesar's yoke, letting Caesar inflict the scourge of civilian conscript service upon them, they are immediately on the low ground of bargaining for indulgence for a small and, in that view, not too principled or brave a minority. Standing on that lower ground they have very little bargaining *power* and results will reflect that fact—

as during World War II. On the other hand, the sufferings which the COs endured in World War I both in Great Britain and in the United States, when there was virtually no legal or social recognition of them, according to all competent observers were largely responsible for the fairly liberal provisions made for COs in World War II. The Army did not want to "be bothered with these fellows again."

This does not mean that, if the imposition of alternative service is accepted, it should be rendered grudgingly or that feelings of hostility toward government officials with whom one may deal are appropriate. Quite the contrary. If we decide to go with Caesar one mile, the Gospel enjoins us to go two! We have the choice of not going along at all or of going two miles, but never a skimpy one mile.

I think it is now generally admitted that there was not a great deal of this glad, spontaneous "second miling" on the part of the conscript COs in World War II, though there was considerable talk about it among older folks. Civilian Public Service, in large measure, simply did not operate on the high spiritual plane that was originally hoped and is still sometimes implied or stated, but for many was making the best of a bad business, perhaps for lack of clear guidance, or of the courage to follow another course.

It will be recalled that a considerable number of Civilian Public Service men declared flatly that it was inconsistent, and indeed hypocritical, to talk of spontaneous service under conscription. "We are here," they said, "not because our desire to serve brought us here. We are here because the government, as part of its war program, passed a conscription law and under that law took us by the scruff of the neck and forced us to do this job. We have no choice but this or the army or jail. That is bound to color this whole experience, except perhaps for those who can shut their eyes to reality. Anyone who denies this is a hypocrite."

It seems to me that these COs placed the finger on an essential point. Compulsion does enter into "service" under a conscription law. It affects the whole picture. Therefore, the evaluation to be made of the IV-E position, and of alternative service under it, is not disposed of by asserting that "service is at least as real a part of Christian or pacifist life as witness or resistance." That statement is perfectly correct. Service to men and fellowship with them on the one hand, and non-cooperation with evil, witness against injustice, nonviolent resistance on the other, are both essential in the pacifist way of life. There is some of each in every pacifist life. The most "reconciling" pacifist refuses to use a gun or even, probably, to put on a uniform. Some of the most extreme "resisters" in prison were known for the thoughtful and gentle service they rendered to criminal fellow inmates. A very discerning English pacifist observed: "For some their witness is their service, for others their service is their witness"—or resistance. Each type needs to be on guard against the temptations peculiar to it, including the temptation to question the motives or underestimate the contribution of the pacifists of the other type.

But the service which is the essence of pacifism is free, spontaneous, joyous, sacrificial, unbought. To magnify or glorify this is by no means automatically to magnify or glorify the IV-E position *under the draft*. Here, as we have pointed out, an element occurs which is contradictory to pacifism, freedom and spontaneity—*the element of compulsion in a context of war and war preparation.*

It seems to me that it is important for pacifists to bear this in mind as we make plans to deal with the problem of alternative service under the amended 1948 Selective Service Act. No matter how "liberal" or "considerate" the conditions for administering alternative service may be in the estimation of government officials or the pacifist agencies, if alternative service is accepted or acquiesced in at all, it will inevitably pose grave problems from the standpoint of Christian vocation and it will not, I think, be possible to escape the contamination or corruption which "conscription" infuses into "service." At the moment it seems possible that Selective Service regulations will permit some individuals to remain at their accustomed occupations. We put aside certain questions, to which we shall return, as to what the act of registration itself implies in the context of conscription for atomic and biological war. Here we emphasize that, once a man has appealed to the State to permit him to remain in his job and has been granted such permission, it is not exactly the same job as before. Others will not be given the same permission, and he should not evade the question of whether he can acquiesce in and, to a degree, benefit from such discrimination. He will have to ponder whether the consideration in his case is because officials regard his work as a contribution in some way to the war effort, or desire to placate and silence an influential person. If he should conclude that he ought to change jobs, he would have to consult the authorities again, and what then?

In conferences with Selective Service officials efforts are being made to avoid some of the features of the wartime Civilian Public

Service set-up which deeply troubled a good many Quakers—such as the close supervision by military men allegedly functioning as civilians and the undesirable and frustrating character of much of the work to which IV-E men were assigned. Even if substantial concessions are obtained, it would be well for us to be on guard against idealizing the situation. It is hoped that a good many young men will in effect be furloughed to projects at home and abroad which will not be exclusively for COs of draft age, and which will have real social value. It will not be the same as if these men had undertaken these jobs out of a sense of vocation and mission, apart from the context of conscription. We will know that for the most part they did not volunteer until conscription came along. The same questions faced by the man who is permitted to remain in his own job will confront these young men on projects. In addition, their term of service and rates of pay will be set by the government.

To sum up this first part of our analysis, it is my conclusion that the one consistent attitude toward conscript alternative service from the standpoint of Christian vocation—if one accepts such work at all—is that which regards submission or non-resistance to the evil which the State imposes upon him when it interferes with his normal occupation, as the vocation or duty of the Christian man. Any other attitude seems to me to involve a considerable measure of rationalization. The Mennonites came nearest to adopting this non-resistant position and the fact that the experience of Mennonite youths in Civilian Public Service was less frustrating and brought better results than was the case with others, save in exceptional instances, seems to me to bear out my analysis. As we have pointed out, those who non-resistantly take up their cross of conscription should bear it joyously and be ready to carry it the second mile.

We turn next to a brief consideration of the arguments for the IV-E as against the non-registrant position which center around the problem of "the immature 18-year-old youth." A number of 18-year-olds, it is pointed out, have a strong aversion to war and a leaning toward pacifism. They are, however, emotionally immature. If they have no choice but the army or jail, all but a few will choose the army and are likely to be lost to the pacifist cause. They could be held and possibly even developed into a radical pacifist position, if they had a third choice, namely, civilian service. On the other hand, the youth who chooses prison rather than the army, in the absence of such a third possibility, may suffer grave psychological injury.

I am sure no one will be disposed to be callous or "tough" in his attitude toward any youth faced with a problem such as we are discussing. Anyone in the position of counselor to an individual will want to avoid "psychological pressuring" to induce him to take this or that course, and will strive to help the young man to make his own decision, in accord with his own inner need and conviction, rather than to impose a decision upon him. But I conceive that it would be my duty as a Christian minister to have this same attitude in talking and praying with a young man who was going into the army. I would have no right, nor do I think it would do any good, to "pressure" him, against his conviction and inner need, to refuse service. But this would certainly not mean that I give up my own pacifist convictions, or refrain from doing all I can in general to spread them or from making this particular young man aware of my own thoughts, and feelings.—This in spite of the fact that, if young men who had planned to submit to the draft are consequently won to the pacifist position, this may entail considerable suffering on their part, anguish for parents who disagree with them, and so on. It is fairly certain, incidentally, that in many typical Southern communities—though by no means exclusively in the South—a youth who chose the I-A-O (medical corps) position, not to mention IV-E, would have as tough a time as a non-registrant in many metropolitan centers. We cannot, therefore, escape the conclusion that, as we have a responsibility to choose the pacifist or non-pacifist position, and to bear witness for pacifism if that is the stand we take, then, if we are pacifists, we have a responsibility to decide whether complete non-cooperation with military conscription is the more consistent, committed and effective stand or not; and if we so decide, then we are required to do what we can to make known our stand and the reasons for it.

I have the impression that a great many pacifist ministers, perhaps even the majority, will work harder to keep a young pacifist parishioner from taking the "absolutist" position and going to jail rather than into civilian service, than they would to get the run-of-the-mill young parishioners to think seriously about not going into the army. They somehow seem to feel that a more awful thing is happening to the young CO who goes to jail than to the 18-year-old who goes into the army. It is my impression that this same feeling is an unconscious factor in the thinking of many lay pacifists when they react strongly against the idea of COs going to prison. This puzzles me greatly. Why should they have this reaction?

To my mind—even apart from the sufficiently appalling factor of being systematically trained for wholesale killing and subjected to the risk of being killed in brutal war—there are few if any more evil and perilous situations to put young men into than the armed forces. I should feel much deeper grief over possibly having had some part in persuading a youth to go into the armed forces than I would over having taken some responsibility in bringing a young man to go to prison for conscience's sake. Are the qualms people feel about youthful COs going to prison in certain instances perhaps because taking the non-registrant position is something very unusual and regarded with social disapproval, whereas becoming a soldier is extremely common and meets with the highest social approval? It may be, therefore, that there are some ministers and other older people who should examine themselves as to whether they feel that they themselves might find life in the community or in the church very uncomfortable if they were suspected of having influenced a youth to take a radical anti-draft stand, whereas all men will speak well of them—or at least not too ill—if they have helped, or at least not hindered, young Christians in adjusting themselves to the idea of going into the army. Is it just possible that we older people are sometimes concerned with sparing ourselves when we think we are solely concerned about sparing teen-agers?

To return to the 18-year-old. There are young men who on physical and psychological grounds are exempted from army service. There may well be COs who should on similar grounds be exempted from any kind of service. If such a physically or mentally ill CO is refused exemption, he should perhaps be discouraged from undergoing the risks of prison experience if there is an alternative for him. This still leaves us with the problem of the majority of pacifist and non-pacifist youth who are not ill.

When we find ourselves concerned about what the teen-age religious CO who goes to prison must undergo, and inclined to think that there is an absolutely conclusive case for providing alternative service and urging most such COs to avail themselves of it, we first might take a look at two other categories of youth who are subject to the draft. One consists of those actually drafted into the armed services; the other of the so-called non-religious COs.

The great mass of teen-agers are going to be put through rigorous military training with all the hardships, the toughening and the temptations which this entails. They have to be ready to undergo battle experience. Many of them will actually experience modern war in combat. Is what the CO undergoes in prison vastly more terrible than this? Is it as terrible? It may be said that the soldier has social approbation, whereas the pacifist, especially the "absolutist," meets social disapprobation and even ostracism. This is indeed a sore trial and many cannot endure it. Frankly, I am still left with more grief and pity in my heart for the teen-age soldier than for the teen-age "absolutist" CO. I am still left with a question of whether we have a right to take any time and energy away from the struggle to lift the curse of conscription from the mass of youth and put it into an effort to secure alternative conscript service for COs.

There are, as we know, teen-age "absolutists" who feel the same way and who have demonstrated that they can endure whatever they may be called upon to endure. Nor is their lot without its compensations. They, also, "have their reward."

Religious COs who accept the IV-E classification and older pacifists who advocate this course also have to consider the non-religious CO. Under United States law, it is the so-called religious CO who is eligible for this classification; the so-called non-religious CO, though he may by unanimous consent be equally sincere, is not. The latter has no choice except the army or jail. The fact that he is only 18 years old does not alter that. Nothing in this entire field of pacifist policy and behavior is harder for me to understand than how religious COs and many of the leaders of the peace churches and of the Fellowship of Reconciliation can acquiesce in this situation and accept what must be regarded as an advantage, a preferred position. The white CO who accepted conscript alternative service when the Negro CO was automatically forced to choose the army or prison would be in an invidious position. So would the Gentile when his Jewish comrade was thus discriminated against. But in my mind the case is far more deplorable when it is the religious and the supposedly non-religious man who are involved. The white man or the Gentile might actually believe in discrimination or not regard it too seriously when the discrimination is in his favor. But for the religious man it surely should be a central and indispensable part of his faith that discrimination—most of all where two men acting in obedience to conscience are involved—is unthinkable and that, if there is discrimination, he cannot be the beneficiary of it.

At any rate, the argument that there must be alternative service because *immature* 18-year-olds must by no means be subjected to prison experience seems to me to become completely impotent in the mouths of those religious pacifists who acquiesce in the arrangement and enable it to work—unless indeed they mean to contend that the average religious CO has less stamina than the non-religious CO, and therefore the former should be given gentler treatment.

Advocacy of alternative service for the teen-age CO is based on considerations relating to the future of the pacifist movement, as well as to the effect on the COs themselves. It is argued that if the only choice young pacifists have is the army or jail, there will be very few pacifists. This argument was not first advanced, however, when the draft age was lowered. It was often heard during World War II, when most COs were older and more seasoned. It has always impressed me as a dubious argument and I wonder where it leads us. What, for example, is the relationship of this argument to the one which is also advanced—sometimes by the same person—that the IV-E position is very meaningful and perhaps to be preferred to the more "absolutist" one, because it is the IV-E man who gives a glorious demonstration of the spirit of selfless service which is the essence of pacifism at its best? These two concepts cannot very well be harnessed together as a team. We can hardly contend in one breath that we want alternative service because most young pacifists are not ready to follow a stronger and more sacrificial course *and* that we want it because it is the strongest and most meaningful course pacifists can follow. It seems to me we have to decide whether our problem is to find shelter for COs or whether it is to find freedom and the opportunity for self-expression and service, even though the price be high.

To consider the matter for a moment from the tactical viewpoint, it seems quite certain that the number of 18-year-olds who take either the IV-E or the non-registrant position (perhaps even the I-A-O position might be included) will, at least at the outset, be small. The draft now gets the young man at the very age when it is most difficult for him to stand out in any way from the mass of his fellows. Even if he is intellectually fairly well convinced of the pacifist position, he is not mature enough emotionally to take it. It is a fair guess that accessions to the pacifist movement, should military service or training become universal, will come mainly from young people who have gone through the experience of life in the armed forces. In other words, the additional number of pacifists recruited because alternative service is provided may turn out to be very small. If so, the quantitative advantage to be derived from the adoption of a less uncompromising pacifism is illusory.

There is one more factor—we live in an age when the role of minorities is an increasingly difficult one. The pressures and actual persecution to which they are subjected are severe. The trend is still particularly obscured in the United States, but if we pause to reflect that not a single bomb has as yet fallen on this country, we will realize that this country is not an exception to the trend toward greater conformity and regimentation. As *The New York Times* editorialized some time ago in commenting on some features of the McCarran Act, if we are resorting to such repressive measures already, what will we do when a real crisis comes? In other words, while we spend a good deal of time arguing that COs should have some choice other than the army or jail, we probably are moving into a time when that will be the only choice that members of minorities, including pacifists, will have. It would seem then that our thought and energy should be devoted to two issues: whether and how this trend toward totalitarianism can be halted; and how we may prepare and discipline ourselves to meet the tests which our fellow-pacifists in some other lands already have faced.

This leads to the third and last of the issues we are trying to explore: the true nature of conscription, of modern war, and of the conscripting, war-making State—and the attitude which pacifists consequently should take toward them.

Participation in alternative service is quite often defended on the ground that our opposition is to war rather than conscription. Except in the matter of war, we are as ready to serve the nation as anybody. Therefore, as long as we are not drafted for combat or forced against our will into the armed forces, we are ready to render whatever service of a civilian character may be imposed upon us.

Is this a sound position? Let me emphasize that it is conscription for war under the conditions of the second half of the twentieth century that we are talking about. The question as to whether sometime and under some circumstances we might accept conscription for some conceivable purpose not related to war is not here at stake. It is academic and irrelevant. The question with which we are dealing is that of conscripting youth in and for modern war.

As pacifists, we are opposed to all war. Even if recruitment were entirely on a voluntary basis, we would be opposed. It seems to me that from this we might infer that we should be, *a fortiori*, opposed to military conscription; for in addition to war itself, in conscription we have coercion by government, coercion which places young boys in a military regime where they are deprived of freedom of choice in virtually all essential matters. They may not have the slightest interest in the war, yet they are made to kill by order. This, surely, is a fundamental violation of the human spirit which must cause the pacifist to shudder.

The reply sometimes is made that pacifists are *not* being conscripted for military purposes and therefore—presumably—*they* are not faced with the issue of the nature of military conscription. I shall contend later that it is not really possible to separate conscription and war, as I think this argument attempts. Here I wish to suggest that, even if the question is the conscription of non-pacifist youth, it is a fundamental mistake for pacifists ever to relent in their opposition to this evil, ever to devote their energies primarily to securing special provisions for COs within a draft law, or to lapse into feeling that conscription has become somehow more palatable if such provisions are made by the State. It is not our own children, if we are pacifist parents, or our fellow pacifist Christians, if we are churchmen, about whom we should be most deeply concerned. That is a narrow and perhaps self-centered attitude. Also, pacifist youths have some inner resources for meeting the issue. The terrible thing which we should never lose sight of, to which we should never reconcile our spirits, is that the great mass of 18-year-olds are drafted for war. They are given no choice. Few are at the stage of development where they are capable of making a fully rational and responsible choice. Thus the fathers immolate the sons, the older generation immolates the younger, on the altar of Moloch. What God, centuries ago, forbade Abraham to do even to his own son—"Lay not thy hand upon the lad, neither do thou anything unto him"—this we do by decree to the entire youth of a nation.

We need to ask ourselves whether such conscription is in any sense a lesser evil. We have all sensed the danger of arguing against conscription *on the ground* that the nation could raise all the troops it needed by voluntary enlistment. Nevertheless, there is a point to an impassioned argument which George Bernanos makes in his book *Tradition of Freedom*. He states that the man created by Western or Christian civilization "disappeared in the day conscription became law . . . the principle is a totalitarian principle if ever there was one—so much so that you could deduce the whole system from it, as you can deduce the whole of geometry from the propositions of Euclid."

To the question as to whether France, his fatherland, should not be defended if in peril, he has France answer: "I very much doubt whether my salvation requires such monstrous behavior" as defense by modern war methods. If men wanted to die on behalf of the fatherland, moreover, that would be one thing, but "making a clean sweep, with one scoop of the hand, of an entire male population" is another matter altogether. "You tell me," says France, "that, in saving me, they save themselves. Yes, if they can remain free; no, if they allow you to destroy, by this unheard-of measure, the national covenant. For as soon as you have, by simple decree, created millions of French soldiers, it will be held as proven that you have sovereign rights over the persons and the goods of every Frenchman, that there are no rights higher than yours and where, then, will your usurpations stop? Won't you presently presume to decide what is just and what is unjust, what is Evil and what is Good?"

It is fairly certainly an oversimplification to suggest, as Bernanos does here, that the entire totalitarian mechanized "system" under which men live today or into which they are increasingly drawn, even in countries where a semblance of freedom and spontaneity remains, can be traced to its source in the military conscription which was instituted in the eighteenth century by the French during their revolutionary wars. But what cannot be successfully denied, it seems to me, is that totalitarianism, depersonalization, conscription, war, and the conscripting, war-making power-state are inextricably linked. They constitute a whole, a "system." It is a disease, a creeping paralysis, which affects all nations, on both sides of the global conflict. Revolution and counter-revolution, "peoples' democracies" and "Western democracies," the "peace-loving" nations—on both sides of the war—are cast in this mold of conformity, mechanization and violence. This is the Beast which, in the language of the Apocalypse, is seeking to usurp the place of the Lamb.

We know that "war will stop at nothing," and we are clear in our recognition that, as pacifists, we can have nothing to do with it. But I do not think that it is possible to distinguish between war and conscription, to say that the former is and the latter is not an instrument or mark of the Beast.

Non-conformity, Holy Disobedience, becomes a virtue, indeed a necessary and indispensable measure of spiritual self-preservation, in a day when the impulse to conform, to acquiesce, to go along, is used as an instrument to subject men to totalitarian rule and involve them in permanent war. To create the impression of at least outward unanimity, the impression that there is no "real" opposition, is something for which all dictators and military leaders strive. The more it seems that there is no opposition, the less worthwhile it seems to an ever larger number of people to cherish even the thought of opposition. Surely, in such a situation, it is important not to place the pinch of incense before Caesar's image, not to make the gesture of conformity which is required, let us say, by registering under a military conscription law. When the object is so plainly to create a situation where the individual no longer has a choice except total conformity, the concentration camp or death; when reliable people tell us seriously that experiments are being conducted with drugs that will paralyze the wills of opponents within a nation or in an enemy country, it is surely neither right nor wise to wait until the "system" has driven us into a corner where we cannot retain a vestige of self-respect unless we say No. It does not seem wise or right to wait until this evil catches up with us, but rather to go out to meet it—to *resist*—before it has gone any further.

As Bernanos reminds us, "things are moving fast, dear reader, they are moving very fast." He recalls that he "lived at a time when passport formalities seemed to have vanished forever." A man could "travel around the world with nothing in his wallet but his visiting card." He recalls that "twenty years ago, Frenchmen of the middle class refused to have their fingerprints taken; fingerprints were the concern of convicts." But the word "criminal" has "swollen to such prodigious proportions that it now includes every citizen who dislikes the regime, the system, the party, or the man who represents them. . . . The moment, perhaps, is not far off when it will seem as natural for us to leave the front-door key in the lock at night so the police may enter, at any hour of the day or night, *as it does to open our pocket-books to every official demand.* And when the State decides that it would be a practical measure to put some outward sign on us, why should we hesitate to have ourselves branded on the cheek or on the buttock, with a hot iron, like cattle? The purges of 'wrong-thinkers,' so dear to the totalitarian regimes, would thus become infinitely easier."

To me it seems that submitting to conscription even for civilian service is permitting oneself thus to be branded by the State. It makes the work of the State in preparing for war and in securing the desired impression of unanimity much easier. It seems, therefore, that pacifists should refuse to be thus branded.

In the introductory chapter to Kay Boyle's volume of short

stories about occupied Germany, *The Smoking Mountain*, there is an episode which indicates to me the need for Resistance and for not waiting until it is indeed too late. She tells about a woman, professor of philology in a Hessian University, who said of the German experience with Nazism: "It was a gradual process." When the first *Jews Not Wanted* signs went up, "there was never any protest made about them, and, after a few months, not only we, but even the Jews who lived in that town, walked past without noticing any more that they were there. Does it seem impossible to you that this should happen to civilized people anywhere?"

The philology professor went on to say that, after a while, she put up a picture of Hitler in her class room. After twice refusing to take the oath of allegiance to Hitler, she was persuaded by her students to take it. "They agreed that in taking this oath, which so many anti-Nazis had taken before me, I was committing myself to nothing, and that I could exert more influence as a professor than as an outcast in the town."

She concluded by saying that she now had a picture of a Jew, Spinoza, where Hitler's picture used to hang, and added: "Perhaps you will think I did this ten years too late, and perhaps you are right in thinking this. Perhaps there was something else we could all of us have done, but we never seemed to find a way to do it; either as individuals or as a group, we never seemed to find a way." A decision by the pacifist movement in this country to break completely with conscription, to give up the ideas that we can "exert more influence" if we conform in some measure, if we do not resist to the uttermost—this might awaken our countrymen to a realization of the precipice on the edge of which we stand. It might be the making of our movement.

Thus to embrace Holy Disobedience is not to substitute resistance for reconciliation. It is to practice both reconciliation and resistance. In so far as we help to build up or to smooth the way for American militarism and the regimentation which accompanies it, we certainly are not practicing reconciliation toward the millions of people in the Communist bloc countries against whom American war preparations, including conscription, are directed. Nor are we practicing reconciliation toward the hundreds of millions in Asia and Africa whom we condemn to poverty and drive into the arms of Communism by our addiction to military "defense." Nor are we practicing love toward our own fellow-citizens, including the multitude of youths in the armed services, if, against our deepest insight, we help to fasten the chains of conscription and war upon them.

Our works of mercy, healing and reconstruction will have a deeper and more genuinely reconciling effect when they are not entangled with conscript service for "the health, safety and interest" of the United States or any other war-making State. It is highly doubtful whether Christian mission boards can permit any of their projects in the Orient to be staffed by men supposed to be working for "the health, safety and interest" of the United States. The Gospel of reconciliation will be preached with a new freedom and power when the preachers have broken decisively with American militarism. It surely cannot be preached at all in Communist lands by those who have not made that break. When we have gotten off the back of what someone has called the "wild elephant" of militarism and conscription on to the solid ground of freedom, and only then, we will be able to live and work constructively. Like Abraham, we shall have to depart from the City-which-is in order that we may help to build the City-which-is-to-be, whose true builder and maker is God.

It is possible, perhaps even likely, that if we set ourselves apart as those who will have no dealings whatever with conscription, who will not place the pinch of incense before Caesar's image, our fellow-citizens will stone us, as Stephen was stoned when he reminded his people that it was they who had "received the law as it was ordained by angels, and kept it not." So may we be stoned for reminding our people of a tradition of freedom and peace which was also, in a real sense, "ordained by angels" and which we no longer keep. But, it will thus become possible for them, as for Paul, even amidst the search for new victims to persecute, suddenly to see the face of Christ and the vision of a new Jerusalem.

Someone may reflect at this point that I have counseled against people leaving the normal path of life too readily and that I am now counseling a policy which is certain to create disturbance in individual lives, in families and communities. That is so. But to depart from the common way in response to a conscription law, in an attempt to adapt oneself to an abnormal state of society, is one thing; to leave father, mother, wife, child, yea and one's own life also, at the behest of Christ or conscience is quite another. Our generation will not return to a condition under which every man may sit under his own vine and fig tree, with none to make him afraid, unless there are those who are willing to pay the high cost of redemption and deliverance from regimentation, terror and war.

Finally, it is of crucial importance that we should understand that for the individual to pit himself in Holy Disobedience against the war-making and conscripting State, wherever it or he be located, is not an act of despair or defeatism. Rather, I think we may say that precisely this individual refusal to "go along" is now the beginning and the core of any realistic and practical movement against war and for a more peaceful and brotherly world. For it becomes daily clearer that political and military leaders pay virtually no attention to protests against current foreign policy and pleas for peace since they know quite well that, when it comes to a showdown, all but a handful of the millions of protesters will "go along" with the war to which the policy leads. All but a handful will submit to conscription. Few of the protesters will so much as risk their jobs in the cause of "peace." The failure of the policymakers to change their course does not, save perhaps in very rare instances, mean that they are evil men who want war. They feel, as indeed they so often declare in crucial moments, that the issues are so complicated, the forces arrayed against them so strong, that they "have no choice" but to add another score of billions to the military budget, and so on and on. Why should they think there is any reality, hope or salvation in "peace advocates" who, when the moment of decision comes, also act on the assumption that they "have no choice" but to conform?

Precisely on that day when the individual appears to be utterly hopeless, to "have no choice," when the aim of the "system" is to convince him that he is helpless as an individual and that the only way to meet regimentation is by regimentation, there is absolutely no hope save in going back to the beginning. The human being, the child of God, must assert his humanity and his sonship again. He must exercise the choice which no longer is accorded him by society, which, "naked, weaponless, armourless, without shield or spear, but only with naked hands and open eyes," he must create again. He must understand that this naked human being is the one *real* thing in the face of the machines and the mechanized institutions of our age. He, by the grace of God, is the seed of all the human life there will be on earth, though he may have to die to make that harvest possible. As *Life* stated, in its unexpectedly profound and stirring editorial of August 20, 1945, its first issue after the atom bombing of Hiroshima: "Our sole safeguard against the very real danger of a reversion to barbarism is the kind of morality which compels the individual conscience, be the group right or wrong. The individual conscience against the atomic bomb? Yes. There is no other way."

Mephistopheles
and the Scientists

Mephistopheles:
*"He calls it Reason—thence his powers increased
To be far beastlier than any beast."*

Goethe

1954 In these terrible days none know better than the scientists who sacrificed their misgivings to the demands of "national security" the fate that frequently befalls those who try to bargain with the devil.

At first they thought that they could handle it, and the early years after Hiroshima rang with the urgent cries of scientists turned prophets. But the warnings have become ever less effective and now these confused Fausts learn to their dismay that they have sold their souls so completely that even their Mephistopheles disdains their protests. They have served their purpose—the murders have been done—and this Mephisto will go so far as to toss them lightly out of the kingdom they have made for him, if the whim seizes him.

If there was any doubt about the scientists' plight, it was resolved with the decision to bar J. Robert Oppenheimer from access to the "secrets" of the very project of which he had been the principal architect.

The findings of the United States Personal Security Board[1] that barred him present a fascinating and disconcerting revelation of the point at which the men who hold the reins of communication and power in their hands have arrived in their thinking.

The majority came to "a clear conclusion" that Oppenheimer is a "loyal citizen." They do not charge him with ever having been a member of the Communist Party. They do not faintly hint at any *specific* instance where he even unwittingly betrayed military secrets. Nevertheless, they were "unable to arrive at the conclusion that it would be clearly consistent with the security interests of the United States to reinstate Dr. Oppenheimer's clearance."

There are two kinds of material in Oppenheimer's record that led to this conclusion. In the first place, Dr. Oppenheimer was allegedly a fellow-traveler of the Communist Party for several years before he took charge of the A-bomb project, in 1942; and he was said to number a good many Party members among his close associates. The circumstances of Dr. Oppenheimer's life were well known when he was engaged. They were reviewed again in 1947 by one of the loyalty and security outfits that are now a part of American life; he was cleared, and he continued in highly responsible and sensitive war work for another seven years. As Dr. Evans pointed out in his minority recommendation, Oppenheimer is certainly *less* of a security risk now than he was then.

Gray and Morgan point out, however, that Dr. Oppenheimer has not cut off personal association and friendship with persons who formerly were Communists. In the past he sometimes held back names from F.B.I. agents during conferences with them when, in his judgment, bringing in these names was not relevant to a security investigation. Thus Oppenheimer, it is stated, "has repeatedly exercised an arrogance of his own judgment with respect to the loyalty and reliability of other citizens." He has, that is to say, exercised his judgment as to what to tell and what not to tell the F.B.I.

Asserting "the right of citizens to be in disagreement with security measures . . . [as] a part of the right of dissent which must

---

[1] The board consisted of chairman Gordon Gray, president of the University of North Carolina; Thomas A. Morgan, former president of the Sperry Corporation; and Ward V. Evans, professor of chemistry at Loyola University, Chicago. Dr. Evans agreed with the findings but filed a minority recommendation to restore Dr. Oppenheimer's clearance.

be preserved for our people," the authorities insist that this does not mean that a person who does not unequivocally accept the security system, and abide by its requirements, should be a part of it.

They agree, furthermore, that *"there can be no tampering with the national security, which in times of peril must be absolute,* and without concessions for reasons of admiration, gratitude, reward, sympathy or charity. *Any doubts whatever must be resolved in the interests of the national security."* (Emphasis added.)

Even this, however, does not touch rock bottom of the conformity required of those who would serve the nation in important war jobs. This was reached in the Gray-Morgan findings on the subject of Oppenheimer's position on production of the H-bomb. In the tremendous debate that preceded President Truman's decision to produce the H-bomb, not only Oppenheimer, but Conant, then president of Harvard, Du Bridge, president of the California Institute of Technology, and three others of the eight active members of the General Advisory Committee of the A.E.C. advised against it. Only Fermi of Chicago and Rabi of Columbia voted affirmatively. It is admitted that Oppenheimer's own opposition was based, to an important extent, on technical obstacles that were eliminated only by *later* discoveries and that, after Truman made his decision, Oppenheimer not only did nothing positively to hinder the program but continued for several years to work effectively on the war program.

Wherein, then, did the learned doctor err? Messrs. Gray and Morgan leave us in no doubt.

First, Oppenheimer and others opined, on various grounds, that it would be wiser for the government to build up defense, such as the radar screen, rather than produce the frightful offensive H-bomb weapons; but "government officials charged with the military posture of our country must also be certain that underlying any advice is a genuine conviction that this country cannot in the interest of security have less than the *strongest possible* offensive capabilities in a time of national danger." (As "they" always say, a strong offense is the best defense.)

Second, there is reason to believe that Oppenheimer was somewhat influenced by ethical and emotional considerations in his counsel regarding the H-bomb; and Gray and Morgan remind him and us that a scientist ought not to mix science and technics with ethics and emotions.

Finally, though the charge is rejected that Oppenheimer hindered the program in any specific way after Truman's decision, he is nevertheless adjudged to be a security risk, because his support was not "enthusiastic" enough for a man with "Dr. Oppenheimer's influence in the atomic scientific circles." As under totalitarian regimes, it is now spelled out that the severest penalties may attach to making an honest mistake, even though three-fourths of your professional associates also make it; and to not being *enthusiastic*, as well as efficient and obedient.[2]

Oppenheimer himself is clearly a man with a highly developed sense of individuality, far removed from the typical, hardened Communist type in which the person is submerged in the Party. It is inevitable that for such a man other people are also "persons," and that he should regard his relations with his friends as somehow inviolate, to be protected against such things as government inquisition. A one-time friend or associate is not to be abandoned when he gets into trouble—perhaps least of all then.

Oppenheimer is "non-political." He had been out of Harvard for eleven years before, "in late 1936, my interests began to change" from physics, Sanskrit, and the classics of literature and art to politics. From then on, his reaction and activities for some years are those of the typical idealistic and liberal fellow-traveler who never knew what was really going on "inside" the Communist Party or the political world generally.

"I had a continuing smoldering fury about the treatment of Jews in Germany. I had relatives there. . . . I saw what the depression was doing to my students. . . . Through them, I began to sense the larger sorrows of the great depression. . . . *I had no framework of political experience or conviction to give me perspective in these matters.*" (Emphasis added.)

He met a girl who had a lot of Communist friends. He gave hundreds of dollars to the Loyalist cause in Spain. He married a girl whose former husband was considered a Communist and had died in the Spanish Civil War. Even "the Nazi-Soviet pact and the behavior of the Soviet Union in Poland and in Finland . . . did not mean a sharp break for me with those who held different views. At that time I did not fully understand. . . ." It is doubtful whether even now he understands 1942 in political terms, and it is virtually

[2] Since this was written, the Atomic Energy Commission's affirmation of the decision against Dr. Oppenheimer expressly disavowed the "enthusiasm" item—possibly in response to the shocked protest expressed by many Americans.

certain that he does not understand the power struggle and the nature of the American power-state in 1954.

But the chief problem Robert Oppenheimer poses for us is the problem of conscience. Oppenheimer is a man of conscience, an inherently gentle person. He shrinks from hurting and killing, even from hurting a man's reputation, or injuring his chances for a job. He actually cannot bring himself to do it, and will take any measures to avoid it, unless in a case of treason. To a reporter for *Time* who, six years or so ago, asked him what was his "formula" for bringing up children, he said: "Just pour the love in and it will come out."

Yet Oppenheimer is involved, as deeply as anyone in our generation, in the colossal tragedies at Hiroshima, Eniwetok and Bikini. He did nothing to interfere with the production of the H-bomb, and indeed worked along at his key job in the atomic weapons field, after the Truman decision was made. And he seeks to remain part of an authoritarian military enterprise, to be adjudged not only loyal but a "good" security risk in a context where the "national security" has absolute priority. Here, where the lives of millions of human beings are involved, he is not a conscientious objector.

Michael Amrine in a very perceptive article on "The Scientist as Hamlet"[3] speaks of our time as "an age which has taken the work of the saintly Einstein and created a weapon ruthless beyond the dreams of Genghis Khan." As a matter of fact, it was the saintly Einstein who wrote the famous letter to Franklin D. Roosevelt that set in motion the machinery for making the A-bomb.

Both Einstein and Oppenheimer were among the spiritual victims of Hitler and the Nazis, and were decisively influenced by the fear that the Nazis might beat the United States to the A-bomb. "We had information in those days," Oppenheimer wrote, "of German activity in the field of nuclear fission. We were aware of what it might mean if they beat us to the draw."

I suppose the chief mitigating factor in the judgment that must be made is that neither Dr. Oppenheimer's Jewish spiritual counselors nor the leading Christian spiritual counselors of our time have guidance to give him. They are in the same place that he is in. Here we are face to face with the still generally accepted doctrine that, where war and the national interest are involved, the ordinary ethical or Christian standards are not relevant. The Christian as

[3] *The Saturday Review*, December 13, 1952.

Christian behaves in one way, the Christian as citizen in another. In the first capacity he "pours the love in"; in the second, he drops the atom bomb, since otherwise the Germans might beat us to the draw, or the H-bomb, since otherwise the Russians will beat us to the draw.

Sorrow over the ordeal to which Robert Oppenheimer has been subjected is appropriate. But it is also appropriate to observe that he and the other scientists who have worked on atomic weapons at Los Alamos and elsewhere helped to brew the bitter draught they now are made to drink. Their compact with Mephistopheles is their own, entered into with their eyes open. They don't like secrecy, but they worked in secrecy. They reject special responsibility for the use of the bombs they produced because in a democracy it is for the people to decide what weapons to use, but they spent two billion dollars of the taxpayers' money, and the labor of thousands of men, in a project about which the people knew nothing until some minutes after the bomb dropped on Hiroshima. More recently, as we have seen, there was a momentous debate over the H-bomb which involved political and moral, not merely technical, issues and not a single scientist has taken the American people into his confidence on these matters.

What kind of age did the scientists think this age of the A-bomb would be? What kind of age do they think the H-bomb symbolizes? An age of secret debates about the issues on which man's spiritual and even physical survival depends cannot be free from spies, informers, secrecy, regimentation, militarization, hysteria, murder, fear and totalitarianism!

It has seemed remotely possible that the verdict on Oppenheimer might be in part reversed. But suppose Dr. Oppenheimer were nominally cleared and merely not hired to work on atomic weapons any more—which some have thought a "better" way to handle the case—it is not likely that any but the most gullible would think that this changed anything.

What, then, are the real choices? Perhaps the best way for Dr. Oppenheimer to approach this question would be to ask himself another: "Suppose I were fully cleared and invited to go back to work for the Atomic Energy Commission and the Pentagon, what should I do?" A possible answer, of course, is: "Why not go back? It would then be evident that the United States is still fundamentally sound and democratic. I would have more power for good, to protect other scientists and liberals, to counsel moderation in foreign policy—and to help produce the super-super-weapon if my country should need it as a deterrent." This, alas, is presumably the way Dr. Oppenheimer might have reasoned if his clearance had not been called into question. Most of what are regarded as the finest elements in the country would have approved and continued to regard him as a great servant of his country.

Suppose, however, that a man like Oppenheimer were to come to the point where, whatever his personal fortunes, he can no longer believe that the world of the H-bomb and the global power struggle really is moving forward toward sanity, freedom and peace—not to mention love—what is there for him but to make a sharp break with the past, regardless of what anyone else does? He could acknowledge that "fellow-traveling" in the Thirties was indeed a "mistake," but not nearly so great a mistake as the work on the A-bomb and the H-bomb, or the notion that war can contribute anything to the destruction of totalitarianism or the salvaging of human dignity and decency. Having thus learned from error once more he could call on fellow scientists and fellow citizens to abandon war, unilaterally if need be, since meeting paranoia with sanity is in any case a better bet than meeting it with counter-paranoia.

It is customary to say that such individual action does not count. But surely this is the totalitarian heresy. Suppose Einstein and Oppenheimer joined in such an action and such a call from Princeton. There would be multitudes to join them.

Moreover, the response would not be confined to this country's scientists or citizens. Otto Hahn, director of the Kaiser Wilhelm Institute for Chemistry in Berlin, in 1938, was co-discoverer of uranium-fission. As a reviewer said, in the *Saturday Review*, of a book of Hahn's that was published in 1951, he "demonstrated that atomic energy was no longer a science-fiction monopoly." Otto Hahn was aware of the military implications of his discovery *but he did not write such a letter to Hitler as Einstein wrote to Roosevelt*—he did not become the Oppenheimer of the Nazi war-machine. Such men as Hahn—and there may be some in Russia, too—would gladly have responded to an Einstein-Oppenheimer call, and even in a Siberian concentration camp would organize a section of an international strike of scientists and other human beings against war.

Is it possible? Can these modern Fausts free themselves from the bonds into which they sold themselves?

It may be. Gounod left his operatic Faust helplessly imprisoned, a demonstration of the correctness of the Mephistophelean cynicism about man's nature, but Gounod never finished the story as Goethe did. For in Part II of the great German poet's work, Faust slowly and painfully redeems himself by acts of unselfish love for humanity and at last demonstrates triumphantly the answer of the Almighty, when Mephisto first laid down his cynical challenge:

> *"A good man through obscurest aspirations,*
> *Has still an instinct for the one true way."*

Getting Rid of War

1959 Every thoughtful person wants to abolish war and the benumbing threat of nuclear destruction which hangs over all of mankind. The question is how to do it. Here is an attempt to state one answer to that question. It is an answer which hitherto represented the view of a minority; but more and more people are beginning to think it is the only one that makes any sense or holds out real hope.

First, we must try to see the nature of the problem. The international political scene today has two main characteristics. It is marked on the one hand by terrific, dizzying movement in the field of military technology, the development of weapons of extermination. There is, on the other hand, extreme rigidity in the political field, at the point of struggle between the United States and the Soviet Union, the Western and Eastern power blocs.

As for the first, the A-bomb now seems like something out of the Middle Ages in the context of missile development, the firing of satellites to orbit the earth, the catapulting of satellites into outer space—all directly tied in with war preparations on the part of both major powers.

As for political relationships, on the surface, of course, changes occur, or seem to occur, tension waxes and wanes and grows again, and it is clear that at the moment neither power wants a nuclear war; neither wants the situation anywhere to get completely out of hand. But no major political issues, as in Germany or in the Middle

East or in the realm of disarmament, get settled. There is no indication that any are on the way to settlement.

I am not impressed in this connection with the struggle that goes on periodically between the White House and Congressional committees over whether a balanced budget or national security is of first importance. These are not struggles between pacifists and militarists, people who want or do not want "genuine negotiation." And however these controversies are resolved, the military budget will still be of astronomical proportions for "peacetime," and intended to enable the United States to obliterate Russia if it should prove "necessary."

Both aspects of the contemporary situation make one think of mass hypnosis, mass hysteria or catalepsy. A short time ago, we were appalled at the thought that some bomber pilot would misread a signal on his radar screen, conclude that an enemy was taking hostile action, and touch off a nuclear war. Now Professor William Pickering, jet missile expert of the California Institute of Technology, points out that it seems inevitable that technological military developments will proceed fatalistically. The calculations now required are so intricate that they have to be made by super-calculating machines. A defect in a tube of such a machine here may lead to a wrong signal being received by a machine in Russia, or vice versa. This will automatically set missiles flying. Even if a human observer realizes in a moment, Professor Pickering warns, that a mistake has occurred, it will be too late to stop the machinery of extermination. Thus, hypnotically, the intricate dance goes on.

In the field of so-called negotiations between the powers, one gets the same impression of mental aberration, flight from reality, in the immobility, the rigid stalemate, the utter failure of diplomats to communicate on controversial issues. Nations simply talk *at* each other like talking machines.

Note that this bound-to-be-catastrophic conjunction of violent movement in one field and stark rigidity in the other goes on, in spite of the fact that the policy makers, generals, scientists, and opinion makers—including the clergy on both sides—know the nature of modern weapons and the character of the war in which they are to be used.

It is essential to note that *in this crucial respect* there is no difference between the leaders in the two rival blocs. Nuclear war is politically irrational and morally an indefensible and hideous atrocity, whoever perpetrates it. Preparation for such war is also politically irrational, and since there is no guarantee that the preparation will lead to anything but war, the preparation itself is an atrocity and a degradation of mankind.

I lay this charge at the doors of Eisenhower and Khrushchev, of Dulles and Gromyko; of the intellectuals of this country and of the Soviet Union and other Communist countries; of the Protestant, Catholic and Jewish teachers of the United States, and of the priests of whatever denomination in Russia.

On each side a claim about the end in view is made by the government, and to a large extent accepted by the people. This claim tends to be absolutistic—that the conflict is an ultimate one, either *the* Revolution which finally will liberate mankind or a war to save "all the values of democratic and Christian civilization." Even insofar as these claims are sincerely made and not sheer propagandist hypocrisy the indictment is not mitigated. Not one of the professed aims of Communism (classless and warless world and the rest) or of the democratic and Christian faith (the sacredness and infinite worth of every human soul, and what-have-you) can be advanced by or salvaged after a nuclear war.

The very arrogance which is revealed in this absolutizing— the infamous notion that *my* regime, *my* country, *my* philosophy is so precious that its defense justifies the obliteration of an enemy people and quite possibly wiping out the population of my own country as well—what can one say of this concept except that it is itself an extreme expression of the mental sickness and the foul moral degradation which has mankind, or at least its present leaders, in its grip?

Note, furthermore, that each of these regimes in the very preparation of nuclear war is alike in displaying the impudence of exposing other peoples and even the future generations of other countries to genetic distortion and death by fall-out and other means. Russia and the United States alike, if war ensues, will doom millions in other nations to death.

This charge, unprecedented in the history of man, lies now at the doors of Eisenhower and Khrushchev, Dulles and Gromyko, and the policy- and opinion-makers of both camps.

In the presence of the stark, central fact of what modern war means, the validity of the talk about defense on both sides—"We do these things because the other side is doing it"—adds up to exactly zero. When mass retaliation is called defense, that is double-think and double-talk on both sides.

Parenthetically, this is not the only point at which both the

United States and the Soviet Union need to see that the enemy is not the other nation, but war.

Nor is this the only point at which all of us need to see that the basic fact of international life today is no longer, if it ever was, the battle of the power blocs. It is increasingly the case that each is confronted by the same problems, perhaps in somewhat different form, including the ultimate problems of how the human spirit is to survive and, surviving, to enter into its heritage in the age of the fissioned and fused atom.

Similarly, most of the discussion about which government is making genuine peace offers, negotiating astutely or stupidly, and so on, is also pointless. All this negotiation takes place in the context of the nuclear arms race, and this is an activity of lunatics and global criminals. Neither side gives any indication of being ready to take any risk by withdrawing from this madness. When they stop this senselessness, then we can begin to apply sensible standards to their interminable negotiations.

The situation is so full of peril that many fall back for consolation on the idea of deterrence: the very fact that weapons are so destructive is somehow going to prevent war. Some assert that we actually have a nuclear stalemate now, since general war has not yet broken out.

If the reader will take a historical stance for a moment, he may reflect on what a brand-new idea it is that weapons—the most intricate, expensive and deadly weapons—are made and stockpiled in an atmosphere of extreme tension, for the purpose of never being used. Each big nation turns out this stuff, we are asked to believe, with no notion of ever using it, but simply in order to keep the other fellow from using his. Surely this is an Alice in Wonderland notion. Raymond Gram Swing long ago characterized this as the theory that "the bigger the danger grows, the greater the safety." General Omar Bradley more recently stigmatized it as "peace by the accumulation of peril." Any beginner in logic would point out that if it were guaranteed that nuclear weapons were not going to be used, their deterrent power would vanish.

Obviously, if there were any substance to the concept that we are now secure behind our deterrent shield, we would feel it, a little bit, somewhere. We would relax, take a deep breath. The fact is that the arms race spells tension and creates fear and tension. Brinkmanship is inevitably the foreign policy that is associated with such an arms race, and brinkmanship is not relaxing.

As a matter of fact, neither great power is seeking to achieve a balance. Each is constantly seeking to upset it. In this realm, perpetual motion is the aim. How little intention the "realists," military and civilian, have of breaking out of the fixed pattern of violence against violence was revealed, perhaps inadvertently, by one of the experts of the Rand Corporation (which seems to be a sort of brain trust of the Defense Department), who wrote that if an agreement were reached to "abolish" the weapons necessary in a general war, the need for a deterrent then would be all the greater. For then "the violator could gain an overwhelming advantage from the concealment of even a few weapons. *The need for a deterrent . . . is ineradicable.*"

There is, then, no built-in, automatic safety factor in the nuclear power struggle. Modern technology is not equipped with a safety valve. The nature of modern war *may* lead to the abolition of war, provided that men face the facts regarding the abolition of war and the rivalries of power states, and act upon the facts.

All this points to the conclusion that we cannot depend on the accustomed, traditional ways of thinking and of political behavior to save us. We have to find a new pattern of action. There has to be an illumination, a vision. This must lead to a moral and political decision, an act of the will.

It seems to me inescapable, therefore, that we have, as a nation, or a people, to be ready to take unilateral action. Disarmament will not come out of "I will if you will" bargaining; it will come when some nation transposes "war must not be" from the conclusion of an analysis to which everybody agrees into the basis for national action.

We may put this another way: neither the Soviet Union nor the United States is going to force or cajole or trick the other into breaking out of the circle of suspicion and exposing itself to insecurity in the military power sense. They certainly will not coexist peacefully unless they change substantially. But the change in each case will have to come from within. The one can induce or encourage it in the other only by example, i.e., by unilateral action.

Something like a revolution, a rebirth of man, is necessary and you cannot say to the man across the fence: "I will be reborn, if you will—first." That's something entirely different: a bargain, a deal, not rebirth.

In face of all this, an important development in the struggle to end war is the fact that C. Wright Mills, Columbia University sociologist, and one of the best informed and most sophisticated analysts of political affairs, has recently come out for unilateral nuclear disarmament in a book called *The Causes of World War III*. He says, for example, that "the United States government should at once and unilaterally cease all further production of 'experimental' weapons" and move to destroy or convert to peacetime uses its existing stocks. Mills similarly calls on the government to "abandon all military bases and installations outside the continental domain of the United States."

At another point, he nails down the case for unilateral action, saying: "It is less 'realistic' to spend more money on arms than to *stop at once—and, if must be, unilaterally*—all preparation of World War III. There is no other realism, no other necessity, no other end. If they do not mean these things, necessity and need and realism are merely the desperate slogans of the morally crippled."

As soon as anyone starts to talk about the United States unilaterally getting rid of its nuclear weapons, the familiar questions bob up: "Are you going to let the Russians or the Communists run over you? Would they try to do it? Could they?" There are a number of answers to such questions. Here we must confine ourselves to a few.

The first can be found in a reference in Mills' book to one of those courageous top physicists who are on record as absolutely refusing to help equip their own country, West Germany, with nuclear weapons. Said Max Van Laue (not a pacifist), justifying his refusal against the charge that he was playing into the hands of the Soviets: "Suppose I live in a big apartment house and burglars attack me; I am allowed to defend myself and, if need be, I may even shoot, but under no circumstances may I blow up the house. It is true that to do so would be an effective defense against the burglars, but the resulting evil would be much greater than any I could suffer. But what if the burglars have explosives to destroy the whole house? Then I would leave them with the responsibility for the evil and would not contribute anything to it."

In one sense, no other answer is needed. It is our contention that, whatever the provocation or the danger, there is no justification in heaven or on earth for our arms indiscriminately wiping out any other people, men, women, the aged and the babies. If we have no words harsh enough for those who would do such a thing to us, what are we if we do it to others?

In the second place, the one way in which the sane and democratic elements in the Soviet Union would be encouraged, and the dictatorship undermined, would be by a United States which dared to risk sanity, which acted for peace, which established a true, racially integrated democracy here at home, and which backed the democratic revolutions in the underdeveloped countries so that their people would not find the Communists their only source of aid and leadership. In such a peaceful democracy, multitudes in the satellite countries would see an alternative to which they would be irresistibly drawn. By such a peaceful and genuine revolution, the faith the uncommitted countries had in us would be restored, and totalitarianism might be transformed—as it certainly will not be by war or threat of war.

Here I want to call attention to a remarkable declaration made by a world-famous political analyst, former United States Ambassador to the Soviet Union, and head of the Policy Planning Committee of the State Department, George F. Kennan. In his *Russia, the Atom and the West*—probably the most widely discussed book on East-West relations to have appeared in 1958—Kennan writes:

What sort of life is it to which these devotees of the weapons race would see us condemned? The technological realities of this competition are constantly changing from month to month and from year to year. Are we to flee like haunted creatures from one defensive device to another, each more costly and humiliating than the one before, cowering underground one day, breaking up our cities the next, attempting to surround ourselves with elaborate electronic shields on the third, concerned only to prolong the length of our lives while sacrificing all the values for which it might be worthwhile to live at all? If I thought this was the best the future held for us, I should be tempted to join those who say, "Let us divest ourselves of this weapon altogether; let us stake our safety on God's grace and our own good consciences and on that measure of common sense and humanity which even our adversaries possess; but then let us at least walk like men, with our heads up, so long as we are permitted to walk at all." We must not forget that this is actually the situation in which many of the peoples of this world are obliged to live today; and while I would not wish to say that they are now more secure than we are, for the fact that they do not hold these weapons, I would submit that they are more secure than we would be if we were to resign ourselves entirely to the negative dynamics of the weapons race, as many would have us do.

If things get bad enough, as the weapons race runs its predestined course, Kennan would advise us to have the good sense and moral courage to take unilateral action, to follow the pacifist, nonviolent way. We would be safer doing that, this statesman contends, than if we "resign ourselves to the negative dynamics of the weapons race."

But surely the fact is that we are caught now in these negative and perilous dynamics. We are less likely to be able to break out if we get in any deeper. As more nations get atomic weapons, the harder it becomes to break out, the greater is the risk of an irretrievable misstep and disaster. This is the best the future holds for us unless we break away now, before it is too late. Now is the time for the American people to stake their safety on God's grace and their own good consciences and on that measure of common sense and humanity which even our enemies possess.

What is Mr. Kennan waiting for? What are any of us waiting for?

One final word. Whether or not the nation adopts any such course, the question of the personal responsibility of each of us must be faced by us and by our fellow citizens.

In unequivocal terms, C. Wright Mills, in his recent book, calls upon all men and women, but especially the intellectuals and the scientists, to become conscientious objectors. As for the scientists, "they ought unilaterally to withdraw from, and so abolish, the Science Machine as it now exists."

To the objection often heard that "if I don't do a certain war job, somebody else will," Mills retorts that "this is less an argument than the mannerism of the irresponsible. It is based . . . upon the acceptance of your own impotence." He concludes:

My answers to this mannerism are: if you do not do it, you at least are not responsible for its being done. If you refuse to do so out loud, others may quietly refrain from doing it, and those who still do it may then do it only with hesitation and guilt . . . To refuse to do it is an act affirming yourself as a moral center of responsible decisions . . . it is the act of a man who rejects "fate," for it reveals the resolution of one human being to take at least his own fate into his own hands.

This challenge to each human being to take at least his own fate in his own hands in this matter of war is what the War Resisters League and other such organizations have been proclaiming these many decades. I submit that there never has been a time when the challenge came more insistently to each man and each woman; or when it was more appropriate to support the organizations which, in an age of anxiety, apathy and conformity, call on men each "to take at least his own fate into his own hands."

Africa
Against the Bomb

1960 During my visit to Ghana, on the morning of December 6, 1959, I witnessed the start of the Sahara Protest Team from Accra. No matter what the future may bring, this project has now unquestionably developed into the most significant in the series of direct-action civil-disobedience projects in which radical non-pacifists have been involved in recent years.

We all had to rise before dawn to be on hand for the farewell rally at Accra Arena. As daylight came, the two Land Rovers (British version of jeeps), the truck to carry water, gasoline and food, and an extra jeep left the bungalows belonging to the Ghana government, in which the Team members from abroad had been housed for some weeks. Ghanaians walking the road waved at the caravan. Everybody in this city knows about the Team. In Ghana "Sahara" now means the Project.

At six on that Sunday morning, although people stay up late Saturday and a good many church services are held at this early hour, a thousand people were in the Arena when the farewell rally started. E. E. Quaye, chairman of the Accra Municipal Council (mayor), presided. Bayard Rustin and Michael Scott participated briefly, the Ghanaian Minister of Agriculture spoke, and then the principal address was given by the Finance Minister, K. A. Gbdemah, who has been the most prominent and active of the local committee members. It should be mentioned that the Prime Minister, Kwame Nkrumah, contributed over $1,000 to the fund of $25,000, which was raised through public appeal by the Ghana Council For Nuclear Disarmament, for the use of the Sahara Project.

Gbdemah held nothing back in his pledge of support for the Team and pulled no punches in his attack on French nuclear policy. He said that he is not against the French people but that "it seems nowadays that when Frenchmen assume high government office, they become mad. This is the only word one can apply to much of French policy today and especially to its fatuous effort to become a nuclear power."

He expressed the deeply felt conviction of Africans that the French have no right to dominance in any part of Africa, and hailed the Algerian struggle for independence. Alluding to the refusal by the French to grant visas to the Team, he said that the French had no right to interfere, on African soil, with "an international team traveling to the Sahara on a mission for all mankind. If the French dare to arrest these people, that will only further blacken the name of France in the minds of decent people everywhere, and make it more likely that world opinion will force France to abandon the test. But even if this fortunate event should not result from this Project, right will win in the end and every bad Frenchman will be driven from Africa."

The nineteen members of the Team were lined up on the high platform—eleven Ghanaians, one Nigerian, one man, President of the National Congress, from Basutoland in the South of Africa, Esther Peter of France, Michael Scott, Michael Randle and Francis Hoyland of England, and Bayard Rustin and Bill Sutherland of the United States. Bill has lived in Ghana for six years and for several of them has been Gbdemah's private secretary.

Gbdemah spoke of the completely nonviolent character of the Team and of the sacrifice the members were making. "Whatever country you may come from," he said, "and whatever your color may be, you are now a part of Africa. You represent the two hundred million people of this continent. We hope you will succeed and that you will not suffer undue hardship. But, whether you come back dead or alive, you are forever enshrined in the hearts of Africans."

Then the Team's vehicles were driven up in front of the platform. At their head was a sound truck supplied by the Convention People's Party, the ruling party of the country. C. P. P. songs and hymns came from the sound truck as a cavalcade of cars got under way carrying Gbdemah, Quaye, and nearly a hundred other prominent citizens. The cavalcade traveled through various sections of the city, where hundreds lined the streets, waving their hands in the beautiful African fashion and shouting, "Sahara! Freedom!"

About five miles from the center of Accra, the procession halted for deeply moving farewells. Then the Team left for Kumasi, seven hours away, where they were to hold a mass meeting in the early evening and spend the night.

The young man who served as my secretary and guide then told me, "Now we are going to Gbdemah's house." Most of the crowd who had escorted the Team out of town went there also. Beer and soft drinks were brought out, but before anyone drank, Gbdemah filled a glass half full of beer, walked out of doors, poured a few drops on the ground, and half chanted a few sentences. There was an approving response to each statement he made. At first, only one or two men made this response; then some women joined in; then more and more people, so that at the close there was a loud shouting. At each new chant more beer was spilled until, at the end, the last drop was poured out. This ritual is a libation poured onto the ground, an offering, I gather, to the soil or motherland itself, to the gods, and to ancestors.

I witnessed a similar ritual later when several Team members and forty or fifty Ghanaians met City Council Chairman Quaye at the airport upon his return from Liberia. References to the Protest Team were woven into the chant then by an enthusiastic supporter whose grandfather, a famous chief, had fought for his people's rights against the British. At the close, passengers at the air terminal stood in wonderment as great shouts of "Sahara! Sahara!" went up, and some of the women moved into a lovely dance in honor of the Chairman and of the Team.

All this indicated that the Sahara Project had been taken up enthusiastically by the people of Ghana. Radio Ghana had mentioned the Team's activities and quoted its statements in almost every newscast during the preceding weeks. The papers carried stories and pictures regularly. But this did not mean that the project was a government undertaking. Obviously, it could not have the participation of Cabinet members (another minister, N. A. Welbeck, also served on the working committee) if the government were not sympathetic. But the Cabinet insisted that each Ghanaian volunteer chosen for the Team sign a statement, witnessed by a police officer, that he was going of his own free will and clearly understood that he was not being appointed by the government or being guaranteed special protection, as would a government emissary or soldier. There was, at one moment during the final stages of preparation, a possibility that the government would insist that the Ghanaian contingent be limited to four members. There is real apprehension here that the French have hostile intentions toward Ghana because of the influence this progressive nation has on people in nearby French African countries. The Ghana government did not wish to give the impression that it was leading some sort of "invasion" into the Upper Volta or to risk demands for "action" from the Ghanaian people if Ghanaian citizens on the Team should be badly treated by the French or their native collaborators.

Any sort of tie-in with a government obviously presents problems for almost any private "cause," and very real problems for a project of a radical, nonviolent character. It would be folly to assume that any government is truly devoted to nonviolence and its revolutionary implications or that there will not be differences of opinion and perhaps eventually sharp clashes between even a progressive modern government and a nonviolent movement—if the movement avoids compromise of principle, as it certainly should.

On the other hand, I am satisfied that a project of the size of the present one could not have been set up, without real, though in this case strictly unofficial, support from persons in government. I am equally confident that no compromise of principle has been made by the Team. The result, in the opinion of a considerable number of Ghanaians, is that something of the idealism and enthusiasm of the hard struggle for independence has been revived among C. P. P. people in Ghana. Moreover, an immense propaganda job for the idea of nonviolence has been done among the masses and a considerable amount of intensive training in nonviolent philosophy and strategy has been given the twenty-odd volunteers who were able to attend training sessions regularly. But the *popular* education in nonviolence has by no means been confined to Ghana. Among the countries where we know, because we have had letters from important organizations, that the idea has become widespread, are Kenya, the East and Central African countries, Nigeria, the Cameroons, Guinea and Basutoland. N. Mokhekle, president of the Basutoland National Congress, and a member of the Team, represents a hundred and fifty volunteers from that country alone, who would have come if funds had been available. Mokhekle, having missed a plane, drove hundreds of miles to catch another one in order to be in Accra on time.

At least an equally important achievement is that large masses of Africans have raised their sights from concern about independence and the building of new regimes to concern about the world struggle against nuclear war. Not that Africans had not been troubled about the Sahara test. Anxiety does not have to be manufactured in such a case. Nonetheless, something was needed to crystallize the sentiment and fuse it into action. The Team has done that on a truly big scale here in Accra. And reports are coming in, from other African countries, of radio addresses, articles in the press, mass meetings, days of mourning, and other activities in support of the Sahara Project and in protest against the test.

The Team's first stop was late in the afternoon of December 6 at Kumasi, second largest city in Ghana, a busy manufacturing and trading center, surrounded by rich agricultural territory. The Team was enthusiastically received, put up at a government Rest House and sent on its way next morning to the next city, two hundred and fifty miles farther north, more than half way from Accra to the Upper Volta border, where French jurisdiction begins. At Tamale (pronounced tam-a-lee, with the accent on the first syllable) the Team was given a rousing rally. Twenty-five young men pleaded to be added to the Team and were prepared to leave their jobs and families immediately in order to come along. There was no vehicle to carry them, but this incident indicates the extent of the propaganda for nonviolence that has been accomplished by the Project. One of the problems which clearly emerges is how these young men can be trained for a permanent nonviolent and pacifist movement. I wish that all activists in the United States and Britain could witness these scenes—the big rallies, the people lined along streets and roads shouting "Freedom!" and "Sahara Team!" as the huge truck and the Land Rovers roll by.

On Tuesday afternoon, December 7, the Team moved on to a place about three hundred miles north, named Bolgo-Tanga, from which one road branches off toward Bawku and another to Navrango, the border villages, from one of which the crossing into French territory was to be made. The Team had asked me to fly in from Accra to join them in strategy conferences. At Navrango, three of us had a good talk with several district commissioners and the Regional Commissioner of the border area about conditions on the French side of the border, the attitude of the people, etc. These conversations made it clear that the Team should make the crossing at Bawku the next day while at the same time Team leaflets were being distributed by volunteers in the part of the Upper Volta adjoining Navrango. One of our workers had already sent leaflets by truckmen into the Ivory Coast, and over the week end a big batch was sent to Togoland, on the other side of Liberia. Copies were also mailed to sixty organizations all over Africa, with authority to reproduce them.

From Navrango, the Team drove fifty miles to Bawku. We were escorted by Amadu Sedou, who is Commissioner for sixty thousand people in that border area. He is about thirty-five, trim and handsome, completely unassuming. On the street, you would not be able to tell him from any other African. He is idealistic and quietly efficient. It would be hard to conceive of a finer type of government official.

At midnight in Bawku he found places for everyone to sleep. At seven A. M. we were having a breakfast of bread and butter and tea at Sedou's. Soon after eight we were driving through the streets of Bawku, lined with typical back-country huts and stores, and with people, many of whom were dressed in African back-country style, which often means no clothing from the waist up. At the open field where rallies are held, there was a mass of two thousand wildly cheering people (in a town whose population is probably one thousand) to greet Michael Scott and the rest of the Team as we drove in.

On a high chair sat the chief of the local tribe in full regalia, surrounded by his counselors and accompanied by his band. Ghana Films had to have pictures of Team members shaking hands with the chief. I would judge from a number of such scenes that the process of transferring authority from the various chiefs to the government representatives and developing a national, rather than a parochial, tribal spirit, seems to be moving ahead, and moving in such a way as not to banish or liquidate the chiefs but somehow to draw them into the national orbit and perspective. For example, the first name on the list of international sponsors of the Sahara Team is the Asantahene, which means Grand Chief of the Ashantis, a very important figure. He publicly received the Team members early in the preparations and gave $156.00 for the Project. The chief at Bawku made a present of two baskets of canned goods to the Team. At the close of the rally, members of the Team who were handing out leaflets were nearly mobbed by people who wanted to be sure to get one.

After the rally we moved to the courtyard of the town hall,

where, from 10 A. M. to 3:45 P. M., a series of feverish activities took place, including a final intensive strategy conference.

Then the team finally set off for the border, with Sedou, four of his assistants, and myself going on ahead in Sedou's car. There *had* been rumors that some Upper Volta people would be hostile to anybody coming from Ghana, and we were on the lookout as we drove the approximately twenty miles from Bawku to the border-line. The border itself is unmarked—the country a near-desert. No one was there except forty or fifty friendly Ghanaians who had come to see the Team off.

Ghana Films took pictures as the truck and Land Rovers moved on into French territory. As Sedou and I learned from Bayard, four hours later in Bawku, the Volta people en route were friendly and cheered the Team. At Bittou, the first French control post and barrier—16 miles from the actual border-line—three white French officers, an unusual sight in this region, stopped the Team at the barrier. Their first move was to collect all passports.

The Team's Committee—Scott, Rustin, Mokhekle of Basuto-land and Esther Peter (interpreter)—were received by the French officers very courteously. They were offered drinks and declined; offered food and declined. Michael Scott stated the Team's purpose. After he had spoken a few minutes, one of the officers interrupted him and said: "You do not need to speak at length. We know all about your group. We know you are sincere people. But we are here *under instructions from Paris* to forbid you to proceed."

Scott said the Team would not go back. "If this means arrest, we're ready for that." The reply was: "As of this moment, we have no orders to arrest you."

"So why not let the Team pass?"

"This is strictly forbidden," they were told. The officers retired for a conference and then stated: "Since you will not leave, we shall have to get fresh instructions from Paris. For this we have to go to Ouagodougou, fifty miles away. We cannot make the journey there and back and make contact with Paris before 12:30 P. M. on Thursday—next day."

Large numbers of Africans stood around, evidently interested and friendly to the Team. This confirmed the impression, that, whether they say so openly or not, Africans are afraid of and are against the Sahara Tests. One of them said: "If it's harmless, why not hold it in the country outside Paris, so all the French people can see the wonder?" If the Team runs into any trouble in French territory, it will be clear that the French provoked it. The officers were plainly sensitive to the friendliness of Africans and asked the Team's Committee not to propagandize while the officers were away. The Committee agreed not to propagandize until 12:30 P. M., next day.

When the officers returned on Thursday, they said they had been unable to reach the proper authorities in Paris but demanded that keys to the vehicles be surrendered. This the Team refused to do.

From then on tension built up. The Africans in the vicinity were plainly friendly to the Team, eagerly sought leaflets (which had a message in four languages: Arabic, Hawza, French, and English), and listened to the talks. Even some of the African police showed interest. The local chief built a hut to shelter the Team from the heat. The local butcher brought meat.

The response of the French officers to this infiltration of the anti-test propaganda into the native population was to tighten control. By the end of the third day at the Bittou barrier there were a hundred police and soldiers on hand, armed with revolvers, rifles, and machine guns. Not only did they surround the Team on all sides, confining them to a space of only 50 yards in diameter, but they also kept the Africans so far away that propaganda by talk or leaflet distribution was shut off.

In the meantime, in Paris, a spokesman for the French government told inquiring reporters that they had "no knowledge" of any anti-bomb protesters being "arrested" at the Upper Volta border—which was technically correct. The policy of the French government obviously is to try to suppress all information about the Team and, if at all possible, to avoid making any move which would constitute news, such as arresting or deporting its members.

On returning to the United States I found that the newspapers and broadcasting agencies here were cooperating with De Gaulle's strategy and have failed to publish dispatches which I know were sent from Ghana, by Reuters and other agencies, because they came back to Accra on the ticker. Both Paris and London have reported more than New York.

Surrounded by soldiers and police, the Team decided to withdraw temporarily into Ghana. On December 17, seven of its members crossed into French territory in Upper Volta a second time and again were stopped at the first control point that they reached, near a little village named Po.

Since this Project protesting against the proposed explosion of an atomic bomb at Reggan in the Sahara Desert by the French government is, I think, the first international, direct action program against nuclear war and certainly the first in which Western European and American pacifists sought to enlist and train people of other continents—in this case Africans—in "positive nonviolent action" (a phrase common in West Africa) it should be useful to outline in some detail the problems the Team faced at Bittou and the course it members resorted to in dealing with them.

For one thing, there was an element of ambiguity in the relationship between the Team and the French officials, especially the three white officers in charge. The problem was in some respects similar to the one which conscientious objectors have in dealing with guards and trusties in prison. On the one hand, the latter must be recognized as fellow human beings. There is always the responsibility and the possibility of getting them to see the true character of the role they are playing and to turn away from it. On the other hand, while the functionary is also a human being, it is equally true that in such situations the human being is a functionary. In order to maintain one's integrity and also the possibility of influencing fellow-prisoners, one must avoid the kind of "fraternization" with functionaries which in effect makes one part of the coercive and brutalizing machinery, or at least enables it to operate more smoothly.

When the white French officers offered drinks and food to Michael Scott and the other members of the Team's committee, they refused them. They did accept an offer that one or two Team members, under police guard, should be permitted once or twice a day to go into Bittou to purchase such things as bread and soft drinks. As time went on, this became less and less satisfactory. The French, who had halted the Team although declining formally to arrest them, avoided the responsibility either of providing for their keep or letting them go through. There was no clear confrontation of an issue.

Another element of ambiguity arose from a special factor in West African psychology: the French are to West Africans what Communists were not long ago to the majority of Americans (and still are to many)—incarnate devils. This is especially true for Ghanaians, who suspect the French of imperialistic designs against Ghana, because of its vigorous championship of complete independence for all Africa. This bitterness stems partly from the general history of French imperialism in Africa; partly from the French atrocities in Indo-China a few years ago and more recently in Algeria. It is also the result of the way in which the French literally stripped Guinea of all administrative equipment and economic support when that country, under the leadership of Sekou Touré, voted for complete independence.

In such an atmosphere some of the Ghanaian youths found it difficult to understand how you could expect to gain anything by any conversation at all with white French officers. They even harbored the absurd suspicion that Esther Peter, the Frenchwoman who served as interpreter for the Team, was somehow "betraying" them when she conversed with the French. In the arguments that took place between Team members and the French, there were times when the latter showed more restraint and good will than the former!

Lest there be any even temporary misunderstanding, two observations should be recorded at once. This was the very first experience of the Ghanaian youths with nonviolent direct action. They had had experience as soldiers and as participants in political demonstrations, where sheer force of numbers dominated and violence was expected or encouraged. They had had no experience of "that other kind of force—patience," as one of them put it to me later. We had carried on daily intensive training sessions for two or three weeks. It is probable that for dramatic situations, such as arrest and imprisonment, the volunteers would have been prepared to function nonviolently. For the hard task of simply sticking it out day after day they were not so well prepared. One of the lessons to be drawn from the Sahara Project is that in similar situations the courses must be longer and more varied. However, as training and simulated situations are never the same for a soldier as the experience of actual war, so the nonviolent resister learns only in actual experience what nonviolence means.

The other observation is that, although it was not always obvious under the severe stress at Bittou, the Sahara Project did much in Ghana, and to some extent in other parts of Africa, to dispel the unthinking anti-French emotionalism. It could hardly have done this unless people like Michael Scott, Michael Randle and Francis Hoyland had records of opposing nuclear testing and armament at home in Great Britain; Pierre Martin and Esther Peter at home in France; Bayard Rustin and Bill Sutherland at home in the United States.

In one of our training sessions shortly before the Team left

Accra, a Ghanaian volunteer suddenly got up with his face alight and said: "Now I know what nonviolence is. It means that if Ghana should decide to test an atomic bomb, I'd have to oppose that most of all."

I think it would be accurate to say that the foreign policy of the Ghana government until recently had tended to be anti-French. But in the foreign policy debate in Parliament in December, the Foreign Minister struck a new note, which Ghana had learned mainly from the Sahara Project. He remarked that one of the members of his own Party, the Convention People's Party, had characterized Ghana policy as anti-French. "This," he said, "is not true. We are against French atomic policy—against nuclear testing by whomsoever carried out."

To return to the dilemma at Bittou, the Team had a huge truck, able to carry enough food, water and petrol for ten persons the last five hundred miles through the desert to Reggan, where none of these things could be obtained at any price. They also had the two Land Rovers and the second-hand jeep. These had been parked a little to one side of the main road since the Team first reached the control post. Suppose now that such a Team wishes to move on, to pass the barrier? How go about it? Assuming you could get to the closed gate, would you crash into it with your big truck? Would this be nonviolence?

An experiment was carried out at Bittou, to see what might happen if the vehicles were moved. It was agreed to move them a few feet, and then to hold a conference to assess the situation, on the basis of the reaction of the guards. As soon as the members got into the cars and turned on the engines, the one hundred police and soldiers closed in, revolvers and rifles pointed at the cars; machine guns were passed to those who were supposed to use them in an emergency. In other words, if the Team's vehicles had moved forward, they would have encountered human beings, not a wooden barrier.

One thing was made clear. As Bayard Rustin has put it, "trucks and jeeps are lethal weapons" in such situations. Can they possibly be used by nonviolent resisters to run down police soldiers who are ordered to prevent passage? Assuming the answer is in the negative, how do people proceed nonviolently to carry the protest to another stage? At Bittou, the Team could not work out an answer to that question.

There was another important factor that led to the decision, after five days, to pull back into Ghana for the kind of analysis and hammering out of program for a second phase which seemed impossible of attainment at Bittou. This had to do with personality problems and personal relationships. I surmise that all who were close to the Sahara Project would emphasize that, in planning direct action projects—especially of an international character—frank and serious attention should be given in advance to the question of the kind of people needed on a particular action; to the selection of personnel from among volunteers; and to the nature of the commitment and discipline required in the given situation.

It will be easy to understand that the withdrawal to Bolgo-Tanga was regarded by some as a gesture of despair. However, it turned out to have been a brilliant improvisation. This is a tribute to the leadership of Scott, Randle, Rustin and Sutherland; to the exceptional qualities of some of the young Ghanaians; and to the spirit which the Project had generated, which to a remarkable degree had fused all its twenty members into a fellowship, and made it possible to work out a program for a new phase that met with general acceptance.

The main decision was to reduce to seven the number of persons who would cross into French territory a second time and attempt to get into the Sahara. The seven selected to cross the border and again risk arrest or injury were Michael Scott, Michael Randle, Bill Sutherland and four young Ghanaians, Arkhurst, Manso, Lindsay, and Akita. Three other Ghanaian citizens remained as liaison men on the Ghana side of the border.

It was agreed that Mokhekle of Basutoland should go back for the elections in his country early in January. Francis Hoyland returned to London; Bayard Rustin returned for a couple weeks to Accra, after which he had to go back to the United States, as he had promised to work in the movement for racial integration here. Esther Peter returned, a week later, to France, where she supplied a much needed push to French protests against the Sahara test. Several other Ghanaians returned to Accra to do educational work there.

It was agreed that the seven who would take part in the second phase should pursue a more aggressive course when they met the French police and gendarmes. They would, for example, make it known to these functionaries that Team members, if not permitted to proceed, would consider themselves under arrest and would hold the police or troops responsible for providing food and water, as if they were in jail. They would insist on using their loudspeaker regularly, and would persistently seek to pass out literature and talk with travelers and people living nearby.

In line with this approach, when the seven, who had left this time from Navrango, were stopped at the first control post, eleven miles inside Upper Volta, they did not park their vehicles off the road as at Bittou, but left them in the middle of the road a few yards from the barrier. Thus "normal passage was not possible," as Radio Ghana reported. All travelers and people living nearby constantly saw the cars challenging the French with their slogan: "Stop the Sahara Tests."

Several times each day the seven walked to the barrier and applied for passage. When refused, they sat down across the road in front of the gate for a considerable time. As they sat, they sang African songs and familiar hymns. At intervals Michael Scott said prayers.

At one point it looked as though the French were about to make a concession. They agreed to transmit a message to the President of the Upper Volta Parliament, although they had said at Bittou that this could not be done. This proved, however, to be a diversion, for in the end the Team were told that a matter of this kind was not for Upper Volta to decide but was in the jurisdiction of Paris. This was another proof that the handling of the Project had been planned and supervised from the start by the highest echelons of the French government. A Ghana official stationed in Washington declared that this exposure by the Team of the illusory character of the "self-government" granted by the French to Africans is one of the most significant achievements of the project.

The Team members were prepared to stick it out indefinitely this time. But in two weeks a Reuters dispatch in *The New York Times* from Ouagadougou, capital of Upper Volta, announced that they had been "arrested by the French authorities and deported to Ghana." From another source it was learned that their loudspeaker had been confiscated, which may be set down as symbolic of the basic fear which animated the French government throughout—the fear that the West African peoples would be reminded of the outrage the French were about to perpetrate on their soil, and might join the protest *en masse*.

Meanwhile, Pierre Martin, leading French pacifist who had been with the Team at Bittou, was carrying out an impressive supporting action. A few days before Christmas, he started a poster walk before the French Embassy in the heart of downtown Accra. On Christmas Eve, he began a week's fast. At the close of his fast, on New Year's Eve, Cabinet Ministers Gbdemah and Welbeck took part in an anti-bomb test protest meeting. Prime Minister Kwame Nkrumah sent Martin a message of congratulation for his courageous action as a French citizen. The message was a big feature of the meeting. Characteristically, *The New York Times* failed to report this at the time but later included an item about the Prime Minister's greeting to Martin in a story from Accra which featured British Prime Minister Macmillan's approval of the French test.

Stories relating to Macmillan's visit to West Africa produced further evidence that the Sahara Project was continuing to bear fruit. The Ghana Council for Nuclear Disarmament issued a statement severely condemning Macmillan's attitude. When, a couple of days later, Macmillan traveled west to Lagos, capital of Nigeria, *The New York Times* reported that thousands of students lined the route of his cavalcade, carrying posters. Some called for independence for Nigeria, which Britain is in the process of granting. The rest bore the slogan: "God forbids the Atom Bomb!" On January 18, *The New York Times* reported that when the French government issued warnings to airlines indicating that the Reggan test might take place soon, "it prompted another upsurge of protests by African states adjoining the region."

This statement is vague and sketchy, as all references by American news agencies to protests against the French policy have been. What is meant by "states adjoining the region"? If this means French West African states near the Sahara, such as Senegal, Sudan and Niger (not to be confused with Nigeria), then this is a development of the utmost importance, and good reporting would give us detailed information. The great political defect in the opposition to the Sahara test has been that, for months, these West African governments which belong to the French Community have not uttered a single protest. They even have permitted De Gaulle's propaganda organs to announce that they "approve" of the French action. This is impossible. No African can at heart "approve" of this violation of African territory by the French, and no African official, except perhaps under the severest pressure, would dare to express public approval of the Sahara test. The resentment against it is visceral in character, so intense that there are informed people who believe that if the bomb is actually exploded at Reggan, Frenchmen will be physically assaulted in many parts of Africa. But all these West African states are involved in complicated negotiations concerning the organization of the French Community. Their economies are dependent on France. They have before their eyes the spectacle of how Guinea was stripped when it voted for independence. So they have kept silence. One of our hopes has been that, at some point, with the Protest Team keeping the issue alive, popular resentment against the test might force the French West African leaders to protest in defiance of De Gaulle.

This brings up one other political factor. It had been assumed that Guinea and its leader, Sekou Touré, would give substantial support to the Sahara Team. Early in December, however, a number of African papers quoted Touré as saying in Morocco that personally he was neither for nor against the test, but that Africa was against it! Touré made no effort to deny this report. In view of the treatment Guinea had received at the hands of France, and earlier indications of Guinean hostility to the Sahara test, it is impossible to avoid speculating as to whether there is a connection between Touré's recent visit to Moscow and his aloofness from the protest movement at a crucial juncture. One inevitably recalls that it is doubtful whether Guinea could have survived, when it boldly voted for independence from France, but for two quick loans, one of ten million dollars from Ghana and another of three times that amount from Moscow.

We had some indications that Communists in Africa had little if any sympathy for the nonviolent action, and it is obvious that Moscow has not made an issue of De Gaulle's nuclear experiment. One may speculate that Khrushchev deems it advantageous that the world should see the failure of the United States and Britain to stop this absurd and dangerous project of its NATO ally. Or one may guess that Khrushchev realizes that the balance of nuclear power is not going to be affected by the explosion of De Gaulle's atomic firecracker in the Sahara, and therefore will permit the latter to pursue his "mirage of nuclear might" in exchange for some assistance to Soviet plans in North Africa, the Middle East, or Eastern Europe.

As these words are written, we may be near the climax of this drama. Indications multiply that the French may explode the bomb any day. The preliminary warnings to airlines, and the appearance of the sinister Jacques Soustelle on the scene in West Africa, seem to show that Paris is getting down to business. Nonetheless, we received a cable some days ago from Michael Randle in Accra saying that, on January 14 or 15, the Team would make a third attempt to penetrate French territory. This time, the Team would travel light and concentrate on means to penetrate much farther in an attempt to arouse the latent hostility of Africans in and around the Sahara to the French plan to make Africa the site of French nuclear missiles as well as to French nuclear politics in Africa and the Middle East.

Saints for This Age

"To all that be in Rome, beloved of God, called to be saints."

Romans 1:7

1962 I spend a good deal of time these days among those who are regarded as unbelievers, and my thoughts constantly shuttle back and forth between the conviction that many of these are the true believers and the wish that I might be able to give them an account of the faith that is in me—and which in some sense they do not have—in language which would be comprehensible to them. For many of us also, religion, or the living of the religious life, is a problem in this age. So, beside those of us who say, "Lord, I believe, help thou mine unbelief," stand those others whose heart's cry, if it could be uttered, might be, "Lord, I do not believe; help me to recognize that nevertheless I do believe."

To put it another way: our age is an age of crisis, and in the final analysis the crisis is religious. It has to do with ultimates, with what it is to be human, with the presuppositions by which men live, with the nature of the resources upon which we draw in extremity, the quality of life men seek, the values which they embrace, the drums to which they march, the commands they dare not disobey. It is essential that we should think about these things.

During the past week, my mind has turned repeatedly to those words of the Apostle Paul, who opened his Letter to the Romans:

"To all that be in Rome, beloved of God, called to be saints." This salutation tells us three things about the people to whom Paul addressed his Epistle. They were in Rome, not in heaven or the desert of the Sahara; they were beloved of God; they were called to be saints. They lived in Rome, a big city, a metropolis, the center of government and in considerable measure of culture. Most early Christians were city-dwellers, as we are. In that Mediterranean world, geographical and cultural boundaries which once had tended to isolate city-states and kingdoms from each other had been wiped out. This was partly because roads had been built, ship routes developed, communication speeded up; partly because the common Hellenistic culture had spread; partly because the Roman Republic, and the Empire which recently had succeeded it, had established its rule and a relative peace throughout that world.

In the old sense, the tribes or families, the city-states or villages constituting close communities in which men were born, lived, and died no longer existed. People were in motion. They were sucked into the cities, especially into great Rome—slaves, merchants, adventurers, sophisticates, evangelists, intellectuals. Concurrently, the tribal and local or regional religions which had related their devotees to a realm beyond the immediately tangible and visible had lost their power and relevance. An assortment of philosophies which intrigued or even fed the mind but did not nourish the heart was offered. Materially, life was easier in that era of an expanding economy. But people were now individuals, on their own, rootless, fragmented. They were individuals, but not persons. The sensitive ones among them who could not live on the surface of life, nor find satisfaction in intellectual cynicism, nor in the moral heroism of the Stoics, experienced spiritual agonies in the search for release from guilt, escape from the bleak prison of the self, release from the terror of death—that is, from the nightmare of the meaninglessness of a life which consisted of the passage of time, of working to keep alive, and of distractions. They suffered agonies in the search for identity and salvation.

It is important to add that the operative religion, to which all were expected to adhere, was the religion of the Emperor, or of the State. It was a prudential, and hence a spurious, religion which was quite content with outward observance, but very suspicious of dissent, intolerant of divided allegiance, even on the part of people who lived the most exemplary and useful and inoffensive lives. Christians and Jews had a God who claimed a higher allegiance than Caesar; they had an experience which they regarded as richer than citizenship in the Empire. Consequently they were regarded as atheists, godless. The State cult had to be enforced and at the same time it had to demand unquestioning obedience, because something had to hold things together in a world where there were individuals but where natural and traditional communities had been dissolved and new ones not yet delivered from the womb of time, not yet revealed by the Creator. Meanwhile the steady tramp of Rome's soldiers was heard on every road of that ancient world.

In addressing the Christians living in that city in those days Paul could use the term "beloved of God" and be sure that they would recognize its applicability to themselves. Let me try to state very briefly and sketchily some things in Christian experience to which that phrase points.

To begin with, these people were not saints first and then and therefore beloved of God. In a way it was just the opposite. It was because they were not saints, because they had looked steadily and deeply enough into themselves to realize that they were not, that there was some subtle corruption within, an ultimate inability to lift oneself by one's own bootstraps, true virtue and pure, understanding love, that in the moment of ultimate despair and self-abasement they found—not the abyss, not eternal darkness, not the Enemy of the Soul—but God, pure grace, possibility. The experience was mediated to them by the figure on the Cross. No doubt, they cried out in much the same language as the medieval hymn writer:

> *O sacred head, now wounded*
> *With thorns thine only crown . . .*
>
> *Mine, mine was the transgression*
> *And Thine the deadly pain.*

I suppose the experience is somewhat analogous to what takes place in psychoanalysis: when the self has been confronted, when the hidden has been brought to the surface, the perhaps paradoxical result is not horror and paralysis—they come when the hidden has not yet been faced—but release and a new birth.

Secondly, there was ecstasy for these uprooted and inwardly torn individuals in the realization that they were "beloved," but it was not the essentially sentimental feeling, that sometimes passes for religious experience, of being a father's favorite child. It was not the feeling, "God loves me, though everybody else hates me" (which really means that I hate everybody else)—individuals were saved but not *as individuals*. They were baptized into the church, that is, they were saved by finding that a true community existed, a community of love, and by finding themselves a part of it. "By this we *know* that we have passed from death into life, because we love the brethren." There is no such thing as being forgiven but unforgiving. On the other hand, people who do not have the experience of being forgiven, that is, who have not been able to accept themselves, cannot be forgiving either, cannot accept others for what they are.

In the third place, then, the crucial development was the emergence of a Christian community, a fellowship, a family which embraced mankind, all men.

The State sensed a threat in this fellowship which meant more to its members than the civic order and their citizenship in that. It sensed a threat in a fellowship which was somehow set apart from "the world," though its members were in their external behavior good citizens, law-abiding. To understand the real situation it is necessary to look at it from the other side, from *within* the church. The fact that, to its members, this "Society of Friends" was profoundly satisfying, real and permanent—"the gates of Hell shall not prevail against it"—meant that "the world" in which they existed was seen by them as deeply lacking, as unreal, impermanent, bound to pass away. Augustine in a later century was to say of the seemingly powerful and indestructible "world," the civic order: "The kingdoms of the world seem able to dominate and destroy everything; but they are themselves dominated and destroyed by their own lust for power." He might have said: by their own will to exist as they are, to arrogate to themselves a substantiality which never belongs to what is, but only to what may be.

The practical result of their feeling of the unreality and inadequacy of "the world" was that the early Christians had broken loose from it, from its allurements; but even more, since it is not too uncommon for men to resist superficial allurements, from its rewards, its threats, its standards, and its version of what constitutes security. They knew in their bones that all this was perishing, "there shall not be left here one stone upon another that shall not be torn down." Consequently, their faces were turned toward the future, a future already present in some profound sense; to the *new* kingdom, of which Christ was king, the *new* society in which all were his brothers and hence each other's. They were not merely, like their uprooted contemporaries, in movement; they were in movement toward a goal.

The concept of history as movement toward a goal is deeply imbedded in the thinking of Western man. Its source is primarily Hebraic. Abraham is not only the progenitor of Israel but "the father of many peoples." He stands at the beginning of both profane and sacred history because in obedience to divine command he left the city of his ancestors. Unquestionably, this represents a great turning point in man's history. It is in one sense the greatest revolution of all, since it is the father of revolutions and of the revolutionary concept of history as the expression of God at work. History and the daily life of man are, therefore, real and not illusory. If God is to be found at all, he must be found here. Men become co-workers, co-creators, and they are in movement toward a goal.

There had, of course, been nomadic wanderings before Abraham. But they were essentially movement of a geographical character. The tribe moved as a tribe and fought as a tribe, for the immediate purpose of obtaining forage for the flocks. When men settled down, cultivated land, and built cities, they conceived of their society as having been founded by the gods of the place or by divine ancestors. The pattern of life was fixed, as if in the nature of things. The individual could hardly conceive of himself or be conceived of by others as having an existence outside this pattern. His destiny and duty were to remain in the city of his birth so that his sons after him could inherit this same fixed and sacred pattern.

But with Abraham the divine command becomes radically different. What makes a man the true servant of the Most High is that he does not remain in the place of his birth. It has its sacredness and importance, but as a point of departure. Through Abraham, man in the Hebraic tradition came to know that his destiny and his God are not ties which bind and confine him. They are ahead of him and are drawing him outward and onward. The crucial thing about men, or societies, is not where they came from but where they are going.

What is of even more significance about Abraham than that he emigrated from Ur of the Chaldees is that there was no city, no society or community for him to move into. Had his journey been simply a geographical one, to another Ur with another name, it would have constituted no part of the source of dynamic Western civilization.

The fact is that Abraham "went out, not knowing whither he went." He was a fool and a gambler. But he was not a little fool; rather he was a big one, whose foolishness consisted in taking on a Herculean task. He gambled for stakes of such a nature that the gambling itself became the pattern of human history. It created Western society and is still its lifeblood and its reason for existence.

Abraham went out looking for a city which existed—and had yet to be brought into existence. It was the perfect and holy city—which had to be built and whose "builder and maker is God." Precisely because it was God who built the city, it could be built only by Abraham's faith and labor.

The creative movement in history is not from any city-which-is to another city-which-is. The reality is not what men tend to call the real. Insofar as it is fixed and has a fixating or binding effect on men or societies, it is already becoming unreal and insubstantial. What matters is the movement from the unreal, because unrealized, city-which-is to the city-which-is-to-be, which is more real because the potentiality of realization and completion remains.

The experience of having broken loose, of being finished with an illusory reality and related instead to the real, was indicated for the first Christians and habitually expressed by them in the concept of the Second Coming of Christ. This is a concept about which there has been enormous controversy. It is certain that the early Christian response to the idea was not that of certain groups who become convinced that Christ is going to return on a certain date and hour, and who leave ordinary work and ties to wait on some hilltop to greet him. Nothing is made clearer, more repeatedly, in the New Testament than that the Second Coming would be a surprise. "Of the day and the hour no man knoweth."

What the concept meant to the early Christians in life, as distinct from dogma or verbal formulation, was that to them Christ whom the world deemed foolish, weak, defeated, dead, was in fact the wisdom of God, the power of God. He was alive, here, and always about to come in power and glory. The divine was always about to break into history.

There was continuity, it is true, but there was also discontinuity. The past did not simply grind out the future through the sieve of the present. The reality was the *new* age, the new fellowship of love. Consequently, change and possibility were the operative concepts with which they worked.

As we look back and reflect on these things, we do so, of course, from our own standing ground in the perspective of the whole history of the Church, of the Western world, the vast stream which issued from those tiny, hidden springs in Rome. The early Christians could not look from this perspective.

We know also that what came about, in many respects, did not resemble their dreams. It never does. Corruption was mingled with the glory. It always it. Nevertheless, there is no doubt that these believers "in Rome, beloved of God," this fellowship, represents a great movement in history, in the dialogue between God and man, in the unfolding of the divine-human society.

The third idea in Paul's salutation—"called to be saints"—did not mean that they were all or always extremely virtuous, ascetic, saintly in the usual sense of the word. Paul, in one of his letters to the Corinthians, suggests that there was quite a variety of saints, not all saintly.

What is clear, for one thing, is that they got a great kick out of being saints, that is, Christians. Joy was an outstanding characteristic of them. On the face of it, you cannot command Christians to be joyous, as if it were a duty. But the Apostle could perpetuate the paradox and shout: "*Rejoice,* and again I say, Rejoice." It was simply inconceivable that the experience of fellowship with one another and with Christ should not produce effervescence. Personally, I always have a certain suspicion of alleged saintliness which lacks this tone of buoyancy and effervescence.

Saintliness expressed itself in *experimentation,* growing out of and demanded by the experience of love and of release, of having cut loose. Experimentation took place in relation to violence: the early Christians did not serve in Caesar's armies—"Our Lord in disarming Peter disarmed every soldier." It took place in economic life, in a religious communism of consumption, though not of production. Such experimentation seemed to follow naturally from their altered view of the nature of history.

Religious people in such a time see apocalyptic visions and embrace an apocalyptic view of history. I surmise that some form of apocalypticism is a conscious or unconscious part of the mentality of those who are drawn into intentional communities, whether they are religious or not. In our own day, many people are attracted to Jehovah's Witnesses and the Seventh Day Adventists. They are growing. I think it must be granted that as dissenters from the prevailing culture they are pretty effective. There is no question that their members find an intense and deeply satisfying fellowship in their movement. It is also that in these denominations there are standards regarding the use of income, and a degree of economic sharing which one does not find in the more respectable churches. But these people do not live in communities of the kind we usually associate with that term. They live much more in the mainstream of urban or rural life, and mingle more constantly with people than communitarians generally do.

The same thing may be said of the early Christians, and it certainly will not be contended that they were not effective or that they did not achieve *koinonia* of a remarkable kind, even though they did not live in some Middle Eastern or Italian Rifton or Primavera settlement, but rather in a second—or third—century equivalent of London, Paris, or New York. "See how these Christians love one another," their neighbors used to remark. In the field of social relationships, perhaps the most amazing thing about these men and women, who also lived in an age of deep cleavages in society, is that they could say, not as a mere form of words, not as an ideal perhaps partially achieved, but as a fact of their life: "In Christ Jesus"—here in this fellowship of love—"there is neither Jew nor Greek, barbarian, Scythian, bondman, free man." It is much as if, in a Baptist Church in the Deep South, whites and Negroes worshipped together—as of course they should—and if attacked for that by the heathen were to shout joyously together: "In Christ Jesus there is neither black nor white, neither North nor South."

Let me now try to relate some of the facts about the condition and the response of the "saints in Rome" to our own condition and response, being mindful of the danger in pressing historical analogies in a mechanical fashion.

It is obvious that there are indeed many resemblances. Even the members of the so-called Historic Peace Churches are today largely city-dwellers. The world is becoming urbanized in the twentieth century.

Old boundaries are being wiped out. The reality at this point is to some extent obscured, for one thing, by the deep East-West cleavage and also by the intense upsurge of nationalism. But the East-West conflict is itself the result of one world coming into being, and evidence that any important development is now a global one. The eruption of nationalism takes place in the larger and dominant context of world-wide communication, industrialization and nuclear technology.

It is a world in which the old faiths are no longer dominant factors. This is true both in the sense that religious institutions are not decisive in fashioning culture or shaping national policy, and in the sense that religious practices do not, for the most part, deeply satisfy church-goers.

Human beings are physically in motion again. Psychologically and spiritually they are rootless. Old traditions and ties have been loosened, new ones not yet formed. It may be said that individuals are emancipated *from* many things, but they are not *persons*, and hence free for living. As the common phrase goes, they are fragmented and alienated. Political discussion and action tends toward taking opinion polls. Life, like much diplomacy, becomes an elaborate minuet performed by puppets.

Another contributing factor is the threat of nuclear annihilation. Those of us who are engaged in "peace work" may feel frustrated because we do not seem to be able to penetrate a thick crust of indifference and to make the mass of citizens aware of the threat. But a closer look makes it clear that this element which shuts out the future, which places the survival of mankind in jeopardy, is having a subtle, corrosive effect in many fields and in the depths of the human spirit.

One more thing has to be noted, namely that in our time, as in Rome of the first Christian centuries, the operative religion, the one in which men actually believe or to which in any case they submit, is that of the State. It is a prudential religion. And as is always the case where there is not a deep inner religion, external enforcement tends to prevail and increase. You have to have the effects of loyalty in human society; if, therefore, human beings are not loyal, you have to force them to be. This phenomenon exists both in the communist and in the non-communist world, though in different forms and perhaps in somewhat different degrees.

After all this, it is no surprise that we can add that the tramp of soldiers is heard on every road of our world as in the ancient Roman one, or, since soldiers tend perhaps to become obsolete, that the missiles and other machines of war multiply, and in this case too, on both sides of the so-called "Iron Curtain." We are indeed in Rome.

In some sense also we know ourselves to be "beloved of God." We belong to the Society of Friends, a community of love, a family of persons. Insofar as we are not just another "denomination," we know also that the salvation of our age is in our keeping; that is, that it lies in the divine-human society which is "rooted and grounded in love." This is the unity which alone can make one world out of "one world," and not one nightmare, one hell, one burned-out cinder.

We know also and in a way we respond to the fact that we have a mission, we are "called to be saints."

Yet we have not, let me put it, experienced Pentecost. The Spirit has not invaded the houses where we meet. We are not on fire. How then wait for the Spirit? How open the door?

First let us recall what we said about the spiritual agony of the early Christians, the confrontation of a person with his own corruption, weakness, aloneness; and the finding of God, love, truth, precisely at that moment of genuine despair. Do we perhaps sometimes tend to obscure this aspect, this spring of religious living by our focusing exclusively on the idea that men are "naturally good," there is "that of God" in every man? I do not mean to deny the truth to which such phrases point, but we always have our "treasure in earthen vessels," do we not? In fixing our eyes on one aspect of truth we inevitably shut out or blur another.

It was surely by the hard road of spiritual agony that men like George Fox and James Naylor arrived at clarity, power and serenity. I am suggesting that we shall achieve confidence and power only in the degree that we do not deceive ourselves about ourselves. This experience of self-examination and repentance is not something which takes place once and for all. It is a state rather than an event.

This is an experience I came to understand when in 1915 as a young pastor I had to face—not academically but existentially—the question of whether I could reconcile what I had been preaching out of the Gospels, and passages like 1 Corinthians 13 from the Epistles, with participation in the war. The problem, as it presented itself to me, was simply one for the Christian conscience. It was a problem which I could not evade because I had been brought up to take religion, specifically the Biblical teaching and Gospel ethic, seriously, and to abhor the sham which enables a person to preach what he does not try desperately to practice. Moreover, my upbringing had given me a definite attitude regarding the struggle which goes on perpetually in the human spirit and in society as to whether the

Gospel demand shall be adjusted to the outward circumstances or the recalcitrant reality shall be made to conform to the high ethical demand. I did not believe that there is a pat rule which one can find in a proof text and apply to a complicated situation, thereby achieving perfection. I had received too solid a dose of Calvinism not to have a strong conviction about human frailty and corruption. It was this that had made me aware, long before Freud was more than a name to me, that when a man is sure that he is honest, he deceives himself; when he imagines himself to be pure, he is impure; and when we bask in the glow of the feeling that we love, the fact is that in subtle ways we hate.

In each psychological "moment" of our lives, in each moment of decision it is necessary for us to know this. It is in the moment when we know how foolish we can be that we begin to be wise. It is when we are aware of our impurity that we are pure. It is when we realize in what subtle ways hate can express itself that we learn to love.

It is salutary, I suggest, that we who are Quakers apply this test to our social activities. We think that in our practice of silence, in avoiding ballots and decision by majority, in depending on "the sense of the meeting," we have a way of overcoming the artificiality, the evasions, the power plays, the rivalries of conventional "political" behavior and struggle. In a measure we do. But it would be fatal to feel complacent and self-satisfied at this point. Evasion, indirection, the play of ambition, the thirst for power, are not absent from our quarterly and yearly meetings, our committee work, the staffs of service committees, and so on. It will help to nourish a religious life in our midst if we think of such insights as are represented in the "sense of the meeting" concept, not as ripened fruit we have produced, but as seed which has been providentially planted within us, which has by no means come to full growth and for which we often furnish dry or even sour soil.

But this does not alter the nature of the demand the Gospel places upon us. The poet who does not agonize in order to translate the vision he sees truly and exactly into his poem is not a poet. The man who does not passionately strive to be honest, pure and loving is not a man. The temptation to pride and self-righteousness is real and pervasive, but the temptation to adapt the Gospel demand to circumstances and to abandon the hard effort to mold one's own life and the world according to that imperious demand is no less subtle and pervasive.

G. K. Chesterton, in a beautiful passage in the volume *Alarms and Discursions*, has stated his version of this law of life:

> Bows are beautiful when they bend only because they try to remain rigid, and sword blades can curl like silver only because they are certain to spring straight again. . . . The foil may curve in the lunge, but there is nothing beautiful about beginning the battle with a crooked foil. So the strict aim, the strong doctrine, may give a little in the actual fight with facts; but that is no reason for beginning with a weak doctrine or a twisted aim . . . Do not try to bend, any more than trees try to bend. Try to grow straight, and life will bend you.

We cannot extricate ourselves from the human condition, which means both that we do not lose the capacity for self-deception and hence the need for self-examination, and that we fail, like the Apostle, to do the good that we would. But we can be safely grateful that it is, nevertheless, the good that we will, and that we, too, can do all things in Christ who strengtheneth us.

In the next place, as a true religious life depends on facing ourselves, probing deeply into ourselves, it also depends upon and is nourished by facing our world, our age. We are called to be saints "in Rome." One thing this implies is that we must face the evil in other men and in the various social patterns which constitute "the world."

Consider Eichmann and his trial in Israel. There are men who perpetrate monstrous evil. There are regimes which permit or even breed monstrous evil. Men habitually deal with such situations as if they themselves were good and therefore entitled to sit in judgment and to cast these criminals into hell or blast these regimes off the face of the earth, and to all such the Gospel says: "Have you seen that monster in yourself?"

But there is also a perverse way of using that admonition into which we sometimes fall. Subconsciously we argue that after all *we* are not so bad, "that bad," and accordingly he is not so bad, this regime is not so bad either. But this really means that we have not yet faced the hater and killer in ourselves. And it will be in the degree that we are sensitive in this area and do not equate love with sentimentality, and child-likeness with childishness, and reconciliation with glossing over and suppressing reality, that our faith in "that of God" in men will be pure and hence efficacious.

The same kind of counsel applies to our dealing with the "realities of power and the power struggle" in the world. Ultimately, as Augustine declared in the passage we have quoted, the power structure is not permanent, not real. It is the house built on sand. Yet in its way the Roman Empire was real enough. So are the United States, the Soviet Union, the H-bomb, the Polaris missile, the arms race. We have to function in relation to such realities and as Martin Buber said in a profound utterance: "It is difficult, terribly difficult, to drive the plowshare of the normative principle into the hard soil of political reality."

We and some of our fellow Christians are continually at cross purposes, it seems to me, because they tend to say: "There is no normative principle, or at any rate it doesn't apply here; the realm of power is autonomous; it develops according to its own laws." We, on the other hand, tend to fall into sentimentalism. We don't realize that the soil *is* hard, that it *is* "terribly difficult" and complicated to make love operative in politics. To a very considerable extent, I surmise the answer to the question whether we can have in our day a Christianity which "speaks to power" authoritatively and yet in love depends on whether we can resist our respective temptations and come together to agonize our way to a common program.

Another thing I have in mind when I refer to realistically facing our world is something quite different, on which I have really no light to throw. Yet it is something we must at least be aware of. I refer to science, both physical and social-psychological, the runaway technology, the "wisdom" of our age. These things represent a great danger—apart from the threat of nuclear annihilation. The inner life of man may be neglected, starved, fragmented, shattered under these pressures. It has even been suggested that man may be threatened with a new Fall, now that he seems to be fathoming the secrets of the universe.

We tend to regard these developments as simply evil or completely mysterious, or to ignore them. But if we do try to evade and escape from the findings and the challenge of the new knowledge, it means that we are afraid, we have not yet experienced the love which casteth out fear. Being afraid and evasive, we shall also be ineffective and futile in trying to bring to the Greeks of our age a wisdom—a "foolishness"—which is indeed wiser than their own.

My last and, I feel, most important observation relates to what I had in mind when I spoke of the early Christians as having "broken loose." They understood that for all its size, seeming stability and power, the "world," the "age," in which they lived was ephemeral, weak, doomed. It was not built on sound foundations. They had, therefore, turned their backs on it in the sense that they were not placing their bets on it, did not give it their ultimate allegiance, were not intimidated by what it could do to them, and did not seek satisfaction and security within its structure, under its standards. They were loose—not tied to "business as usual."

I wrote at the beginning of this essay of my present experience among those who are considered "unbelievers." Some of my fellow Christians are unable to understand why so much of my life has been spent among such persons and groups, and more particularly why, at one period, I counted myself among them. Perhaps it is in this area of "looseness" that one can find the key to this experience . . . it was on the Left—and here the Communists of the period cannot be excluded—that one found people who were truly "religious" in the sense that they were virtually completely committed, they were betting their lives on the cause they embraced. Often they gave up ordinary comforts, security, life itself, with a burning devotion which few Christians display toward the Christ whom they profess as Lord and incarnation of God. Later I was to mourn the wastage of so much youthful devotion, and its corruption among Communists and others, which I had witnessed from the inside. Yet the beauty and attractive power of commitment to that which we profess to believe remains—and it plays a considerable part in the contemporary world struggle.

Besides, the Left had the vision, the dream, of a classless and warless world, as the hackneyed phrase goes. This also was a strong factor in making me feel that here, in a sense, was the true church. Here was the fellowship drawn together and drawn forward by the Judeo-Christian prophetic vision of a "new earth in which righteousness dwelleth." The now generally despised Christian liberals had had this vision. As neo-orthodoxy took over, that vision was scorned as naïve and utopian. The "Kingdom" was something to be realized "beyond history." And again, the Communists are those who are today able to convince vast multitudes that they do cherish the ancient dream of brotherhood realized on earth and have the determination to make it come true. This is a measure of the fall of what is called the Free World. The liberal Christians were never, in my opinion, wrong in cherishing the vision. Their mistake, and in a sense, their crime, was not to see that it was revolutionary in character and demanded revolutionary living and action of those who claimed to be its votaries.

The other aspect of the experience of the early Christians was that they *did* feel the reality, the authority, of the fellowship which they had found. It had the keys to the future. They lived in *this* world and by its power. Perforce, therefore, they were *experimentalists*, seeking to live out the implications of the love they had experienced, of that "love of God and not of self" to which they were joyously committed.

This quality of looseness from the world-that-is, of experimentation, creativeness, characterizes all the great periods of religious history. This is certainly true of Early Quakerism. It is from this same spring that our religious life will have to be nourished.

There is no doubt that our world is doomed. I do not mean by this that I think nuclear war and resultant nuclear annihilation are inevitable. It would be even more risky, I think, to assert that they will not happen. But I am not here making a political judgment or calculation. In a much profounder sense, the world we have known is passing. The uncovering of nuclear secrets, other developments we might mention, make this certain. Mankind *has* to find the way into a radically new world. Mankind has to become a "new humanity" or perish.

If we are true at such a juncture to the seed of love which is in us, that light of faith which neither inner nor outer storms have put out, then we shall be loose and experimental. We shall set less and less store by the world's gifts of money, success, respectability, comfort. Most of all, we shall then truly live *in* the Society of Friends, the fellowship of love, shall truly believe that the divine-human society is real, is the future. We shall be aware that we stand at the end of an era, but much more basically that we stand before a new beginning.

It is surely in this context very significant how many Friends experienced a refreshment, a nourishing of the inner life of the Spirit, when recently a thousand of them "cut loose" and "experimented," standing in silent vigil around the Pentagon.

By grace, if we continue in this way we shall daily love more deeply. Daily, in the freedom of the Spirit, we shall build in our homes, neighborhoods, cities, the city that is to be, whose builder and maker is God.

We shall do it not because we are wise, strong, politically astute, but because the Spirit dwells in our hearts and the Lord is coming, will reveal himself. His kingdom is *ever* at hand.

For us all it is as yet unbegun; but where the Spirit of the Lord is, there is liberty and possibility.

All this was movingly stated some ten years ago by an American poet, Muriel Rukeyser, who did not come at the matter primarily from a Christian approach. In a volume entitled *The Life of Poetry* she said: "Now again we see that all is unbegun. The only danger is in not going far enough. If we go deep enough, we reach the common life, the shared experience of man, the world of possibility. If we do not go deep enough, if we live and write half-way, there are obscurity, vulgarity, the slang of fashion, and several kinds of death." Let us mark the dangers if we do not go far enough: "obscurity," confusion as to our goals; "vulgarity," the resort to clever and evil means to achieve our ends; "the slang of fashion," such as succumbing to the ways of "Madison Avenue." For us, too, no doubt "several kinds of death" will be available if we do not realize how clean the break must be, how loose of the "world" we must be, how thoroughly experimental, how profoundly convinced of possibility—if, that is to say, we do not go far enough.

Rifle Squads
or the
Beloved Community

1964 Everyone who is at all informed about the civil rights struggle seems agreed that the summer of 1964 will be critical and quite possibly tragic. The present situation is a product of forces which have been piling up for years and even centuries. The changes that will come about in all spheres of American life if integration is achieved will be profound. The political patterns, the economy, the culture, the ethos will be affected. The issues facing individuals and organizations are highly complicated and emotion-laden. Yet all sorts of individuals and groups (including advocates and practitioners of "nonviolence") have to act—do act and make decisions —without adequate information to guide them, and for the most part are able to calculate the consequences only tentatively and partially. It is clearly important that we try to discern such guidelines to action as may be available.

The Georgia Council on Human Relations, with headquarters in Atlanta, has just issued a pamphlet entitled "Albany, Georgia— Police State." Readers may recall that this city was the scene of bitter episodes in the civil rights struggle in 1961 and 1962 and of an encounter between the Albany authorities and townspeople, on the one hand, and the Quebec-Washington-Guantánamo Peace Walk, on the other, early in 1964. The pamphlet begins as follows:

The white majority in Albany is living in a dream—a one hundred year old, segregated dream. In the dream, everybody dwells contentedly. Negroes are happy in their child-like singing and dancing. Whites are loving, understanding and paternal. Listen to some white people in Albany talk:

"We love our Nigras and they love us."

"We're making a lot of progress here. I can't tell you how much we've done for our colored folks."

"Many's the Monday morning I've gone downtown to get our yard-man, Joe, out of jail. I take care of my own."

"My maid told me herself: 'Oh, no ma'am, I don't want to be integrated. I wouldn't be happy in with all the white folks.' "

I can testify on the basis of my own recent visits to Albany and other Southern cities that attitudes and statements such as those are to be found even among religious and other leaders. Moreover, the parochialism which sees the situation essentially in terms of annoyance with Negroes who suddenly don't "keep their place" and become "aggressive," and with liberal dreamers or radical and "Communist" subverters who mislead Negroes, is not confined to the South. Many people have no realization that we live in a world upheaval which is "happening" to all of us, white and Negro alike, much as a natural phenomenon like a hurricane or tidal wave asks no by-your-leave and makes no distinctions based on character, color or anything else. To change the metaphor, there is no awareness that, on an important level, various people and groups are playing parts which they did not freely choose in a drama which they did not write and are not directing. One thing we are powerless to do about it is to wish away the problem. Change and disturbance are as certain as "death and taxes."

In this context it is pertinent to point out that insofar as one can speak of "responsibility" in such historic developments, the white peoples of West Europe and North America have brought the present situation upon themselves and the rest of mankind. These people developed the technology which made large-scale industry possible and revolutionized agriculture. For several centuries, they spread their rule over the world, by direct or indirect conquest, while preaching doctrines of freedom, equality and even love. They are now developing automation. The white nations are still militarily dominant and remain the nuclear powers. They made the mistake of engaging, mostly among themselves, in two colossal World Wars during the present century, as a result of which their hold over colonial peoples was broken.

The psychological aspect of white conquest should constantly be kept in mind these days. One of the great chasms in the world is that between the peoples who have known humiliation as peoples and those who instead have humiliated others. The white peoples are the ones who shoved other peoples, especially the colored, off the sidewalk in Western and in Asian and African countries alike; but no one could push the white master off the sidewalk anywhere.

The tide began to turn some time ago and is now flowing strongly in the other direction. The colored peoples are asserting themselves; the white people are having to make room and to abandon theories and practices of superiority. This is never easy and seldom, if ever, has backing down from a position of superiority and domination to one of something near equality been done gracefully. But there come times when it has to be done.

We may here remind ourselves that it is a part of American tradition to hold that freedom cannot be handed to people on a silver platter, that real men and women stand up for their rights. "Don't tread on me!" is thought of as a typical American slogan. To be ready to defend your own house and shoot the man who invades it, and would perhaps insult or attack your womenfolk, is commonly considered a laudable attitude, especially in the South. Are not Negroes following in this American tradition when they resent being patronized, when they do not have the "feel" of being free until they have taken hold of freedom? One often hears men of standing say that it would be different if Negroes asked (begged?) for their rights, but that "we're not going to be bullied into granting them—don't push us." In much the same way, many Englishmen, in the time of George III, thought of the colonials as upstarts and insolent boors for "demanding" rights and independence. There are many generations of humiliation and oppression behind the upsurge among Negroes and the belligerence now asserting itself. The results are not invariably pleasant. They are often bizarre, and in some cases horrible, as revolutions always are. Perhaps at least we might not be so surprised that the usual accompaniments of mass change are manifesting themselves in the United States today. We might even take some satisfaction in the realization that once more people are "demanding" that beautiful thing, freedom, and that their leaders are saying: "Let my people go." Perhaps whites could derive a measure of intellectual objectivity and reduce the intensity of their anger by realizing that these things are "happening" to us (as similar surprises, mysteries and disturbances have happened to others in revolutionary periods) rather than being "inflicted" on us by some mad or evil persons who live in the Negro sections or flood out of New York's Harlem, for instance, to tie up highways leading to the New York World's Fair.

Other cases might be mentioned that show a tendency on the part of whites to apply a double standard and to find reprehensible among Negroes what they condone or even practice themselves. Take the resentment of Southern senators, as well as a good many ordinary citizens in all sections of the country, against what are stigmatized as illegal, undemocratic and obstructionist tactics on the part of Negroes and their allies in the civil rights struggle. The senators are presently engaged in the obstructionist tactic of a filibuster. It is usually possible for men in positions of power with the machinery of government in their hands, working to maintain the *status quo*, to obstruct measures they oppose in a respectable and outwardly legal fashion. Southern senators do not have to display themselves on streets in Washington or in the states where their civil rights senatorial colleagues live. They do not have to commit "trespass" or distribute leaflets on the streets, or "disobey an officer's command." But the results seen in the Senate today, and the shocking business of these Southern senators being elected to power by a small minority of voters, in direct violation of the Constitution, are no less obstructionist and undemocratic, and even more effective. People who have not realized this, or worked to change it, are not in a position to press the issue of obstructionism against the civil rights movement.

Another case in point is that of ordinances in Southern cities and towns which limit civil liberties and are patently contrary to decisions laid down by the Supreme Court. The only recourse for citizens (of whatever color) who want to exercise their democratic rights is to take each unconstitutional ordinance all the way to the Supreme Court, only—in many instances—to see a slightly altered but no less repressive ordinance adopted in its place. In Mississippi a whole series of measures has been enacted for the avowed purpose of preventing or indefinitely delaying change in the racial pattern. Yet a good many people—and not all by any means poorly educated or simple-minded—have a more negative and intense reaction toward the proposed "stall-in" at the World's Fair (which I am not endorsing at this point) than to the colossal and enduring "stall-in" which is being staged in Mississippi.

A word needs to be said about the attitudes people take toward violence and nonviolence. Many act as if they thought Negroes had a peculiar obligation to be nonviolent, and especially in the civil rights struggle, the struggle for emancipation, for Freedom Now. Yet in the very sections of Georgia and other states where any but the most pacifist, not to say submissive, conduct on the part of Negroes is regarded shocking and where one frequently hears discourses on how readily Negroes resort to violence in their day-to-day life, one finds little espousal of pacifism or nonviolence. There is less concern there than in some other sections of the country about the nuclear arms race and the danger of nuclear war. There is only the most embryonic peace movement. The Peace Churches are almost non-existent. The military virtues are extolled. And, of course, one encounters practically no opposition to the location of missile bases and various other military installations in this region.

Until one has faced these facts, one is in no position, either politically or morally, to speak to the Negro community or the civil rights movement. This is pre-eminently true of those of us who advocate nonviolence.

Turning now to the relevance of nonviolence, in face of an undoubtedly growing tendency among Negroes to be suspicious of it and to feel that the movement has to become more militant and resort to more "realistic" tactics, it seems to me at the outset that there is confusion about the use of the so-called "right to self-defense" and the call to exercise it which needs to be cleared up. If one is talking in terms of legality and prevailing *mores*, then the right of an individual to defend himself, his home, his family— even to shoot a man who threatens to shoot or otherwise injure him and his family—undoubtedly exists in American and Western society. So long as that is the case, the Negro should have the right to self-defense as well as the white man. The pamphlet issued by the Georgia Council on Human Relations states: "Everywhere in the streets of Albany you see white men carrying firearms. 'If you are white and can see to sign your name to the application, you are given a permit, no questions asked,' a white businessman observed. Of course, no Negroes need apply."

But the problem now before American society and in particular before Negroes is not so simply or automatically disposed of. For one thing, it is not generally assumed that a good community, one where people can live peacefully, is one where all or even many citizens go about with guns in their belts, or keep guns in their homes. Quite the contrary. As a matter of fact, Malcolm X and other "leaders" who call on Negroes to exercise the right of "self-defense" are not talking about that "right" as commonly understood. I suspect that some of them at least are aware of this and use the term as a demagogic and manipulative device. If they are not aware that this is the case, then they are not qualified to be leaders. People who do not know what an explosive or a poison is should not handle explosives or poisons.

What is meant by certain leaders in the present context is, only to a small degree, that an individual Negro might have a gun and, under circumstances of great danger, use it against another individual, white or Negro, who attacks him or his family. What is meant is that Negroes generally around the country should provide themselves with firearms and organize rifle clubs wherever there are conflict situations, and where the agencies which are supposed to provide safety for citizens and enable them to exercise elementary rights fail to do so for Negroes. This tactic is thought to hold good more particularly in sections where whites are armed, and where they have bullied and, very likely, actually injured or killed Negroes. It is this reasoning which has to be evaluated, not a simple case of "self-defense" or a spontaneous action of one individual toward another in a tense moment.

I have heard it said more than once by Negroes who are reluctantly turning to the idea that "nonviolence" may not be enough that if in a few cases Negroes were to use force, or even threaten it seriously, this would cool down the Citizens Council people and the white hoodlums. It is suggested that this also would convince the wielders of power in the South that it is no longer possible to keep Negroes down or to delay integration.

It seems to me conceivable that in some local situation a shooting might have what could be called a questioning or catalytic effect in that isolated local instance. But, putting pacifist considerations aside for a moment, one cannot think realistically of the problems raised by the tendency to become belligerent and violent in isolated local terms. What is very likely to happen (and indeed is expected by people like Malcolm X and those who go along with him to greater or less degree) is a summer series of mass demonstrations and rioting in which Negroes will "fight back." Whitney Young, junior, executive director of the National Urban League, commented on the restraint exercised up to now by Negroes in recent testimony before a Congressional Committee as follows:

I think Negro citizens in the face of the years of provocation, in the face of the historic abuse, have shown an amazing restraint and an amazing loyalty. This from a people who have so little reason to have this kind of faith, who have all the provocation, the abuse, the murders, the years of want, of poor housing, of rats biting their children.

I trust I have made it abundantly clear that in a sense things "happen" to people, even the things they themselves do in situations of social turmoil, and that it is absurd to expect that Negroes will be exceptions. But this does not absolve individuals and especially leaders from the necessity of making choices as to tactics and not allowing themselves to be the pawns of historic forces or of social hysteria. On this level and in this context the current trend away from nonviolence is certainly subject to suspicion and criticism.

One basic question that exponents of this trend have not considered seriously, in my opinion, is whether Negroes plan to become, eventually, an equal part of American society. While I do not necessarily mean society as now constituted and organized, truth compels us to observe that this is probably just what large numbers of Negroes want. However, as I see it, a desegregrated American society would be quite radically different from the one we now have. I believe that, whether America is radically transformed or not, Negroes as a people want to live in the United States; they don't want to migrate and they don't seriously want to live in a Negro nation-state in some corner of American soil. Parenthetically, the desire of Negroes to control their own civil rights movement and not to have it run by whites is legitimate. But in this, as in other movements, demagogues use nationalist appeals, or proclamations of Negro racial superiority, to overcome social inertia and evoke a response from those who rightly want to be free from various forms of white domination or condescension. At the same time, the demagogues run the risk of helping to precipitate tragedy.

If Negroes do plan to become a genuine part of the American community then they will have to live in a community to which whites also belong. To think lightly of deepening the rifts between the races; to create new psychological wounds, which may take long to heal, in numerous cities and towns; to polarize existing enmities seems clearly dangerous and might be laying the groundwork for eventual elimination of that multi-racial or *truly* integrated society which is the object of the civil rights movement and the goal of the Negro community. The race problem is psychological and social, not merely one of economic or political structure. It is necessary that the reality and the shame, the deep causes, of the present rift be exposed and not slurred over. But this must be only for the purpose of obliterating the rift, not for deepening it or making it permanent and unalterable.

In an even more narrowly political sense there is a problem here which has received too little attention. Important sections of the Negro movement look to Federal action, specifically to the intervention of Federal troops at critical moments, to contribute to the advance of integration. Many seem to have espoused a strategy which could lead to the intervention of Federal troops on a mass scale in Mississippi this summer. The wisdom of this dependence on Federal agencies and especially on Federal armed force can be questioned on various grounds. But in the present context it seems clear that the civil rights movement cannot expect the support of Federal agencies that are supposed to hold society together, whose duty is to keep the situation from getting utterly out of hand—and this is precisely what can happen in a desperate situation like Mississippi—if at the same time the movement were to work for the (temporary?) breakdown of that society or, more accurately, accept such collapse as inevitable.

To put it in another way, it is one thing for Federal troops to intervene at some point in order to protect Negroes from police brutality or vigilante violence. A quite different situation would exist if it even appeared that whites should have to be protected from Negro violence, even when born of frustration and intolerable emotional pressures.

The Johnson administration certainly is going to try to have a civil rights bill adopted and then will try to avoid creating a bad image of the United States in the minds of other nations and of colored peoples throughout the world. But I do not see how anyone for a moment could entertain the thought that the Administration would welcome a call to send Federal troops to Mississippi or anywhere else during an election campaign; or that one could assume confidently that it would decide to do so at all.

There is another aspect of strategy to which very little serious consideration has been given as yet. There is no doubt that those who have been denied freedom and equality have to struggle for them in a way that will "disturb" society, or else things will remain as they are, or get worse. This involves "social dislocation." But when tactics are devised—and the proposed stall-in in connection with the opening of the World's Fair seems to me probably to fall in this category—with a view to creating inconvenience and disturbance in general, merely as an outlet for pent-up emotion, then a vast problem area is opened up. The same problem is raised when people like Malcolm X ridicule "nonviolent revolution" as spurious and contend that in a real revolution blood has to flow.

A phase of traditional revolutions has been disintegration of the old order in various ways and through various means. One of the most important factors in the disintegration of Czarist society in 1917 was Lenin's counsel to the Russian soldiers to "vote with your feet" and go home. He told them that the defeat of "their own nation" in war was a lesser evil. Now, in such a situation, there is a certain practicality in general dislocation *provided* that there is a group that wants to take power, and may perhaps be able to, and is ready to undertake building a new society and a new center of power. The Bolsheviks were in such a position in 1917.

Assuming for the sake of argument that such an overturn were desirable, who are the elements that are to accomplish this in the United States today? Malcolm X and his followers? Even moderately well informed people know that the civil rights issue, the economic or job issue and the Cold War issue are linked together. They know that without labor and other elements joining in the struggle even integration as such cannot be achieved. But any such cooperation of these various elements exists today only in the most embryonic sense. To base the tactics of the civil rights movement on the assumption that a traditional revolution is imminent in the United States is either mad or criminal. In the present state of things there has to be some fairly obvious connection between a demonstration and a specific not an infinitely remote goal.

In general, there is no coherent or generally recognized theory as to how or whether a revolution like the historic ones can take place in a country like the United States in the nuclear age. For all thoughtful people, and certainly for those who espouse nonviolence, or at least conceive of its possible relevance, the question of what "revolution" means in our time is posed.

The traditional revolution centers around the transfer of power from one class or social element to another, and results in the setting up of a new power structure. It is well to remind ourselves at this moment, when a good many seem to think that nothing "real" is taking place except where there is shooting, that in their early stages traditional revolutions were often remarkably free from violence. Essentially, the old order collapsed and the new element moved in to fill a vacuum. The large-scale violence was likely to occur when counter-revolutionary efforts were being staged.

It is also the case that revolutions were in their beginnings idealistic. They were to bring in a new order of "liberty, fraternity, equality" or "a classless and warless world." In no sense did the masses realize in the early stages that a new power structure was going to be set up to dominate society. There would not have been sufficient emotional motivation for the great venture and arduous labors of revolution if people had not believed that liberation was in sight and not just another variety of bondage.

The believers in nonviolence (and at least some who do not think of themselves in those terms) do not see the task of our age as that of seizure of power by a new social element and the setting up of a new power structure. They see the task of our age as that of building the beloved community. No one can have a fairly close contact with the civil rights movement and the people in it, including the young people, without feeling that, in spite of all contrary appearances and even realities in the movement, deep near its center is this aspiration for a beloved community and the faith that this is what they are working for and already in a sense realizing now. "O Freedom, Freedom over me. . . ." "Deep in my heart, I do believe that we shall overcome some day. . . ."—Overcome not the white man, but overcome all that stands in the way of man, each man.

In the meantime, regardless of whether or not one embraces nonviolence, either as revolutionary strategy or as a way of life, all available evidence points to the conclusion that nonviolence as basic strategy should not be abandoned by the civil rights movement. Rather, mistakes should be corrected and new possibilities of developing nonviolent action should be diligently explored and experimented with. It seems essential that the decision to adhere to nonviolence be a firm one and that it be clearly and openly proclaimed. The present situation, where there is considerable difference of opinion in various sections of the movement and a tendency for many of the adherents of nonviolence to weaken in their stand, while the advocates of "self-defense" and "true revolution" are (or seem to be) certain of their stand and aggressive in their attitude, is the worst possible. If the latter are right, their strategy should be generally accepted. Some of them might be shocked if it were accepted. If their policy is not adopted, those who reject it should not be intimidated by its advocates.

It is not my intention here to make detailed suggestions as to tactics. Moreover, the civil rights movement has, in the leaders of the Student Nonviolent Coordinating Committee, CORE, and in Bayard Rustin, persons who are brilliant and masterful in this field. Three general suggestions do seem to me worth noting.

The opponents of nonviolence tend to gain a following among the more depressed and poverty-stricken elements in the Negro ghettos. There are a number of reasons for this, but a principal one is that the "nationalists," and others, pay attention to these people and at least appear to offer programs they hope could improve their condition. I think more attention to these people, as against what might be called Negro white-collar elements, might produce important results. Rent strikes and unemployed actions presumably would appeal to them more than actions related to education or electing Negroes to Congress or even voter registration.

Secondly, there are indications that training for nonviolent action is being taken more seriously than it has been, but much more needs to be done immediately in this field.

Thirdly, while there is a tendency among sections of the white community to become polarized into a hostile or disillusioned position because of alleged "extremist" action by Negroes, there are also many whites who have become increasingly troubled and are eager to help. Very large sections of the nation are capable of experiencing deep moral revulsion against racism and segregation, especially when Negro nonviolent demonstrators are brutally treated, as was shown, e.g., in relation to the Birmingham struggle. In my view, that moral revulsion may have been the main factor in impelling Kennedy at last to submit a civil rights bill and the House finally to adopt a stronger one than Kennedy's. It is my impression that the nonviolent movement may have been distracted from paying sufficient attention to the involvement of whites on this moral ground.

In closing as in beginning an analysis of this kind, attention must be focused on the white community. I referred earlier to the chasm between the peoples who have known humiliation as peoples and those who have not, but have humiliated others. The latter are the West Europeans and the Americans. The chasm has for the most part kept the peoples, colored and white, separated from each other. It is so no longer. The chasm is going to be bridged somehow. From the side of white men a bridge of understanding, repentance, reconciliation and love might be thrown across the chasm. If this is not done, a bridge of pent-up frustration, vengeance and hate may be thrown across it by the majority of the human race. Those who over centuries dug the chasm would hardly be in a position to quarrel with the effect. But this would not be building the beloved community either. It would be opening another familiar cycle of domination and eventual corruption. This might prove suicidal for all in the nuclear age.

Therefore, Negroes of whom love cannot be "demanded" by whites—love is in any case not subject to demand—may nevertheless give it. Those who have so long known what it is to be shoved off the sidewalk by whites may possibly understand what it means to the latter to be shoved into the street. If, by discrimination and hate, Negroes are driven to discrimination and hate, what, after all, have they done to themselves? There is no virtue or healing in following a bad example. There are Negroes who know this; whites are not needed to teach it to them. It was in Jackson, Mississippi, last year, that the widow of Medgar W. Evers said to her fellow Negroes at a Memorial service for her slain husband: "You mustn't hate; you must love."

The poet Mark Van Doren was asked recently to read his poem entitled "Born Brother?" to a gathering of writers. He first exclaimed: "Ah, yes. Equality—the greatest of all doctrines and the hardest to understand." Then he read:

> *"Equality is absolutely or no.*
> *Nothing between us can stand.*
> > *We are the sons*
> *Of the same sire, or madness*
> > *breaks and runs*
> *Through the rude world."*

The venerable Jewish philosopher Martin Buber, referring mainly to relations between nations, uttered an appeal some years ago which is applicable in a peculiarly poignant way to the race situation. He spoke of those in whatever camp who "carry on the battle again the anti-human," and said: "Those who build the great unknown front shall make it known by speaking unreservedly with one another, not overlooking what divides them but determined to bear this division in common."

The Fall of Man

1964 The peace movement is in a period of transition, a period of groping for a valid analysis of the conditions under which we live and for a program based on such an analysis. This is true for all sections of the movement in all countries, East, West or essentially unaligned.

In seeking some clarification of our problem today, I want to go back to a crisis which occurred exactly fifty years ago, with the outbreak of World War I in 1914. Europe, which at the time contained all the major powers of the world—the United States joined the ranks during that war—had witnessed the rise of a powerful labor and socialist movement during the late nineteenth and early twentieth centuries. This movement had its left, right and center, and controversies were often intense. It had important trade union, political, cooperative and cultural institutions. Individuals might devote themselves to one or another activity but the movement constituted a working whole such as we have not experienced since 1914.

I think it is accurate to say that there were two dominant elements in the thinking, or ideology, of the movement. One was Marxism; the other was the prophetic idealism of the Judeo-Christian tradition. Marxism of course contributed the materialistic interpretation of history according to which religion was "the opiate of the people," and other such concepts. But, in spite of possible appearances to the contrary, Marxism was essentially humanistic.

In liberating itself, the working class was to liberate mankind. The goal to which history moved and to the achievement of which the workers and all honest men were summoned to commit themselves was "the classless and warless world," which was also the goal of Judeo-Christian prophecy. Large numbers of the adherents of the social application of Jewish and Christian ethics and faith were drawn to the socialist and labor movement.

For our present purpose it is important to underscore that this movement intended not only to bring in a "classless" world, i.e., one free from exploitation, discrimination and injustice, but also a "warless" one, i.e., one free from organized violence and cruelty. The two were as closely tied together in the thinking and the emotions of their adherents as the command to love God and to love your neighbor are tied together in the Christian ethic.

It can be argued plausibly that the abolition of war as a major factor in historic development was a possibility in 1914. In spite of the arms race under way at the time and minor wars in the Balkans and elsewhere, which indeed proved to be the prelude to World War I, sentiment was fairly widespread that a major war was inconceivable. Many held that civilized people would not resort to mass slaughter. Men like Norman Angell wrote books "proving" that no economic objective could be achieved by war among major nations and since this was now self-evident, massive war really could not occur. But of greater practical importance was the fact that the idealism and humanitarianism which forbade war on moral or spiritual grounds was backed by a powerful labor and socialist movement which commanded mass support and was capable of wielding serious and quite possibly decisive influence on the course of nations.

This movement was profoundly anti-militarist and anti-war. It proclaimed that the first allegiance of workers everywhere was not to their respective states but to their fellow workers in other states. In the English labor movement and to some extent on the continent of Europe, many rank and file members and leaders were out-and-out pacifists. Should war be decided upon, the workers and their allies in each country would strike and make it impossible for the armies to move.

War did break out in August, 1914. It precipitated an agonizing crisis in the labor and socialist movement. The outcome of the struggle split the movement apart. In every Western European country, though not in the United States where the Socialist Party was relatively insignificant, the majority in the political parties went along with the national policy and supported the war. So far as the labor unions were concerned, not even the United States furnished an exception. The national tie proved stronger and more deeply imbedded than those which bound workers, idealists, humanitarians, and Christians together across national boundaries. Christian apologists furnished rationalization for support of wars fought under the Kaiser, the Russian and Austrian Czars, Clemenceau, Lloyd George and so on.

Ever since then, the labor and social democratic parties and the trade unions have been identified primarily with their respective national establishments, and have taken part generally in the military build-up in various countries, with rearmament after defeat in war, etc., though at times exercising a moderating influence.

There were minority Socialist parties which opposed the war. Lenin emerged as the principal leader of these minorities. To them, support of the war was a base betrayal of the working class and of humanity as a whole. With few exceptions, the leaders of the minorities were not pacifists, Lenin certainly not. However, one of the ways in which Lenin and his Bolshevik party undermined Czarism and the old order generally in Russia was to urge Russian soldiers to desert, and go home to their farms and cities. Lenin advocated a doctrine of the "lesser evil" exactly opposite to that commonly held by Christian theologians. "Defeat of your own country in time of war" is the lesser evil, he proclaimed. If workers in various nations were to support their respective nations in war, the power relationships among the nations might shift as one country won and another was defeated. But the basic pattern leading repeatedly to war would continue; whereas, if workers in one country refused to fight, this would introduce a revolutionary element into the situation. Other workers might follow the example and so a new pattern of political and social relationships, as well as a new economic order, would become possible.

Under pressure of Allied intervention from without and violent attempts to scuttle it from within, the Bolshevik regime turned to military action. A powerful Red Army was organized. Under Stalin, a vast state machinery was built up and effort was concentrated on developing a modern military establishment. All this took place under the familiar generalizations: they had "no choice"; what was vile when used to defend "Christian civilization" or "imperialism" was noble and heroic when used to defend "The Revolution," and so on. It is one of the ironies of the contemporary world that the two nuclear super-powers, each equipped to exterminate the human race several times over, should be anti-Communist and "Christian" United States on the one hand, and Communist Russia on the other.

It seems to me impossible to reflect seriously on the developments which followed or, to put it the other way round, to contemplate what the world might have been like if the labor and socialist movement had met the 1914 crisis differently, without concluding that what actually did take place was the major catastrophe of modern times—perhaps of all history. This was, in a real sense, "the fall of man."

It may be difficult to imagine just what the world would have been like if the dereliction had not occurred. Consider that modern science had attained a development which opened the way for all that has taken place subsequently in that domain. Technology and economic organization were making the abolition of poverty a realizable and not too distant goal. Man's knowledge of himself and of his history on earth had likewise developed to a point where men were able to a considerable degree to shape their own future. There were social elements, such as the modern working class and many intellectuals whose immediate needs tied them to a movement with revolutionary aims and possibilities. There was a long, deeply ingrained prophetic tradition. There was a belief that men could decisively influence their destinies and there was hope in contrast to the present day apathy and the feeling that all problems are so complicated that they have to be left to the "authorities" and "establishments" to decide. Western men had not experienced the orgies of hate and slaughter which marked subsequent decades.

This leads us directly to the first horrendous result of the 1914 collapse of the great anti-war and anti-militarist movement—namely, the emergence of the Fascist and Nazi movements. Both were expressions of resurgent nationalism which regarded the labor and socialist movement (together with the Bolsheviks) as responsible for national humiliation and their members as traitors. Both sought national revenge and consequently had to cultivate hate. Both repudiated the humanitarianism of the past, whether Judeo-Christian or secular, and consequently undertook deliberately to cultivate the anti-human and to release the sadistic urges in men. It is unthinkable that such developments could have taken place if resort to war had been repudiated.

Communism, at any rate in its Stalinist form, would not have developed.

If democratic and humanitarian socialist regimes with an internationalist orientation had been established in Europe, Western imperialism and colonialism would have been abandoned in principle and to a substantial extent in practice. The education and enlistment of native leaders to take over control of economic and political organization in the colonies would have been put into effect. "Revolution" in these cases could have been basically nonviolent and more profound than when one power structure (foreign) is simply replaced by another (native). Such abominations as the long support of the Chiang Kai-shek regime in China and Taiwan or the French colonial wars in Indo-China and Algeria could not have taken place. It seems self-evident that relations between the colored and the white races generally would be vastly different from what they are now, and less likely to lead to further catastrophes.

It will be recalled that it took a long time for the United States to become involved in World War I. The nation was pacific in its mood, certainly in the sense of wanting to keep aloof from the wars of Europe. As late as November, 1916, Woodrow Wilson was elected President on the slogan, "He kept us out of war." Being dragged or slipping into the war opened the way for United States expansionism and "neo-imperialism," to involvement in World War II and to the atomic bombing of Hiroshima and Nagasaki. How different life in America might be now if these had not taken place.

But for the dereliction of 1914 there would have been no World War II. This is not necessarily to say that no wars would have occurred but, because of technological and other factors, a war like World War II could not have occurred had the European nations been joined in a labor and socialist federation with a universal rather than a nationalist and power-oriented basis.

It is virtually certain that the course of science and scientists would have been radically different if the crisis of 1914 had been met differently. Science in the pre-World War I world was still universal in its outlook rather than nationalist. Scientific research was primarily oriented toward peace rather than war. At any rate, scientists thought of themselves as engaged in a common pursuit of truth to be shared across national and other boundaries by all members of the fraternity, not in the pursuit of military secrets. Consider all the ramifications of this development, not excluding the risk of annihilation to which the race is now subjected, and again we are impressed by the tragedy of the turn Western and so-called Christian nations took in 1914. Again we are forced to ask ourselves what the world might now be like if another road had been chosen; and even more, how may we now meet our own crisis in a more creative way.

Turning then to the problem of war in our own time there are a number of considerations which make the abolition of war, especially wars of mass destruction, more necessary and in a sense more feasible than fifty years ago. The argument that was made then by Norman Angell seems feeble indeed beside the argument that can be made in the age of atomic weapons in support of the same contention—that war can no longer achieve rational economic and political objectives. To some extent even military men, on both sides of the Iron Curtain, reckon with the factor of unsupportable and inadmissible losses that would be sustained in any major war. Furthermore, in repeated instances, such as in Korea, Cuba, Vietnam, United States policy makers are confronted with the fact that nuclear weapons, which supposedly are the embodiment of superior power, cannot be used in combat. (Some use is made of them in the game of "brinkmanship," but even this resort may prove ineffectual if it becomes generally recognized that it is not intended for the weapons actually to be used.)

Secondly, modern technology has placed the abolition of poverty and the general elevation of living standards within reach of mankind and thus removed one of the major reasons for war. This could be more or less clearly discerned in 1914. It is self-evident now.

Thirdly, man's knowledge of history, of his evolution, of himself, has greatly increased. The means of communication are vastly improved. Were these factors devoted to solving man's problems, they would provide our generation with an enormous advantage over that of our grandparents.

We have not, however, abolished war and it is far from clear that we are on the way to doing so. There are certain respects in which it appears that men have deteriorated since the outbreak of World War I. For one thing, a growing revulsion against cruelty and violence was certainly a characteristic of Western society after the Enlightenment. It found expression in education, in the treatment of the mentally ill and of law violators, as well as in a revulsion against the mass slaughter of war. After the Nazi nightmare, two World Wars, the dropping of atomic bombs on defenseless cities by a supposedly highly civilized nation, we are, alas, more accustomed and so less sensitive to brutality, cruelty and mass slaughter than was an earlier generation. Horrors that would have raised a popular outcry a decade or a few decades ago pass well-nigh unnoticed. "Better dead than Red," "Better no world than a Communist world," are typical of the thinking of many today. What politician today could get away with Woodrow Wilson's pronouncement that Americans are "too proud to fight"?

There is a second great difference, it seems to me, between the intellectual and political climate today and that of the first quarter of the century. In general during the earlier period men believed that a better human order, a classless and warless world, a socialist society, if you please, could be achieved. Man could in some decisive sense shape his destiny. Or, while truth might forever be on the scaffold and wrong on the throne, "behind the dim unknown," God stood "within the shadows, keeping watch above his own." A substantial element in one's loyalty to his nation or culture was a sense of responsibility for helping transform it.

More specifically, as we pointed out earlier, there was the powerful labor and socialist movement which did not identify with the state and the capitalist culture. To its members, war was the result of machinations of governments and social elements which were exploiting mankind, and to which workers were hostile. Now, on both sides of the Iron Curtain, the masses tend to identify themselves with the state and the culture. At any rate, the state and the economy are vast institutions which individuals accept, or feel that they have to accept, willy-nilly. In relation to foreign affairs and war the state is an institution with which they are inextricably involved, which can manipulate them but which they are not in a position to influence appreciably, much less manipulate or transform or overthrow.

As tends to happen, philosophical and theological rationalizations have emerged which appear to justify this attitude. Former radicals write about "the end of ideologies" from chairs in vast educational institutions a big part of whose activity is devoted to research in nuclear weapons and related matters. Theologians emphasize "power" as the motive force in social life, decry utopianism, place the realization of the beloved community "beyond history," and refrain from condemning actions which would have met anguished condemnation a few decades ago. Contrast the excitement about integration in church circles today with the prevailing inattention to the threat of nuclear war, to Cuba and to Vietnam.

For the moment, in the spring of 1964, there is still in the United States on the whole a feeling of confidence that the situation, so far as war is concerned, is under control.

Nobody in these days brings up the fact that until quite recently Americans were sold the idea that there was a large "missile gap" to the disadvantage of the United States. Thus the American people for the most part supported the government in colossal expenditures to equip itself with "overkill" capacity, the capacity to wipe out the human race several times over. Surely this is what should be seen as The Absurd. The fact that we were tricked into it—or whatever the verb should be—should make us skeptical about the leadership which carried out this action, essentially the same leadership as we now have, and about the reliability of the grounds for our present optimism.

The nuclear "kegs of dynamite" are still standing around all over the place. The risk of accident has certainly not been removed, perhaps not really reduced. The world was forcibly reminded of this on the very day in May, 1964, when this essay was being written. On that day *The New York Times* reported: "Because someone forgot to throw a switch, the Atomic Energy Commission has lost one million dollars' worth of lethal plutonium somewhere in space near Africa. The loss was at first concealed. . . . The exact fate of the radioactive material is not known. The Commission hopes that it is floating safely in the upper atmosphere." After many paragraphs "explaining" why the matter was kept secret for a month, and why many features of the occurrence are still secret, the *Times* states: "Plutonium 238 is one of the most toxic and costly materials ever produced by man. It now costs four hundred and fifty thousand dollars a pound." Shall we now have a mass campaign, perhaps initiated by Women Strike for Peace, to scrap all nuclear weapons at once? What are we waiting for, as someone said a long time ago?

At about the same time as the news leaked about the lost plutonium, President Johnson was making a speech in which he quoted President Eisenhower as having said in 1963: "This we do know: a world that begins to witness the rebirth of trust among nations can find its way to peace that is neither partial nor primitive." President Johnson followed this immediately with a statement of his own about building bridges between the United States and Eastern, i.e. Communist, countries: "We will continue to build bridges across the gulf which has separated us from Eastern Europe. They will be bridges of increased trade, of ideas, of visitors and of humanitarian aid."

The speech was made at the Virginia Military Institute to the assembled cadets of that institution. He did not give the cadets or their faculty any hint that the institution might before long, as disarmament and peace drew near, become obsolete. As a matter of fact, he said: "Throughout our long history, our long glorious history, when the day was in doubt and freedom seemed to falter, the voice of V. M. I. has always helped lead our nation to victory. . . . I will go back to my tasks with a heart, knowing as did my predecessors that the men of V. M. I. are at my side in the service of our country."

The dilemma in which President Johnson and the American people find themselves today is very explicitly stated in a *New York Times* editorial of May 24, 1964, dealing with the crisis in Vietnam and Indo-China generally. The United States at present is engaged in a war in South Vietnam for which the people of that country have little stomach. For a long time the United States sought to maintain its power position in South Vietnam and Indo-China by supporting the corrupt regime of Ngo Dinh Diem. Recently, both in Vietnam—in spite of additional United States military aid—and in Laos, Communist forces have been gaining. The United States accuses these forces and also those of North Vietnam and China of "intervening" in the affairs of these countries. But what, then, is the United States doing there, seven thousand miles from home? Now, observes the *Times,* "neither side can realistically hope for total victory in the area because the Communists do not have the power and the American people would, wisely, be unwilling to pay the price of the all-out war that would be necessary to achieve it. Our task right now is to convince the Communists that they, no more than we, are going to attain such a victory." The *Times* continues, "It may well be . . . that to teach this lesson a further substantial investment of American forces in the area will be needed" and it believes "the people of the United States are prepared to accept such additional sacrifices."

This is the language of polite society. It means that the war in the jungles of Vietnam will be stepped up. Much reliance will be placed presumably on Moscow's either keeping hands off or giving the United States some backing because for its own power purposes it now wants to check Communist China.

What if Peking wants to be as free from any necessity to reckon with American power in Asia as we wish to be from having to reckon with Chinese power on the American continents? What if Peking is bent on becoming a nuclear power in the end? Is the United States in a position to forbid any big power to attain that eminence, any more than it was able to forbid the Soviet Union to do so? How many men, our own, Vietnamese and others, are we ready to sacrifice to keep up a war which postpones the possibility of peace, in order to "teach the Chinese the lesson that they cannot win a total victory"?

The *Times'* suggestion that the American people would "wisely" be unwilling to pay the price of all-out war sharply points up the hard choice that must be made, and made soon. We cannot use our nuclear weapons, except in a game of bluff, in the situations we now face as in Vietnam or Cuba. If we were, for a second time, to perpetrate a Hiroshima, especially on a non-nuclear power, it would be the end of us. This would stamp us finally as the interloper and warmonger from the West. In the meantime we continue to operate in world affairs on the (nuclear) power basis. But almost certainly we shall not be able or willing to supply enough manpower and weapons at long distance to win out and be in a position to impose a compromise which will satisfy us, i.e., not weaken our power position. Inevitably we play the role of interloper, "the foreigner," the "white man." If self-respect, the feeling of being manly and of defending our rights and freedoms, depends on being able to assert military power to maintain our power position, then a time is bound to come when we will feel overwhelmingly that we must drop the bomb to save our honor—"Better dead than Red"—or be crushed by the feeling that we have chickened out. Either would be an unutterable horror.

No problems will be solved really under the pattern of balance of power and nuclear war or threat of war. Temporary or even long-term balance of "hardware" does not automatically spell peace. Peace depends on political decisions and action, not balance on a seesaw.

The revolutionary "class" today consists of the masses among the underdeveloped, mainly colored, peoples of the world. The West, and this includes Russia, dominates them in only a limited sense now. Before very long even the United States and Russia and the rest of Europe combined will not be able to dominate them. If these great sections of mankind should be arrayed against each other, then the West will not be able to withstand the rest of the world.

Back in the 1940's, Robinson Jeffers in a poem entitled "Prescription of Painful Ends" spoke of an ancient "great republic riding to the height whence every road leads downward." He used the image of a faltering horse:

> There is a change felt in the rhythm of events as when an
>   exhausted horse
> Falters and recovers, then the rhythm of the running hoof-beats
>   is changed; he will run miles yet
> But he must fall: we have felt it again in our own life time.
> . . . And now perceive that come peace or war, the progress of
>   Europe and America
> Becomes a long process of deterioration . . .

There is one thing that can save the West, and the United States in particular. It is to recognize that their day of power and domination is over. It is for the United States to avoid interjecting its supposed power interests as against the Communist "enemy," with whom nevertheless one gladly consorts if it appears to suit one's power interests. In place of this, the American people and the West generally must become concerned, as President Johnson suggested in a recent speech, almost surely without fully realizing what was involved, about the "quality" of their lives in the age of nuclear power and automation. Along with this, the American people must become sensitive to the world revolution that is sweeping over Asia, Africa and Latin America, and become a humble and creative supporter and friend of these efforts of multitudes to rise into physical well-being, political independence, and spiritual freedom.

The conviction that war must be abolished, that in every available way we must break with it, must become again central in our thinking and our desire. Then we shall be nonviolent within and various ways will open to us to develop nonviolent activities and brotherhoods.

The labor and socialist movement of a half century ago, which had such great promise and, alas, did not fulfill it, was a movement which sought economic well-being, social justice, humaneness in all human relationships, equality and the end of war—all of these together. It believed in man's power to determine his own destiny and to build the beloved community. We need such a movement in our own time and it is not easy to see how it can be gathered in such vastly changed circumstances. But one condition may be emphasized here. That great earlier labor and socialist movement had no doubt that the abolition of war was essential to its program and goal.

Any social and radical movement today which thinks that its goal can be achieved by, and in, an America which does not break sharply with war and devote itself instead to facing its own life problems and helping to advance the emancipation of the disadvantaged masses throughout the world is deluding itself. It tells its followers in effect that they will attain freedom and peace in an America as it is today, an America which fails to devote itself to freedom and peace for all men.

In conclusion, let me include the peace movements of the Soviet Union and other Communist countries and the peace movements, here and abroad, which are favorably inclined toward the Communist countries, in the appeal which I am making here. We all go back in one way or another to that labor and socialist movement of the late nineteenth and early twentieth century, that remarkable combination of mass power, prophetic idealism and utopian hope. All of us in one way or another are the spiritual if not physical descendants of those who in various ways failed to meet the challenge, or perhaps we should say betrayed that shining dream. Our respective nations are trapped in the rivalry of power and in an absurd arms race. We are enmeshed with these nation states. It is not impossible, as I hinted earlier, that our countries may go down to a common doom as empires have in the past, even if a nuclear war between the present super-powers is somehow avoided. The present so-called balance or stalemate does not automatically guarantee security or peace for you any more than for us. Perhaps the survival of mankind and even more its ability to devise a creative life for itself in the nuclear age depend on each of us breaking with war and war preparations unequivocally, breaking with what passes for "realism" now in each of our countries.

In 1947 Albert Camus wrote an essay which sets forth the challenge of breaking with murder and violence, and suggests how that may be done. His is a voice that will be listened to not without a measure of respect on all sides of the lines that divide men into warring camps and sometimes lead to a proliferation of violence on so many levels as to make us wonder whether mankind is dominated by a wish to die.

Camus' essay is entitled "Neither Victims nor Executioners." Crudely paraphrased, it points out that in a world saturated in violence we may not have a choice as to whether or not to be victims but we can still choose not to be executioners. "For my part," he concludes, "I am fairly sure that I have made the choice. . . . I will never again be one of those, whoever they be, who compromise with murder." The basic decision that must be made, he elaborates, is "whether humanity's lot must be made still more miserable in order to achieve far-off and shadowy ends, whether we should accept a world bristling with arms where brother kills brother; or whether, on the contrary, we should avoid bloodshed and misery as much as possible so that we give a chance for survival to later generations better equipped than we are."

Camus, in 1947, assumed that only a few at first would take the course of rejecting murder as a social instrument and of embracing nonviolence, the course of "discovering a style of life." Even so, he felt that precisely such a minority would exhibit a "positively dazzling realism." But may it not be that in the nuclear age multitudes on both sides of barriers indeed may be driven both by necessity—the need for bare survival—and by moral passion, to commit themselves to nonviolence? In this way a movement adapted to our own time but reminiscent of that imposing and noble radical movement of an earlier age might spring into life.

Even Camus a decade or so ago could not reject the possibility of such a development and accordingly concluded his essay with this beautiful expression of hope that "the thirst for fraternity which burns in Western man" might be satisfied. He wrote:

Over the expanse of five continents throughout the coming years an endless struggle is going to be pursued between violence and friendly persuasion, a struggle in which, granted, the former has a thousand times the chances of success than those of the latter. But I have always held that, if he who bases his hopes on human nature is a fool, he who gives up in the face of circumstances is a coward.

The Civil Rights Movement and the American Establishment

1965 Two days before the New Year began, James Farmer, national director of the Congress of Racial Equality (CORE), set out on a journey to nine African countries. *The New York Times* gave an extended report of the press conference which he held before his departure. Farmer described his trip as a "fact-finding tour" and added that his "mission" was neither as an anti-American nor as an apologist. It "would be foolish to hide the fact that we have problems here." Africans know that. However, "in some cases their picture is not entirely accurate."

Accordingly, Farmer said, he will not hide the gains that have been achieved in civil rights here, including the passage of the Civil Rights Law, "the massive desegregation of public places in the South" and the war on poverty. He said his tour will have four major purposes: (1) to foster a close liaison between the civil rights movement and the new African nations; (2) to interpret to Africans what is happening here; (3) later to interpret to Americans what is happening in Africa; and (4) to seek to have "some impact" on United States foreign policy in Africa.

Another major contribution Farmer felt he could make was in pointing out to Africans that white Americans have joined in the civil rights movement. He also planned to offer the services of trained Negro specialists in a "type of Peace Corps operation," but stressed that no American Negro would be sent unless a request was made by the African nations.

The *Times* further reported that James Farmer stressed his role as a "free agent," representing the American Negro Leadership Conference on Africa, which was established a year or so ago by the National Association for the Advancement of Colored People, the Urban League, the Southern Christian Leadership Conference, the National Council of Negro Women and CORE. However, he also stated that on his return he would present a report with recommendations to President Johnson and the State Department.

Shortly before this story appeared, two pronouncements by other figures associated with the civil rights struggle came to my notice. One was in a *New York Times* account of a meeting in Harlem addressed by the black nationalist leader Malcolm X. Earlier this year he had written from Mecca, Arabia, to a friend here that he had renounced black racism and had embraced the brotherhood of man, but "his words yesterday bristled with militancy." Specifically, Malcolm X told his audience of several hundred, a third of them white, that "we need a Mau Mau" to win freedom and equality for Negroes in the United States. The Mau Mau, he declared, were "the greatest African freedom fighters" and would hold an important place in history.

He went on to accuse President Johnson, Vice President-elect Hubert Humphrey and Mayor Wagner of "playing the same game as the Southern crackers." Having in mind, perhaps, his earlier communication from Mecca he stated:

"I'm for anybody who is for freedom, justice and equality. I'm against anybody who tells black people to be nonviolent while nobody is telling white people to be nonviolent. . . . A black man has the right to do whatever is necessary to get his freedom. We will never get it by nonviolence. . . . Let the Klan know we can do it, tit for tat, tit for tat. We have brothers who are able, equipped and ready to do that."

The other utterance appeared in a report by Jack Newfield in the *Village Voice* (New York) of an interview with Le Roi Jones, the young Negro playwright, poet and critic. Jones states his philosophy and orientation in the following terms:

"My ideas revolve around the rotting and destruction of America, so I can't really expect anyone who is part of that to accept my ideas. But ninety percent of the world knows they are true. That's what counts. They know the West is done. . . . America is the West because it owns the West. America is the source of Western culture . . . a culture whose time has come and which is rotting at the roots."

The theme of one of Jones' plays, *The Slave,* is that Western culture is coming down during a war between blacks and whites. So he told Newfield:

"It is all a struggle between good, useful life forces and those which are ugly and exploitative. That it shapes up as black against white is the way it is: it's not my doing. . . . Guerrilla warfare by blacks is inevitable in the North and the South. History has neutralized the West. You can't use nuclear weapons against us when we kill a few cops. The same goes for the South. Even S. N. C. C. [Student Nonviolent Coordinating Committee] doesn't realize this because they are just a bunch of middle-class vigilantes. Their middle-class allegiance and values may be unconscious, but they lead S. N. C. C. to value America's existence, and there is no way of saving America. . . . Every black is a potential revolutionist. There are a lot of Tshombes—black traitors—but no matter what kind of fool the middle-class Negro is, he knows he is black."

These contrasting statements by Farmer, Malcolm X and Jones provide a useful starting point for an analysis of the civil rights movement and its problems. (I hope it will be clear that I am dealing with ideas and programs and not with personalities.) Though CORE and S. N. C. C. are not thick-and-thin supporters of the Democratic party under Johnson's leadership, the tie between the Johnson administration and the civil rights movement, except for its black nationalist and allied sections, comes out clearly in James Farmer's "mission" and his observations in connection with it. The very fact that he made a point of saying that he was going as a "free agent" and not as an "apologist" for the United States or the Administration underscores the other parts of his statement in which identification with the "cause" of America and with the Administration is positively presented.

There can be no mistaking the intention to do a service to the United States and the Administration in connection with the current power struggle over Africa in Farmer's remark, during that press conference, that twenty million American Negroes constitute a "great reservoir of goodwill" and could be used with greater effectiveness in various diplomatic posts in African countries. The same applies to the idea of offering new nations the services of trained American Negroes in a type of Peace Corps operation. It was not necessary for Farmer, after all this, to say that on his return he would present a report with recommendations to the President and the State Department, but his having said it serves to nail down the political character of his mission and indicates the extent to which the civil rights movement, except for the left and the fringe elements, is tied in with the current American regime and in no small measure is its tool.

Let us take a brief look at the Johnson regime. James Reston in his column in the New Year's Day issue of the *Times* stated that "the President believes that the major conflicting forces in the nation have reached a level of maturity that reduces the friction between them and opens up the prospect of greater national unity." He goes on to cite several fields in which the President assumes this to be the case: (1) acceptance of the theory that rich and poor stand to gain by a faster expanding economy rather than "merely taxing the rich to help the poor"; (2) labor and management agree they have more to gain by increasing production, wages and profits than "in fighting one another for the more limited benefits of a sluggish economy"; (3) there is a wider acceptance of the need to work toward equality between the races and between urban and rural sections of the population; (4) there is a new spirit of religious tolerance here and in the Western world generally; (5) in the foreign field, the rising power of nuclear weapons has brought about a "new realization of the necessity of cooperation at least in limited fields and for limited ends." Both the United States and the Soviet Union, for example, have a common interest in arms control and in limiting the spread of nuclear weapons.

When nowadays the question is raised as to how this "progress" can be maintained and eventually lead to more radical measures to meet the profound changes taking place in the world—how something in accord with the manifesto, the "Triple Revolution," which ties together the issues of race, poverty and war, might be achieved—the common answer is that we must look to a "coalition" of forces in which the labor and civil rights movements will be joined by intellectuals and "progressive elements" generally. For the present the tendency among those holding this point of view is to contend that the Democratic Party is the instrumentality to work through. The labor movement, A. F. L.-C. I. O., has operated for some years on that basis, but, for obvious reasons, only in the years since 1954 has the civil rights movement been undergoing a development comparable to that which the labor movement experienced from 1932 to 1941.

In the case of both the labor and civil rights movements, identification with the contemporary American regime takes place in an economy which has been expanding rapidly for some years and, as the familiar phrase goes, in an affluent society. It would be unusual if those who benefit from present conditions—and this now includes a considerable number of Negroes—did not tend to think well of the regime under which they prosper and were not disposed to serve it in various ways and to look to it for further benefits. Recent advances in the struggle against racial discrimination, such as the 1954 Supreme Court decision and the 1964 Civil Rights Law, have accentuated the tendency.

When this has been said, however, it would seem elementary for all sections of the civil rights movement to keep in mind that until recently the political machinery of the country, and not least the Democratic Party, worked against the Negro people and in fact constituted the instrumentality by which they were kept in a state of servitude and humiliation. Their determination to tolerate these conditions no longer and to disregard laws which fettered and debased them was responsible for the advances which have been made. While from one point of view these advances have been considerable, a calm survey of the situation will certainly not lead to a verdict that justice and equality for the Negro people have been substantially achieved. On the contrary, there is still a long way to go. Accordingly, it is not a time to abandon genuine militancy or in any sense to yield to the comfortable notion that Washington will now take charge of the campaign.

Young Thomas Hayden, one of the leaders of Students for a Democratic Society, in the November, 1964, issue of the magazine *Fellowship* has furnished a profound description of American society today. "Dissent and protest," he points out, "exist either within a framework of accepting the mainstream institutions, or they are relegated to isolation or the underworld society. This grim picture is of an encroaching trend. . . . To the extent that the trend is transformed into dominant reality, the United States will be advancing into a qualitatively new phase of history: the phase of *post-revolution*." Recent developments, he continues, "at least in capitalist society . . . have tended to flatten out class conflicts and other contradictions typically expected to foster polarization and change. What has developed is a very complex corporate state in which all major organizations are openly or tacitly coordinated in support, extension and defense of the interests of the largest institutions: the private, state-supported corporations. The debates which take place in this 'corporate state' are *not* between conscious opposites, but rather between proponents of more or less welfare.

. . . Above all, the real clue to the corporate state lies in its ability to undercut or isolate all positions of potential revolt."

Ponder this description of the contemporary politico-economic regime in the United States, the soundness of which will hardly be questioned by informed and thoughtful observers. Then place beside it President Johnson's evaluation that there are no "irreconcilable conflicts in the United States" and James Reston's description of the President's guiding principle—"that the major conflicting forces within the nation have reached a level of maturity that reduces the friction between them and opens up the prospect of greater national unity." It is surely obvious that the President regards as "mature" the society which Hayden describes as being in the phase of post-revolution, welcomes the fact that debate is not over conscious alternatives and believes that the existing politico-economic regime can be the instrument to achieve "the great society."

Even James Reston points out that there are "honest men pessimistic about the capacity of this country" to deal with the problems of automation, for example, and who differ with the President's assumptions. Others are better able than I am to deal with specific questions such as the adequacy of the proposals dealing with "war on poverty," urban slums, and inadequate housing. But it would seem to me elementary that instead of identifying with the Establishment, representatives of the Negro people should regard it as their appropriate function to make radical inquiries into these questions and to use the power they and their people command, when in motion, to press for fundamental solutions. The debate about "more or less welfare," however it is decided, is not likely to result in meeting the problems of Negro workers and the youth of the slums.

Le Roi Jones, in the *Village Voice* interview, declares unequivocally: "My ideas revolve around the rotting and destruction of America." He sets forth the view that Western culture is coming down in a war between blacks and whites and "does not hide the fact this is his vision of how it will really happen."

There are forms of expression used by Jones which seem to me open to question, but his basic view about America's role in the world today should be seriously considered, and comes nearer, in my opinion, to the realities of the present world situation than the point of view which prevails among Americans, including probably most Negro Americans.

Ninety percent of the world, Jones told Newfield, knows that the West and America are done. This is probably an exaggeration (though if by "know" you mean what people "feel in their bones" and if you take account of the comparative population figures for the non-white and non-Western peoples and the rest of the world, it may not be a gross exaggeration at that). Patently the Western colonial powers have had to retreat and grant political independence to their former colonies. This has not as yet meant full economic independence, as the current struggles in the Congo and elsewhere testify. But informed people are pretty well aware of which way the tide is running.

Now the role which the United States is playing is essentially that of trying in somewhat altered form to maintain Western economic, political and military hegemony in Asia, Africa and Latin America. The United States conceives of itself as engaged in a global struggle to contain Communist power, primarily Russian in the past, primarily Chinese now. But under the circumstances, as a very rich and powerful nation, the United States is constantly in the position of trying to prevent revolutionary movements aiming at national independence and radical socio-economic change in the non-Western world, or at the least to push the brakes down heavily on them. It is, so to speak, seeking to enforce a Monroe Doctrine turned upside down. For the Monroe Doctrine in its inception told European powers to keep out of the Western hemisphere, among other reasons because other peoples in this hemisphere had the same right to independence from foreign powers that the United States had achieved in its Revolutionary War. Today the United States represents established power and the *status quo*. Communist China may be said to be insisting that the United States keep out of Asia and not seek to prevent or control revolutionary movements there. The war in South Vietnam, which incidentally the United States is not winning, furnishes a vivid symbol of the accuracy of what we are saying.

Two points need to be stressed in passing in order that Le Roi Jones' viewpoint may be fully understood, as well as the influence it is bound to command in most of the rest of the world, if not in this country. The first is the disparity, becoming greater rather than less, between the standard of living in the highly developed Western nations and the underdeveloped parts of the world where the non-white peoples live. Because of its preoccupation with the power struggle, the arms race and the economic interest of its corporations (and despite its contributions of economic aid as distinct from military) the United States is doing nothing substantial to bridge that gulf. But that disparity will not be permitted to last and the advantaged nations are bound to be on the losing end of the struggle that will be waged to wipe it out.

The second point that must be stressed has to do with racial attitudes. To Negroes and other Americans committed to racial justice and equality, Mississippi is today a symbol of evil, injustice, terrorism and shame. What people like Le Roi Jones are underlining is that Mississippi represents on a small scale what has obtained on a vast scale for several centuries in other parts of the world. In Asia and Africa white men have proclaimed and lived the doctrine of white supremacy and have humiliated the non-white peoples. I sometimes think that the gulf between the peoples who have experienced humiliation as a people and those who have not is the deepest and most significant we have to face, and that contemplation of it and awareness of its meaning are the chief essentials for dealing with contemporary problems. When one undertakes to do that, one comes to see that most people are on one side of that gulf, and that almost alone, perhaps, on the other side are the white Americans. They could shove other people off the sidewalk in their own country and virtually anywhere else in the world; no one could shove them off the sidewalk—until recently. It is this, I take it, that Le Roi Jones is talking about when he speaks of "a struggle between good, useful life forces and those which are ugly and exploitative"; and when he adds, "that it shapes up as black against white is the way it is: it's not my doing." (I assume he would include yellow and brown as well as black among non-whites.)

It is probably time for me to observe that I am not becoming an apologist for "black nationalism" or some similar position. Briefly, many spokesmen for this position seem not to regard white people as human beings. This is racism. Furthermore, though in many cases they may not intend to do so, many spokesmen for this position in effect line up on the anti-American rather than the pro-humanity side in the power struggle and the arms race. Anti-Washington means for them pro-Moscow or pro-Peking and not anti-war and pro-mankind. It is hardly necessary to say that their advocacy of violence and guerrilla warfare is a position which I do not accept. As I have suggested in another essay, I think that apart from the general case for nonviolence there are special reasons why the advocacy of violence in the United States, at least at this juncture, is adventurist rather than revolutionary.

But this is not what, in my opinion, needs most to be said when we are considering the program and strategy of the civil rights movement in the United States and especially that of the section of it which is committed to nonviolence. I think it is a mistake for the Urban League, the N. A. A. C. P., the Southern Christian Leadership Conference, CORE and S. N. C. C. not to take seriously certain criticisms by the black nationalists and similar groups relating to the domestic situation, such as their allegation about the phony, or "token," character of what has been achieved so far in the integration field; their questioning of the role of the Kennedys, Johnson, Wagner; their allegations about the middle-class character of most of the civil rights movement. Most important in my view, however, is that men like Roy Wilkins, Whitney Young, Martin Luther King, junior, James Farmer, Bayard Rustin, and the S. N. C. C. leaders, should at this time contemplate what their attitude is toward the United States as a world power, toward the role it is playing in Vietnam, the Congo, and Cuba.

It seems to me it cannot be contested successfully that the role of the United States in the South Vietnam war is stupid, politically inept, wicked. *The New York Times* daily provides the evidence. It seems to me extremely difficult, to put it conservatively, to contest successfully what I have been saying about the general role of the United States in relation to the popular movements of our age, the power struggle, the obscene build-up of nuclear weapons. This should have the attention especially of those in the civil rights movement and elsewhere who profess commitment to nonviolence. How can the leaders of a movement which is based on nonviolence associate themselves, tacitly or openly, with the nuclear build-up of this Administration or the war in South Vietnam? Are we truly moving toward a peaceful world and a nonviolent society when we ignore these aspects of national life while occupied with the violence in Mississippi, Alabama and New York? Are these really separate matters so that a movement can attend to one and ignore the other?

There is, of course, the general consideration that if the nations continue on their present course the nuclear catastrophe will overtake us. And what will racial equality mean for Negroes in a world living in fear and doomed to annihilation? But there is another way to state the issue in the context of this essay. The civil rights movement seeks the end of white domination in this country. Perhaps it should be said that it remains to be seen whether this is indeed the goal of the movement or whether it will rest satisfied with improving the status of a section of the Negro people in a society which continues to be based on the pattern of domination-submission. But let us for present purposes accept what the movement says about its goal. Then it cannot fail consistently to back the struggle for that goal on the part of non-white people anywhere. In other words, the civil rights movement for Freedom Now has to be for *liberation* of subjugated and humiliated people everywhere, or carry a cancer in its own body. To be for liberation means that you cannot side with any force that obstructs liberation; certainly you cannot give support to that force. But the role of the United States in the world today is largely that of obstruction. If the civil rights movement does not dissociate itself from that role and support the liberation movements it will in the end stultify itself. Obviously this presents a grave problem for the civil rights movement: how can it be involved in the Johnson regime and look to it for aid in the struggle here at home to the extent that it does, and at the same time dissociate itself from the role of that regime in Asia, Africa and Latin America?

James Farmer makes a tour of nine African nations to "interpret" the United States to them. One might ask whether this means telling them that "massive strides" have been taken though we still have "problems." Presumably Le Roi Jones and Malcolm X would dwell on the fact that this is the country where for nearly a hundred years after the Emancipation Proclamation the Negro was humiliated and kept in subjection; they might dwell on "token" integration, etc. Who would be the true "interpreter"? Moreover, what will be Farmer's "interpretation" of the American role in South Vietnam? What can it be in his report to the President and the State Department?

There is no reference in *The New York Times* report to nonviolence as one of the themes Farmer was to expound. It is probably safe to conjecture that it was not stressed by him at the press conference. In any case, it is difficult for anyone to talk nonviolence to black Africans today. How shall it be done at all by anyone who is not clearly dissociated from a regime which has equipment to wipe out the human race several times over and which is waging a "dirty" war in South Vietnam?

Some will be thinking that the United States has no alternative until the Russians and Chinese are ready for disarmament. In no sense do I whitewash the Moscow and Peking regimes in these matters: they are not pacifistic. But it needs to be said over and over again in these days, that one of the crucial obstacles to peace in the world is American self-righteousness, our feeling that we have never sought anything but peace, that our invention and building of a nuclear arsenal was in the interest of peace, and that it is always the "others" who are the disturbers, aggressors and troublemakers, no matter how many miles away from home we may be. The main point is that so long as nations generally accept the pattern of power and war, things will go on as they have. And this will mean that the West, including the United States, will not be able to dominate any more; its day is over. It will be pushed back. The vast impoverished masses will demand food and dignity. In one way or another they will sweep aside those who stand in their way, unless indeed the nuclear armed nations play the role of Samson and take the whole house of mankind down with them. The new nations will continue to turn for aid to one or the other Communist regime. In the United States, the civil rights movement will have to reckon with the Le Roi Joneses, the James T. Killenses and the Malcolm X's.

That is why we have to embrace nonviolence now. But this means *true* nonviolence, which is the opposite of passivity. It also precludes rejecting violence in, let us say, the racial struggle at home and supporting or acquiescing in the unlimited violence of a national nuclear military establishment. It means seeking to find ways in which oppressed peoples may be helped to liberate themselves nonviolently, which necessarily requires withdrawal of support from the violence of one's own country which is an instrument of oppression. These, I submit, are questions which those of us who profess nonviolence, including the leaders of the civil rights movement, have now to wrestle with and that will involve agony.

Statement Made on 12/21/65 to the Federal Grand Jury

It is impossible for me to cooperate with the Grand Jury in its present investigation of draft card burning by certain individuals and my own activity in that event.

This is not because I have any desire to hide what I have done, nor do I think any others involved in this action have any such desire.

So far from wishing to hold back anything from my fellow-citizens and fellow-religionists, I freely state that on November 6, 1965, I was present at a meeting in Union Square, New York City, where five young men burned their draft cards. I addressed that meeting expressing full support of their action and calling on others to dissociate themselves from support of United States military action in Vietnam and the foreign policy of this nation which led to this war, to military intervention in the Dominican Republic and to similar actions.

I now hold the same views that I did then. I continue to advocate them. I plan to do my utmost to bring home to my fellow-Americans the truth about war as I see it, and about the war in Vietnam and current American foreign policy, and to call upon them to face the question whether reason and conscience do not require them to withdraw all support from these policies and in particular to call for an immediate halt in American military action in Southeast Asia.

I am unable to cooperate in the Grand Jury inquisition into my belief and actions because it is an element, though perhaps a minor one, in the prosecution of the Vietnamese war and in the militarization of this country. It relates to a law about burning draft cards which is clearly intended to induce conformity in wartime, to discourage dissent, and to intimidate those who cannot in conscience support the war, from expressing and acting upon their convictions.

Demanding conformity and penalizing dissent is a pattern on which all governments tend to operate in wartime. Totalitarian governments seek not only to impose complete outward conformity but to obtain unequivocal inner conformity from their subjects.

But it is precisely in wartime and in relation to participation in war that freedom of thought, expression and association is most needed and most precious. In war, vast material resources are drawn upon and destroyed. Incalculable suffering is imposed upon vast numbers of human beings. The youth of the nation are called upon not only to sacrifice their own lives but to engage in the slaughter of the youth of another nation and even of the babies, the mothers, the children, the aged, of the national adversary.

The idea of the freedom and dignity of the human being, of his responsibility to God or his fellows or to history, is an empty mockery if precisely in such matters each individual is not free to think and to decide for himself, and free to obey or disobey orders of so-called superiors. In the presence of these ultimate issues, no man is superior to another.

Few Americans have any question that this was the case with the Germans under Hitler. At the Nuremberg trial we formally took the position as a nation that it was the responsibility of Germans to disobey orders to do evil deeds, not to obey them because a government demanded it or because the nation was at war. Shall we deprive ourselves of the privilege and the responsibility of being autonomous human beings?

To have dissent and opposition in wartime may create a problem for a democratic government, but if it does not have citizens who refuse to be coerced and regimented, it is no longer democratic.

The conclusion may well be that war itself, certainly in the nuclear age, is inhuman, undemocratic and irrational and that we should lead the way in rejecting it. As it is, we lead the world today in piling up the weapons of mass annihilation, and this nation daily dishonors itself by a war in Vietnam which has not been constitutionally declared, which violates our international obligation and in which we slaughter a people on behalf of a dictatorial puppet government which could not exist but for our support and which proclaims its refusal to negotiate.

To reverse this course would be, perhaps, something of a miracle. It would surely be to our honor to pioneer a new future for mankind by performing that miracle. As one of our foremost philosophers and writers has said: "Man has the faculty of interrupting and beginning something new, an ever present reminder that men, though they must die, were not born to die but to begin."

Crisis in the World
and in
the Peace Movement

1965 As these words are written, early in May, the United States is rapidly escalating the war in South and North Vietnam. The hopes that a good many people felt, after President Johnson's April 7 speech at Johns Hopkins University, that the Administration would be moving toward de-emphasis of the military approach and toward attempts at a political adjustment of the conflict have vanished. The bombing of North Vietnam has been severely criticized even by academic and political figures who, on the whole, are backing the Administration. What characterizes the reaction of the President and of intellectuals such as McGeorge Bundy among the policy-makers is irritability and impatience over all criticism, especially that made by academic and professional figures and students.

Making allowances for the formidable pressures and choices with which men like Bundy are confronted, one still would expect them to welcome public discussion and "involvement" (even if critical), especially on the part of youth; or at least to try to figure out why so many of our best informed people are critical. Part of their impatience may no doubt be ascribed to human weakness; some perhaps to the fact that university professors are not accustomed to being contradicted.

I am not inclined, however, to make too much of such considerations because I think the phenomenon has deeper political roots. As I have pointed out on other occasions, the prevailing American attitude is essentially a self-righteous one, which regards others (our "enemies," the Communists) as the source of trouble in the world and maintains that the United States has no desire for territory or power, is peaceable and on the side of the good. When we intervene, it is because somebody else is creating a disturbance and we move in to restore "order." As a result of this image we have of ourselves, we are impatient with those who oppose us and insensitive to the way they look at things. Thus it apparently has never occurred to the American people as such or to the government that our possession of a nuclear arsenal is anything but natural and proper. No country has any reason to be disturbed over this, or over our military presence on her borders, although we will not tolerate the military presence of another power on our borders. An attempt by China to achieve an atomic arsenal and a disposition to resent our military presence on her borders is regarded as outrageous and incomprehensible. This is an instance of stupendous insensitivity on our part. The Administration's insensitivity to criticism at home is simply a reflection of this national attitude. People who execute national policy in such a context are not naturally stupid but behave stupidly because they are carrying out a stupid policy. Their behavior is irrational because the national course is irrational.

Let us turn for a moment to a controversy taking place within the American peace movement, a controversy which in my view is directly related to the national psychology which we have been describing. Those people in the peace movement to whom I refer are, in a number of cases, pacifists and accordingly are opposed to military action by the United States as well as any other nation. Some of them regard themselves as nonviolent revolutionists. Others are non-pacifist, but nonetheless people usually characterized as liberals or progressives, and accordingly critical of many features of current United States policy in Southeast Asia and in the Dominican Republic. All of them are deeply disturbed because they believe that others in the peace movement are one-sided and prejudiced in their criticism of the United States and its present foreign policy. They charge a failure to criticize other nations, especially, of course, the Soviet Union and Communist China, or failure to criticize the latter countries "equally" in every instance with the United States.

Another charge is that some elements in the peace movement and in the burgeoning youth organizations are psychologically "alienated" from American life. For the most part, those making these charges think that basic social change and abolition of war can be achieved within the American political structure and the institutions of American society generally. They tend to be critical of those who are "anti-Establishment." Unless I misunderstand them radically, they see the conflict between the Communist and the "free" world as the main issue which is decisive for the future of mankind. Accordingly, a "victory" of some sort for the "free" world is desirable and in a sense necessary, though it should be achieved by nonmilitary means if possible. What this all adds up to, as I see and feel it, is that these peace people in the final analysis are in some sense pro-West, pro-United States, pro-Washington.

My first observation is that we have passed through a period when a moderate, non-revolutionary policy seemed plausible and successful. Roughly, this was the period following the passing of the crisis with Moscow over the missiles in Cuba. The limited test ban had been adopted; there was an easing of United States-Soviet tensions, and some liberalization in many Communist countries; the developing Sino-Soviet controversy could be regarded as a way to bring Moscow and Washington together, thereby tipping the balance in favor of "peace"—which, to most Americans, meant in favor of the United States and the West. Things were thought to be under control; there was time to "educate" people, to move— slowly and painfully perhaps but nevertheless to move—toward disarmament. In Kennedy and Johnson we had new and forward-looking leadership. Goldwater was overwhelmingly defeated. Some fairly substantial progress was being made in the civil rights field. What need for being "revolutionary"?

It is not necessary to set forth details to show that this period has passed, that we are now in a grave crisis, and may be swaying at the edge of a precipice. In view of daily developments in South and North Vietnam, and now suddenly in Santo Domingo, what place now for complacency, equanimity, or illusions about peace and the Great Society?

The next observation is that the United States course in South-east Asia and basically throughout the world is both untenable and indefensible. Much has already been said on this point by those who are neither pacifist nor radical in other respects, and I shall confine myself to stating some considerations which perhaps have not received general attention and which in any case seem to me of decisive importance.

For example, putting aside pacifist considerations, and starting from those premises on which relations between nations ordinarily proceed (such as maintaining a balance of power), and assuming that it is possible to contain and perhaps eventually overcome Communism by military means—a fairly formidable set of assumptions —a kind of case can be made out for maintaining stability in international relations by holding on to the present United States positions in Japan, Taiwan, Okinawa and the Philippines. But what the United States is trying to do in effect, despite the fact that we signify our intention to withdraw troops from South Vietnam as soon as a tolerable settlement has been arrived at and the aggression (!) from North Vietnam overcome or withdrawn, is to establish a power base in Southeast Asia and have a voice in the affairs of that part of the world. Considering the bases the United States already has off mainland Asia, the overthrow of the British, French and other colonial empires in that part of the world, the huge nuclear build-up, and the power of the Air Force and the Navy, this effort to broaden the land base of American power is surely indefensible on any terms—unless Communism must be wiped off the face of the earth even at the price of nuclear war. This course is inevitably regarded by the Peking regime as naked aggression, and if the roles were reversed and the North American continent surrounded by Chinese bases, there is no question of what our attitude would be. Witness the profound excitement whenever a precarious foothold of "Communism" seems to threaten the Western hemisphere.

Even if, by some combination of circumstances, negotiations take place over Vietnam and a "settlement" is arrived at, so that the United States is not immediately subjected to the humiliation to which the French were subjected—and why should we not be? —such an arrangement could be only a temporary and artificial one. The notion that we can serve as policeman in East Asia is utterly absurd.

To look at the matter from another angle, we justify our military action in Vietnam on the ground that North Vietnam is a foreign power invading an independent state, South Vietnam. Even if this were anywhere near the truth, surely there would still be a question as to whether North Vietnam might intervene in the affairs of a near neighbor with more justification than the United States from thousands of miles away.

But this is in no sense the case—France sought to impose colonial rule on Indo-China after World War II in defiance of the alleged aims of that conflict. The United States put billions of dollars into support of France in its nefarious war to defeat the popular revolt led by Ho Chi Minh (an admitted Communist but not a Chinese puppet, and probably much more a Titoist than a Maoist). The Viet Minh forces were victorious. France was driven out. Incidentally, this did not destroy or cripple France—or even end its political influence in Indo-China, as the Johnson administration is painfully aware. The Geneva settlement divided North and South Vietnam, but only temporarily, and with a provision for an election in the nation as a whole. The election was cancelled by Diem, with United States acquiesence, because it would have resulted in a victory for Ho Chi Minh. Under the National Liberation Front and its military arm, the Viet Cong, the battle to overthrow a series of puppet regimes has followed. None of these regimes could last a week without American military support. Even so, at lowest estimate, sixty percent of the country is under Viet Cong control. The number of American troops thrown into this civil war constantly increases, and even Administration supporters are not heard to claim that a victory is possible, let alone certain. Consider the horrors—napalm, defoliation and so on—which admittedly are perpetrated by American and South Vietnamese forces. (War is not a tea party, we are told; "the other side also perpetrates atrocities.")

Let me insert at this point some evidence concerning the effects of this policy. At the end of April, I attended as an observer a two-day session of the Presidential Committee (executive board) of the World Council of Peace, in Stockholm. The leading Chinese delegate at that gathering was a Protestant clergyman, with close ties in the old days to liberal and pacifist Christians in the West. He is now a liaison man between the churches and government, and high in the circles of the Chinese peace movement. In his statement to the meeting he declared that the sole responsibility for the situation in Vietnam rests on United States imperialism. He characterized it as "the most arrogant imperialism the world has ever known" and likened its leaders, though not the American people, to the Nazis. Peaceful coexistence with the United States, he said, is impossible. The world peace movement must be centered on fighting United States imperialism. He went on to say that the Vietnamese are already victors in the war, so why spread panicky ideas about danger of nuclear war? The situation in Vietnam "is not a tragedy, but a heroic epic of the Vietnamese people."

At the Stockholm gathering, in contrast to other years, the Chinese rather than the Soviet point of view prevailed. The resolution which was adopted emphasized support of the Viet Cong in the war as the primary duty of true peace workers everywhere and made no mention of peaceful coexistence or of disarmament.

I am not propagandizing for the Chinese point of view. I think the development which took place at Stockholm was appalling. But as I listened to the North and South Vietnamese delegates recall their struggle against French colonialism and all the humiliation Asian peoples have suffered at the hands of white peoples, as I heard the daily reports of American bombing of North Vietnam and considered the spoliation of their country by war, I could understand that these people who make no claim to being pacifists could not vote otherwise than they did. Americans like John K. Galbraith have warned that to follow the President's Johns Hopkins address with stepped-up bombing of North Vietnam was bound to result in driving the Russian position closer to that of the Chinese. The Stockholm meeting has confirmed the accuracy of that prediction. How could it be possible for non-Westerners, with any kind of Communist orientation, to be hesitant or lukewarm in support of the rebels in Vietnam? For that matter, how much support does the United States have for its military action in Vietnam among Asians generally, with the exception of those whose economic and military ties are such that they have to be, or must appear to be, pro-Washington?

All this, it seems to me, has an important meaning for Americans generally and peace workers in particular, namely, that if we consider the situation objectively, we cannot be for an American victory in the war in Vietnam, and cannot give any voluntary support to that war effort. In line with our Declaration of Conscience we have to dissociate ourselves from support of the American war effort and strive in every possible nonviolent way to put an end to it. Americans of good will who are not committed to nonviolence have the same kind of responsibility to oppose American military action in Vietnam and the Dominican Republic as Frenchmen had to oppose the French government in the Algerian War a few years ago. In doing so, they would be taking a position comparable to that of people in England, in 1775-1783, who were against the British crown and for the American colonists in our Revolutionary War.

It became even more necessary to speak these harsh truths when the United States poured troops into the Dominican Republic. The revolt in that now devastated country broke out as an attempt to overthrow a military dictatorship which, late in President Kennedy's administration, overthrew Juan Bosch, the first President of the Dominican Republic to be democratically elected in decades. Bosch, it is universally admitted, is not a Communist but a socially minded democrat. Many competent observers, including Bosch, hold that the United States troops were rushed into Santo Domingo at the moment when the democratic rebel forces were on the point of victory and Bosch, the legitimate President, might have returned. *The New York Times* has pointed out repeatedly that from the beginning the Administration made it clear, *behind the scenes,* that it was out to prevent "another Cuba" in the form of a "Communist take-over" in the Dominican Republic, though publicly it stated that the rescue of United States and other endangered nationals was the only object in sending troops.

Now President Johnson makes emotional statements such as: "We don't intend to sit here in our rocking chair with our hands folded and let Communists set up any government in the Western hemisphere." He adds, regardless of the contradiction involved in asserting virtually equal power in *distant Asia,* "They actually thought pressure on an American President would get so great he'd pull out of Vietnam. They don't know the President of the United States. He's not pulling out." (The speech, *The New York Times* reports, "was surprisingly acclaimed by 4,000 labor leaders.") This is another startling illustration of a mood and policy which can only lead to disaster.

In contending that we must dissociate ourselves from any support of this policy and from American war preparations and activities in support of it, I am not unaware of the complexities and risks involved. I am not speaking from a pro-Moscow or pro-Peking point of view, any more than from a pro-Washington standpoint. But American policy in Vietnam makes no sense. It cannot even achieve the power objectives of the American state, not to mention the defense or extension of freedom in the world. There are, moreover, moral limits beyond which national interests and the power to slaughter may not go. I come back, therefore, to the assertion that reason, conscience, and loyalty to the professed ideals of America compel us to call a halt to the military activities of the Administration in Vietnam and the Dominican Republic, to dissociate ourselves from any support of these activities, and to place our bodies, as it were, in the path of our own military personnel and war machines. There will no doubt be those who call this treason.

If there are those who feel this way we can only say that, to us, to act otherwise would be treason of the most heinous kind to humanity, here and in all the earth.

I am not so simple-minded as to suggest that the United States can decide tonight to call back its troops from Vietnam and have them all on the way out in twenty-four hours. What I am saying is —to use a phrase of Martin Buber's—that a "naked" or "unrepeatable" decision has to be made, resting on the premise that our troops must be withdrawn from Southeast Asia, and recognizing that as with any such decision, ways and means to carry it out have to be devised.

Even if we thus provide for a time process, for thoughtful Americans—and especially all who have any claim to be called progressives or radicals—a paramount, in a sense even the paramount issue, is war—meaning the rejection of war as a tolerated way of human behavior and the abolition of the implements of war.

Dealing decisively with war and corrupt American foreign policy is not something that can be put off now, not even for the civil rights struggle. With the course which the Johnson administration is following, the issue cannot be put off. It is upon us. It will sweep us away if we do not summon all our energies to resist.

I am serious and mean to be precise when I talk about revolutionizing our foreign policy, rejecting war and scuttling our war establishment. This is not to write off completely and in advance the possible value of moderate measures or to suggest that some amelioration in the situation in Vietnam would be deplorable. But it is to declare emphatically that we cannot afford to relax attention and effort toward the renunciation and abolition of war because of such developments. It is not possible to continue on the road the United States is on now and at the same time to be moving toward peace and human well-being. Nothing is really gained if we *seem* for a time to be moving more slowly toward the abyss only to learn presently that this was an illusion. It is not possible for a great modern nation to be both in and out of the arms race, any more than a woman can be pregnant and non-pregnant at the same time. If a major power is in the arms race it has to be fully committed to it. We may see in the actions of Johnson and Bundy and in the American position in the world today where this gets people who "want peace," but stay in an arms race.

The waging of peace, the renunciation of the practice of war, is as much the attribute of national sovereignty today as the "right" and the ability to wage war conceivably may have been in an earlier period of human history. To possess and use or threaten to use nuclear weapons is to abdicate sovereignty and to confess to being trapped, along with other nations, in ancient habits, in illusion. The power to destroy the human race is not the power to make others behave as we wish, but quite the opposite. The power to influence the behavior of other peoples and especially those in Asia, Africa and Latin America will be given to us when we attain the courage, wisdom and realism to lay down the power to destroy them. The only thing that will restore us to respect and genuine power to influence history will be the renunciation of our nuclear arsenal and a foreign policy oriented toward supporting the popular revolutions in Asia, Africa and Latin America rather than opposing them as we habitually do, or giving them at best dubious and lukewarm support.

Let us return to the controversy within the American peace movement over collaboration or non-collaboration by pacifists and pacifist organizations, with non-pacifist organizations of various kinds. I think the issues are serious, and I do not think that the problem is solved by the formula quite frequently put forward: namely, that in a given demonstration or other form of action, we welcome the collaboration or co-sponsorship of any organization which accepts the objectives and the slogans of that particular demonstration, and is willing to adhere to a nonviolent discipline on that occasion, regardless of what other objectives such an organization may have or what its behavior standards on other occasions may be. This kind of collaboration has an attractive and non-sectarian sound. But it is politically naïve as used by some and a Machiavellian device on the part of others. I like Martin Buber's observation that members of "the great unknown front across mankind" who are called to carry on "within each people the battle against the anti-human . . . shall make it known by speaking *unreservedly* with one another, *not overlooking* what divides them."

The controversy about "fronting" recently came to be centered on the March on Washington of April 17, and the part played in it by "supporting organizations" such as the Du Bois Clubs, the May 2nd Movement and Youth Against War and Fascism. Involved in the problem is also the situation in the San Francisco Bay area, where a concurrent demonstration to "End the War in Vietnam" seems to have evolved into two parts, one mainly led by the DuBois Clubs (essentially adherents to the Moscow line in contemporary politics) and the other by the May 2nd Movement (Maoists?), along with Trotskyists and African Nationalists, leaving many pacifists and others merging merely as individuals or else sitting it out.*

In a memo written by friends of mine in San Francisco, groups who "seized" the peace movement there, at least temporarily, are characterized as "not" opposed to war *per se*, not critical equally of military policies on all sides, and not opposed to totalitarian forms of political organization *per se*. As a rough formula for use by pacifists in dealing with the sometimes complicated and delicate problem of "co-sponsorship" this will do. At another point this memo recommends both "a clear turning away from all forms of united fronts with Marxists and fellow-travellers," and "a stronger, more alert concentration of pacifists and non-totalitarian liberal groups open to nonviolence."

A thoughtful consideration of these statements in the context of the facts of life in the United States today seems to me to suggest that pacifists of all kinds, and certainly all nonviolent revolutionists, ought to ponder whether the danger does not lie in "fronting" with questionable groups on what may for convenience be called the right, quite as much as with groups on the left. When it comes to "opposition to war *per se*" is that not just the point at which large numbers of liberals and liberal groups do not go along with the pacifist position?

Being critical *equally* of the military policies on all sides often is laid down as another criterion, but there certainly are large numbers of "liberals," as well as whole groups, who may be ready to join in specific demonstrations, but who in political terms do not devote *equal* criticism to, let us say, American and Russian and *a fortiori* Chinese military policies. "Equal" is a sweeping and essentially a mathematical term which needs to be handled with some care when applied to morals and politics. Basically, I am in accord with it, but then we surely must face the fact that in the United States our main problem is with those who do not accept the idea that this nation is "equally" guilty.

There is another criterion for joint activity which is related, if somewhat indirectly, to the issue of war. Some of us regard "nonviolent revolutionary" as the best simple description of our position,

---

* I am relying here on a memo from three friends living in that area. I am attempting to deal with what seem to me general principles, not with details of current developments, knowledge of which is inevitably very limited.

and I have always thought that to be a Christian pacifist included being a revolutionist, though one who had put away his sword. There are not a few, such as Dorothy Day, who share that position. In any case, from this base it is as important to ask whether activities, including "joint" actions, in some sense advance (or perhaps divert) revolutionary objectives as to ask whether they are nonviolent. There are differences among pacifists and other peace elements at this point. This problem needs to be discussed at length; meanwhile, in our controversies and activities, we should try to be clear about whether it is the soundness and purity of one's adherence to nonviolence that is at stake or some other question. Certainly we should not regard too readily, as natural or preferred allies in the struggle against war, people who are far from radical in their general orientation, or not opposed to war *per se*, simply *because* they are not radical and may have gentle dispositions.

One other pair of observations requires to be made in this general context. We passed not so very long ago through the ordeal of McCarthyism. It is in my opinion valid to be sensitive to this fact and to guard against falling into McCarthyist attitudes or practices. There are still enough obscurantists and hysterical "anti-Communists" in the land to warrant caution at this point. Secondly, the Communist world as a whole and the Communist nations are not what they were during the Stalin era. The degree and character of the change are matters for informed discussion but the known facts should not be ignored, and neither should Pope John's thesis as to the possibility of change in the future. I firmly believe that the "dialogue" with the Communist elements and Communist countries must be maintained.

I think it must be clearly understood that critical examination of the political and military policies, and of the "systems," of Communist countries is in order. The same holds true of Communist parties and any movements or organizations which follow one or another of the Communist lines. It is valid enough, within certain limits, to say that we must not emphasize our differences and must work together for "peace" or for other supposedly common objectives. But actually the limits within which this holds good are quite narrow. *Seeming* to work for the same end and actually doing so are not necessarily the same. Basically, in human relationships of all kinds, reconciliation and understanding do not grow out of ignoring or trying to cover over differences, but out of bringing them to the surface and facing them. We should not be intimidated into refraining from criticism of warlike or other wrong activities in Communist regimes by the cry that this is "Red-baiting," any more than we should be tempted into any form of real "Red-baiting," or let ourselves be intimidated from acting radically in order to avoid being *labeled* as Reds.

Secondly, I think that we should not obscure or basically compromise our utter rejection of war and our commitment to nonviolence. There are a good many today who question both, many who think that nonviolence has been shown to be non-workable.

Our total rejection of war and our witness to nonviolence are our distinctive contributions—in the final analysis our reason for existence. As to rejection of war, one cannot possibly be for the victory of the United States in Vietnam or the Dominican Republic. But to say we cannot be for victory of one nation is not the same as being for the victory of another. A brilliant Italian commentator, a dozen years or so ago, made the observation that "the problem after a war is with the victor. He thinks he has just proved that war and violence pay. Who will now teach him a lesson?" As Camus demonstrated in *Neither Victims nor Executioners*, this holds good in a peculiar sense for all wars in the nuclear age. From one important angle, we should work so tirelessly to disarm the United States and so to prevent it from being victor over others, precisely in order that the tragedy of "victory" may not be imposed on this country.

Nonviolence in a broader sense is not our weakness. It is our strength. Violence in a profound sense is *the* evil, *the* temptation of our time. Nonviolence—"gentleness," as a leader of the French Resistance put it in a meeting which I attended in 1947—is what the victims of war and all mankind cry out for now. Nonviolence is in fact "weak" partly because we waver in our own allegiance to it. It is "weak" in practice because our practice of it is sentimental, dogmatic, abstract, and not imaginative, creative and revolutionary. But for nonviolent revolutionaries, it is *equally* imperative to be nonviolent and revolutionary, to be revolutionary and nonviolent.

The main requirement of the "peace movement," the nonviolent revolutionary movement, is to plan and execute its own job more wisely and efficiently, rather than become absorbed in and divided by a controversy over "fronting." But I do not mean by this to evade the latter question. Rather, I hold that as we define and carry out our own task we shall, on the one hand, see clearly where to draw lines and on the other hand, find that "the opposition" on the right and on the left, in its various forms, is weaker.

With this background, I made a brief and somewhat tentative comment on specific matters. The Committee for Nonviolent Action, nationally and in New York and New England, has followed essentially the policy I have just described of trying to do its own job. It does not require documenting here that it has never weakened its stand against totalitarianism or against militarism in any nation. Joint activity has for the most part been carried on with the War Resisters League, Catholic Worker groups, Student Peace Union, Women's International League for Peace and Freedom and recently on occasion with Women Strike for Peace.

It is clear to us that as a general policy we cannot engage in joint activity, co-sponsorship, with organizations which have as part of their basic philosophy support of certain types of war; or nuclear military build-up of some countries; or a tendency to condone military action by some countries, or revolutionary violence. On this general ground, when the Committee for Nonviolent Action has organized demonstrations in New York we have not sought or accepted sponsorship of DuBois Clubs, the May 2nd Movement, or Youth Against War and Fascism. (We have made it clear, however, that no individuals would be excluded from action based on our program and under our nonviolent discipline.) At a recent meeting of C. N. V. A.'s national executive committee, however, it was agreed that it was necessary to get more extensive and accurate information about the ideology, the activities and the spirit of these groups than we now have. Arrangements have been made for a sub-committee to make such a study.

Let me add here that if, as is not unlikely, persecution of organizations labeled as leftist and regarded as "dangerous," develops in the United States, pacifists must, as in the past, pursue a policy of unequivocal and vigorous defense of the civil rights of these organizations and individuals who may be connected with them.

As I have indicated previously, radical pacifists or nonviolent revolutionists also need to face the question of whether their position is compromised and their effectiveness diluted by collaboration with movements and elements which are free from any tendency to alignment with Communist nations in the power struggle or with Communist ideologies but which in practice are aligned with Western nations and are less sensitive to factors of violence, suppression and evil in American and Western culture than in the non-Western world.

Students for a Democratic Society is in a category of its own.

Like S. N. C. C. in the civil rights field, it is a genuinely spontaneous movement of youth, mainly out of the colleges and universities. So far from being the creature of any foreign agency or political tendency, it is not the product of any movement of grown-ups out of the American past either. *De jure*, it is the youth section of the League for Industrial Democracy, which is certainly not tainted with "frontism," and which is not altogether happy with its child. S. D. S. is deeply experimental in its approach. It has very great potentialities. By all but universal admission, it did a magnificent job on the March to Washington to End the War in Vietnam. The March turned out to be an "event" in some sense comparable to the March on Washington for jobs and freedom some years ago.

This is not to say that S. D. S. does not have unresolved problems. One of them is its policy of including groups like those mentioned above (DuBois Clubs, etc.) in the invitation to take part in its activities. This involves political issues whch in my opinion S. D. S. will certainly have to face at some point, and I have made that clear to some of its leaders. But I have no evidence that these organizations are dominating or manipulating S. D. S. Spokesmen for the political view of these organizations were not on the platform at the Washington meeting. For the time being it is my opinion that radical pacifist groups such as C. N. V. A. have to recognize that the S. D. S. policy in relation to these organizations constitutes a problem which ought to be discussed whenever it comes up in planning for any joint action. But for a "break" to occur between S. D. S. and radical pacifist groups would be tragic and senseless.

It is obviously time for very serious discussion of philosophy, program and strategy in the peace movement and among progressives and radicals generally. I do not think that the question of whether or not to engage in a "united front" with certain elements on the so-called left is negligible. I still doubt after a good deal of reflection whether it is the main issue. Furthermore, in spite of what I reported earlier about what I regard as the deplorable development at the Stockholm meeting, I remain clear in my own mind that part of the "dialogue" which must take place in this most revolutionary of all times has constantly to be with Communists, and the members of Communist movements, who also face problems, live amid furious changes, and are tempted, as we are, to live amid unrealities.

Who Has the
Spiritual
Atom Bomb?

Introductory note: It seems advisable in an article which has to do in part with controversial matters to begin with a personal note. I do not feel "alienated" from American society, in the sense of not feeling a part of it or having a deep resentment toward it. I think of myself as a part of it. That is why I have and am fully entitled to have grave indictments against it. Nor am I unpatriotic in the sense of being pro *some other existing society or nation as against the United States. In saying what I have to say I feel that I am being patriotic in the only sense of that word which I consider relevant or in accord with human dignity. The other personal remark I feel moved to make is that I believe passionately that I am right in the position I hold, in presenting it, in calling others also to embrace it, and in arguing against those who do not. But long ago I heard someone—I cannot remember whom—say: "A man may be right in a situation, but that does not make him more righteous." I was deeply impressed. I do not consider myself more righteous than those with whom I am in disagreement on the matters dealt with in this essay.*

1965 The greatest task of the people of our day is to get rid of war. Certainly there is no greater or more urgent one. The fact that war of any dimension now, in the nuclear age, directly or indirectly threatens the survival of civilization, even perhaps of the race itself, is obvious proof. Furthermore, all the great powers which are capable of waging war declare that war must be abolished and that they are for "general and complete disarmament."

My next proposition is that insofar as it is possible to speak of one nation as being more of an obstacle to peace, more responsible for the failure to abolish war, than another, or others, the United States must bear the brunt of the charge today. I phrase it in this way because I do not think that it is sound or ultimately helpful to think of the international situation today in terms of conflict—this nation versus that—or in terms of praise or blame, angels versus devils, the relatively good versus the relatively bad. It is more in accord with what I believe to be the realities of the situation to think of us all as trapped in the heritage of the past, including the wars of our century, in the technological revolution, the arms race and so on. We are not—Americans, Russians, Chinese, Vietnamese and the rest—in separate boats trying to run each other down. We are all in one boat needing to outride a monstrous storm. To put it in another way, we confront a set of problems in common, and all peoples, as Dr. Eric Erikson of Harvard University put it, need to "find a common denominator in the rapid change of technology and history and transcend the dangerous imagery of victory and defeat, of subjugation and exploitation which is the heritage of a fragmented past."

It happens that a major and very outspoken contribution to the discussion of virtually all aspects of the international situation, including the world revolution, the war in Vietnam and related matters, has been recently made in an article written by the Chinese Communist Minister of Defense, Marshal Lin Piao, which was published in all major Chinese newspapers on September 3. It was made available by Hsinhua, the official Chinese press agency. A full page of excerpts from this official translation appeared in *The New York Times* the following day.

The opening paragraph of Marshal Lin's statement refers to what it calls "the famous thesis" of Comrade Mao Tse-tung. The thesis is that "political power grows out of the barrel of a gun."

War, Lin's statement continues, is the product of imperialism and "the system of exploitation of man by man." Here the authority of Lenin is invoked: "War is always and everywhere begun by the exploiters themselves, by the ruling and oppressing classes."

It follows that so long as imperialism and the system of exploitation exists, imperialists and reactionaries will "invariably rely on armed force to maintain their reactionary rule and impose war on the oppressed nations and peoples." This, Marshal Lin declares, "is an objective law independent of man's will."

Under these circumstances the test of whether one is seriously bent on revolution and ready actually to embark on it is "whether one dares to fight a people's war." This is the test which distinguishes "genuine from fake revolutionaries and Marxist-Leninists."

Marshal Lin turns next to the problem of the military (including nuclear) power of the imperialists. Here again he cites a "famous thesis" of Mao, namely, that "the imperialists and all reactionaries are paper tigers." They may seem and even be formidable from a short run point of view, but in the long run it is "the people who are really powerful." A people's war may meet with many difficulties but "no force can alter its general trend toward inevitable triumph. . . . Without the courage to despise the enemy and without daring to win, it will be impossible to make a revolution . . . let alone to achieve victory."

Lin's next main point sets forth the Maoist strategy of establishing the revolutionary base in rural areas, on the peasantry, and carrying out "the encirclement of the cities from the countryside."

Not only must the revolution within each Asian, African and Latin American nation be conducted along Maoist lines, but Lin adds the intriguing and important thesis that on a global scale the revolutionary struggle is now between North America and Western Europe, which can be called "the cities of the world," and Asia, Africa and Latin America, which can be said to constitute "the rural areas of the world." In a sense, Lin suggests, "the contemporary world revolution also presents a picture of the encirclement of cities by the rural areas."

The United States, Lin declares next, has actually "stepped into the shoes of German, Japanese and Italian Fascism and has been trying to build a great American empire by dominating and enslaving the whole world. It is the most rabid aggressor in human history and the most ferocious common enemy of the people of the whole world."

The crucial struggle in the world today shapes up, therefore, as that between the people of the world on one side and "United States imperialism and its lackeys on the other." This means primarily the United States versus the masses in the vast areas of Asia, Africa and Latin America *"where the people suffer most."* (Italics mine.)

The argument continues with the contention that the United States cannot possibly win this struggle. It is "stronger but also more vulnerable" than any preceding imperialism. There is a great revolutionary upsurge, on the one hand, and on the other a general weakening of the capitalist-imperialist system which the United States now leads. The United States has to fight wars at a distance against people in their own homeland. It has to fight in numerous spots. It cannot cope adequately with all these developments; hence it relies ultimately on its nuclear weapons. But these "cannot be used lightly." The people of the whole world condemned "the towering crime" of dropping atomic bombs on Japan. "If the United States uses nuclear weapons again, it will become isolated in the extreme." Moreover, the monopoly of nuclear weapons has been broken. If the United States resorts to nuclear war it will itself be exposed to nuclear attack.

Lin next contends that even if nuclear weapons are used, the outcome of a war will be decided by ground forces, fighting at close quarters. Here follows another of his striking formulations: "The spiritual atom bomb that the revolutionary people possess is a far more powerful and useful weapon than the physical atom bomb."

The statement then takes up the Vietnam situation. The United States has made Vietnam a "testing ground for the suppression of a people's war," and it is doing badly after many years of effort.

At this point, Marshal Lin makes his main assault on the Russian doctrine of revisionism and peaceful co-existence with the United States and other Western powers. To intimidate people from waging war by pointing to the United States nuclear threat, he argues, is tantamount to saying that a people without nuclear weapons is destined to be bullied and annihilated, and has to capitulate to the nuclear-armed enemy or seek the "protection" of a nuclear-armed power. Lin asks: "Isn't this the jungle law of survival *par excellence?* . . . Isn't this openly forbidding people to make a revolution?"

Who has been involved in wars costing millions of lives, who is now destroying women and children as well as men in Vietnam, if not the United States? "*It is the imperialists and reactionaries who have taught people the arts of war.* We are simply using revolutionary 'bellicosity' to cope with counter-revolutionary bellicosity. How can it be argued that the imperialists and their lackeys may kill people everywhere, while the people must not strike back in self-defense or help one another! What kind of logic is this?" (Italics added.)

From this it is easy to move on to the assertion that though war causes destruction and sacrifice, these will be much greater if no resistance is offered to imperialist armed aggression and "the people become willing slaves." The sacrifice of a small number in revolutionary war brings security for whole countries, and "even the whole of mankind's temporary suffering is repaid by lasting or even perpetual peace and happiness."

There follows another impressive formulation: "Revolutionary people never take a gloomy view of war. Our attitude toward imperialist wars of aggression has always been clear-cut. First, we are against them, and secondly, we are not afraid of them. We will destroy whoever attacks us."

Marshal Lin proceeds to make the point that though revolution in any country has to proceed from the demands of its own people and "in this sense, revolution cannot be imported," this does not exclude support from other countries. The process will continue and the people "will wipe off the earth once and for all the common enemy of all peoples, United States imperialism and its lackeys."

Unshakable determination on the part of the Chinese people to support the Viet Cong war is proclaimed. Lin asserts that the United States imperialists are indeed clamoring for another large-scale ground war in Asia. Even if the United States commits "a few million aggressive troops" to such a war, several hundred million Chinese in arms will submerge them. *"If you want to send troops, go ahead. The more the better. We will annihilate as many as you can send, and can even give you receipts."* (Italics mine.)

On such grounds the dawn of peace is envisaged as not far away: "We are optimistic about the future of the world. We are confident that the people will bring to an end the epoch of wars in human history." This is followed by another direct quotation from Mao Tse-tung to the effect that the monster of war "will be finally eliminated by the progress of human society. And in the not too distant future, too. But there is only one way to eliminate it and that is to oppose war with war, to oppose counter-revolutionary war with revolutionary war."

There will be a strong temptation on the part of groups and individuals in this country to use this frank and specific declaration as a justification for their dim view of Communism, or at least of Chinese Communism, and as a justification also for war of some sort or degree against Communist nations. Certainly the Marshal Lin dissertation will be used to justify the current United States policy in Vietnam and toward Peking, or even to demand a harder line than the Johnson administration is pursuing at the moment.

In non-governmental circles, individuals and groups that are critical of some aspects of the Administration's Vietnam policy and of its civil rights and economic measures as "not going far enough," but who are also highly critical of many aspects of Communism, and inclined to regard the "free world" as essentially superior to the Communist, will be strengthened in their position by the Lin manifesto. So will peace-minded people and those pacifists who, when it comes to assessing addiction to "violence," regard Communist and democratic regimes as equally guilty. Some of these may be confirmed in the conviction that Communist regimes are virtually identical with Fascist regimes and more openly and deeply committed to violence, whether in their domestic affairs or foreign relations, than democratic countries.

I have no desire to play down the oppression and violence which are to be found in the Communist regimes. I am puzzled by those who seem to think that Communist regimes are led by angelic beings who are committed to pacifist programs and methods. These regimes do not really make such claims for themselves, as the Marshal Lin dissertation clearly and forcibly reminds us. When, as is often the case, these regimes or their supporters do make out that their national policy is inherently and integrally a peace policy (we are the "peace-loving nations") and their ways the ways of peace, one must conclude that they deliberately resort to "double-speak," as so-called statesmen have done so regularly through the centuries, so that they are victims of "double-think," the rationalizing tendency to which leaders of thought and action, as well as ordinary human beings, also have been prone throughout history.

But reasonable people will draw from such an observation the warning that, especially in a war situation, the primary and most subtle danger is that of minimizing the evils and magnifying the virtues of one's own nation or culture. The American tendency to self-satisfaction, to be convinced that it is always the other people who are violent and make trouble, is indeed very powerful and in my opinion is one of the greatest obstacles to peace in the world today. The worst sin, according to a great scripture, is that of the Pharisee who dared to stand in the presence of God and say: "God, I thank thee that I am not as other men are, or even as this publican." How often Americans, especially white Anglo-Saxon Americans, have prayed, in effect: "God, we thank thee that we are not as other men are, these immigrants, Negroes, Jews, Nazis, heathen, Communists, or even as these Chinese." President Johnson indeed gave a ghastly illustration of the tendency in his famous Johns Hopkins address. "We often say," he remarked, "how impressive power is. But I do not find it impressive. The guns and bombs, the rockets and warships are all symbols of human failure. . . . They are witness to human folly. . . . A rich harvest in a hungry land is impressive. These—not mighty arms—are the achievements the American nation believes to be impressive. . . . The time may come when all other nations will also find it so." The next day he ordered more bombs and bombers to Vietnam. A few months later, he gave further evidence of our low opinion of "power" by providing for Manned Orbital Laboratories to be built by the Air Force at a cost of billions.

Let us elaborate on this phenomenon in the context of Marshal Lin's speech. Take the blunt statement, in Lin's opening paragraph, ascribed to Mao Tse-tung: "Political power grows out of the barrel of a gun." This concept of "power" is not unknown in Western, democratic and Christian countries. It is in fact the basis of politics in the West and has been for centuries. "Power" in this sense is not regarded as the sole attribute of a regime. But our political and theological "realists" do not tire of rebuking pacifists and others for alleged failure to reckon with the "realities of power," as applied to both domestic affairs of societies and foreign relations of states.

Consider next the question of war itself, organized violence on the part of states or other social groupings. Certainly, the Communists have not been around for enough centuries to have invented or practiced war. The history of Western or Christian nations has been marked by war and violence at least as much as that of any other section of mankind. The responsibility for World War I cannot be ascribed to Communists. There were no Communist nations at all then. Nor by any stretch of the imagination can any major responsibility for World War II be ascribed to the Soviet Union, to the Communist movement, or to the present Chinese regime, which was then non-existent. It is, however, a fact that, as Marshal Lin observes and John Foster Dulles observed before him, World War I was followed by the emergence of the Soviet state and World War II by the emergence of other "Socialist" countries and in many lands by the end of colonial rule by Western nations. In one of his more perceptive moments, Dulles suggested that this should teach Western nations a lesson. I happen to think that, in turning to setting up military establishments as large as possible, these "Socialist" regimes followed a bad example and perpetrated a fatal misstep, but there can be no question whose example they were following. As Marshal Lin, in his own terminology, remarked: "It is . . . the imperialists and reactionaries who have taught the people the arts of war."

It is difficult also, unless one adopts a different view of such matters from the prevalent non-pacifist one, to quarrel with Lin's contention: "How can it be argued that the imperialists and their lackeys may kill people everywhere, while the people must not strike back in self-defense or help one another? What kind of logic is this?"

Nuclear weapons have introduced a new dimension into the world situation. In this field also there is no basis for the charge that the Communists effected this new departure and then "forced" others, in "self-defense," to equip themselves with nuclear capability. The United States pioneered in this effort for "reasons of state" that the American government and many of its people regarded during World War II (and still regard) as sufficient. Moreover, the United States actually atom-bombed Hiroshima and Nagasaki for reasons that were and are regarded as sufficient by many in this country, though in the rest of the world there is widespread doubt.

Just now one of the indictments against the Peking regime, especially in the United States, is that it has not signed a limited ban against nuclear testing and has proceeded to acquire the beginnings of a nuclear arsenal for itself. The danger of proliferation is declared by many experts to be the worst the world faces today. It is one about which, however, American authorities did not think before *they* produced the A-bomb, except to speculate that at least for a long time the United States would have a monopoly on the grim weapon. Obviously no moral credit can be derived from that. Nor were American policy makers deterred by the proliferation danger from producing the H-bomb, although it was already known by that time that they did *not* have a monopoly on atomic weapons.

How the heavily armed nuclear nations, such as the United States and the Soviet Union, can with a straight face ask or demand self-denial of other nations, before they take drastic steps to eliminate their own nuclear capability, has always been beyond me. It seems to me sheer effrontery for the United States to make a case out of the Chinese tests in view of the more than three hundred tests of mega-weapons it has conducted over the years and its failure to make any substantial effort to prevent France from going in for atomic weapons production.

If one thinks for a moment in geopolitical terms, one is led to much the same conclusion. If anyone is entitled to a "sphere of influence" in Southeast Asia, on what are called "security" grounds, it is China, certainly not the United States. The latter would regard a military presence of the Chinese in Mexico of anything near the size of United States presence in Japan, Okinawa, Taiwan, the Philippines and South Vietnam as a mortal threat to its security and indeed its existence. Add to this the history of humiliation of Asiatics by Western peoples (not least the United States); and Americans who want to understand their world and how to deal with it would do well to ask why a Chinese theoretician like Marshal Lin should *not* say: "Since World War II U.S. imperialism . . . has been trying to build a great American empire by dominating and enslaving the whole world. It is the most rabid aggressor in human history and the most ferocious common enemy of the people of the world."

Let me pause to emphasize that these are Lin's words, not mine. For the moment I am concerned that my fellow Americans should understand him and the regime and the people for whom he speaks and thereby see themselves as others see them.

What is clear to those who are willing and able to look dispassionately and honestly at the world scene is that we cannot look upon others—the Chinese, e.g., or the Russians—as violent and addicted to violence but ourselves as essentially nonviolent. We cannot look upon others as the originators of war in the modern world and ourselves as seeking to put an end to war, people who would be peaceful if only other nations were not constantly stirring up trouble in which we have to intervene in order to quiet things down. It would mean quite an advance toward sanity and peace if we could get that into our heads—and into our bones, as it were.

If we accept that and take another look at Marshal Lin's pronouncement, I think we have to say that it presents a logical, integrated case which is very appealing to many thoughtful people around the world as well as to multitudes of those "who suffer most." There are peoples reaching out for national independence, for human dignity, for economic well-being, for a brotherly society, for "a classless and warless" world; peoples who are most of all, perhaps, in deep psychological revolt against the humiliation to which they as colored peoples have been subjected for centuries. In their countries there is only a semblance of democracy, if even that. The old colonial powers suppressed any effort at fundamental change as long as they could. The policy of the United States today is essentially one of suppression, allegedly because Communists are involved in the social revolts, as witness the actions in Vietnam, the Congo, the Dominican Republic. There has to be change and, historically, such changes do not come about without violence, as we know from the American Revolution of which we boast. In an age in which the leading nations have shed so much blood and fought so bitterly to suppress revolt, "how can it be argued that the imperialists and their lackeys may kill people everywhere, while people must not strike back in self-defense or help one another? What kind of logic is this?"

This is said in relation, among other things, to the war the United States is waging today in Vietnam. I think it must be said that, by contrast, the case the Johnson administration presents today is much less logical and coherent and holds out no such clear prospect for the "resolution" of the basic problems in Vietnam or elsewhere. In substance, its objective in the frightful and daily escalated war in Vietnam is simply, to cite the formulation used by James Reston in *The New York Times,* to make possible "a negotiated settlement in which American power can be withdrawn from the peninsula." This and other aspects of the current administration program constitute a vast retreat from the earlier position; namely, that the United States was responding to the call of a little people, under a democratic government, being invaded by a foreign power, North Vietnam, instigated to do so by Red China for no reason except to wipe out democracy in South Vietnam and to extend cruel Communist rule all over Asia. In such a situation there could be no negotiation except on the basis of complete victory for democratic South Vietnam, selflessly backed by the United States. In taking its present position, the Administration has pronounced a devastating verdict of political ineptitude and moral shabbiness upon its earlier stand and presents all who accepted and backed the earlier position with the need to re-examine their whole view of the United States role in the world. On the other hand, as Walter Lippmann has repeatedly pointed out, the Administration has no clearly defined objective now for the future of Southeast Asia. It hopes to "buy time" without any clear idea as to what the time would buy.

In this dilemma, the Administration is now experimenting in another direction and in doing so provides support for our thesis that it must resort to a radically new approach if the United States is to maintain its honor and self-respect, is to serve mankind, and even perhaps to survive.

Recently the Johnson administration has recognized and proclaimed that while the military struggle against North Vietnam and the Viet Cong is necessary and must be carried on, the social or civic struggle to meet the legitimate needs of the Vietnamese peasants is more important than the military struggle. Thus it appears, at long last, that there are grave doubts about the legitimacy and virtue of the Saigon regime—not to mention its viability—that the peasants have real and great grievances, and that the National Liberation Front and the Viet Cong have their roots in these grievances, whether or not they are the agents that can or will redress them.

Let us note briefly James Reston's analysis, in an article written from Saigon and appearing in *The New York Times,* August 23, of what the new approach comes to in fact. Reston is commenting on the dispatch of Henry Cabot Lodge to Vietnam as Ambassador for a second time. Lodge is supposed to emphasize the non-military aspect of the American program in that country. In this context, says Reston, Lodge is "expected to cooperate primarily with any government here that is anti-Communist. The present South Vietnam government certainly meets this test. . . . But at the same time it is essentially a Saigon group, remote from the problems of the people on the land and in the hamlets and backed by the urban upper class, which is undoubtedly anti-Communist too. That class is opposed to the social revolution the peasants want and the Communists promise."

Reston continues his analysis by pointing out that the United States government claims to be aware of the need for social change, which presumably would provide the masses of the people with what they need and desire with less social turmoil and at less cost than a Communist "take-over" would entail. He quotes the Eisenhower directive of 1954, on which President Johnson now bases his case for the proposition that we are in Vietnam for the good of the Vietnamese people. That statement emphasizes the "needed reforms" to be undertaken by the Diem regime. Mr. Reston then states flatly: "None of this requirement has been carried out." He accordingly concludes that Ambassador Lodge "has to work within two policy guidelines which may well be contradictory"—the military directive which has to do with the power struggle, and the political which has to do with "the social revolution that the peasants want."

It is difficult to believe that the new proposal will prove to be anything but another hoax, whether it is so intended or not. An unusually well informed and perceptive New York *Post* columnist, Joseph Kraft, in the issue of August 25, points out that the man who is to back Ambassador Lodge in carrying out the "political" assignment is Major General Edward Lansdale, who is put forward for this delicate and "revolutionary" job by men like Senators Mundt and Dodd. "The essence of the Lansdale doctrine," says Kraft, "is that a nationalist army can be trained to filch, on behalf of the free world, a revolution that is being used by the Communists for their purposes." General Lansdale calls the instrument for this "civic action," through which, "besides fighting the enemy, the army also helps the underlying population through such projects as building roads and schools, etc." In this way, according to the General, "the national government, the army and the general population become welded together in an anti-Communist, pro-people fight."

Lansdale's reputation among liberals rests upon the idea that some years ago a similar program helped President Magsaysay of the Philippines subdue and wipe out the pro-Communist Hukbalahups. But Kraft makes the devastating comment that "the pro-people fight faded as soon as President Magsaysay died. Now the Philippines are a prime candidate for the role of the next Vietnam." Moreover, Lansdale previously operated also in South Vietnam, of all places, in collaboration with Diem! And, as Kraft points out, there "the pro-people fight lost momentum and became a family fight as soon as President Diem was established in office."

Kraft further points out that the central factor in Vietnam now is the American military force and "with Americans running the show the prospect that a revolutionary current of idealism will somehow transform the South Vietnam government and army is obviously diminished. . . . The history of the past four years alone teaches that the more Americans are on the spot, the more the Vietnamese are corrupted." Other observers have pointed out how American aid tends to enrich what Reston calls the anti-Communist

"Saigon group" and the middle class, and not to reach the peasants. Kraft concludes with the startling but, on reflection, sound observation that "if the American military somehow convince themselves that they have a crusading mission in Vietnam," that will be a misfortune since it will serve to postpone rather than hasten peace.

I have not introduced into this discussion any specific details about the role of the Central Intelligence Agency. Americans will have to take into account the notorious role this secret agency plays in all such situations if they are to understand, for example, how the Chinese and many other people can regard America's role in the world as they do, and above all understand the nature of the job Americans must perform, if they are to play the progressive and peace-making role which the Administration professes, and which most Americans probably believe in and want.

When it comes to the question of "what to do" in Vietnam and in the larger international context, we are faced with the fact that a grave and often heated controversy is going on over that question within the peace and pacifist movements. This controversy is strikingly illustrated in my mind by the document called an *Open Letter to Faculty Participants in the Vietnam Day Committee*[1] (at the University of California, Berkeley). I trust that what I have to say here may be taken for what it is meant to be, a comment on what seems to me typical of the prevailing American approach to Vietnam and related problems, and what is at the same time wrong and dangerous in the *Open Letter*. I am aware that there is more than one point to the controversy. I trust readers will keep in mind that I am not dealing with all of them here.

At one point, the *Open Letter* speaks of "the moral scandal of what is now wrong with America." This is after Guatemala and the Bay of Pigs were mentioned and agreement expressed with the Vietnam Day Committee on the point that "the constructive side of the American record is now being *undermined* by events in Vietnam." (Italics mine.) The letter accuses those who would escalate the war in Vietnam of giving little if any "serious thought for the fate of the Vietnamese people." The letter then, however, takes

[1] The Vietnam Day Committee was organized to sponsor the 36-hour "teach-in" on May 21-22, 1965. It was attended by some thirty-five thousand people, including faculty members of the University of California at Berkeley, who represented every shade of opposition to the war in Vietnam. The participation of the Berkeley faculty members came under criticism by another group of the Berkeley faculty in the so-called "Open Letter," which Dr. Muste analyzes and discusses in this essay.

the position that American policy in Vietnam should be looked at
as "the project of specific international conditions or . . . errors of
political judgment" rather than—and here it attempts to paraphrase
the Vietnam Day Committee's position—"as the logical projection
of some all-pervasive moral and social iniquity in American internal
life." The paragraph in which this sentence occurs concludes with
the observation that "America, like all historically significant societies, is complex, offering accomplishments in which we may take
pride no less than deficiencies (*sic*) against which we must
struggle." When I read such a sentence I think automatically of
Arthur Schlesinger's famous phrase about "the bland leading the
bland."

Let me cite another instance of what disturbs me profoundly
in the *Open Letter*. The Vietnam Day Committee is accused of insensitivity to the "tragic ambiguities of the present situation." We
should understand "the dilemma of a President who has done more
than his three immediate predecessors to promote social reform in-
ternally, yet now finds himself embroiled in dubious (*sic*) war
externally. What we must understand is the tragedy of a nation
with the traditions of the United States . . . which has now, *in part
through an accumulation of errors,* become involved in a conflict
which is *obscuring the genuine achievements and promise of this
country.*" (Italics mine.)

To take one other troubling instance, the *Open Letter* attempts
to deal with the race situation in this country. It begins by characterizing the condition of the Negro, in North and South, as "clearly
a scandal and an outrage." But then it quickly suggests that there
is another side to the story, such as the "Warren Court" and the
voting registration act. From there it goes on to criticize sharply
those who pick out the worst elements in a situation and "then
maintain that these form a pattern, or rather *the* pattern."

Frankly, that highly informed, intelligent and socially sensitive
intellectuals should be able to write about the race situation in this
country as if it did not in some decisive sense show *a pattern,* as if
indeed there were not something about it which had to be called *the*
pattern, leaves me appalled.

One would have expected that perceptive and sensitive people
dealing with the race situation, in the context of a controversy about
how change comes about, would have emphasized the fact that,
when it comes to political and psychological factors, progress has
been made only when a deep change in the psychology and attitude

of the Negro people took place (granted, of course, that objective factors such as the transformation of Southern rural and industrial life were involved). "Freedom Now" became the slogan. There developed a large-scale civil-disobedience movement which involved multitudes of whites—youth, women, church people—as well as Negroes, and then things began to happen in which we can now "take pride." Perhaps we are now tempted to take too much pride or self-satisfaction, thereby losing the sense of urgency which is precisely what counted for so much in the achievements that have been made.

The situation in respect to Vietnam and United States foreign policy in general is considerably more complicated than the internal race issue. Nevertheless, it is almost as difficult for me to understand how people like the signers of the *Open Letter* can talk about American foreign policy in Vietnam or elsewhere as the result of specific international conditions, "errors of political judgment," a mixture of "accomplishments in which we may take pride no less than deficiencies against which we must struggle," and can contend that there is not a *pattern,* or even *the* pattern, in our foreign relations which is bad, and which is misrepresented if we speak merely of "counterbalancing errors" in a course about which, on the whole, it seems to be implied, we need not feel too badly.

If the signers of the *Open Letter* have in mind that Johnson has "shown restraint" by not actually following the advice of the hawks in the Pentagon or the psychopathic anti-Communists in the country at large to drop atomic bombs on China now, then my amazement and depression are further intensified. It seems to me like saying that a regime which pursues a policy of brinkmanship somehow amasses political and moral credit because it does not quite shove the nation over the precipice. I do not mean that I am unaware of or insensitive to the "tragic ambiguities" of the present situation and the "dilemma" in which Johnson as a person finds himself. But he was also in a "dilemma" some years ago when he was still voting for segregation.

In the United States the opposition to war and the efforts to achieve peace have in the main proceeded from a basis similar to that of the signers of the *Open Letter,* i.e., within the framework of American institutions, by means of conventional methods of influencing legislators and public opinion; eschewing what are regarded as radical measures; perhaps opposing war up to the day the government declared war and then going along, even in very messy situations like the one in Vietnam today, doing nothing further than "registering public dissent," balancing deficiencies against accomplishments, tending to regard expressions of disgust and repulsion with the basic trend as indicating unhealthy "alienation," as "systematic anti-Americanism indulged in for its own sake," and so on and on. The plain fact is that these conventional means have not availed; and, while it is undoubtedly the case that there are some persons who are in the anti-war movement here because they want to help the Viet Cong win, it is also true that multitudes of Americans are, objectively speaking, supporting the American government in measures which it is taking to win a war against the Viet Cong. Certainly these people are not, to use a phrase of Thoreau's, "clogging with their whole weight." We are living—let us reflect—at a time when the Chairman of the Senate Foreign Relations Committee, on the basis of an exhaustive investigation by that Committee (composed of people none of whom is "alienated" from American society or infected with "systematic anti-Americanism, indulged in almost for its own sake"), can issue a formal statement constituting a sweeping indictment of the whole United States policy in the Dominican Republic. Other Senators of hardly less standing can make comparable indictments of United States policy in Vietnam. *And nothing happens!* Senator Fulbright, as recently as September 15, said: "In the Dominican Republic, hope must be tempered by the fact that the military continues to wield great power—power which it would not now have if the United States had not intervened to save it from defeat."

When concerned people call for negotiations in the traditional manner and do not somehow clog with their whole weight, they are in a dilemma the gravity of which they may not realize. In a sense, talk is always better than what Martin Buber poignantly calls "the speechlessness of slaughter," and talk—"negotiation"—must follow a war if the slaughter is not to be universal and final. But negotiation among nation-states does not really lead to peace, only to what can more accurately be designated an armed truce based on the power relationships of the moment. Munich may serve to remind us that when a settlement occurs, we have to inquire very carefully as to what has been settled. Something quite beyond "negotiations" in the conventional sense will have to take place if we are to achieve peace or general and complete disarmament.

Moreover, while the appeals for negotiation are made, frequently month after month, the slaughter goes on. It often happens

that when an administration has in effect virtually rejected negotiation for a time, and then takes a stand in favor of it, this is regarded as a great advance. How little can appease our outrage in the
macabre world in which we live. *The slaughter goes on.* In a certain
sense we are all thus trapped. But there is at least sense in demanding that a nation act, cease fighting, and go on from there, rather
than let it be implied that there is some justification or excuse for
slaughter pending the start of negotiation. And the question of
how to bring "total opposition to further pursuit of the war" has
to be faced by each of us.

In France, after the debacle in Indo-China, at a point in what
they came to call the "dirty" Algerian War, thousands of Frenchmen, including intellectuals, clergy, both Catholic and Protestant,
youth of almost all parties, and workers, got to the point where they
could stomach the war no longer. They made it known in a way
the government could not ignore. So the Algerian War was ended
in spite of the fact that the reactionary army threatened to revolt.
The multitudes who finally called an unequivocal and peremptory
halt to the moral scandal of the Algerian War did not "alienate the
very society they sought to convince." The society went along and
to that extent saved the "honor" of France. Nor, be it noted in
passing, has France suffered an economic or social collapse because
it was forced out of Indo-China and Algeria.

The writers of the Berkeley *Open Letter* do not deny "the moral
scandal of what is now wrong with America." They do not deny
but rather assert that "the constructive side of the American record
is now being undermined by events in Vietnam." It is a little difficult for me to understand what is meant by "exploiting" a moral
scandal, which is what they accuse the Vietnam Day Committee of
doing. I should think it was the scandal that did the harm rather
than pointing to it in an offensive manner or with mixed motives,
assuming for the sake of argument that this has taken place. In any
case, those who do not want to see the nation's shame "exploited"
can dissociate themselves decisively from the moral scandal and
summon their utmost efforts to terminate it.

The opening sentence of the *Open Letter* states that its signers
are deeply concerned about the war in Vietnam. The next sentence
states that "some of us are totally opposed to further pursuit of this
war." I suppose this still leaves some room for differences of opinion as to how one expresses "total opposition" to an action of one's
nation which is undermining its own constructive activities. If the

opposition is to be political in character, it must dissociate the opponent in some public manner from any form of support which he is in a position to withhold. For young men of military age, whether faced directly with the draft or not, it presumably would mean refusal to render any military service or any form of cooperation with the draft. This is what a considerable and growing number of young men have concluded. There are those who submit to induction in the armed forces, but then carry on anti-war activity of various sorts within the military establishment. One may have criticisms or questions, as I do, about this approach, but I think it cannot be denied that it may be an expression of a truly conscientious objection to a war and a means of resisting it.

If there were enough young men who could not stomach participation in the war in Vietnam and who perhaps in a number of cases had been brought to the stand of conscientious objection to any war, then the government would be unable to pursue the war. This would be so because if so many men of draft age took this position there would be wide support for them among other elements of the population. The government would be in the position of the French regime some years ago when it *had* to terminate the Algerian War.

Dr. Norman K. Gottwald, distinguished member of the Faculty of Andover-Newton Theological Seminary, posed the question which is suggested by this analysis. In *The New York Times* of August 26, he wrote: "In the weighing of American honor in Vietnam, account must be taken of the dishonor which the escalated war is heaping up: breaches of international law going back to 1954; failure to submit the dispute formally to the U. N. for action; backing up a series of undemocratic puppet regimes; prosecution of a brutal and politically inept war which alienates more Vietnamese than it kills or defends." He concludes with a statement that will undoubtedly shock some but which certainly cannot be dismissed offhand: "By the usual tests of honor it is no longer clear that the United States deserves to win or to achieve a stalemate." In other words it may be that the United States "deserves" defeat. I take it that Dr. Gottwald probably does not regard this as automatically or simplistically equivalent to plumping for a military victory of the other side.

What seems to me clearly implied is that the United States should call a halt—unilaterally if you please—to its military activities in Vietnam as the course which is required by its sense of "honor" as well as, presumably, other considerations. The United

States should order its troops to cease fire and should take immediate steps to have them withdrawn. I am aware that these things take time, but a decision has to be made. The United States is now making daily decisions to escalate the war and to pursue it until a military victory or at least a stalemate is gained. I am proposing a decision to cease fire, to withdraw the United States military presence—and then to proceed from there.

Withdrawal has world-wide implications. It is followed logically by the proposal that the United States disarm unilaterally. Let me be more specific. I am not here advocating that all or even most Americans should become pacifists in the sense in which that term is usually used in the United States. What I propose is, briefly, that the United States abdicate the role of a big (nuclear) armed power and divest itself of the armament which enables it to wage war (as it is doing in Vietnam) and to threaten other peoples (as President Kennedy threatened the Soviet Union at the time of the Cuban crisis). So far as the present argument goes I am not objecting to the United States' disarming *only* to the extent that Ireland, Denmark, Norway, or Sweden, for example, have done; but I am insisting that it should disarm *at least* to that extent and, of course, with the understanding that it would not be in any military alliance with other big powers, as are some of the countries named. None of the Scandinavian countries is a major power. They are nevertheless cultured, highly respected peoples and perhaps more secure than most nations, or in any case not less.

The responsibility to disarm unilaterally rests equally upon other big powers, including the Soviet Union and the Chinese People's Republic. The Committee for Nonviolent Action, a few years ago, sponsored a San Francisco to Moscow Peace March which actually carried the appeal to disarm unilaterally to England, Belgium, West and East Germany, Poland and the Soviet Union. The only country the team did not get into at all, except for a dramatic demonstration at the Le Havre harbor, was Gaullist France. However, in each nation its own citizens must do the job.

I am aware that there is the grave problem of a transition during which the American people must prepare themselves for such a step. I am aware that, even if they were prepared, such undertakings as disarmament take time and involve complicated planning. We seem quite competent to do the most intricate planning and to carry out the most stupendous operations when it comes to war. Why should one assume in advance that these things cannot be done in order to carry out a decision to cease from war-making? As it is, we are deciding daily to remain in the nuclear arms race, to keep ahead if we can, to escalate our forces where they are engaged, and so on. What is needed is a decision to reverse the course. To use again a somewhat crude figure, we are on the edge of a precipice. We call for a decision to stop and turn around, recognizing that then we still would have a long way to go.

In making a proposal for unilateral disarmament as a follow-up to withdrawal from Vietnam we have opened up a highly complicated subject. Only a few of the questions raised can be touched upon here, and these only in a sketchy fashion. I am, of course, aware of the fact that to many, perhaps nearly all, the proposal seems unrealistic, utterly fantastic, even perhaps mad, unthinkable. I trust that the reader who may feel this reaction will read on for a few more sentences.

A few years ago, Herman Kahn, formerly of the Rand Corporation and now head of the Hudson Institute, a research agency which does a lot of work for the Defense Department, insisted that Americans had to face up to thinking about the unthinkable. He was referring to the fact that many considered it inappropriate or scandalous to discuss the strategy of modern, nuclear war which might terminate in a nuclear catastrophe. He characterized this attitude as that of the ostrich sticking his head in the sand. As realists and people living in a scientific age we, or at any rate our leaders in the Pentagon and the White House, should calmly examine the many possible developments, the alternative strategies which we and the enemy might follow and so on. Dr. Kahn looked into such questions as how many deaths a United States government might consider permissible in a nuclear war before surrendering. He found that, as a group, the various people he interviewed who might be competent to judge or at least typical of official opinion, ruled out a hundred million American deaths as too many—sixty million might be tolerable. Dr. Kahn is only in a minor degree responsible for it, in my opinion, but the fact is that the White House and the Pentagon are now thinking in such terms, with the help of computers, no doubt, and in the main the American people accept this. We are thinking, if it can be called thinking, about what is or should be "unthinkable" in another sense from what Dr. Kahn perhaps had in mind. Now I raise the question of whether our present behavior in this whole field of war and foreign policy and the various phases of it, is not precisely the behavior of an ostrich with his head in the sand; whether we are not in fact living in a world of phantasy. As is the case with people afflicted with certain forms of mental disease, we may be firmly convinced of our sanity, as we are of our righteousness, and may in fact in the general context of our diseased state be able to perform amazingly logical operations. But we may, nevertheless, be living in a world which does not exist.

In any event, taking into account the revolutions which are now under way in many fields, it would seem absurd and extremely hazardous to bar from our minds the idea that a revolution in the behavior of peoples toward each other may also have to occur. It is fairly safe to assume, to change the figure, that if people who have been living in a dark cave come out into the light, the world on which they open their eyes may seem at first utterly unreal. In fields of human experience and adventure other than the one which occupies us here—let us say those of the physicists and space scientists, on the one hand, and those of large sections of modern youth, on the other—exactly this experience of living in another world which is virtually closed to others is taking place.

To turn to what will be regarded as more practical matters, it is generally assumed that if, for example, the United States were to withdraw from the arms race (not just say that it is willing to talk with other governments, which generally comes down to saying: "I will disarm if you will first") the world situation, the opposition of power would remain the same, and the Communists—Chinese or what have you—would take over everywhere. As far as the Communists are concerned—again Chinese or what have you—everything also would remain the same.

Such reasoning, to the effect that you can radically alter a *causal* factor, and that this would have no *effect,* would seem patently absurd to any fairly intelligent person if we were not trapped in intellectual and emotional patterns which rob us of common sense! The big Communist take-overs, as Marshal Lin pointed out—and John Foster Dulles long before him—took place in fact in the midst or the aftermath of big wars like World Wars I and II. Dulles actually said on occasion that if we were to win another World War, that would be the end for the West and we could leave what remained to the Communists.

It is said that if the United States were to stop shooting and withdraw its troops from Vietnam, the Viet Cong would then stage a great purge of the people whom we have been seeking to protect—

have pledged to protect. First of all, so far they have been getting precious little protection from us. The Vietnamese people as human individuals have been shot at by the French, by us, by Communists, by guerrillas for years. Maybe, if only somebody would stop shooting at them that would be something to the good.

Next, I cannot get it out of my head or my guts that Americans are away over there, not only shooting at people but dropping bombs on them, roasting them with napalm and all the rest. Do we really want to proceed on the proposition that as long as others do the same or similar things, we are exonerated or are in a "tragic predicament" over which, however, we should not lose sleep? A good many knowledgeable people make out a convincing case for the proposition that many of our acts in Vietnam constitute war crimes under the Nuremberg pattern. What do we do: continue to commit them on the assumption that the criminals are to be tried, when the war is over, by ourselves?

But above all, I do not think for a moment of a cease-fire by American troops as necessarily or probably a signal for a purge by the Viet Cong. God is my witness that I do not want that to happen. While we are on the subject of purges, by the way, why is it that some people never seem to think that non-Communist elements might undertake them? Chiang Kai-shek certainly did in Taiwan at a certain stage. I don't see how any informed person can unequivocally assert that a purge is certain to take place or deny that it is possible that if the United States stopped shooting and bombing and made it clear that it firmly intended to withdraw its troops (the latter is now, at least on paper, a part of our avowed policy) this would be precisely the break-through that would lead to a general cease-fire and to serious negotiations. A strong case can be made out, in my opinion, that it is highly probable that this would prove to be the case. In a situation in which a number of people may feel the need of "saving face," someone who is not that insecure or juvenile may hold the key to the solution.

Next, I want to observe briefly that the charge of isolationism brought against the policy we are proposing for Vietnam and unilateral disarmament generally is utterly without foundation. The United States is of course very choosy about intervention, as are all nation-states in their turn. We do not intervene in South Africa where a horrible evil exists which threatens the peace of the world. Our corporations "intervene" in many parts of the world and are backed by our diplomats and armed forces. We habitually consort with elements that represent the *status quo,* the Communists with those that represent the forces of change. We did not intervene against Trujillo in the Dominican Republic or Batista in Cuba. Where we intervene militarily, as in Santo Domingo, or in Vietnam, and earlier against Castro in Cuba, this is done in such a way (as many competent non-Communist observers, among others, have pointed out) as to cause the discontented elements to turn to the Communists for counsel and aid. The process of revolution then becomes painful, violent, at times often ghastly. The results are not altogether satisfactory, but this is the movement of events at this stage in history.

Now if a power like the United States voluntarily withdraws from the arms race and makes the changes in its own social structure which this entails, this would constitute "intervention" of historic dimensions. It would be a revolutionary development comparable in one sense to the Russian and Chinese revolutions themselves. It would, to use Marshal Lin's phrase, be "a spiritual atom bomb . . . far more powerful and useful than the physical atom bomb." The United States would be able to address itself and to devote its vast resources, human and technological, to aiding the impoverished and exploited masses to lift themselves to independence, to human dignity and to a life where the simple human needs of food, clothing, shelter and beauty would be met. Moreover, the spell of conflict might then be broken, as somehow it has to be before long if the human race is to survive; and the peoples of East and West, North and South, could together deal with the problems of automation, cybernation, the possible move into space, and the problem of man himself in the so "unthinkably" new conditions of this age. If we wish to speak of the American Dream, this is surely closer to it by far than anything which can come out of our present course and mood, out of business or politics as usual, out of the war in Vietnam, out of the continual embroilment in the arms race and the power struggle.

In closing, I want to invoke the help of Hannah Arendt in backing up in a philosophical or "ultimate" way the call for a "miracle" which I am in a sense sounding. I am referring to a chapter in her book *The Human Condition* entitled "Action" which is subtitled: *A Study of the Central Dilemmas Facing Modern Man.* In Miss Arendt's book "action" is distinguished from "labor" and from "work." It is essentially what we think of as political action by which men or human communities intervene in their own destiny.

If without action or speech [she suggests], without the articulation of natality, we should be doomed to swing forever in the ever-recurring cycle of becoming, then without the faculty to undo what we have done, to control at least partially the processes we have let loose, we would be the victims of an automatic necessity. . . . We have seen before that to mortal beings this natural fatality . . . can only spell doom. If it were true that fatality is the inalienable mark of historical processes, then it would indeed be equally true that everything done in history is doomed. And to a certain extent this is true.

Miss Arendt continues with the thought that this process of man toward doom would continue "if it were not for the faculty of interrupting it and beginning something new, a faculty which is inherent in action like an ever present reminder that men, though they must die, are not born to die but to begin. . . . Thus action, seen from the viewpoint of the automatic processes which seem to determine the course of the world, looks like a miracle. In the language of natural science, it is the 'infinite improbability which occurs regularly.' Action is in fact the one miracle-working faculty of man."

Miss Arendt concludes this chapter with a reference to the event of birth, the fact of "natality." She may, she surely does, have something to say to all of us, whatever our place in the controversies of the moment relating to modern youth, and to modern youths themselves:

The miracle that saves the world [she writes], the realm of human affairs, from its normal, "natural" ruin is ultimately the fact of natality, in which the faculty of action is ontologically rooted. It is, in other words, the birth of new men and the new beginning, the action they are capable of by virtue of being born. Only the full experience of this capacity can bestow upon human experience faith and hope, those two essential characteristics of human existence which Greek antiquity ignored altogether, discounting the keeping of faith as a very uncommon and not too important virtue and counting hope among the evils of illusion in Pandora's box. It is this faith in and hope for the world that found perhaps its most glorious and most succinct expression in the few words with which the Gospels announced their "glad tidings": a child has been born unto us.

The Movement
to Stop the War
in Vietnam

1966 As the year 1965 draws to a close the Johnson administration is clearly on the point of a further escalation of the Vietnam war on such proportions that the character of the war itself may change from one which can still be regarded as in some sense limited, to one which approaches global proportions and which may well get out of control. At the same time serious dialogue over the Johnson policy continues in this country, and opposition is, in my opinion, still mounting or at least holding its own. "Patriotic" counter-demonstrations and public opinion polls indicate that there is backing for the President but not anything like enthusiasm for the war. In these circumstances reflection on the war itself and the foreign policy of the United States and on how the opposition can be developed effectively is needed. What follows is a contribution to the discussion of these matters.

They were discussed also in an article which appeared in the November 25, 1965, issue of the *New York Review of Books* entitled "The Vietnam Protest" and was signed by Irving Howe, Michael Harrington, Bayard Rustin, Lewis Coser and Penn Kimble. It was a thoughtful contribution to the discussion, free from invective, and seems a convenient starting point from which to state some of my own views.

The signers of the statement declare their belief "that the present United States policy in Vietnam is morally and politically disastrous." Very welcome, also, in view of the contrary opinion

frequently expressed, is their categorical rejection of the argument
that recent demonstrations against the war may persuade the Chinese
and the Vietnamese Communists to prolong the war because
they might be misled into supposing that the American people do
not support the government's policy: "It is the kind of demagogic
appeal characteristically advanced by governments embarked upon
adventures in which they do not have full confidence."

It is when the signers undertake to set forth their own proposal
and the arguments in support of it and to criticize aspects of the
developing protest movement that questions arise.

For example, a "significant protest movement" such as they
propose, which would appeal presumably to a broad public, should
"clearly indicate that its purpose is to end a cruel and futile war,
not to give explicit or covert political support to the Viet Cong."
It is argued that "this is both a tactical necessity and a moral obligation,
since any ambiguity on this score makes impossible, as well
as undeserved, the support of large numbers of American people."

Similar questions are raised by the argument that an effective
protest movement cannot be organized around a full-scale historical
and political analysis of the Vietnam situation.

The kind of difficulty with which we are faced, in my opinion,
is illustrated by the fact that the signers immediately criticize as
"vague and unfocused" the slogan employed in the October 16
New York parade: "Stop the War in Vietnam Now." It provided
"no guidelines for action." (Spokesmen for various points of view
were represented on the platform on that occasion and organizations
were free to distribute leaflets of their own which were quite specific.)
The program of a protest movement must, then, after all,
be somewhat focused, and it has to take considerable account of the
historic background and political context, as indeed the signers do
in their opening section. The problem then arises of how the movement
is to be focused.

To tackle a delicate question: the purpose of the movement
is to end a cruel and futile war, "not to give explicit or covert political
support to the Viet Cong." Many Americans will hold that for
the United States to declare, as the signers propose, its readiness
to negotiate with the National Liberation Front, the political arm
of the Viet Cong, does give explicit, *de facto* political support
to the Viet Cong. The Saigon regime, which recently has explicitly
rejected negotiation with "the enemy," will certainly also regard
this as giving the latter political ' encouragement" if not support.

Similarly, when it is proposed that assignment of historical responsibility is ruled out, does this mean that the National Liberation Front—North Vietnam, on the one hand, and the United States intervention in Vietnam, on the other hand, are placed *politically* on the same basis? The resort to violence and slaughter on either side, as a pacifist I must and do condemn. On the basis of the corruption and ultimately self-defeating character of organized violence, I am prepared to appeal to either side to disarm unilaterally. But to leave out of account the political wickedness and stupidity of United States military intervention in Vietnam and the Dominican Republic, either when campaigning for an end to the war or in connection with negotiations, seems to me wrong and impractical, even "utopian" in its way. It seems to me that socialists or progressives have to take account of the problem of United States interference with popular revolts and cannot deal with the problem of stopping the fighting in abstraction from this factor. If, as is true, this will at first call forth opposition or skepticism on the part of many Americans, we have to face it and in any case will not be able to evade it.

The first proposal made in the *New York Review* article as a basis for common action is that "the United States immediately cease bombing of North Vietnam." Presumably the United States is to take this step unilaterally, and adhere to it whether or not this leads to Hanoi withdrawing troops from South Vietnam. As an unrepentant unilateralist, on political as well as moral grounds, I am of course all for this move. But is it going to be argued, explicitly or inferentially, that ceasing to bomb North Vietnam does not seriously affect the military position of the United States? If the projected movement does take this stand, it will have to prove its case to the satisfaction of the military and of informed civilians. I doubt that it can. If it fails, then it will have to decide whether to withdraw that proposal because it does not want to be "responsible" for a military defeat of the United States and because Americans generally will not welcome it; or whether it will argue that taking a risk which, from a military standpoint, is inadmissible is still required on political and moral grounds. In the latter case, the whole question of the role of the United States in Southeast Asia and as a power state in the atomic age has to be faced, including the very crucial one of whether the United States has to give up trying to play a traditional big-power role in this era.

A similar dilemma arises in relation to other proposals in the statement under discussion such as that the United States propose to Hanoi and the Viet Cong a cease-fire and urge them to accept that proposal and declare themselves ready for immediate and unconditional negotiations. Up to the President's Johns Hopkins speech in April, the United States would not negotiate. "Negotiation" in the relations between warring nations is something that is based on an estimation of the power relationships of the moment; each government is ready to negotiate when it deems the situation favorable to itself. The Johnson administration is making a good deal of the (alleged) fact that it is now ready to negotiate but Hanoi and the Viet Cong stand in the way—"It's up to them now." I am sure that the signers of the present statement do not intend to help the Administration to make capital out of the situation, but they will in that case have to devise ways to guard against the Administration's doing just that; and this will hardly be possible without going into the historical background and other delicate matters which they propose to avoid in order to make peace proposals more palatable to Americans.

Assume that Hanoi and the Viet Cong refuse to negotiate, which they well may, perhaps on the ground that the United States has no business in Vietnam. Will the proposed movement to end the war collapse at that point and, in effect, take the position that under such circumstances the United States "has no choice" but to keep on fighting and quite possibly to further escalate the war? Escalating the war *is* what the United States is doing. There are those who regard the idea of whether or not the United States is to proceed to kill more babies, children, old people, and adults generally is subject to "negotiation" as gruesome, inhuman and dishonorable.

One other plank in the platform of the proposed movement is that the United States "recognize the right of the South Vietnamese to determine their own future, whatever it may be, without interference from foreign troops, and possibly under UN supervision."

The tentative tone of that last clause both covers up and hints at a basic problem. The proposal is that the Vietnamese be their own masters and free from inteference from foreign troops. This suggests, for one thing, that United States troops have no legitimate business there now. Certainly their presence has not in recent years left the Vietnamese people free to determine their own course and it has been the instrument for terrorizing and killing many of them. The argument for withdrawing foreign troops, leaving the

Vietnamese free, but maintaining some kind of "presence," possibly UN, is that otherwise there may be a purge—a purge of people whom we have pledged to protect. It hardly can be said that we have afforded them much protection up to now or that if we keep on fighting longer we eventually shall save lives, after having destroyed more in the interim. Again the question arises: do the signers of this statement propose that fighting continue if Hanoi and the Viet Cong do not accept its provisions? It is such considerations which lead to the question of whether the way to begin to end the war is not for the United States to plan for a cease-fire of its own, a cessation of adding to the troops already there, a clear declaration that it will withdraw them—and on that basis proceed to what might prove to be genuine negotiation. This is not to indicate insensitivity to the problem of retaliation which might be resorted to by either side after a bitter civil war, but to insist that if we are fighting for self-determination for the Vietnamese people, we have to start at that point and that an international "presence," whatever form it may take, cannot be imposed on them.

The United States is deriving little, if any, honor from its role in Vietnam now. It is not altogether fantastic to suppose that for the United States to recognize that the day of Western military intervenion in Asia is at an end and that to act on that assumption would accrue to its honor, would save lives there and in other parts of the world, and would be a much more efficacious way to stop "Communist or Chinese" expansion than the course we are now pursuing. Both George F. Kennan, the American political analyst, and Enoch Powell, the defense expert of the British Conservative Party, are on record to the effect that the longer Western nations try to maintain their "presence" in Asia, for example, the longer it will be before indigenous resistance to Chinese or Communist expansion develops in those regions. I am not for a moment suggesting that it is a simple matter to carry out the approach I am advocating, any more than is that set forth in the *New York Review* statement under discussion. I am suggesting that it is politically and morally a sounder one, that we may be forced to take it in any case and that it will be to our honor and a boon to mankind if we choose to take it.

In the light of what I have said and of the situation in the country, what the *New York Review* statement has to say about civil disobedience and other aspects of the protest movement seems to me in part beside the point and in part mistaken and unfortunate.

For one thing, I could wish that those who are critical of the end-the-war movement, as hitherto conducted, would not only make alternative proposals as to program but would be explicit as to how a more effective movement could and should be built. Do they, for example, expect that the labor movement can be won away from its present position of support for the Johnson program to anything remotely resembling opposition? Since a power factor is involved in actions which influence government policy in an immediate sense, do they anticipate that unions might be called on to refuse to produce or transport war material? Similar questions could be asked about what support for an end-the-war movement might be expected, and how to go about getting that support, from the various sections of the civil rights movement.

As it is, the *New York Review* statement devotes itself largely to criticism of forms of protest and resistance which have hitherto been resorted to. With some of the criticisms I am in agreement, but not with others. Before dealing with some specific instances, there is a general observation. The statement begins with the assertion of the belief that the debate in this country about Vietnam is by no means over, that "the protest movement has an important role to play" and that "there is now a genuine opportunity for the movement that wishes to change United States policy in Vietnam." But, it is contended, this can become true only if the movement adopts some such program and methods as the signers advocate. Otherwise it will not gain the approval of "more than the small band already committed to protest."

I already have said that these proposals should be taken seriously, but it surely should be noted also that we do now have a debate and at least a substantial beginning of a protest movement. Immediately after the October 16 demonstrations there was a series of attacks on them and not a few predictions that the protests had "failed." This clearly has not proved to be the case. Even those who argue that the parades, demonstrations, draft card burnings, and self-immolations did not in any way help the situation, cannot possibly make a case for the proposition that they destroyed a protest and a debate which obviously exist. Admittedly the "patriotic" counter-demonstrations have been poorly attended and have produced no evidence of popular enthusiasm for the war. There is, as a matter of fact, a lot of evidence that the various protests have had an impact on public opinion and in Washington. The Johnson administration has had to take notice of the various forms of criticism and protest during the past year even though, in spite or in defiance of them, it has continued its escalation. It is also significant now that almost universally a distinction is drawn by the press and other mass circulation agencies between pacifists and conscientious objectors on the one hand and other kinds of protesters. I cite this fact merely to meet the criticism made by some that pacifism and nonviolence have been submerged. The fact is that they have never before received so much attention in this country. The evidence seems to me, therefore, all in favor of continuing the forms of pressure which have been used rather than abandoning them—by which I do not mean that all the things that have been done should be continued, or that there is not room for other forms of pressure.

I turn to the deprecation, in the statement, of resort to civil disobedience. Take the reference to recent efforts to stop the operation of troop trains in California. I, too, questioned the wisdom of that action, but not on the grounds that these efforts involved "an action by a small minority to revoke through its own decision the policy of a democratically elected government," etc. This implies a characterization of the war policy in relation to Vietnam as "democratically" arrived at, which Senators Morse and Fulbright—judging by their utterances—would not share. Would it not rule out the men and women who operated the Underground Railway a century or so ago? To get at the question from another angle, do the signers rule out strikes of transport or munitions workers on the ground that they cannot any longer take an active part in what they may come to regard as a "dirty" war? Presumably all of the signers who have a history of support of labor would back up a strike of such workers for higher wages, or of Negroes against discrimination, even if the strike interfered with war production. Or would they rule out strikes in wartime?

I do not mean to suggest that the situation is simple; nor do I approve or condone any and every act of protest however bizarre, or adventurist "revolutionary" actions in what is not, I grant, in the Marxian sense a revolutionary situation. But surely great care must be exercised in statements relating to the "democratic" character of our regime and the role of direct action and civil disobedience. The role of the latter in the civil rights movement has obviously not been eliminated by the gains so far achieved.

Finally, a word about the discussion of conscientious objection. It is true that there is a difference between individual moral objection and a political protest movement against the draft, but perhaps not so clear and sharp as the signers of the *New York Review* statement seem to think. For example, if there were enough young men who, on essentially religious or moral grounds, could not stomach participation in any war or in a particular war, if the number of such individuals went beyond a certain point—taking into account the inevitable side effects of such escalation among youth—it would become impossible for a government to wage war, especially if the dissenters included—as would almost certainly be the case in such a climate—some scientists and engineers in key positions. Such individual conscientious objection would constitute a political action of profound impact. The government would undoubtedly regard it as political and subversive if it went beyond a certain point. Presumably the signers of the *New York Review* statement would not argue that conscientious objection is permissible only if there are not enough objectors to interfere in any way with the smooth operation of the war, but should be ruled out as being "political," or "action by a minority to revoke through its own decision the policy of a democratically elected government," if the number should pass the critical point. Would they not agree also that unless there are a good many conscientious objectors, a movement to end the war is not likely to get very far?

I agree with the criticism of using the conscientious objector provisions in the Selective Service Act "as a tactic of the protest movement," and of filing as a C O merely in order to delay induction, because I think both individuals and movements are built by openness and not by evasion or what amounts to trickery. There are other tactics which have had some support that I would strongly oppose. It goes without saying—and the signers of the statement need hardly have taken the space to say it—that organizations should scrupulously inform young men of the possible consequences of a course they might take. An immense amount of such counseling is in fact being given these days by organizations such as the War Resisters League and the Central Committee for Conscientious Objectors.

But, granted that such conditions must be observed, I cannot understand why an anti-draft movement should not be a legitimate and highly useful part of a movement to end the war. Where else would a young man "vote," i.e., exercise his democratic duty, if not at the point where he is called upon to do what he holds is unwarranted and injurious, not only to himself but to society? What does the Nuremberg trial mean if not that young men do not obey, but disobey, orders at that point? And what is wrong about acting concertedly in such a moment? (I would agree with those who contend that opposition to the draft board should not be carried on in such a way as to divert attention and energy from opposition to the war itself.)

Lastly, I think it is most unfortunate that the signers of the *New York Review* statement should have made a plea to young men who refuse to serve in a war of which they disapprove to "recognize their responsibilities to authentic conscientious objectors, that is, pacifists who refuse on principle to employ violence under any circumstances." The former are urged not to claim status under the Selective Service Act since "the present status of conscientious objectors, achieved only after long and hard struggles," might be endangered!

In the first place, this is to define "authentic conscientious objection" in a narrow way which would be rejected by great numbers of C Os, and also by many ethical and religious teachers who are not pacifists themselves. If the government is to make provision for C Os, the definition of conscientious objector should by all means be broadened, not kept narrow and in effect discriminatory. A young man may be a sincere and genuine conscientious objector to a *particular* war, though not to every conceivable war. Strictly speaking, a Roman Catholic can be a C O on only one of two grounds: either that he has a special vocation to pacifism, as a monk or nun would have to the monastic life, or that a given war is "unjust." Would anyone argue, to cite another instance, that there were not in Germany, under Hitler, men who were not "authentic pacifists" according to the above definition but unquestionably sincere in their opposition to Hitler and war, perhaps even more so than the "authentic" pacifists?

Above all, any notion that pacifists ought to be protected or given special consideration under the law should be firmly rejected. The law affecting conscientious objectors at present is limited to those who refuse participation in any war on grounds of religious training and belief, and it defines "religious belief" as implying belief in a Supreme Being. The courts have, to all intents and purposes, eliminated the Supreme Being clause, ruling in effect that anyone to whom pacifism is a matter of deep conviction comes under the law. Personally I have always held that when religious C Os were offered special *status*, religious bodies should have refused it and insisted that government agents were not qualified to distinguish between one man's conscience and another's in such a context. Religious believers above all should not seek privileged status.

Furthermore I deny the right of a government, certainly in a military context, to conscript a man for so-called civilian service. The place where he is may be the place where he ought to be, the work he is doing may be what he ought to be doing. It is presumption and an invasion of human dignity for a government, because it happens to be waging war or preparing for it, to order him against his will to drop what he has been doing and do something else which it deems useful and fitting. Some of the proposals which have been made in statements issued for consideration by Students for a Democratic Society have, in my opinion, disregarded this important consideration. Moreover, they have not always made clear that they are not proposing "alternative service," in the context of the Selective Service Act, which seems to me only to make it easier for the government to administer the draft and carry on the war.

In conclusion, we are experiencing an unprecedented development of open opposition to a war in the midst of that war. That this opposition has not been suppressed so far by governmental action; and that, for example, in New York city, Park Department authorities issue a permit for space in which draft card burners may perform a supposedly illegal act; and that the Police Department provides protection for such an assembly is heartening evidence that American society is in some degree democratic.

It is to be expected that in the midst of this upsurge of anti-war sentiment and of a war such as the one in Vietnam, proposals for an "end-the-war movement" should emerge and efforts to build such a movement—*the* movement which would do the job—should be undertaken. It also is inevitable that the question of whether the "end-the-war movement" might not be made the starting point for a new political alignment, a new "revolutionary" line-up, and what have you, should be broached, and that various groups should think they have *the* answer to that broader question and proceed to act upon it. All this is obviously too vast a matter to be discussed in detail here.

I am not at the moment sanguine that *the* "movement" is about to come into existence. But I am convinced that movement, revolt, cannot be suppressed and that this in itself is a "revolutionary" development. If the revolt is to express itself in various ways, and not in a single "movement," then it is my hope that the adherents of each tendency or program will work very hard at their job as they see it and, while not abandoning political dialogue, will not dissipate energy in personal or organizational attacks on each other. The issue will in any event be decided largely by forces and developments over which none of us exercises a substantial measure of control.

Notes on Previous
Publication

1. *Sketches for an Autobiography* was first published serially in Liberation (1957-1960).

2. *The Problem of Discontent* was first published in the Hope College Anchor in 1903.

3. *Pacifism and Class War* was first published in The World Tomorrow in September, 1928.

4. *Trade Unions and the Revolution* was first published in The New International in August, 1935.

5. *Return to Pacifism* was first published in The Christian Century on December 2, 1936.

6. *Sit-Downs and Lie-Downs* was first published in Fellowship in March, 1937.

7. *The True International* was first published in The Christian Century on May 24, 1939.

8. *The World Task of Pacifism* was first published as a Pendle Hill pamphlet in 1941.

9. *Where Are We Going?* was first published as a Fellowship of Reconciliation pamphlet in 1941.

10. *War Is the Enemy* was first published as a Pendle Hill pamphlet in 1942.

11. *What the Bible Teaches About Freedom* was first published as a Fellowship of Reconciliation pamphlet in 1943.

12. *Germany—Summer 1947* was first published in Fellowship in October, 1947.

13. *Theology of Despair* was first published in Fellowship in September, 1948.

14. *Pacifism and Perfectionism* was first published in Fellowship in March and April, 1948.

15. *Communism and Civil Liberties* was first published in Fellowship in October, 1948.

16. *Korea: Spark to Set a World Afire?* was first published as a Fellowship of Reconciliation pamphlet in 1950.

17. *Of Holy Disobedience* was first published as a Pendle Hill pamphlet in 1952.

18. *Mephistopheles and the Scientists* was first published in Fellowship in July, 1954.

19. *Getting Rid of War* was first published in Liberation in March, 1959.

20. *Africa Against the Bomb* was first published in Liberation in January, 1960.

21. *Saints for This Age* was first published as a Pendle Hill pamphlet in 1962.

22. *Rifle Squads or the Beloved Community* was first published in Liberation in May, 1964.

23. *The Fall of Man* was first published in Liberation in June-July, 1964.

24. *The Civil Rights Movement and the American Establishment* was first published in Liberation in February, 1965.

25. *Statement Made on 12/21/65 to the Federal Grand Jury.*

26. *Crisis in the World and in the Peace Movement* was first published in Liberation in June-July, 1965.

27. *Who Has the Spiritual Atom Bomb?* was first published in Liberation in November, 1965.

28. *The Movement to Stop the War in Vietnam* was first published in Liberation in January, 1966.

About the Author

NAT HENTOFF was born in Boston and educated at Boston Latin School, Northeastern University and Harvard Graduate School. He attended the Sorbonne in Paris on a Fulbright scholarship. Mr. Hentoff is on the staff of *The New Yorker* and is a regular contributor to *The Village Voice, Evergreen Review, Playboy, The New York Times* and *Jazz & Pop,* among many other periodicals. He is also on the Board of the New York Civil Liberties Union and is the author of a number of adult books as well as the widely acclaimed young adult book *Jazz Country,* which won the Herald Tribune Spring Books Award. Mr. and Mrs. Hentoff live in New York City with their four children.